Passages

The Complete Trilogy Box Set

Sandra Waine

Solstice Publishing - www.solsticepublishing.com

Passages: Touch Me from Afar

Sandra Waine

Chapter One

"*Bona sera, signore, parla inglese?*"

"*Si*, signora. How can I help you? Are you checking in?"

The look on the manager's face said it all. The hour was late, near eleven o'clock, and the possibility of erasing that frown from his features seemed impossible. Sam's already frayed nerves shifted into high gear.

"Well, I'm hoping to. I just can't seem to locate a room. I tried several along the plaza. I realize it is very late, but could you possibly help me? Venice is busy with large tourist groups. Or, so I have been told over and over and well…"

"*Signorina*," he interrupted, "I wish I had better news for you. But we find ourselves in the same situation you have previously encountered elsewhere on this night."

"Please, it's *Signora* Arnesen, Samantha Arnesen. Anything you have will be perfect. A closet or even a bench." She swept her hand around the room. "I am not particular given the late hour."

Eyes beseeching, she leaned closer. "I can't go back out there; it is so late. I know it's not your fault. It is entirely my own. But, if nothing truly exists, would you permit me to find a corner and make some calls and check around with other establishments? I will be quiet as a mouse." Clasping hands tightly, her voice quivered. "For you see I am at a desperate point now, *signore*."

Crooking his head slightly, she felt a spark of hope arise. He spun around, hands flailing, speaking rapid Italian to a perky young lad sporting a crisp white and black uniform, who seemed to have appeared from thin air.

As the lad turned and dashed off, the beat of her heart collided with the breath in her lungs. It was deja vu all over again.

"*Signore*, pardon the intrusion. I could not help but overhear the lady's distress and wondered how I could be of help. Allow me to suggest a reasonable solution that should be agreeable to everyone."

Paralyzed, Sam found it difficult to breath. The only part that did move was her lower lip as his midnight blue eyes locked with hers.

"*Signore* Riozi." The handsome stranger addressed the manager. "I can move into the small room I stayed in previously. I know it's vacant. I am only here for the night, so I will give my room to the *signora*. If you agree, I shall return in less than ten minutes for that key and will leave mine."

Her eyes never left his features while that deep, penetrating voice surrounded the air she was trying to breath. She shook her head. Did he just say something else? Immobile, her mind drifted to her ex-husband. Never would he have performed such a gallant act as this, woman in distress or not. He was selfish head to toe.

Unable to avoid it, her eyes raked him from top to bottom. The gray, tailor-made, designer suit was snug around his shoulders. A soft sigh escaped her lips. She housed no doubts that beneath it all was a masterful and strong physique. Sam's imagination took flight as his voice faded off into the distance.

He was standing to close to her. But she could not move away as distant memories came back to haunt her. An ancient call to prayer, the winds rustling the reeds on the banks of a wide river, a camel's grunt.

Then there was silence. A darkness in her mind as reality rose from the past to present. His eyes shone bright, then turned dark. She swayed suddenly toward him.

As her knees buckled, his strong hands were there.

"Are you okay? Here, come and sit. Surely you are exhausted from tonight's ordeal. Rest, while I go and pack. Just give me a few minutes, then you can be comfortable for the night."

A feeling of knowing this handsome stranger made her spine tingle. Did he feel it too or was she just overtired from the train trip earlier today? Perhaps she had pushed it a bit much with jamming a long hike and a cycle into the countryside into her last day in France. Yes, she was convinced. It was just too much. The sooner she was tucked away, the better it would be for all.

Glancing at his retreating back, she felt like a manner-less idiot at not letting him know how much she appreciated his assistance. Indeed, he had come to her rescue. Fumbling in her cross-body bag for a tissue, a wave of anxiety and excitement coursed through her veins still feeling his warm, strong touch.

Signore Riozi had been standing there a few seconds eyeing her skeptically.

"*Signora* Arnesen, here is your key. Would you like Luigi to help with the bag?"

She reached up and took the old-fashioned key, moving it around in her hand. "What floor am I on?"

"*Sette*, room *settantasette.* It's a fine room; you will like it. Fresh sheets are on the bed and linens in the bathroom. If you need anything else just ring the desk."

Just like that he was finished with her. But the hour was very late and she could not blame him for wanting to finish up his night.

"*Mi scusi, signore*, but where is the gentleman that is taking my room? I wanted to thank him appropriately."

"Luigi already met him upstairs and gave him his key. If you request, I will be sure to extend your gratitude when he checks out tomorrow. *Buona notte.*"

She rose clutching the key while lifting the bag.

Damn, I am tired, she thought. I can't remember what room he said I am in. Great, I will just wander the halls.

She grinned reviewing the now vacant reception area. Glancing down she chuckled, smiling gingerly at the two sevens on the key.

"Right, got it. Seventh floor, room seventy-seven. Come on, Sam, you can make it."

The bellboy peered out from behind the desk, watching her get onto the single elevator, relieved she was not in need of assistance.

Locating the room, she unlocked the door and entered. Was this for real, she thought, assessing the two lovely large rooms suitable for a couple, or one very handsome man. All the same, it was a bit much for her tastes.

"My gosh," Sam said aloud. "He gave up a suite for me. I must be hallucinating. I need that bed and pillow now."

Throwing the bag up on a chair, she took out her things and wandered to the bathroom marveling at the exquisite marble tiles with sparkling gold everywhere. She stopped, pressing the side of her head against its coolness.

"Sam, you have to get your shit together." She mumbled to no one. Then took the last two steps towards the pedestal sink, washing her face and brushing her teeth.

Then something strong stirred inside her mind.

A voice.

It sounded like his but echoed with another.

Her fingers lifted, touching the mirror, noticing how bright her eyes shown back in the reflection. Yes, her thoughts had wandered back to a different time long ago. A place from the past long ignored. Shaking her head slightly, she picked up all the items, placing them back into the bag.

Climbing into the bed, tugging the fluffy, down comforter beneath her chin, Sam was suddenly afraid to close her eyes.

Would he haunt her again tonight?

The voice with no face attached; the one that sounded so much like the man who had been in here. Heavy lids won out as her brain finally shut down. At last, she slept.

A loud pounding at the door nearly sent it off the hinges making her jump. Biting a hand to hold back a scream, she momentarily sat there staring at it. Quickly glancing at her bag, she wondered if perhaps it was the attendant from the front desk and she had left her credit card in error. Slowly, she got up. Walking over, keeping the dead bolt slid in place, she opened it only as far as the chain allowed.

Two men dressed in dark suits were standing there. Fear raced throughout her body, while mentally chiding herself for being so stupid. She should have just asked who it was before opening at all.

"Yes?"

"Pardon the interruption, madam, but is *Signore* Weaver here? We believed that this is his room. Perhaps we were given the wrong information?"

Sam looked perplexed. "I do not know who that is. Perhaps the front desk could assist?"

Without awaiting a reply, she closed the door and snapped the deadbolt securely.

Was that his name, *Signore* Weaver? Odd, that would not have been a name she'd associate with this guy at all. Something more old European, rich family money and a long heritage. As she slid into bed, her mind conjured up all kinds of mysteries surrounding him.

"Whatever," echoed around the large rooms, "I'll never set eyes on him again. Tomorrow I move on and will leave this behind."

She grinned, squishing the pillow, and settled her weary head down onto its softness. Many hailed Venice as one of the most romantic cities in Italy. Yawning, the smile faded as lids slid down, while she rolled over and drifted off to sleep.

Early the next morning Sam stretched languidly, happy it had been an uneventful rest of night. Rested and refreshed, she was relieved no one else had come knocking. Just as the sun was drifting in through the open shutters, she rose, showered, dressed, and repacked the few items removed last night. Grabbing her bag, she hurried along hoping to find him before he left. She'd made up her mind. She wanted to pay for the difference in the rooms, knowing that was the very least she could do. If he was already gone, she'd ask the clerk to refund his card the difference.

Sliding the key up onto the beautiful mahogany counter, the lobby was quiet. Shrugging when no attendant came out, she swung the tote up to a shoulder and rolled the other bag behind her in the direction of a delicious smell. They would have breakfast staff and someone would be able to help her. Along a narrow lantern lit corridor, she continued, reaching the entrance.

La Calcina's sumptuous breakfast was served overlooking the *Guidecca* Canal. Sam smiled, surveying the beautiful surroundings of this third-generation hotel, restored to its grand splendor of years past. Surveying it further, it was a bit too romantic for her single stay. Setting her bag down, she pressed hands to the windows imagining his face in the reflection back.

"You are up early."

She did not have to even look up to know who it was. Afraid of what she may do this time. Perhaps she'd just melt into a puddle on the floor right at his shiny, Italian leather shoes. Or, continue to appear like an idiot with no command of the English language.

Shaking her head slightly, common sense and her voice returned.

"I'm glad you are still here. I wanted to give you the difference in our rooms. I'm sure yours were a hefty cost compared to where you ended up. If you would be so kind to let me know the amount?"

Heaven please help me, she prayed, having managed to get that all out before his dark gorgeous eyes swallowed her up.

"Was it okay? You don't seem any worse for the wear this morning."

He chuckled.

"It was small," he admitted. A smile spreading across his full lips. "But absolutely suitable."

Sam stepped closer subconsciously placing a hand on his arm feeling the softness of his silk dress shirt.

"Honestly, nice gesture that it was, it does not feel proper paying for less and getting more.

He grinned, eyes boring into her very soul. Her brows drew in, not able to look away as he kept her captive for several seconds.

"I have a different thought on that. I want to make sure you remember what I did. Who I am. So, I'll claim payment in a somewhat offhanded manner. It appears I have a point to prove this morning and only you can help me with it."

She had no idea what the hell he was talking about.

With that, he pulled her into his strong chest, lowered his head and stole a long, sweet kiss. Then turned and walked away.

As she leaned against the dark paneled wall, feeling its coolness with the palms of both hands, Sam watched him leave.

She touched her lips. Yes, they were still warm as a satisfying smile appeared. Sliding her bag under a table, she noticed she was completely alone as the waitress approached.

"*Buon giorno, signora*, coffee, tea?"

"Tea, *grazie*."

After helping herself to the buffet, Sam shot down the last of her tea, paid the bill, and then headed out into the back alley, met by a brilliantly sunny day in Venice. Where to? She had planned on staying here just a day. Keeping that in mind, there was time for one major sightseeing excursion. Then the late train to Milano would be in order.

Knowing exactly where she wanted to go, she approached the *Basilica dei Frari* as excitement coursed through her blood. Loving to get off the beaten path, Sam had read a short online article about the history of this basilica and the strange goings on that had been recorded over the years. Intrigue filled her thoughts.

Stopping to let a small group of school children pass by, she glanced up and spotted him engaged in conversation with the two men. The very same that had visited her room last night. Their new addition was a friar. Her mind reeled. Who was this rogue who had stolen a kiss? Now he seemed draped in further mystery.

Was he here on business or living here? Was she frigging crazy, she pondered, stopping to hide behind Japanese tourists. Invisible to discovery but close enough to eavesdrop, she listened intently to their hushed Italian conversation picking up only a few words.

As they dispersed, the two men accompanied her handsome stranger inside the Basilica. How coincidental it was that they were heading in the same general direction? Lifting the bag, Sam entered, watching them head down the long nave toward the front altar. Strange, she thought, watching them. They were assessing the place. Why? As a pulsating force coursed throughout her body.

As she moved back, bringing them into vision, they disappeared toward the left side of the altar towards a small cluster of confessionals.

Wait a minute, her mind screamed. What exactly do you think you are doing? Would he appreciate you stalking him like this? An internal voice rose strongly up. *Sam, get over yourself.*

Yet as this brain battle was going on, a shiver spooked the hairs on the back of her neck and arms simultaneously. Moving behind a pillar and out of sight, she listened in squashing that pragmatic voice.

Their words were faint but she could make out English and Scottish accents. But, it was just not clear enough to distinguish the full conversation from this distance.

Then it dawned on her. At the *Pensione* he had spoken in perfect American English. Ear turned, she honed in. Yes. Indeed, that was his voice. Placing a packet inside his suit jacket, the men exchanged handshakes as they left heading toward the rear entrance. She stuck her nose out briefly. It was the two from last night. Confirmed.

Then everything turned bizarre.

Out of the corner of an eye, a priest appeared from behind a lovely, hand painted, three-dimensional screen depicting the Resurrection. Patting the handsome stranger's back, they exchanged smiles and entered adjoining confessionals. She moved closer and glanced around nervously. But all she heard were muffled voices. As the priest's door opened, Sam turned looking away as he walked toward the main altar. She stood there, waiting, thinking he was praying, or something. Feeling foolish and awkward, she removed her camera and took a few photos, all the while staying close to that all important confessional door.

Pulling out her cellphone and checking the time, it had been over fifteen minutes since he'd gone in there. Was that unusual? She started to laugh softly into the nave. Maybe he had a lot to atone for. She chuckled harder drawing glances; perhaps he did indeed. Brazenly she walked over and knocked gently on the door.

There was no answer.

An about face was in order and right now. Surely, he must have come out while she was locked in thought or taking pictures and had missed him. Then again, what the hell would she do once she found him? Ask him why he had kissed her?

Strangely enough, a voice inside her head urged her on, to go ahead, open the confessional door. See for herself. Or embarrass them both by interrupting a very private moment. Eyeing the confessional at length, a voice loomed over her shoulder followed quickly by the face of the priest. His eyes pierced her soul and in that instance she truly felt like an idiot. Anxiously, she glanced about for the fastest exit.

"That one is empty, *Signorina*. Go on in. I'll be with you shortly."

Then there it was. The moment of truth. Did she dare do it just to prove some stupid point? Smarter yet would be to shrug it off and leave. This was her chance to flee. He did not know who she was. Oh, fuck it, nearly came out of her opened mouth. Knuckles white, fingers wrapped tightly around the knob, Sam walked in rolling the bag. Then set it down at her feet. Leaning over, she closed the door.

A hint of his cologne remained in the air. How had he come out and she was unaware? She could have sworn her eyes never moved off this confessional for more than a couple of seconds in a row. Minutes passed. Where was the priest? How long had it been? She refrained from taking out her cellphone to check again. That would be rude. Especially if he was opposite waiting for her to speak.

Then the other confessional door creaked. She heard sounds of shuffling and could faintly make out his silhouette.

Voice crackling with nervousness she began.

"Father, I've not done this in fifteen years. I am sure. Where do I even begin? Do you need to know I am divorced, but never married in a Catholic Church? I don't really remember the prayer I'm to use to start all this." She stopped feeling like a fool and gathered her thoughts. "I have to be honest, father. The only reason I am here is to inquire about the man you were speaking with earlier. I know you may not be able to tell me much, but is there anything you can?"

Taking a breath, she wondered why he had not said a word.

"Father?"

A door creaked then it was silent again.

"Anyone?"

Relief washed over her. It must have been a tourist just peering inside then moved along.

"That was close." Opening the door, she stood for a second then rolled the bag out in front of her. Suddenly whispers and stares were all around.

Sam's few minutes of enjoyment at her verbal dialogue with the non-showing priest was short lived. Feeling more than ridiculous, she was glad she had not found him. Really, she had been stalking him. A slight blush cased her cheeks as she smiled to no one except herself. As she glanced around the smaller church, her stomach tightened.

What the hell was going on?

Nudged suddenly by a passing nun, who apologized softly, Sam's apprehension exploded noticing she had twitched her head to one side as if silently showing the right way out. Her hand met the coolness of the large stone pillar, as it penetrated through her skin.

This was not the *Basilica dei Frari*. The women and men speaking in hushed tones all around her were not Italian at all.

They were every bit British.

Stunned, she looked back at the confessional. Was this a dream? Had something happened to her sanity? Was she still at the *Pensione* safe in that nice room? Would her eyes flutter and she was tucked on a sofa having not been able to secure one? Was he a fantasy as well?

Sam pinched the top of her hand, wincing, feeling it acutely along with a tingling apprehension. Had that nod meant something, telling her to move on? But to where? Had the nun meant to do that? Thoughts jumbled together making no damn sense. Nor did the fact that the next person who went to open the same confessional door halted, finding it locked.

Locked? Yes as she watched the same man try one next to it with the same results. Turning, he walked away but not before engaging her in a smile. She was losing it now. First the handsome stranger, the priest, the nun, and now this guy. Fresh air. Yes, she needed to get outside. Eyes brimming with tears at not being able to understand this at all, she tugged the bag along as the whispers increased.

"What?" She bellowed towards a woman staring her. Who turned anxiously and hurried away. Sam closed in quickly on the nearest exit as people moved aside providing a clear channel out. To let the crazy woman out.

Chapter Two

Sliding the handle of the wheeled bag down and securing it from sight, Sam lifted it up and carried it out of the church. Stopping, her eyes gingerly shifted down to the hem of her long dress. Setting her bag on the ground, she hesitantly lifted it up a few inches stunned at what was on her feet. Boots, very gentile, leather boots.

She softly mouthed, "What the fuck…?"

The dress slid from fingertips as a horse drawn carriage halted a few yards away. As if being pulled over by some unknown force, Sam walked over as a door pushed out.

"You look at bit disoriented. Is this an unexpected visit? Perhaps you should come on in and sit. I may be able to help you."

Silence prevailed. The words would not come as Sam stood rooted for several minutes taking in the street scene. Finally, one of the stranger's sentences penetrated her confused mind. Only one sentence made it. Is this an unexpected visit? Disbelief shadowed her features. Then in the upheaval, she heard it again.

"Madam."

Sam reached down and picked up her bag, as a simple gloved hand extended out helping her into the carriage. Sliding a hand over the soft leather, her eyes finally rose to the woman.

Smartly attired, the lady's eyes seemed kind giving Sam short-lived comfort.

"Nice piece of luggage you have there. Now, where can I give you a lift to?"

The woman banged on the top of the carriage as the horses jolted, moving them forward while pushing Sam further back onto the seat.

"I don't know exactly where I am. I know that sounds strange, but I only just arrived." Trying to calm her frayed nerves, Sam glanced down, opening the small bag in her lap. British pound notes and coins filled it.

"What the hell happened to me?"

The woman reached over, patting her hand. Sam pulled back sharply, fear clear on her white face.

"Love, don't worry. You seemed very flustered. I can help you. Don't try to figure anything out right now. Once we reach the estate, I can help clear some things up for you. For now, just sit back and try to relax."

The rocking motion of the coach was somehow soothing as Sam listened to the hooves hitting the dirt road.

"This is real. I am not in some dream having bumped my head in that *Basilica*." she mumbled. "All because I wanted to know more about... Oh, well. I guess that's just not important now."

"Yes, you should not have followed him. But, I think there is more at work here than we both understand right now. The fact is you did. Now we figure out what's next and how to deal with it. He will need to deal with it."

"He? He is here and you know of whom I am speaking?"

"He sure is, and, Samantha?"

Sam's head swung around facing the woman.

"You know my name?"

"Yes. That and a bit more. Try and stay calm. Answers are not going to come as fast as you want. All the same, it's important to stay rational until you do know more. Don't worry, I'll help you to make sense of this. Now, if you continue to fret, your head will hurt more than it may already. Possibly until you have taken a few more passages. It affects us all in different ways, passing through. Just close your eyes and rest."

"Passing through? Am I dead and this is what it's like?"

She laughed, a soft comforting sound to Sam's ears.

"No, you are quite alive, my dear. More alive than you have been since your existence. Enough. Now let those lids drop."

"Just one more question, please? Well two. Who are you? I recognize you as the nun that bumped me in the *Basilica* back in Italy. But, how are you here?" She paused, reflecting. "Oh, I understand. You came through after that to be here to help. I get it. So, what is his name then?"

"You are an observant one, I must say. Which is quite refreshing compared to whom I sometimes assist. I am Mrs. Hoyt. The main housekeeper for Lord Adam Griffin, the sixth Earl of Ard Aulinn."

"Oh, my, a real Earl. I thought they did away with those titles long ago? Anyway, never mind." Realizing by her attire she was not back in 2015, nor did Mrs. Hoyt acknowledge being the nun. "Where is the estate?"

"You did say two questions, Samantha. But I'll give you one more answer. Then enough for now. It lies outside the village of Chester, near the Welsh border."

Sam smiled, feeling slightly more comfortable and settled back internally acknowledging the housekeeper's firm tone. But then nearly jumped from her seat again.

"But wait! Can't I just go back into the church and transport back to Venice? I know the man after you could not open the confessional door. It was locked. Maybe now it would open?"

Mrs. Hoyt patted her hand. "No, child, you are here for a reason. We have to figure that out before you go anywhere else."

Sam sat back and let the swaying motion of the carriage lull her into a more agreeable state of mind. It was better than another option of freaking out. As it came to an abrupt stop jolting her forward, Mrs. Hoyt's arm prevented her from hitting the seat across.

"Damn, this is not a dream. I am here. Shit."

"I beg your pardon. But, you had better watch your tongue around the men. Hearing it as such may arouse more attention than bargained for. They will think you are a tavern wench speaking such foul language." Mrs. Hoyt's eyes were ablaze. Not with condemnation, rather mirth.

Sam bore no apology. "Are we there?"

"Indeed, we are. Now come along and quietly. Bring your bags and follow closely. We are maneuvering around the rear of the estate in a roundabout manner. This way, I can get you into the room unnoticed."

Shuffling along at a snail's pace, the man appeared by Sam's perusal to sport quite a limp. She had to wonder if it was caused by old age or by battle. Winding up the uneven slippery stone steps, holding a torch, they continued behind until they reached a large, medieval, wooden door. It was cold, damp and housed the smell of piss and mustiness, nearly causing Sam to wretch as they stopped.

The man disappeared as Mrs. Hoyt reached into her heaving bosom, expanding rapidly from the exertion, and produced a large skeleton key. Ironically, it resembled the one Sam had held just hours before at the *Pensione La Calcina.*

She swept aside, whispering, "Get on, woman, now hurry." Sam moved through as the large door creaked shut. "We have to keep our voices very low. Set those bags over near the bed and let's get you into it. We can talk tomorrow. Tonight, you must stay here. Bolt the door after I leave or you may find yourself woken during the night by a lost and lonely drunken soldier."

Glancing about at the simplicity of the room, she had to wonder who stayed here. The blazing fire warmed it into coziness, with softly lit candles producing dancing shadows about the room. The four-poster bed looked inviting enough and comfortable. She could hardly wait to climb in and see if maybe in the morning she would wake up someplace outside of Venice, laughing that she must had drank too much wine the night before and did not remember a thing on her train journey to *Milano*.

"I'll leave you to your thoughts, Samantha. I'll bring your breakfast early. When you hear my raps, open up straight away."

"Sounds fine, Mrs. Hoyt. I assure you I'll be up and about if I even sleep tonight. Would you prefer I call you Mrs. Hoyt or something more formal?"

Mrs. Hoyt laughed softly, eyes amused. "Mrs. H will do. Then you will fit right in as everyone else does. Now, go about your business and do as I have said. There is someplace I must be." Silently she moved from the room checking the handle to make sure Samantha had engaged the sturdy iron lock into place.

"Son of a bitch," Sam whispered, bolting the door then turned abruptly straight into the corner of a dresser with her right hip. For a few seconds it hurt like bloody hell. "Dammit, I really thought this was a dream, but that smarted. Reality check, I guess. Now, what do I wear to bed?"

Her curiosity won over as she pulled open a dresser draw and out a linen nightgown. She changed and was relieved to wash off the day's dirt and make-up from her face using the pitcher and bowl.

Opening the tote, she pulled out face cream and applied it liberally. The room was too warm and dry, but she dared not see if the windows opened. That would entail pulling aside the heavy drapes and could pose a threat. If anyone outside was curious, they may indeed wander up here to investigate. Extinguishing all the candles, firelight washed the room with a soft glow as she burrowed under the blankets, marveling in how soft they were, then drifted off to sleep.

***

Meanwhile, Mrs. Hoyt quietly worked her way back outside through the nearly silent Great Hall. Tonight, there were only a handful of passed out soldiers, who had indulged in too much alcohol. Moving along, listening to snores, she passed through two long corridors before closing and locking a door behind. Now she was back in the main house.

Hand raised, she knocked on his library door then without hesitation, entered.

"What happened? Why were you delayed?" His voice was curt as he glanced at her briefly, acknowledging with his eyes an apology of sorts. She knew something was clearly bothering him.

A hunch formed in her mind. "You seem irritated. Did your day not go as scheduled?"

He shook his head. "It went just as planned." His eyes glazed over, but he was to smart to let her see to much. Regardless she was fully aware something was amiss. He had always been a stubborn lad, so the time of toying with him would be short lived.

"We have an unexpected visitor, my lord. I waited after you rode off on your mount as something delayed me from following straight away."

"Go on."

"A lady came out of the church within minutes of your departure. Standing there dazed and confused."

"Not another transient. Did you get her moving along?"

She watched his face intently. "No, she's here. Came through the church door directly to my carriage and I knew. She's up in the Lancaster Tower Wing. I'll find out more in the morning. I wanted you to know."

"Do you have a name? Where she's headed? What's her reason is for being here?"

"Not much to go on right now. Clearly, she is new. I could tell that straight away. Dressed properly enough though. But one thing stood out clearly. She handled a very expensive bag that does not belong in our era. *Italian* to be sure. From the future."

"Is she?"

"No, she's British and quite comely, I must say. All I've received in advance is her first name. It's Samantha."

Silence permeated the room.

Staring up at the Lancaster Tower Wing, his head moved slightly.

"Find out what you can in the morning. I ride to Shrewsbury for a meeting with the Duke. I may be a day or two. I'll expect more details upon my return."

Hand on the knob, she nodded.

"I will find out what we need to know, Lord Adam. Are you okay?"

He ran his hand through thick hair. "Yes, why do you ask?"

She scrutinized him carefully. "Just making sure." As she waited on a reply.

"Mrs. H, bring her into the house. I don't think that's an appropriate place up there for her."

She smiled softly closing the door. This time it was different. She could feel it. Something electrifying was in the air. With a heightened sense of alertness, she sauntered down toward the kitchens then beyond into her rooms.

This was not the first time a woman had followed him back. But she was always kept tucked away in the Tower until things concluded. Then sent along on her way. Yes, this was getting interesting. She was looking forward to Lord Griffin and Samantha's first face to face meeting here. What had the young buck done now? Moving on, grin spreading with each step, Mrs. H knew the tides had indeed changed. That this time he'd get his just due from that lady tucked away up in the Tower.

Chapter Three

A persistent rapping rattled Sam out of the chair and dashing for the wooden door. Up early and settled into a pretty day dress, she opened it up to a stern look on Mrs. H's face as she rushed in with tray in hand. Sam slid the lock firmly back into place.

"Good morning, Samantha, come and sit. Let's get you fed while we chat. I have a lot of things to take care of today. So, we need to figure out what we can in short order. Then get moving on what's next for you."

"Is he here?"

"You can start by calling him Lord Adam. No, he left at sunrise on business and will be back in a few days."

"Okay. Well, I have a lot of questions. Can you tell me how my clothes changed between the confessional in Venice and that church? Also, how my bags came with me? I checked them this morning and I have everything I had there. But this is strange, I also have a small purse with lots of English currency in it."

"Hm. That is interesting and perplexing. I must admit. I've seen dozens come through over the years. But you have me puzzled Sam. You are different than the others and I need to figure out why. I wonder if your purpose is more complex than what I am familiar with? We may need some outside guidance. Don't you agree?"

Sam looked confused. "You are asking the wrong person, but I understand what you are saying. What others are you referring too?"

"Okay." She grabbed her warm hands. "This may take a bit to digest. All I ask is that you are patient until I am through. Are you ready?"

"Yes, go ahead."

"There are special people who can move between time and space. We are referred to as old souls. We do not question how or why, but we know we have a purpose in being here. You for instance, came with the appropriate clothing. But, also traveled with baggage from your era. That's unusual. It has never happened on my watch before. That makes me wonder if you are going to be able to return at will. I guess we are going to have to wait that one out."

Sam disengaged one hand and put it to her forehead. Closing her eyes, she hoped it would do the trick; when she opened them, she would be back in Italy or even better England. Her true England.

It did not work.

"How much money is in that purse?"

"Not counting the coinage, there is about eleven thousand pounds in notes. That seems like a lot for this time frame. But it means I have plenty to take up a room at the local inn until we get to the bottom of this."

"I'll let his Lordship decide when he returns. Do you have any ties with family history in this period?"

"I don't know, probably. I think we all do. But I don't even know what year we are in."

"Eighteen-hundred and sixty-five. Among your travels in Italy, or before, did you meet anyone that may have said anything to you that made no sense. Perhaps it makes sense now that you are here?"

That brought out a laugh. "I chat with a lot of people along my travels. It helps to pass time since I go alone."

"We may not get too far, Sam. It may take a while for more of the puzzle to unravel. We need to strategize. A story as to why you are here to prevent any unwanted nosing about by gossip mongering locals. How old are you?"

"Forty-four. Mrs. H. I'm no spring chicken."

She smiled. "You look younger than that. His Lordship has eight years on you, if it be of interest." They shared a grin.

"We will keep it simple. You are the spinster daughter of a friend who passed away last year. That is easier than having a husband and children in lieu of the circumstances. This allows free rein of the estate. Just keep yourself clear of the stables and the soldiers. Queen Victoria has a garrison on the border of England and Wales. Often they pass through to water their horses and spend a night or two along their journey to London. His Lordship is well received at Court, so they are welcome here."

"Mrs. H how many of us are there around here?"

"I know of only a handful. For hundreds of year's stories have been handed down. Some say a few of us go back to Egyptian times. Are you familiar, Sam, with ancient Egypt?"

She shook her head, eyes large and bright.

"It was the birthplace of the original Nine Gods of Egypt, Isis being one of them. Surely you've heard of her?"

"Ah, yes, of her I have. But I still do not understand; am I an old soul? Are you?"

"Yes, dear. It seems we have a lot of work to do before we can complete all our earthly tasks and move on for good. Anyway, let me continue. As far as I know, we never work knowingly with each other and rarely discuss where we have been. You need to be very careful. Although the witch trials and tribulations have long passed, there are those that are here to block our progress, trying to affect history in a different way."

"So, I affect history?"

"No, to assist. Often, we are passing documents, providing money, securing a passage or assisting in a recovery. It could be as simple as a nun nudging you, if you know what I mean."

Sam eyed her recalling that nun's habit.

"You need to always remember one important thing. If you affect a historical moment, it will alter your life as well. You and others of historical importance may never exist after that. So be very careful."

Sam shuddered, having not even given that possibility a thought,

"Holy shit. So, it's basically go in, get the job done and get out? How do you know where to transport and when to transport next?"

"That's going to be tricky for you. What year did you come in from? I came through so quick I was not sure."

"Twenty-fifteen."

"You did follow Lord Adam out of Italy after all. I thought you may have." She smiled figuring out a bit more. Deciding that was enough for now, Mrs. H asked one more question. "Did you have family there?"

"An ex-husband, that's it. Both my parents have passed away. I was an only child. Any distant relatives are just that. We have no contact."

"Okay, then I'm going to move you into the main house. Pack up your bags and come with me. I'll have more time this afternoon to show you around the grounds. Until then you are free to roam."

She picked up the serving tray. "Where did you live in England?"

"Exeter. I had a small cottage outside the city and when my mother passed, I retired early to travel. I've been divorced for quite a few years. It's probably stupid to think that I could just hire a carriage, grab up my things and just go, right?"

"Oh, you can do that, dear. But you will be in 1865 and not 2015, so it won't matter."

"This is so frustrating, Mrs. H."

"Come on now, let's get you re-settled. Soon a trip to town will be in order to purchase a suitable wardrobe. The clothes kept in that room were for a few of his Lordship's former mistresses. I doubt you want anything to do with those."

Sam closed the door behind, scowling. So, indeed he was a rogue after all. That explains why he stole that kiss from her and then disappeared. Well, one thing was clear. Under his roof or not, until she figured out why the hell she was here, he'd not lay another finger on her. As they moved down the tower and outside into the courtyard, she had her first real glimpse of the expansive estate.

"Mrs. H, holy... Ah, my goodness. This is not just a home. Hell, a person could go missing for days and no one would be the wiser."

"True it may take some adjusting. But it is yours until we figure things out. Another benefit of staying is that you should not have any trouble avoiding certain people, if that is your desire." She was toying with the lady and enjoying it as much as she had the Master.

Catching that look Sam contemplated what the housekeeper was hiding. It was plain as the nose on her face it was something. As they entered the rear of the house, the eccentric interior reminded her of artwork she'd seen at the Victoria & Albert Museum in London. She'd enjoy staying and exploring centuries of statues, wall hangings and furniture.

A servant took the tray from Mrs. H as they ascended one the staircases, then a second, before she swung down a long wide corridor opening a set of double wide, wooden doors.

"Here you go. I'm sure his Lordship will not mind you in this wing. It's opposite his which are down the other side. Normally only guests are housed here. We don't have any this time of year, so you will have plenty of freedom."

Sam set her bags down mesmerized by how large the rooms were. Quite grander than her humble cottage back in Exeter.

"I don't need this much space. Although it is quite lovely. I would prefer something smaller. So, if you do not mind." Sam turned, speech halted. Mrs. H had already departed and the doors tightly shut.

Okay, so she was on her own now. Quickly, she unpacked and headed out, laughing inwardly, sorely tempted to leave a trail along the hall toward the staircase so she'd know the way back later. Sam was quite sure, walking along all the handsomely painted faces of the current Lord's ancient relatives, that many were in conspiracy smiling down at her. Believing she was totally nuts, she moved on.

Tucked in her small lady's reticule was her Fuji camera and some of the money. With a spring in her step, she suddenly spied a young housemaid moving about.

"Excuse me. How far are we from Chester by foot?"

The perky young maid looked at her with clear anxiety. Sam was quick to realize by that review what it appeared like. She was one of his lordships mistresses gone astray inside the estate. She pursed her lips to hide a smile.

"Oh, miss, pardon me. I walk from town every day. I know it's about two miles each direction. You can leave out the back of the kitchens through the field. Just keep going. You will come right into the greens at Chester. When you return, if you need assistance finding your way back to the tower, let anyone in the kitchen know and they will help you."

"You probably have not been told by Mrs. Hoyt since I just arrived, that I am visiting. I will be staying in the West Wing while I am here. Anyway, thank you for your assistance. Is there any shopping, lady's shops specifically, that you may suggest I visit?"

Sam knew it would be shocking of a true lady of the time to ask a servant for such information, but she did not give a fig right about now.

"Why, yes, my uncle runs a shop there."

"Well, then, that's settled, I shall go pay him a visit. And your name is?"

"Molly, miss."

The servant nodded, curtsied, then abruptly hurried off a bit red in the face.

Oh crap, was she not to have spoken to her at all? No, probably not. Sam knew history like the back of her hand, like who reigned and where, but as for estate etiquette, well, that was a different story. Most of the novels she could recall from her twenties involved men removing women's clothing and clandestine meetings.

She was laughing as she pressed on.

Twenty minutes later she arrived to the lower floor kitchens noticing Mrs. Hoyt was doing paperwork. Others were milling about prepping food, canning vegetables, plucking the feathers off a pheasant as she approached.

"I'm going for a walk into town. Is that okay? I've received instructions on the best route." She kept her voice low.

"Fine. Watch for darkness if you take the field and be back before the sunset."

Nodding, Sam left through the side door and was outside on the path heading to Chester as a sudden quiver ran from shoes to head. Was she alone? Whistling, she spun around and nearly hit the chest of a tall man of the cloth.

"Good day to you, mistress. That's a lively tune you were whistling. It's a shame we never hear more women in our society having such confidence to do it in public."

His comment did not go unnoticed by Sam.

"It appears we are headed in the same direction. Do you mind if I join you?"

"Not at all father, please do. I'd welcome the conversation along the way."

"Are you staying at the Earl's estate?"

"Yes, I am visiting a friend of my mother's, Mrs. Hoyt. I just arrived last night."

"Where are you from?"

"Exeter."

"Did you find your journey here pleasant enough?"

Sam felt it again. A quiver. An important message was passing between them. Was he a contact of some sort? Is that how this works? Get to where you need to be and await instructions; is that what Mrs. H had been alluding too?

"Well, this is me." He held out his large strong hand. "Father Godwin at your service. I think you should come for a visit tomorrow. If you arrive at half-past eleven, we will have plenty of time to chat before I have a later afternoon parish meeting. See you then?"

"Sure, father, I can think of no other who can give me the run-down on the town's goings on than you. To make sure I don't make myself too obvious being new in these parts."

He grinned, nodding, as she extended her hand.

"Samantha Arnesen, father, and thank you. I should like to do that."

Nodding, he disappeared out of sight down the path toward the graveyard and church. Glancing ahead, she saw the green and sighed. It was a lovely, old English village thriving with carriages, horses, people and life. She already felt at home here.

Carswell's Shop housed a large, handsomely decorated, display window with several items of interest lying just inside. Stepping up off the cobbled street, Sam opened the rickety door as a tin bell chimed overhead signaling her arrival.

"Yes, miss, what can I do for you?"

"I was wondering if you may have any day dresses in my size and a riding habit as well that I may see?"

"I believe we do. Come this way. Let's take your measures and see what we can find."

Two hours later, packages loaded on a hired wagon, Sam paid the driver to deliver to the estate as she sauntered through the lovely old medieval town. Dark brown and white Tudor buildings lined each side as Sam appreciated the great beauty of a time that was gentler. No electricity yet, no cellphones or the loud annoying honking of car horns. Yes indeed, this was quite pleasant.

A gentleman and lady came out of a tea shop as Sam thought, well, why not? Sitting alone, it never occurred that it would cause a stir as she sat down at a small table facing the street.

"Tea, mistress?"

"Please. A tray of cakes as well." She smiled to the attendant. How very proper, she thought, sporting a lovely day dress, cute boots, bag, hat and gloves sitting down for a 'spot of tea.' Very English.

Finished, settling the bill and rising, she stepped outside. It quickly became apparent the sun had set. Briskly moving up the hard-packed dirt street, she quickly located the path that headed back through the fields toward the estate. Darkness descended as the glow of gas lights on the property illuminated all the grand buildings.

Slipping through a side door, Sam was out of breath after nearly sprinting up the stairs. Washed up and changed, a quick about face was in order as she headed back down to find the main dining hall. Why was she eating in there if the Lord of the Manor was absent?

Coming down the final flight, she stopped to appreciate the ornate beauty of this level. Tomorrow after visiting with Father Godwin, she'd come back and explore the inside with more thoroughness.

"Mistress, if you do not mind, with the Earl away this evening, Mrs. Hoyt asks me to assist you to a smaller dining area. If you would come this way, please."

Sam startled slightly. Just where had the maid come out of so quickly? Nodding, she followed down a beautiful hall passing lit candelabras gleaming softly against hand carved busts.

"Ah, there you are, Samantha. I hope you don't mind the breakfast room since his Lordship is away. I thought it would be more suitable with just the two of us. Come now, sit so we can be served."

Sam sat down at one of the four place setting.

"Is anyone else joining us?"

"No. It's just the two of us tonight. Sometimes when the Earl's brother is here, or his sister, they like to dine in a less formal atmosphere."

"Thank you for taking care of the shipment of packages. I hope it was no trouble?"

"Not at all dear. I'm happy you found Mr. Carswell's shop. I would guess that all your purchases will be suitable enough for now."

Mrs. H seem to have a well-planned script for all ears that may be near, as Sam hid a smile behind a starched white linen napkin.

"I happened upon Father Godwin along the way to town. He's invited me to visit later tomorrow morning. I hope you did not have plans for me as I readily accepted."

A sharp glance passed between them.

"Absolutely, you will be here for a spell. Making acquaintances will be nice, dear. I hope there will be no gossip about you not being married by your age and all."

Sam giggled, moving her utensils up on the plate as they finished dinner. Rising, taking Mrs. H by the arm, they exited the room,

"Why don't we walk out into the night air before retiring? I do not think it is too chilly." She shut the double wide French doors behind them as they started arm in arm.

"You must be very intuitive tomorrow, Sam, as the good father will have plenty to say, so do pay attention."

"So, he does have something to do with this. I'm seeing a pattern now. First the priest at the *Basilica* in Venice and now Father Godwin." She grinned adding, "I best watch out for those men of the cloth and a good nun or two in following, eh?"

"You hush now, young lady." She laughed softly as well. "Get yourself up to bed and make sure you nod to me on your way out and find me when you return. I just want to know you are back. Unless I hear differently, I fully expect tomorrow night you will dine with the Earl. Best be prepared."

"Woman to woman, Mrs. H, will you give me more details about what type of a man he is? I'd like to be forewarned and forearmed if I can. Remember, I am a modern woman from a modern era."

She patted Sam's arm gingerly.

"Best you discover that yourself so my opinion does not cloud your best judgement of him. Now get yourself along and sleep well."

Sam eyed her skeptically letting it ride for now. It seemed like an eternity before she finally found the correct corridor that led to familiar territory and that soft cozy bed. Lying there with one of the French doors open toward the expansive gardens, she could hear night sounds somewhat similar to her cottage from the future.

The night crickets were chirping a soft repetitive song along with a babbling fountain off in the distance. It reminded her of how much she loved to be outside, free from all and making her own choices. She was indeed a lost soul, or Mrs. H had said an old soul. But she was also a loner and a wanderer.

Then a thought occurred. One thing would remain the same from 2015 to today and that was the farmers market. She'd enjoy going there soon and wandering around aimlessly, getting her feet wet. Meet others. It was nice to not see apartment buildings, sports centers and malls.

As her eyelids finally became too heavy, she heard the sweet song of a lovely songbird out on the balcony nestling inside a weave of ivy. Smiling, that song lulled her into a sound sleep.

Chapter Four

"Father, is all of this for me?"

He chuckled. "Sam, if I may call you Sam? We have this after every Tuesday service, brought in by the lovely ladies of our faith community. Now sit, we have a lot to chat about."

"I think I've figured out some of it. If I may be so bold?"

"Go right ahead. I want to hear all you have to say."

"Passages are used for special people to move something of importance from one location to another. Back in time or ahead. I think it's done at religious sites like the *Basilica* in Venice and the church in Shrewsbury. Is your church part of this as well?"

"I'll answer you all at once. Go on. What else do you think?"

"Well, I came here with all the possessions I had with me back in Venice. Mrs. H says that's unusual. I also have a large sum of money on me in today's currency. I wonder why I came with so much? I had quite a tidy sum stowed away back in 2015."

"Did you bring your purse with you?"

"I did, but I spent a small amount of it yesterday on clothing."

"I want you to take out five thousand pounds and keep the rest in there."

She counted it out, rolled it up and held her hand out toward him.

"Am I here to deliver this to you?"

"Nope. You keep it. I think the best way is trial by fire, so to speak. I'm going to send you on a journey. Are you ready to start?"

Sam was momentarily taken aback. So soon? Then ignored all apprehension forming inside her stomach.

"Okay, I think you are right. Let's get the ball rolling. Yes, I am ready."

"Good. Then the money is for the Iona Abbey. Are you aware of its location?"

"Yes, Scotland, just off the coast. Am I going by a certain route?"

"Indeed, you are. Once there, I want you to wait in the confessional until Father O'Malley comes in. He will speak to you in Gaelic, *Dia Idir Sinn Agus Gach Dochar*, which translated means God between us and all harm."

"That's beautiful. I'll remember that. Do I have any special reply?"

"Yes, *Bealtaine e a rai I gconai*, which means may it always be said. That's it, then you always know who your friend is. If, for some reason, you do not receive that reply, get out. Seek cover and use your wits. An opportunity will always arise providing you with safe cover until you are contacted again. Sam, it's not as easy as it sounds. You are going back in time during the Jacobite uprising. The King's Army is all over the place. If you are stopped, you will need to find a way out. If that happens, there is a secondary passage at *Sithean Mor*, it's...."

"I know it. I've been there. It is the Fairy Mounds."

He smiled. "Yes, you were chosen because you are a smart thinker, have few family ties and are independent in means. If you come back that way you may reappear here in Shrewsbury. Or, someplace close to here. We have no control over that."

"What specifically should I take? Will my wardrobe adjust along the way like it did when I arrived here?"

"The pouch, a dagger or small pistol is always a benefit. Remember you are not there to change history. If you need to delay any pursuer, you must do so with careful thought."

"I understand completely. When do I go?"

"Shortly. Now I need your full attention. This is the most important message I can give. If you end up in a different location than I explained, don't think you are in the wrong country. It means you were rerouted prior to your arrival for a purpose. Normally it is for safety. You still are required to complete your journey to get back. If you do not, you are stuck there until you do. So, it's necessary to find a way. That's why you need to keep that purse private, so if the time or need warrants, you can use it to buy yourself out of any predicament. As we both know, everyone does indeed have their price when it comes to turning a cheek."

"Father, I'm nervous yet excited. Show me where to go and let's do this." Her bravado was rising and she was glad it was squashing the anxiety of what was to come.

"Step into the confessional. But, before you do, are there any last questions?"

She nodded.

"God speed, Sam." With that he closed the door and went about his business inside the church, softly singing Ave Maria.

Thankful that the contents of her bag contained modern day items, Sam sat on the wooden confessional, lifted the dress and fastened a small pistol to one leg and a dagger to the other. Sliding her purse up on her right forearm, she clutched her parasol in her left hand, shoved the door open and stepped out into pouring rain.

Momentarily perplexed, she glanced around the area as rain began to fall dampening her hair. Internally, she was thankful at bringing the parasol along while silently wondering what was next.

She glanced in all directions then looked up at the worn, wooden road sign. Then started the short walk on the Road of the Dead leading toward the Abbey.

The harsh weather and bone chilling wind drove a shiver up her spine as she ditched the parasol, pulling the heavy hood up over her cascading hair. With both hand's free, Sam approached the front entrance with trepidation. Beneath the cloak her breasts were heaving as breathing became labored. Silently, she calmed her frayed nerves and glanced about. Stationed outside was a carriage with four horses. But, where were the soldiers and which side were they on?

The heavy wooden door was slightly open. Silently she slid inside and shook out her hood, but kept it on. Swirling around after hearing voices growing in volume, she watched with increasing trepidation at their quick approach. Shit, she silently thought, it was the King's soldiers. She recalled from past readings of this era they were referred to as the bloody Redcoats. Ruthless cutthroats in his majesty's service.

Suddenly, one was standing at attention before her.

"Oh, I am so happy to see you. I was riding with a small party when my horse lost a shoe. Then to make matters worse, she bolted in this nasty rain. I had no choice but to leave my group to come in here to get dry. They are sending a carriage for me when they get back to our accommodations at *Fhonn Farraig*. I find myself grateful for this respite."

The officer surveyed her top to bottom. "Well, madam, we are at your disposal, of course. In just a few minutes we will conclude our business with the good Father O'Malley. Let me introduce myself, Lieutenant Jarred Banks at your service. We are completing rounds before heading to our encampment. My men have nearly completed our search. If you do wish to engage Father O'Malley, he should be with you shortly."

With a click of his boots, the lieutenant turned and disappeared behind a back door at the rear of the Abbey. She stood by taking a few minutes to gather her thoughts, lower her breathing rate and take in the artistic and historical grandeur of the interior. It was indeed a work of art and a momentary welcomed distraction.

Father O'Malley appeared placing a hand gently upon a shoulder.

"My dear, I heard of your plight. How can I help you?"

"Father, I wonder since I'm here if I may ask you for a quick confession?"

"Of course, dear child. You go ahead in while I'll get my vestibules and be right with you."

Sam went into one of the confessionals and shut the door, quickly lifting her dress. Pulling out the roll of five thousand pounds, she slid it inside the tight bodice of her dress and readjusted the cape. The adjoining door creaked open as he sat in his chair, sliding the small screen over.

"Dia idir sinn agus gach dochar."

"Bealtaine e a ra I gconai."

She slid the money into his hand which promptly disappeared as he placed the screen back between them. Thoughts of this process came back momentarily; attendance at mass on Sundays was mandatory with her parents.

"Bless me father, for I have sinned."

Suddenly doors swung open on both sides as two soldiers looked towards Sam and the father a bit apologetic.

"Sorry mistress, father. But, the lieutenant beckons you to his carriage. He wishes to extend his services in returning you to your party. He had no idea you were receiving confession. My apologies. Could this wait for another time?"

Rising and nodding to Father O'Malley, Sam knew an alternate plan needed to be put in place as over the soldiers shoulder another man in red was staring at her with something akin to open interest. Her stomach tightened.

"Thank you, father. It appears my confession shall need to be heard another day. Now, soldier, show me the way. I'll not keep your lieutenant waiting any further."

As the carriage door closed and she settled in opposite the commander, she realized this was her golden opportunity to see what she was made of. Adrenalin coursed through her veins, as she had to try and make out the fairy mound with rain streaking her vision off the windows of the coach.

"Are you well, miss?"

"I am, sir, and want to thank you so much for returning me to my group. I also wish to extend my apologies for delaying you. I thought I may take advantage of the good priest and have a confession." She smiled warmly as he returned one of his own. For a split second, something stirred again about that second soldier back inside the church. Had she seen him before? Biting the inside of her mouth, she refocused on this passage.

"Perhaps I did not have that many sins to abolish since I've been on Iona, after all. Such a holy and sacred place."

He chuckled. "It will be a short ride and we will have you back in no time. I thought you may prefer that as well as your friends in having to send someone out in this foul Scottish weather."

"That is very considerate of you." Apprehension churned as she knew it was now or never.

As the carriage swayed she felt a bit nauseous. "Sir," she lifted her gloved hand up to her mouth, briefly shutting her eyes. "Might I impose once again? Could I please be let out, to… well, it's delicate. My stomach is quite upset suddenly. It must have been our picnic earlier on local food brought in from the sea…" She let that trail off, lowering her head slightly.

He banged on the carriage and bellowed, "Halt, stop the coach. The lady needs assistance."

It grinded abruptly as her stomach truly lurched into her throat as she was assisted down.

"If you would but give me two minutes, I will pass over there by that mound and hope to return shortly."

As she walked away, a brisk breeze removed her hood. Not stopping nor caring, she located the largest mound, *Sithean Mor* and moved around the back side. An opening appeared just as she heard voices coming up behind her. It was the Lieutenant and the other soldier getting closer and closer. Quickly stepping in, within a split second she was back in 1865 sitting in the cold interior of Father Godwin's Church of St. James.

Standing, she exited the confessional quite full of vigor with a large smile displayed across her face. The lighting was fair enough with moon beams streaming through the stain glass windows. She reached over and removed a candle, laughing softly.

"Sorry, Lord." she muttered. "I don't know how to even light it."

She placed it back in its holder and felt her way to the side entrance. But, knew the door would be locked with one of those skeleton keys.

She sighed. "I guess I can't send a text to Mrs. H and tell her I will not make dinner. But perhaps I shall make breakfast." Settling into a pew near the front, she curled into a ball. With a satisfied smile and the moonlight streaming down, drifted off into a sound sleep.

Suddenly, someone was shaking her. Really? At this unholy hour?

Faintly, she heard him. "Sam, you are back. Sit up and come to the rectory. We can have tea and then I will bring you to the estate. They must all be wondering where you are by now."

She sat up adjusting her cloak and checked ensuring everything else was where it should be.

"Oh, hello, father, I'm fine. A good night's sleep I had even though your pews are a bit hard. I was warm enough with my cloak."

She rose, smiling at his grin while taking his arm as they left the church. They were sitting inside the warm rectory before he inquired about her journey.

"It went well I can tell. But, you did have to divert?"

Her eyes were ablaze with a voice just as passionate.

"I did, he has it and yes. A plan b was enacted and worked. You were right, I did encounter a small group of soldiers. But all is well. As you can see, here I am."

She grinned tipping back the cup, "But I have to go. I'll walk through the fields. It will give me a chance to digest what just happened. Father, how will I know where and when to go again? I wonder why I did not end up back in Venice."

"Sam, I think you possibly may not be heading back there. If it was the case, you would be there now and not here. Besides, you arrived with all your possessions. There is also one more bit of detail that makes me think you are staying here. For now anyway."

"What's that?"

"I'll let you find out when you get back to the Earl's estate, by which you had better get going now. Mrs. H came herself last night to inquire on you when you did not come back. I did not tell her your passage details, but she was most anxious you were taking one so soon."

"Thank you, father, I'm sure to see you very soon. I appreciate everything you've done for me." She wanted to hug him, but halted, not wanting to overstep any boundaries of propriety.

Quickly leaving, she ran the whole way back. Reaching the rear entrance, she opened it taking the few steps down to the now active kitchens. No one seemed to pay her much attention except Mrs. H.

"Did you enjoy you early morning walk, my dear? Come, I've a tray of tea and crumpets for you in the drawing room. Hurry now, you must be a bit chilled and hungry."

Sam did not dare to try and get two words in edgewise while following along, cape slung over an arm, until they reached the room. Sipping the tea, she took a bite out of a warm, buttery crumpet and sighed. Oh, yes, this was just what was needed. It tasted so delicious.

"We can chat later, dear, but you have a letter that came yesterday from Freedman's Bank in Chester. I thought it may be something urgent for your quick review."

Sam ripped it open as her mouth gaped. It was a request to come into the bank as soon as possible to discuss her draft account balance and possibilities of investing. It matched exactly what was in her account back in Exeter before all this began. Suddenly, her whole world began to tip upside down. Then on top of this detail, his voice once again permeated to her soul.

"Mrs. Hoyt, good morning. You as well, Miss Arnesen. Mrs. H, I wonder if you'd pardon my intrusion and give me a few minutes with our house guest?"

Sam was just tipping back the last of her tea as her hand stopped in mid-stream. His dark eyes locked with hers as a volcanic shiver passed through her frame.

"Miss Arnesen if you are finished, perhaps you'd accompany me so we can engage in a private conversation?"

Chapter Five

It was an eternal walk of what seemed like miles down lengthy corridors as Sam tried to remain calm. To make matters slightly worse, she glanced over and saw that he housed a slight grin on that damn handsome face. Right about then, she wanted nothing more than to just stick her boot out and send him down to the hard, Italian, marble floor.

When they arrived to their destination, he waved her to a chair, helped her sit, then sat opposite. Even though there was distance between them, she could feel the intensity flowing in great strength.

She did not want to look him straight in the eyes right now. Was that even necessary, she thought, suppressing a grin and twisting the top of her day dress into a ball.

"Considering we've known each other for one hundred and fifty years, should I just start with, hey, Sam, what's new?"

She broke out laughing,

"That's a hell of a way to begin our conversation. But, I can tell you, I'm adjusting. Thinking this is really bizarre dream, but I'm going with it for now."

"Mrs. H was a bit put out last night when you were nowhere to be located. She was forced to take action going over to the good father's place to search you out."

"Yeah, well, my cellphone doesn't come in here, so I was in a bit of a pickle, right?"

He laughed. "So, what's your agenda now? Do you want to ride in the *barouche* with me to Chester this morning? I have business at the bank as well. Give us a chance to get caught up, so to speak."

"Yeah, that actually sounds good. I wanted to talk with you about a few things I could use your help with." She rose, placing both hands on the table top for support. "What's good for you?"

"An hour, be out front."

On her way to the rooms, it occurred to her that with all this money at her disposal, she did not need to stay here. Was that part of the design, to find a place of her own? That thought was quickly shrugged off realizing she needed Adam and Mrs. H's guidance until more was revealed.

Then it became clearer.

Changed and back in the large foyer, Sam smiled warmly at the butler as he opened one of the two large wooden doors. Walking out into the warming day, she glanced down feeling positively pretty in her local Victorian attire. Yes, indeed. One would think she was a proper lady.

"Something got your mirth again? Seems like you are about to break into a laugh at any second." He extended a gloved hand toward her assisting her into the *barouche*.

"I kind of feel like that. I have to admit I like the clothes of this period. You know it's funny. When I was a young girl, I loved reading history about this time. It always fascinated me."

He settled beside her as the coach and horses started down the dirt drive.

"It appears all of our backgrounds and interests combine in special ways to assist us in what we do."

"What I find really astounding is how I took care of my first passage. It's also neat how my clothing altered along the way. My British accent was impeccable."

She seemed so amused. Not wanting to burst her bubble so fast, Adam knew he had no other choice. She seemed to be taking it all in stride. He'd never met any soul like her. Was she in shock? He did not think so, but needed to warn her of the ups and downs. What he wondered deep down was how long would she be here? Would she eventually just disappear one day and he'd have no way of knowing where she was, again?

This may be amusing for her, but it was not for him. This was the very reason he had kept mistresses over the years and no long-term relationships.

"Hello? Did I lose you?"

"Just for a second. So, what are your plans now?"

"After the bank, I will know more. I was thinking it may be a better idea to secure my own place. But then again, I don't know how long I'm here. I don't have a clue what's even next. So maybe that's not a great idea. What do you think?"

His brows raised. "Well, are you comfortable with your accommodations in my home so far?"

"Who would not be? It's lovely. To me it's like a true fantasy and it probably is. I wonder what will ensue when the other shoe falls."

"Sam, it will. It has too; it is not all easy. There are many dangers, diversions and, yes, you can throw in a few pleasures too."

"It's just you and I in this carriage with no danger of being overheard. So, I'll be frank. That explains why you have mistresses. I actually get it."

He nearly choked at her bluntness.

"Hey, it's better than even trying to have a long-term relationship and then disappearing all the time and trying to explain to her you are not cheating."

"Okay, from a lady's perspective we'd naturally think you are lying and cheating." But she wanted to say, if you kiss them like you kissed me, we'd hardly care!

"Are you inadvertently asking me if there are any gents like us that I can introduce you too?"

"Nope, not interested just yet. I want to figure things out a lot more than this before I even consider that."

She nudged his shoulder slightly. "How about getting back to my question?"

"About my mistresses?"

"Don't be an ass, you know what I mean."

His laughter filled the carriage. "I think you should stay put so we can help you. If you take a place and make friends too fast and then disappear, that may raise the awareness of the local law. If you are here and disappear, we can just say you returned to your home in Exeter or have gone off on your own personal holiday jaunt."

"That makes sense, but I would like to pay my way and will not take no for an answer. I am a woman of means."

He crossed his ankles, leaning forward and was met by her very own gloved hand.

"But, Lord Adam, not in the way that was collected previously when you left me in Venice."

She watched as an arrogant grin appeared on his devilishly handsome face causing her jaw to clench. The air inside the carriage filled with a deafening silence and yes, intimate tension.

"Agreed, why don't we take care of our banking business and I'll show you around town before we head back."

"Sure, that sounds fine. But first I need to know something important. In front of your staff, and in public, how do I actually address you?"

She was right, needing to know what to do to acclimate to 1865.

"Either my lord or Lord Griffin, and I prefer the latter. But when we are alone, Adam will do."

"Do I curtsey or is that just reserved for higher aristocracy?" He laughed, patting her hand. "Why don't I let Mrs. H help you out with lady's etiquette stuff. So I don't screw it up."

The carriage pulled to a halt as one of the coachman opened the door and assisted her out. The Earl quickly followed and addressed both men.

"Go have a pint or two. We require about three hours. Meet us at The Red Lion." The coachman nodded as they drove the coach and horses off.

His hand rested at the curve of her back and that slight pressure ripped right through to the other side. They both felt it and knew this was not going to be easy.

"Good morning, Lord Griffin. We were expecting you, so please come this way with your companion." She bristled. Did he always take his mistresses along to the bank? She bit back a snide remark.

"Mr. Jackson, let me introduce you to Lady Samantha Arnesen. She is in possession of a letter from your establishment regarding her accounts. She's a guest at Ard Aulinn, so I hope you do not mind I brought her in with me today without an official appointment."

Yeah, she thought, extending her hand in a firm grip, surprising the banker.

"Lady Arnesen, yes, of course. Let me get you settled with my partner, Mr. Hanlon, straight away. He will be happy to discuss all the options with you."

Seated in a secluded office, she glanced over to Adam in an opposite one. Their eyes met as she smiled. He returned one as her attention then focused on Mr. Hanlon as he came into the room.

"Well, Lady Arnesen, your account is at quite a sizable amount. So, shall we discuss how you may want to invest?"

It took the better part of an hour and a half before they shook hands and she walked out satisfied. Adam met her in the lobby as she placed her hand on his arm and strolled out together. One big perk was that she knew in the future what was big, who built it up that way and how it would turn out for investing. Well, this was a good start in moving back in time.

"You are looking like the falcon that snared the rabbit, madam."

"Feels something like that. Why was the exact amount I had in my bank in Exeter the same as what was transferred here? Any idea on this?"

"That's not something I can explain, Sam. It's just one of the many things that will happen where you will just shake your head and move on."

"I'm obviously going to be sticking around for a while, I'm thinking. Have you noticed all the eyes following us about?"

"Yeah, but the gossipmongers will quiet soon when someone from the bank gets the word out that you are Lady Samantha Arnesen. A guest of the Eleventh Earl of Cheshire. An independent woman of substantial means."

She stopped momentarily as he gazed down upon her beauty.

"Wow, that's pretty cool you can trace your roots that far."

"We actually go back to William the Conqueror. My great ancestor was given extensive land rights and this title, when he served as a general in that army. I can show you his portrait in the ancestry hall at some point."

"I know we all have lineage, after all, there was only one Adam and Eve, right? But, that's impressive, Lord Griffin."

"Very nicely said, Lady Arnesen. Now put your very best aristocratic nose up in the air, for I'm going to take you shopping. We host a ball in a month and if you are still around, you will need a few gowns. What do you say? Are you ready to spend some of that money?"

Together, arm in arm, they entered a very exclusive lady's shop.

Later, her head was so full of muslin this, you must have French lace, oh, Lady Arnesen, you must have ruffles on the sleeves, and hats! Finally, they were finished as she had to admit to being darn hungry.

Strolling back out onto the street, the aroma of fresh bread caused her stomach to react in a most unfashionable way.

"I'll pretend I did not hear that," he chuckled. I have a great idea. Why don't we pick up a hamper so on our way we can picnic? Would you like that?"

"Oh goodness, yes. But, is that proper? No one would think it inappropriate without a chaperone?"

His gaze blazed a heated path right through to her stocking feet as he leaned closer than was proper, that was for sure.

"At our age, we can do what we want. Here or anywhere else."

She blushed as he chuckled, tipping a hat or raising a hand to several whom passed them by. Although a rogue in her eyes, it was clear in this area he was royalty. Grudgingly, she had to admit that the more she was with him the more she enjoyed his company.

"Good day to you both, Mrs. Baker, Mr. Baker. I hope you have been well?"

"Indeed, Lord Griffin. Good to see you again. What can we do for you and your companion?"

There it was again, Sam thought. He must bring his damn mistresses all around town. Morning, noon and night. Irritated, she took over. The hell with etiquette.

"Mrs. Baker, could you please put together a hamper for us? I'd like two of those crusty meat pasties, a wedge of your Cheddar Gorge cheese along with a pair of those delicious looking apple tortes. I think that will do."

Adam stood against the wall glancing out the window letting her have at it. A few minutes later Mrs. Baker brought around a small wicker basket fully stocked.

"Lord Griffin, shall I put this on your ledger?"

Sam wanted to pay but she knew that would cause some unneeded gossip.

"Absolutely and thank you Mrs. Baker."

"Okay, so we need something to drink. Should we secure a bottle of something? I don't know what that would be or where to find it." She was laughing again, softly, leaning precariously close to him as the shopkeeper watched on with a sly grin as they exited the stop.

"Or wine? I don't even know what's proper for this time of day. I've not had my full etiquette lesson yet as you know. But, I will come clean. I never drink during this time of the day. If we do, I am sure I will require a nap in the fields before we go back."

He had no choice but to grin. "Watch yourself woman. Grown men in this day are not supposed to enjoy a lady's company this much in broad daylight. Nor be invited on such short acquaintance to a nap in the field."

She raised a sassy eyebrow at him.

"Fine, stay here. I'll go into that shop and purchase a bottle of wine and two glasses. I will be right back." He opened his mouth to stop her, but too late, she was already scurrying away. He watched her swaying backside enter a different shop wondering how long this would take. Glancing around, the streets were filling up with people and he wanted her quick return so they could get moving along. Looking down, the urge to kick at a stone was strong as the time she was away lengthened.

Then felt a slap on the back. Turning, Adam was greeted by an old friend, Jonas Westman.

"Nice looking basket, old chap, but where's the unwitting snit that you are taking on a picnic?"

"Turn around, she's walking our way now."

Jonas was silent for a second.

"You are just friends, I take it? For I've known you for years and you would never bring any of your mistresses out during daylight hours."

"She's acquainted with Mrs. Hoyt and staying with us for a duration. She needed to come to town. I'm showing her around."

"Including a picnic? I think I should impose and tag along."

"My ass you will and shall get lost just as soon as I introduce you."

"Is that any way to treat a friend? Aren't you still seeing that amazon mistress from... Hell, where exactly is she from?"

"No, she was getting a bit too demanding for my taste, so it was time to bid her *au revoir*."

Both gentlemen turned as she approached with a fancy pouch in hand.

"You were successful, I see."

She smiled giving a swift glance to his friend.

"Lady Samantha Arnesen, let me introduce you to a longtime friend of mine, Lord Jonas Westman. Jonas has an estate down toward Shrewsbury."

She allowed him to take her hand a bit longer than even she knew was proper.

"My pleasure, Lady Arnesen, may I assume you will be at Adam's ball in a few weeks?"

"I am planning on it."

He did not let go of her gloved hand as she smiled warmly up into his golden, brown orbs. She liked him instantly! Was he one of them?

"Let's catch up with a pint soon, eh, Adam? Lady Arnesen, it will be a pleasure to see you again."

She finally had her hand back and had just a second to say, "Thank you, Lord Westman." Over her right shoulder as Adam hastily led her away towards The Red Lion.

The *barouche* and two coachmen were ready as one secured their parcel and the other assisted her inside.

"So, can I ask you a question?"

"About him I presume. I'll tell you right up front he's single and if you think I'm open about mistresses, he's even more so."

His voice was masked well, but she still heard the tenseness in it. "Not that, Lord Griffin. I was wondering if he is one of us like you and I?"

"He is. But you need to be careful. Although we are long standing friends, an ancestor from his past turned out to be a dark horse. There were consequences on both sides."

"This is precisely why you are so important to me. I have a lot to learn between you and Mrs. H. But now, how about a change of subject. Just exactly where are we going for our luncheon? I hope it's near for I really am quite hungry."

"At times you are a bit short on patience, I see. Look, we are already there." Just as he spoke, the door opened. A firm grip on her upper arm kept her from leaping out like a jack-rabbit.

Releasing a disgruntled sigh, she took the coachman's hand, stepped down and politely stepped aside while he got out. Basket and wine in hand, he held the other as she placed her hand over it.

"You were doing good until that appetite of yours got in the way."

"Dang, I'm not about eating like a bird as a lot of women do here. I like my food. Now can we sit and make work of it or not?"

She took a glass of wine from him.

"I'm not sure why I am here, but I am sure it's all your fault. In fact, I am positive about it.

He smiled. "Here's to answers."

He clunked his glass to hers. "Well said. Okay, I know you want to ask, so go ahead."

"Am I that easy to read? Well, the hell with it then. How many are there around here?"

"Mrs. H, myself, Jonas, Mrs. Baker's daughter, Anne, and you are all that I'm familiar with directly. But like I said, you never know who else."

"Aren't Father Godwin and Father O'Malley?"

"No, the priests, reverends and fathers are protectors of the passages. If you ever are in trouble, make sure to locate a nearby church or abbey."

They rose, walking a bit further down a well beaten path as the coachmen took care of the picnic items.

"Can you and Mrs. H do a condensed course, spend some time with me? Is that possible? Or, do most just show up here and there muddling along until they figure it out? I don't suppose there's a manual, and I am not being sarcastic."

He matched her smile. "No manual included and yes, we will help you. The sooner the better as I have no idea when you will head out again. I have a feeling it's going to be soon. You are different, Sam, more so than anyone I've come across."

Even though the men were several yards away, he could not help but notice the effect the wine was having on her. Shit, he did want to kiss her but was a bit worried what could transpire here, out in the open.

"Do you think we can get started when we get back, or am I being a bit too pushy?"

"You are fine, but I cannot tonight. Possibly Mrs. H can. I have plans overnight and will be heading out shortly after we return."

She immediately assumed that meant a visit to his latest vixen.

"Okay, I see they are all packed up and waiting for us. Shall we?"

As they sat opposite each other in the coach, the invisible barrier went up between them. Just as well, he thought, knowing it was the right thing to do. A bit of separation from the chit was required to avoid any unnecessary feelings, that he clearly wanted to avoid, from arising. Tonight, he'd go and enjoy cards, some booze and a good smoke. Let her think what she wanted.

"You okay? You got a bit quiet."

"Yeah, fine, must be I'm not use to drinking wine in the early part of the day. I did warn you I may need a nap, so I guess I can say I was really not joking." Her eyes transmitted asshole, but her words were sugar coated.

He grinned, letting it go.

The coach halted as she nearly jumped out, but remembered her manners just in time; sitting still until the magical white gloved hand appeared. Once they walked through the main doors, she dislodged her hand from his arm.

"Thanks, Adam. It was an educational day and I appreciate you bending the rules for me to see the banker. I'll go now and find Mrs. H. We've got work to do and I'm ready to get it done."

As she swished off, he smiled, not taking his eyes off until she disappeared down a long hall. Whistling, he headed to his study knowing it was a matter of time before he'd need to kiss her again. Regardless of how much distance he wanted to keep between them.

***

But Sam's thoughts had turned in an entirely different direction. Mrs. H had told her she was an old soul. Was there anyone she could talk to about where she originated from? Here there were no computers and internet, so she could not investigate the mere meaning of being one, which would provide much more detail.

Then a thought occurred to her; the House of Record and Deed must be local considering the size of the village. Perhaps there she would be able to secure more details about her ancestry. Mrs. H would know where she could go.

Moving along the hallways, Sam halted, glancing at the beautiful countryside paintings. Hanging side by side, Adam's distant family members were elegantly encased in gold frames. She had to marvel at how wonderful it must be for him to know who he was and where he came from. She sighed, hearing it echo back as it moved through the long hall.

"What's got you sad, Sam?" She spun around to the approaching Mrs. H.

"Just that I wonder about what you said earlier. You know, my being an old soul. Is there any way I can find out where I came from and just what that means? Is there someone I can talk to about this in more detail? I was thinking about the local hall of records, but now that I think about it, would there be by any chance a local gypsy?"

Mrs. H smiled taking her by the arm as they walked to Sam's rooms.

"There is a woman I know in the next village. She is a Tinker. Her small caravan has been welcomed here on Lord Griffin's land for many generations. They return late summer and early fall just before harvest time and leave before Boxing Day. They are here now. If you want, I can take you to her so there is no mischief. They may try to take advantage of you being a strange lady to this area and all."

"I'd like that. Can we go today or tomorrow? You said she's a Tinker, what is that?"

She laughed. "A Tinker is what we British call a gypsy and I don't actually know where that originated from. Maybe we were trying to make it sound less obtrusive and more romantic. You never know. But anyway, we can go tomorrow. I have things to take care of. Plus, some of your parcels have arrived from your trip today and need to be settled. I've sent a maid up to your rooms; she's awaiting you now. If you want to give her instructions, you are then free to do what it this evening. Lord Griffin advised me he will be out tonight. I can have a tray brought to you if you wish."

"I think I'm good. We had a large picnic on our way back. If I want to eat later, I can always meander to the kitchen and find something, right?"

"As you wish, dear. Now go ahead in and let the maid know where you want your things. Tomorrow we can go and see the Tinker."

Wondering what had brought that on, Mrs. H left her at the doors. Sam helped the maid put things away and then dismissed her. Properly attired in a warmer day dress, Sam headed outside for a stroll through the lovely gardens, enjoying the cooler summer evening.

As she walked along the banks of the winding river, Sam kept aware of her surroundings, memorizing the way back. This time though, she had taken her small flashlight and would only use it if necessary since there was no way to replace the batteries when they wore out.

Faintly off in the distance, she heard voices. From out of the brush a young girl emerged with buttercups woven into one long braid. Reaching, she took Sam's hand like a fairy waif. Sam glanced down into the softest brown eyes, smiling, as the little girl smiled back, speaking softly,

"Come, my mother is expecting you."

Stunned silent, she was led to a caravan brightly painted in green, red and orange. The air was thick with the aroma of smoking meats. A plump woman rose and walked slowly toward her, extended both her hands, clasped Sam's tightly and turned them up glancing down at both palms.

"Come, we have a lot to talk about, Samantha Arnesen of Exeter."

They sat inside one of the caravans as Sam's excitement grew at being inside a true gypsy encampment. The noises of preparing food, cutting wood, kids playing and music moved to the recesses of her mind as the woman began to speak. It was her voice. Familiar, reaching deep inside of her being.

"You are an old soul indeed, Sam, I saw your arrival ahead of time and knew you'd be here today. I see many lives on both your palms, so you have been on this plane for thousands of years." She looked deeply into her eyes and held them for several minutes, neither one pulling away.

"You want to know more about where your soul comes from and how old you are." She released her hands and reached behind her, opened a dark velvet pouch and pulled out a beautiful, clear, crystal ball.

"Here, take this and cup it in your hands. It is heavy. Rest your hands on your lap; it will be more comfortable for you. Now, close your eyes and be very still. Let your mind speak to me slowly and ask me your questions in silence. Be patient while I seek your answers. If things do not make sense right now, soon all will be clear. They will unfold for you at the right time and you will completely understand. Are you ready to begin?"

Sam nodded, eyelids dropping.

"I see you lived before in Italy where water is in abundance. I see bridges, artists and seafood. Yes, I believe it was Venice. I see you before that in Norway or Sweden, it's hard to decipher which it was. I see a family crest of an old design. No faces come to me. Oh, yes, they are. It's a man and a woman, married and she's about to give birth. Twins."

She paused.

"Take heed of a soul that is joined to you but not in a romantic way, although this person loves you. I see a cloak with a hooded figure. Wait, the mist is clearing and I see it is a man and he will be diligent in trying to reach you. He is already in your life or will be soon. Beware. But, know he means no undue harm."

Sam thought that must be Adam.

She rushed in a breath and let it out slowly before continuing.

"I see your handsome tall man who does what you do and he's special as well. Almost like your guardian and your lover, combined. You will not marry him. At least as things are now. You have too much to learn, which will discourage him. Be warned, you may drive him away if you do not tell him what your feelings are.

"I see you moving through many destinations and destinies. When you arrived, I glimpsed the land of the Pharaohs in your life. When you go there, more of your past life will unravel. You may be tempted to hold on to this and stay. You will have choices then.

"I see children in your future, but they are not borne by you. But you will love them as your own." She glanced up at Sam seeing the furrow on her brows and continued.

"You made the choice long ago to take passages and you will need to decide in your future where you wish to stay. I see two men you will love, but somehow the love is different. I do not see who you chose. I see both in your life. Yet I see a third man from your past who still haunts you. You must put him to rest and let him go to truly have happiness and closure."

Sam felt strange; the pulsating energy from the crystal ball raced through her arms and energized her entire being. It prevented her from opening her eyes to see if she was through, not wanting these feelings to stop.

It was magnificent.

"I see your numbers are seven-seven-seven. This dates to ancient Egypt and biblical times. You are indeed a fortunate and blessed soul. I do not see danger by your hand or others in your future as you are protected by this long-lost love. Sam, when you two are reunited, you must make sure you do not lose his protection then or in the rest of your lives. If he stops loving you or does not pass that on to another, it could destroy you."

Sam shuddered as the gypsy's voice penetrated her thoughts.

"Look at me now."

Sam's eyelids fluttered, so empowered, as the crystal nearly rolled from her palms onto the wooden floor. She glanced up at the gypsy.

"I cannot go on. Your spirit is so strong. We will finish this another day when it is right. I will see you again, but it may be a while before this happens. I can't tell you more right now."

Sam handed her the crystal, which she rubbed, wrapped and put in the silk pouch and tucked it right away. They stood, eyes locked.

"I feel so strange now, very different, almost like I'm not even in my body but hovering just outside of it."

"Yes, that may stay with you for just a few minutes or for several days, even weeks. It depends upon how much your spirit is attached to the world beyond. You will know when it leaves you. Just like you will know when he leaves you."

Sam reached inside her reticule pulling out some pounds when her hands stopped her.

"No, a time from now a different form of payment will take place. Until then I cannot accept it."

Sam was clearly dazed walking down the three small wooden steps. Feet finally planted firmly in the grass, she began her walk back hearing the parting comment.

"Sam, when it's time to go to Egypt, just go, and remember you are always protected."

She stopped, but did not turn around. In a complete haze, her boots seemed to know the direction back to the estate. Those words echoed. Her body and mind reacted.

Egypt. The land of the Pharaohs, mysticism, scribes, ancient customs and belly dancers. Glancing down her hands shook, as she moved on, taking the secluded walk back through to her room. Right now, she was glad Adam was not here. She was glad Mrs. H would have a tray sent up to her, but mostly she was glad to have started her true venture. The one that would give her final closure.

Chapter Six

The gypsy woman's remarks remained with her. Some made sense, some did not. She was thankful that no further passages took place as time ticked by. Mrs. H was still smarting about her taking matters in her own hands and going to visit them without her knowledge until after the fact. She promptly chided her for being a bit of a rogue herself. Although Sam had to admit, her own version of what rogue meant leant more toward Lord Griffin than her taking an adventure.

Adam had been conveniently absent. But had heard him a time or two and saw him out in the fields riding with a woman dressed in a very expensive habit. So, had his roaming and mistresses returned? She hardly gave it much thought in lieu of what was ahead of her. Keeping him out of her life right now seemed vital if she was to succeed in discovering more.

He had merely given her a reason to not seek him out. That stolen kiss and their one day out in the town was now quite behind her.

Then it was the weekend before the ball. Her gowns had finally arrived giving a needed diversion. As she opened the large boxes and unwrapped the soft tissue paper, she admired each of them side by side. She grinned, knowing how much she'd enjoy the preparation in getting those on just as much as wearing them.

Leaving them as they sat for the maid to attend, Sam stood at the double-wide French doors overlooking the grounds and smiled, believing a spirit was sharing these rooms with her. The presence of another woman.

"I know you are with me madam. I can smell violets." Slowly she turned around leaning against the railing.

"Go ahead. I give permission. You can shuffle them around when I leave and I nor the maid will be any the wiser."

All she had been able to learn about her strange room partner was from a few of the hesitant, older staff members. She was a woman who liked the soft flowery perfumes of a by-gone era and still enjoyed running her hands along a dress sewed to perfection using the finest silk.

After spending the last few weeks in these rooms and time with Mrs. Hoyt and Father Godwin, today she felt like a walk to town to visit Mrs. Baker.

Resplendent in her day attire, Sam threw a shawl over her shoulders, grabbed her reticule and parasol and headed out. She was getting antsy though now; she wanted to find Adam and insist he let her move into a cottage she'd found abandoned on the property. She was going to offer to pay for renovations and a nice sum for monthly rent. She'd hire someone reliable to help her with these tasks. Now all she had to do was get him to agree. That would, of course, rely on when a moment could be snared from his dalliances.

Just as much as she'd avoided him, he had been doing the same. That was quite clear. But with a plan now in mind, she wanted to move forward. If it took cornering him at the ball, then so be it. It was the perfect solution. Secure and reclusive. But, where the devil had that bloke been?

Shrugging her shoulders, she nodded to the doorman in passing and left out the front entrance. It was nice now she did not feel the need to advise her comings and goings to anyone.

Opening the parasol and heading down the main lane, a smile lit her face as the Baker's daughter, Anne, speaking rather loud, was fast approaching.

"I was just on my way to see you. Are you set on a particular task or just a stroll?"

"Nothing too important. You have that look in your eyes. Do you want to go back to my rooms and have a chat?"

"We need to."

Tingles began in Sam's body. "Good, come on. I take it your parents are fine?"

"Yes, they are. I come with a hello from them both." The butler eyed Sam as he opened the doors and let them both in.

"Is that one of your new dresses from the shop?"

"It is nice. I think he does excellent work. I just got my ball gowns. Do you want to look?" The two exchanged glances as they hit the upper staircase. Their pace increased.

Glancing quickly down both hallways, Sam closed her doors soundly.

"What is going on?"

"Father Godwin thought it may be a good idea for you to come with me on a bit of an adventure. Not quite sure what it is yet. You know how that goes. It involves France and a hat shop, that's about all I know."

"A shopping trip?" Sam smiled. "And you need an experienced shopper because you are too young to make good choices? Oh, I get it." They both shared a laugh. "When do we go?"

"Now. Do what you need. I'm ready. Then we can finish our walk in an entirely different direction."

Sam never left the estate without her pistol, knife, extra ammunition and a small hand bag. Everything else was unnecessary. Suddenly, she halted. A nagging sensation resonated throughout her body as she heard a faint voice inside her head questioning what she was doing. Was it intuition or the spirit sharing her rooms? Heaving the shawl down, she grabbed a small backpack and a hooded cape instead.

"Anything else you think I need?"

"No, let's go. I'm going to try and get you back for your first ball at *Ard Aulinn*. We never know how long any of these trips will take."

Sneaking silently out of the servants' entrance, they chatted quietly through the field. Instead of the familiar left bend toward the church, they went right toward an abandoned rectory long ago left for ruins from the Saxon days.

"I did not even know this was here. Is this on the Earl's property, or are we off it at this juncture?"

"Still on it. They keep this building intact for obvious reasons." She smiled.

"But, there's no confessional. I only see that cellar hole which looks none to inviting."

"Oh, come on. There will be some cobwebs. Pull on your cloak and hood, hold my hand, and follow me."

Stumbling a bit down the few stone steps, the brightness of the day quickly faded into total darkness. Continuing along and up, loud shouts were heard as gunfire rang out. The earth shook with explosions. The dark gave way to light as they climbed the last few steps then halted in disbelief. The streets were in rubble as men in uniforms rushed by them, seemingly unaware of their presence.

Sam watched as a horrified look come over Anne's features which forced her into swift action.

"Get low. Do not under any circumstance let me go. Now run! We need to reach a safer area!"

Crouching, they stumbled over the debris and sped toward a large pile of rubble as bombs continued to explode all around them. Sam's body shook down to the core.

Never had she felt so removed and surreal as she did right this very moment.

Tugging Anne's hand, she pulled her down an alley just as the corner of the stone building was nearly leveled by another bomb. "Quick, this way!"

As the blistering noise started to recede, she turned down a small side street. Then she knew what they were looking for. There it was surrounded by so much wreckage. Staring at the sign hanging on one chain, she read the fading words: *LaBonte Magasin de Chapeau.*

"In here now." She pushed in the door tugging Anne along then secured it. As they moved toward the back of the shop, she saw it.

"Oh, my God! It is a baby in that basket. Sound asleep even through all this noise." Sam crept over and moved the rough, woolen blankets aside, appraising. "It's a boy and a note written in French. It asks us to bring the baby to Nancy. There is a great battle about to begin in Verdun and he needs to get to safety. It's very important to his future."

She handed the note over to Anne who crumpled it into a ball then slipped it inside her dress pocket.

Sam knew she had to take control of this situation. Now.

"You will be the mother, I your lady maid. I am a bit old to have a young one. But, you fit the bill. Look. There are supplies, water, powder milk, cloth diapers and pins. God, am I glad I brought my backpack."

She shoved everything into it, slid off her cloak, draped it over a shoulder and put it back on. Ann suddenly broke out in laughter. Sam glared at her.

"You look like the hunchback of *Notre Dame.*"

"Oh, shut up you chit. This is no time to crack jokes." But Sam did smile realizing how hideous she must look. "I don't want to wake the tyke to check his diaper, so let's get him up and going. I can't even begin to see how we are going to get to Nancy. There must be a way already awaiting us and we need to get the heck out of here and find it."

Outside the building Sam glanced frantically for some instinctual direction to come to her. Seconds ticked by when finally her feet started to move. Grasping Anne's arm tightly with one hand, she kept the baby close with the other.

"Shit."

"What? Do you smell horse dung or something?"

This brought Sam out of near panic.

"No, I am looking for some kind of a sign to help us know which direction to take. Hold on, I've something in my reticule that will help. Here is the baby."

Steadying her shaking hand, she removed a circular compass on a key chain.

"What is that?"

"A directional device called a compass. Okay, I have a reading. It is down this street. You hold tight onto him and stay right behind me. Grasp my cloak; if I move too fast I want you to tug it. Don't you dare let go, I mean it!"

Passing quickly by a dilapidated shop front where only the beams remained, Sam glanced down pulling out a bundle. It was a wrapped block of cheese, or smelled like one. Slipping it under her cloak into the side pocket of the backpack, they hurried along never losing pace.

As they moved out of town she took compass readings. Periodically glancing up at the darkening sky praying it would be cloudy as hell tonight. Silently, they crept along keeping parallel to a stream.

"Stop. Hush. I need to listen. But come closer. Let's stay in this brush for a few seconds." A short paused ensued. "I knew it. I can hear voices, but I need to make sure they are French so we need complete silence." Precious moments ticked by as just on the other side of the steam she made out a small band of French soldiers. She threw a stone their direction speaking rapidly.

"*Soldats, nous avons esoin de votre aide.*" [Soldiers, we need your help.] That got their attention as two of them waded through the stream and crouched down in her face.

"*Ou devez-vous aller?*" [Where do you need to go?]

"*Nancy.*"

"*Venez avec noir.*" [Come with us.]

One stood helping Anne and the baby. Miraculously, he had not caused a fuss at all. A lengthy silence followed as they joined the band of men. As the pace quickened, Sam was near begging them to slow down when she saw soft flickers of light up ahead. They were swiftly ushered into a makeshift tent.

"*Notre commandant va vous parler, eu de temps.*" [Our commander will speak with you, shortly.]

Sam nodded as both women simultaneously expelled a deep sigh.

"He's gone to get his commander who will speak with us shortly."

Anne nodded and whispered so softly, Sam had to lean right up to her quivering mouth to hear. The poor girl had clearly never been in anything like this before. Now it was completely clear why Sam was along.

"I think we should feed and change him soon."

"Agree, as soon as we speak with the Commander. Do you, by any chance, speak French?"

"No, I've never been out of England before, Sam. I'm scared as hell."

"Don't worry it appears I do and quite fluently. So, I guess we are all set. I'll tell him what he needs to know."

The flap parted as a rather rugged, tall soldier entered. His presence filling the small tent. Bowing, he removed his hat addressing Sam.

"Bonsoir, Madame, Je suis Commandant Philippe Petain, vous avez un problem?" [Good evening, madam. I am Commander Philippe Petain. You have a problem?]

"Commandant, vous etes un grand soldat que j'ai entendu parler de vous. Ma pupillr est avec le bebe et son pere est moty. Nous cherchons le transport de Nancy." [Commander, I have heard that you are a great soldier. My mistress has a baby and his father is either dead or injured. We need transport to Nancy.]

"Oui, nous avons un hospital, il y a un camion peut vous prendre." [Yes. We have a hospital. There is a truck that can take you.]

"Combien de temps pouvons-nous partir?" [How long?]

"Encore trois jours." [Another three days.] He nodded, secured his hat and left the tent speaking to the soldier posted outside. Believing they were out of danger, at least for the moment, Sam let out a heavy sigh of relief.

"What did he say?"

"In three day's a truck will take us to Nancy where they have a hospital. I do believe, my friend, that is where our little bundle will be left. It's just a hunch, so it is very important that we keep our eyes and ears open and mouths shut while we are here. Especially you. As I don't want them suspicious of your obvious British accent, even though the country's men are here fighting alongside the French."

She slid the cape from her shoulders and took out a small glass baby bottle filled with water. Let out a little and put in the powdery substance. Known in the period as *Mellin*. It looked utterly distasteful. But once she shook the bottle and handed it to Anne, the baby latched on with a bit of a smile. Glancing back and forth to them both.

Did this little boy have any idea what his world held in store? That was hoping they got him to Nancy and it worked out right.

As Anne fed him, Sam disrobed his lower section and put a new diaper on. Secured with pins, she held up the old one wondering what the hell to do with it. She hardly could throw it in the laundry and have it warm and clean in forty-five minutes. Unfortunately, there was a short supply and it was needed.

Knowing the soldier was posted outside, she opened the flap. Unflinchingly, he poised his gun in front of her preventing further movement. It was the shine of his bayonet that mesmerized her for a second.

"*Je besoin de quelque chose dans lequel se laver sa couche.*" (I need something in which to wash diapers.)

The soldier smiled, jerked his head to indicate she was to go back inside than walked off.

A couple of minutes later he produced a large tin can with hot water, placed it inside the tent, lowered the flap and disappeared.

She grinned. "Maybe he thought I'd ask him to wash it." She dunked it inside the pot swishing it around with her hands until it looked clean enough. The rope supporting the tent was a great place to start a laundry line.

"I am so glad you are with me, Sam, I'd not know what to do. You are so smart. No wonder F.G. wanted me to get you."

"F.G., now is it? You make me smile. But, we are a pair, so don't give it another thought. It is very clear we need each other, that's why we were teamed up. Look. He is now sleeping. Why not try and get some rest yourself? I am going to. We have no idea how far we are from the front lines. But, it seems pretty quiet right now."

Having recalled a history lesson long ago about the Battle of Verdun, Sam was not going to tell Anne why she knew they were probably closer to enemy lines than either would like. Hopefully, they would be in Nancy before the bloody battle took place. Their little bundle safely tucked with whomever, and could about face back to jolly old England.

Two days passed and the best they could do was dig holes to relieve themselves, knowing the encampment was busy as hell. At one point, the guard did not stop her as Sam took a chance and peeked out and saw the strangest looking contraption off in the distance. It was not a tank. Or, she had the wrong year in her head. Rather a jalopy with a back bed and canopy.

Inside, she watched Anne who was becoming quite fond of the little guy. What a gem he was hardly fussing at all. He seemed to know it was important to behave. If Sam had known kids could be like that, she may have considered having a few of her own. But as time and divorce took over, she realized her chance to having them had passed.

"One more day Sam. Should we make sure they remember we are still here? It's been nice of them to provide a pot of food every night. "

"If we don't see them come sunrise, I'll ask the guard outside if I can speak with someone. Commandant Petain seemed keen to see us there, though, so I trust him."

She was right. The next morning before sunrise, the flap opened startling them both as their guard motioned them out.

"*Guardez le silence, mesdames.*" (Keep silent, ladies.)

They both nodded yes. Glancing down at the still sleeping baby, Sam was pleased they had him in a fresh diaper and a bottle of milk powder already mixed.

Ushered up and into the jalopy, they both eyed the large red painted cross on both sides. Flap closing, the driver ground the gears as the strange contraption moved forward. Normally, these vehicles were neutral to ambush and bombings. But, perhaps it was not a sure bet and that was why their departure was so early before sunrise.

She wanted desperately to peer out and see how many were accompanying them, but did not dare. They had been so good to them. By the enormous sounds rumbling off the earth beneath the truck's tires, she estimated it was a large ensemble moving on.

Anne rested the baby on her lap while reaching into a side pocket and produced a wrapper.

"That soldier put this in when he helped me up. Look. We have some chocolate."

As if on cue, Sam's gut grumbled. For never had something looked so good. As she ate her piece, she glanced down at her hands. It was hard not to notice they were dry and cracked from cleaning nappies in the hot water. She did not care.

"You have been hogging that little man, but at this point I'm nervous to take him. I think he's adjusted to you so well. Someday if you have kids, you will make a wonderful parent."

"Why did you not have any? Oh, I'm sorry, Sam, I should not pry."

How was she to tell her about divorce? They had that back in 1865. Heck, Henry VIII was a pro at it long before, but it was just not worth discussing at this juncture.

"I was so busy with my life by the time I realized it... well, here I am. A bit too old to begin. I did not want to raise kids and have their friends think I was their grandmother not their mother."

Anne laughed. "Sorry, but that's a really good point."

"I'll make sure you pay for that later."

A bump nearly sent them all to the roof of the truck and back as they steadied. The baby's eyes opened as both waited with baited breath to see if he'd scream bloody hell at being bothered so.

But he smiled.

Unfortunately, that bump caused a tire to puncture as they stopped and were ordered out to wait between the vehicles while it was patched and re-inflated.

Then all hell broke loose as soldiers started yelling. The threesome were thrown to the ground and held there by two other armed men as shots ricochet all around. Suddenly Sam's confidence evaporated. What should they do? Crawl beneath the vehicle? What if they threw a grenade? Should they stay put and be in the line of fire? When a hot, searing sensation pulsated up through her leg. Lifting her dress up slightly, a small pool of blood had formed.

The gunshots finally stopped as they were helped back up by a small band of French soldiers who had reappeared from the brush. Quickly, they were ushered into the back, the others boarded and the transports started moving again.

"Oh, to all that's holy, Sam, you are shot! I see the blood forming on your dress. We need to do something right away. You could be in real danger and I need you!"

Anne's voice was reaching a fever pitch as the baby started to cry and Sam knew she needed to act fast, both for her leg and calming Anne down.

"Stop it, I say. You stop that right now. It's only a scratch." She leaned down ripping the ruffle from her petticoat beneath and tied it around her leg, staunching the flow. "Now you sit still and calm yourself. The baby has been through enough already. He hardly needs hysteria right now. We are on our way, aren't we?"

That worked, harsh as it was. Sam held her hand up halting Anne's apology.

"Nope, don't do it. It's done. We are fine. Learn a lesson from this Anne. You leave your emotions at home. Let's move on. Surely by now he must be hungry. Give him a half feed. We will cap the rest for when we get to our location. Just in case we need to keep our supply running longer."

But the stinging from the wound reminded Sam it required attending. The bullet needed to be removed, leg sanitized to avoid infection. Clenching her jaw, she knew it could not wait any longer. It had to be done.

"I am going to get the bullet out now just to be safe. I have perfume in my reticule which has alcohol to sterilize. Then I'll bandage it back up. The only reason I'm going to do this now is so you can see my process in case you ever need to know. You pay attention and don't go squeamish on me, girl."

It was the tip of the knife going into the wound that made her eyes water. Clenching her teeth, she continued along until it popped out onto the floor of the truck bed. Once the wound was cleaned and bandaged, she wiped the knife, placed it back and lowered her dress.

"You are so brave, Sam."

"Hogwash. It's just a precaution. I'd better hurry. I think we are starting to slow down."

Sam refused to glance up at Anne during the process and finished just in time lowering her dress.

The vehicle had come to a stop and back flap opened and they were assisted outside.

"Nancy?"

"*Oui, Madame, l'hopital est la.*"

"*Je vous remercie.*"

She grabbed Anne's arm and headed. The streets of Nancy were still smoking from last night's bombs. Locals that remained picked through debris searching for what she hoped was pictures or clothing and not deceased family members.

They had to find out who was going to take this baby. As they walked down the steps and into the infirmary, Anne halted. Neither had ever witnessed so many wounded, bleeding soldiers. Cries filled the air as blood streamed on the cold cement floors.

"Get a hold of yourself, there's a nurse coming toward us and she looks like she's about to burst into tears."

As the woman approached she spoke to them in a mix of French and English. "Mon bebe, oh, you bring him safe."

Anne held him out as the woman clutched him so tightly, a squeal emerged from his tiny mouth. Lowering her head, she kissed both his cheeks as tears streamed down her face.

Sam had to know. "*Est-il votre neveu?*" [Is he your nephew?]

"*Non*, no, he is my son. How did you know it was me he belonged to? How to find me?"

Sam cried. Anne cried. The mother cried.

"I did not. We just needed to get someplace safer than Verdun and came here." She knew not to ask or say more. "*Ou est l'eglise?*" [Where is the church?]

"*Deux rues plus loin.*" [Two streets away.]

They hugged as Sam moved on with Anne. "Come on, we need to get the heck out of here before all hell breaks loose. Our work is now done. She told me there is a church two streets down. That has to be our exit point."

"Oh, my goodness. How will I ever be able to get used to not knowing where I am going until I get there? Then respond in horror if I am ever anywhere like this, Sam?"

"You are special, girl. Do not sell yourself short. You were chosen, remember? You need to look beyond all of this and always focus on what needs to be done and go about your work. That's it."

As they walked into the church, glancing around, their arms locked while descending. Both were amazed that the stairs were still intact walking down into the crypt. Torches lit the dank, stone corridor. As they came out the other side, Sam nodded to Anne. They had made it and were back at the ruins on *Ard Aulinn.*

"We did it! Oh, Sam, I wish I could tell F. G. and my parents. I must go; I need to go. I want to see them and my room and… well, eat!"

Sam laughed waving her off. Then headed toward the side entrance of the great estate.

The house was ablaze with light and even though she was in the back, she could hear voices wafting toward her from the front. Oh, my God, she thought. Had so much time passed? It became imperative to get to her room, clean the wound and then locate Adam.

Determination set in. She was going to have that needed conversation tonight and that was that. Period.

Chapter Seven

Into the shadows, she slipped. Hiding a few times to avoid servants until she made it into the bedroom. Gas lamps were lit inside. Her handmaid Abbey was anxiously awaiting her arrival. Pacing, clearly in a tither.

"Lady Samantha! Oh, my goodness. I am so glad to see you. His Lordship had been here three times asking about you."

Sam smiled. "Abbey, I can't explain why I am tardy and a bit messy right now. We have no time to waste. I need to get into the tub. But more than that, I would like you to go and get a few things right away. You must pledge to do it quietly. I need plasters. I had a bit of a spill this afternoon. Nothing too serious. I require it for my leg before I can get dressed."

"Oh, yes, miss. I will be right back. Go ahead and get into the water. It is warm. I had it poured a while ago. When I return, I will help you get dressed. You will be late, but make it."

She was such a cute little thing, Sam thought, as she disrobed, removed the make-shift bandage and slid into the refreshing water. "Ah, this is just what the doctor ordered." Scrubbing vigorously with the thick lavender soap, she rinsed and dried off. The wound looked pink which was a good sign. It would heal properly. Foot resting on the side of the porcelain tub, she poured alcohol over it.

Yup, it stung like bloody hell as she flinched, teeth clenched tightly while finishing the task.

Grabbing the healing balm out of the bag and smothering the area, she slid back onto the fainting chair trying to suppress a grin as Abbey strode in.

Her cheeks were as bright as her eyes.

She was enjoying this!

"How should I wrap your leg, mistress? Oh, that looks horrible. Shall I go get Mrs. Hoyt, or fetch a physician for you? No one saw me. I made sure of it. But, now I am thinking you could use some assistance."

"Heck, no. I can do it. Here, watch me in case you have a child someday and you need to wrap a bandage. There, see, it was so easy. Now where do we begin? I see you have both my gowns pressed and out. Which shall I wear?"

"You want my opinion? Well, they are both so lovely, but I think the soft creamy yellow will look so nice since it is still summer."

"Okay. Let's do it."

A full stream of layers came one after the other: white silk stockings up over her knees secured with garters, cotton drawers, a sleeveless chemise. More ensued. A corset which nearly had her gasping for breath, then petticoats followed at last by the gown.

"My, gosh, Abbey, I'll be in a sweat before I even get down the stairs. Please be a dear and open a window while I put on my slippers. Oh, these are lovely."

As Sam went over to have her hair done up in a swirl, she glanced down at unfamiliar rectangular boxes on her dressing table. "What are these? They are not mine."

"I have no idea, mistress. When I came to wait earlier, they were already here."

Sam opened each side by side then gasped. They housed a set of gorgeous, sparkling jewelry that matched whichever gown she chose.

Sliding her fingers over each piece, she knew it was Adam as her eyes misted.

"Let's get my hair done. Then I'll put on the citrine set."

As Abbey fastened the gorgeous necklace, Sam put in the drop earrings. Both women's eyes met in the mirror.

"Let's do something fun before I go down. Here." Sam turned to Abbey with the other set in her hand. "I want you to put these on so you know you could wear them too. They are not just for rich types like me." She smiled.

"Oh, mistress, I could not... but, oh it's so tempting. If you are sure?" Sam stood and helped turning her toward the mirror, "See? You are just as beautiful, Miss Abbey."

As the box was restocked and placed in the upper draw, Sam grabbed her evening bag. With one last smile toward Abbey, she closed the door. Feeling a bit out of sorts now, she wanted a different entrance than the large grand staircase straight into the path of the aristocrats below.

Slipping down a side entrance and weaving slightly from her stiff leg, Sam finally found the hall leading to the dining room. Beyond was the great ballroom. She had made it. From here she'd find him and hopefully a few other faces she may know. Halting in the shadows, she removed from her clutch a small flask and took a hearty swig of rum. Ironically that did the trick. She screwed the silver cap back on and tucked it neatly back inside.

The moment she entered, a swarm of older dowagers descended all demanding answers. Where did she come from? How long was she staying? Did she come from money? How were she and the Earl acquainted? She smiled, ready to answer with a bold outright lies.

Then she felt his close proximity and scrutiny.

Turning, she weaved through throngs of couples and halted in the middle of the large dance floor.

As if on cue, the orchestra began a Strauss Waltz.

"You are the most beautiful woman in the room."

Her heart hit her throat with a thud, but this was not the time nor the place her inner thoughts reminded.

"That's kind of you to say with so many lovely ladies here. I do have to apologize for being delayed to your festivities tonight, Lord Griffin. But, with all this going on, I'm sure you did not miss me."

Her barb struck.

Looming over his shoulder, a tall brunette eyed her with open and apparent venom. Oh, yes, one of the mistresses was in the house tonight. Sam grinned up into his eyes, but what she truly desired was to give him a good swift kick in a shin.

"Ah, Lord Adam, there is a woman over your shoulders who looks a bit put out that you are engaging me in conversation on this dance floor. I do not think this is such a grand idea if you two are to be acquainted later. That is, to continue dancing with me. But, of course that is just my opinion."

He smiled.

"I can feel her eyes in my back. Or, they are daggers? So, shall we? As my guest in this house, it is my duty to take the first dance with you. She should know protocol by now.

"Oh, I see."

Taking her gloved hand into his, he settled the other on the small of her back. Swirling around faster and faster, Sam finally winced, squeezing his hand for a brief second.

He did not stop, but slowed, "You are hurt. Where?"

"Leg. It is fine, should be fit as a fiddle in a few days."

"We can talk about it later. Would you rather sit or come around the room with me and meet some people?"

"My mind is busy, Lord Griffin, so I do apologize again. For I am not the most suitable partner for you at this moment." Halting at the far side of the room as the music ended, Sam nodded to the brazen brunette then released his grip.

"Lord Griffin, I do think this is your partner. I thank you for taking a spin with me and performing your perfunctory duties. Now you are free to enjoy the evening."

Adam's eyes darkened as their gazes locked. She looked boldly into his. With a slight curtsy and a satisfied grin, she swished off toward a gathered group of lades she was acquainted with from town.

He turned towards her knowing it was coming.

"Leah at this point I'd prefer you not utter a word. She's my house guest. Actually, that it is not entirely true. She is under the guidance of Mrs. Hoyt. They are acquainted. So, let's not make a show of it right now."

He was clearly agitated by what that chit had done. But as he swirled his latest mistress around the room, the sparkle of the gems resting against Sam's soft skin nearly had him missing a step as he contemplated wringing her beautiful neck.

Sam was deeply engaged with two men he knew to be clear rogues and was having a time of it. He housed no doubt she was retaliating. Or was she? As his mind worked, his body responded like a robot out on the dance floor. Did she think of him as just a situation she found herself in? All because of that kiss and what followed?

Ah, hell, he concluded. Let her act up. Right now, he had other things to take care of.

"Really, Adam, this is tedious. You are not even listening to a word I've just said. I'm not that fickle that I don't recognize your eyes wandering to where she is. Am I wasting my time here?"

Lowering his eyes down to the pretty woman, he knew it was time to get rid of this one as well. Damn.

"You know I don't apologize, so don't look for one. If my lifestyle does not agree with you, then I can send for a carriage and have you taken home. It's of no consequence to me, Leah."

"I'm fine right here. I'll let your man know when I want that carriage. But be assured I'm ending it now before you do." He shrugged as the music ended, bowed relinquishing her hand. "Of no consequence, like I said. You do as you will."

***

With the next three rounds under her belt and three different handsome partners, Sam had to admit she was glad when this last jig ended. Followed with the bell ringing for dinner. Her leg was smarting, but it was her own damn fault with that last dance. No one would be the wiser. But, she was in enormous discomfort.

Except for him. He knew.

Settling her hand slightly on his extended arm, she subconsciously touched with the other the beautiful gems encircling her neck. "These are beautiful, are they family heirlooms?"

"Yes, my great-great grandmother. You do them justice." She was being directed into the large dining hall. "I have you sitting opposite me, Jonas will be on your right and his sister, Annabelle, on your left. Just make sure you keep your conversation light." As he pulled her chair out she settled as a finger grazed a right bare shoulder. An uncontrollable shudder passed straight through. His eyes raked her forcing additional discomfort as her eyes followed him until he sat.

Glancing down the long rectangular table, Sam saw his mistress sitting precariously close to a middle-aged soldier dressed in full British regalia. Adam caught her questioning gaze before quickly looking away. Was this how he treated all his women of love interest? Or, was it lust interest? She was not going to be a part of his probably long list. No frigging way, but there was a bit of chemistry existing between them and she was determined to extinguish it right now before falling prey to his insurmountable charms.

It was as if they were already lovers sharing many private thoughts and moments. For they did indeed have this peculiar and special gift in common.

Minutes ticked away as she felt the heat of Adam's gaze sweep over her. A twinge of something unfamiliar weaved through them both as their eyes locked. It was there. Something very tangible.

"I take it your delay was unavoidable, Lady Arnesen, but I am glad you arrived. Let me introduce you to my sister, Annabelle. Annabelle, Lady Samantha Arnesen, from Exeter."

She nodded a hello.

"How long are you here? Do you mind if I use your given name?"

"Of course, you may. I am not sure exactly how long I will stay. I believe it will be of some duration at this point. Lord Griffin has kindly given me free rein while I visit with a close family friend."

"Someone we know?"

Sam was not sure she should say who in this crowd of snobs, glancing at him for guidance. His sly smile said she was on her own, testing her again - the damn bloke!

"No, I'm sure you would not know her. Tell me, Annabelle, wherever did you have your gown made? The workmanship looks positively Parisian."

His foot grazed her right leg as she winced slightly, but still managed to keep her attention on her companion. Vain, the woman was vain, but it had worked. On and on she droned discussing the gown, the custom lace made in the same shop as the Queen, the button fabric - blah, blah, blah - as Sam worked her way through the courses. Thankfully, no one else got a word in edgewise.

As the Earl rose signaling cigars and port for the gents, the ladies left in clusters to the drawing room for coffee, sweets and a full platter of gossip. This was the part she wanted nothing to do with and he knew it.

Great, she thought, as three old crones came her way plastering a smile on her face.

"Lady Samantha, we have a small wager going on. I think the jewels you are wearing are from London, Mrs. Tuttle thinks Paris and Miss Christie thinks they are from America. So, you need to settle this for us. Rarely have the three of us seen gems so beautifully set."

"Actually, they belong to Lord Griffin's family. He lent them to me this evening. I believe they are from his grandmother's side, which is Welsh." She smiled, waving her fan for a few seconds. "They are lovely, aren't they?"

The expression on their faces was priceless.

"If you will please pardon me, ladies, I am a bit parched. I think I'll go in search of refreshment. Can I offer to get something for any of you?"

Moving around the chatter, Sam felt a dire need to bolt. Screaming all the way at the top of her lungs. Thank heavens the butler rang for rejoining in the ballroom. Great, a few more dances and the evening would be over, she realized when suddenly he was there, blocking an exit.

"I insist, my dear, you dance the next with me." It was of course, Jonas,

"I'd be delighted. But not a jig or reel. It would be lovely if it was something a bit gentle, if you will, as this night has taken its toll on me."

Shit, she wished she had not said that. Not wanting to lead this dude on in any way. As a matter of fact, she did not trust him at all, even though Adam's report on him previously only said to be cautious.

As the waltz started, he danced her out on to the floor and swirled them around the room. Heat radiated throughout her leg and it was clear enough was enough. Tempting as it was to just walk off leaving him there, Sam stuck it out. He turned out to be one of those pompous aristocrats, blathering on about something. Exactly what did he do, anyway, when on a passage? Kill someone, steal, just be a jerk? With amusement, she let him just babble on.

"Jonas, mind if I step in?"

"Not at all my friend." As he stepped aside, tipped a finger in a mock salute then sauntered off to sip a scotch off an offered tray.

"I'm actually grateful for your interference this time. Thank you. I'm going to have to sit soon or go back to my rooms and put my leg on a chair cushion."

"Can you hang on a bit longer? I can walk you up as there is something I would like to ask you. I believe this is the last dance. Then the staff will start to usher the guests out."

"I can do that."

"Then wait for me in the foyer toward the side stairwell. It will be closer to your rooms."

Never taking her eyes from him as he thanked people as they left, she sifted between ladies putting on capes and gentlemen their hats. Maneuvering unnoticed until reaching the location he spoke of, an appealing chair beckoned. Slumping down into it, exhausted, it took only minutes before she drifted off into sleep. Then she felt him. Again.

Kneeling, Adam placed hands over hers on a lap covered with yards and yards of silk. He did not want to wake her, but she needed a bed. There was no way he could successfully carry her the country mile it was up to her rooms without that happening.

"Sam," he softly shook her as sleep-filled eyes opened slowly. She smiled, silently rising as he held her hand and they headed up

She opened the doors realizing that Abbey would need to be rung to help her with all the back buttons on the gown.

"I do have something I want to talk to you about, if you have a couple of minutes. First though, would you please undo these? Tonight, I've no patience to wait on Abbey. Surely she is already snugly tucked into bed. Also, I want to give you back both sets of jewels."

Turning, presenting her back, she gave him no time to protest. Chuckling, he started at the top and slowly worked his way down.

"I was thinking tomorrow, if you are up to it, that we'd ride to Wales. I have business to conclude and I think you would benefit from meeting this couple. Is your leg up for it?"

He had finished helping her out of the gown as it fell in a swirl to the floor. Her breathing was shallow. Words way too soft. But, she found the nerve to speak.

"I'd like that. What time?"

"Do you think you'd prefer to ride with an English saddle rather than side saddle, or take the coach instead?"

"To ride, no side saddle. You saw me a while back. I nearly got dragged. I'm not sure I ever want to try that again, lady or not."

"Much safer for us all if you don't." He moved away taking both jewelry boxes. "I already know the rules, Sam, and you are quickly learning them. If what you want to discuss involves my mistresses, then we can save it. She's on her way."

"Adam, that's your business. I'm not in a frame of mind to think about your dalliances and could give a hoot. I've enough on my plate right now. You would prove to be a big distraction if I even let it happen. So, it's best we both forget about that kiss in Venice. I want to talk with you about moving out." She held up her hand. "Before you protest, I need you to hear me. I have a plan that I think would work best for both of us, even Mrs. Hoyt."

"So, you are going to ignore it, are you? How long do you think you can hold out? My guess is that you are stubborn and it may take a while. But, mark my words, the mistress stuff is done. No point. So why don't you tell me about what you want to do tomorrow along our ride. I'll settle for being your friend, for now. Do you think I could start by seeing your leg?"

If the night had not finished her off, his dialogue sure would have. She sat down on the bed in a heap, shoving up her petticoat enough to expose the bandage. It was a bit bloody, but the crinoline had kept it from seeping through to the lovely gown.

He touched it, unwrapped it and held her leg in his hand. "A bullet wound, eh? You packed it with something that looks appropriate and the color is good." He reached to her bedside table and took the other dressings and wrapped it.

"Looks like you had some practice with this." Concern shaded his handsome eyes. "You do know you don't have to do this, right? You are here, nothing will make you go back if you stop taking passages."

How dare he? When she was most vulnerable and at the point of total exhaustion. Especially when his voice turned deep holding true concern and eyes held hers captive.

She touched his shoulder, resting both hands and smiled, "What would I do? Become a woman with no ideals, bored out of my mind? I don't think so. At last I have a purpose. I had no idea I could stop, but I don't want too. Do you? I doubt it."

Rising, he sighed placing hands on his hips, "I know. It was just something I needed to say. I'll see you in the morning. Let's plan on ten o'clock so you can sleep in a bit and have breakfast. Goodnight, Lady Arnesen." His smile was warm and inviting as he slid the backside of a hand against a soft cheek, "Sleep well."

"A good night to you as well, Lord Griffin."

As her doors closed, Sam slid out of the layers and into her nightdress. Lowering the glass lamps, she got into bed and once her head hit the pillow, sleep took over.

Chapter Eight

"A bit of a gimp, I see, but you do look well. Did you get a decent breakfast in you?"

"Yes, to all. Thank you. So, shall we roll?"

He drew in a frown. "Roll? What the hell kind of nonsense are you jabbering about now, woman?"

She chuckled. "Really, Lord Griffin. That's not very gentlemanly, I must say. But, to educate, roll means let's head out. You've been to the future. Surely you must have at one time or another been in an unfavorable area where the slang is entirely different."

His voice was a bit stern. "Sam, you have to watch what you say and when. Not everyone around here understands where I go when I am away for longer periods of time."

"Understood. Would you please give me a hand up? I'm just not that coordinated with all these yards of cloth on."

"Okay, woman, up you go." Sam grabbed the reins in gloved hands, steadying, then clicked her tongue as the mare walked on.

"Where are we headed and how far? Mrs. Hoyt warned me that a storm is brewing off the River Dee and we'd better make haste to make it back before it curls inland and soaks us all."

"So, she's a weatherwoman as well? I wonder more about her every day. Plus, she never seems to age. What magic potions are stored in that cottage of hers?"

Sam laughed as they picked the pace up to a trot. "Okay, so let's get down to business. I've been exploring your grounds and found a cottage that's in need of some repairs. It is solid from thatched roof to stone foundation. I had your groundsman give it a thorough evaluation. So, I would like to propose an offer."

"Go on. There's no stopping you when you get a notion in your head. I'm listening."

"I'd like to fix it up inside and out. I'll pay locally so I won't take up your staff's time. I can pay a fair wage. I'll hire on a maid combined as a housekeeper who I can trust. There I may need Mrs. H or Father G's help. I'll hire a gardener to come once a week to keep the place tidy in case I am off somewhere."

"You've got your mind set on it then?"

"Indeed, I do."

"Why now and what's the rush?"

Their eyes locked, but damn if the real reason was to be revealed.

"Seems logical, don't you think? I may like to have a personal life out from under your roof, so to speak. Especially if I'm to stick around for a spell. I can let Mrs. H know a specified spot at the cottage where we can correspond. Then she will always know what I'm up to."

Their legs touched as he moved closer. "Not liking that, Sam. I know I've not been around, but I've been giving you room to expand your horizons, breath and take it all in."

"That may be partially true, but you've been occupying your time elsewhere. That is your business, not mine. I want to have my own place, Adam." She softened her harsh words with a true grin. "I think it would benefit us both."

"I suppose I have no voice in this, even though I own the grounds and the buildings, right? No, you don't have to answer that. I already know I'm going to agree. So, how soon do you want to start this project? Have you even been inside to see what else is already living in there?"

"If they can get in, they can get out and stay out. I'll make that known fast. I'd already have someone lined up in the village. Two men that need work. One older and one younger and they know how to build."

"Mr. Bruce and his son, I suppose, and if it's them, then you have made a proper choice."

"Good. They are started today. I'm glad we agree. Now let's settle on a monthly rent sum. What do you collect from your other properties around here?"

"Since you are going to take care of repairs and all upkeep how about we say ten pounds a month. I know that does not sound like a lot, but you are going to have your hands full."

She eyed him suspiciously knowing he was already up to something.

"Agreed, Lord Griffin." She reached over extending her right gloved hand. "Do we have an agreement?"

"Aye." He shook her hand. "Now what's next? For sure as this road is dirt you have more on your mind."

"So true. Okay, I'm going to break a rule. How long have you been taking passages?"

He eyed her trying to figure this woman out as her sweet perkiness won over yet again. "Maybe fifteen years. I'm surprised you've barely been here a month and have gone out twice. Makes we wonder what's in place for you. Far as I know, we are out half a dozen times a year."

"Oh, so is there a chief? Someone that sits high on a perch in their castle overseeing all the lands and centuries? I'm not being sarcastic either. How the hell does this work and who manages it?"

"No one knows. That's the big mystery. Fables and myths abound in this part of the country about 'people like us'. There are even children's books written. But, it all still remains as to who and how."

"I'm going to change the subject before it causes us to go all intellectual. I just don't feel like it today. I can tell you after what we did over the last few days, I realize how important it is to appreciate every bit of my life whether I understand it or not."

His brows drew in. "We? You did not work alone?"

"Your turn to break the rules. No, I had someone from here and we worked together."

"Shit, Sam, there must be something I need to know, but I can't figure out what the hell it is yet."

"Two swears in one sentence, Lord Griffin, now you are finally speaking my language." They both laughed.

"I'm glad you are along. It sure makes the ride a lot more pleasant. How's the leg holding up? It must be a bit stiff."

"It's okay. Is that the town we are going to?" She pointed up ahead as the road forked viewing the top of a small spire.

"Indeed, you are going to meet my tenants and good friends. You will like them."

Even as they rode into town, Sam refused to identify the feelings coursing through her. They were out of Chester, away from prying eyes and someplace new. Besides all of that, she was enjoying her time with him. He was easy to be with. Raking him with her eyes as they halted, she slid gingerly off the horse right into his arms and he lowered her slowly to the ground.

Diverting those impetuous emotions, she released but frowned as he seemed reluctant to let her go. Chuckling, he took the reins and tied the horses up in front of the Prancing Pony public house.

"It's safe enough here, but bring your small bag just in case." She unlatched it from the rear of the saddle.

The smell of polished wood and cigar smoke assaulted her senses as soon as they entered. A burly man and rounded woman were quickly on approach as Sam stepped back right into his body.

"Ah, Lord Griffin, you made good time. It is great to see you both." The woman was brazen, shoving him aside quick enough, "Damn, you are still a handsome devil. Come now and give me a big squeeze."

He laughed reaching back for Sam.

"Lady Samantha these are the Hywels, Alwen and Baglen. Alwen has operated the Prancing Pony for our family for nearly forty years."

Enveloped by Alwen right away keeping a firm grip on an arm, Sam was paraded away from the men. "I insist we are on first names. When I am away from the estate, I really like to keep things simple."

Her catlike eyes were sharp and piercing, yet warm and inviting. "Samantha, it is. What's your fancy? A cup of mead, ale or wine?"

In this era, one would not normally drink this early in the day. But, water was hardly stored for more than cooking, bathing and washing clothes. "Ale. It is lovely here. How many rooms do you have upstairs?"

"Ten. We seem to fill them often being in such a good location. We are close to the river and a garrison of British soldiers. They will be here soon enough, though, then we will get busy. I'm glad you two came before that happens. So, dear," she patted a bench seat beside her while she waived a bar maid over, "two pints of ale, Elizabeth, if you would please. So, how long have you been in these parts?"

Sam's stomach tightened staring into the women's green eyes. A picture of not long ago flashed quickly through her brain. Her facial features tightened, leaning close. "I saw you. You were the cloaked woman that left the Labonte Magasin de Chapeau in Verdun."

"Ah, the little hat shop and *la bebe, oui madame*, that was me. You have very sharp eyes."

Sam raised her glass. "To you. If you had not done that..." She let it trail off.

Alwen clinked her glass. "To us all."

"Now, ladies, what are you toasting to already?"

A sharp quiver weaved through Sam before she even glanced up.

"Pardon this interruption. But we met a long time ago in Scotland. On the Isle of Iona. I am sure. If I am mistaken, I apologize."

"Ah, yes. You are correct." She knew who he was. It was the unnamed soldier that was in the church who had stood back watching her a bit to intensely. "I am so sorry. As I recall it was very rainy. I am amiss, soldier, for I do not remember your name."

Every hair was standing at attention on Sam's body.

"Correct, Lady Arnesen, for if I recall I never provided it." He swept his hat off. "Major Victor Savoy."

"Well, let me thank you again for your assistance. It was much appreciated. Tell me. Are you posted here or just passing through?"

Their eyes locked. Sam knew he was one of them, the 'others' she'd heard about. What was his game and where the bloody hell was Adam?

"I am passing through to an appointment and stopped here last night. I saw you and wanted to acknowledge our acquaintance. I hope you pardon my boldness."

Her mind was screaming, what the fuck! But, her smile was sincere. Eyes unreadable. Causing his gaze to become piercingly unrelenting.

"Why, not at all. Have a safe journey, major, and thank you again for your assistance on Iona."

They both knew what she had done in Scotland.

He bowed. "Lady Arnesen, Mistress Hywel, a pleasant day to you both."

Silence prevailed as two sets of eyes watched him leave without a backwards glance. Sam raised her glass swigging down the entire contents. "Alwen, have you seen him here before?"

"No, last night was a first. You know I can't ask. Are you safe? I saw his cold, calculating look and I know he's in passage. You'd better be on your guard. Have you been appraised that both good and bad are at work here?"

Sam shifted on the bench watching them getting closer. Had Adam seen this? She could tell something was not settled with him. But Baglen looked jovial enough. The men sat as talk changed to the arriving storm coming in much earlier than anticipated.

"I've secured two rooms for the night Samantha. The skies are black and the winds howling off the river. Our return back to *Ard Aulinn* will be delayed.",

"And good timing. Indeed it is. For we have elk tonight and fresh rosemary bread. Nothing tastes so grand on a stormy night than a hearty stew. Don't you think?"

"That sounds great, Alwen."

When it was time to light the gas lamps, the innkeepers stood leaving Adam and Sam.

"How's your leg? Do you want to take a short stroll through town before the rains begin? May feel good to stretch a bit."

Nodding, they stood and walked over.

Hanging on a peg at the door was her cloak. Adam took it down and placed it around her shoulders, sliding up the hood. Then gestured her ahead. In silence, they continued along stopping at the church and graveyard.

"Who was he?"

"I wondered if you saw."

"I did. Something did not feel right. I walked Alwen out from behind the bar and saw him engaging you both."

"This is not fair Adam. I want to tell you. Who's to know if I do?"

"Under the circumstances, I think you should. How can I protect you if you don't?"

"But what if I do speak of it, of him and it spirals into something awful for us both?" Stopping, she turned into his arms, eyes locking.

"I have an idea. Come. I want to see if the church is open."

"If you are thinking of involving the priest, I don't believe that to be a good idea."

"No." She opened the door, smiling and moved away from him rather quick for someone with a leg wound. She had her back to him and was doing something as he glanced around the church noticing only two people sitting in prayer.

Smugly, she walked back. What was this beautiful lass up to now?

"Here." She handed him a folded piece of paper ripped out of the back of a hymnal book. As he read it, his face masked over.

"Come." He whispered. "We'd better head back before it gets too foul outside." Once around the rear of the church, he took out a match and burnt the note down. Ashes flowing down onto hallowed earth.

Grabbing her hand, the wind suddenly whipped around them lifting her hood. He moved quickly walking in front of her. They stopped. Suddenly facing him, inches apart, he lifted it back up resting his hands on her shoulders.

"I know him. You are in possible danger. I don't know when or where. But we need to make a pact right now. If you ever find yourself in trouble, real trouble, where you have no way out and have exhausted all your means, I want you to make it somehow to the nearest priest, reverend or father. Write a note. Give it them. It just needs to say 'help' and I will find you. Do you understand?"

She was speechless, partially because he was so close. What had he said? Oh, yes. She had heard him. A note. A priest. Come and get me. But why had he not kissed her? She wanted him to kiss her again and probably again and again and again. What was his delay? Where was her staunch back bone and resolve now?

Reaching up, Sam pulled his mouth down to hers taking fate into her own hands.

He could not resist as their lips met.

Finally.

The intense pleasure was felt down to her toes as somehow the rumble of thunder above reached her thoughts as she pulled back.

"Thank you."

His head moved slightly, eyes briefly closed. "I need you well and safe. What kind of a person would I be since you followed me here, if I did not protect you? And Sam, the next time you kiss me like that, it will end differently. I assure you. You had better keep that in mind."

Her own boldness brought color to her cheeks. How long did she even want to keep him at bay? Keep a protective circle around her heart? Not for much longer, that she knew. This thing between them was inevitable.

"We'd better go now. I hear thunder and it's getting closer and closer. But as for running, I can't do that. I'll walk as fast as possible."

He eyed her, glancing at their surroundings. There was a path from the graveyard that would bring them to the inn.

Sweeping her up into his arms, he chuckled at her reaction. "Nope, keep it to yourself. I am saving us both a good drenching."

Arriving back, Adam set her down opening the door just as the sky exploded.

"Over here you two. I've a nice table near a roaring fire. The food is hot. Would you care for wine or ale?"

Opposite they sat, her cloak hanging on the peg close to their table as Adam replied. "Ale for us both,

Alwen, thank you." She patted his shoulder quickly disappearing toward the kitchen.

"So, what kind of games do they play here? Darts? Cards?"

He laughed. The mood lightened between them. "Darts are played in encampments between soldiers. Cards are played here. It will be much later and you will be long upstairs tucked away when those types of men come in."

"What if I am a natural card shark? Wouldn't you want to have me tweak their ego by sniffing out their weakness and taking some of their money? Maybe it could be a profitable side business, Lord Griffin."

"You and I both would be in big trouble. First, they'd never let a woman sit in on a game. Second, if they were stupid enough to do that, and you won, we'd have to hire protection back to the estate tomorrow to make it safely. Don't forget, we are still in the prime era of highway men, rogues and robbers."

She sighed. It was a dangerous yet exciting time. "Fine. I'll be upstairs. I don't want them getting frisky with me thinking I'm a tavern wench."

His appraisal gave away his thoughts. Sam grinned, cheeks turning a pretty shade of pink. "I can assure you they'd know you are a lady head to toe. But what would, as I have heard out of your mouth before, 'shock the shit out of them,' would be what you have secured inside of your thighs."

She gasped. "What do you know about that?"

"When you showed me your leg, I saw the strappings and figured you were packing something. What are they?"

The blush increased.

"Cat got your tongue, Sam?"

"Stop teasing me right now." She leaned slightly closer as he met her right in the middle, noses inches apart.

"A knife and a pistol. I keep backup bullets in my corset. You did not happen to see those, did you?"

He sat back crossing his arms across his chest, eyes turning a dark blue while a roguish grin made its way across his lips. "Samantha, you watch yourself. I am a man after all."

Tit for tat was what she thought. Raising her spoon, she tasted the stew, moaning softly. "Oh, you have to taste this it is amazing."

The subject was officially changed.

They ate in relative silence as the room filled with smoke and cantankerous voices. Adam knew it was time for her to go.

"You all set?" He rose, taking her cloak while clasping one of her hands leading them over to the front desk. Alwen was ready handing over two sets of keys.

"You two are toward the back so the noise will hardly be heard. If you need anything, Adam can come down."

"Alwen, thank you very much. I will see you in the morning."

As they took the hallway toward the back of the inn and up the rickety stairs, Sam had to let go and move up ahead. At the last door he halted, inserted the key and had the lamps lit before she blinked twice. Parting the drapes a few inches, he peered out.

It was pouring, the wind howling and whistling between the beams. But, inside it was warm, dry and safe. He unlocked the door between their rooms and slid it open a few inches.

She eyed him questioningly.

"Just a precaution. If anything did happen, you lock this side and get downstairs. I'm not trying to frighten you, not that I think I would, I just like to be prepared."

He slipped through the middle door.

"No worries. Tonight I'll sleep with my friends on."

He stopped, smiled then disappeared to his own room.

"Goodnight, Adam."

"Goodnight, Sam."

Chapter Nine

There was a knock on the adjoining door. "Would you be decent?"

"That's a matter of opinion, I suppose, if I am or not."

He chuckled shaking his head. "I mean, is it okay for me to come into the room?"

"Yeah." She was struggling to get her dress over her head. It was stuck. His grin grew, stretching across his features. "Need a bit of help, mistress?"

"Shut up. I can't see your face and that may save you a good kick in the shins. Yes, dammit, I need your help."

"There you go," he tugged it down over her petticoats appreciating every inch of this curvy lass. Spinning her around, he began the task of fastening buttons. Standing erect, Sam was trying to contain some unruly curls.

"You know, I like Abbey. But, I must admit you make a fine lady's maid when I'm out on the road."

Brows raised. "You know we are going to have to discuss this eventually."

"What, you being a lady's maid? Is there a secret hiding inside of you, Lord Griffin?"

Laughter echoed around the room. "No, damn that creative mind and mouth. I already feel too familiar with you and not receiving the benefit of sharing your nighttime bed chamber seems wrong."

The brush stopped in mid-air as their eyes locked in the mirror.

Long seconds passed. Finally, composure was restored. But the mark had been made. Her skin burned for want of this man. "I am afraid I don't know where I'll be tomorrow. I don't know where you will be tomorrow. At least like this, I can think about what it could be like. But, if something goes wrong, I don't want to think about what it could have been and will never be because we took things a bit too far."

"See, I look at it the other way. We should do this. Take it for all we are given. Because who knows if I'll ever see you in another lifetime again."

She shook her head in realization that what he said was so damn valid. "I think no matter how strong I am, I will not be able to resist what's between us. Unfortunately, I am just not ready yet. I feel like I need to find the key to a hidden door first. Am I making sense?"

"In a way, yes. But at least you acknowledge this exists between us."

She laughed. "I never doubted that at all. If you had not kissed me like that in Venice, I'd not be here right now, Lord Griffin. It is indeed entirely your fault."

He conceded, knowing there was much more at work here than a kiss. "You ready to have a bite and leave? We need to get back before the afternoon. I have somewhere to go."

"A passage?"

"Yes. I will be gone a few days."

"You know upfront where and when? Why do I not get advanced notice like this? Do they not know where to send the memos?"

He shook his head giving up. "To coin a phrase from your era, because you are a newbie."

She shut her door as they walked down the hallway. "Oh, stop it Anyway, how many centuries have you been in?"

"Too many to count."

"Do you have a favorite so to speak? Where you like being more than any other?"

"Here. This really is home."

"So, do I. But I admit I liked Scotland in the 1700's. I did not like France during the Great War." Stopping abruptly on the rickety stairs, he grabbed her just in time before knocking her down them.

"We'd better keep this kind of conversation to more private locations now, Sam."

"I got a bit carried away. Sorry about that. I'll zip it. Oh, look, there's that soldier. Still here. That's ironic, isn't it? He gives me the creeps. I just don't trust him at all."

As they approached, he nodded. "Lady Arnesen, nice to see you and Lord Griffin this morning. I take it you passed the night here while the storm surged outside."

Adam stepped in front of her defensively. "We did and are on our way. A good day to you, major." As Alwen rushed up to grab Sam's arm, the two men exchanged long, hard looks.

"That bloke gives the hairs on my arms quite a ride."

Sam laughed. "That's one way to put it. But I'm going to forget about him for now. As they say, forewarned is forearmed."

"You'll do just fine, mistress. But if you ever need anything and are out on the road, especially to the north, you make sure you trust anyone you encounter that is a true Norse."

Sam found that extremely strange since she'd not been anywhere near Norway, Sweden, Iceland, or the real north countries. Shivering slightly, she recalled a similar message from the tinker.

"I've got a nice breakfast for you both. Now sit and I will bring tea."

She shifted gears so fast, Sam had to stop and digest it as Adam slid in opposite. "When I'm back, I'm going to take you out to shoot and teach you a few things. I want to make sure you are fully equipped to outmaneuver the likes of him."

"Well, hello again to you too." She leaned closer. "Did I tell you that back in my time, long ago, I learned how to shoot a shot-gun from my adoptive dad and my heritage is Norwegian. Arnesen derives from the eagle. I am an amazing predator and hunter."

He could not help but smile at this intelligent and sassy woman. "All the same, I want to test your prowess and see how I can help you. I have a feeling that at some point you will be tested beyond your knowledge. I want to give to you an edge. It may save your life someday."

Thank heavens Alwen arrived with two heaping plates of eggs, sausage and toast. For she was tempted to fire back how she had survived on her own all these years. Hundreds, so to speak.

"Here you go, my lovelies. Eat up. The day has dawned bright and clear and you should have a pleasant enough ride back."

Sam was keenly aware of how close that Savoy was to their table. She made sure they kept the conversation a bit on the menial side until bidding their hosts good-bye and were mounted on their horses outside.

"How often have you gone back to 2015?"

"Three times. Sometimes finishing business is required. Then there are times where once is enough."

"I feel like I'm not done in Scotland for some reason."

He shrugged. "That could be. Time will tell. Shall we pick up the pace a bit? Is your leg up to it?"

"It is. I think these two deserve a good run. Let's have at it."

After nearly two hours he finally slowed to a trot. "Can you stay close to the estate while I am gone unless you are called away? I'd feel more comfortable if you would consider it."

"I am planning on spending a lot of time at the cottage, driving the Bruce's crazy with renovations. Other than a few trips into the village and spending time with Father G, I will keep my adventures local."

"If you see him looming about, feel free to shoot him between those unruly brows. I'm the lord in these parts. No one would question if you did."

She laughed. "I don't think he's stupid enough to come and pay me a visit."

"Perhaps not. But all the same, keep those friends of yours on you no matter where you go."

"I can assure you other than when I sleep in my bed here, they are always on me."

The stable hand was awaiting them as they turned up the lane behind the estate. They dismounted and went around the side terrace and entered his study. When inside, she headed toward the door. But he halted her.

"Sam." he hesitated as their eyes locked, his filled with an unasked question.

"I don't know what it is yet. So, I can't tell you and that's honest. It's just a feeling that has come over me. If it's something you need to know about, I'll pass it along."

Then added as an afterthought, "Safe travels, Adam."

She closed the door behind her heading at a clipped pace to the rooms. Something of great importance was there as she pushed open the door closing it with the back of a boot. Leaning up against a perfume decanter it sat. Reaching for the paper, she turned it over eyeing the royal red waxed seal.

"Lady Arnesen, I need you to come to Norway. Seek passage to Northern Scotland. From there the journey will be clearer. Go to the ruins on Adam's property as soon as possible. Your instinct will provide more detail."

She turned the hand note over then back again, but there was no signature. Looking at the seal, she realized it was from the House of Olaf II Haraldsson.

Oh, my, she thought, recalling recent discovery of her true family lineage. This was a forewarning of the time-period she would be travelling to. Sometime in the first century.

Who had left this?

Damn, her heart was racing!

"Oh, my gosh. I'm off to the dark ages."

Her grin spread and voice quickened. "This just gets better and better." Quickly she threw some dressings, balm and extra base layers into her bag.

With hand on hips, Sam stood back evaluating everything. A quick bath, new bandage and change of clothes were in order. It was late summer here, but as she was travelling north, cold weather clothes would be a necessity. Hastily, she rang for Abbey, began removing her gun and knife setting them under one pillow while preparing to leave right away.

"Yes, mistress." Abbey stood just insider her door.

"Oh, good. Please bring me a kettle of hot water. I need to refresh and change and then I'll be heading out. When you come back, I will have a letter for you to give to Lord Griffin. Make sure you hand it to only him. It is critical he receives it straight away. There will be another to deliver by early light to Mr. Bruce in the village. "

The maid closed the door and rushed off returning minutes later with three other servants all carrying large pots. The tub was quickly filled to half and it was enough for a fast bath and wash of hair.

"Abbey, you are a godsend. I'll dry off while you hand me my clothes. The letter for Lord Griffin and Mr. Bruce are over there on my dresser. Take them both. If you would run down his Lordship's now, I want to ensure he receives it before I go, please."

"Yes, mistress, I'll be quick. I know you are in a hurry."

Sam put the necessities back in place. Reached into the dresser and removed extra bullets and slipped them into one boot. Partially dressed, she sat and awaited Abbey's return to finish the buttons. Glancing around the room, she decided to bring her small Vera backpack and put in tissues and a few other things just in case.

"Mistress, he was in his study. I handed it to him. But did not wait. I returned straight away."

"Wonderful, remind me when I get back to take you to town. We should go shopping for a new dress. Also, I wanted to run something by you. Would you be interested in coming to come work for me at my new cottage when it's livable?"

"Oh, mistress, what? You are leaving us? Oh, of course. The letter to Mr. Bruce. It is about renovations, correct?"

"Yes, I am letting a cottage on the grounds and Mr. Bruce and his son will be updating it. If I am gone a while, I'd like to have someone keep him on track. Do you think you may be interested in doing this for me? We can revisit this again when I return. I spoke with Mrs. H already and she is leaving this to us to decide."

"I would! What do you need me to do beside give him the letter while you are away?"

"Just go over and check his progress. I've written up a short list of things he's to work on first, which matches what I put in his letter. It is over there. Just be my eyes and ears while I am away, okay?"

"I will, mistress, and thank you."

"Excellent. Then it is agreed. When I get back, we go shopping. Will you also let Mrs. H know I had to go out?"

"I will, anything else?"

"No, you can go. Thank you, Abbey."

Stepping out the back entrance, Sam lifted the hood on her cloak and walked on. Missing Adam by mere minutes.

***

The sky was lit with stars as the full moon guided her steps toward the ruins. Somehow this time was different, she could feel it. Walking down the stone steps, Sam, felt prickling alertness as she began the descend up the other side. Immediately, she was propelled onto a horse, quickly grabbed the reins tightly to avoid falling off and beneath their pounding hooves.

Fast approaching was a league of Anglo-Saxon soldiers. Glancing, while the stead ran at a break neck speed, their uniforms appeared to be under the rein of King Athelstan. Damn! Glancing over her shoulder once more, she caught sight of none other than Major Victor Savoy.

Arrows were flying as the mare raced, barely keeping ahead of the charging group. Loud voices were getting closer and closer as fear and adrenaline intermixed. Their voices rising one above the other. Yeah, it was Savoy. Demanding she halt in the name of the king.

A wry smile creased her lips.

Like hell she would!

That's when a piercing pain racked her shoulder nearly knocking her off the mount. Placing a hand there, a warm stickiness seeped into the glove.

"Oh, mother of God. Not again! Really? What the fuck was that?"

Thoughts streamed through her brain faster than could be processed. Realizing the best course of action would be to dismount, Sam pulled the reins tightly, rearing off to hide in the thick forest. The bleeding needed to be staunched. Jumping to the ground and slapping the mare's ass, she and the animal disappeared in separate directions into its denseness.

Slowly moving further in, she listened acutely for their approach. An arm, out of nowhere, reached out. Grabbed her roughly, strongly, then slapped a hand across her mouth.

In vain she tried to bite it.

"Shut up, woman, I am trying to help you! "He hissed. "The way I see it you have two choices. Scream and they will find you, in which case as I will move away unnoticed. Or, you can trust me. Do you want to leave your fate in their hands, madam, or in mine?"

She nodded her head.

"Wise choice. Now, I'm going to remove it."

Turning around as his other arm held her body tight against his, she tried to gain freedom. His grip was iron tight wrapped around her.

"I am shot, you ass. I need you to let me go so I can check if it passed through and get a bandage on right away."

"Let me look," He could see the blood forming on her under garment. "It has passed right through." She stood hands on hip ready to wage a dark war with this man who was apparently here to help her.

"How the hell did you know which shoulder? I did not tell."

"Because I shot you with an arrow, lass."

Her face blanched. "You what! For heaven's sake, why did you do that?"

"I needed to get your attention. Now, keep yourself calm. I know what I'm doing. I am here to assist you."

Laughter burst out. "Oh, really? How nice of you to shoot me then offer assistance. That's just grand of you. What else are you planning? Mind telling me up front so I can be more prepared?"

He weaved the bandage over her shoulder and ripped off a piece stuffing it under the wound.

His silence pissed her off. "How about we start with a name. Who are you?"

"Gunner Gudrun at your service, mistress."

This was just uncomprehensive. Why he'd shoot her to help her out of a chase from those soldiers? Hovering on her lips were a large stream of vulgarities. "And you know who I am?"

"I do. Now, if you don't mind, I'm sure by now they've caught up with your mare and are doubling back. My stead is back a bit so we need to move on and get him."

Walking beside his tall, robust frame, her mind did wander taking quick glances at his clothing. For sure he was a manly man as she caught sight of his horse just up ahead. He was enormous! As if she was as light as a feather, the stranger lifted her up setting her before him, then mounted taking up the reins. His large frame enveloped her body, making her feel quite small, all of a sudden.

"Where do we go?"

"Northern Scotland. There's a village where a woman will help us. She's a Beaton. Then we move on to Stavenger."

"Norway? That's in Norway. How the hell are we going to do that?"

"I needed you injured to enable us entry into this village. It is highly protected. With you a Scotswoman and requiring the services of the healer, they will allow us in."

"But won't they stop us because you are from an invading territory? Is not that too dangerous?"

"I can speak with a Scottish brogue, so they won't have any idea. Besides, my clothes are just servants as to not raise suspicions. I go by the name of Shamus Dougall and have our papers secured if needed. You, mistress, are Lady Elles of Kincard. A long standing family in the Highlands. We were put on by those damn Saxons, who are short on any dignity, the bloody heathens."

"You speak well, but better curtail using words like dignity. I doubt in this time servants speak like that. Right? I suppose if I look in my bag, I will see my own papers?"

There was no comment as his warm breath permeated threw the layers of clothing. Brows drawing in, Sam had to wonder why he was affecting her so strongly.

"How long before we get there? I would really like to know that damn band of unsavory cutthroats will not get their hands on me this night."

"I was warned your tongue could be foul."

She lowered her head, glad for the darkness as she felt the heat on her inflamed face. "I apologize I offended you. I will curtail my vocalization of what is really the truth."

He chuckled. "Spirited too. Nothing wrong with a spirited woman."

"Anyway, how long before we get there?"

"About five hours of riding. Are you feeling well enough? I tried to give you a clean wound. But if you start to feel feverish, we will stop and I'll clean it out."

"I think we'd better muddle on and leave it. Then the guards at the village won't think we are up to something."

"That's your choice. But, you need to make sure to tell me if it gets worse. I hear you have quite a stubborn streak in you."

"I won't ask who fed you all these lies. So, is Kenneth II still King?"

"Yes, although his health recedes."

"Oh, my goodness," she said out into the dark night, "I'm in the year 995. The Dark Ages."

"Mistress, women don't speak out like you did earlier, or now. They stay behind their men well out of sight doing women's work. It's going to be hard for you to not be verbal when you see village life in this time, but you must. Remember we have a higher purpose."

"You said what I see for village life in this time. I surmise you are on a passage as well?" Answers were needed and time was of the essence.

"Yes, to guide and assist. No further discussion. I will not disclose what is burning to be asked."

She smiled, unwittingly leaning back into his strong chest and felt protected and safe.

"Get some rest now, mistress, you will need it."

She had to get the last word in before sleep closed in.

"That's an interesting word."

"What is?"

"Mistress. Some men use it in a polite way. Some to hide their inability to commit."

Her eyes closed as his arms tightened around. A thought suddenly sprang to life. Was he the other one the tinker had spoken of?

Body sagging, breathing quieter, he knew although it was dark, that she rested a bit easier. Pulling her closer to ensure she did not fall, he lifted a hand up tugging on his beard. All the warnings about her had been accurate.

Chapter Ten

"Mistress, rise and look awake. We are fast on approach to the village perimeter and are under observation."

Moaning, Sam's eyes did not fully open. The burning in her shoulder increased, forcing her back into unconsciousness. Placing his cheek to her forehead, he quickly slowed the stead. She was burning hot.

"Damn."

Two armed clansmen stepped out of the woods, halting progress. "Identify yourself."

"The name's Dougall with Lady Elles of the Clan Kincaid." He held her and the reins with his left hand while reaching under his cloak for his packet of papers.

Swords were drawn in a flash.

"Easy there, Dougall." One of them moved forward slightly and halted, clearly recognizing a man of their own. "What ails her?"

"Shot by a band of Saxons, led by that bastard Savoy."

Both men eyed each other briefly.

"We need a warm place I can lay her. I need to look more closely at the wound. She has the fever in her." He threw down the pouch as it landed at their boots. Once reviewed, it was handed back up to him.

"Do you have papers for her as well?"

"Aye, on her. If you want me to set her down, I can provide them."

"Of no matter. Go ahead slowly."

As Gunner kicked the sides of the mount and moved on toward the castle, he glanced around knowing this settlement would eventually become the thriving City of Aberdeen.

Even in her sleep she moaned, as concern became etched on his bearded face. As they entered the inner courtyard, they were detained a second time.

"Stop there and wait."

He pressed his mouth to her ear. "If you can hear me, we are inside. I hope to have help soon." She pressed a hand against his chest. She had heard.

One of the men returned, followed by a small, heavy set woman. Her hair and hands flailed madly in every conceivable direction.

"Come along and follow me." As she gave Sam the once over. "Oh my, she's a lady. No dragging your muddy boots, now get on with it!"

Gunner smiled. Yes, this was the woman they were hoping to find. The great Beaton.

"Put her on that bedding. Now hurry, take the cloak off and turn your back. I need to ask you questions while I work."

Instantly he did as bid.

"Oh, bless her, but praise all that's holy. You got here just in time. I will mend the devil's work. Go. Get yourself some bread and wine in the hall. I'm sure the Laird will want a few words before you come back here to your mistress."

Glancing cautiously around, Gunner strode up the stone stairs, weaving his way back toward the Great Hall. The second he sat, a wench sauntered over settling a foamy mug of ale and plate of meat before him. Her grin said it all as he provided one right back.

Under apparent observation, he dug into the food not stopping until the plate was empty. Pushing it away, crossing his ankles and leaning back, he watched as a gangly youth approached.

"The Laird will see you now, follow me."

With few exterior windows and thick wax candles lit, the room still appeared to dark for him.

"So, Shamus Dougall, how is it that you are here with the lass? What happened and where?"

"She is my charge. I was transporting her to Kierloch when an attempt was made by a band of Saxon soldiers to detain us." He stopped, leaning cocky to one side smiling. "I managed to get us on our way, but not before the lass was hit."

"Kierloch, you say? She's Mistress Elles of Kincaid?"

"That she is."

"Kincaid once assisted my very own wife at a time of need. 'Twas before we were wed years ago. I am foul in not extending my hand to you. Rupert Donald of the Clan Donald and Chief Laird of Castle Druim."

The two shook hands. "I will extend our full hospitality while she recovers. I assure you that the Beaton will heal her. She performs incredible deeds."

Gunner nodded. "I'm sure in this case I can say we appreciate your assistance. I was in a bit of fear for the mistress, as she took a fever. I'll go back to see if I can gain access. Your Beaton looked hell bent on keeping me out while she worked her magic."

He chuckled. "We don't know if she's a witch, but her healing powers and knowledge of the herbs are amazing."

Nodding, closing the creaky wooden door behind him, Gunner circled back down to the Beaton's room. Hand poised on the latch, it suddenly swung open causing him to start.

"She's high in fever and has lost blood. It's up to her now and the good Lord above."

She rushed passed as he glanced watching her hastily retreating form. Was she leaving Lady Elles alone with him? Returning? What a strange little woman she was. Roughly tugging on the closest chair and pulling it over to the makeshift bed, he glanced down at her face, dewy with fever. Gently he took a small hand in his large, calloused one.

"I'm here." Was all he said. Feeling a tinge of remorse that he had to do such a thing to get them into this village.

Thirty-one hours passed. Still he did not leave her side except for private matters. In between, she weaved between gibberish, talking about a man named Adam and cycling. That did bring a smile to his face. Once he was placed at a very important place in time. In 1960's Europe during one Tour de France. A time of peace and love.

It had indeed been the golden age of psychedelic images, wild parties and some interesting music. All the while, he was glad he had finished his tasks and had left with all brain cells miraculously still working.

As he lit more candles, she stirred at last. Quickly, he went over sitting down. "So, was it worth it?" she whispered. "Shooting me with that arrow or whatever it was."

He clasped her hand tightly. "Indeed, it was. For the woman that is attending you is the very woman we seek."

"Well, she'd better be damn important," she hesitated a bit breathless, "Shamus Dougall."

"Quiet up now, lass and rest. Do you want anything? You've been lost to us for a few days."

"Yes, I am parched and hungry."

'He rose and took his own platter off a rickety table and brought it over as she gingerly sat up. "I won't have you feeding me, I may choke." She grinned, no longer mad at this handsome rugged stranger. Yes, he indeed did have charm lurking beneath the surface of that strong body and wild beard.

Darn, if he wasn't even more alluring with the heavy Scottish accent and kilt. A question did burn, but not one she dared to ask. Was there anything else in the way of garments under it?

"Point well taken. Here eat. I'll go up to the hall and let the Laird know you are awake. He's been asking about you daily."

"Do we 'know' him?"

"Aye, I do. But only as I have the history of Castle Druim and his clansmen. He does not know who I am, mistress. But beware. Long ago your father assisted his wife before they were wed. That's why he's extended his hospitality to us."

"Shit, do you know what my father did? He's bound to engage me in conversation and I have no idea."

"The Laird assisted her and her lady in waiting when they were hindered by a group of unruly drunken men at an inn in Blackburn. It is a distance away from here. But you could always say your father did not regale of his earlier tales with your mother present and be done with it."

"This is not good, Shamus. We need to get on our way. I have an idea. I will feign my weakness longer than it affects me. So how are we going to get the woman to go with us? Maybe she's content now."

"She has no choice. But that task falls on you. Get to know her and find the right time to tell her we are here to take her home. Whether she wants to go or not."

She sighed. "I suppose you have already secured us passage and a ship's journey it will be."

"It's all arranged. But, take notice. We have only five days. By that time, you must have her ready for departure. Any further recuperation can be done on board. It is a Viking vessel."

She slid the platter toward him as he picked it up and set it on the table, turning back. "I will..." his voice trailed off as he saw she was tucked back in and already fast asleep.

Moving about the castle in complete freedom, Shamus took care of what he needed to do. Lady Elles, on the other hand, felt cooped up in the alchemy chamber and wanted out. Some fresh air and yes, she wanted to get going.

Finally, after nearly three days an opportunity presented itself.

"Mistress, I don't even know your proper name so I can thank you. My strength improves daily." Lady Elles stood to be assisted in dressing.

The Beaton, hands on plump, rounded hips stared into her eyes for several long seconds. "Mistress Elles of Kincaid, I know why you are here."

Apprehension sprouted as she placed the shift back over her head and the Healer buttoned it up. "In fever, you spoke in a foreign tongue. Don't worry, Lady Elles, I am packed. Let your burly man know. Be forewarned, we are going to have a hard time getting out of here. It is well guarded around the entire area, inside and out, tight as a cork in a jug."

"Perhaps your knowledge can guide us. Is there a weakness? A tunnel? Something that can help achieve success?"

"There is. But you two will need to trust me. I won't speak about it, even though we are safe enough here to discuss it without being heard. There are not any vents for our voices to pass along or keyholes to peep through." She smiled.

"I don't know how that will go over with my companion." Turning towards him as he came down the stone steps.

"Mistress, you are up. Is that a good decision?"

"Is the door closed above?"

"It is." He eyed the two women warily. "Why?"

She gathered him in as they spoke in whispers. When finished, the Beaton added, "Mistress, the Laird will want to at least meet you so you can extend a proper thank you for his generosity and kindness. I suggest you come up tonight for the meal?"

"That's appropriate. I agree."

"Now, come, fresh air is needed. You." She pointed a finger at Shamus. "Make yourself busy until then. Perhaps take a wash?"

He eyed her sternly, flashing a warning at the excitement lurking beneath the surface of her tone. "Healer, you are different. Even I can see that. Keep those emotions under control or they will know something is amiss."

Both women watched him leave. Disappearing up the stone steps and through the door. The Beaton gave one more look over her shoulder once outside to make sure he had indeed gone about his own business as Lady Elles's voice brought her back to the present.

"This garden holds wonderful healing properties. I've not seen some of these plants where I came from."

She smiled. "My name is Gerda, it sounds better than Beaton or Healer."

"Are we being watched?"

"No, I've been here too long for anyone to care much when I leave the Keep."

"You must miss your home and family a great deal." Lady Elles touched her arm.

"Aye, mistress I do." Her eyes welled up as she quickly shook her head, warding the somber mood off. "I've never even thought about escape. It always seemed so hopeless. What I don't understand is why you two? Who sent you?"

"I can't tell you. Even if I knew. Rest assured we will get you out. I promise."

"Okay, well come along. The sun has set so we had best go inside and prepare. I will route you by his table. Do you know what to say?"

"Yes, I am ready."

As they maneuvered through the populated Great Hall, a heavy Scottish brogue halted their progress, "Ah, Mistress Elles, it must be. At last we meet!"

Cool accessing eyes swept over her as he bowed slightly. She nodded. "I am glad for a bit of fresh air finally. Your Beaton has worked amazing healing skills on me. I am very thankful for such hospitality lent toward myself and my charge, Dougall."

He patted the chair beside him. "Here, you do look a bit tired. The Beaton told me you had lost a fair amount of blood. Come and have a bit of wine and meat with me."

He stood, pulling out a chair as Lady Elles walked around the long wooden table. Every step came with scrutinizing stares from all around the candlelit room.

Gerda nodded. "Laird, I need to get these herbs set properly. I will take a platter with me this night." He watched as the Beaton disappeared from the great hall.

Sipping the wine cautiously, with a stomach nearly empty, Lady Elles stayed on high alert. "I heard of your ordeal with that blackard, Savoy. An ugly sort under the protection of the King's rein."

She grimaced, nodding. "I agree completely. He is a foul Norseman hiding under that imperial soldier creed of his."

"Fear not. When the time is right, we will take care of our friend from the North."

He meant Norway, for many had come to this area of Scotland plundering and then hiding, taking to the highways and being funded by some organization of rogue soldiers called the Imperials.

"Let us not speak of him for now, mistress." As he patted her hand she feigned a yawn.

"Oh dear me, I do apologize. But, if I may be so forward. I believe my own good father mentioned assisting your dear wife once. Will I have the privilege of meeting her?"

"No. She is in Perth with her sister who's expecting their fifth child. I will not see her back for quite some time.

But you are right. Your father did do her a service. I do believe it was at the Inn at Buckthorn, if I recall the story."

She peered into his eyes never flinching. "I beg your pardon. But, I believe it was the Inn at Blackburn that she and her lady's maid were assisted, if I recall correctly."

He relaxed immediately. "Yes, dear, I do believe you are right. So, do not laugh. For an old man, I am becoming and with that my memory fades."

An old man, my ass, she thought. His eyes were clear, strong and bright and his strength noteworthy against the tightness of his cloth shirt.

She rose. "I'm sorry I am of little company and conversation tonight. Perhaps another day will find me a bit livelier. I would beg your pardon so I can have a rest."

He pulled her chair further back. "Why of course. Make sure the Beaton looks you over. If you feel more rested tomorrow, I shall have you moved to a more suitable room." She smiled, moving away toward the spiral stone stairs back down to the alchemy.

As she slowly walked down them, she saw Gunner and the Beaton deep in conversation.

"What are you two plotting? I must have my say in it. Now give me what you are discussing."

They both swung around having not heard her arrive. "Damn, lass, you must not do that again. You move to silently!"

"So?"

"Here, put your cloak on. Dougall is going to close our exit and then double back to the forest and meet us down at the beach." Close to the burning fire in the hearth, her foot pressed down on a floor stone. A small chamber door slid open. "I found this months ago. It goes down to the beach. Unfortunately, I never located a latch to know how it closes. So, if anyone came in while I investigated, they'd realize what I was about and sound the alarm. I wanted to keep it private. I walked it just the other night. A day prior to your arrival."

"But wait, didn't Rupert have this keep built? Surely he must know about this passage."

"Aye, he did have it built. But, this room and two above were already here when a battle was fought and he took it from the Norseman. He should not even know of its existence."

"How long will it take us to get to the beach?"

"I can only measure it by my candle, about two fingers wide." She pointed to Gunner. "His journey will be a bit further. I've already outlined a route that should get him outside the castle and to the woods unseen."

"That part is not guarded, Gerda? This place is like a fortress. Even I noticed the men in the woods at different locations when we were out in the garden today."

She smiled. "You both make a good pair, I daresay. He asked me the same thing before you came down from supper."

Lady Elles grew stern. "Enough of that. It is imperative we all make it to the beach. Shamus, when do we go?"

He pulled the cloak over her shoulders and spun her around fastening the clasp under her chin. "How about now, mistress?"

Nodding, she let Gerda go first. Each lit a torch that the Beaton had procured early that day. Down the cramped, cold, dark passageway they went. The light was their shining star as the heavy door closed behind them. Rats scurried blinded by the flames shadowing off the stones. It seemed like minutes turned to hours before she could see over Gerda's head the cloudy night sky.

"Stop." She whispered. "Give me your torch. We need them extinguished before exiting the passage. There can be no chances taken that guards posted above will see them."

"Oh, mistress, you are clever, for I had not thought of that. But what about signaling the boat?"

Lady Elles laughed softly putting both out in the sand. "Hush, I hear someone just outside the cave. You stay back. I'm going to investigate."

Lifting her gown, she removed her revolver.

There he was. She squinted her eyes to be sure. Yes! It was the outline of Savoy! Slouching down, she caught him by surprise and kicked the boots out from beneath as he hit the deck. Quickly, she leaned over with the butt of the gun and gave him a good enough slug to keep him down for the count until they were safe away.

"Come out. Watch out for this ass. Hurry!"

"Oh, mistress!"

Lady Elles grabbed her arm rather roughly, tugging her along down the path. "Now, did Dougall advise where we wait?"

"Yes, down there. At the crop of large rocks. The longboat will be coming in now so we can board. His orders were explicit. He told me not to tell you until we were this far."

"Go on."

"He said, if he did not show up when the sun fully sets into darkness, at the boats arrival, we were to sail without him. Under no circumstances are we to wait."

She felt a prickle of anticipation at those words, as in the now growing darkness she took Gerda by the arm. They moved along the beach toward the approaching longboat. It was very difficult for her to grasp how time was read without an actual watch. This was a very weird experience and one that taught her she needed to learn more about it at some point in her future.

As the boat came in, guided by the gently rolling surf, the oars were raised by the men. Standing on a large rock, she grabbed the tossed rope, giving it a needed tug and winced at the pain in both her shoulder and leg. At last, it was partially up onto the beach.

"Evening, mistress, I see our cargo. Where is your companion? It was advised there would be three." His heavy Norse accent was simultaneously threatening and stimulating.

"He should be here within minutes."

He jumped out of the longboat, lifted Gerda up and placed her in as she was helped further back.

"Mistress." She turned looking up at the cliff as loud voices and unfamiliar noises could be heard. She stiffened. He had been discovered!

"We must go. Take my hand and get in so I can shove off!" Clasping it, he pulled her quickly on board. Sitting in the bow she suddenly realized something needed to be done. They could not leave without him. She would not allow it.

"Can you shove the boat off but we wait a few yards off shore?"

He pushed the boat, jumped in and sat taking up an oar while they hovered momentarily. Then, nodded to the other men as they began rowing out toward the ship.

"Wait! Please, stop! Let him swim out to us!"

Longbows and crossbows were ricocheting off the boat, whizzing into the water as he dove in and began to swim.

"Mistress! We are jeopardizing our mission and the lives of us all if we remain here any longer!"

Watching his progress, emotions bordering on hysteria, Sam leaned over nearly falling into the swells of the water.

"I know. But he is almost here! Look! If you don't wait a second longer, I will jump in!"

His gaze warned her, as he noticed Gunner was just about to grab the front of the boat.

"A few seconds more is all you have!"

Reaching the longboat at last, Lady Elles, with the assistance of another man, pulled Gunner up and in.

"You had specific orders not to wait for me!"

"And you are grateful I don't listen to orders. I knew you could make it, Gunner, so perhaps a word of thanks we did!"

He nodded to the men taking up an oar, as they were safely out of the bay. She glanced over nearly being eaten alive by the darkness of his eyes.

As they approached the ship, she grabbed the netting and started climbing up.

"Gudrun, is it appropriate for you to have your hands on my bottom half? I don't recall asking you to help me up the riggings."

He grinned into the moonlight. "Just trying to help, mistress, with your injury and all."

"That's BS and you know it."

"I'll not reprimand you on use of that. For I wager no one else that may have heard would understand what that means."

It was her turn to grin as she lifted a leg and was pulled over the railing. With everyone on board, the anchor was lifted and sails hoisted. Never had she seen such a swagger as the one being done by the approaching Captain.

"Gudrun, *du gamle J'vel*!" [Gudrun, you bastard.]

He turned to her, a broad grin on his handsome features.

"Mistress Arnesen, you will need to block your ears when this man speaks. He's already referred to me as a bastard. Let me introduce you to Captain Knutren. Captain, Mistress Samantha Arnesen and Mistress Gerda."

He bowed smiling gallantly. "Ladies, our pleasure to have you aboard. You will find your shared room is tidy, but, quite comfortable for your journey. Mistress Gerda, you will be home soon. But first you need to see to the birth of a special baby."

She grinned, knowing It had been in her palm reading.

He extended his arm, "Shall I show you your cabin?"

Sam hovered back, a strange look on her face.

"You were Lady Elles back there. On our journey to Norway, you will hold the same name you were born with in England."

As she started to mouth what the fuck, he stood with hands on hips towering over her. "If you continue to use such language, I will have no choice but to kiss you." He turned, laughing boldly over his shoulder and joined the men on deck.

"But wait."

"Shit." He mouthed out loud, then stopped. It was the tone of her voice. Soft and inviting. The temptation was too much to know what she would ask. Turning, he walked back.

Chapter Eleven

"If we already know what she's going to do and she's keen on it, why can't I return now?"

He leaned close to her and, for a split second, her heart stopped as she thought he was going to kiss her.

"Mistress, you still have other business here, that's why."

He saw her bright eyes become brighter and the flush on her cheeks and smiled, raising a brow, then leaned in and did just that. He met with no resistance at all.

"Don't tell me there's another. I won't believe you for a minute."

She stomped her foot on top of his boot as he grinned. "Did you even give me a chance to tell you there was? I did not realize I had to fill you in on my personal life. The Captain was right. You are a bastard!"

Somehow, he had steered her from above to below deck and they were at her door. Opening it, Gerda was already lying down with a huge smile on her face. Why should she not? She was going home. Sam apparently was not and needed to get away from this obnoxious man.

Turning, he was still there, smug as all hell as she kicked at the door, slamming it shut in his face. His laughter resonated through the thick wood infuriating her further.

"What did he do, mistress? Your face is bright as the noonday sun!"

"Stop it, Gerda, he's an ass."

"Your reaction says something entirely different."

"*Det er dritt.*" (It's crap, I say.")

Gerda threw her quite a belly laugh. "That's crap you say? Since when do you speak Norwegian?"

Sam stopped moving up onto her berth. "I'm really not sure. Can I tell you a truth since we are bound together on this ship? I'm thinking when we are through, our paths will never cross again?"

Gerda nodded crossing hands over her chest when there was a loud rap at their door.

"Who is it?"

"Mistresses, I have a tray for you, open up."

It was a young lad, a deck hand trying to carry successfully a silver tray holding a feast. Gerda jumped up and took it. "Relay to your Captain our gratitude, lad." She closed the door setting it on a rickety table and glanced at her to continue.

"My real name is Arnesen, Samantha Arnesen and it's ironic that I'm headed to where my name originates from. I've never been there before."

"You will discover quite a bit on this trip. If I had my spearmint leaves, I could make you a tea and read them. But I don't have any on me. I left behind everything."

"Tea?"

"I can do things that show me what has not come to pass using tea leaves. There are other means too. But I must be cautious. If discovered. I could be labeled names and improperly imprisoned

"Like witchcraft and sorcery?"

"Keep your voice down. Let's not mention that again. I am not one of those. But I have unique gifts as well."

"Sorry, I did not mean to offend you Gerda. Were you truly trapped in Aberdeen? Did you never have a chance to escape?"

"Once. We were invaded by my own people. They locked me away in the Keep when that happened. When the Norse were driven away, I knew all my hopes were lost. I have to say, the Laird and his people always treat me with respect, though."

"Did you ever have any doings with that Savoy person?"

"The one you knocked out at the cave? Yes. That man made my hairs rise, he is a leering bastard to say the least. I prayed to Thor asking him to come from the sea and swallow him up. He was in the village once and tried to detain me. But, one of the Laird's men was with me and persuaded him that would not be such a good plan." She grinned. "There was a confrontation. Savoy ended up with a knife wound to the face. He was alone, so he was forced to allow us to move along our way. But, I wonder if he's like a demon reappearing to take revenge on some lost soul."

Sam shuddered wondering the same thing. An immediate change of subject was in order. "Do you have family back in Norway?"

"Aye, I do. Lots of them if they are still alive. We live in a small village near *Stavenger*. As soon as I help with the births, I will go to them. It will be wonderful to be back in my home country."

"Do you happen to know how to read palms?"

She grinned, sitting beside her, taking the right one and studying it. Her brows furrowed. "Mistress, have you been married and released from that marriage?"

Sam smiled. "Yes, a while ago. What else do you see?"

"Two other men. One I think you know, or maybe you know them by now. Both are handsome, strong and quite persistent in their interest in you. But they are from different times. Oh, you are in for quite a ride! But, I also see another woman who has given you advice. You must heed what she has said."

She pulled her hand away. "Shall we have some wine? I don't know about you, but I want to eat and then sleep. Maybe in the morning the captain will let us up on deck." She stuffed a piece of meat in. "Oh, you have to try this. It is delicious. I wonder what it is?"

"It's actually not meat but salted fish. Smoked then pulled off the bone. It's very traditional in Norway."

"Well, it's good. So, you had better help yourself to some before I devour it all."

As they finished, Sam took the water from the wooden bowl and washed her face. She was not going to put on any night cream until candles were out. This woman was already a bit astute, two men, great. Now confirmed by a Tinker and a Beaton.

As her head hit the pillow and Gerda blew out the candles, she was lulled to sleep by the rocking and pitching motion of the ship. "I'm happy for you, Gerda, sleep well."

"Mistress, I'm happy for you as well. For when your choice is made, you will be very high in spirits."

Sam rolled over and closed her eyes not wanting to think about either of them right now. She was exhausted. A leg and shoulder still smarted and her heart was torn between one left behind and one here. Yes, a good night's sleep was in order.

When the day dawned bright, Sam rose, glancing out the small porthole. As she stretched, Gerda was nowhere to be found. Quickly cleaning up, she grabbed the cloak and headed topside.

On deck, she saw the captain, Gunner and the second mate who had the helm in hand. She took her time walking toward them as her sea legs were waking up themselves. As she started to pitch, Gunner was there taking her arm. "Good to see you up and about mistress. You've been asleep for forty-eight hours."

"Are you kidding me?"

"No, we were going to wake you to eat, but left you alone. You should have some food and wine and let Gerda, or, the ship's surgeon check your wound and put on new bandages."

"Oh, my goodness. I'm up here six seconds and you are bossing me about already! Can you give me a chance to catch a breath?" She tried to tug her arm away but his hand held fast with that annoyingly handsome grin on his face, again. Damn him! He was all those things Gerda said and more!

"See you are feeling better and you've found your tongue. What's gotten into you today?"

"Maybe the feeling that everyone else seems to know what the hell I am still doing here. That may have something to do with it."

He leaned in. "You can swear all you want in front of me, but keep your voice low. Others don't need to know what you are about." Glancing around, it was clear the deckhands were close enough to have overheard the tirade.

"Yeah, dressed like a lady, but the mouth of a tramp."

She laughed. "Well I must have woken on the wrong side of the berth, that's all."

He would not release her hand. "Apology accepted." He stared at her boldly, eyes daring her to spew off another round.

"Fine." was all she muttered as they moved along and stood next to the captain.

"You are looking better, mistress, the sea air must agree with you."

"I think so too as well as the good food and wine. How long will it take us to make land in *Stavanger*?"

"We should make port tomorrow midday."

"Your ship is beautiful. It has been a long, long time since I have been on one so fine." She took Gunner by the hand unexpectedly, "Would you take me around so I can see more? Gerda, care to join us?"

An obvious slow smile lit her face as she shook her head.

"What was that for?"

"Who knows, she's a mischievous sort, that Gerda. You seem right of foot on board."

"Yes, I've been on a few over the years."

"So where do you live? Where do you hang your longbow when the day's work is really done?"

He pulled her toward him, holding both her arms.

"A day's sail from the main port. You would not be interested."

"Do you have a ship of your own?"

"I do. It is anchored off shore."

"Will I get home from where we are headed?"

He shrugged his shoulders, noncommittal, leaning back against the port side rail. "What if you are not to go back? That you are to be here for quite a long time? I sense you are leaving behind someone you care about."

"Damn it, I don't even know where the heck I belong to know if I should have a relationship with anyone." Her voice had turned annoyed. Why could no one just tell her and be done with it? "This may be the only time I apologize. So here it is. Sorry. I appreciate your help. Not the fact you shot me. But, I will leave that one be for now."

An apparent nerve had been struck.

"Come on, Gerda is waving us down. It must be time to eat. With food in your mouth, that language can be curtailed."

She jabbed his ribs knowing he was fooling around, but was right. The less she said right now the better. As they ate, good ole Gerda chatted away about her homeland. The fish, market, her mum that had passed away, father still alive, brothers, all seven of them and two sisters. Yes, before they had all finished, even the captain was smiling having not uttered a word himself.

"Mistress, we should look at that bandage now. The ships surgeon has given me fresh ones to apply."

As she followed her down to their cabin, Sam, glanced back grateful Gunner had moved on with the captain and had not seen her do it. What was this all about? Did she have leave to have a relationship with him? In truth, he had been born centuries before Adam.

"Samantha Arnesen!" She hissed out into the cabin.

"What is that you say, mistress?"

"Nothing. Just spurting out loud. It's nothing."

"There, that new bandage should be suitable for the next few days. I am so excited. Tomorrow I will set foot on my home soil again!"

Sam laughed caught up in her excitement. "I know it. Once the duties are taken care of with the birthing, you will be reunited with your family."

"I was forward, mistress. I asked the Captain to have a plate brought to us tonight. I did not feel like small chatter. I hope you don't mind."

"Not at all. You know you can call me Samantha or Sam. It is just us down here."

"No, I cannot. If I get comfortable doing that and it happens in public, there will be a lot of explanations expected. None of which can be answered."

"I understand."

Staring out the porthole, she was thinking about Gunner as Gerda worked about the room humming away. She never even heard the knock at the door or plate being set down on the table. Finally, the aroma reached her nostrils. Glancing down, her eyes raised back out to the glistening water watching the light of day fade over the ocean. It was beautiful. Yes, she could not deny it. Her heart was stirring.

Directly above, Gunner stood with one booted foot up on the cross rail, while he swigged down the rest of the ale, glancing out over the water. Those stirrings reached topside to him.

Chapter Twelve

"Who are those men?" Gunner had a solid grin planted on his face. "Those are from the House of Arne, they are here to give us safe passage to Randaberg."

"Where the hell is that?" she was close to him, his ear down to her mouth. "Where the mother is about to give birth."

"Did you say *Arne*? I know my real parents' name derived from that." She held him back with a strong grip, surprising him for one so petite.

"Yes?"

"Did you hear me?"

"I did. Now come along with no more questions, do you understand? They just have to wait."

Cantankerous slaps followed strong handshakes as Gunner spoke in hushed tones to the large band of guards. To Sam, they did not look welcoming at all. It fit a historical picture she'd viewed from previous studies.

She knew them to be a mixed breed without scruples. Pagans and savages who pillage, plunder and rape leaving a swathe of fear and dread behind. A shudder passed through her as she was hoisted onto a large gelding. Gerda on the other hand, seemed to enjoy a burly man's touch on her as she flirted with him shamelessly. Sam was all too amused at how comfortable she looked in their present company. In any event, they were safe.

Holding tight to the rope, they galloped off at a rapid pace as she wondered how long before she simply fell off. Gerda seemed right at home on hers. Which Sam found amusing.

Gunner was ahead as suddenly two of the men came up, one asking a question. Or, perhaps by the way they were looking at each other, she was their discussion and no question had been asked. Keeping her eyes forward, Sam attempted to ignore them.

"You English?" She stared at her inquisitor for a few seconds. "No, my last name is Arnesen." His companion spoke. "What village?"

Damn, now she was in trouble. Was the village her ancestors hailed from even in existence yet? "It was burned when I was small. I do not know the name. I was taken to another land. This is my first time back."

Shit! Would that work? She glanced straight ahead not wanting to engage in any further conversation. Her mind beseeched Gunner back to her side, right this very second. But, it did not work

"She," he pointed ahead to Gerda, "we knew when she was young. Are you friends?"

Too many questions were being asked. "Yes."

His thigh brushed up against hers. Although he nodded as if in apology while his eyes were keen at taking her in. This was enough. She felt completely ill at ease. Finally, at her persistent silence, they moved up as a small village came into sight.

But, something was amiss.

Gunner, turned and came back.

"You stay with these two men over there under cover. Keep quiet. Mounts stable and absolutely no speaking."

Gerda came close. Horses side by side as the two men raised shields and weapons. A distant whistling came from behind as cold fear gripped Sam.

"Gerda," she barely got out, "stay close to me no matter what happens. If I tell you to get down, do it fast and keep low. I can't protect you if you wander off." She seemed to hear her but what worried Sam was how her eyes had glazed over.

Sam shook her arm roughly. "Get a grip, woman, I need you to have your wits about you."

Suddenly, the guard to her left fell, arrow piercing right through his back and protruded out the front. Gerda was on the verge of screaming as Sam quickly reached over and placed a hand over her mouth. Gerda nodded she was okay. Sliding down off her mount, landing with a thud on the rough gravel, she whispered. "Get down, now."

Pulling on her leg, forcing her to slide off, they crouched as both horses pranced nervously. Crawling on their bellies, the other guard followed them toward the brush. "Stay close to me," he pointed to Gerda. Then glanced at Sam. "You are not so important."

She understood while clutching the coldness of the knife just as two men jumped out of nowhere, seized the guard and were inches from slitting his throat as Sam threw the blade hard as possible, hoping for the best.

Backwards he fell, embedding it further, eyes closing as he passed out. Right about now, she cared less if he was dead or not. By her quick action, the other man had time to draw his sword, killing the other attacker.

He nodded. "Stay here. Pull your knife out of him and prepare. Guard the Beaton with your life." Both women watched him scour the area searching for more of them.

Sam turned the man onto his stomach, put a boot on his back trying to pull it out, but slipped, falling onto him. He did not move as horrified, she put a knee on his back and pulled it. The gross sound nearly caused her to vomit. Using the grass, she wiped it and stood to a petrified look on Gerda's face.

"Are you hurt? Is that his blood?"

Sam glanced down and shook. Had she killed him? He had not moved at all. A lot of blood had soaked her and the ground under him. She had to know. Reaching down, she placed a shaking finger against the hollow of his neck to check for a pulse. It was there but very faint.

Someone was approaching fast as she spun around, poised, knife raised ready to strike again. Her motion was brutally stopped by an iron grip.

"Woman, are you injured? Where is the other man?"

"He's there." she pointed. Just as he made his way back to them. "The other one was pierced by an arrow."

He shook her roughly. "Dammit! Answer me. Are you hurt?"

"No. No I am not. He is though. Do we just leave him here?"

"He tried to kill you, mistress. What would you do now? Bandage him, leave him off in the next village so he could stalk and kill you?"

"No, but he is still alive, although barely."

Gunner was pissed off, speaking briskly. "Gerda, is there something you can quickly do? The rest of the men have checked the village. It was pillaged by the Normans. They must have been part of it and are still close by. We need to divert. Do something now. They will be back here shortly."

She pulled up some moss and spit on it several times, placing it on the wound under his shirt. She took her elk skin horn filled with water and placed it beside him. "It is in his hands now if he lives or dies."

Sam picked up her cloak from the grass and threw it over her body just as the men reappeared. They all stood near and glanced down at one of their own dead. Conversations took place but neither women could hear. Once concluded, Gunner approached.

"Let me get you onto your mount." She put a leg up and took the rope. He was watching her closely now knowing she had never been in a situation like this. "I'll ride with you both."

Sam nodded, but remained quiet. As they moved on and darkness took over the day, it started to rain. He reached over and pulled the hood up over her head and handed over a piece of dried fish. Taking it, she clicked her heels into the mare's side and moved up next to Gerda. "Are you doing okay?"

"Mistress, I'm more worried about you. I've seen plenty of savagery in my time. But I don't think you have seen the likes of what occurred today."

She handed her the fish. "I'll be okay. I'm adjusting my thinking that he was alive when we left. If any bit of magic will heal him, it will be what you did. I'm going to keep that thought because I may never know."

"Better that you are long gone if he does live and heals. No man would want to be knowing he was bested by a woman." She smiled, patting Sam's hand. "You are a lethal weapon with that, mistress."

"It is a benefit to carry certain items of comfort Gerda." Sam nodded to her slowing the mount as Gunner caught up. "You are not hungry. But still need your strength."

"I can smell his blood on me, Gunner. I can't eat right now. How much longer before we get there?"

"Daylight. Do you want to ride with me? I'll tie your horse to mine so you can rest."

"Of course not. Then I'd appear weak."

She smiled as they exchanged a long look.

"They won't say it, mistress, but they think you are a warrior from the House of Arne and have the blood of the Goddess Freyja coursing through your veins."

"Frey what?"

"Freyja. The Goddess of love, fertility and battle. I'd say that about sums you up."

Thank heavens it was dark, for she was sure her face was flamed again. "Funny I did not know that. I am more familiar with Thor, Forseti and Hoenir."

He chuckled catching himself. "Hoenir, the Silent God? Mistress that's priceless."

"Glad I could lend a bit of humor to this dark night." Ironically, they were both smiling as the soldier from earlier rode up beside her.

Sam locked eyes with him.

"You fought well, Arnesen."

Nodding, she did not reply as he clicked his heels and continued up ahead. Now, at least in this group of men, she'd be left to her own devices and was safe.

Gunner took out his skin and drank of wine, handing it to her. She took a large gulp, swallowed then took a second before handing it back.

"It will warm your insides in this dankness."

"I don't suppose there is a hot shower waiting for me when I get there?"

"You don't quit, do you? A true picture of you is forming in my mind."

"Do you think we could disperse with the formalities in lieu of what we've been through? Do you think it would be permissible to call me Samantha?"

"It took you long enough to ask."

She gave up at that point and just shut up. As they rode through the night and the sky was returning to daylight, she saw the village and Keep. "What is that?"

"Where hopefully we won't be long. It's Castle Berghus. Just a note here. You need to pay attention to not being alone in halls, rooms or grounds. Either I am with you or Gerda. I can say the men from this area are ruthless and would not hesitate to take you in broad daylight in front of their wives."

She nodded appreciating his frank candor. As they dismounted, the group dispersed as Gunner took her by the arm, motioning Gerda to move up ahead of them. Apparently, she already knew where they needed to go.

In the great hall, Gerda halted taking Sam by the arm. "We need to go up there. Don't let go of me. Now come along. Time is ticking away."

Turning to speak to Gunner, Sam stopped as a wench with heaving cleavage launched herself into his arms and planted a hearty kiss on his lips. Quick enough she had tugged him into a secluded location. Jealousy, strong and undeniable, sprang to the surface as Gerda dragged her up the remaining stone steps onto the second landing.

Bastard, she thought! How dare he? But then again, what the hell was she thinking, anyway? If this was what men who take passages do, then she'd think long and hard about having any kind of relationship with Adam if she ever got back there again.

"Mistress, why are you making this so hard for me? We need to hurry!"

"Gerda I'm sorry. Where do we go?"

"Into a bedroom to help with birthing. Asta does not even know she's having twins. But I do. I saw it in the leaves. We must be quick about getting into her rooms."

She swung a large door open to a rush of ladies in waiting coming over to halt her progress.

"Stop, I am Gerda the Healer. Listen to me so we can help Mistress Gud. I need a large kettle of hot water, a knife, clean linen and some silk twine. Now, please go and get what I have asked!"

People started hustling from the room as she slid her cloak to the side and rolled up her sleeves, sitting down beside the Mistress Gud.

"There, there, I will help you. How much pain are you in?"

She was sweating as Sam took a cloth, wiping a brow. "Who are you?"

"I am Mistress Samantha here to help Gerda." She placed a hand under her shoulders and lifted. "Here, take a sip of some wine."

Sam was afraid to take her cloak off for fear the woman would see all the blood. That just did not seem like a good idea since she was about to give birth. As the ladies started coming back with the necessities, one came over and tapped Sam on the shoulder.

"Mistress, Master Gudrun asked me to give you this. He instructed me to wait while you changed and to take your dress with me." Sam turned expecting to see the wench from downstairs that had accosted him. Suddenly relieved it was not. Great, she thought, it was probably one of hers, though. Regardless, she stepped back behind the barrier and hastily removed it, rolling it into a tight ball, then came out and handed it over.

She whispered. "You take that and burn it without talk, am I clear?" Her voice commanded complete authority as the maid nodded and hurried from the room to do exactly that.

"Mistress, wash your hands. I need you to take the white cloth and fold it into fours and have it ready. I am going to lift her up and I want you to put the knife beneath her spine, halfway down."

Sam nodded working quickly.

"Mistress Gud, are you ready to start pushing?" She nodded, clenching teeth as the pains increased. "I'm ready. I have instructed a servant to wait outside the door for news to take to my husband." As the moans increased in earnest, her delicate hands clutching tightly at the bedding. "Tell me when…" Her voice quivered in pain.

"Push. Yes, harder. One more mistress, I can see the head! Oh. It's a red-haired girl." She handed her over to Sam as she cleaned and wrapped her snugly.

"But wait, there is another on the way!" Gerda's excitement radiated around the room. "Push, my lady, push again!"

The squeal of a second arrival brought Sam closer, ready to take the newborn.

"It's a boy! You have a handsome son, and a comely girl." Gerda handed him to Sam as she quickly had the twins nestled side by side in a basket.

"Oh, Mistress, they are indeed beautiful and listen to them talking to each other. They will always be close. Do you have names for them yet?" Sam knew she was rambling on. But, since she had no children of her own, seeing this process was amazing.

"We had not thought of two, but the boy is going to rule someday. So, his name is Olaf II Haraldsson. I think his sister should have the great name of Gerda."

"Oh, how lovely of you to do that. I am honored."

Listening to them, Sam crept over to the door and opened it. "Go and tell the King he has a fine, healthy son and daughter, Olaf and Gerda." Closing the door, it dawned on her why she was here.

Her head began to spin slightly, mouth going dry. When she had paid for her family ancestry, she recalled seeing this name. Asta Arnesen Gudbrandsdatter. This was a long distant relative. Her ancient family.

Creeping over toward one darkened corner, she wept. Finally, as the tears diminished, she wiped away the rest and found a true smile emerging from inside as it ended up on her lips. This would be a time she'd remember all the rest of her days.

There was a soft knock on the door as the King came in. Proud as a peacock, love shone brightly in his eyes as he quickly moved over to his wife's side. Gerda had placed both children in their mother's arms, as he reached down gently touching both with a fingertip.

"We must go." Closing the door, Gerda, took her by the arm and squeezed it. "I heard you crying. Are you okay, mistress?"

"Yes, it was the first time I'd seen a child born, let alone two. Gerda, you are indeed a miracle worker. That was beyond words."

"Thank you. I will stay on a few days to help them. Then I will leave to join my family in the village. You will be leaving sooner, I believe." As she moved off suddenly.

Feeling him before he even arrived, Sam glanced up as he approached with a servant in tow.

"I'll take you to your room where there is food and wine. Gerda, go with the servant and she will show you where to sleep this night."

"Wait." Sam spoke. Turning towards Gerda's arms. "I will think of you often, Healer."

"And I of you, mistress." Quickly Gerda was around the hall, out of sight.

"This way, Samantha."

He opened the heavy wooden door stepping aside to let her pass. "I see you got changed in time."

"Thanks for taking care of it. I hope you did not remove it from that wench you were locked with and left her standing someplace cold."

"A bit jealous?"

"Nope, not at all." She went quiet, but the urge to hurl something harmful at his head was absurdly strong.

"I'm going to be sharing your room tonight. There is a rough crowd down there celebrating the King and Queen's new additions. So, I want to prevent any issues with delaying our departure tomorrow."

She spun around, furious, staring him down, but was instead met with his hard, muscled chest.

"Calm down. I will sleep on the floor in front of the hearth. It is only one night." She closed her eyes to will her heart from pounding as his hands moved slightly down to the curve of her waist.

"Are you afraid to look at me?"

If he had said look at me, she would have bristled, but instead he was daring her and she was no coward.

As she raised her eyes to him, her toes lifted and met his lips. The braided rope belt fell to the floor as he hoisted the shift over her head and stopped at the ties crossing over her heaving bosom.

He took her lips again. Not so gentle this time as she weaved her arms up around his neck and grabbed his long, unruly hair. If he shaved the beard and cut the hair, would he be truly handsome as imagined?

"Samantha, if you were just the wench downstairs I'd not hesitate to have you on your back right now. But, you are not. We've been through a lot. Here tonight is not where I want it to begin for us."

He lowered her to the bed. She turned and eyed it. Yes, she internally thought, it would serve them both.

"So why don't you just go and do that, with that wench down there. Get it out of your system and then return. You can knock and I'll let you in."

He grinned expecting a retort of such. "Because I am protecting you and she is more than likely already entwined with another. Possibly two."

She scuffed up the dirt on the floor with one shoe. "All right, then come over and sleep here. There is plenty of room for us both. I promise you I will not try and seduce you in the same manner that you use. Especially during the lateness of the night."

She slid under the furs, laid back on her side of the straw mattress, closed her eyes and was asleep in minutes.

He chuckled, settling down opposite following her lead and was also asleep in short order.

Chapter Thirteen

Oh, this dream was delightful, she thought, resting under his chin. Then, an exploration began while weaving an errant hand beneath his tunic to feel the heat of his skin. He was a chiseled being, as gentle fingers cruised over the hard plains and valleys of his chest. As her hand moved slightly lower, she felt the hairs, sighing, as suddenly her body was swung swiftly backside with his lips possessing such searing passion, it forced her toes to curl.

She wove her hands up under his thick long hair, clasped them behind his neck, noticing a crevice. His hand cupped a breast long before it had peaked, hurting against the rough shift she was wearing. When his lips left hers and he leaned up on elbows, his deep raspy voice penetrated her sleep induced brain.

"That's a hell of a way to wake a man up, mistress." Her eyes shot open, cheeks inflamed. But where could she go with him holding her down like this. So, she smiled, which threw him off guard. He truly had expected a knee to the groin. One eyebrow cocked as a crooked grin appeared on his handsome face.

"What, no fighting? No slugging or throwing me to the dirt floor?"

Instead, she wiggled, knowing that caused him much more discomfort.

"Samantha, I'd take you here, right now and you know it. Don't fool with me. Besides, it is nearly first light. As much as we would both enjoy our tryst, we need to head out of here before the King and Queen want to see you. I'm sure sooner or later they will have more questions. We cannot stick around to answer them."

She looked put out that he was making so much sense. But, he had not budged an inch.

"You had better let me up then. So, we can prepare to exit before any of that can take place."

He slid off her and sat on the side of the bed glancing toward the now brightening sky. "Yeah, we have to go. Can you be ready in a couple of minutes?"

"Yes." She rose throwing the tunic over her head and picked up the rope, tying it. "That's it. I can put my hair up on our way out." Sliding the cloak on, she glanced about the room. "Let's go."

They crept down the stairs and through the hall. Moving slowly against one far wall, he surveyed the scene. Everyone was sleeping. Slowly, they continued along taking the safest exit. Once outside, he lifted the hood, reminding her instantly of another man at another time.

"We just need to go to the Chapel. It's a short walk. Stay close and be quick with your steps."

Nearly jogging to keep up with his long strides, they arrived outside the lovely, old, stone chapel. Halting to glance up at the beautiful workmanship of the stain glass windows, he tugged her inside.

"No confessional?"

He grinned. "No, they did it face to face in this era. Those came a few centuries later."

"How do we get out then?" As if in a trance, Sam glanced about at the cold, stark beauty. She turned toward the altar as a soft, golden beam encased it.

"Go, we don't have all day!"

She moved into it, walking down a long tunnel brightly lit with torches.

"Well." she said out loud noticing he was not behind her. "This is very different."

Up ahead, the paths forked. As she walked by the path to the right, she halted and looked back.

"Hmm." she said continuing. "Maybe he was staying or his beam took him a different route." Shrugging, she continued along the path to the right.

The announcement was loud and clear.

"Mind the platform. The train to Exeter is now approaching the platform."

Exeter. Momentarily dazed and confused, Sam watched the train approached. The doors opened and she got on, found a vacant seat and fell onto it. Pressing her forehead against the cold glass, the countryside passed quickly and she knew it well. The train stopped as she rose and got off.

"Holy shit, am I really back?" She mouthed rather loudly.

Up ahead parked exactly as remembered was her red Spark. Sitting in the car, a grin formed while turning the car key. She tested the wiper blades. Even though it was not raining.

One of her favorite songs, Karma Chameleon, blared from satellite radio. Which quickly brought her mind back to the present.

Clicking in the seatbelt, Sam shifted through the gears, depressed the button so the sunroof opened and burned some serious rubber out of the parking lot. The attendant smiled, waving to her. She knew him! It was Dave. Damn, what the hell had been going on? Did someone throw a mind-altering drug into her lunch drink? While she tried not to think about it, or anyone for that matter, she was pulling into her driveway.

Lifting the wreath on the back door, she took out the spare key, unlocked it and walked in. A loud sigh escaped as she moved through the utility room removing her Sperry Topsiders. Her Pinarelli road bike was straight ahead, leaning against a wall. It was indeed like a long-lost lover. Oh, if this was real or not, she was going to take a ride. Throwing her clothes right there, she changed and was out on the road in five minutes.

Glancing down at her speedometer, she knew exactly what route to take. Pedaling down a lovely, English, country lane, one she knew so well, Sam released a hoot that sent a bouquet of pheasant scampering from the brush as she sped by.

Weeks, had she been gone weeks or longer? The date on her Garmin said it was 16 September and she had left for Venice in May!

She spewed out loudly, "Oh, Mother of God. I was gone almost four months? Could that be?" Glancing up at the puffy clouds, Sam noticed they were beginning to turn into angry storm faces. "I'd better get my ass in gear and head back. That's not a pretty looking sight at all."

She pulled the bike up on the porch and brought it back into the utility room. But, did not put it away, "You and me, my friend, tomorrow. I sure am glad to see you again."

That night she was restless, tossing and turning endlessly, it seemed, for no apparent reason at all. Here, she was safe from the likes of Gunner, Savoy and even Adam. If they were even real. Fluffing the pillow and turning a cheek, she glanced out the open window watching the storm come straight for her. All she could think about, as sleep claimed her body and mind, was Dorothy in Kansas.

Birds were singing, had she not heard the same song at Adam's estate? She opened one eye slowly to check, and then the other, a smile on her face. Nope, the harsh storm winds had passed and this morning she was indeed inside her cottage in Exeter.

Three days of riding ensued which had her spirits soaring high as she tucked the bike in the closet. Dripping sweat, she started walking up the stairs peeling cycling clothes, bit by bit, until she was naked at the top then started a bath.

Sliding in with a sigh, Sam settled back, head resting on a pillow, and closed her eyes. This was heaven. These were the two things she missed being anywhere but in this century. A bath and bike. If she was stationary in the latter part of the 1800's when bikes were invented, it would have suited her a bit more. But alas, this was a nice treat!

"You really should lock your doors, you know, although I have to admit I was looking forward to finding you at the end of the clothes trail."

She reached for her gun, pointed it at Adam, then lowered it slightly as the movement spewed water all over the tiled floor. Her lower jaw dropped as she put the gun back behind the pink fluff and reached for a large towel, standing.

"This makes me wonder more and more who you really are because you found me."

"When you did not come back, I had to."

"Did you ever think maybe I needed a bit of time alone?"

She watched his eyes rake her over. Slowly taking in her wet, reckless curls then finally reaching her toes. She let the towel slip, putting on the robe and tugged the straps tightly keeping it shut.

"I really wanted to make sure you are okay and my cellphone in 1865 is not as savvy as yours in 2015."

"Very funny." She walked over having pulled the plug on the bath and stood within fingers reach of him. "I'm well, as you see. So, do you want to tell me how you can come here if you are not on a purpose?"

He leaned against the door jam. "Well, Sam, it's like this." His finger found its way to that tie, eyes steady with hers. "I have liberties that not everyone else does. So, I took one and came thinking you may be here. If you were not, I was going to head to Norway."

The tie was undone. "Do you know all my moves? Honestly, were you aware of me before we even met in

Venice? Did you have anything to do with it not being by chance?"

She felt that one roaming finger touch her right hip.

"Yes, to all three."

His left hand moved up her curvy waist as she leaned toward him. The robe slid away into a heap on the floor.

"That's not fair." Her voice was hoarse.

"Then make it fair."

She unbuttoned his shirt, closing her eyes as she stood on tip toes and kissed him. His shirt went to join her robe as she pressed her breasts into his chest. His breath into her mouth was warm and rushed, then she stopped and leaned back.

"Gunner was you."

"Yes."

"You were with me in Aberdeen and on the ship and you slept with me at the castle."

His warm lips caressed the curve of her neck lowering his mouth down and sucking on a puckered breast.

"Yes."

She left her body then, not just by the power of his touch but by the power of his love. She slid his belt off as his jeans followed.

"Glad I took my shoes off downstairs so I could creep up on you."

"Why did you not tell me?" They were head to toe naked.

"Because how well would it go over if I told you I had to shoot you to get you to help me?"

She managed a small smile.

"So how did you know it was me?"

"The notch in the back of your neck."

He leaned down and positively possessed her mouth lifting her up as her legs wound around his powerful hips. "And your kiss. No man has ever kissed me like you do."

He found her bed and slid them both onto its downy softness.

"But you let Gunner kiss you when you have feelings for me."

"But as him, you let a wench in the hall kiss you when you have feelings for me."

He smoothed her hair back brushing her cheek with the back of his hand.

"She caught me by surprise. In short order, I disengaged her and went in search of a dress for you."

Her hands slid over his hips, his ass as she rose slightly pulling his lips back to hers. She did not care about what he did or she did. When or where and under what name. Gunner there, Adam here.

"Sam."

"Stop all this talk now, Adam…"

His finger found her moistness and swirled around, as her body slightly arched. Reaching down and enclosing his enlarged manhood, she stroked him, running her finger over his tip, causing a shudder to stream through them both.

In a swift motion, he opened her thighs up more as she brought them high up his back. He entered her, moving slowly in and out as her nails dug into his back. Their momentum increased so fast she released him to clutch the pillow, moaning into his mouth.

He leaned down, clasping her hands in his as he forcefully plunged, until their release came in such a rush, that emotions so strong rocked right from her loins into his.

He cupped her chin with two fingers, lifting her mouth up taking more of her sweetness.

"You are small. I must be too heavy on you." He started to lift but a strong grasp stopped him.

"No, stay right where you are."

He lowered back moving to his side. She did not want any conversation; the need to digest all of this, all of him, more important. Staring into his eyes, a soft smile would not be denied.

"So, are you ready to come back with me?"

"Well, not quite yet. How much time do we have?"

"A couple of days, why?"

"Because here, it's just you and me. There is no Savoy, no demands and finally no wenches and mistresses."

He had no choice but to grin at all of that. "Sam, why don't you bring the things you want with you on our return?"

"How am I going to get my bike and other items back and not be reviewed as a bit odd ?"

"Yeah, well, the bike won't work. Plus, our roads are not conducive to having those thin tires. Leave it here. You can come back when necessary. The important thing is knowing when it's time to go. If you do not, then there may not be another opportunity. Unless, someone comes to intervene."

"Can you always see where I am?"

"Yes. It seems I can. I do not have such an option with others."

She was confused, not understanding what he was saying. He leaned down, kissing her lips softly then pulled back knowing there was more.

"Then how come I can't see you?"

He laughed. "Well I am here right now, woman, but when I go, you will be able to."

"If you needed me to save you, how would I know where and when to get to you?"

That caught his fancy. "I suppose. But I can't see you coming to my aid, but you never know." He pinched a nipple as she pushed him onto his back. "Well, maybe you will want me to come to your aid." She slid warm kisses down over his stomach, then lower still.

"Sam."

"Just relax, Adam, I promise you won't need anyone to save you now."

Chapter Fourteen

For two days and nights, they spent all their time together. But when duty called it was time to go.

"Sam pack up what you want. We head out this morning. I have to get back before tonight."

"I'm ready now if you want. Should I get my keys or are we walking? The closest church is about twenty minutes away on foot."

His hand curved over her butt, appreciating every single inch he now knew so well.

"Keys. Yes, we will go back the same way you came in. I'm really surprised you did not get towed having your car there that long."

"You think it's invisible, like our passages? Maybe I should call up a cab and leave it here? Yeah, I'm going to do that it. It won't delay our departure but a few extra minutes. Here, ring this number and tell them to send one. I'll just take a walk through and make sure everything else it taken care of."

Placing them up on the hook, she checked all the windows and doors. He was outside waiting with the few things she was taking in a small backpack when the gravel under tires indicated the cab was pulling in.

They both got in as she spoke to the driver.

"Exeter Station, please."

He nodded and sped off getting them there in less than twenty minutes. Paying the man, Adam grabbed the backpack from the trunk.

"You use this for hiking? It looks like it could tell a lot of stories."

She got their tickets as they waited for the train. She glanced up at the electronic sign and back at him.

"If it could talk, I'd have to kill it. Besides, the other one I have back at your estate is one I'd like to keep around. This one could be handy with some of the places I've been going of late. The next train is in four minutes."

"Would it tell me about all the past romances?"

She gave him a sour look. Had she told him about the ugly divorce?

"Did I tell you I was married before? Perhaps it was not you. It was Mrs. H., damn, I can't remember now."

"No, it must have been Mrs. H. Is it a subject off topic for further inquiry?"

"Hey, it's over. He was a cheater and a liar and I was too busy with my career to give a damn until it got nasty. So really, it was my fault. I could have paid more attention to what was happening. I don't think I cared enough. Makes me sound cold and callous, I know."

"Sam, you are none of that crap, so let that be. It takes two to tango. If you insist on taking any blame at all, make it no more than fifty percent."

She smiled. "This, Lord Adam, will be our horse and carriage."

The train arrived as they boarded and sat and he looked up at the train map on the inside of their car.

"We are off at the next stop. So, how long ago was it?"

"It was finalized earlier this past winter. When we met in Venice. I had just quit my job and decided to run wild and travel. Just find the girl I pushed aside a long time ago and rekindle that relationship."

"You found her, that's for sure, or I think you did." He put an arm around her shoulder and squeezed, leaning down to an ear. "You know the saying, right? His loss my gain."

She smiled snuggling with him as the automated voice announced the next station. Side by side they exited the train as he pushed open a stairwell and they climbed up a secluded set of steps and were now back at the ruins of Ard Aulinn.

"Stop." He grabbed her arm. "Tell me what you feel this very second."

Her face was lifted toward the warm sun as she inhaled the fresh air.

"Peaceful, I feel very peaceful." They continued along toward the estate.

"So, when you are on a passage and you know there is something you must do, like kiss a wench or kill a person, you just settle it within yourself and get it done, right?"

"Right. But where are you headed with this?" Skepticism was written all over his face.

"Well, I did two things you do not know about on my last passage."

He did not miss a step. "How can that be? You were not out of my sight for more than a few minutes in total. What is it?"

"Savoy. He was waiting for us at the exit of the cave. I slugged him with the butt of my gun. I'm not so sure he was alive. I think so, but hell I don't know. The other one is I know that the Queen is an ancestor of mine."

"That's a tall order of events especially for Savoy. He's going to hunt you down for sure, Sam. We need to take extra precautions right away. As for the visit, did she know your name?"

She shook her head. "Gerda promised not to mention me by last name. Simply introduced me as Mistress Samantha. The King did though, does that count for anything?"

"Technically, no, because he is not an Arnesen. The queen is. You are fine. We need to find out why Savoy pursues you. He's going to be mighty pissed off, especially if he has a lump to keep reminding him."

He held the back door open as they walked down the hall, into his study and up the winding stairs to her rooms.

"I want you to move into my rooms." He held up his hand as if he knew a protest was to follow. But what was odd to Sam was how he towered over her right now. Weird. He had never been like that. Dominating. He had always treated her like an equal.

"Listen, there are several reasons. More staff are on that side. I can keep track of you and I think it's time you carry something a bit bigger than that dagger. I know your accuracy. But some of the people you come across are burly and stronger than you."

She was not buying any of it. He skirted around the true reason. For now, she'd let it go.

"Maybe I should go ahead in time and spend a few days in the company of the Special Services? Perhaps a few days with the Royal Navy's elite force would do the trick?"

He raised an eyebrow. "Yeah, not likely. You'd enjoy yourself way too much. But I do know a devil of a rogue from Ireland that would be up for that job in a heartbeat once his gaze rested on you."

She smiled raising both brows. "Is he as handsome and tall as you? Perhaps we should get in touch with him?"

"Woman, you need to remember whose touch you prefer above all else and quit thinking you can flirt with all the good-looking blokes you are going to encounter."

"Well, considering the last bloke was you, posing as another, I guess I'm pretty safe, aren't I?"

He laughed. "Enough, you win. This time, anyway."

They had reached her rooms as he closed the doors behind them.

"Pack up what you don't want Abbey to see and let her move the rest. It will give the chit something to take care of. If you do it now, I'll help you. I don't think you even know where my rooms are, right?"

She laughed, shaking her head.

"No, I don't have any idea in this huge place. So how many are there here anyway? Rooms I mean."

He was at one set of large windows glancing out over the gardens.

"Adam?"

He turned. "Thirty-two."

She walked over surveying outside, but found nothing amiss.

"What's up?"

"It is fine. I was just gathering wool. You ready?"

That was bullshit and she knew it. Something had drawn his attention. Handing him the larger bag, she pulled the small roller.

"All set."

As they left her wing and entered the center halls, she walked along the family portraits and glanced at them one at a time. This was one place warranting a return visit. It took nearly fifteen minutes before they halted at his doors. Opening, she stepped around going in.

"Oh, this is nice."

Ancient coverings adorned the walls with two intricately carved marble fireplaces strategically placed on both ends. Leaving the bags, Sam walked over to gaze at amazing views of the lake and expansive gardens. But, it was the large, king size, four poster bed, plush to the nines, that gained her attention.

"Think you will be comfortable? Look in here. I have a writing room I don't need. I prefer my study. You can use it for anything you desire."

She glanced in. It looked suitable enough for now until the cottage was ready. Her mind went to Abbey. She'd need to seek her out and get an update, then take a walk down and see the progress.

The room was silent as they both seemed preoccupied right now.

"I'm going to leave you to unpack. Tuck the bags in the armoire, they will fit. I'll send Abbey up in short order to get the rest of your things. Oh, that door leads to the bathroom."

Her eyes met his, steady and studying. Something was wrong.

"Does that hallway lead down a back stairway to your study?"

"Aye, it does. You should explore this side of the house. There is a lot of history."

"Sounds cool, will do. As soon as I finish I'm going to the stables and a ride."

He pulled her into his arms. "Sam, just for the rest of the day will you stick around the house, or, in the veranda area? Don't be stubborn about it. I need to make sure everything is in order outside before I leave. Will you do this for me?"

She kissed him, feeling the softness of those lips that could wreak havoc on mind and skin simultaneously.

"Okay, I will."

He grinned, easing her discomfort. "What, now? I don't have to go until the morning."

She laughed glancing around his body toward the large bed.

"So, we can christen this together tonight?"

"Indeed, madam, we can. I'll go see to Abbey. You get things done here. I want you well settled before I go. Come to my study when you are through." He kissed both her hands and walked out of the rooms.

She moved over to one of the large windows and wondered if he saw someone outside? Was that why he wanted her to move into his? Or, did he see something coming her way he could not tell her about now? Indeed, he was an enigma.

A light rap at the door preceded Abbey's arrival. Same gave her instructions as, bless her soul, someone must have told her in advance. For she arrived with a tray of biscuits and a hot pot of tea.

"Ah, Abbey, you are a gem. Thank you. I'll come and help you pack up the rest of my things."

"Oh no, mistress. I was advised to not trouble you with any of it. I will take care of it myself."

"Very well." she halted placing sugar and cream into her teacup, poured the aromatic blend and sipped, "Thank you. We can talk later about what's been going on."

As Abbey rushed out of the room, closing the door softly behind.

His bear claw porcelain tub was a glory to behold. It reminded her of the night he crept through her Exeter home, into her bathroom and took from her what he wanted. Her body felt the heat even now. Glancing up, she noticed Abbey had returned more than once. Where the hell was her mind? She knew. It had been lingering on Adam.

"This looks like all of it, right?"

"Yes, mistress it is. I'll finish unpacking it all for you."

"That's okay. By the way, I still plan on moving into the cottage. Have you been able to view their progress by any chance?"

"I have. It is coming along nicely. They have cleaned it all out, plugged all the holes and were fixing the roof yesterday. Today, they were going to whitewash the walls and clean the floors. Mr. Bruce thought it may be ready in another week or so. We need a good rain to make sure the roof does not leak at all."

"Wonderful! Let's not mention this to anyone just yet? Lord Griffin wanted me to move in here with him for reasons I can't explain. But it's more than what is obvious, I can assure you." She glanced at Abbey's blushed cheeks and bright eyes and nearly laughed out loud.

"But, as soon as it's all set, we will move. Do you still want to come? I promise to not work you hard and there will be plenty of time to yourself. Every night you can go back home to your parents."

"When will I start, as soon as we move? I think I need to say something to Mrs. Hoyt."

"Don't concern yourself with that. I'll take care of it. Now, go ahead and take the tray to the kitchens. We can discuss this more over the next few days." Sam nodded needing the conversation over. He'd be pissed she knew, but she was going to hold fast at moving in there. Both would eventually benefit from this decision.

Winding down the private staircase, she suddenly felt a bit odd. Hesitating, she glanced over at him before entering. He was penning a letter as she leaned on the corner of his gorgeously carved mahogany desk. Not speaking, she let him finish. He set the quill into the inkwell, shook the paper to dry, then folded it up, dropping wax onto it, sealing it with his family crest.

"These traditions have been taking place throughout time. I hope they never stop and I'm here long enough to witness more of them."

He found that thought unsettling. "You do belong here. There's no doubt in my mind about that."

Sam shrugged her shoulders. "I'm all settled. I don't want you to get angry with me, but tomorrow I am heading to see Father G and Mrs. Baker." She decided not to discuss the cottage right now. "I've missed them both."

"Let me suggest you do that in reverse order and absolutely. I think that would be good for you."

"So, we have until morning, right?" She moved resting down, straddling his hips. Her lips met with no resistance when pressed to his. "Correct."

She moved off as his hands let her go, undoing his trousers, sliding them down. Grabbing her back, close, his fingers moved her dress up into a heap.

"Ah, madam, no undergarments today. What is this?"

Seductively, she moved onto his lap and took him inside of her in one sweet, quick motion. He started to move but she stopped him.

"No, sit still."

As their eye's locked, it was felt by them both.

"What are you about?"

She kissed him long, hard, as the heat of her moistness seared his soul. She held him tight not allowing movement as deep within a wave of ecstasy flowed.

Moaning into his mouth, the kiss evolved into its own form of lovemaking. The pleasure spread through them as if they were one. He pulled her closer, harder against him until it swept them both into a dimension so beyond, they shook together.

His arms nearly crushed her as she sagged against his hard chest.

"Oh, my God, how is it we can do this?"

"I don't know." she could barely get out.

"You have me spellbound. Lord, I can't even imagine not being with you."

She kissed him deeply, craving more.

"I just wanted to make sure if any wenches were in your midst, you'd remember what you have back here." She grinned coyly.

"Oh, I hear that warning and understand, mistress. It is look, but not touch, right? Well, I remember when it was not apparent I was holding you in my arms back in Norway. So, in your reality you were kissing another man."

She stood so fast, much to his chagrin. "Yes." she smoothed her gown down producing quite a grin. "But you were always toying with me. You got what you deserved, Lord Griffin."

"What the hell am I going to do with you?"

"I expect you don't need a comment for you have no idea."

Laughter bellowed out as he slid his boots up on the corner of the desk.

"Really, Sam, could you think of yourself with anyone but me?"

As she swished her skirts away from the desk, he eyed every bit, shaking his head. The need for her again growing apparent. This woman had indeed bewitched him and he'd have it no other way. Shit, it took into his early fifties and her to do it.

"I'd be a fool to say it's not true." As a cold shiver suddenly doused the passion they had just shared. Was this a warning? What had the Tinker said then the Healer?

In a few quick strides, he was at her side, pulling her into his arms, claiming her lips with near brutal force.

"I was just talking to you and you were a thousand years away. What's up?"

Sam's hand moved up his trousers, over his enlarged manhood. Not uttering a word, rubbing up against the fabric, the other hand tugged his head down to awaiting parted lips. Like a thief in the night, she took everything he had left.

"Black magic woman, that's what you are."

"That's right and don't turn your back on me, ever."

He grinned. The knock at the door only separated their bodies, but not their souls.

"Sir, pardon the intrusion. But I have a letter for you." The butler handed him a sealed envelope, which he quickly opened, read and placed back in it. He opened the desk draw and slid it inside.

Sam did not bother to ask. If he wanted her to know she'd know. Period.

"Shall we go to dinner?" Switching gears, Adam took her hand, heading them out of the study toward the dining hall. "After we dine, I'm going to take you someplace special on the grounds you've not seen."

"I keep finding these secret places, so I can't wait. How much land do you actually own?"

"On the estate, over two hundred acres."

"Well then, it may take a long time to explore it all."

She stopped talking to eat. He would always know when she was truly hungry. She got quiet. As they finished he rose, laughing, while Sam, placed her linen napkin up beside her plate.

"Come, it's a bit of a walk. But, a fine night it is all the same."

As they journeyed through the woods, she absorbed how peaceful it was, then stopped, mesmerized.

"Oh my, who designed this?"

"Capability Brown years ago."

She was speechless. It was like stepping back and being transported to Rome; the Acropolis lit at night where she had once been when roaming around Athens.

"It's beautiful." All other words failed her.

"Well, remember this place. It will deliver you to a safe place when needed. Plus, there is a bonus near your cottage. But I'll let you discover that on your own if the shrubs and plants have not overtaken it."

That piqued her curiosity as she turned toward him and slid quite neatly into the fold of his arm. Warning signs interfered with this reflective moment. Apparent and unable to ignore it any longer, Sam knew something big was coming her way.

Chapter Fifteen

Running her hand over his still warm pillow, Sam kept her eyes closed knowing he was gone. After she rang for Abbey, she took out what would be worn today. Glancing out the large windows toward the gardens to a bright blue sky, a sigh escaped her lips. Today would have been an outstanding day for a cycle through the countryside. Instead, she'd settle for a jaunt to the village to see the good father, then she'd stop off at the cottage.

Abbey, knocked and waited.

"Come in."

Sliding open the door, she was quickly followed by two man servants carrying hot water.

"Mistress, do you want me to get you a breakfast tray?"

"Is there still food down in the kitchen? I know I rose a bit late today."

"Eat in the kitchen? Oh, mistress I don't know about that."

Sam smiled. "Abbey, it's fine. You can let cook know I'll be down as soon as I bathe. Can you take out the rest of my things? I'll be just a few minutes."

Dressed and prepared for the day, she left Abbey to drain the water and make up the bed. Humming down the stairs to the kitchen, she entered to a lively Mrs. Lilly, smiling.

"I could hear your jaunty tune all the way down the hall. I have a warmed plate of eggs and crumpets for you."

She slid up on a high chair and nodded eating at an unladylike pace. "Sorry, Mrs. Lilly, but I was famished. Would you happen to know where Mrs. Hoyt is?"

"Roaming the rooms making sure things are in order. You want me to pass her a message?"

"No, just wanted to say hello. I'm headed into the village to the Bakers. Do you need any orders placed? I'm happy to bring them with me."

"Mistress, I surely do. Let me get the paper for you. I'll just be a moment." She reached over with floured hands and wiped them off on her apron. "Let her know she can deliver these on Thursday. There is no rush at all."

Nodding, Sam dabbed her lips with the linen napkin, washed her dishes then placed them on the rack to dry. Mrs. Lilly shook her head and continued kneading the dough

Today, Sam took the main lane down to the village, preferring to be seen rather than take any chances on the back path to the church. She opened the side rectory door and found him immediately.

"Hello, Father Godwin."

He stepped back having filled the daily wine.

"Ah, Samantha, come in. I've missed you. I gather you've been busy."

She shook his hand. "I have. But you are indeed a face I've quite longed to see."

"Things have gone well, my child. I'm sure you are just tired from all your travels." He grinned. "Come and sit so we can have a nice long chat. I think a lot has changed for you since we last spoke."

They sat opposite each other. "It feels like a hundred years." Then she realized how that sounded and started laughing as he joined in. "I hope I'm here for a bit before I'm off again. I need some downtime."

"Don't get to settled, Sam, you do have some place to go. But it will be nice and warm place. You will be welcomed there."

"Why can't people just come out and say, Sam, you are going to Ireland next. You will meet so and so and do this and that and then come home."

He patted her gloved hand. Sounds too programmed for me. I think you would be bored knowing all that up front, right?"

"Maybe it would be just good to know how long I'll be here before I leave."

"You are really unsettled, aren't you? Why is that?"

"Savoy. I don't know why. But I feel like I need to find out what's up with that man. Father, I've seen him in Scotland, here and Norway. I don't know how to find out why he's always around wherever it seems that I am."

"So, to use some futuristic language, it is some recon you desire. Well, first you need to know his background and that can be tricky. You can't just show up where he was actually born and start asking a whole batch of questions."

"Well, I have to start someplace. He seems to know about me. I need to return the favor. Besides, with Lord Griffin away now appears like a good time to put idle hours to good use."

"Seems to me he'd like you to hang about a bit longer, Sam, to rest up."

She knew he was referring to her recent wounds, but all the same!

"What does everyone know about my business?" She grinned not expecting an answer.

"Why don't you wait about for a few days. I'll see what I can find out. I do have a few resources to tap into."

She rose.

"Okay then have at it and trust I'll run into you when the times right. I'm off to see Mrs. Baker and Anne. Then I think a spot of tea in the village is in order. Do you know where he is by the way?"

Pondering if indeed Savoy was dead back in Norway.

"Not exactly. But he's not here now. I think you will have a little bit of freedom, Sam. I don't always pay attention to his comings and goings. But I'll be more diligent in focusing on this for you."

She patted his shoulder,

"Father G, thank you. Any news, you know where to find me. Well, most of the time anyway."

She grinned, as she stood and closed the rectory door. The late summer day was warm and pleasant as she continued toward the bakery with passersby nodding a greeting. Smiling warmly, Sam knew this part of England, this era, was quickly becoming her home. Grudgingly, she silently admitted to liking the lovely estate and even the bloke who owned it.

Opening the shop door, she was quickly embraced by the short, stalky arms of Mrs. Baker.

"Where have you been, mistress? I've missed you in the last few weeks. Have you been away?"

"Indeed, I have. I smell the aroma of heaven in here. What is it?"

"A new pastry I've created with fresh berries, cream and other ingredients. I'll box a slice up for you to take back."

"Can you please make it a whole pie so I can share it with everyone? You may like to have several opinions if you are going to put it out in your shop window. Perhaps if it's as delectable as it smells, you will offer it at the Tea Room?"

"Me, branching out? I don't know about that."

"Why not? You have the shop. You could increase your revenue and if you are making them anyway, why not a few more?" Pondering that, Sam shifted gears.

"How is Anne? Is she about?"

"She just left to run errands. If you don't see her, I'll say hello for you." Tightly tying the string around the box, Sam slid a shilling on the counter. Mrs. Baker gave up long ago telling her not to pay.

"Oh, I nearly neglected to give you Mrs. Lilly's order. There is no rush. The next delivery date will be fine." She pressed it into her hand. "I'm off. I will be back in town soon. I'll let you know the polling results on your new creation."

"Mistress, wait. One more thing. I see clear sailing for the next few days, if you know what I mean."

Nodding, a bit more frustrated, she closed the shop door spewing out loud. "Okay, enough of this. It would be wrong of me to get pissed off at good, sound advice."

"You were fortunate it was just me looming about, Mistress Samantha, with that mouth of yours."

Smiling, Adam pulled her right into his arms nearly knocking the box down. The desire to place a hearty kiss on those lips was so very tempting, as she glanced around. No, this was not the time as she took his arm.

"I thought you were going to be gone for a while?"

"Plans change sometimes and I must say it was welcoming. For some reason, getting out of bed this morning was a bit of an issue."

Their eyes locked.

"I was going to the Tea Room. Perhaps that's no longer a good idea and we should return to your estate?"

Her body was on fire. She needed to get out of the public eye before everyone else could see it.

"Shall we take a different path along the meadow, or have you discovered it already?"

She grinned coyly. "Busted, but let's go that way anyway."

Strolling from town and down the path, he went ahead of her over a stile, then lifted her down by the waist.

On tiptoes, she let her boots touch slowly to the ground as their bodies touched, lips very close.

He took her gloved hand as they continued.

"I hear you have Father Godwin researching a matter for you."

She stopped, stomping a foot. "Bloody hell! How did you know that? I only left there thirty minutes ago! Were you that close to my heels?"

"Aye, you had left the kitchen and headed out when I came back. If we had cellphones, I'd have texted my arrival."

She smiled, truly glad he was here. As the trees grew thicker, he stepped in front of her blocking the path. Somehow the box was removed and set down as he pulled her roughly into his arms, lips taking total command of hers.

His hands cupped her buttocks, as Sam clutched his back feeling every bit of him against her. She unbuttoned his trousers as he lifted her onto him. Falling gently into the tall grass, a moan escaped their slightly parted lips.

"I don't know if I can let you go next time."

He tossed her onto her back. "Next time we go together."

He kissed her neck then trailed a heated blaze back to her lips as she felt him grow hard inside of her again. Arching, taking all of him, their bodies met and melded into one as the outside world faded around them both.

"Did you hear that?"

He stood, pulling her quickly up. "Yes. Be quiet. Quick. Grab the box and come back into the brush."

Crouching, she pressed her gloved hand to her mouth to stifle a sure laugh as his stern look nearly broke her down completely. They watched two riders off in the distance pass by them unnoticed.

"Damn, that was close, woman. Next time we'd better take a good look around first."

"As always, it's your fault. You grabbed me leaving me with no other choice but to succumb to your charms, Lord Griffin."

He chuckled. "Madam, your hat has come off." Picking it up and brushing the grass off, he placed it back on just at the correct angle. She tipped a shoulder in the cutest motion.

"If anyone sees us, they are going to know we've been up to something." He took the box in his hand. "Especially if this is all scrambled. Shall we make sure it's not?"

She untied the box and flipped open the cover. "Oh, this does look magnificent. Straight from a patisserie in Paris. Look."

He was tempted to pick a piece off but she closed the cover and tied it snugly.

"I brought this back for all of us to try. It is Mrs. Baker's latest concoction and I, for one, could have a piece right this very moment. So, let's hurry."

Deep into their own conversation, Mrs. Hoyt and Lilly's talk immediately halted eyeing the handsome pair.

"What have you there, mistress?"

"Something we can all share tonight after our dinner. Now no peeking until then."

She slid the box onto the counter. Sam went about business pouring hot water into a pot, grabbed everything else they needed and set it all on a large silver serving tray.

"Lord Griffin, I don't want to start gossip or worse than that a scandal." She glanced at both ladies faces, surprise clearly written on both. "But would you carry this tray to your study for me?"

"Bossy lass, isn't she?"

The two women went nose deep into conversation as soon as the door closed. But Sam did not care. That was fun! Sauntering down the halls she opened his study door and closed it, as he came through.

"Liked that, didn't you?"

"Yeah, I did."

"Just remember that I pay staff to do things like this because they like to work. Don't go taking all their tasks or it will leave them idle."

She shrugged. "After tea, can you take me on that grand tour inside? Remember, you promised a while ago and I think it is long overdue. Are there dark passages? Dungeons? Any ghosts?"

He laughed, taking the saucer and cup.

"Exactly what I was thinking. But we don't have a dungeon here, Sam. But, plenty of dark secret passages. Perhaps you will want to change into your jeans and more suitable shoes."

"Sounds smart. After we can both go up and change." She watched his eyes darken and knew they were on the same page. "Then you can show me and along the way, we can have a talk about my good friend, Major Victor Savoy."

Chapter Sixteen

Her hair was a tousled mess as they dressed, the glances toward each other were both intense and humorous at the same time.

"Good thing I did not know you in my younger days, Adam, we'd have twenty-five kids by now."

He broke out in laughter. "I suppose at some point I should do the right thing by you."

She shrugged her shoulders.

"That's the nice part of being slightly older, people are less interested in your private lives than the young scandalous ones."

"I can tell you the two clacking hens in the kitchen are enjoying keeping an eye on us."

"True, but they are sweet and harmless. Nothing like some of the so-called ladies in the surrounds and you know it."

"Bitches are more like it. That's the very reason why I kept the few dalliances I had to villages outside this area. You never know when one day, one of them is going to decide they had enough and speak up."

Hands on hips, she cocked a brow.

"What?"

"Oh, your mistress, right. So how many will I run into along my adventures? I wondered if that was why you gave up that large suite in Venice? Because you were ditching one."

He ignored that part. "Sam, that's possible. Do you think we could change the subject?"

"You brought it up, you know, but sure. I am ready. Where do we begin?"

"Right in this room." He stood inside the bathroom door. "In there, look."

"Are you kidding?"

He grinned, twisting an intricately fanciful knob at the bottom of a wall sconce. The wallpapered panel opened, producing a very nasty set of narrow, rickety stairs.

"Great, spider webs and who knows what else. Hang on a second, I'll get my cap."

Racing back with it firmly in place, hair tucked up inside, she walked down them gingerly not wanting to touch a bloody thing, catching up with him. When they reached the end, he felt for the release panel.

"You know you may have a bit of trouble if you ever needed this exit. The panel may be out of reach. Here, put your hand on mine, so you know how high it is."

She had to go on tiptoes but she could feel it and pressed against it, as the wall opened inside toward them. She gasped. They were down under the first floor in the wine cellar.

Creeping along through the eerie space, Sam wondered who kept this place up. Stopping for a second, she listened. There was no sound of water dribbling nor could she feel air coming through of any kind. A shudder passed up her spine, raising the hairs on the back of her neck as the flames of the closest lit lanterns danced about, nearly flickering off.

"Are there any spirits here, Adam?"

He patted her ass as he moved along to the opposite side.

"Do you really want to know how many, or just if there are any specifically where we are?"

Damn jerk was baiting her and she knew it.

"No, not really. Better I don't. But, what about evil ones?"

"One or two are a bit more spirited than the rest. I'm sure you can handle them. If you have outwitted Savoy and take passages. I've always thought they knew what we all are about anyway, leaving us to our devices."

Stopping, he leaned against one of the stone walls.

"Try and find this exit yourself."

Tugging on her baseball cap, she eyed it knowing where he was leaning it was not. Glancing at the large kegs she knew that would be too obvious by turning a knob. It had to be on the floor, or perhaps it was not that wall at all!

Sam moved back and glanced at the entire end of the room, the three walls, then moved left behind the kegs and saw one stone slightly discolored. The lighting was not helping and it was well planted, so larger frames would hardly notice it.

Pressing the corner panel, it opened.

"Excellent, I thought we may be here a while."

She grinned. "That was cool." As she vanished up ahead leaving him standing there alone. Moving quite a bit ahead he jogged to catch up remaining quiet as they approached the end of the dark corridor. Sam halted, placing a hand up to stop him from speaking, inhaled sharply then smiled.

Glancing above, little was in view. But, when she stretched out an arm, the roughness of the wood caused a slight wince. She had snagged a splinter. If the ceiling was this low, there had to be a release up there somewhere. As she felt further, her fingertips caught a latch. It opened automatically producing a few short steps up.

Once inside, she spun around like a little kid who had found the pie on the windowsill with no grownups in sight.

"The stables, how frigging bloody brilliant! You must have had such a grand time as a kid living here."

"I did. Now that's the best route because it gets you quite a distance away from the house and to a fast means of escape. Can you ride bareback?"

"Indeed, I can. Not well, but in a pinch I could do it. Let me make sure I've found them all. There's one from your study up to our suite, this one, but surely there are more?"

"There are a few others. One to the attic, one under the kitchen to a cave toward the river and one in the other side of the house where your rooms were."

"So, you've shown me the best one. How about giving me a clue where the one is under the kitchen. You go and wait where it exits and let's see how long before I find you."

He shook his head laughing. "Okay, chit, bet's on if you can be there in less than thirty minutes. How about I allow you to ask one thing of me that I will not refuse you. If it is after thirty. I do the asking."

"Damn, it's a deal. Tell me where it is."

She bolted from the stables with breakneck speed, running quite unladylike into the building, sliding to a stop as she passed the butler, and thought about what he had said. Turning down the hall of ancestors on the first floor, Sam stood in awe; there were so many different things she could try! Damn, caution had to be used here with this many valuable items.

Wait, she thought, hadn't he said, "Not all that glitters is gold?"

A large embossed fireplace struck her fancy. Staring into the eyes of the lion, intricately and quite beautifully engraved, she pushed simultaneously with both pointer fingers into his eyes. The trap door to the right slid open.

Feeling quite smug for withholding information from him, she removed her small pen light from her jeans pocket and switched it on. As she quickly walked, it was apparent the kitchen was receding as the clang of pots could be heard then faded away. Onward her progress went until the corridor became rougher, with water seeping onto the floor rising an inch or so up over the sole of her boots.

The eerie noise of things crawling about did not slow the pace. Further up, a pinhead of light started to grow bigger and brighter as she carefully picked up the pace. Stepping outside, glancing up to a darkening sky, she saw him leaning against a tree chewing on a blade of grass. Creeping over, she tapped his right shoulder while moving to his left.

He grabbed her up over his shoulder and swung her down into the grass moving on top.

"Damn, Sam, that was less than twenty minutes."

"Darn good, don't you think? So, let's see. What shall I ask of you? Do I have to make the request right this second? Or, can I bank it for when I decide exactly what I want."

"Woman, you are too smart for your own good." He swept her up on her feet as he grabbed her hand. "While we are here, let me show you one more thing. Then you can take me back the way you came out."

"Is that an old boat down there?"

"Yes, I won't even ask you if you know how to row. But, your toughest challenge may be pulling up the anchor. It's quite deep in this part of the river.".

"Hopefully, I won't have to do that. So, are you ready to go back? I need a bath, change of clothes and dinner. I am really hungry."

"Well, lead on then."

As they entered the cave, she pulled out the penlight and smiled, shrugging her shoulders as laughter vibrated around the tunnel.

"When did you even have time to grab that? Oh, I get it. When you went to retrieve your hat. Right."

"That's about it." They had reached the floor hall of ancestors. "There are some really handsome portraits of your family, in particular this one." She was standing looking up at one of him.

His hands wove around pulling her back against him, then settled his chin on top of her cap.

"That's my brother to the left, James, and in the smaller portrait is his wife, Anna, and their daughter, Catriona. You will meet them soon. Just before I met you in Venice, we were all in Ireland. My niece just married a bloke from there, but in essence he's a good sort."

"What a handsome family. Is he older or younger?"

"Two years' younger. That is why I am the grand owner of all this." She knew the aristocracy's diplomatic order. His brother would inherit all when Adam was no longer around. Then it would follow his niece.

"Isn't Catriona an Irish name? Does your family have roots there as well?"

He moved her to the center of the hall.

"Yes, my mother was Irish. My father a split between English and Welsh. That is them. They have been gone for a few years. The rooms you were in were my mother's; she passed away a few years after my father did and it's said that she still has a presence in there."

Sam turned into his arms staring up into his dark blue eyes.

"I know, she liked my lace and handkerchiefs. I did not know whose room it was, now that makes sense."

He kept his mouth shut. "Let's get cleaned up so we can eat. If we don't get a move on, Mrs. Lilly will leave us scraps as punishment for making her keep our food warm."

As they reached their rooms, Abbey, and a few other servants were hurrying their exit having left the hot water in the tub. She blushed, head bowed low, and rushed by them.

"Poor girl. Do you think she's pondering two people, unmarried and one tub?" Sam laughed, sliding out of her shoes, clothes quickly dropping down to the floor in a heap. A quick glance over her shoulder proved amusing, he was quite naked and closing in fast.

Sliding into one end, the hot water and coolness of the porcelain tub brought a sincere sigh of gratification out of her mouth. Submerging, she soaked her hair, put in cleanser and rinsed it out. Soaping up, she crawled over, sliding on top of his warm skin.

Kissing him was just as easy as breathing as he pulled away, sliding inside of her. He sat straight, eyes locking as she resisted his lips on purpose.

Sliding over him again and again, back arching, he gripped her strongly as water spilled over the tub onto the tile floor. As they climaxed together, it was only then she allowed his kiss.

It was powerful.

"You are getting cold. We had better get you dried off."

"It's not cold, Lord Griffin, of that I can assure you." She stood over him reaching for a warming towel on a rack placed in front of the fireplace as he kissed a breast.

Her warm smile drove his heart to skip a beat.

She dried off, wrapped her hair, then stepped out handing him one.

He caught up with her as she reached the dresser, spun her around playfully, hands roaming over hips while lowering his lips to claim hers once again.

Finally, they pulled away.

"I should have left you in my mother's suite. It's pretty clear that with you here, we may never leave this room, woman."

She smiled that special smile. When a woman is sure she has a man. But the truth was he had her too. Suddenly, the idea she was sharing his rooms under the presence of the entire household had her feeling a bit annoyed. What was the difference with her being in the tower, his mother's suite or here? The bottom line was clear, with her own admittance and acceptance, she had indeed become his mistress. But that would be less obvious when she moved into the cottage and paid rent.

Then things would be different. She'd not be so available as she was right now. Truth though, she liked being in close proximity to this man.

"Is that my imagination or can I actually smell our dinner from the kitchen? It can't be. It is nearly a mile between there and here."

She laughed. "I think that's my cue we need to go down. I am truly starving."

She had been quiet, mood changed. Even though she tried to mask it, he knew. It was not until the berry concoction from Mrs. Baker was finished that she perked up.

"I need to let her know how spectacular that was, don't you think?"

"Another one could come this way any time. She could make a fortune with those."

"I'm going to make sure that happens. I insist on arranging some to be present on the ladies' menu at the Tea Room. If I need to use your name to push this through, I will. I'm going to go see her tomorrow and get it moving along. I was thinking if they did not readily have the funds for multiple production, that this may just be a great idea to present to them the possibility of my being a partner. A silent one, of course. But I'll see what they think tomorrow."

"Tomorrow, you say? Well, that's not going to be possible."

She took his arm as they headed for his study, he was going to take a smoke out on the veranda.

"Why is that?"

"Tomorrow we leave for New Orleans in the United States of America."

"Oh, my goodness, I love New Orleans. I've had a lot of fun there in the past, well, the future. Ah, hell, you know what I mean. Have you been there before?"

"Not in a few years. We have a joint mission that's not completely clear yet."

Suddenly, she felt the need to get to the cottage before full darkness emerged. A quick little white lie was in order.

"I want to hear more about that, but I just remembered that I have something to do of importance. I'll see you in a bit."

Quickly, she disappeared out of sight just as he was forming a question. Soon, the gardens beyond swallowed her up as his brows furrowed. His cigar finished, he stomped it out, irritated, beneath a boot then picked it up and put it in the bucket.

Walking back in, he closed and locked the double wide French doors. Up in their rooms, he strode out to the balcony listening to night sounds. Still she had not returned. As the sky turned from red to orange and darkness took over, it was then he gave up, sitting down in one of the chairs. Finally, she came in through the hall door.

Her grin was mischievous. Unfortunately, any inquisition was to be left for later. There was something that needed to be addressed and it was now or never. Actually, he thought about it. Damn, he silently mouthed. It would have to be now or if it came up later, he was sure to be in big trouble.

She was undressing in the changing room when he finally spoke.

"Sam, when I was in New Orleans last, I had a mistress. I was there for quite a while. Anyway, I just want you to be aware in case she's still around."

"Is this your way of telling me you are going to reacquaint yourself with her, or just a warning in case she expects that of you?"

He knew this was not going to go as planned. It was the tone of the question that was not right.

"I have no plans to do either." To him that was a declaration that he would not. To her it was a declaration that he did not plan on it, but hell, it sure could happen.

"We all have pasts, but thanks for the warning. Do you think Savoy already knows we are headed there?"

"He seems to turn up wherever you are, so we had better assume he's going to be."

She yawned, crawling in bed beside him noticing he had turned down the gas lit lanterns.

"Are we going back or forward?"

"Back. By now, Sam, you should be able to see what will transpire." He fluffed up his own pillow placing one arm under his head. "Don't you?" He paused. But, not long enough for her to answer. "Anyway, I wanted to ask you where you went earlier. Care to share?"

Glancing over by the silence in the room, he quickly realized she was sound asleep.

Chapter Seventeen

Stretching like a panther, she slid from bed and pulled aside a heavy drape before he could reach for her.

"It's going be a lot warmer and sunnier there than it is here today, that's for sure." She let it fall back and slipped into a robe and slippers. With a messy mop, she went into the bathroom to get cleaned up.

She seemed all business this morning. Like she had something on her mind and it sure as hell was not him.

"We head out as soon as you are ready." He called toward the closed door.

"Uh huh."

He dressed and put together a few things. But basically, he knew where they were going, staying and they would be taken care of completely when arrived.

Suddenly she appeared out of the dressing room ready to go. He eyed her warily. When had she done that? Did she have time to put her clothes in there last night?

Pinning up her hair and taking the bag, she turned looking at him. "I'm set, shall we?"

He strode over as she opened the door. He followed as they went down a different hall toward the rear entrance. Once they were outside, he moved in front, walking backwards.

"Lord Griffin, I'm ready to get this going. I can now see a lot of very interesting things coming my way. Why are you deterring me?" Her voice was quite playful as he wondered where this shift of gear came from.

"So, you are getting visuals?"

"Yup, I sure am."

He moved in step beside her, as they descended the stairs of the ruin and back up, right onto deck of the

Angeline, owned by Captain Jean Lafitte. The schooner was in the throes of outrunning a British frigate, cutting sail at a quick pace through the choppy Atlantic. It was in a race, and winning, toward New Orleans.

Adam glanced down, presenting a smashing smile, and quickened his steps as he reached the first mate, clasping hands.

"Damn, you old, salty dog. I knew I'd see you again. But figured it would be in a rift over some bar wench, not here. Damn, how the hell are you?"

Adam glanced over his shoulder laughing as the cannon fire was having less results as the sleek schooner moved on.

"Bastard. You have always been a bastard Lord this or that, matters not to me." They both laughed.

Suddenly, he glanced around. Fuck. Where was she? Striding around up on deck, he took a good, long look.

She was nowhere to be seen. What the hell? This was unique. When they walked up the stairs together there had been only one exit. Strange, he did not have an option for two passages, but she must have. A good shove brought him around in a flash.

"Ah, Lafitte, seems as if you've avoided another issue with the British again. How are you, my old friend?"

"A little of this and that. It's good to have you on board. But, your arrival always means extra trouble for me. So, come clean. What's this all about?"

"Well, it's not entirely clear. But, it appears I have lost someone upon my arrival. You have not seen a handsome woman roaming on board, have you?"

"I assure you, handsome or not, if a woman was on the Angelina, someone would have accosted her onto her back by now and we'd know she was here."

He grinned, flashing a devilish smile. Was this why he could not see as much as normal and she woke this morning to what seemed like a clarity of vision? Shit, this was not good.

"You putting into 'Orleans?'"

"*Oui*, should be in about an hour and then you and I, my friend, will go ashore and see what we can turn up before my mistress even knows I am about. Now, come below. For I've good Jamaican Rum to share."

***

Sam, on the other hand, was climbing up a set of rickety stairs outside an old inn. It had rained, she noticed glancing down. Street mud was adhering to her boots. Opening the door, she slid through.

"Yeah, I've been waiting on you. Come, get yourself over here and be quick about it. Close that damn door."

"Who are you?"

Sam stood with hands on hips, nearly falling over at the reflection staring back across the room in a framed floor glass. Dressed like a tavern wench, breasts barely contained under a fluff of lace, her grin expanded. There was but a breath between her and flesh expelling out in total freedom. Damn, this was getting better by the second.

"Molly's the name." She eyed her attire, nodding in approval. "I understand you need a bit of assistance. Specifically, how to fend for yourself. The crowds here about get pretty rowdy at times."

Sam felt an instant kinship to this woman. Eyeing her head to toe. No, she was more than just a bar wench. This person was her own special training operative. Oh, how funny, she thought, moving closer.

"Yeah, will be my first night in a tavern actually working. I need you to set me straight so I know the trouble before it finds me. As shit smells, it will."

"Well, sweetie, hike up that skirt and let's see what you got under there."

Eyebrows raised in surprise, Sam picked up the hem.

"Higher, honey, I know you are strapping."

Sam eyed her bag briefly knowing in there was a gun. A real one and a knife.

"That is not good for you. What you think is in that bag may not be and you and I both thought you would arrive with protection."

Glancing down, Sam was astonished; both upper thighs were indeed missing them. Molly tied a sheath encased with a knife high on the inside making sure it was secure.

"Open the bag."

Sam reached down and untied it.

"Damn it, Molly, I've never been anywhere and not had more than this."

"No shit. There must be other means you are to use, dear, if you get my drift." Inside her dress pocket, she produced a small corked glass alchemy bottle and slid it between Sam's breasts, tucking it down low.

"What's that for?"

"A magical blend of herbs and rum that will burn the eyes of those that think they got you. All you do is tell them you want to be on top, take it out, pop the cork and throw it right at their eyes. That will give you time to get away."

"Is everyone around here pirates and privateers?"

"There are a few that roam these parts, now and again, that aren't so bad. Take Lafitte and his salty crew. They can be a bit rough, but they always leave a hard coin or two for you to get by with." She winked.

"Issues with the girls?" Sam was having a hard time not cracking up laughing at her true southern belle, 'Orleans' accent.

"Watch out for Lucinda. She is quick to recognize and pretty to be sure. Oh, but wait until she catches a glimpse of you. The fur's going to fly."

Oh, a bit of territorial competition, eh? Well, Sam thought internally, she was up for it after their conversation last night, feeling the need to be independent and in charge.

"When they pinch your ass for the hundredth time, you may get a bit testy. But, remember your tips come from the likes of them and other things of importance. Don't let them follow you to the back taps, though, or you may get more bargained for. At times, the bar keep is too busy to notice if you need a bit of assistance."

"What if I have to stab one? Won't that evoke more trouble?" Her mirth was shared.

"Depends on who you stab. If it is a local grub, no one will care. But, if it's one of Lafitte's men, then you had better be prepared. You will get no support from anyone. Just keep to yourself in the main room or go back there with one of us."

She sat down on the corner of the bed.

"Here, drink this. It will warm you. Settle the nerves and prepare you for what's ahead." Swigging it down, she bit back a choke as it burned from throat to gut. Damn, it was not smooth but bloody potent.

"Here, have another."

The two tipped glasses and swigged down another two-finger shot.

"Whoa, no more of that or I won't be able to walk."

"Honey, you had betta get used to it. Sometimes, it is the only way to get by. Now, let's get that hair tied back so no bloke can grab it, because they will try. We need to get our asses down there, now."

The red ribbon matched the red in her itsy, bitsy dress and seemed laughable that a portion of her hair was pulled back and tied in a bow. A nice little ladies' bow, even though she was nearly naked. Oh, hell, she thought, pinching cheeks and putting some stain on her lips Molly handed her. She had always wanted to be a bar wench.

Check mark. Fantasy fulfilled.

Downstairs, she was quickly immersed into the ill lit, smoky tavern. This was a bar room brawl waiting to happen. Flashing some pearly whites, she exaggerated the swish of her hips and focused straight on a table overflowing with an unsavory lot. Sliding a boot up on the curve of the bench, she exposed a bit of leg.

"What have you, gents?"

"Well, hello, my sweet. Rum it will be. Damn, make it a round for all!" He beat a fist on top of the table as she took her large tray off toward the bar keep. He slid the tankards up onto it.

"Ah, another new one. Well, get your skirts a swaying about the room, we've money to make."

His toothless grin and the way he raked her over proved a point with Sam. Yeah, some men were just plain ole stupid.

Sliding the mugs in front of each, the language turned cantankerous as calloused, hardened, groping hands began getting more adventuresome.

"Now gents, give the new girl a chance. She won't come back if you keep touching her like that. She's the third one in a week."

Turning an appreciative nod to Molly, Sam's face suddenly froze.

It was Savoy.

"Be a love, honey, get me one of those."

Emotions ran through her so fast, she nearly lost her sight as her whole body turned stiff before moving on.

Composure, Samantha, she screamed inside her head. Calm the fuck down!

The barkeep slid a mug and a small cup.

"For you, drink up lass, you are doing well. Pay them all no mind."

The fiery liquid worked magic settling rattled nerves.

Collecting the money and pocketing it, Sam maneuvered through the crowded room, serving other tables when her gaze locked with piercing green eyes. Although shorter than Sam, she was pretty with flailing red hair. Yup, sure as the sun sets over Egypt, this was Lucinda.

A nod of agreement passed between them.

Lines were drawn. Sides acknowledged.

Turning, she wafted back toward the group to check on refills. Eyes narrowing briefly, she watched intently, listening while ducking into the shadows paying close attention to two men deep in conversation.

"The Angeline pulled into port a short time ago. My source tells me they are heading here now. We'd better drink up and go. If he lays eyes on me, he will know no good is about."

One waved Sam over. "Here you go, missy. Buy a new ribbon for your pretty hair."

"Why, thank you!"

Leaving the coinage up on the bar top, Sam knew something was amiss. My, how their language had changed when they thought no one was keen on hearing. But, it was apparent from the shine of their boots that they were not harbor riff-raff. Rather, spies, possibly officers under cover.

The room grew rowdy, filling with electricity as emotions ramped up. Everyone felt it. Every damn soul was drunk as a skunk as Molly stopped next to her.

"This is when you need to pay extra attention."

She nodded, staring down Savoy; the rum having its effect. In her eyes was a clear warning. *You fuck with me and I'll fuck with you.*

He grinned, tipped his hat and slugged back a tankard, slamming it down on the table.

"Wench! Get your ass over here now. Refills!"

Her grin was lethal as she leaned over him displaying every bit of her creamy flesh.

His eyes briefly raked her over.

"Seems like you've been neglecting us, woman. We need another round. You see it is like this. I was with a rather reckless woman a bit ago and she left me with a lump on me head. I need that rum to ease the pain."

She laughed.

"You got what you deserved, I'm sure!"

The bloke opposite grabbed her as she tugged out of his alcohol weakened grip just before he planted a foul breath kiss on her mouth. The man stood, weaving, then slid back onto the bench, his head hitting the wood, before he passed out.

Then the shit hit the fan.

"Griffin, did not see you there, man. Warning, my friend. This wench isn't for you tonight. Even though I'm drunk as hell, I can see Lucinda heading your way."

Sam was halfway to the bar when she heard the dialogue; she watched, as the redhead used every charm, claiming him long before her body got there. It was apparent the affect it had on him.

The bastard!

Over in the corner of the room, she saw a group of men, knowing now who he had come in with. Damn, that explained why they were separated upon arrival. He was with Captain Jean Lafitte, the infamous pirate of the high seas and true Governor of New Orleans in the eyes of the locals.

Using her wits, it was apparent the two that left were important. As to why they were all here, that centered around one lofty pirate. Hell, now all she had to do was find out what the heck that was.

As she swayed by Adam, who was disengaging his mistress from his arms, the whole tavern could not help but hear her tirade as he held her back.

"Two years and not a bloody word from you. Now, you just show up and what is this? No kiss? How dare you treat me like that? So, who is she? Surely you must have another woman? Are you thinking about bedding that new wench right under this roof? I will slit your throat before you..."

"Woman, shut your mouth."

He pulled her close, whispering into her ear.

"There may be time later. Right now, I am on official business and can't be detained. Even by your loveliness."

She smiled up into his eyes.

Sam, truly pissed off, moved behind a door with Molly in tow.

"You know him?"

That was the cold water in her face she needed.

"Nay, just thought I may have a go at him. Handsome as sin and probably as evil as the Devil by listening to Lucinda's tirade. But, I know it's her man. So, I'll keep my thoughts to myself. When is closing?"

"For us, soon. For the girls coming on shortly, it will be early morning. You are coming with me to the inn. I have two rooms and will grab you when it is time to leave. Go back out there and finish collecting from your area."

"Thanks, Molly."

Sam slid back out and at several tables had to just pick up the coin spewed about carelessly, collecting the bills. Bringing it up to the bar keep, she nodded no to one more shot. Reaching for a cloak to wrap around, Sam looked to where Savoy had been. He had since vacated and replaced by another. Where had he gone this time and why did he keep showing up where ever she was?

Answers were needed and fast. As they left through a side alley, Sam never looked back to see where Adam and his mistress were, or what they were doing. To ensure sanity, it was clear there was a purpose to them both being here. Until that was understood, she was going to damn well remain clear of that man. Heaven help him if her hands found their way toward his neck!

"We'll be there in ten minutes. You stay close to me. These streets are filled with unsavory types, especially now that Lafitte's men are back in the city."

Sam stopped and grabbed Molly's arm whispering, "Hey you are speaking differently now, what's up with that?"

"New Orleans is filled with those who look like aristocrats and are slum dogs. Then there are wenches like us working in the darkest corners, who are here to do a task other than serve ale and rum. I'm here to help you in the tavern and make sure whatever is needed is done expeditiously."

Sam grinned. "You know, I like this. You had me fooled. But you knew what I was all about all along. You are one of us too?"

She nodded. "Don't worry about your man. You did not see how he was watching every swish of your hips when you were working the room. Those eyes caressed every inch of your body. Between you and me, he sure did like you in this outfit."

"You have a way of making me feel a whole lot better, Molly."

"Well sit tight, honey and pay good attention because there's a lot coming your way over the next few days. Tomorrow, we have a day off. I'll take you around the city and lend some helpful suggestions."

"Will I be working the tavern again?"

"No, we will go over that soon. There are other plans for you that I think you will find quite exciting."

As they reached the inn, Sam was glad it was away from the rowdy, waterfront pubs and quite a bit nicer. As they climbed the steps, Molly stopped in front of her door. Sam's was three down.

"Sleep well, you will be safe here."

"Thanks, see you in the morning."

At the end of the hall, Sam found her door and inserted the key. As she turned the doorknob and automatically adjusted her eyes to the darkened room, suddenly there was a hand over her mouth. Stomping a boot as hard as possible, raising an elbow and landing a hard jab, she spun around, swiftly lifting her skirts and pulled out a knife.

"Samantha put that away. It's me."

Feeling quite smug, she smiled at how quickly she reacted. Lighting a few candles, she put the glass domes back over them. A few seconds was all that she needed feeling calmer. Then turned toward him.

His heated gaze swept her head to toe.

"You have to bring this one back when we leave here."

The back of his hand smoothed over her exploding breasts. Pulling his head down, Sam took complete control swiftly unbuttoning his trousers and had her hand surrounding him before he knew what hit.

He moaned into her mouth before lifting her to the bed, roughly removing her dress.

"You have to be gone before sunrise."

He started to question her, but the roaming of possessive hands halted his speech. Then he felt her warmth surround them both as it quickly spread. Had jealousy spurred this on?

He'd get to the root source and get rid of it for good. There were never going to be any secrets between them ever again. But, right now, it was only the two of them.

Chapter Eighteen

Sunrise streaked in through sparse curtains as she stretched. It was early and Molly had said they were not working. Today she would learn more about her story and what was to come next. Then her brow furrowed, recalling Savoy. Ironically, as their other meetings were dissected, Sam realized he did not seem to pose a threat. Laughing inside the meager surroundings of the room, it was apparent an analyzation of events had to occur. He needed to be figured out, especially after she had left him for dead and he had not tried to settle the score. At least, not yet.

"What's your story?" she posed to dead air as her hand smoothed over where Adam's head had been.

He grumbled when nudged to get up and out. Her smile grew. Sure, he knew she was a little jealous about Lucinda. But, that admission would never leave her lips, ever. Then again, he could barely speak as she took control of their lovemaking, turning it into quite a flurry last night.

The floor was cool to the touch beneath her feet as she washed and dressed just as there was a knock at the door. Peering, opening it up a crack, Sam smiled.

"Hello, come on in."

"You look sprite and spirited this morning. Have a good night's sleep, did you?"

"How did you know?"

"Not much gets by me, missy. Besides, yours was the last room. So, when I heard the boots hitting the planks, a whistle along with it, I knew. Was it the bloke from the tavern?"

"I can't tell a lie, it was. We are acquainted."

"Glad I was a few doors down then. You sent him along the way before daylight. Smart move."

"Much to his chagrin." she winked. "But he'll get over it soon enough."

"You are quite a confident woman, I'll say, and comfortable knowing about his past with Lucinda."

She was. "Yes, because two can play at this game and here I feel like I have the upper hand."

Molly, grinned patting her on the arm.

"Well, let's get going then. I truly think you are going to find today damn interesting. We must fetch ourselves a couple of nice evening gowns. The night after next we are serving drinks and smokes to some society blokes at a high stakes poker game. I daresay your gent and Lafitte will both be there."

The warm morning air greeted them as they stepped outside.

"I've been here before, Molly, at a different time. This city's vibrancy never fades. I just love it."

"Twenty-four-seven it sure does. That's why I call this place home. A while ago I was given the opportunity to make an important decision. If I wanted to return to my dark, dismal flat in London or remain here. Obviously, you know the results. This was an easy choice."

Sam leaned closer. "What period are you from?"

"Nineteen-fifty. A blast from the past. No joke, right? Here, it's thriving morning to night and I do have tucked away a gentleman friend that comes to visit time to time. Calling this my home suits me real fine."

"You said you had a choice; do those only come once?"

"Well, I've heard for most indeed they do. You may be the one that's different. I'm not sure. But when yours does, it will be at the right moment in your life. It always comes during a passage. So, take warning of this now. A decision will need to be made soon on where you really want to be."

"They said for me it was unusual. When I arrived from 2015, I had all my bags. The few who I've been allowed to discuss this with have no explanations."

Molly halted, steadying eyes into Sam's.

"Well, then, that does paint a different picture. From all my travels, I've not encountered any stories such as you have described. I don't know what to say. You are different. Whether that makes it harder or easier for you, well, time will tell. Ah, here we are at Madame Thereault's Dress Shop. What do you say to going in and spending some loot?"

Sam's mouth gaped open as they entered the establishment. The proprietress swished toward them, producing a large, inviting smile.

"Surprised, mistress, at the variety? Well, Monsieur Lafitte made me aware of your arrival. Ensuring I was up-to-date with the finest Parisian fashions available. He's such a love."

Sam smiled, "And a good friend he is to have by the looks of all your choices, madame. Do you mind if I poke around? Or, would proper etiquette dictate I sit as a gentile lady, point at what I desire, and one of your shop girls would assist?"

The three women broke out in laughter.

"Madame likes you. Tell me, Molly, where ever did you find her?"

"Oh, don't allow her to give any airs. She's just a comely tavern wench, new to town, quite unique in her ways of travel and in need of a few special gowns."

Madame nodded, grinning. "Why that's just excellent, ladies. I shall be at the counter taking care of papers. You have my girls' undivided attention with all the fittings. Any alterations will be done on premise and delivered to you in plenty of time for your special event." She winked, crinoline and silk swishing off.

"Oh, I like her. Molly, look at that periwinkle silk dress and all that lace. The hat, I must have that hat. If I needed an additional weapon I could remove it and poke out an eye. Oh, yes, this works for me!"

She never even gave her companion a chance to voice an opinion. Quickly waving over one of the girls, they hastily disappeared behind a curtain.

Nearly three hours later, boxes tidied up and set on the seat of a hired carriage, they ladies stopped and took stock.

Should we have kept the driver a bit longer? What if we buy more?" Molly was completely pulling her leg.

"I can't imagine needing anything else. I know I purchased more than necessary, but I could not resist."

"What the hell. Anyway, you won't be in the inn much longer. Our plans are to move out this afternoon to more suitable arrangements. I have an apartment for us right in the heart of the Quarter. There is another bonus, my dear, no one will know you have relocated. So, if a certain gent comes a calling, he will find a new resident in that room at the inn and much to pay for!"

Sam burst out laughing, raising a gloved hand to her mouth to stifle further response as passers eyed them both.

"Oh, my gosh, did you see the looks on those faces? Are we not to laugh in public here?" Sam, waved off a reply not caring. She was enjoying this way too much. "Is there a reason for all of this? Something I should be made aware of upfront by any chance?"

"Of course, you little chit. But we will let that all unravel in due time. Enough of that. Shall we go back and get our things? We can be settled and out exploring by lunch."

They hailed a carriage and were back at the inn, packed and met in the hallway minutes later.

"Tell me about this poker game. Surely, there is more at stake than money."

"First things first. Let me pry a moment. Exactly how old are you and why this lifestyle?"

"In my forties. I was married. But, he decided to swap me in for a younger model. I basically said screw it and chucked it all in favor of travel. I was vacationing in Venice when I met up with my gentleman friend and then found myself transplanted to his England. I've been around for three months. I did not actually choose it. It seems to have chosen me. It seems to come with pretty nice benefits, if you know what I mean."

Molly must have bobbed her head up and down four or five times before lending a thought.

"How are your resources?"

Sam knew she was referring to finances.

"Ironically, my bank account was magically deposited into a local bank in the village near his estates."

"Blimey, that is rather odd, I must say. You know I have an idea. If you are up to a bit of fun. There is a woman living down on the bayou that's a bit eerie, but reads a good palm. If you want to go and check it out, we can."

"Sounds like a voodoo priestess. But, I must admit I'm intrigued. Sure, why the hell not? Let's do it. May be cool to hear what her story is about all of this. It seems like I am always one step away from discovering something, then uprooted again in a different direction. Yeah, I'm up for that. Sounds like another adventure." She chuckled. "Can we go before the poker game?"

"Yes, I'll send the servant with a note to her this afternoon and what the reply is." She laughed. "He hates it when I do that, thinking the old crone is going to cast a spell on him every time."

"Well, we all have read stories about these women. I won't pretend I am not a bit nervous already. Does an orange and white poisonous snake dangle about her crinkled neck?"

"Sam, it's a dark place for sure. But, we don't have to go. There are others here in the Quarter who have that special gift. But take caution. Most are hoaxers only interested in taking money. It's up to you."

"Oh, no, I'm game. I admit all that voodoo talk would give any good Christian woman the creeps. Good thing I'm not one of those!"

Halting in front of a tall black iron fence, Molly inserted a large skeleton key, turned the lock, opened the door and waved Sam ahead. "Welcome to your new home, at least for a while. Shall we?"

Excitement weaved through her as they strolled in. Senses at full alert, she gasped at the inner courtyard. Tranquil and inviting as it was, the water babbling at the statuesque fountain was soothing to her ears as the sweet smell of blooming magnolias wafted through the air. It was delightful as cozy metal tables, chairs and beautiful tile work surrounding the entire inside walls.

"This is your permanent home?"

"Indeed, it is. Come on, our parcels have been left in our rooms. I have you on the opposite side of me." She led the way up an outside set of stairs and through double-wide French doors. "Our rooms open up to this corridor. Remember, even though we secure the gates at night, you need to make sure you lock your doors as well."

"I will. This is gorgeous. I may never want to leave."

She set her bags down, unwrapped the parcels and began hanging the new dresses.

"I'll leave you to it then. If you pull the cord over there next to your bed, a servant will come help with anything you need. As soon as you are through, lock the doors and come through the interior hall. Take a left down the stairs and another into the morning room. I will meet you there with tea and snacks. That should tide us over until supper."

"Molly, I can't thank you enough. This is just lovely."

"Honey, you are going to be real busy, real soon, so enjoy it."

With everything neatly packed away and her bags in the mahogany armoire, Sam pulled the drapes, clicked the locks and exited the room. The hallway was light, airy and decorated in soft pastels. She found the morning room quickly stepping aside as a handsomely dressed servant dashing out clutching an envelope tightly in his white knuckled hand.

Grinning, she entered the plush parlor. "Yeah, I just saw your man looking none too happy."

"He will get over it. I've sent him on this type of an errand a few times. He's always worried he will not return and no one will know how to find him." She laughed softly. "Hugh, has been with me since I bought this place and would do anything for me. This sets his teeth on edge. Come sit. I have goodies."

As they chatted away for the next hour, Hugh, reappeared knocking on the door then reentered the room.

"Madame Molly, that woman is spooky. I say it every time. She handed me a note before I could give her yours. Seems she expected your request in advance, creepy woman."

"Thank you. Would you please have the carriage brought along the rear? We will be leaving shortly."

Molly stood taking out a small pistol from the top desk drawer and put it in her reticule.

"You are all set, right?"

"Yes, I am. Oh, my goodness. My nerves are on edge. Cripes, she's going to know I'm scared like bloody hell before I even arrive! By the way, what did the note say?"

"She's expecting us, that's it. Shall we?"

They slid into the carriage as the driver closed the door hiding them from pedestrians. Both settled back on opposite seats against the plush leather. Several minutes ticked by in silence, each in their own thoughts, when the coach halted.

"The driver will wait here just in case it's dark when we get back. Come on, we have a boat to catch."

Sam eyed the rowboat curiously recalling a time not that long ago when she was sitting in one watching for whom she believed was Gunner. Her mind drifted to him. What was he doing now? Where was he? With Lafitte or back at the tavern with that wench?

As the oarsman slowly rowed them up river, the air transformed into thick and steamy. Sam's stomach lurched up to her throat. Glancing down in near horror, she watched a long, poisonous snake weave its way downstream. When a gator slid off the bank into the murky water toward them, she nearly passed out in earnest.

She could whack a man in the ribs, stab him and even hit one over the head leaving him lifeless and unconscious. But the thought of her being swallowed up by that snake or thrashed and chewed up by the alligator, had her biting a lower lip.

Emotions played heavily across Sam's features as she contemplated today's visit deep into the bayou of the infamous swamp witch.

As the boat slid up against the nutrient rich grassy bank, she woke up as if in a deep trance. The oarsman helped them ashore, tied the boat to an overhanging branch, then stepped under a tree and lit up a smoke.

She could tell he knew this drill well enough. It was time to wait.

Sam clutched Molly's arm tightly, nearly causing her to blurt out to ease up. Cats seemed to appear out of nowhere, not all black as Sam had imagined. Their throaty chatter sent ripples of concern up both their spines. Hissing, they dispersed in several directions, vanishing into the cover of thick brush. Sam swatted at a bug on her neck, flicking it to the ground, stomping it in a very unladylike manner, as sweat from the humidity grew on an upper lip. Face moist to the touch, she felt her unruly hair. It had now coiled into an ugly mess.

The solid old Cyprus door swung open, but no one was there. As they stood on the stoop, both mouth agape, a hand came out encased partially by a ruby red robe. But, it was the strong voice that surprised Sam the most. She had expected a creaky, frightening one.

"You," she pointed to Sam, "come in. Molly, you stay put on the porch."

Sam shook as Molly disengaged her grip, giving a bit of a shove.

"Go, Sam."

Walking into the room, looking around, her brows drew in as a frown formed. It was warmly lit with candles and sunlight. Suddenly, optimism filled the air.

"I surprised you, didn't I? But I admit, Samantha Arnesen, I wanted to see you in person and have been looking forward to meeting you for a long time. Here, sit across from me so I can read your eyes."

She slid onto a wooden chair, clasped hands as their eyes locked. They were the darkest unreadable orbs she had ever seen.

"Come now, dear, you need not fear me. I know more about you than you think. My sister, Anna, told me you would be coming to New Orleans. Not all your journey here is to assist Lafitte. Let me hold your right hand."

Shaking slightly, Sam held it out forcing confidence she did not feel at all right now. Then realization dawned. So, the Tinker and swamp priestess were sisters?

This whole situation just went from frightening to bizarre in zero to sixty.

The room went quiet as the old woman moved her fingertip over the lines, stopping, contemplating, when at last she finally began.

Chapter Nineteen

The door creaked open as Sam came out, face blanched. Molly rushed to her side grabbing her just before legs gave way. Apprehensively, Molly glanced up at the old woman as their eyes fastened on one another.

"She has a lot to digest." Was all that was said before she slipped back into the shadows and closed the door.

Silence prevailed on the walk back as Sam's hand clutched Molly's arm tightly.

Sam glanced up noticing Hugh was waiting, having heard their approach. She was grateful no words had been uttered along the walk, nor now. As they all got back into the boat, she drifted off in time hardly realizing until the boat was being pulled up on shore, that they had returned.

"When we get back do you want a tray sent up? Anything in particular?"

Sam stepped down from the carriage as the door was opened.

"No. Aren't we going out to that swanky place you were talking about? We have time to wash and change before, don't we?"

They entered the rear courtyard.

"It's unavoidable, Sam, I'm going to ask you questions. But, I can see that now is just not the time. When you are ready, meet me in the study. It is opposite the morning room. Bring a shawl. It will get cooler. I expect we will be out late tonight."

Sam nodded disappearing behind a potted palm frock. With a quick glance, she took the stairs at a run. Unlocking the door and closing it with a boot, she jumped onto the beds downy comfort. Damn, that experience was stranger than being with the tinker.

Would he believe what she had just been told?

Did she?

Pulling on the cord she rang for her handmaid. Who was smart enough to show up with two gents in tow carrying hot water. As they exited, she slid into the hot water. It was just enough to shock the senses and reboot an overloaded brain.

Now, a whole hell of a lot made sense. Even Adam. Having the next two days free was going to be a needed benefit. A focus on her purpose. Making it clearer. She rose as the maid toweled the water off. Wrapping up her hair, Sam slid into the newly purchased, illegally imported, silk stockings.

"Manny, there's nothing like a lady putting on a pair of these lovelies that alters a whole mood. Do you own any?"

"Oh, no, mistress, I surely do not!"

"Go into the top drawer and pick yourself out a set. When you go back to your room tonight, you put them on. Then you will know what I am talking about in earnest."

The maid stared at her with bulbous eyes.

"Mistress?"

Sam laughed. "I'm not crazy at all. Even though I am aware the whole household knows I went to see the old crone on the bayou today. Now, be a good girl and do as I say. Take a pair. If anyone questions you, send them to me. I will take care of it."

As she tied her boots, shawl handbag and gloves, a smugness took over watching the maid. Good, the girl was following instructions. It was a priceless moment for Sam,

"You have the night off. When we get back I will take care of my needs. Go and do something fun. You hear?"

She pulled the door closed leaving the maid to clean up. When she entered the study, Molly had two shot glasses out filled with amber liquid.

"If that's rum I may pass. It caused me havoc last night. That is for damn sure."

"Ah, Sam is back..." she patted the swooning seat beside her chair. "It's not. We get this from Lafitte on his ventures to Mexico. It's referred to as Tequila. Have you ever tried it amongst your journey's?"

Sam groaned. It was her modern world poison of choice. It along with a few beers, would probably land them in jail. Or enslaved on some rogue ship toward the southern Caribbean islands. Who the hell cared anyway. Tonight, was ladies' night out and they deserved it.

She took the crystal glass in hand and held it up.

"You are a novel woman, Sam, of that I am sure. Let us raise glasses at our successful day of shopping, making it out of the swamp and the laughs to follow. To good friends." They clunked glasses swigging back.

"Oh, that's smooth. How about another because I have one more toast."

"I'm game." Molly filled the glasses again. "The floor's yours, Samantha."

With a somber face, she raised it.

"Here's to the men we love, here's to the men that love us. If the men we love don't love us, fuck them all and drink to us."

Molly burst out laughing, glasses touching.

"You are going to have to repeat that a few times to me, so I can share that with a few of my acquaintances."

"Can do. But, no word of the source. Long ago I had two very close friends and we traveled together all the time. Back then, we certainly lived by that mantra!"

She grinned, nodding.

"The carriage is awaiting us. Shall we go? Ricardo's should be entertaining by now. Great New

Orleans music and a fine dinner are awaiting. Just be warned, this is not ball room dancing. Get prepared for grabbing hands. This place is barely one step up from last night. Keep your wits if you saunter off."

"After experiencing the tavern, I'm using all my senses. Which may be a bit dulled by both those shots. Oh, this will be fun. Damn fine Tequila, Molly. We'd better get out of here before I do one more and we settle in and get drunk."

Rising, they went outside.

"Will Lafitte or Griffin be there?"

"You are feeling spunky, aren't you? No, I don't think so. Word on the street was they had cargo to move. Your man was helping Lafitte. He has new contacts lined up. It appears the last two disappeared rather quickly. But you will like this one, Sam. I heard that a certain wench wanted to run along with them on this trip. To keep your man busy. But, Lafitte stepped in and said no damn woman would be on his ship without one for every man. Then I heard he asked if she was up to the task. I guess she decided not to pursue it further."

They both laughed.

"Okay, funny enough. But, I refrain from comment on that one. If he decides he needs to use her to gain an advantage that's important, then he should. So long as I am oblivious to it, I mean. Anyway, what happened to the double agents? Did they get away with it?"

"No, they set up cargo to be confiscated, arranged it to be sold and it was all bogus. Lafitte took them on a bit of a ride up the river and, well, they haven't been seen since."

She nodded, now understanding. "Good, I'd like a bit of time before I see him again."

"The crone, did she frighten you?"

"Actually, she opened up my eyes to a lot of things."

"I hope she told you he loves you. Even my eyes can see he does."

Sam smiled lowering her gaze, but would not say a word. Molly leaned forward as if she knew in the dark night exactly where they were.

"If we get separated, make sure you don't go outside with anyone. There's much amiss about this night. I can feel it. Stay alert"

"The old crone got to you too. Even though you did not sit with her, eh?"

"No, this is New Orleans; mischief flows through the streets just as much as voodoo magic. You will recognize the difference when we get in there."

As if on cue, the carriage halted and the footman helped them out. Molly parted with final instructions.

"Three a.m. no later. We will be right here."

Taking Sam by the arm, they strode inside. Sweeping her eyes around the room. A smile formed as she surveyed the gas lit lamps, dark mahogany tables, thickly padded wooden chairs and crisp linen. How bad could it be, she pondered, looking at the lovely fine china and tableware.

"Is this for real?" she whispered, as the *maitre d'* nodded to Molly. They followed him to a table neatly tucked into a cozy alcove. Perfect, here they could chat unabated by nosey neighbors with ears listening in.

"Sam, you can have Cuban, Creole, Spanish and island food. But try to avoid anything with a heavy wine sauce. Regrets will come later if you mix that with drinks." She winked.

"Where does the wine come from?"

"Lafitte would have to tell you. Next time you see him, you ask."

Giggling, Sam lowered her face leaning closer to Molly. "This is utterly too much enjoyment. Don't look now, but we are being watched. I wonder what's going through all those inquisitive minds?"

"Yes, no one here knows you were a tavern wench last night. Tonight, tongues will wag believing you to be an aristocrat having just arrived. A steamy socialite with a large pocketbook. Be diligent. There are snakes here as well as the in the bayou swamps."

"Shit, I recognize those two over there. I saw them last night in the tavern. Oh, damn. This gets worse. I see someone else I have had previous dealings with."

Tilting her head right, Molly glanced over.

"I've seen them as well and I know where and when. They were there last night. All of them. Are they following you Sam? Surely this is no coincidence."

"Savoy, I know him as Savoy. I've had a few run-ins with him. I need to find out what they are up to."

"You will have your chance tomorrow night. All three of them along with your gent, Lafitte, and many diplomats from New Orleans will be at the poker game."

"Perhaps. But I will have a word with him before then."

Their dinner arrived as they kept the conversation light and flowing. Their minds engaged in different ways.

Molly signed the bill as both rose placing the linen napkins on top of the table.

"Through that hallway by their table is the entrance to the nightclub. Most of the so-called ladies in this room are not allowed entry; it could prove scandalous. Truth be told, it's because their husbands go in there and send them home in carriages. Otherwise, they would not be able to truly enjoy themselves with their mistresses, or gents. Whatever the flavor is." She let that trail off.

"Oh, *risqué*. I say. Well? What are we waiting for?"

As they strode along she made eye contact with Savoy. A silent message passed between them. It was as if she was daring him to follow.

He enjoyed dares.

As the double wide door closed, they found a table close to the stage and small dance floor. Yeah, this was hardly Saturday night rocking the Casbah. It was seedy, dangerous and just where she wanted to be. This was the real beat of New Orleans after dark.

They ordered up drinks. Sam picked hers up, nodding to Molly as they scoped out the interior inhabitants. A quartet walked up on stage, picked up their instruments and began playing a whizzing jazz piece as Sam's hand was grabbed. Swinging around, she found her hands in the iron tight grip of none other.

Savoy.

Surely tonight he was going to put her to the test.

"Shall we wait for a slower one?"

"Nope, this suits me fine."

As that piece ended, a much slower one took its place as the floor suddenly teemed with pairs.

"So, mistress, what has you in New Orleans? Seems our paths keep crossing. Now a gent like me can't help but wonder why that may be?"

Would a double fist to the ribs or a knee to the balls be appropriate about now? Sam internally contemplated which as a lethal grin formed.

His eyes narrowed.

"Stop plotting to maim me. I think we need to come to a kind of truce. I mean not to detain you. But I am quite sure we need each other's help."

"Now, why would I believe you? I've escaped from you a time or two and more recently hit you pretty hard and left you to your own devices."

He grinned, a devilish one at that. It worked, softening her resolve a bit. Damn, he was an enigma!

"I've never tried to hurt you, mistress, it's been entirely one way."

She knew that was true.

"So, do we have a temporary one?"

She locked horns with him until the tune ended.

"Can I get back to you on that?"

He took her hand into the crook of his arm as he walked back toward the vacant table.

"Just where are the blokes you were with at dinner? Are they no longer here?"

"No, they had prior arrangements. But they will be at the game tomorrow night. I understand you will as well."

She leaned toward him. "How the hell do you know all of my plans? Do you have someone following me?"

"I think you already know the answer to that and are the one baiting me, Samantha."

"Fine, I'm not in the mood for any of your antics. If I decide to join forces with you, I will give you a nod tomorrow night when I see you. Are you sure they don't recognize me from the tavern?"

"No, it was dark and they were deep in conversation. I'm sure all dolled up like you are now, they would never think you were that tavern wench." He chuckled, grinning roguishly.

"Oh, shut up."

She released her hand from his arm and swished away without so much as a goodbye not seeing the smug look of satisfaction on his face.

She sat down, smiling. That had gone exactly as planned. Perhaps a bit too neat and tidy. Yes, she'd work with him. It was important to make him believe they were on the same page, so more information could be gathered. Plus, he was her ticket to the other two gents. Yup, she needed Savoy. Damn if his timing was not perfect.

"So, I think we've accomplished all our goals this night," Molly asked. "Do you agree? Shall we head out? It's near three."

Sam rose taking her cloak. A sly smile hovering across her lips.

Yes, I want to make sure I get plenty of sleep for our main event."

"Absolutely, it's going to be quite a dandy. These old bones can feel it. You get up tomorrow when you are ready. Make sure to keep to the courtyard just in case. We can dine at seven before leaving to go to the club and Sam, wear the periwinkle dress. It's quite grand. We all want you to stand out."

"Oh, Molly, after all of this ends will our paths cross again? I've really enjoyed getting to know you."

"Probably not, but you never know. Maybe a visit back to the crone is in order so we can be enlightened?"

"I'll pass." she grinned. "You can go. Wow, that was a quick ride back. Good, I'm beat and looking forward to that plush bed I can evaporate into."

"Sleep well, Sam."

"You too. Thank you again. For everything."

Nodding at the top of the stairs, they parted ways.

Chapter Twenty

Sauntering into the kitchen unannounced, Sam quickly realized the error of her ways. Indeed, it was not Ard Aulinn where roaming free as a bird was allowed and completely tolerated. There, the staff just turned an eye to her comings and goings.

"Mistress, did you ring for your maid and she not come?"

She plopped a cherry into her mouth.

"Oh, no, I was just strolling and thought I'd come in and see what I could wrestle up for a snack to take out in the courtyard."

The two cooks eyed her briefly.

"What would you like? We will have it brought to you."

It was clear the emphasis was on 'you.'

"Bread, cheese, fruit and meats will do. Nothing too fancy and a pot of tea please."

She nodded knowing a hasty retreat was in order. Quickly, she caught up with Molly, who was holding some paperwork and appeared headed toward the study.

"Ah, you made it. When I get in I'll ring for some food brought to you. Would you like it served here?"

"Well, here is the thing. I screwed up and went in there already. Now, I am properly chastised and put in my place." She giggled. "I now know where I do and don't belong."

"Serves you right for crossing that boundary. Even I don't go in there.

"Yes, I've been sternly disciplined by your staff."

Watching her disappear inside the study. Sam picked just the right spot to sit. Viewing the street and the hub of activity brought much needed diversion at a time when it was needed. The fountain's water cascaded over forming a pool and the sound was indeed soothing as a palm tree provided shade.

Placing her feet up on an opposite chair, she hastily removed them sitting ramrod straight. Damn, she thought, this was the land of pirates, voodoo and lusty men. Yet she felt she needed to be more prim and proper here than back in Victorian England.

Attentive on her approach, the servant brought a large tray of food.

"Thank you. I'll serve myself. I'll leave this here when I am through so you can take it back to the kitchen."

She smiled, hoping to relay an apology of sorts for having crossed that imaginary boundary earlier.

"Thank you, mistress. I appreciate that." The maid curtsied hurrying away.

Diving in completely famished, Sam stuffed her mouth while watching the comings and goings out on the busy street. It was enjoyable indeed being smack dab in the middle of the Quarter. Off in the distance, the air filled with the sounds of clarinets and horns. Yes. The city was wakening up from the previous night's slumber.

Stomach filled, happy, sipping on the hot tea, she decided the hell with it. Those boots went up on the opposite chair as she poured another cup.

Mentally, a picture formed on how tonight's events should unfold. Toying with it over and over, a plan formed. Sam felt confident it would work. There would only be one opportunity to fulfill this passage. On top of that, a big decision had to be made. There was no way out now.

Lips slimming into a firm line, eyes narrowing, determination rose as her spirit matched. Yes, now she understood what needed to be done.

Molly suddenly plopped down in one of the other chairs producing a green concoction.

"Want one of your own?"

"Is that the infamous mint julep? If so, I'll pass. One thing I never touch is colored drinks; they can make for a fun time until they wear off. Then its hell to pay in the head."

"Damn true. What's on your mind? You were deep within your own thoughts."

Sam leaned close. "I'll tell you more in the carriage tonight on our way to the game." She sat back in her chair. "I decided on the periwinkle dress. You were right. It is a good choice. What time do we leave?"

"We need to be there by nine. Basically, we hover all night around our dedicated tables, ensuring the servants keep the drinks filled. There will be a lot going on. Your focus is different than mine. Only you know what that is. Money will flow like the alcohol. Don't be astonished at who arrives. A few familiar faces from the history books will be there."

"Can I make sure I'm assigned to the tables where Savoy and his cohorts will be seated?"

"Already taken care of."

Locking eyes with Molly, Sam raised a brow. "Will the mistress be there?"

She laughed. "Ah, the green monster does live in you. No, she will not. A more comfortable place for that wench is in the tavern. We'd not want her about on such an important night as this, now would we?"

"True. I do not see you in my future after tomorrow."

"Correct. I will miss you. It has been fun having you about."

Sam reached over and squeezed her hand. "There won't be time later so thank you for everything. Will you take care of my things left behind?"

"Yes, already have a place for them. Indulge me for a moment. I need to know something. Do you have everything in case later you find an unexpected situation has come about?"

Sam laughed. "I'm prepared. Do you think we should start to get ready? It's going to take the maid a few hours to finish my hair. Those Parisian hairdos are quite the rage, but I'm not going with that awful powder in it. Don't be startled when you see me."

Molly stood grinning. "And I'd expect you no other way than doing your own thing. Have at it no matter what. You will stand out in any room, especially tonight."

Reaching over, Sam hugged her tightly just before leaving to go up to her room. Swinging open the doors, she was greeted by the servant.

"Mistress, I have your bath ready, dress pressed. But, we'd better hurry. It will take quite a long time to wash, dry and curl your hair."

"Okay. I know it is a bit tardy of me. But, what is your name?"

"It is Sofia, mistress."

Taking the sponge and lathering it, Sam cleansed then handed it over so she could do her back and neck. "That's a pretty name. How old are you?"

"Twenty, mistress."

"Did you enjoy the stockings?"

She grinned raising the skirt up a few inches, producing one silk stockinged leg.

"Indeed. They are just like you said. Completely wonderful."

"Well, how about another little gift. I am leaving soon and won't be able to take everything with me. I want you to pick out a day dress along with petticoat. Write down where you live so I can have it boxed and sent. I can assure you no one will question how it was obtained. I will not accept no for an answer, Sofia. I insist."

"Oh, honestly? Well, all right then, I will! It will bother my two other sisters and shall be worth it. They will be quite jealous I received a gift!"

"Good, then it's settled. Now hand me that warm towel. I will dry off while you take care of the rest. I need to get this whole ordeal done with."

Sitting at the dressing table, Sam was amazed at what had to come next. "Mistress, we need to put your gown on now. It is time to do your hair."

Luscious yards of silk slid down over her shoulders settling in a voluptuous heap at her hips to feet. Sofia buttoned while Sam lowered the top so it rested above the shoulders. A puff filled with lavender pearl powder was the finishing touch. Oh, how she wished this could be taken along when it was time to go. Extravagant, yes, but for this night it was entirely worth it.

"Your skin glows like a full moon rising up over the river."

"It does. Why don't you take it tonight? I cannot chance it in my satchel. If for some reason it opens, it will make a bloody mess of the rest of my things. I can always buy another when I get resettled."

"Oh, I was going to say I can't take any more. You have already been so generous. But, I will take that."

Sam laughed sitting back down. For the next two hours, Sofia worked magic on her hair. It was piled high with sassy ringlets swaying and one unruly but delicious curl lying softly down her back. Slipping on the amethyst and diamond earrings, bracelet and ring she borrowed from Molly, Sam dabbed lavender rose oil onto the pulse points. Later, the groomsman would retrieve these gems and bring them back to her.

"Well, shall I do?"

Silk swirled as she marveled at the reflection shining back from the mahogany floor mirror.

"You are lovely, mistress. Here, take your gloves and shawl."

Sam set the gloves back down.

Sofia gasped.

"No worry tonight. I am going to set a new fashion trend. I want to show off my beautiful jewelry. The gloves can stay behind. I will not need them."

Placing the shawl over her shoulders, Sam swung wide the double balcony doors throwing over her shoulder,

"Please lock everything and do not forget to set out what you want. I've sent a note to the housekeeper what's left on the bed will be sent to your address. Write it out and leave it on top of everything. And Sofia, thank you."

Not awaiting a reply she closed the door. Lifting the hem up from the ground, she walked down the stairs and outside to where Molly was already sitting. A gloved hand reached out, extended, as *de ja vu* took over. It was a time recalled when Mrs. H did the same thing. That was then. In his England. Now, new business needed to be concluded.

A deep saturated smile lifted Sam's lips while clasping that hand. Climbing in and sitting comfortably, the door closed as the coachman drove the horses on.

"I can tell you are ready. Your gaze says it all. This will be our last chat, Sam, anything you want to ask before we get there? We only have about fifteen minutes."

"No, but I want to thank you for setting up my meeting with the crone. I know now who asked you to do that and why. I have more than one task that befalls me that's crucially important over the next twenty-four hours."

They clutched hands.

"You left your gloves on purpose, didn't you? Oh, dear girl, I'm going to miss you a lot! We'd really paint this town bright red if you were here longer."

"I think we can still do a bit of painting tonight, don't you?"

"Lass, I'm just along for the ride. It's your show completely."

As the carriage came to a halt, Sam was assisted down first. Glancing up at the three-storied antebellum home, she realized they had quickly reached the outer perimeter of the Quarter. Drapes were drawn, but light was creeping out from behind, as she lifted her dress up a bit and was escorted inside by a handsomely dressed attendant.

"Mistresses, welcome. Follow me and I'll show you your stations and who will be under your management this evening. We have a full house. It's the who's who of society and government. With an added tip for flare with a few, umm, privateers thrown in for good measure."

The adrenaline heightened throughout her system as she observed Molly being escorted by a very handsome gent; one whom she already had engaged in a lively conversation.

"Mistress Samantha, these four tables are under your care. A quick nod to either of your two attendants will bring them quickly to your side. They will be responsible for delivering drinks and smokes to your section."

"When do they start to arrive?"

The shawl slid off as he retrieved and took care of it.

"In about thirty minutes. Walk around and get yourself familiar. Should you need to have a few minutes to yourself at any time during the evening, just make eye contact with me and I'll send backup."

"Excellent. Is that water?"

"Yes. It will be filled when you need it. Remember, there is no eating on the floor. If you are hungry, we have small snacks in the back hallway away from normal traffic. You can help yourself." He nodded, heading off then stopped briefly to chat with the gent with Molly.

As the two ladies' eye's locked, Sam smiled. Very happy her friend was situated in the next group. Sipping on the cool water, it was settling against the increasing warmth of nerves pulsating through her stomach.

Refraining from anxiety was not easy. Especially as the two guys from the tavern stood at the entrance. Their eyes raked Sam's attire. Under normal circumstance, that would have pissed her off. But, it was a clear indication, and a good one, they had not recognized her at all.

Taking their order as they sat, she nodded passing it off to the servant nearly laughing at how fast he hurried to get their booze.

Suddenly, the room filled with electricity.

Swinging around, Sam knew well before the ruckus hit the infamous Lafitte had arrived. Entourage in tow. They dispersed to separate tables. As if dividing they could conquer more, save one.

Years ago, when planning a visit to the Jazz City, Sam had googled places of interest and discovered much about the sea fairing Captain Lafitte. Including some artistic renditions. He was that mirror image. Handsome and roguish as he sauntered toward her.

There was a tour of his haunts, so to speak, she had taken and enjoyed immensely. Funny how knowing about him then brought her closer to understanding how he operated now.

It all made sense.

But where that tour left off, he began.... She was trying in vain to suppress a giggle.

His eyes rested on the handsome lass, smiling devilishly all along his short walk to where she stood. A hand roughly grabbed an arm halting forward progress.

"Lafitte, don't even go there."

"Ah, my friend. She is the one you've been searching for. But, I could swear to the swamps witches she's the tavern wench."

His eyes gleamed raking over her attire so boldly. Yet, with a familiarity only a lover truly knew.

"Ah, damn."

Adam swatted him on the back moving toward his chair, a roguish smile hovering on his face.

Seated, Cuban cigars lit, drinks served, Sam had every intention on causing chaos tonight as she leaned just close enough to him, eyes tempting, taunting, then moved away.

"She must keep you busy, my friend."

"More than I can say."

Both men belted out in laughter as she moved over near Savoy's associates happy Adam and Lafitte's banter had not been overheard.

Here was a conversation she wanted to hear.

"He should be here shortly. Still, we need the room to fill up before taking the document."

"Agreed. But doing this under the nose of Lafitte? As I said time and again, I'm still not sure this is the right move. I think it's a bit too risky?"

"Not at all. Here we can maneuver with more freedom and less observation than if we were just out on the street in some dark alley or in one of the taverns. You know he has spies all over the city. Here he has no idea who we are. Look at him. Completely oblivious and relaxed. Just what we want."

"Well, we both know how he' has contacts all over. There is the proof. The governor just arrived and I can bet you he's not sitting at our table."

Sam had no clue what their names are, but needed little more from them. Moving away, she needed to make sure the timely arrival of the governor was met with satisfaction. The astute waiter already had his drink of preference set before him. At Lafitte's table. As she passed by, he glanced up, momentarily taking in her beauty then finished engaging the gents at the table at how pissed off his wife was she could not attend.

Sam grinned, weaving around the outside perimeter of tables glancing quickly at Adam. Damn the man! His eyes were burning the clothes off her back!

Turning toward another table, Savoy came into focus weaving through the now smoked infused room. Nodding at him as he passed, she escorted him towards his two tavern associates. Leaning down, Sam placed a bourbon on the rocks beside his right hand, lightly grazing it as their eyes locked briefly. She knew he understood.

Doors opened as several dealers came out opening fresh decks of cards at each of their tables. The night of gaming was officially under way. Hours they played. Voices grew louder as the alcohol flow increased like the water pounding over Niagara Falls.

But time was of the essence and quickly running out. Something had to happen soon. Finally, it was one of the two men she had been observing closely that got it rolling along.

"Jackson, I call."

Eyes squinting, the other threw a silent dare out to the entire table.

"What's it going to be." He glanced over to his companion and grinned knowing he won this round.

"Someday I'll spit on your grave. Mark my word on it, Lee." There was a deafening pause at their table as he toyed with a choice. "Dammit, fine. I take the bait. I call."

Simultaneously, both flipped over their cards. The others at the table having folded theirs over in defeat.

Jackson slapped the table forcing cards to fly. He quickly realized his friend had pulled a fast one. "Damn, you shithead. I was sure to have you dead to rights in a bluff and you threw one over on me. Good move, ass."

Laughing, hitting both on the back, Savoy stood as the chair grated against the wooden floor.

"Deal me out of this round. I'll return shortly."

As Sam observed, smiling, Molly seemed to have a different plan for him. Hardly a klutz, she bumped into him slightly, the contents of a glass full with whisky landing on his suit jacket.

"Pardon me, sir, I do apologize. You," she pointed towards an attendant, "bring a warm cloth. Quickly now. I've spilled a drink on this gentleman. One up until now was having such great luck."

Savoy indulged humored by the move.

Molly nodded as Sam walked by stopping to look over a shoulder. Leaning in to pick up empties between Lafitte and Adam, a strong, yet familiar hand slid up a thigh. It halted when it was met by the strap engulfing a knife. Just as quick as that, he slid it back down.

Really? Had she felt that? Glancing at him with a twinkle in her eyes, Sam shifted out of reach and moved away.

Adam sat back watching, eyes roaming up Sam's delicious backside. What a surprise was in store for her later. Surely the lass had seen it too. What Molly had done? Picking up the refreshed drink, he refocused attention on Savoy, who had returned to his gaming table. Leaning slightly towards, he was trying to catch an earful of the conversation taking place with the men there. What he heard next was music to his ears.

"Did you decide not to leave it?" Jackson asked quietly.

Savoy threw him a quick glance. "No, I thought the incident of the drink being spilled on me may be a diversion." Pulling the chair in, Savoy swiftly moved the document into Jackson's hands. His job was now done. Well, almost.

"Deal me in," Savoy said, glancing quickly at Sam. "The night's winding down. It may be too late to recoup my losses. You gents seem to be damn lucky tonight."

Relief swept through Sam at Savoy's silent acknowledgement. But, now she was in a true dilemma at which cat to chase first?

Savoy? Lafitte? Adam? Jackson and Lee?

She needed all of them!

A bell rang signaling the gamers that the night's events had ended. Shortly, the room started to clear out as servants cleaned up tables. Lines of carriages formed outside as gentlemen shook hands and headed in that direction.

Sam was already following behind a group of them then noticed Molly's servant.

"Oh, hello. You are the mistress groomsman? Please make sure you place this in her hands right away." She handed him a small pouch containing the borrowed jewels.

"Indeed, I was advised earlier to expect it. I see her coming out now. Pardon me, mistress, but I must go."

Both ladies' hands shot up in the air in a wave as Sam turned weaving between departing carriages. Waiting briefly, one rolled up, halted, a hand extended as she laughed. This was becoming a habit!

She got into Lafitte's carriage and sat opposite him as his hand released hers.

"Here." she slid onto his lap an envelope. "You will want to look at this now."

He ripped it open, unfolding a large piece of parchment.

"How the bloody hell did you get this?"

"That's not important. We must get back to your encampment as fast as possible. Time is not on your side while we just sit here. I know for a fact that fast on your heels, the militia is following. They only have one mission. To kill all your men, loot all your bounty and confiscate the Angelina.

Someone from your crew, Lafitte, has turned traitor on you and only I know who it is. Well, rather how to sniff him out."

Chapter Twenty-One

Lafitte banged roughly on the inside carriage roof. The driver hastened with quick action as it jerked into movement, pitching and rolling. Holding tight to the seat, Sam felt like her teeth were going to crack and fall right out of her mouth. The reverberation was so intense.

"Where is Griffin?"

He grinned. "I sent him up ahead on his stead. I wish I had been advised about this before. He could have ridden with orders. Then again, the knowledge of who this traitor is lies inside your pretty head, mistress."

"Anyone new to your party or disgruntled lately?"

"Aye, a few. So, it will be interesting to discover exactly who it is."

He eyed her keenly. "You must have a plan?"

She grinned, growing fonder of this handsome rogue pirate.

"I do. Are you willing to trust me completely? The fate of all of you hangs in the balance."

He locked eyes, clasping gloveless hands.

"You are steady, lass. Either you are a conniving wench, or Griffin has you pegged right and I must believe in you both completely."

"I'm here to help you. I give you my word and life on it."

"Okay, all that's good and fine." He removed a flask of rum and handed it to her. "Let us seal this alignment by sharing a drink."

It was a welcome sight to her as she swigged back a gulp, handing it back a cough spurted out.

"Yeah, took a bit much."

He laughed. "That wench Lucinda could very well be involved in this Samantha. I hope you don't mind my addressing you so informally?"

She shook her head. "I think you are right. A visit to her will be in order when this is done. Too bad we may not be here to see her face when you walk into that tavern. I wager she's expecting news of a dead man."

His eyes bore into hers. "What's your connection to Savoy?"

She took the flask right out of his hand and took another sip. "Finding a renewed fondness for this fiery liquid."

"You don't have to answer me. But Griffin will demand answers. You won't be able to keep his intentions at bay that long."

She shrugged her shoulders. "How much further? I hope we are close. My teeth are rattling around inside my head with this quick pace."

He knew the rum had settled nicely into her system.

"Okay, back to the business at hand. Is your entire encampment easily seen from where the coach will stop? I need it to be. I must have a full view of all your men. Shit, what if the one I seek is not there? I had not thought of that."

His grin grew.

"All of them were posted here tonight. If any of their snarly asses are missing, then they are dead men anyway. How will you point him out?"

"You leave that up to me." As she finished a final swig and handed it back to him, the carriage came to an abrupt stop. Not looking back, Lafitte stepped out shutting the door tight. From this vantage point, she could see the area well. The roaring fire was an asset. Yes, this worked as she quickly reviewed the entire encampment.

It took her no time to zero in on him.

Yes, she was right. Hand on the handle to get out, the opposite door opened as in slid Savoy. The cool steel blade of a sharp knife was pressed to her throat. Sam was rendered temporarily motionless. Quite in shock.

"Get out and go easy, mistress. Or, I slice up your pretty face. Then no man will want you."

Sam slid slowly as he shoved her forward. They both came into full view of the gathering as fear lit her eyes. Adam came out of the shadows, gun pointed right between the brows of Savoy.

Now it came down to this, who wanted to die more?

Silently, Sam's eyes beseeched him, begging no shot be taken at this range. Especially with the type of gun he held. It was old. The shot accuracy sucked and she knew it from reading stories about them.

Seconds ticked by.

Finally, he lowered it slightly. Eyes dark as the blackest pool.

Lafitte glared at him. "Savoy, what the bloody hell are you doing here? What's your grief with this woman?"

The air filled with tension.

Weapons were drawn.

A bat swooping by was heard so deafening was the silence.

But no one budged an inch.

"I'm feeling might generous tonight, Lafitte. How about the girl lives if you drop the keys to the storage barn at your boots? I'm giving you a chance. Kick them toward me now."

Lafitte eyed him as if he was an errant child.

"You think the lass means anything to me? She may to Griffin, but not me. It's not my issue."

The whole group laughed except one man. It was what Lafitte had been waiting for, but could hardly believe who it was.

"Vashon?" Was all he said, approaching at swords length. "You bastard. Why would you do this to your men? A traitor to us all?"

Vashon panicked and pulled his pistol aiming it directly at Lafitte.

"If I go, so do you, my arrogant, bastard friend. All these years and you treat me no better than the hands that swab the deck. Equal divides of the loot, my ass! I am your first mate. I should have claimed a higher reward!"

Glancing briefly at Sam, amazed she knew of this all, Lafitte stepped into the pistol, daring him to pull the trigger. Anger grew in Vashon's eyes. Hatred. Pure hatred.

A finger pulled back on the trigger, cocking it.

Suddenly out of nowhere, fast as lightning, a knife grazed his hand as the weapon dropped to the ground. Quickly set upon by two mates, Vashon realized he was fucked.

All eyes were suddenly on her as Adam aimed to shoot Savoy.

"No!" Sam Screamed, arms expanding out to block his frame.

"Madam, explain yourself! Now!"

"Well." Turning, Savoy reached down, grabbed the knife and handed it over. He and Sam exchanged broad smiles. His gun and knife now tucked back inside his belt.

"Because he's my brother, that's why." Sam spoke loud, proudly, out to them all.

Lafitte stopped, standing still, watching this escapade unfold. This woman was much more than a chit to be reckoned with. Hell, more than any three men could handle. He glanced over at Griffin, face tied up in a knot, trying to figure this all out.

Lafitte broke out in laughter.

"Men, while they sort out their business let's get the ship down river and out to open water. Looks like we need to find a new place right away! You three, do you need my carriage to take you to someplace safe, or seek passage on my ship?"

Adam lowered his pistol and in short strides was standing with Savoy and Sam.

"I don't know what the fuck is going on here, but there's a lot of explaining to do. If you are not a part of this," he jabbed a finger into Savoy's chest, "advise what needs to be done and be quick about it."

"Oh, the militia will be looking for me in a fiery hurry. Especially when they realize the locked barn is empty and the ship and Lafitte are nowhere to be found. I say we run like hell and board, they are preparing to ship off. I can explain the rest on the fly!"

Sam hoisted her skirts way above lady-like level and ran just as fast as they did, out of breath and smiling, just before the plank was tossed into the river.

The breeze picked up as the ship creaked, sails expanding moving it downriver. In the distance, the sound of hooves approaching was growing louder. In this darkness, they would not be able to locate the ship until they were at the opening of New Orleans harbor and well on their way out to sea. Once there, the fate of the first mate would swiftly be dealt with.

Sam marched over to Lafitte, smiling and held out one hand.

He grinned, a devilish one it was, then placed the flask in it.

I'll need it more than you. There's going to be a brawl and if I get damn good and drunk they won't be able to irritate me more than they have already."

He laughed pulling her up against him, kissed he fully on the lips, then released just as fast.

"Take it and keep it. My thanks to you, Mistress Samantha. Wait. Is there anything else I need to know before you all leave here?"

"Ah, yes there is. The two men setting this up with Vashon are with the British Militia. I do know their last names are Jackson and Lee. They were at the games earlier tonight sitting at Savoy's Table. I know you were keeping an eye on them. Make sure you become acquainted pretty soon."

As she turned to join her newly discovered brother and the man she loved, Adam's rough chest halted progress. He claimed her lips in a fierce kiss. Both breathless, he released Sam only when he felt he'd done just duty.

"Shall we head down the stairs now? It's time."

She glanced at them both and nodded, handing him the flask.

"Wait. Will we all end up back at the same place? Savoy, will you be there as well? We have a lot of things to discuss."

Adam looked down at her.

"Do you know something that I don't?"

"I'm not actually sure. The old crone told me my biggest decision was about to come and to pay attention to it. So now I'm actually nervous about leaving the ship."

Adam tried to reassure her, "We have to go, it's time. Either that or we pay the price and will all be stuck here. So, it's now or never, Sam."

She nodded, feeling with each step the anxiety mount as darkness suddenly engulfed her entire being. As her eye's fluttered, voices sounded in the distance.

But they were not familiar voices at all. Nor the accent.

It was Italian. Yes. That's what they were speaking. Furrowing her brows, a softer feminine voice penetrated her brain.

"Look, I think she's awaking. Her eyelids just moved."

Sam gingerly opened them.

Glancing in total dismay, growing sadness filled her heart. She was in a hospital room.

A hand lifted her head up offering a sip of water through a straw.

A straw! Damnit all to hell, she was in modern times.

"Oh, my, miss. We are so happy to have you back amongst us. It was a nasty fall you took at the *dei Frari*! Do you feel well enough to speak? To tell us your name? We did not find anything on you for identification."

Sam tried to sit up but was refrained.

"No, you must rest. Can you tell us who you are?"

"Yes, Samantha Arnesen. How long have I been here?"

"Nearly ten days, dear. You had a nasty fall and have been in a coma since you were brought here by the good priest. Several days ago."

Tears formed in her eyes. Oh, my God, she felt such horrible sadness. It had not been real. It had been a dream. A very awful, nasty one. Quite suddenly it overtook as she wept openly. Tears streaming down her cheeks.

"Oh, don't cry." The nurse was applying a cold compress to her warm forehead. "You are safe now and all is well. Is there anyone we can ring for you and tell them you are better?"

Sam shook her head no, not able to utter a word.

"How much longer do I need to stay? My home is in England. I'd like to go back there as soon as you say I am able."

"I'll let the doctor know you are awake right now. If you are okay with me leaving you? It is very important that you eat. We have had you on liquids for a long time. Without strength, the doctor will keep you."

"Then bring me a pizza, spaghetti, I do not care. I am very hungry."

She was not; the pit in her stomach was as large as a cantaloupe. Adam, Mrs. H, her newly found brother. It was all just a dream. She shook her head again, pushing the pillow higher.

Suddenly, she felt lifeless.

"Wait. Nurse, just so I know I am not nuts, it is 2015, right?"

She smiled back at Sam. "Yes, it is."

Thirty minutes later, she was eating a hearty meal when the doctor came in, took her vitals and evaluated her chart.

"If you can keep the food down and we remove the IV, I'll discharge you tomorrow night. But, all your tests need to come back clear."

Thankfully, they did.

The next afternoon, with money donated from an unknown source, Sam took the train from Venice to Paris, through the Eurostar Channel Tunnel to London. At last, she arrived back to her home in Exeter.

Sitting in her car, engine running, she started to laugh uncontrollably. Shaking her head to on one at all, she shifted the car through the gears and left the train station.

"Damn, that was one hell of a coma, that's for sure." She said loudly, flicking the car blinker on just before pulling into the driveway. Everything dropped onto the sofa while she took the stairs slowly, recalling how he had showed up in her bathroom and what followed.

"Stop it, Sam!" she yelled into the hallway. "He is not real, none of it was real!"

But just to punish herself more that night, she ran a bath, waited until the water promoted shriveling and shivers, before she toweled off, eyes pooling and climbed into bed.

It was a lonely bed. It was a lonely house. It was a lonely life.

Fluffing the pillows in frustration, she rose going room to room praying for some damn sign he had been there.

But found none.

Sliding back into bed, roughly pulling the covers up to her chin, she spent the whole night just staring out at the night sky.

Chapter Twenty-Two

Four days slid by as she moped about, hardly being able to get herself out of the cottage, except for the small enjoyment of cycling. Eyeing her laptop, she finally opened it up and noticed it was already on. How could that be? Surely having been gone for so long the battery would be dead by now?

Emails filled the screen. Most of little interest until one caught her eye. It was from ancestry.com. Suddenly, it dawned on her! Grabbing at a pile of paper on her desk, strewing them quickly, shoving them aside, one held high interest. It was from her parent's attorney. One she had reviewed a while ago then left forgotten.

Glancing toward the stairs, thoughts of the ruins haunted every thought. Feet hit the wooden floor.

Dressed, keys and bag in hand, she and the Spark sped off heading on the motorway toward Chester. It was getting late. Would she arrive at Adam's ancestral estate before it closed?

Pressing the accelerator down and watching closely for the police, hours later she was exiting off the byway toward *Ard Aulin*. The large National Trust sign showed their hours. The parking lot was empty. It was four-o'clock which meant thirty minutes to closing.

In the gift shop, she found an attendant.

"What time do the grounds close?"

"Half past four. I won't charge you if you want to roam until then. But, we lock the gates after that so make sure you are off the property."

Sam nodded heading around the familiar backside of the house and found the path she was looking for.

As the ruins loomed up ahead, suddenly her brisk pace turned into a steady run. There it was. Ivy had woven thickly as she pried enough apart until she could slip through the opening of the ruins.

As she descended, wave after wave of strong vibrations reverberated through her being. Even before she climbed up the other side, she knew it completely.

She was back!

Running, breathless, her lungs positively burning, Sam flung the kitchen door wide, stopped briefly with pure delight hugging both Mrs. H and Mrs. Lilly. Strange glances followed her backside as she disappeared from their sight down toward his study. She stopped in front of the door. Halting briefly, eyes filling with tears, it was then their voices could be heard.

Sliding the door open and stepping in, her eyes flew to his. Quickly the distance was closed between them as she launched into his arms, wrapped her legs around his waist and kissed him.

Minutes passed and neither cared.

A clearing of the throat could be heard as Sam pulled back reluctantly.

"Victor?" She slid her feet to the ground and slipped out of Adam's warm, strong arms to stand in front of her brother, clasping his hands.

"I thought you were lost to me." She turned as Adam stood next to her. "Both of you were lost to me forever."

"Samantha," Victor's voice quivered slightly so full of emotion, "we both thought the same of you. That had to be the big decision. When you arrived back in 2015 to Exeter, you had to discover whether it was real. Then make your choices. I am so happy to see you here." He grabbed her hand and hugged her tightly, then stepped aside.

"I want you to meet the rest of your family while you are at it. This is my wife, Melinda, and our two children Vincent and Louisa. She's got your middle name, sweet one."

Sam dropped down to her knees, throwing her arms wide as both seemed to feel how special she was.

"And how old are you two?"

"I'm five and my sister is three and we are going to have a brother or sister soon, Aunt Sam."

She reeled. Aunt Sam. Her heart swelled with love at hearing those words.

"You are? Well you are both going to have big responsibilities you know? Being an older brother and sister. Are you ready for that?"

She tickled them both, standing as their hands clutched hers. Walking over with them in tow, she spoke to Melinda.

"I'd hug you. But they are holding on so tight. I don't want to let them go."

Melinda reached in and hugged her.

"They seem to have the will of you both. Heaven help me with not knowing who this one will take after." She patted her protruding stomach.

Sam turned to Victor. "We have so much to catch up on. Where do you all live?"

He laughed, lifting his son into his arms as Adam lifted Louisa.

"Why don't we go eat and talk about it more there. I think now that you have returned so will our appetites."

He glanced at Adam, knowing he had not fared well since she disappeared.

"After we do, we will leave you two alone. Our place is close. I think some catching up is in order, but can wait a bit longer." He slapped Adam on the back. "We can reconvene tomorrow later in the morning, Sam. I wondered how long before it would take you to find out about me and our true past together."

"Well, Victor, you see that's the question I still have burning. It all started to dawn on me. But, there are still pieces of the puzzle I do not have. I acted quickly and drove here without reading what would explain more. Anyway, I will leave that up to you. One thing I want to know right now is how old I was when they gave you up?"

He grinned. "Three. They sent me to live with Aunt Irene, who you probably never met. She was Mom's sister, a renegade and well, just like you. If you know what I mean."

"So, this merry goose chase is about you both, right?" Adams arm was wrapped tightly around her shoulder.

"It involves a whole lot more than that, I can assure. Sam, this is just a beginning for you. One of which will hold many twists and turns."

"I suppose that will do for now. By looking at the kids' faces they are positively bored by our adult conversation. Right?"

"Well, I think so." Came Louisa's soft reply.

Sam laughed. "True we can do that pretty well. But, you may grow up and do that like us."

"Do I have to?"

Victor reached down to his daughter, flouncing a long braid and laughed with the others.

"We will see. You may have no choice."

As they finished their meal and a pie from town, Adam took the bull by the horns, standing and placing the napkin on his plate. Victor grinned, knowing his patience had evaporated and wanted nothing more than to have his sister alone.

At the door, they hugged. "I'll come by tomorrow afternoon and we can sit down and go over a few things, alright, Sam?"

"Yes, please do. I can't wait." He tugged on her hand once, then let it drift as they got into the awaiting carriage.

"I have to tell you the God's truth. That was one hell of a four days I just spent. And woman, I don't want to ever go through that again." He claimed her by the hand as they went in the large front doors.

"Times like this that make me wish your home was not so big, Lord Griffin. It will take us fifteen minutes to get to your chambers."

They both understood.

Finally, they arrived as he closed their bedroom door.

"It's our chambers and our home, not just mine, Sam." The blouse came up over her shoulders, plush breasts teaming over a silky French bra.

"Oh, I like this one."

Lifting his chin, their eyes locked. "No mind about that right now. I want to tell you three things in order of importance."

He stopped after unhooking her bra, sliding it off creamy shoulders.

"What, now?"

"Yes, now."

The shirt fell to floor as his britches followed suit.

"Go on." His voice was beyond gruff, he needed her and she knew it.

"Now don't get pissed off until you hear it all. First, this is your home. I don't have any clue where I will end up. But I know you will be a part of my life wherever I am. I decided if you ask me, I do not want to marry right now."

"What the hell?"

She held up a hand to silence him and for once he stopped. But, not without raising both eyebrows with a very stern look of disapproval.

"I like being your only mistress. It leaves no room for anyone else." She was smiling in that way that wound right around his heart. It was fruitless to balk at this right now. But, it would come up again, soon.

"Second, I'm going to be moving out. I paid for those renovations and I want to fully enjoy having you court me properly. As your continued mistress, of course, by visiting me at my own home. How much more convenient can I make it for you and still be happy if I am here on your lands, right?"

"Oh, now, wait a minute…"

"Thirdly, it's easy for the rest of the world to see this, but I need to make myself clear to you so you never have to think about it again. I am in love with you. Whether we marry someday or no day. I will always be with you until this world, of which I don't fully understand, dictates otherwise."

Pushing her backwards, they fell onto their large bed. "Is anything negotiable with you? It seems all the men you've blazed a trail with since you left Italy all have given me the same advice, love. That I will always have my hands full with you."

She grinned, never wanting to be anywhere without him and wondered what her future would bring. But, until more was disclosed, she was completely content for their relationship to be like it is.

"Well, what can I say, Lord Griffin, other than please, let's stop talking so we can make love properly. I've sorely missed you."

Her smile was slight, her eyes bright as he leaned down absorbing her further into his life, mind and body in a lovely, wonderful kiss.

"Oh." She pulled back attempting to add in one final thought. But this time he'd had enough of their chatter.

"No, Sam, no more until later. I love you. But, now we need this more than further conversation."

He moved inside of her as she wrapped her legs around his strong back and did indeed give him as he asked.

Chapter Twenty-Three

"Mr. Bruce, you and your son have done a magnificent job with all the renovations. I apologize for having been away for so long. It was unavoidable. All the same, I am so happy with the results." Handing him a velvet pouch brimming with sterling pounds. "I'll let you know if I see anything else I want done and thank you both again."

"Mistress, it's been our pleasure. We now have several positions lined up with great thanks to your recommendations in the village. We much appreciate you as well."

He tipped his cap to her as they finished loading up the carriage and headed down her dirt drive.

It was a great day. Sam was feeling on top of the world. The good people in the heavens had allowed her a bit of time off from passages. Perhaps to absorb it all.

Around the back, she followed a beautifully discovered path as it wove between roses, honeysuckle, lavender and foxglove all which would soon depart as fall gave leave to winter.

Moving toward the sounds of a babbling stream, she could hear a voice. It was faint, but with each forward step it gathered strength. Closing her eyes and raising her head upwards, Sam felt the warmth of the day against her skin and listened intently.

Interesting, she thought, continuing along the intricately designed stone path. Surely this was mother nature's creation. Reaching the other side, her smile grew. It was a short walk when she halted in front of a beautiful statue of the Egyptian Goddess, Isis. This gorgeous replica had been discovered during the renovations of the grounds and brought Sam much pleasure.

Who knew when or why this was placed here. No old documents had been discovered at the big house or at the cottage to lay claim to its history. But, she loved this area. Lately, she imagined hearing the wind carrying a delicate voice calling out her name to come here. Sit. Pay Attention.

Just beneath the base, a carved stone bench beckoned. It was here as Sam sat down, that a tremor started in her head and worked with mighty strength through to her toes. Gripping the cold sides, visions of places long ago played in her mind as she tried desperately to keep a balanced reality.

Then she heard her. A voice that was strong and commanding.

"You must listen to me. It is time. You are well prepared. Now, you must go."

Sam refused to open her eyes.

"He needs you more there than you are needed here. You must lay your past to rest and give him great peace. Otherwise, many will be destroyed if you do not move swiftly. Do not worry about what you leave behind. That which is yours will be, when you are ready to reclaim it."

Sam blinked, nodding, as she stood as if in a trance. Yet with each passing step back to the cottage, sensations of such a grand nature flourished throughout her being. Her soul was alive, spirit happy and mind reeling to a time so far back in her lives that she must have suppressed it for a purpose.

She could see visions of him. As clear as if it was a cloudless day in her mind's eye.

He was powerful, tall, rugged and handsome. With chiseled features and a strong will and heart. He was a warrior in the highest sense and had been her lover.

Bands of gold wrapped around his upper arms. His was a time steeped in the traditions of an ancient empire.

One so vast and superior, when it moved to the heavens and stars, all traits were scooped up by new races and religions.

Coming around the back of the cozy cottage, Sam spotted a note that had been placed by her maid on the table in the hall. Turning it over in her hand, she saw Adam's seal. Ripping it open, she read his print, smiling.

This was as the Gods would have it.

Perfect timing.

"Sam, I'm away for a while to Canada. I can't tell you when I will return. I see a trip coming for you. But not to where or for how long. If you depart before I return, send a note up so I can get it when I come back. Love, Adam."

She placed it back where it was left and journeyed up the stairs to change. Then returned to the kitchen and ate the food already prepared. Finished, dishes washed, dried and put away, she headed back to climb those stairs.

Then it started.

Eyes blurred as a lightness began, becoming so strong she felt like passing out.

At last at the top, moving as if in a dream, Sam reached for the bedroom door handle, turning it. As soon as she opened and walked in, it was clear.

She was no longer in England.

She was in Egypt. In a bar with a hell of a scene unfolding!

The End of the Beginning…

Passages Book Two:

What Have You Unearthed?

Sandra Waine

Dedication

This second book of three is dedicated to my sons, Nick & Tyler. You are amazing guys and I hope you view all the craziness I am with open amusement. You know what I mean!

Chapter One

"I can't believe you let Amen maneuver us out here."

Derek Clash had been thrust into her life suddenly upon Sam's arrival in Egypt a short time ago. She knew they were still trying to figure each other out as she glanced over at him with a smile hovering on her face.

"What? Resist a challenge? Especially as vocal as the one he made to us last night at the bar? He's an idiot."

"We may be the idiots. Who the hell knows what is in store for us now, Sam? I still do not think this is a good idea." They both watched Amen and his sidekicks get out of their vehicle.

"Derek, you are filming, right? I don't see the light on."

"Yeah, I have a camera locked on us up on the dash. Using a new roaming device so when we move it does. Just so he does not get any asinine ideas, I'm going to lower this camera so he focuses on you and not me. Try to stay close. We need this footage to back up what I took last night."

"Oh fuck. His face is beet red. Great, he's preparing to do battle. Perhaps you are right and you should have thrown a chair at my head last night. It could have prevented me from pissing him off. You jackass. This is all your fault." Sam grinned, then swung around, preparing to do battle with this ego-inflated tyrant.

"Arnesen. Glad to see you. Rather, that you took the bait. Stupid woman. But it sure works out for me. Then you and your lackey there won't need to be rounded up later."

"What the hell are you talking about, Amen?" She was keen on playing him along.

His eyes darkened to piercingly black, lips in a thin line as he tried to hold his anger in check. "I warned you.

This is my territory. You messed with us last night; today I am returning the favor."

Sam glanced over her shoulder at Derek, who seemed quite casual, leaning off to one side, very relaxed. She grinned at him as he nodded.

"Still a bit touchy from last night? Well, love to say I'm sorry but those words just don't want to come out right now."

He stepped a bit closer, towering over Sam, a muscle twitching in his cheek.

Sam watched, quite amused despite the situation she and Derek now found themselves in. "Got some kind of plan in place for us? Going to dispose of us here and now and think no one will be the wiser?"

His lecherous grin made her own grow bigger.

"Nope. Something better. Someone better."

"What's your timeframe on this, my friend?"

Behind her she could hear Derek's groan—which, of course egged her on.

"Or is this just more bullshit? Imagining friends in places they just do not exist?" She felt a rock hit the back of her boot. It was Derek, trying in vain to get her to shut up. The urge to shove a fist into Amen's ugly face was nearly overwhelming.

"Look over your shoulder," Amen shouted. He pointed a shaking finger at her.

"At the dust bowl?"

"You got it. Politically I carry some weight. You are about to feel the force of it. No one is going to help you now, bitch."

"Oh. Bitch, it is? I can't help but wonder if you were ever educated, Amen. All I have heard out of that foul mouth is foul words. Your mother must be so ashamed."

Derek shook his head, moving between them in a hurry. He raised his hand, his eyes locking with Sam's. "Stop it."

She scoffed, hearing him but refusing to back down an inch. *Damn,* she thought as the oncoming vehicle reached their destination, *I'll not let that ass get the upper hand here.*

All bodies turned in the direction of the large four-doored diplomatic black sedan. As soon as the view cleared from the rising sand, Sam relaxed her stance, Derek by her side. The tenseness from his body radiated over toward her own. Scoffing it off, she reached over and placed a reassuring hand on his arm.

Amen, along with his two men, stepped toward the now halted vehicle. The doors opened. That was when Sam noticed his entire demeanor change as he watched who got out.

"Mother of...," Clash began, wavering in midstream, amazed at who was coming towards them.

Sam held up a hand, squashing further comment. "Enough. Hang in there," she whispered. "We both know who she is. Bahati Asenath. The prime minister's right-hand confidante and long-standing mistress. So behave."

In step behind her commanding figure were two burly bodyguards. This, they both knew, was a woman not to be trifled with under any circumstances. She could raise bloody hell with the minister.

Blinking rapidly, Sam maneuvered around them all and nearly laughed out loud at the surprise on Amen's face as they awaited the arrival of the threesome. "Ms. Asenath."

"Ms. Arnesen." The two women clasped hands. "I apologize—" Ms. Asenath glanced at Amen, who had been moving toward them until he was met by the brick wall of her escorts. "—that we do not have more time to stand here and exchange small talk." A grin creased the corners of those brightly painted lipstick-red lips. "I've spoken with the prime minister. We have decided that it may be of benefit for you and your cohort to leave the area as soon as possible. In the contents of this envelope, more details are provided. I am fully aware of that which you seek. Both of you. Much needs to be done with little time to spare."

The coldness of Bahati's eyes belied the warmth of her smile as both women glanced over at the frustration on Amen and his men's faces.

"Conflicts are endless in Egypt's streets now. Let me give you and Clash a bit of advice. I suggest you get rid of your vehicle as soon as possible. I can keep Amen at bay for twenty-four hours. After that, he and his band of criminals will be back on the streets looking for you both. Word has reached me about last night's, ah, events. You really liked stoking his fire, didn't you?"

Sam's gaze did not falter as she shrugged one shoulder. "You know it was his fault. He's an ass. They all are. I could not resist. He wanted something I was not going to give. Period."

"If I had my way, he'd have those balls cut off and woven into a band hanging around a lamppost in one of the squares. To serve up a good dose of humility to these men that have no respect for women at all. But for now, anyway, this will ring them. He will be looking for you. Of that I am sure. He has a score to settle. Even if it is just with his freaking ego."

Sam nodded, tucking the envelope under one arm. "I don't know how you pulled this off. But I owe you and the prime minister our gratitude. I know Amen did not enjoy my hands-off verbal onslaught last night in front of a room full of drunken men. But it enabled Derek to film a few of them making an illegal black market sale. That's invaluable to his cause."

The understanding was clear between both women.

"Possibly not. But in the end this will lead us further into his dealings. Clash will remain in touch with a special contact. For now, we cut him some slack. That's why I can't buy any more time than that for you. In truth, we need them all back on the streets."

"We will move out shortly then."

"Good idea." Bahati nodded to her guards, tilting her head towards her sedan and Amen's car.

As she started to walk away, Sam placed a hand on her arm. Leaning close, she whispered, "I recognize you. From the Exeter train station. Night attendant. We have spoken before. Or, rather, back then."

Bahati laughed. "Good luck on your journey, Sam." Nodding, she headed toward the men. "Amen, come with me. What the hell were your parents thinking to give you the name of our God of Peace, Amenhotep?" As his mouth opened to reply, she held up her hand. "Forget it. Get your ass in gear. No further crap do I want to hear. Now let's go."

Glaring venomously, he deliberately nudged Sam on his way by. "I don't know how the hell you pulled that off. But be warned. I will strike back with a hot iron when the time is right."

Her arrogant grin matched his own. "Doubt that. Feeling comfortable our paths will not cross again. As a matter of fact, I am quite sure of it. Enjoy your ride."

Clash stepped up beside her and they watched as Amen and his two men got into their sedan, along with a heavily armed Asenath guard. As the two vehicles sped away, they left in their wake a sandy vortex.

Clash and Sam turned toward each other and broke out in laughter.

"Well, that's a good day's work already, isn't it?"

Clash grinned. "How the hell did you pull that off? We have barely met. It has only been two days."

"Frig, how do I know? How does any of this work? You do not happen to have any information to share on this whole process, do you? It irritates the hell out of me that I can't get more assistance." Laughter smothered the true frustration Sam felt inside. "I ask everyone I meet—" They glanced back to watch the vehicles disappear. "—if there is a user's manual. Always I receive the same reply. Basically, that I just need to fly by the seat of my pants."

Clash lowered the camera. "Yeah, I hear what you are saying. It does take time to figure things out. In the beginning we all feel the same way. Unavoidable. You hang on to the fact that we are cut out for this. Not a whole lot of people are. So, chief, what's our next move?"

"Let's bug out of the city and public eye. I've got a feeling this envelope contains a lot of detail we need. Especially where we are camping out tonight. Once we get moving, I can review it and see what's up."

"I suppose you want to drive?"

"You are starting to paint me as a rather aggressive and dominating female, Clash. Now, where are you getting all this shit from?"

It was his turn to laugh. "Truth is given. When I headed here I was told you'd be unpredictable, sassy and a bit high-strung. To expect just about anything and be ready for it. Seems it is all correct and sums you up in a few sentences."

"Do you know Adam?"

His expression was questioning.

"Who, then, or am I not to ask?"

"A woman named Anna."

She stopped dead in her tracks. "Shut the hell up. Where did you meet the gypsy?"

He placed the camera on the back floor of the Land Rover, climbed into the driver's seat and turned the key. She was opposite, glaring at him. "Do you need help getting in?" Her look back said it all before she chimed in.

"Jerk." She climbed in. "So, you know her? I take it she knew exactly what to warn you about? That's not fair. I did not receive any advance details on you. I'm going to file a complaint with someone when I get back."

He smiled, patting her knee while quickly shifting through the gears. As they maneuvered out of Cairo she clicked in the seat belt, closely watching a huge hole up ahead grow closer and closer. She glanced over at the intent look on his face and knew he was going to take it. Sam clutched the roll bar just in time as the SUV sank in and then sprang up the other side. They both broke out in laughter.

She yelled over the wind and roar of the engine, "We are going to have to talk about this over drinks, I think. Or a good Egyptian smoke."

"You had better stay away from the smoke. Where we headed? If you look over your right shoulder the sky is darkening. That's not from the sun setting. A bomb has just gone off. Cairo center is under siege again. We need a plan now, Sam."

"That won't be our location tonight then." She opened the envelope and sieved through to what was important. "Cosmopolitan Hotel. Turn left up ahead. I think we should be able to safely navigate around the city going this direction. Best be quick about it. Look. Angry mobs are forming again."

"Agree. They are either on the hunt for something or someone. Not a good situation for us. All hell's about to break loose. I'm glad you are my commentator, Sam, for the recordings. What are your thoughts about the intro? I need to get as much in the can as possible so I can transmit to my contact and the station. London's been on my case to get them something. We are right in the middle of breaking news at every turn, it seems."

"Do you want me to start now? Then you can filter out the crap and background noise after we get to our rooms."

Clash extended his hand, palm open, and offered the recorder.

"Okay. But first, who else told you about me besides the tinker?"

His quick glance brought a smile to her lips. "Later. You had better get that started. Look up ahead. We may have a hell of a time getting through that mob. Suddenly it has tripled in size."

He clicked the door locks as she pulled her Crystal Palace soccer cap lower over her head. "Does that help?"

He laughed. "Hell, I do not know. Don't you have something to do? And no, dammit. That hat does not help. You are a traitor in my eyes. Shocking you are not rooting for Manchester United."

Laughing, she pressed the button, bouncing around like crazy in the front seat as she started the recording. "During a divided country's constant conflict, valuable Egyptian artifacts, many yet to be studied, were stolen by an unknown band of looters during a recent seventy-two-hour rampage in Cairo." She paused, briefly staring at the uprising. Guns were raised, flags flying and several wore dark full-face masks.

"I hear your thoughts loud and clear. We will be all right. Anyway, keep going. You even had me listening with open curiosity."

She glowered at him. "Articles of lesser value have already hit the booming black market business. A business that reaches far beyond the city and country's border. Confirmation of several priceless items has been confiscated by various authorities, who have identified two additional mountain towns in Yemen that are knee deep in this illegal trade."

The vehicle hit a bump and the unit popped out of her hand and hit the floor. Reaching down, she grabbed it and continued. "Yemen is a divided country. But it has one thing in common with its close neighbor, Egypt. Both have extended unlawful dealings with ancient antiquities. The transfer of valuable artifacts will never cease when there is such a strong lust to obtain them. In this report, I've located a few renegades that want to see these gems of history returned to their native Egyptian people. Should the myths told over the centuries be true, then a few souls also need to be laid to rest in the process."

Pulling quickly on the steering wheel, Clash maneuvered by burnt-out cars and piles of debris. There were obvious signs of looting everywhere. Finished, Sam clicked the stop button and placed it in his top right T-shirt pocket.

"That will do. Shit, Derek, this is a bloody war zone. Where exactly are we? I have lost track of our route."

He stopped the rig inside a long alley. "At the back door of the Cosmopolitan. So be quick and grab your gear. Let's get in there."

"Not feeling too comfortable about parking in that garage I see over there?"

"Figure this is about as safe a place as any. Maybe here no one will try to place a bomb under the rig. Besides, too much happens in those garages. We can't take a chance. These wheels are too valuable right now. Especially if a quick extraction is in order."

"Okay, Major, I get it."

He swung the camera up on one shoulder, engaging the key remote to lock the doors. "You lied earlier! You did a background check on me. How the hell did you find the time to do that? I've barely left your sight."

"Didn't you do the same for me?"

She pulled the knob on the outside door. It did not move. Setting down her bag and reaching inside, she brought out a small case.

Clash leaned up against the wall, a lopsided grin encasing his handsome features as he watched her pick the lock. It took only a few seconds.

"There, that will do. It is always a good idea to stay in practice. I would just hate to lose my skills." Her boot kept the door open. "You coming in? Or just standing there? I'm not the frigging doorman."

Grabbing it just before it closed, he followed, making sure it locked. "With all these boxes stacked it looks like we are in the basement. Look over there. An exit sign. Let's see if that staircase is usable. Make note of our direction, Sam, just in case we split and need to meet up back here."

"Roger that."

"You know, if I had a hand free I'd swat that ass of yours."

She raised a brow while heading up the rusty metal stairs. "Ah yeah, I don't think so. Besides, who the hell said I was high-handed and aggressive? You seem to like being in charge yourself."

Pushing against the door, her gaze shifted quickly around, noticing the absence of anyone else. Reaching, she pushed one of the two elevator buttons and awaited its arrival. The door opened and they got on. "We came in from the west and up two flights of stairs. My guess is if I had taken the first one, we'd have come out in the lobby."

"I'll refrain from commenting since my hands are full." Sam pressed an elbow against floor one's button. It closed and opened exactly where they both thought.

"Yeah, the less I hear from you about now would be a benefit," she mouthed quietly.

He chuckled, nodding her toward the weathered front desk. The clerk hardly looked better. His clothes were rumpled, as if he had not changed his attire for a few days.

"Two rooms. Names are Clash and Arnesen."

Sam pulled out her Egyptian passport with a wad of cash. The clerk eyed the cover briefly, then the money. "Yes, here are your keys. Your rooms have been prepaid. You are all set. If you want mini-bar service that's additional."

Sam slid 800 Egyptian pounds toward him. "Will this cover it as well as our rig parked outside in the alley?"

He grinned, sliding two keys over. As subtly as possible, the money disappeared and he nodded that they were through.

Once the elevator door closed, Sam noticed a change in Clash as he slid the cellphone into a back pocket.

"I have to get this story filed ASAP. I'm starting to run out of options. You are on your own tonight. What time do you want to bug out tomorrow?"

"Before sunrise. Then we can drive to the airport. We've got confirmed tickets on a cheap early morning flight on Yemenia Airways."

He glanced at her. "Yeah, sounds lovely. Heard of them. I'll see you at the Rover at zero four-thirty."

"Works for me."

"Good, then we can have a nice chat about where your nose has been, little woman. I suggest you prepare those lies tonight. I'll want some answers tomorrow on how you gained access to look up anything on me."

They exited the elevator together and were now standing in front of her room. She had no comment to give him. Instead, she laughed, inserted the key and nodded at him before closing the door in his face. Upon quick review, it was clear the room was shabby but clean. As the bag slipped off her shoulder, she placed that and a small purse on the bed. She stepped over toward the windows as a long sigh escaped.

It was still bothersome how she'd arrived in Egypt. Modern Egypt. "Damn," she said to no one else in the room but herself. "I wish I could have just left Adam word." But powerful forces had been at work, she silently concluded, to not even allow her that small privilege. Why? Her mind continued to search for a bona fide reason.

Along the brief walk up the cottage stairs, no preamble of what was to come had been available. Then there was a bright flash as suddenly Clash had reached out and grabbed her, delivering them out of harm's way from an angry group sweeping by. Part of which was that asshole, Amen, and his band of thieves. Hastily they'd joined forces and followed the group into the bar, watching and listening to what illegal dealings they were in.

He told her his vision of her arrival had streamed inside his head so fast he hardly had time to realize it before she was there. They both had an agenda separate from each other. That was clear. But they needed one another at the same time. It would be a relief when more unfolded. He had acted strangely in the elevator on their way up to the rooms. Then again, she pondered, perhaps it was not Derek that was acting odd, but her.

Closing the room-darkening shades, she changed into yoga pants and a top to sleep in. In the event of a hasty retreat, they would serve a twofold purpose. Between brushing both rows of teeth, she stared at the reflection in the mirror, contemplating why time travel did not alter her looks in any way. "You don't look younger and you should. It's 2013, not 2015." She chuckled into the small, dimly-lit room then spit into the sink and rinsed her mouth. Flicking the light switch off and throwing back the covers, Sam moved her purse and bag to the opposite pillow, keeping them close.

In the quietness of the room, her mind buzzed with chatter. "Okay," she whispered softly into the darkness. "I'm going to try this again. No ruins or church was required to depart on this passage. Which is strange. But I was aware in advance of my arrival to Egypt. Although I thought since Isis was involved, I would arrive back in the time of the Pharaohs. Maybe somewhere in my bag are clues?"

She reached over, tapping the light switch on, and unzipped the bag. Sifting through, she got frustrated as nothing seemed apparent. "Damn it. There has to be something." Her voice mirrored what she felt into the empty room. She slid a hand back in slowly, and a couple of fingers pierced through a hole in the lining, catching something. It was a plastic card. Looking it over, she grinned and set it back.

Really? An ambassador for women's rights from Great Britain? She found great humor in that, believing someone upstairs was poking fun at her. Farther under the lining was a parchment. Pulling that out, she read the details twice. Now it was apparent what the next move was. Folding it back up along with their flight itineraries, Sam's adrenaline heightened, pulsating through her veins.

"I need to settle down. Keep my wits about me." She glanced around the room rather anxiously, making sure no one was indeed there. Then it all started to filter through her brain as she finally settled back onto one pillow.

A vision came into sight of an older man dressed entirely in white, holding out one hand. The white contrasted starkly against his dark brown skin and eyes. His mouth was moving, yet she could not hear his words. But there was a message. A special message, just for her. As her mind received it, a quiver ran up her spine. Shaking her head, Sam sat motionless for several minutes, barely breathing. He was waiting for something to be returned to him. Something of utmost importance—and she was the key to making sure he received it.

What, she internally contemplated, is it?

Giving up, she zipped the bag and placed it on the pillow in case a hasty exit was needed. Fluffing up the other, she lowered herself down onto it as thoughts of Adam suddenly entered her mind.

Was he pissed at not knowing where she was? Try as she might, her visions could not provide a location for him. He could be home. Or on a passage himself. She had no flipping idea.

"Oh, fuck it," she spewed into the dark room. At last giving way to exhaustion, her eyelids finally dropped and then closed. Sleep came at last but was short lived.

The wailing screams of sirens wafted up into the darkened room as her eyes fluttered open. Smiling up at the ceiling, she listened as they grew steadily louder before finally diminishing. Finally, silence prevailed.

"So, Lord Griffin," she whispered. "I wonder if our paths will cross here. Will I run into that new brother of mine along these roads less traveled? It's almost every passage where one of you are with me. Ironically, I don't think so this time. Let's see how good I read my own crystal ball."

She fluffed the pillow, turned sideways facing the door, and fell back asleep.

Chapter Two

"Dammit." She bolted upright at the insistent banging on the door. She hit the carpet, ready to do battle. *What the hell is going on?* resonated through her mind as the knocking persisted. Creeping over, she kneeled, glancing between the gap, and saw weathered black boots.

His boots.

She was sure he'd heard what she had done and that was confirmed as soon as she opened the door. He was standing there laughing at her.

"Great move, ace. Grab your gear. We need to get out of here fast. The army is assembled and headed toward a large mob gathered in the square nearby. If we don't, this could detain us much longer than we want."

Marching over, she grabbed the bag and closed the door fast on his heels. She followed, attempting to keep pace with the breakneck speed he set as they quickly entered the stairwell and took the steps down, her lungs burning.

He called out over his shoulder, "You always sleep like that? With boots on and bag packed?"

She pushed against the stairwell door so hard it banged against the brick wall. She laughed. "Not until I was lured into this new career." He pulled out of a pants pocket the keys and unlocked the doors. They threw their bags inside and got in.

"I've learned. Situations like this just keep right on reminding me."

Clash started up the vehicle and sped them away from the gathering. The side of the vehicle scraped against an alley wall as Clash turned a sharp left.

"Once outside the city, I know a route to the dockyards. When we are that far, it should be smoother sailing. These people just don't quit. I heard during the night there was more vandalism and deaths. I guess thousands of years of this just does not penetrate into their brains that there may be other ways to get things accomplished."

"Ah, Clash, you are an optimist after all...." She laughed, holding tight to the door rail. "But it will never change. Is it any different in the States, Britain or how about Africa?"

He shook his head no. "Fuck, Sam, I think we are screwed. This was the safest route I know. Look ahead. The road is blocked." He pulled over to the curb, engine running, and opened his door. Raising his body toward the top of the rig, he glanced around, brows drawn in concern.

Curiosity got the better of her. She stood outside the door frame, holding the rooftop. "Shit, I am not tall enough. Tell me what you see!"

"It sucks. Looks like our options have run out. We will need to hoof it." He glanced over and their eyes locked. "We have to make a decision right now. Either we take our chances through another approaching mob, or abandon the vehicle and weave through on foot. We need to find out what happened overnight. What caused this. I hope the dockyards and airport are not affected."

"My friend, I say we make a run for it. Come on!"

They grabbed bags and went street side. Right away a crowd, hell-bent on destruction by the makeshift weapons they carried, swallowed them up. A thick-waisted, burly woman was pushed right into Sam. Grabbing her arm, Sam seized the moment and hollered out, "What happened?"

"Six men were accosted last night by the government. A neighborhood search is occurring now. Stores are being broken into and buildings torn apart as they look."

"Who has them?"

"No clue. But we are being held accountable until they are located." She pushed past Sam as bodies thumped bodies.

Sam reached Clash. "I have no idea if the docks are affected. I would assume they are or soon will be. I could not find out. Did you have any luck?"

"I did. They are open right now. The boats are still running and flights coming in and out of the airport. So let's see if we can get someone to take us there by cab. I would like to avoid being on a vessel right now."

"Little chance of that with cars burning all around us. We may have run out of luck if we can't take the ferry across to the airport dock."

He halted, clutching her upper right arm tightly.

"Hang on for a second. I've got an idea. Follow me."

Derek grabbed her hand and she winced. He was using a bit too much force, but she refrained from yelling at him right now in light of their situation. He tugged her hand harder.

"Pick up the pace. I can't carry you and all this gear."

That was motivation enough. She pulled her hand free and raced along beside him, ignoring the pain building in her legs. Finally he stopped, reaching out an arm to halt their progress. Her lungs were close to bursting but she managed to utter a question while resting her hands on her knees, slightly bent over.

"Why are we stopping here?"

"I'm aware that recent activity in this area caused a certain high-profile New York businessman to have an evacuation plan in place. We are just going to borrow something temporarily. It will be back before he even knows what happened."

"Who is it?"

"I'll give you a hint. He has hideous hair. Need more?"

Sam broke out in laughter. "Nope. I know exactly who you are talking about. So how the hell do we get access? It must be tight with security."

"Leave that to me. Stay close and follow my lead."

They walked casually into the hotel as workers frantically rushed about, attempting unsuccessfully to keep the panic from their stricken faces. Clash bumped into one, apologizing well after the clerk had moved on. Alerted immediately by his tell-tale grin, Sam knew something else was up.

He shoved her into the elevator just as the doors opened and inserted a security card, pressing the penthouse button. As the door opened, their movement was immediately halted by two heavily-armed security guards.

"Damn. I never thought I'd see you in this neck of the woods, Clash."

Keenly she watched as the two men shook hands and the other looked away, feigning disinterest. She stared at them, wondering what the hell...?

"Got your text. She's all fired up and ready to roll. Grab that little lady whose mouth is catching flies and follow me."

Sam's jaw slammed shut as Derek nodded. They all broke into a hefty run toward the awaiting helicopter. Throwing her bag inside, Clash lifted her up and then dashed around the other side of the chopper and got in. Sam clicked the seat belt in place and settled back as Clash and the pilot put on headsets.

From what she could view but not hear, it must have been quite an animated conversation the guys were having. The noise intensified as the blades gained momentum and quickly they were airborne. From up this high, all three of them received a clear picture of what was occurring below: billowing smoke, burning cars, riots, and looting.

Sam expelled a thankful breath when, ten minutes later, they touched down beside a storage hanger. Glancing around, she became aware they were on a more secluded side of Cairo Airport. Bag slung over one shoulder, she jumped down and ducked beneath the blades. Clash waved back to his friend, gave a thumb up and moved her farther away as the helicopter took off.

"Who the heck was that?"

"We go way back. From military days. I knew he was here so I called in a marker. Groovy, eh?"

She had to smirk at that. "You two clear now?"

"Not in a long shot. He married, then divorced my sister. He will always owe me one. My parents are still ungrateful to this day about that. She ended up moving back in with them."

Laughing, they entered one of the hangers, glanced at each other and then toward an awaiting sedan. Both rear doors were open. "Ah, well. Seems like you must have quite a bit of shit on the dude, I'd say. Nice work, Clash. I could not have done this without you. And by the way, that is the last damn time I say thank you."

He choked back a laugh.

"Have your passport handy. We need to show it before clearing this area."

Tucked neatly inside Sam's British passport was a wad of Egyptian currency. He took it and gave both to the security personnel. The guard evaluated both passports carefully and handed them back as the gate lifted. The driver maneuvered the vehicle through heavy traffic and had them outside of the departure terminal without delay.

"You know, I like this. Not the part about people dying for causes they can't explain. Especially since they have been doing this for thousands of years. The part about being extracted from that rooftop by a mysterious driver who asked no questions. All so we can simply make a flight."

"Princess, don't get used to it. I see plenty of shit ahead of us both. I hope you are prepared, Sam."

"Why does the whole frigging world keep saying that to me? It's like showing a young kid the candy store window filled with sweet concoctions and not letting them go in. F that."

He let that last comment slide. "This is not the time nor place to delve into that."

She released a loud snort as side by side they printed their boarding cards. Walking silently together, they passed through several security checks before finally arriving at their gate. Their flight was up on the board, scheduled to start loading passengers in fifteen minutes. They had made it in the nick of time.

"Nice job."

"You can buy me a beer when we get there."

He was referring to their jaunt to Yemen.

"Is our transfer on that side as interesting as the one we just took?"

"Truth be told, I have no idea what awaits us. I was thinking you'd know more than I do at this juncture. Can you 'see' anything?"

She shook her head as the loudspeaker crackled to life with the gate attendant making an announcement.

"We will begin boarding flight number 1913 from Cairo to Sanaa. Those in premium economy or needing assistance, please come ahead. You may board now."

Sam glanced down at her boarding card and at the one in his hand. They were in premium economy and seated together. He extended a hand, offering her to go on board ahead of him. As she found their seats, she leaned forward tucking her bag beneath and whispered, "Quite an adventure so far. Don't you think? Any clue how long we will be together?"

"Nope. Do you want a cocktail?"

"It's before 9 o'clock, mister!"

He nodded to the flight attendant. "Two beers, please."

She nudged his shoulder. "I'm a bit perplexed. I believed what I truly needed would be in Cairo. Apparently not."

"That is not entirely true. You got what you needed there. You got me."

Her expression made him chuckle.

He was right. She pulled out her small laptop and accessed the Internet for the few minutes they had until boarding completed and it would have to be stowed. A headline from the Yemen Times caught her interest. She read through it, a smile forming on her face. Exiting the website, she powered down the computer and set it back in the bag at her feet. As her head rested against the seat cushion, their eyes locked.

Two beers were set down, picked up, clinked together and drank in one clean chug. He took them both and placed them on his tray for removal. Leaning his head back, he closed his eyes. Sam followed suit and soon they both had dozed off.

Yet it seemed like only minutes before the loudspeaker startled them awake. "Can I have your attention please as we prepare for our descent into Sanaa. Return your seats to their upright position and place your tray tables back, secured."

Sam opened her eyes and moved the seat forward. "Just enough time for a power nap. How are you doing? Ready to be dragged all over creation?"

He was zipping up his bag on the floor. She had seen what he was up to, though, filtering his film down to a flash drive just in case. "Probably more of me covering your ass than anything else. I know we both have things to take care of. But I admit the footage I have on what's going on where we came from is damn good. It won't matter once you have moved on. But for me, it will open up new doors while ticking off a few government officials in the process."

Her brows drew in. What was he talking about? His cameraman career, the journalistic side or the hidden agenda she knew he was on? It did not matter. Here on the aircraft, it was not the time to inquire.

As the cabin door opened, they were close to the first travelers to disembark. She pulled out a Saudi passport and tucked it in her front pants pocket. With his dark skin, Sam knew Clash would have no trouble. But she knew for her a full burqa was required to pull this off. It was clear from glancing around at other Middle-eastern women that a pair of jeans, T-shirt and soccer cap would not work at all.

Unintentionally, she bumped into a short Asian man and then quickly apologized. Over his head she caught sight of the ladies' room. She knew his bump had been intentional. Damn, she internally thought, still in awe at how controlled every step she took had become.

As she entered the ladies' room, a woman coming out of one stall gave her direct eye contact. Nodding, holding the door open for her, Sam went in and closed and locked it.

Hanging on the inside hook was a change of clothes. She brushed a hand against the soft fabric of the full burka. Quickly donning it, Sam wrapped the veil properly and then rolled her clothes into a tight ball. Unlocking the door and turning the knob, she exited, glancing about with open curiosity to see if anyone had noticed this transformation.

Outside, she moved back over towards Clash and shoved the clothes into a bag. Straightening back up, she nodded to him as he picked up his own bag and they walked on. A different passport was tucked in one of her hands hidden beneath the dark, heavy, black robe she now wore.

"Not quite you. But all the same an appropriate touch." Middle-eastern culture dictated she remain silent in public and they were both aware of that. As they waited in line, she flipped open the passport to her picture, easily hiding a smile under the thick face veil.

They were married.

Smirking, she wondered where the hell her wedding band was. Was he that cheap? She'd have to have a word with the bloke, she thought as her grin intensified.

As if reading her mind and sensing the mirth beneath the garments, his hand slid beneath her left sleeve and placed a ring in her palm. She put it on, unable to hold back a laugh as they stepped up to the passport officer. Clash's eyes issued a stern warning to shut up as the attendant stamped both, handed them back and signaled with cold, calculating eyes for them to move along.

"A few more feet and we are clear. Stay close. Try to be quiet. Who knows if you have a British accent or not? I don't want to be halted now when I can see our exit."

Once outside the doors, pulsating heat from the tarred pavement enveloped her entire being as sweat beaded on an upper lip. "Oh, my God. This won't suit me to maneuver around in this forsaken heaviness. What am I going to do?" She stopped, realizing how her voice sounded. "Oh good. My accent is appropriate. How lovely I sound."

Derek was relieved as well. "Suck it up, sweetheart. That's your garb until we leave here." Glancing around, he seemed pleased to finally locate whom he was looking for. "Great, I see them. Come along now, wife, our ride awaits."

A long line of Mercedes Benzes brought Sam relief. They would indeed have air conditioning. In this money-pit part of the Middle East, she should have known they'd be all set.

He broke out in laughter. "Nope, not those, honey. Those."

"The motorbikes?"

She wanted to punch that smug look right off his handsome face.

"Sling your bag up over your shoulder and hop on. She's not going to wait if you don't get moving."

Assessing the motorcycle, as well as the woman straddling it, dressed like a man, Sam threw caution to the wind. "Yes, dear husband. Love of my very life. I am doing as you bid."

The woman sped away so fast it nearly knocked Sam off the back. Weaving rapidly between pedestrians and traffic, her driver had them quickly up to top speed while maneuvering through the ancient city of Sanaa.

Piles of rubble were visible and Sam surveyed it all. Earlier in the year, Saudi-led air strikes had caused all of this. For what? People were still living here. Going about their daily business and walking around the debris as if it did not exist. Disdain filled her being.

Men. They caused this with their overblown egos. Recent peace talks in Geneva had halted them, but continued signs of war were apparent. Would it ever end in this war-torn Middle East? She doubted it. Or that many westerners even knew this was taking place.

All the same, the medieval walled city and grand architecture of Bat at Yemen was a sight to behold. Suddenly and without warning, the driver squeezed the brakes, bringing the bike to a rather abrupt halt. Boots lowered to the pavement as she pointed one finger towards a tall building. It was beautiful, Sam thought, examining it top to bottom before the still running engine's noise penetrated her brain.

They got off the bike and stepped onto the cobbled curb, Clash's hand on the small of her back, directing her inside. The interior was plush, much to her surprise and pleasure. Rich-hued carpets lay beneath her booted feet and carvings over 2,500 years old adorned the walls. They entered the elevator and ascended to the top floor, without seeing a soul along this route. Where were they all?

As Clash opened the door, Sam entered, setting her bag down on the dark, marble-tiled floor.

"We will be sharing this suite. Go ahead and look around and pick a room that suits you best. When you are through, come and find me. It looks like we have quite a pad here. I want to take you up to the rooftop for a bit of fresh air and conversation."

She nodded. Did he think the place was under surveillance? A cold shiver passed up her spine, providing an instant acknowledgment. As she walked down the long hall, her hand wove its way over a beautifully carved mahogany table, along the coolness of the tan stucco painted wall, rough to the touch, then let the frocks of a palm tree slip through fingertips.

In the distance, babbling water was streaming from a statue of Isis. She stopped, dumbfounded. Isis. Here? This was not traditional Yemen decor. If her memory served her correctly, most of the buildings would have a touch of Moorish and Turkish design. With a hand she shoved open a large wooden door, then stopped in open astonishment while her eyes devoured the splendid Louis XIV chair and the extremely luxurious fabric housed on it. Having viewed one being sold at a recent estate auction, Sam knew in today's market it would bring a hefty sum.

In awe, she continued a steady perusal. Someone had substantial money and had just simply opened their home to them. She found this extremely interesting.

A beautifully crafted wooden cabinet was layered painstakingly with lacquer. Intricately laid on its magnificent doors were combinations of precious lapis lazuli, agate, and marble with ancient silver inlays. It was beyond priceless, Sam thought, and absolutely gorgeous.

Then all of a sudden the bells rang off inside her head. Three of them in succession.

"Oh, my God," she whispered, raising a shaking hand toward it. Then she halted, adding, "Only a few of these were supposed to have survived from his reign in the 1600s. One in a private English Lord's collection, one I saw in the Louvre and another that remained unaccounted for. Until now."

She moved closer. Then she slid a steadier hand up the details. As she pushed against a smaller Lapis stone, one of the two doors opened.

She eyed the empty shelves and slouched down in front of it, sitting on a wooden stool. Something about this piece was bothering her. What the hell was it? Standing, she moved her bag to the inside and closed it, knowing it was secure. Taking her purse and placing it under the burka, Sam took a long, slow walk back by Isis in search of Clash.

"Your room must be fine. You took your time."

"Strange enough, it is. Shall we head to the roof?"

"Yes, follow me. I must say Yemen agrees with me. But I have something to say that may piss you off." He surveyed the area, making sure no one was about. "Just hear me out. You will want to watch what you say in public. I know you are aware of how suppressed women here are. But it's important to us both you curb that tongue. Their rules, not mine, Sam."

Her eyes bore into his as she pursed her lips, restraining a comment.

He laughed. "Exactly. Like I said. This place works for me."

Standing aside, she moved out into the hallway, eyeing for the first time a guard posted at the elevator.

When had that happened? As they exited out onto the roof, he took her by an arm over toward a secluded corner.

They both glanced out over the scenery together and then back at each other. The view was mesmerizing.

"We are right in the middle of the old city. Over there is the Sarawat Mountain Range. They are the largest on the Arabian Peninsula. If you ever find yourself in a pickle, locate them and you will then have your direction."

She knew he had no idea that in her possession was a diplomatic immunity card if she ever needed it. A get out of jail quick pass.

"Beautiful. Far beyond what I imagined. This is a gorgeous part of the world, isn't it?"

"I have to agree with you. Now, are you hungry? We can do one of two things, wife. Have the servant make us a lunch, or stroll to the market. From that vantage point, I can provide landmarks. They may prove helpful later."

"Sounds like you may be heading in a different direction than I am, hubby. Preparing me to be out on my own."

"I'm sure I don't need to remind you to watch that tongue of yours, right?"

"Hey, you started it. I'm game to finish it. Anyway, I prefer your second option. Under this garb, no one will know the hand signals I am making your way."

"Even with your last breath, I think you will still be fresh."

She laughed as the elevator door closed, but refrained from commenting.

As they reached the ground floor and headed outside into the old quarter, the call for prayer resonated around the city. Still to this day she found it appealing. It reached deep within her soul. Where exactly did this originate, anyway? She toyed for an answer while they streamed between throngs of men and women all moving about their business. None paid them any heed, as she was dressed properly and kept a suitable distance from her husband.

The dark dialogue in Sam's mind had to be suppressed as she watched all that was going on around them. Who the hell did these men think they were, anyway? Treating women so horribly. Did they truly believe they'd just landed here on this earth without being born from the womb of one of them?

Shame on the lot of them, she thought, as a booted foot smacked the living daylights out of a stone. Rapidly it moved with such ferocity it ricocheted off the back of Clash's shoe. Glaring down, his eyes relayed a stern warning, knowing full well what was roaming through her head. She knew it was exposed in her eyes that she did not like what she saw.

Grabbing her by the arm rather roughly, he tugged her into the Alshaybani Restaurant. Daringly, she reached up and pulled his head down towards her as if a kiss was in the works.

"I don't care what you order me. But make sure it is dead, spiced properly and cooked to at least medium, got it?"

He laughed and then turned away and spoke in Arabic to the waiter.

Hands on lap weaved tightly, she pondered what the hell was bothering her about that piece of furniture. Obviously, it was beautiful. But quite empty. Then a thought took hold. Sure! That was it. There must be someplace inside of it that housed her next message. The key to where she was to go and when. Her leg swung with velocity, unintentionally meeting his shin. This robust action nearly spiraled them both backward.

He leaned in. "What the hell was that about?"

"I just realized something. How long will we be out?"

"A short while." He eyed her suspiciously. "Just want you to get some bearings. Landmarks. Just in case. Why? You got a hot date?"

"Nope. Something's bugging the crap out of me. I think I now know what it is. I need to look into it as soon as possible. By the way, why are those men watching us so intently? Do you recognize any of them? I thought you may since you seem to have friends all over God's green earth."

He glanced over his shoulder, taking a good look. "Yeah, I do know them. I'm sure once we leave here our paths will cross again."

"Good or bad, Clash?"

"I'd prefer you refer to me as husband, and good. It's all good as a matter of fact. Ah, here's our food and it appears to be cooked to your exact specifications."

The second kick hit its mark. They both smiled at each other and ate in silence. Once the bill was paid, he rose and came around, pulling out her chair as she stood. Weaving their way throughout the busy market area, Sam was getting a bit more accustomed to the heavy material of the burka. Suddenly Clash halted and engaged two men in Arabic. Sam stood back, truly not having any idea what they were saying. So, here she did not speak the language. Even more interesting. Damn, was someone up there playing around with her? Making sure she kept her mouth shut? That, she thought, glancing up towards the heavens, was just not fair.

He shook hands with them and turned toward her. "Don't get yourself too comfortable in our digs, madam. It's not going to be long before we head out. You had better locate what you are looking for straight away. Can you find yourself safely back to the building, or do you want me to escort you?"

***

She was already turning away from him with a quick wave and was on the way. He smiled and headed towards a back alley. One more glance back, satisfied she was now out of sight, Clash opened a large metal door, latched it and then dashed up the stairs. Glancing about, he noticed that the room was sparsely furnished. He viewed a couple computers, chairs and a single printer.

"Clash, over here. This is the secure network I was discussing with you. You can file your story here. When it is done, I will transmit to headquarters."

"Good. Edge, Sam's a nosy bird. She's going to want to know what is going on here besides my filing a report with you."

"So she's in the dark about all the reasons you are here?"

He shook his head. "In essence, I am still in the dark about all of them." They both laughed. "She has her own private agenda as well. I've kept my nose out of it."

"I'm going to leave what she's advised to you. The less the men and I are involved, the better."

"Fine. I assume since you were aware of our whereabouts that you had me monitored?"

"You know the business. Everyone is under observation. But I was surprised to see you walk into that restaurant with her. I was thinking it would be someone else. Anyway. We need to get down to business. You got that story from Cairo ready?"

Clash nodded. "Yeah, here." He handed him the flash. "She's damn good. You will hear it for yourself."

"Excellent. If your work here is finished, you can ditch."

"That's the issue. I don't think it is. There is a part two to this you must not have been told about. I am to see her safely to her next stop." He slapped Edge on one shoulder. "Especially if the likes of you and your unruly band of thugs are the asses transporting her."

Sudsy beers appeared out of nowhere and were set down by one of Edge's men. Mugs raised, they clinked and polished them off. "Right then. So what is your next move?" Edge leaned back against a wall, eyeing his friend warily.

"I head into the seedier part of town and see what else I can turn up. If something does happen to me between there and later, just go ahead and extract her as scheduled. Tell her whatever comes to mind. She may be more open to listening to you than me."

Both grinned.

"Clash, keep your head down over there. It is damn nasty. Right now, everyone is selling everyone else out. The body count is on the rise."

"Since I've been in worse spots, I think I can handle this one. All the same, do as I say about her, okay?"

"Don't recall you ever being this bossy, but you got it."

Clash grinned. "Yeah, well there's a lot going on right now. I guess you and that pretty attitude I always remembered rubbed off on me after all those years behind enemy lines serving our country."

Edge laughed. "Go on and get your sorry carcass on its way."

They shook hands as Clash headed back down the stairs and outside. Into the late steamy afternoon, he descended upon the fetid slums on the outskirts of Sanaa. Dark-skinned men in faded orange jumpsuits descended here during this time of day, returning home from squandering their time in the old city.

Normally unsuccessful in their daily pursuit of work and food of any kind, they arrived in time for their well-worn women to exit for a night of prostitution. "*Al Akhdam*," they were known as—the servants. They were reportedly the descendants of a very old Ethiopian army that were rumored to have crossed the Red Sea to pillage and plunder Yemen before the arrival of Islam.

How much of history was accurate was never revealed, as this sort never felt much need for recording accurately their true dealings. Indeed, they wanted to vanish into today's civilization unbranded by ancestral acts. As far as social classes went, Clash was aware they were at the bottom of the chain. A thick slew of grotesque muck was how they were viewed locally.

Weaving toward a worn café, he sat down, fully expecting solicitation. Hanging around to see what the next move would be, he glanced off toward two female bodies. His eyes moved past them and then returned, watching intently.

One was Sam sitting three tables down, fully engaged in conversation nose to nose with some other woman he could not identify.

Clash had to be certain. Was it? Then the bright sun reflected brilliantly off her brand-new wedding band and he had confirmation. Quickly he flicked on the surveillance camera housed snugly beneath his headdress. A live stream was being transmitted back to Edge's crew where he had just departed.

Two full breasts barely contained in a partially shredded cotton top filled his vision suddenly as he quickly scraped the chair legs backward.

"What can I get for you?" the waitress asked, moving closer to him. His stomach twisted into a tight knot. *Damn*, he thought, rapidly appraising the thin threaded wardrobe. She was indeed a poor soul.

"Beer."

She walked off and returned with it. He nodded, never taking eyes off Sam and her companion.

Warning signals went off in his brain as he honed in, catching enough of their conversation to realize women in this part of the city did not speak with such an educated voice. A British voice. His eyes darted about, making sure no one else seemed as interested in them as he was.

As he was about to rise and go over to make his presence known, she and the woman stood and walked by. With a slight nod, he let them move ahead a safe distance. Lifting the beer and polishing it off, Clash threw down some cash. Then he headed behind them farther into the cesspool of this dismal place.

Now it was clear. This was his part two. It was Sam and this story. She was leading him straight into it. He would follow and film and not care about why she was here. He would be able to get a dialog attached later. But he would also be a bodyguard, off in the shadows, in case she needed it.

Chapter Three

Humanitarian work, getting the message out through readily available media, was his constant personal mission—one that Clash took with every step and breath. He was a hidden ambassador for the United Nations, silently going behind the scenes into areas where few journalists were allowed entry.

Opportunities like this normally had to be well thought-out and planned. This portion of his passage was apparent. Someone upstairs had thrown a gem into his life when they assigned him to Sam. What she and the woman were doing right now, and what he was witnessing and recording, would be invaluable to the U.N. in upcoming humanitarian work. He'd leave it up to others who would view this piece if war crimes would also be filed.

Once it went viral and all the proper sources received what was needed, he'd move on to the next war-torn location. This journey was not so much about the artifacts in Cairo, although that was part of it. The real crux here was the high levels of immoral acts being spewed upon the heads of the *Akhdam*. Those who ignored it in politics were going to be called out globally on this. Explanations would be demanded.

The last journalist here had been an American. Discovered and never seen again. Long denied by the Government of Yemen and their military, this full story would bring it all out in the open. Here it was. A new mission. A new creed needed to be written for these men, women, and children whose daily existence was no better than a gutter rat.

As she and the woman moved onward, Clash suppressed rage watching children play with a dilapidated soccer ball. Their hollers of happiness belied what surrounded them. Windowless buildings, shards of glass and bloodstains littered the streets. For these young kids, it was just a game. But in his eyes, it was so much more. They should not need to seek their enjoyment in such an environment. It was just too dangerous. They should be on a nice grassy field, enticing other kids in their neighborhood into a fun match.

Or maybe better yet, in school. Learning.

Instead, they hit the ball off walls until it disappeared inside a windowless, abandoned storefront. "Get the ball!" one screamed out. An unknowing young boy would go and fetch it and then finally reappear, throwing it back to his friends.

Clash glanced up, seeing the dangers that lurked here. All these dwellings were unstable—that was apparent—while these kids continued playing with their well-worn sandals in all this debris. Ignoring it all.

When had the world truly turned so dark? he wondered. But there was hope. This footage would help. He knew it. His passages were not as extreme as Sam's. He hardly ever left this century. But between the United Nations and the news service he worked for, he was sure his part in this was making a difference.

As Sam and the woman halted, heads bowed together, he realized that he had all the film he needed to file his report with Edge and get it out there.

Later, the streamed dialogue would come from her. She had a knack. Once that was done, he wondered if they would part ways. Something continued to nag at him while watching the kids. Moving over, he hung out on the corner, glancing into one of the abandoned buildings. Ripped blankets were strewn around and two men, reeking of alcohol even from this distance, lay on them, snoring loudly and oblivious to what was going on. Their stench made Clash's eyes water. He moved to the opposite side of the street just as the soccer ball landed at his feet. Leg raised, he gave it a good, swift kick, much to the delight of the kids, as his eyes roamed back toward Sam, who was now on approach.

"Glad to see you, husband. Care for a walk? It seems as if you got the memo, knew how to dress and where I was headed today. How smart."

He ignored the sarcasm.

"I really did a double-take when I arrived and saw you. Who was the woman? Just someone you were directed to meet?"

Sam grinned. "I'll tell you. It's a bit of a story, so be prepared."

"Go on. We have twenty minutes or more before we reach our digs."

"I had no idea why I was here. Now it's all clear. In my room is a gorgeous Louis XIV armoire. That piece has been bugging me since we arrived. I thought there was a missing compartment or secret passage. Then I stood back and took a good look. It has beautiful stones on it. That's when a thought occurred to me. I don't even know how that happened. It is the design on the front. I thought it represented something."

They crossed the dilapidated street. Slowly the neighborhood turned to what was entirely more pleasing to the eyes and senses. "So I took the names of the stones on the four corners and looked them up on the Internet. I wanted to know if any street names have Lapis as part of their names in Arabic. I found the Lapis Café. Coincidence? Anyway, I headed there and that's where I met her."

"Still not getting it, Sam. But that's got all the makings of great detective work."

"I know that piece in my room and two others are the only remaining ones of their kind from this period. But it was not the antiquity of the piece. It is the stones. I reached out to a friend in Paris and found out they date back over five thousand years to an artifact stolen from Luxor. When it was confiscated on the black market, the stones were sold off to a private bidder. The actual artifact remains someplace in Mecca in a storekeeper's neat and tidy little shop."

Pausing, she glanced about, making sure they were not being monitored.

"I need to reunite the artifact with the stones. Get them fixed and take it safely back to its resting place in Egypt. I still do not have the name of who it belongs to. But found out it was a big-wig general in the days of the Pharaohs. As my story goes, there is a bigger mystery behind this warrior that needs to be investigated."

"And you are tied to this how?"

"I am not sure. You already know from talking with Anna that I am an old soul. So, besides traveling through these passages, somewhere along the way I stayed long enough to have put down roots. Just that I can't recall that far back and know exactly what the hell that is. I guess it is true that the mind does give way after you reach such and such an age."

He had to smile at her lengthy dialog.

They arrived back to their building and walked in.

"You need me for something so you can have closure here. What is it?"

"How the hell did you know that? Picking my thoughts now as well? But, as a matter of record, I do. We can tackle that tomorrow. It will be soon enough. I'll have the servant prepare us a late dinner up on the rooftop if that suits you?"

She seemed tongue-tied and quietly preoccupied. "Yeah, okay... yeah, that will work for me. About eight o'clock?"

***

Not awaiting an answer while nodding him off, she swung down the long hallway. Once the sandals were removed, she stood barefoot, staring eye to eye with Isis. Hands on hips, her voice sprang out. "It's you. Something about you or your time, isn't it? What am I to do after I get to Mecca?"

Silence.

Sam gave up and continued the last few steps to the room.

Drawing a cool bath, she slid in, recalling the day's events. The vast bleakness of the *Akhdam* people. Amongst it all, a pleasant memory came to sight. Happy kids playing soccer. Which made her realize one more thing. Him. Clash. He was reporting on this area just like he had in Cairo. But there was more. Someone else he was working for?

Sam's mind left Clash, drifting back to the woman she'd met today. Yes. Now she knew who she was and where they had met. It was the waitress at the Pensione back in Venice. "Damn," she mouthed softly. "This just gets freakier by the second!"

Drying off, she slid into a pair of shorts and a tank top. This ensemble would be a whole lot cooler up on the rooftop and safer far away from prying eyes. Smiling, she moved the heavy burka from the bed, tossing it onto one of the chairs. After tomorrow or maybe the next few days, it would no longer be a necessity. *Hall-e-freaking-lujah*, she thought, running hands over the cool stones. Based on the picture a friend had emailed, caution would need to be taken in dislodging them.

Would the owner care? Were they just a part of this whole scheme? Would a servant rat her out before she could escape to Mecca? How were they going to transport and—even more frightening—get them across the border between Yemen and Saudi Arabia? She'd seen the headlines in Arabic and had asked her contact earlier, Almira, what it all meant.

It was very apparent that the rubble around certain parts of the city indicated things were not good. But the stories locally and soon internationally would disclose how tribal defiance, pig-headed politicians and the unruly supporters of exiled President Hadi were all in conflict. It was always the people of the land who would suffer. The proof was all around. Indeed, they were suffering immensely.

Just seeing what it had continually been doing to the *Akhdam* was positively cruel. A sudden loud rap at the door was followed by an eerie silence. Tucking the security documents beneath her shorts, Sam slid on her sandals and left the room.

"Dinner is ready for us on the roof."

Internally Sam felt relieved. It was Derek.

She nodded, scrutinizing him thoroughly. Her eyes drilled right through his back to his soul, trying to find answers to questions not yet asked as they sat down.

Nodding to the waiter to proceed, he poured two glasses of deep red wine from a finely etched glass decanter. "This stuff is potent. Black market goods imported from Saudi, ironically. My best advice is to go easy on it. Or tomorrow you may find your head glued to the pillow."

"Thanks, I'll be mindful. So, when do we leave?"

"I'll let you know shortly. I can see you have a lot on your mind. It is written all over your face. But I have a favor to ask. That dialogue you provided from Cairo was outstanding. I wonder if you can look at some footage I took today and add your version to it?"

"I can do that for you. It won't be hard at all. We both saw the same bloody work by the hand of man in that awful place. Are you helping them?"

"Yes, this story will get worldwide coverage right after I send it. Humanitarian networks need to get in here. But there is another story unfolding and we both know it."

"Yeah, up at the border. It's nasty and I'm headed right for it. Don't you want to tag along and see if you can add more to your plight? I'd feel better if you did."

"I think we are in a hold pattern. I have a feeling that's part of the plan. I just don't know enough about it yet so we have to wait it out."

"Okay. Then let's get your story wrapped up. I take it we will be headed to see that dude you know?"

"Edge, his name is Edge. He's one of the three that will be transporting you. My recommendation is to get on his good side. I've seen the other one and it isn't too pretty." He grinned, sipping the wine.

"F that. I don't have to get on this or that with him at all. He has a job to do just like I do. So, there, take that…"

"Who was the woman?"

"My added coverage. She explained what she could to me about customs, process and how the hell we hope to get me and some valuables out of here across the Al-Wadia Border and into the 'Kingdom' without detection."

"When did you learn Saudi was referred to as the Kingdom?"

She smiled. "I'm smarter than I look, mister. You know, there are hundreds of thousands of people on both sides of the border who are in the throes of this mess. Just like Syria. Someday, the aliens from the galaxies are going to come back here and wipe out all the tribes and just keep us women. We do not fight, we shop. We are not killers. Well, most of us are not. We are lovers. What good is man if all he can do is kill or make weapons that do?"

"That's a bit of a rant, although part of it is true. When I was in the forces I saw plenty. Sam, some of it involved women and children doing things you will not want to ever see. Now I'm on the other end of it. All I want to do is get the word out. Help in ways I could not before. There will always be plenty of places I can go. Including my own country where injustices are being performed on human beings daily."

"We could go on about this for a long time. But—" She reached over and grasped his hand, inwardly feeling compassionate. "—sign me up. You are making a difference. Just one soul getting helped means you've done a hell of a job. Right? Remember that. Now it's agreed. Unless you are pulled away before I go, you come with us. Then I know if you get your sorry ass in trouble, Edge will be there to get it out."

He leaned back in his chair, raising his hands and crossing them behind his head, totally relaxed. "I have to wonder if our paths will ever cross again. Anyway, I have a question. Not because I think you and I should, but I am curious. Have you ever dallied on a passage? What I specifically mean is had an intimate moment during one with the person you were with?"

She choked, spewing the wine toward his face as he leaned farther and grabbed the linen napkin, laughing.

"Yeah, that's how I got here. If I had a week I could tell you how it all happened. If our paths do cross again, you will want to stay the hell away."

"I doubt that. But good fortune to the guy you need to get back to. I'm sure there is one."

He watched as her eyelids lowered slightly.

"Hey, sorry. Just was talking away. Meant nothing by that."

"There is someone. You reminded me. I got so caught up in what I'm doing here I forgot I left him there. He had no idea before I left where I was headed. It happened so fast."

"He's one of us?"

"Yeah. It's all his fault, really."

"You'll get there eventually. I'm sure he's figured it all out. He must be a smart bloke if he lured you from someplace else."

She was taken back. "You had that experience?"

"Yes, twice. Same woman. She's now in Belgium on a so-called relocation process. I have no idea who the 'powers to be' are, Sam. But they keep close surveillance on our jaunts and a steady hand on our progress. Just keep that in mind."

"Holy crap. I had no idea. I consider myself still in training. I've only been doing this for about nine months. They must be having a field day with my docket."

He rose, taking her arm as they headed back to the elevator. "I can only imagine what it looks like. Where they are. A big planet with immense amounts of data transferring like crazy between all of us special people. A grand mission control."

She smiled. "You have to wonder who is behind this and what they look like. Sometimes I wonder if they are here too. Moving between. We are pretty cool people, Clash."

The elevator opened as they entered the suite and simultaneously nodded to their guard, who stood with a straight back and a bored look on his face.

"They are probably having a lot more fun watching you than me, Sam. Have a good night. You need anything give a loud holler or throw something. I'm not that far away."

She grinned, walking down her long hallway, and nodded with a slight smile to Isis. In the room she disrobed, washed up and climbed into her bed, not bothering to pack up the bag. Tonight she was totally safe.

Chapter Four

Rising to a beautiful sunrise, Sam washed, dressed, and then sauntered down the hall to the elevator, taking a cup of tea off the tray the servant was holding. He must have heard her rousing and had it prepared knowing she would head up to the rooftop to join her companion. Indeed, Clash was already there with a mug of dark, aromatic coffee in hand.

"Never figured you for a sleep-in today for some reason."

"Same for you. This is the place to be in the early morning, isn't it? What a sight."

He appreciated the vibrant colors as they lit up the mountain range off in the distance. "Yeah, not bad. Unfortunately, we won't be here much longer to enjoy another one. Last night I instructed the cook to have our breakfast ready at seven. Soon after, we rendezvous with Edge and his men. Once you record the storyline, we bug out. We need to be on the road before noon."

"How long a drive is it to the border?"

"Just under twelve hours if we are extremely fortunate. Today's going to be unlike any other day you've had. I guarantee it." His eyes were alight. Sam glanced at them as the adrenaline somehow passed from his body into her own. It was suddenly coursing through her veins like a powerful river charging towards the sea.

They both turned toward a noise behind them and noticed the servant holding the elevator door open. "Guess that's our sign, woman. Time to eat. Come on. Let's get this ball rolling."

They sat down at the small table, eyeing the simple spread, and ate in silence. Not once did they make eye contact. Both of their minds were engaged elsewhere.

"Grab only essentials. We travel light. Anything you are lacking will be provided when it is time. You know the deal." They both rose, placing the napkins on their plates. "Sam, can you be ready and downstairs in ten minutes?"

"Yup." She turned toward the hall and then stopped. "Wait, I have a quick question. Who are the bodyguards for? To guard this property and what it houses? If they are, how will I get what I need out?"

He raised both brows. "They are with Edge's team. The question you will want to ask next should probably not be bothered with."

She was waiting for him when he arrived downstairs. He nodded to the guard as they left the building and out into the already sultry heat of the early morning.

"You should have told me they are part of your team. I would have stopped thinking about them."

"Did you really need me to give you that detail? I was pretty sure you would figure things out."

"Okay, true. But that makes me wonder if the person that owns this building is already aware of what I am about. Removing objects of great value." She took a quick glance up to his face, but nothing would give away what he was thinking. "Hmmm. Oh, I know. You don't have to tell me. That was the other part of the question I was not supposed to ask."

His finger pointed toward the door as they made their way through the throngs of people selling their chickens, spices, and clothing. All of a sudden, without warning, Sam was engulfed by a fierce, emulsifying emotion. It nearly caused blindness as an intense touch with destiny, or déjà vu wove a heavy spell over her senses. Unable to move forward, she halted, placing a palm against her chest and feeling the heavy beat of her heart. Glancing anxiously around, she tried to locate the source.

A call to prayer suddenly rang throughout the ancient city of Sanaa and the hairs on her arms stood at attention. A slight breeze wafted over, lifting a few unruly tendrils under her heavy burka as she raised her face, eyes closed, towards the heavens, listening with ears perked.

Then it came. A voice.

Subtle at first. Then it grew in strength. It was a man. A heroic man of great power and passion. She could feel him inside her body and mind as if he already possessed her. Senses heightened and nearly out of control, she felt her hands warmed now to a soft stickiness, her breathing labored. No longer grounded to Mother Earth, Sam lost it as this unknown male force took complete control.

His voice was strong. In total command. "Mistress, I await your return."

Frightened, she immediately realized it was not Adam. It was someone else. Familiar yet unfamiliar. This man was from her past. An Egyptian.

A longing pulsated from her toes up through her scalp as she felt a hand on the fabric of her heavy burka. Face lowering, eyes opening, she looked directly into the scrutinizing eyes of Clash.

"What the hell was that about? I was five minutes ahead of you before I noticed you were not there. You can't do that to me again."

She could hear both men as their words collided. The Egyptian's finally faded in her mind—but he had left an imprint on her heart.

Clash shook her slightly. "I don't know what's gotten into you. Move, Arnesen. Do I need to pick you up and cause a scandal in broad daylight?"

She laughed softly, thankful his tone had brought her back to reality in a flash. "No, ass. But while I have your complete attention, tell me why it took five minutes to know I was not there? What the hell were you doing?"

Relief spread across his face. "Well, fuck me, right? Come on. We are nearly there. Try not to give Edge any shit. Okay? Shit, Sam, I've never witnessed anything as strange as that in all my years. Can you try and not put me through it again?"

"Can't make any promises there. It somewhat freaked me out too."

They stopped at the large metal door, exchanged looks and walked in. Clash went ahead, extending a hand to Edge and Sam followed suit.

"Okay." She quickly surveyed how bulked-up they all were. Yup, and quite a handsome a lot too. "Glad to have you all assisting me. Can't trust Clash to get this done on his own and all."

They shook hands as Edge nodded to Clash over her shoulder. His grip was so tight it broke her mental barrier in two.

"Damn straight. Good to know you too, Arnesen. That's Gunner to your left and Fresno opposite. You will be in the safest hands possible with us, rest assured."

"Groovy. I understand we are on a tight schedule. Where is this feed and how do you want to handle it?"

"Sit here. Put these silencer headphones on and the feed will stream up on the monitor in front of you. It is seventeen minutes. How do you want to go about it?"

"Do we have enough time before departure to record then do a second review to ensure it's what you all want?"

He did not even glance at his watch. "Yeah, that'll work."

She put on the phones and started the recording. It was all her eyes had seen yesterday and a no brainer. This dialog was ready in her head. Stopping the feed, she rewound it and hit the button, talking into the mic.

"These are the faces of a sorrowful and forgotten people. People without arrogance marching on to forge a new Yemen. Fearless, they migrated here to fight a raging battle."

Both men stood back, arms folded, side by side, motionless as they watched the feed and listened to the softness of her voice. She spoke with passion about this tortured society, long ignored and hated by the country of Yemen. As the reel ended, she pressed down on the stop button, set the headphones on the desk and swiveled around, facing them both. She did not ask if they liked it. She knew. They knew. No additional review was needed.

"We have a change of clothes that may be a lot more to your liking down that hall. Second door to your left. Bring the burka out and stuff it in your bag. You will definitely want that in Saudi."

She nodded and left them, excited to see what awaited.

***

"Damn, she did that justice, Clash."

"Yeah, she has a definitive style about her that's very different than anyone I have come across. Can't quite figure her out."

"Agree with you on that one. I'll get that sent now. Then we need to vacate asap. Gunner and Fres are outside waiting." With a click of the mouse, he sent the feed. "A new crew is headed here now to disengage the equipment. We have received intelligence more air strikes may be taking place. They are relocating everything. So as soon as she's ready, bring her down."

When she reappeared he started to laugh as she walked towards him. "Don't say it. I can see it written all over your face."

"But I have to. I like these!"

"Yeah, not bad, Arnesen. Now come on. They are waiting on us. Get that stuff into your bag so we can head out. They will review the agenda on the road. Make sure you keep that cap on and as much of your hair tucked up inside."

She zipped the bag. "Any idea of our route? Can't be straight up to the border and just say hi to the patrols and saunter across?"

"Actually, I have no idea. Remember I was not to come along at this juncture." They headed outside into the hot sun. "I reckon we will find out together."

***

Sam climbed into the old relic of a rig, smiling as it reminded her of a Beachcomber from years long past. Something straight out of a surfer movie back in the 1950s and '60s along the coast of California. But one thing was clear: it had been reinforced. In this, they were less obvious than a Hummer decked out with extra Kevlar and machine guns mounted on top.

"No seat belts on this trip, fellas?"

Leaning back from the front seat, Edge produced an engaging smile. "Get comfy, princess. It's going to be a long journey. A long, close journey in these confines with the likes of us." He started the engine, shifted into gear and blazed a rapid path out of the alley north towards Route 5.

"When do you pipe in the entertainment?"

Edge looked over to his co-pilot and laughed. "She fits right in. Pay attention, Sam, we've got goodies for you on board this trip."

"Oh, I see that."

"Strap this around your leg." Fres handed her a holster and she followed his instruction. "You know how to fire this Sig?"

"Oh, you mean that gun? In the vehicle or outside of it?"

He eyed her with a slight warning.

"Yes, I do." She took the knife and sheath from him and pulled off her jacket. Then she slid it cross-body, securing the Velcro and tying her jacket in case she needed it in a hurry. Unbuttoning a top flap on her shirt, she took three mags housing bullets from his outstretched hand and slid two in there and one in her pants pocket.

Fres laughed as Edge watched on in the rearview mirror.

"Done this a few times, Arnesen?"

"Something like that. What else do you have for me?"

"That's it. You are prepared. What documents do you have for crossing the border?"

"Little. But aren't you going to bribe our way? If so, I will not be needing a Kingdom passport if I have a British one."

"Good reply. But if that goes south, you need to know where we are and how to get around. Someone will find you if that happens and get you moving in the right direction." He took out a surveillance air map, settling it on both their knees.

"Here." He pointed. "Al-Tinh is our border crossing in Gizan. We have been advised today seems like a good day to enter. It is quieter than Al-Wadia. Last night air strikes came in. Today nearly two thousand people have been detained from crossing the border from Yemen to the Kingdom."

"Well, that sucks for them. What's our plan if we are stopped?"

"Between here and there? Well, that's obvious, seeing the firepower displayed in this rig. We take to the range and fight our way out. Then cross the border in a new spot. Let's just hope enough money was passed to keep us in the clear."

She was handed a bottled water and quickly unscrewed the top, taking a swig. "What happens next?"

"You will be on your own at that point. Our job done. I guess you figure that out. Do you have any ideas just in case?"

"Well, I need to get to Mecca, so that's my next point of interest. I guess I head there. That is why I needed to keep that awful burka. Good thing to know in case we do get stopped. I need that damn bag."

They were three hours into the trip when she slid her head back and allowed the vast emptiness of the horizon, beautiful in its dusty bleakness, to lull her mind into a simpler place. The Exeter cottage.

Was there any other place she wanted to be right now but there? In truth, no. Who was the voice that had spoken to her? That had taken control with such force and possessed her body and mind earlier today? It was a voice she still could hear resonating in the recesses. Calling. Asking. *Where are you?* How long had he been there inside her soul, restless and needing? Why had she suppressed this for so long?

Eyes closed, the bumpy ride tossing her around, Sam felt the presence on both sides of her rugged companions. A true sense of safety and security enveloped her mind into a relaxed level of security. Like last night, right this minute she knew she was safe and protected.

Chapter Five

"Shit! Fres, move Arnesen to the cargo area and open the top. Looks like we are about to get some visitors!"

Nudged awake, Sam clumsily climbed over the seat into the rear. Yelling ensued. Out his side window, Clash had a sub-machine gun ready. Fres was on the rooftop, setting up while Gunner dangled out with a grenade launcher.

Thrill and fear mixed through her senses. What if the back of the rig was hit? She would be the first to go. Not wanting to succumb to anxiety and freak out, instead, she took in a deep breath and held on for dear life.

Edge swerved the vehicle around in a circle, out of control for a split second. Then he righted his direction, heading straight for the two heavily-armed vehicles fast on approach. Sam could see through the large hole all that was happening in front of the vehicle. But her imagination had to take over listening to them holler where she could not see.

"There's no fucking way they were tipped off. They'd not be so aggressive this far from the border. This is just a band, mates. Why don't we just have some quick fun with them and get it done?"

A shot ricocheted off the side window. Watching the crack form, Sam kicked it out with her boot before it shattered inside the vehicle.

"I got a visual on the second one, Edge. Gunner, how does it look?"

"I have a clear on the first. Don't lift your head or I'll have to shave the top."

She peered over, momentarily paralyzed at the expression on all their faces. They were enjoying this!

"Edge...?"

"Fire!"

Shots rocked every inch of the vehicle, nearly lifting it up off the ground by the massive force of firepower coming from the threesome. Edge swerved sharply to the left, circling back to their original direction toward the border as two massive explosions lit up the sky. Metal flew in every direction as God himself only knew what else.

Sam heard someone yell as the car came to an abrupt stop. Sand kicked up all around, forming a protective cloud.

"Damn good work as always. But we have a slight problem."

The rear tires were spinning, digging a quick hole. They were stuck. Sam slid back into the seat and got out with all of them to examine it.

"Men can't drive. This is all your fault, soldier."

They all broke out in laughter.

"Arnesen, get into the driver's seat and shift into first. Easy on the gas while we give it a hoist."

Sam got in, recalling eons ago her father having a shifter on the steering column of their family car. Laughing to no one but the otherwise empty rig, she felt it being lifted. Gingerly she pressed on the gas. Nothing happened. She pushed harder. It was a bit too much. She and the car sped off, leaving a dustbowl encompassing the guys.

Complete laughter engulfed them all as she spied them with hands either on hips or across their massive chests just glaring at the rear of the car. She ground the gear, put it in reverse and halted, the engine in idle, arm resting on the window frame.

"Need a lift?"

Edge could not keep a grin off his face. "Get out, wench. I'll take over from here. Your driving days in the desert are officially over."

She smiled coyly, patting him on the shoulder as she hopped out. "Got a bit of dust on that face, soldier. I think you need a bucket of water and a rag before another woman sees it." She winked at Fres, who motioned her ahead of him back inside the car.

"You okay, Arnesen?"

"Could not be better unless I had a cold beer and a shot of tequila, Edge."

"Smart move kicking out that window. I gotta say it. You did well under pressure."

She shrugged that off.

"Do you know who they were? Could you tell from this distance?"

Edge quickly replied. "Houthi forces."

"The local rebels?"

"They are more than that, but affirmative. You aware of them?"

"Not much. Just what I've read in papers. Anything I need to know now?"

"Nope. The less the better. Especially if you get disentangled from us. Just you use your smarts, that's all." He shifted and drove onward.

Eleven hours into the journey, darkness descended. Pulling over, doors opening, everyone disappeared with guns in hand to relieve themselves.

Sam came out of the dried brush just as Clash did. "Feels like I've hardly spoken to you since we started out this morning."

"Yeah, I know. Been meaning to ask you what happened earlier. You know. When you went all blank in the face?"

She knew exactly what he was talking about. "I really have no idea. It was like some force took control of my mind and body at the same time. Have you ever had that happen when you have absolutely no way to explain it?"

He stared at her a few seconds as they got back in the car and Edge drove off. "No, not like that. Arnesen, if we do get separated, get yourself across and don't look for the likes of me, you hear? If we both head to Mecca and are supposed to rendezvous, we will. I meant to ask you and now's just a bit too late, I might add. Did you get what you needed from our stay before we bugged out?"

She grinned. "Yes. Tucked snugly away. Even if they strip me they won't find it. If you get my drift." His face said it all as she cracked up laughing.

"What's so humorous back there? You two up to something we need to know about?"

She leaned up in between Edge and Gunner. "Nope. But I got a question. What are you here for? Counter-intelligence? It can't be just to help a mate file a story and get me across some damn border."

Edge patted her hand before she moved back between her two companions.

"None of your damn business, nosy woman. All of you are the same. Can't keep it where it does not belong."

She laughed harder. "Yeah, and if it was not for all you men, guns, ego and the power struggle amongst each other, I'd probably not be sitting here right now. So way to go, sport."

He tilted his head, locking gazes with her in the rear mirror. "Smart ass."

"Well, I'm right and you all know it. So how much longer now? I see brightness up on the horizon. Is that where our crossing is to take place?"

"You are a pain in the ass for sure and yes it is. About an hour, I suspect."

As everyone checked their pistols, getting them ready, there was a tenseness radiating through the interior of the rig that could not be denied. Fres jabbed her in the side. "You remember what I showed you?"

303 • Passages: The Complete Trilogy Box Set

"I do. See the outline of it along my right flank? Are you feeling what I'm feeling? Like we are going to ditch the car and hike it?"

"Yeah, something is up. Stay alerted."

As they closed in on the border, Clash turned to her. "Sam, move forward. Crawl back underneath where the tire was and stay put until one of us opens it up for you. I've seen this before. We are going to have to make our presence known in a most irritating way."

"What?"

"Just do as I say and get in there."

She turned and crawled into the small space, stretching out as much as the cramped quarters would allow. "But I can't see what's happening! How the hell will I know what to do?"

"Shut up. We are nearing the border. Take out your gun and cock it. Just make sure you don't shoot any of us in the back."

Silence engulfed the vehicle. All she could hear was the humming of the engine. Out of nowhere the tailpipe bellowed out a choke and she startled, bumping her head in the close confines. She could not hear clearly what the hell they were saying. But voices were thick with an unfamiliar accent. Then as she listened on more closely, she could make out their conversation.

"Passports seem in order, here take them and proceed up to the gate and wait. They will let you through shortly."

She heard the gear grind slightly as Edge moved the rig further.

Then it all went silent. A very deafening silence.

Fuck, she thought, *that was way too easy.* Her gut knotted, tightening up. Her gun was ready and she was fully prepared to poke her head into the rear seat area when Clash spoke back to her.

"We've made it through the main checkpoint gate and are on the other side. But now there is a soldier from Saudi waving us over. Sam, get ready."

The sound of doors being pulled opened and dragging noises indicated to Sam that all was very wrong. Something had to be done and done now. There was no way she'd be cornered like a sitting duck. Scrunching to the rear corner of the space, she realized how rusty it was. Peering with limited vision into the busy street, she saw a small group gathered. It looked predominately like civilian detainees.

This was her chance.

Kicking fiercely, she leaped out, pointing her gun at the first guard, who was frisking Gunner, and let off a round at his boot. That got his attention just long enough for the guys to take out the guards, grab their guns and at a run follow her into the thrush of detainees down an alley.

"Brazen woman! You could have gotten yourself killed!" Edge was more than pissed off.

She stopped, completely out of breath, lungs on fire from the steady excursion and smiled, leaning down resting both hands on knees. "And you are welcome."

He grabbed her by the arm. "So, what's your plan?"

"Have not a freaking clue right at this second. How about all of you?"

"Suppose we need to see you someplace, right?"

"Nope, this is where we part ways. I'm sure of it. Look over there. I see a few dudes you may fit well in with if you head over."

"How the hell do you know they are 'our kind,' Arnesen?"

"I don't. It is just a hunch. But they are eyeing you and not killing you. I'm banking they can get you a lift. So, guys, thanks a lot! Bye!"

With a quick salute, Sam was engulfed by a group of passing sisters, who did not seem to mind she had joined them. As she kept herself lower than their taller frames, she started the task of removing clothing. When they reached their destination, she was in full burka.

"Come with us. We can provide safe shelter while you find your way."

Sam nodded internally, knowing the nuns' assistance was timely and appreciated. There always seemed to be a nun or good priest around when she needed them the most. *Praise the Lord*, she thought, thinking back to her first appearance in Italy, England and the Chapel at Iona. Yeah, this worked.

"Thank you, sister. I would be honored." She turned around and caught a glimpse of Clash going inside a door a few buildings down. The rest of Edge's team was nowhere to be seen. *Good*, she sighed to above. They were all safe.

The Mother Superior turned the large lock on the strong wrought-iron gates and swung them open. The group passed through. After they were all in, she relocked them from the inside, catching a questioning look from Sam.

"Do not fret, my child. You are not a prisoner. From this vantage point, we can get you further away from the border. It's not just the guards that are a threat. There are militants on both sides that would see harm to anyone who was in their way if they were set on killing. It's all around us."

"I see that. It appears that you, your group and I all seemed to be in the right place at the right time."

"Don't you love it when it just works that way, Sam?"

That comment did not come as a surprise. "Are you here to help me? Or, on your way someplace else after you do so?"

"Are not both the same?"

"Not really. But you know what I am asking."

"I do, and no. I am stationary here for now. By my own choice. Later inside the walls after you clean that dirt off and are fed, we can talk more. I have an address for you in Mecca. A visit there you must make."

"Ah, how sweet. Thank you."

"This will be your room for a short time. Then we will get you on your way. No one will come inquiring about you until well after you have left. They try to avoid us. We are a hospital for lepers. You know what people think of them even to this day, don't you?"

Sam nodded, setting her bag down quickly and reviewing the windowless room. No ornaments were on the walls. Although it was barren of any frivolity, it was clean and she welcomed it.

The Mother Superior watched her careful examination. "No window prevents those outside seeing inside. Stay to the interior only. Do not go out into the courtyard or onto any of the balconies. It's not confinement. Rather, a stay house until you move on. Just look at it that way."

"No worries. I don't plan on rocking the boat here. I promise. You probably already have a word of some kind I can potentially cause trouble. Although, I hardly try."

She smiled, touching Sam's arm. Then she stepped away with her hand poised on the knob. "Yes. That detail came to me before your predicament did. I was advised you sometimes are quite creative." Her grin grew. "But what the hell, right?" Then she shut the door.

Sam's brows shot up. Had she just said that? Her laughter resonated around the small room as she removed the burka, layer by layer. Underneath it, all her attire was fine and would not cause the good sisters upheaval at exposing too much flesh. Closing the door and noting the location, she set off for a needed stretch.

That's when she met Sister Meg.

They smiled at each other the moment their gazes locked.

It was Anne.

"Oh, my bloody word. It is you. Isn't it?"

"Shh. Yes." Anne moved them aside, taking a long, dark wooden hallway and then halted, opening a beautifully carved door as they walked into a divinely small chapel. "We are safe to speak here."

"What are you doing? I have to admit I did not notice you in the cluster when I was swept up by the good sisters."

"I was not amongst them. But I knew of your arrival. I happened here myself a week prior to prepare."

"Damn, you are a sight for sore eyes! How are you?" She paused, looking at the holy cross. "Sorry, Lord." Then continued. "To see someone I actually know from a real place! How is Lord Griffin, everyone?"

"I'm not able to answer some of your questions. It's not my purpose in being here. But I'm sure one word of 'fine' will suffice. I don't think they will give me holy hell for at least giving away that much."

"Okay, I get it. But how frustrating. Anyway, I am still happy you are here. Are you going with me to Mecca?"

"Yes. I will make sure you and the craftsman meet. Shortly after that, I will leave. I'm to ensure safe passage to him."

"That's it? Why do you get all the easy jobs?" Both women clasped hands and softly laughed. "So where is your room in case I need to know?"

"I'll show you, come on. I'll take you to the dining hall as well. Those who eat at this time are fully aware we are your transient home for a short spell. They will not ask you any questions. Everyone is completely trustworthy."

They stood, heading out in a new direction. "These halls don't just run north and south, do they? They seem to stream out in many directions. Like being in a Harry Potter plot. That's kind of neat. Glad to hear everyone is trustworthy. But does that mean I can't write you a note so when you go back you can give it to him?"

"Exactly. You cannot. I stick to the task and so do you. Sorry, mistress."

"Hey, that's not what I told you before. Now that you are coming to assist me I insist we keep it informal. Deal?"

Anne nodded, opening the dining room door as six sisters came over and shook her hand. Not one uttered a word. Was this like a Buddhist monastery? Was no speaking allowed? That would work out perfectly for her. *Wouldn't Clash find that amusing?* she internally thought.

As they sat down, two sisters brought food and wine. Suddenly Sam felt a moment of pure contentment.

"Welcome to our guest and good blessing to your travels. Would you care to say our prayer this evening over the meal?"

They all clasped hands. Sam took in their serene faces while glancing quickly at Anne on her left. "May your bounty always be plentiful, wine sweet and smiles warm those who are in need. Thank you for taking me in with these glorious women, Lord. Amen."

"Amen."

The meats, cheeses and fruit were passed as her glass was filled with their homemade wine. Eating and sipping, she wondered what the guys were having tonight. Was Clash enjoying comfort and safety? Great food? A different type of company? A sigh of appreciation escaped. Indeed, Sam was happy. For the fact was a friend was here for the next part of her journey.

But a note to Adam was not possible? Okay. She could live with that. There was no way Sam wanted to jeopardize Anne's mission. It would have to wait. But what was he doing? Did he miss her? His note said he was off to Canada. Was he back now?

Glancing over at Anne, she realized how raw her emotions truly were. Her young companion seemed to say with her eyes that she understood how frustrating it was. A silent message passed between them. Somehow Sam felt that all was well with Adam as relief washed over her.

"Are you full to your heart's content now?"

"Indeed, Sister Meg."

They rose as Sam thanked each of the sisters personally on their way back to her room.

"When do we go?"

"Tomorrow evening after dusk. We are taking a different route away from the border to a safer location. From there we will get a lift to Mecca."

"How long is that journey going to take?"

"You in some kind of a rush, Sam?"

"That's better, Anne! No. Well, truth be told, kind of. But I must admit I am still perplexed. When I arrived from the cottage I thought I'd be in Egypt. But not in modern times. Rather long ago during one of the Pharaohs' periods."

"Have you any idea why?"

"All I know is that I have to get some valuables back to where they belong. I think I am safe in telling you. Beyond that I do not have a clue. I'm sure once I meet the craftsman, more will be made clear."

They arrived at her room.

"You don't need to worry here. It is safe. All the same, keep things ready just in case."

They hugged as Sam's hand rested on the latch. "See you for breakfast. Probably bright and early." Then she closed her door.

A wash basin and fresh towels had been brought in and she cleaned away the rest of the dirt and removed her boots. Lying down on the soft, single bed, moving hands up beneath her head, she stared up at the ceiling. With a socked foot she pushed down the wall switch. The room went completely dark except for the soft light penetrating in through the eight-pointed cross cut out in the upper door. "Hmm," she mumbled out loud. "That's a Templar Cross."

A tingle slid up her spine.

It was strange to her as she shut her mind down, allowing sleep, how she could be so in love with Adam— yet have days on end where she did not even think about him. It was like another force was at work here. One that gathered strength and was pushing other thoughts from her being. Her mind. Her body.

A rush wove up through her. Not as strong as earlier today, but it was apparent something of great magnitude was coming. What the heck was it? Or who might be a better question?

Lids fluttering shut at last, she housed no dreams this night. With much relief, the silence of the monastery, combined with exhaustion, finally took its toll.

Chapter Six

"Sleep well, I see. You appear completely refreshed this morning."

"I did! Can we take a stroll around the interior? I need to stretch. You know me. I can't stay idle for too long. That's probably one of the reasons why I was selected for this type of work."

"Possibly. Let's go and get some breakfast. It's early. I'm sure we can rustle up something. The good sisters rise with the sun. They probably already have dishes, chores and prayers finished. Although not in that order."

They both laughed as Sam grabbed her arm.

"You're a changed woman, Anne, I can see it. I know you can't tell me all the details. Has it been as eye-opening for you as it has for me? You seem to have gained a lot of confidence. I'm glad to be witnessing it."

"Yes, I believe it is true. I've been on a few simple trips. This is my fourth since you and I visited France. I'm more than getting my feet wet now and ready to accelerate my future passages to a bit more exciting."

"It's cool not knowing what's next until it just simply is. I was so surprised, as I mentioned last night. Not where I showed up, but when. They will keep us on our toes. That's for sure."

They had sauntered onward through an adjoining sitting room before heading into the eatery. "Hey, they left us food and drink. It's like they are invisible angels. Necessities just appear and disappear. In fact, you never even hear them scuffling off or know where exactly they go."

"Well, whatever they are, it's a sight to see. My mouth is positively watering. Let's sit and do the deed."

Sam deposited a piece of smoked meat into her mouth with a wedge of cheese right behind it. Chewing fast, she still managed to produce a grand grin. "Man, that's good. Do we wait until dusk to exit? What exactly do we do between now and then? Are there chores to perform so we can assist the good sisters?"

"I already inquired. They did not want to chance us going into the infirmary helping with the lepers. Just in case any are planted as a spy. You never know who is aware of your adventures crossing the border yesterday."

"Ah, good thinking. So what do we do?"

"The library. There are books to be cataloged and placed back in their proper place. They lend out to local schools. There are also donations that need to be acknowledged."

"They don't have computers, I suppose?"

"Sam, they are modern here. Of course they do. We will not be handwriting stickers and placing them on the binders. You are funny as heck this morning."

"And you, missy, are growing up! How long before some gent's eyes catch yours?"

"Well, I have to admit one has. You have been gone a while, haven't you?"

Sam let that slide. She did not want to let Anne know how very much that had struck home. Smiling, she raised eyebrows at her new sassy friend. "I guess when I do get back we'd better scheme a more efficient plan around letting each other know where we are headed. Don't you think?"

"I do. Perhaps we could move that ceramic chicken you have on your counter filled with candy from the shop. Something like that. I had no idea. I think it's normal for us to come and go. That's why we don't get hitched with someone that would not understand."

Again, that struck home. Again, she ignored it.

Sam swigged down her second cup of warm tea. "It's a rooster, dear girl. Anyway, shall we get this day rolling? The more we can do to help the sisters the better I'll feel. I much prefer to clean the slate before I move on."

Each taking a tray, they stacked the dishes, cups and remaining food on them. Taking it all to the kitchens, one washed and dried dishes and the other put the food in containers.

Anne glanced around to make sure the area looked in order. "I'm sure they will appreciate we just did that."

"Probably. They are good natured by spirit and soul, right?" They both broke out in a giggle.

"Yeah, I guess that comes along with deciding to wear a habit. One that does not have a designer label sewn into the back."

Snickering at Anne's humorous reply, Sam had to silently admit she was indeed growing up. "Yeah, we got to see a lot of designer clothing when we were in Paris, didn't we?"

More laughter followed as Anne could not resist adding, "Right, designer nappies!"

"Shh," quickly followed a somewhat stern look as one of the sisters passed them en route to the library.

"Properly chastised we are, Sam, so we'd better watch ourselves."

"Agreed. Ah, we've arrived. What a lovely library. I see two laptops over there. I'll take one and the stack next to it and you take the other. Mother Superior left us each a note. Cool. Let's get cracking."

For three hours Sam logged and shelved the new acquisitions while Anne took care of the ones being returned. Their combined efforts were quick, efficient and streamlined. By early afternoon, three-quarters of the work was done.

Rising, Sam stretched her arms high and went over to a small shelf, tilting her head sideways to review the titles. These books were old and quite valuable. She let her hands run over the bindings ever so slightly, until one sent a tingle up her spine. Her eyes settled on the title.

"'Ancient Pharaohs and Their Commanding Generals.' Hum," she said softly. "Let's see what happens." Testing, she pulled it slightly off the shelf as the electrifying vibration inside her body rose. Removing her fingers caused it to rapidly decrease.

"What the hell?"

Sam gazed quickly over at Anne to see if she had heard her and then stared at the book again. Grasping it firmly, Sam pulled it from the shelf. It burned her hand as it slid from it to the floor. As if in a dream, she watched it drift slowly down, hit and open. Glancing at her left palm, she was startled, hardly able to move. It glowed bright red.

Kneeling over, she reached slowly down with a slightly shaky hand, halting just before touching it. Crouched, arms resting on both knees, she read the first two paragraphs softly out loud.

"It was during the New Kingdom (1570 BC–1070 BC) that Egypt's military dominance flourished. A rich class of noble warriors joined the army. Charioteers. These powerful men now had mobile platforms. Which launched Egypt back to being a commanding empire once again."

Gingerly, two fingers slid down the side of the ancient binding. It was now cool to the touch. Now sitting cross-legged on the floor, she read on in earnest. Stopping at the bottom of the first page, she cast a quick glance over toward Anne, who was heavily enthralled into her own corner of work.

"Hey, do you think they would let me borrow this book?"

"Nope, not a chance. You cannot get it back to them here and you know that. What is it?"

"Just on ancient Egypt. But something about it has me quite interested."

Anne looked at her. "Really, what would that be?"

"Don't know. I will jot down the name of the book and author and see if I can grab a copy along the way to Mecca."

Anne laughed. "That may be easier than stealing from the good sisters."

Lowering her head, Sam read further. Something was important here. Between the lines. Unfortunately, time was against her. Soon they would leave. Standing, she reached for pen and paper, took down the details and slid the paper into a back pocket. Leaning against a large pedestal, she flipped ahead to the next page:

"Advances were made with increasing a stronger infantry. An iconic new sword was introduced by a hired mercenary. His prowess and strength on the battlefield as well as intelligent tactical mind quickly moved him up through the military ranks. He became one of the greatest Egyptian generals of all time."

This piqued her curiosity. Her mind created a tall, dark, handsomely tanned man with enticing muscles, dressed in leather sandals, a gold belt and tunic. Thinking that if the breeze off the Nile blew just right, well... hm. Kind of like a Scottish kilt. Exactly what did they wear under those?

"Hey, where are you? I've been standing here talking for two minutes. You have not heard a darn thing I've said." Anne glanced at the book. "What's that you are looking through? Sam, you looked a thousand miles away. But it must have been amusing. There was quite a smile on your face. Was it something regarding Lord Griffin?"

It felt like cold water had been splashed on her face.

"No, but I must get my hands on a copy of this. Somehow. Lucky for me this is the only one left. It's a reprint over three hundred years old." Realizing what she'd just said, Sam placed it back on the shelf and turned to Anne.

"You should have poked me. I was in distant lands and that was no place I should have been. What were you saying?"

"That I've finished. Looks like you have as well. What do you say we go to chapel and pray? May send us off in the right direction. Can't hurt, right?" Anne's eyes were filled with sincerity. Sam could tell she really did want to go in there.

"Yes, I think a few moments would do me good. Come on, I hear the bell. We had better get a move on."

"Who was he?"

"Clash? You talking about the dude that helped me get here?"

"Clash, eh? That's quite a name. But no. The one that had you mesmerized when you were looking at that book."

"Truly it was nothing. I just let my mind wander and never has that been a good idea. It usually gets me into trouble. Come to think of it, in those instances, it has landed me in interesting places. I got to meet my real brother. So, I guess my wild imagination is a good asset after all."

They had reached the lovely chapel, blessed themselves with holy water and then knelt a few rows from the rear. Clasping hands, both women lowered their heads in earnest prayer. Sam's was entirely in a different direction than Anne's as her eyes raised above the cross towards heaven and spoke internally.

"Lord, why am I drawn to someone I do not know? Who was that man that controlled me yesterday? If there is a way you can get me back to Adam, please hurry it up. I don't believe I want to keep thinking about this man or imagining things about him when he's not real. Even if he was, I do not know him. Or maybe I'm about to know him. I don't know, do you? I am sorry I am rambling."

She pushed up off the pew and nodded to Anne as she left the chapel to roam the silent halls. Not a soul came into sight. As she finally turned a bend and found her room, she went in and packed up the few items. Waiting had never done her any service. But now she had no choice. Having Anne show up with the nuns and finding that book in the library was all part of the grander scheme. This time, though, seemed different. She was anxious and needed to get moving toward Mecca as soon as possible. Find the craftsman. That was that. She glanced up as her door opened, launched the bag over a shoulder and closed the door behind her.

"This way. There is a special room we will eat in and then leave quietly. It is time. You are ready."

Sam knew Anne was not referring to the bag being carried. Quickly appraising her jeans and T-shirt, a comment could not be resisted. "You fit right in here. In this era. Let me ask you a question. Now that you've seen modern technology, which do you prefer?"

Anne opened a door. Inside was a tiny room with a simple square wooden table and two chairs. It was softly lit by one lone waxed candle. On top of the table was a long handmade wicker basket filled with food and drink.

"Both. I like roaming, Sam. Who knows what will be next? Did I tell you the guy I have a fancy for is one of us too?"

"Is he someone I am acquainted with?"

"Yes, your builder's son."

"What about his father?"

"He is also. Well, was up until his son was twelve and his mother passed away. He then retired to take care of him."

"Sorry about that. But good for you in a way. Then he will understand more about what is going on. Just as Lord Griffin does."

"I think it's the only way. But we are going to have to be careful with kids."

"What! Don't you think you should date him a while and maybe get married before you mention them?" Their heads lowered closer as they giggled. "I meant I was thinking that I already know. Sort of. You understand what I am saying? It will just be easier if it does happen like that between us."

"Well, you are still learning the trade. But it is true. Girls from that generation married young. Do what feels comfortable. Otherwise, your pop will be fishing out his hunting rifle." They laughed. "If you are finished, I'm full. Going to take along a few pieces of fruit. They are too delicious to pass up. So where is this exit?"

"This way. We need to be quiet. What I am about to show you is an infrequently used point of exit. Not all the nuns know about it and it has to stay that way."

Sam nodded, following in silence as they moved to the corner. Selecting the correct wooden panel, Anne pushed against a protruding knot and the door partially opened.

"Cool," Sam whispered as they entered. She turned the tip of her shoe back against it, forcing it closed. Anne flicked the switches on two flashlights and handed one to Sam. Both were forced to duck under the low ceiling.

"How far is it?"

"It is quite a way. Remember we need to move from the monastery. Away from the border. One of the sisters told me that patrols are all over the city looking for you."

"Shit. Okay. It is just a bit confining down here. I feel air but do not see any vents. How's that possible?"

"I'm trying not to think about that and avoid hitting my head at the same time. Who knows? Then there is the thought of what may be lurking around at my feet or crawling over my hair right now. I need to remember to pack a hat next time."

Sam appreciated her humor, wondering what had just brushed against her leg. "Damn. Good point! I have one in my bag. But hell if I'm going to stop and get it." She smiled into the semi-darkness. "Perhaps I should turn on my cellphone and see if the GPS works and I can get a grid of where we are?"

"You do sometimes chat a bit much, you know. All the same, I'm glad we are together. Oh, that did not sound sincere at all. I'm sorry, Sam. I did not mean that; it's just…"

"Now who's talking too much?"

They both laughed as they stopped at a junction looking ahead, left and right.

"It's your ballgame, girl. Which way?"

"My instructions were repeated several times then memorized. Mother Superior did not want a paper trail. I guess they do not use shredders here."

"My, oh my. You are getting quite a saucy way about you."

"Must be you rubbing off on me."

Sam nearly choked, missing a step.

"Left. It is left at the next juncture. Then straight. Remember that."

"How are your parents? Have you seen Mrs. H? Is she well? I imagine she is a bit pissed off not knowing where I am. She really likes to keep track of my comings and goings."

"Everyone is fine. Mrs. H will get over it. Nothing can be done now." Anne kept trudging along with Sam in tow. At last they came to the next juncture and both turned left, not missing a beat. Fifty minutes passed until they reached the next one and kept moving straight.

"Now?"

"Our exit, I believe. If the calculations are correct. We should be coming to a dead end shortly."

Then there it was.

Feeling along the wall for a loose board and locating it, Anne pressed against the side panel and it opened. Peering out slowly, she hastily glanced both directions, making sure the coast was clear. "It's an alley. This is good. I can smell the salt air off the water. We are close. That is what she told me to expect. Dammit, we have done it."

Sam patted her on the shoulder while closing the panel. Then halted as they stood face to face.

"So?"

"We head toward the water. A boat is waiting. Let's shut off the flashlights. We look a bit suspicious with them still turned on and street lights here as well. Someone may think we are bandits."

"Now, that's my girl. If you were truly modernized, you'd have used burglar or thief."

"Very funny. Look, I see it. The boat we are to board. It is just over there. It is the Lady Ru."

Sam glanced at the modern, sleek longboat with crisp white sails and smiled. Yes, this era's technology was good indeed. "Looks like a fine one. I'm ready. Let's go find the captain and get on board. The sooner we are sailing up the Red Sea the better."

He was leaning against the ship's side chewing on something. As they approached, he shifted but did not move. Sam could not help but smile as they neared.

"Clash. Damn, it's good to see you. Are you sailing on this lovely vessel with us?"

"Yup, sure am. Who's your companion?" He could not seem to take his eyes off her. Anne's cheeks flushed a bright pink as Sam bit her tongue to stop a laugh.

"Anne, this is Derek Clash. Derek, this is Anne Baker." Sam nudged her forward, spotting the captain coming their way. "You two excuse me for a second."

"Arnesen?"

"Yes, Skipper, with two companions. I believe you are expecting us."

"Indeed. Grab them and board. We shove off as soon as you do."

Sam glanced about, noticing a police car parked in an alley too close for comfort. "I see that."

He already knew it was there. "This is not the time nor the place to hang out. Get a move on." He turned and left her there, striding up the gangplank. She rushed over to Anne and Clash.

"Hurry. We need to get on board. They are preparing for departure."

As they neared, a shipmate approached. "Best you three follow me. We are motoring off. Once the sails are set and we are away from the harbor, you can come above deck. Until then, it's the captain's orders you remain below." He stopped at a small wooden door, opening it up. "You two will share this berth." Then he opened the door opposite. "This is yours." He nodded to Clash. "You will be advised when it is safe to leave them."

Three sets of eyes watched him disappear up the small steps. "Feels a bit like a pirate ship I was once on. Well, not quite a pirate ship but a Viking ship. Come to think of it, this is nearly a replica except that one was larger and wider and this one is more like a raiding longboat. What do you think, Clash?"

He was listening to Sam, but watching Anne. "Sounds like another story unfolding in that mind of yours."

He slid his bag inside the small room, closed the door and ushered them into theirs. It housed twin beds and a porthole. "This looks efficient enough for your needs. We should not be on board more than twenty-four hours before mooring off the coast of Jeddah. From there it is forty miles or so to Mecca."

He turned back toward the women.

"Do you have appropriate clothing for the crossing?"

"I have my burka so I can get into Mecca. But, Anne, we need one for you. It is off limits to anyone that's not a Muslim."

"I wondered why this was in my bag when I arrived at the monastery. Now I know." She unzipped it and removed the heavy, dark cloth. "I see yours is just as ugly as mine. Good, we will be Muslim sisters."

They both laughed as Sam observed Clash and Anne darting glances at one another. She was properly amused. Try as they would, Sam knew someone upstairs had planned their meeting just like they were watching hers and Adam's.

"This will do." Sam broke between them. "I'm ready for a bit of shut-eye."

Clash took the bait.

"Well, ladies, I have some work to do. See you up on deck later. If not, tomorrow. It will be an interesting transfer into Mecca after we land. Sam, got a second?"

She followed behind him and closed the door, whispering, "Why don't you ask her yourself?"

He eyed her and smiled. "No, not that. I do not have time for it. But she is cute. Albeit a bit too young. I was surprised to see you. Exactly where are you headed in Mecca? You know if you do one thing wrong there, you will be thrown in prison and never seen again. I have a strong hunch I'm to stick around and make sure you both get along your way."

"We are going to meet a master craftsman who's going to put the jewels I borrowed back where they belong. I have a contact to find when we get to the market on

Saturday who will take me to him. After that, I have no idea. But I fully plan on keeping myself concealed, as well as Anne. I've got to watch out for her. I think her exit will come there and mine will continue along."

"Good. I'm following another story. I'll see you two where you need to go since it's in my direction. That was not made clear to me until I met a source who redirected my travels."

"Filling in the blanks. I get it." Her hand was on the doorknob. "Okay, great. See you when I see you. Glad it worked out for Edge and the guys back there."

"Yeah, I'm sure he is too." He grinned, repeating her exact words. "See you when I see you." Turning away from one another, they both entered their respective rooms and closed the doors.

Quite comfortable, relaxing on her now chosen bunk, Anne seemed lost in thought. Sam knew. She was already replacing the face of that cute young man back in England with the handsome, older face of Derek Clash. Presenting her back, feigning a look through her bag, she wondered just how long it would take them.

Chapter Seven

The only light shining in through the porthole was from the moon streaming in. "Is he single?"

"Look at you. Just a few days away from home and your thoughts wander." Sam smiled, turning over onto a side, puffing up the wafer-thin pillow. "I see well enough what is going on here. He could not take his eyes off you even as he spoke to me. Then again, maybe you did not notice. But the color on your cheeks even now would indicate indeed you had."

Anne's flush increased. Sam could not help jabbing. This was no crush. It had the stirrings of true love and it was written on both their faces.

"Shut up and sorry I asked. Anyway, I can say anything I want. Here you are not my boss. This time you need me."

They both laughed.

"Yup, and I'd take full advantage of it too if I was you. He's headed, by the way, along with us tomorrow to make sure we get to Mecca safely. I think he deviated for some reason. Perhaps it was you and not me. For now, I will take your advice and shut up. I'm going to get some sleep."

"Good night, Sam." Anne flicked off the battery-operated light.

"Pleasant dreams, Anne."

The night passed in a rush as the bell above deck rang twice. Sam was already up, washed and changed into jeans and a T-shirt when Anne's eyelids fluttered open. "What's that noise? We in some kind of danger?"

"I haven't got a clue. Let me knock on Clash's door and see if he knows."

She turned the knob, pulled their door open and was startled to see his smiling face filling the frame. "Breakfast is ready for anyone that is interested. The second mate came down last night and told me when the bell rings twice, we can go above deck. It means we are now in safer waters. I think fresh air would benefit us all."

"Great! Let me get her moving. Can you hang out a few minutes?"

His glance maneuvered around Sam's body, watching intently as Anne shuffled around like a mad hen. "Yeah, sure. I'll be right here." He pointed to the very spot his shoes were routed.

"You even wake up a smart-ass. I like it." She grinned, closing the door and taking in Anne's appearance.

"I'm ready. I did not think he'd see me in the corner behind the door."

"Well, perhaps he did through the crack?" Sam produced a huge grin.

"I hate it when you say something that makes so much damn sense. Like always. It infuriates me in a way that I don't catch on quicker by now."

"You skin will get thicker as you get older and get more experiences under your belt. You do leave yourself wide open for my comments. I don't mean to keep picking on you, though. I'll try to curtail it. But it may be difficult seeing you two clearly have a connection already in the works."

She opened the door and smiled back over her shoulder. "We can eat then go above deck. The captain's given Clash the all clear. Are you hungry?" Sam was trying to release the friction in the air between the two of them. 'Like it or not, Clash,' she wanted to verbally declare, 'you are interested in the chit.'

Instead she pointed her thumbs in opposite directions, inquiring which way.

He nodded, leading as Anne shut the door. He opened one further down after listening to the sound of loud male voices. "I sure as shit hope I have the right berth." They all shared a laugh as he opened it farther.

"Ah, you brought us sunshine this morning." One of the crew spoke openly. "Come in. Don't hover over there, ladies. We have space for you and your gent at the end of the table. The food is hot. You can lie while you all eat and tell the cook here how fantastic it really is."

That set the tone for the day.

"Will the captain be joining us?" Sam was more than curious.

"No, he eats in his cabin with the first and second mate so they can go over charts."

She nodded, in a way glad. "How far are we from Jeddah?" She was rarely shy around anyone.

"Mistress, about three hours at our speed. We have a strong north wind and are making good time."

She shoveled a heaping portion of eggs into her mouth and then sipped on the hot tea. "This is good."

Anne too was breaking out of her shell as Sam focused keen eyes on her two traveling companions. "It is good; my thanks to you, Chef."

He rose. "I appreciate your comments. Well, duty calls. I understand you are leaving us today. Safe travels." They all watched him leave the room, tugging slightly at his belted trousers. Turning before exiting, he produced a pearly white smile, saluted and then left the cabin.

Everyone remaining in the room broke out in laughter. One of the crew members spoke up. "Mighty fine of you to say that, ladies. You possibly made his day. Perhaps his good mood will keep and tonight he will give us a fine feast."

He glanced over to the rest of the men. "All right, you blokes. Let's get to it before the captain comes below and hurls our asses overboard for not doing our jobs." The crew rose and exited, leaving them to their own devices.

"I don't know about both of you, but I'm stuffed. A spot of fresh air in my lungs is needed. I'll leave you two. Join me when you are through." Sam stood, not looking at either one, and rushed from the room, a sly grin on her face. "Welcome, Anne," she released softly while heading toward the stairs, "to the grown-up world of dalliances and desires."

The steps pitched high as she clung tightly to the boards, heaving up the last few. At mid-ship, Sam viewed the magnificent longboat. She was at full sail. Crisp white canvases filled with wind expanded out beautifully above. Pitching at quite an angle, the distinct sound of wood on water brought a flashback to Sam's mind of another beautiful sailing vessel.

It was Egyptian.

Much to her liking, no one paid her any heed as she continued along to the bow, holding fast to the railing. The sea was a brilliant blue and sparkled like highly faceted diamonds as the early morning sun beat down. It was going to be hot today, she thought, releasing a peaceful sigh into the evaporating mist off the water. Mentally, she made a note to remind Anne they both would need to don those awful burkas before going ashore.

But right now she would enjoy the saltiness on her tongue and the moistness on her face. Reaching into her pocket, she took out a pair of dark black Oakleys and slid them on. They cut back on the sun's glare and afforded her a better view of the sandy shoreline off in the distance. Long, inviting stretches of palm tree-lined beaches greeted her observation as other vessels of varying sizes trudged along in their own shipping lanes.

Dozens of other ships, some cargo, dotted the horizon along this chartered way. Her curiosity was piqued as to what Jeddah would look like. She knew absolutely nothing about the demographics of Saudi Arabia. But something about being in the Middle East was stirring deep emotions inside. The two companions below deck were now long forgotten.

***

"You don't have to be shy around me. The best way to get to know someone is simply by talking."

"I'm just new to a lot of things. I don't even know what to call you to get a conversation going."

"Derek, and see, you just started one."

Anne smiled as he took in her pretty features. Damn that Sam. This was not the right time at all.

"Okay, let me ask you how long have you been involved? Where are you really from?"

"England. I'm from 2018. In essence the future."

"Wow, Derek, that's really cool. I have not met anyone from that period. Do you actually know in advance when you will be leaving and where you are going?"

"I sure do. Don't you?"

"Not all the time, no. I just get an idea in my head of what I need to bring. Not where. Is that unusual? Did you start out that way?"

"Everyone's baptism into this is different. Seems like you are handling it all in stride. So how old are you?"

She laughed. "In this year, I'm well dead."

He grinned. "I set myself up for that one."

"Twenty-three and from 1865 England."

"Well now, you do look exceedingly well, don't you? Does your family know about all of this?"

"Yes. My parents were both 'involved' at one point or another. But since, both have retired. We own a bakery in Shrewsbury. Where in England do you live?"

"London. I'm not familiar with that part of the Isle. Seems like I'm always on the road traveling. But never had an assignment in that neck of the woods. What is your last name?"

"Okay, you are going to laugh. But, what the hell. Everyone else does. It's Baker."

Indeed, he did. "No apologies for that. It is amusing. You have to admit it." He rose, pulling her chair out as she stood.

Anne suddenly turned quite bold. "I hope you don't think it's too forward of me, but I hope our paths cross again after this. I hear when a task is completed it is normally c'est la vie."

Both brows raised. "You never know." He wanted to smooth his hands around her saucy little butt and help her up the steep steps. But possibly she'd not see the humor in it as Sam would. "You got this?"

"I think so. Man, this ship is really pitching. We must be making good time."

Both stood on deck, glancing about for Sam.

"How about we go this way and see if we can locate her?" He'd seen her hair blowing up at the bow, but led Anne to the aft.

"This is beautiful. Have you been back and forth to this area often?"

"Yes. I seem to get a lot of itineraries that lead me in this direction. I'm a reporter and cameraman rolled in to one so it's convenient for me to do most of my work alone. You know. It's a lot safer that way. Most of my passages involve needing coverage media of some sort. Although this time I used Sam as the reporter and I as her cameraman to do most of what was required."

"It's a lot more complicated with some. Like Sam, you and Lord Griffin. You all seem to take on higher, more important roles than I do. Did you start out where you are?"

"I did. Who is Lord Griffin?"

"He's the reason Sam came from her era to ours. I think she may be permanently in my time now. I am not sure how that's even possible. Even her first passage was harder than all of mine combined. Even this one has not proven to be difficult or challenging at all." One hand clutched the rail, preventing it from smoothing back an unruly strand of her soft hair.

"Remember, we all have a role to play. Think of it this way. We are all part of a cog. If one is broken or missing, the whole operation stops. No matter what your task is, it is equally as important as the rest of ours."

She stopped, placing a hand on his bare arm. It was warm to the touch. It was right then he wanted to kiss her. But he refrained. What had gotten into him? This was not the chit's fault; she was young and did not know the ways of the world, let alone men and relationships yet.

"So Sam and Lord Griffin are friends?"

"Friends with benefits is what I've heard people say here."

He laughed loudly as a coy smile appeared across her lovely lips. "Was that not appropriate? Because it is true."

"No worries. It is quite in with modern times. In truth, I've not run across anyone like her. I know you can dally in an era. But I thought it was important to not hang about or you could get caught up and stuck there. Interesting. So, what do you think of the Red Sea?"

"It's really beautiful. Oh, I see Sam. Do you think we should go up there?" He did not glance over his shoulder, already knowing her whereabouts. A strong gust of wind blew Anne's hair about and he caught a small amount, allowing it to sift through his fingers.

"Sam's a strong lady. I think we both recognize that. You will come into your own as time moves on." Clash extended his hand to keep her from falling against the rocking and rolling of the ship, but she shook her head to ward further actions off.

"Come on," Anne insisted, "let's join her."

***

Glancing briefly at them both, Sam was pleased by what she saw. Excellent. There had been progress. Staring off the port side, she could see the high-rise buildings become more visible and knew their next destination loomed on the horizon. This stop would bring them all to more choices, more answers and hopefully closer to the master craftsman and that book she so needed to get her hands on when her boots hit dry land.

On the wind, even from this distance nearly two miles off shore, the call to prayer was clear and distinguishable. Intently, they all locked gazes as her two traveling companions came up beside her.

"Wow." Sam spoke to them both. "Look at that tower. I thought it was the outer perimeter of the airport. But I see specks of what appear to be yachts. They are using that for the call for those out on the water. This truly is amazing."

In silence, they all watched as the crew sprang out of nowhere like spiders from their caves. They began lowering sails, battening down the hatches and preparing as the motor sprang to life, jerking the boat slightly. Sam steadied Anne at the same time Clash was grabbing on to her other arm.

They all laughed.

"It will be good to get rid of you both. I'm sure I can walk on my own without you holding me like a child." Her voice was stern, a warning that she was indeed growing up beneath their eyes.

They all watched as one of the deck hands approached them. "We anchor in fifteen minutes. Two mates will be taking you and your belongings ashore in the dinghy. Best go and get your gear then regroup above deck."

Back below deck, Sam zipped up her bag, swinging it over her shoulder. "Can't wait to get rid of this thing once and for all. Even now men still control women."

"I've never been in one. I'm already too warm. How do you do it?"

Sam grinned, lifting it up to expose bare legs. "By keeping on as little as possible beneath it. Now finish up and remove what you don't really need and stow it in your bag. I've not heard the anchor drop so be quick about it."

Anne hurried as Sam opened the door, meeting Clash. The sound of grinding metal and splashing signaled the anchor had dropped into the water and they had arrived at Jeddah Harbor.

"You ladies feel stable enough in handling your own gear down to the dinghy?"

Sam nodded, not even bothering to look at the netting they had to climb. Or how the dingy bobbed up and down like an apple in a barrel filled with water. She climbed over and started her descent, pausing upon nearing the water's level. She glanced up to a determined look on Anne's face. 'Bravo, girl!' she wanted to holler out.

As soon as they were all in the dinghy, the crewman started up the motor. As it went from idle to slow speed, everyone's demeanor changed. Three people with three different goals and three different outcomes looming ahead.

Their landing area was moving closer into view as they looked on in awe at the multi-million dollar yachts lined up as if they were a dollar a dozen. Damn, it was indeed the playground of the rich and famous. Greedy and devious. The land of commanding, arrogant men and contained, stifled women.

Chapter Eight

"Wow, is that my ride? I don't know how you are all getting to Mecca, but I'm taking that red Jag." Sam took the outstretched hand of the deck mate, swung her bag around and walked up the boat launch to wait for Anne and Clash.

Anne, positively stubborn, refused Clash's assistance. *Oh my*, Sam thought, *when those two finally hook up, fireworks are going to brighten the sky up to Venus.*

Derek seemed to feel obliged to burst her bubble. "That's not your ride. That is."

Sam did not want to look. "The Lamborghini?"

"No, smart... one... the Rover. But at least it's not rusty and probably has floor boards."

Sam grinned under her burka, taking Anne by the arm. "You aren't going to resist my aid, now are you, little one? You just stick close to me. We need to look like feeble females. The stark reality is we need to remain behind him. Keep quiet until inside the vehicle. He gets in first. Only then can we talk."

The shocked expression in Anne's eyes said it all. She'd had no idea of Middle Eastern etiquette. "Thank the Lord we have these monstrosities; at least it hides my smile."

"Exactly. Stupid men. Don't they realize we are not suppressed at all? Idiots. I am near naked under this and they have no freaking clue. Perhaps that woman over there is not listening to prayer time on her cellphone? Rather, it is vulgar American rap music. Who the hell knows?"

"Stop it. They will hear you."

As soon as Clash was comfortable in the front they slid with their bags inside the back seat and closed their doors. She had already given him their Saudi passports so there would be no issue with him handing them over before exiting the port for entry into Mecca.

That was it. Now she realized why he had rejoined her. *Cool beans*, she thought as the air conditioning blew at full tilt. Its noise was deafening. So loud she had no idea what the conversation was about. But where was his camera? Small as it was, was it tucked neatly into his leather duffle? Lifting her own bag and steadying it, she slid the zipper partially and looked. Damn sneak. He'd taken it apart and portions of it were stowed in her bag. When the hell had he done that? Crept in during the night, heaven forbid, and put it in? She'd bring that up with him later.

Zipping it back, she settled against the distinguished leather seat and refrained from conversing with Anne at all. The scenery was too interesting to even bother. She had never seen so many mosques in all her life. Having been in Istanbul a few times, Sam had no idea they would be pretty much on every street corner. Something akin to Starbucks in the United States.

Ironically, there were no other signs of religious culture outside of this. No crosses adorned ornate Catholic buildings or Russian Orthodox churches. None of the sort. *Wow*, she thought. *This is extreme.* Although she had read in The Guardian Newspaper once that Jeddah was considered a tourist area and fancy resort destination. Signs of that were abundant back in the harbor.

As they passed through a portion of the old part of the city, stopping at a street light, she wanted to put the window down and engage a small group of women clustered in the dark ensemble waiting to cross the street. What were their days like? Were they in university? A private one for women only? What was taught? Would they like to know about her? Did they have pre-arranged marriages already on the books with some bloke better than double their age?

Eyeing Clash up in the front, mouth moving but words not distinguishable, she envied him. Briefly. Imagine that. She envied his sitting in the front seat being allowed to engage the driver in conversation. Learning, asking, receiving and being respected, while they sat back here in silence. Wrapped in a shroud of suppression even though they had a specific reason to be in such a get-up.

Tapping her foot on the floor, Sam's irritation mounted. She wanted to grab the driver by the throat and make him stop. Change seats. Then she would drive like a maniac through the busy area. No, not to hurt anyone. But to take charge. Be in command.

Finally her foot stopped. *There*, she thought. That was better. She felt better. Settling back, she rested her gaze on the passing scenery.

She wanted to learn more. Hoped her master craftsman was amiable and would help to get her hands on what she wanted. First that book and then some other local information.

Then the light bulb lit. She had a story for Clash. Another one.

She glanced up ahead. He did not hear her silent command to look back. Damn, she silently proclaimed, glancing out the window. It would have to wait.

As the old parts of Mecca came into view, she steadied her thoughts and glanced at Anne, nodding. The car pulled down a small, cobbled side street and then halted curbside at a small, white building. Dangling from an iron hanger, the single shingle read: *Quasor Ale Tamaoy*.

Clash got out, bag in hand, and stood to wait for the ladies as he nodded his thanks to the driver. "We have two apartments. I guess I'm here for a spell. Shall we get our keys? Then we can speak privately." He moved ahead of them inside and handed the passports over to a clerk, signed paperwork and was handed keys.

"I've got yours. It is this way."

It was a small boutique hotel appearing to be clean and comfortable. He led them to the elevators and up two floors to their respective apartments, which were opposite each other.

He unlocked their door and placed two keys inside on the table. As he did, he removed a small object and began walking around their rooms until he finished and came back. "You are clear. Let me go take care of mine then I'll return so we can talk. Sam, I think you want to tell me something." He strode out, closing the solid wood door with a thud.

"Which room do you want? I don't know about you, but this damn thing needs to come off now! Hey, look out at the view. We can see parts of the older section." Anne removed her burka and left Sam to find a room.

"How long do you think Derek and I are here?"

So, Derek it now was as Sam came out of her own bedroom. Boots now off and burka long gone.

"No idea. We'll figure that out shortly."

He rapped and entered. "You are to start locking this from now on."

"Oh, but we can't lock it. That is against Muslim law prohibiting our husband to enter at his mighty will."

Anne broke out in laughter as Sam plopped down on a comfy chair. "This place will do, hubby. I applaud you!"

"Cut the shit, woman. Now, what do you want to tell me?"

"That I want a divorce. You are starting to get on my nerves. How did you know I wanted to speak with you about something urgent?"

"Your eyes bore into me on the drive over. What is it?"

***

She leaned forward. Clash sat opposite, beside Anne on the loveseat.

"You are right. I've got some thoughts. I remember women cannot enter Mecca unescorted. But a hubby like you, brother or uncle can bring them in. If they do not adhere to this strict law, then they are moved to a detaining station until exported. So, you are here to help us. But, also to report about oppression that continues today. I recall a fantastic speaker at Oxford, a Professor Livingston, who gave quite a speech on how Mecca has been destroying hundreds of buildings rich with antiquity to make room for new rise hotels so that more pilgrims can come here and be taxed. I believe it's been referred to as the Vegas of the Middle East."

He ran a hand through his hair. "Brilliant! I've got to admit it. Not what I normally report on. But I like the angle. You did all that while in the back seat?"

She grinned. "As we move around Mecca and separate, I'm quite sure I will be halted and detained. More than likely questioned why I am not with you. I can have them call you for verification that you gave your permission and are aware of where I am and what I am doing. I heard that's allowed. We need to make sure that our cellphones are always charged. Volume up or on vibrate at all times."

"Don't you think you should move to London permanently and take over MI6?"

"Oh, I'd love that!" She got up and went to the large window. But she refrained from opening it, knowing how hot it was outside.

"I need to shower. Then we find the craftsman. We have most of the day. But I really need to locate him. In the meantime, Clash, love of my life, why don't you make sure Anne here has all your contact details in her cellphone? She may need a condensed course on how to use it."

"Hold off there, woman. You have a diversion from previous plans. You will not need to go to the market to meet your source. I have been advised by our driver that the master craftsman is a mere two blocks away. I can take you there as soon as you are ready."

Sam jumped up and disappeared in a flash.

"I have to admit that damn burka was uncomfortable. Sam seemed to handle it better. But she's been in one longer than I have." She smiled, placing her phone on the table in front of him. He stared deeply into those beautiful eyes of hers and knew.

"I'll bring this back with me. I think she has the right idea. A quick shower is in order. Then if you need me to show you how to use it I will when I come back."

Anne blushed a cute shade of pink. "Mother Superior showed me at the convent back there."

He laughed as Sam re-appeared. They met in the hall. "I've got a short errand to run after I drop you ladies off at the shop. I wanted you to know up front. That's where I will pick you up, so don't saunter out. I need to ensure we are not being followed or watched. Not that I suspect we are, but nothing about this journey has been normal."

"What's his name?"

"*Ahrmed Abdul Fres Alismaad.* I know. A lot to recall. When you are introduced do not extend your hand or move into his space unless he approaches you first. Just a nod will do. I'll be back shortly. Taking a quick shower and programming that phone." He glanced over, noticing Anne had left the room. "Be ready."

"Yes, dear, I'll make sure we are both back in our burkas. I'll go over some things with Anne before we do."

He nodded, leaving her.

***

Fifteen minutes later he rapped on the door and both women came out, properly attired. They left out the front entrance and turned sharply right around the corner directly into an alley. That seemed to be a large part of her life recently, Sam thought, being in alleys.

It was busy and they were nearly shoved aside by two men carrying a wrapped carpet. Or perhaps it was a dead body, Sam thought, nearly breaking out in laughter. She glanced over at Clash, who seemed to have read her mind.

"Don't say it, woman."

Anne missed that one completely. Just as well. If she had caught on and started to giggle, Sam would have lost it.

There was no shingle over the small wooden door as he opened it. A polished copper bell rang out, announcing their arrival. The small room facing streetside was adorned with shelves filled with holy relics, bracelets, beads and statues. A tourist trap dream come true. They were essential. Pilgrims coming here always found it necessary to pick up dust collectors to take back home. This historical building was well positioned, being one of the last before entering the more modern venue of Mecca.

But how the hell did anyone know of his place? Was this just a cover? Sam stood behind Clash as a younger man came out from behind a woven curtain, moving closer. She recognized what he was saying as he signed in Arabic and Clashed signed back.

"We are here to see the master craftsman. I have something I cannot identify. Rhaoul advised to come and enlist his expertise."

He nodded, hand waving them forward to follow.

Clash needed to make an important point. "My wives cannot be left unattended. I insist they come with me."

Pointing towards a side door, the man turned and left them standing there going back out to the front of the shop.

Knocking once, Clash turned the handle and opened it. Then he stepped aside, allowing the ladies to go ahead.

Eyes nearly bulging out, Sam absorbed this masters interior workshop with stunned amazement. Out front was for street people or goods sold at a stall at the market on the way to *Majid-Al-Haram*. Inside this area was the workings of a true genius.

"Salam, Master Clash. I was expecting you with your wives. Welcome." The craftsman shook his hand and then extended the same courtesy to both women. Sam shook it last, taking in his white linen top and baggy pants. His feet were encased in a nice pair of leather men's sandals. As their hands parted, she set in his a small velvet pouch.

This brought a smile to his weathered, dark face.

"You can rest at ease here, ladies. Although I am a true Muslim, I also adjust to more modern times. Only in this room can I and you meet as equals."

Sam boldly asked, "How would you like us to address you?"

"Use part of my last name, Ali, then the connection to me is hard to make. It's safer for us all just in case." He opened the pouch, sliding gently out the rare gems. "Ah, yes, eleven gems from the New Kingdom. Perfect. You have done well. What is your name?"

"Samantha. Please call me Sam. This is Anne, my traveling companion, and you are already aware of Master Clash."

"Speaking of me, I have someone I need to meet. Would you mind if I left the ladies with you? Or would you prefer I take them and we return at a more convenient time?"

"No, they can stay until you come back. I will be working late tonight. In fact, this process will take me a few days. I need to mix an ancient paste to reinsert them into their proper location. Then it must dry at the correct temperature to remain attached. It may well be a week before this is complete."

"Will they be safe enough to leave and return to our apartments? I assume you know how close we are in proximity to your place?"

"Yes. That will be fine. Should the hour turn late, I will escort them myself. I see no issue with them coming and going. They must remain paired and properly attired."

"Good enough. I will leave you all then. Ladies, I hope to see you later this evening." Clash paused briefly, glancing at Anne before leaving their company.

Ali stepped closer to them both. "You can remove your burkas if you wish. There is tea brewing. Help yourself. Just through those two curtains are the restroom and a small study. Perhaps something in there will be of interest? The other door leads to a shared courtyard with my son and his family. No one else. You met him earlier. He does not speak and has not since birth. So we use sign language with him. Anyway, I think you both will be comfortable while here."

Sam was too nosy to not ask. "I had to admit I was curious but did not want to inquire. About the sign language."

"Ask what you will, Sam. Here we speak freely. I will work away."

"Thank you. Your English is excellent. Did you study abroad?"

"England at Oxford under a good friend and former colleague that has since passed on. I was there the night, Sam, that he spoke and you were in the front row. I remember you."

She was astonished, stammering a reply. "You were?" She could see him now in her mind's eye. "Yes, you were off to his left, sitting at the table that housed his overhead projector. Heavens me. I am by all means without words, Ali."

He laughed as Anne stood back, watching the engagement.

"Why don't you both get settled? I'm sure you will want to see how this process works and have questions. I will be right back. I need to go and retrieve the item these belong on. I shall return in a few minutes."

Sam turned to Anne. "I can't believe sometimes how all this works. You never know who down the road will be involved in your life and in what way. I loved that professor. Every time he gave a talk I was there. Darn amusing how all of that has brought me here. Like I was not being educated for journalism at all. But for this."

"As I listened to you both, I realized how exciting this really is and how special all of us are. We walk between periods, people of all types and places of all kinds and few even know what we are about. It's really dumbfounding."

"I don't think it ever will stop surprising us at all."

"He's pretty cool too. Quite relaxed with us. I don't feel at all threatened by him. I think he's the real deal."

Sam smiled, truly feeling tugged in an opposite direction. "You okay—" She pointed toward the curtain. "—if I ditch you for a few?"

"Sure, go ahead."

It was as if a GPS in her brain was leading her directly to where she needed to be. Examining the books, her hand halted short of picking one up. The few inches of space between fingers and binder sizzled. "Oh, fuck it." She softly spoke, quickly taking it as lightning bolt shivers raced through her entire being. "Oh, my," she barely managed to get out.

"Is that the same one you had read in the monastery library?"

Sam nearly jumped out of her skin, having not heard Anne's arrival.

"Yeah, and it's speaking loud and clear to me. I need to read this. Do you mind? Is there something you can do while I leaf through it?"

"Sure. I am going to take my tea out there in his work area. I want to see what he comes back with. I'm assuming it's a statue of some sort."

That got Sam's curiosity. "I'll go with you. Tea for me can wait. I did see a few large pillows we can relax on in his workshop."

As they settled in, Sam rested on one, removed her boots, crossed her legs and opened the cover, allowing her hands to glide over the old pages gently. She was so engrossed that considerable time had passed before she glanced over to Ali. A broad smile was on his face, but his body blocked what he had been working on from her vision.

Anne was gone. But a slight noise in the direction of the study confirmed the location. Lowering her eyes, she continued to read. It was a particular section on Thutmose III and was fascinating. He was considered the Napoleon equivalent of his era. During this time, he expanded Egypt's army and forged great success to merge their vast empires as Egypt reached its peak in wealth and military domination. He reined 1479 to 1426 BC and many of his artifacts were displayed at the Luxor Museum. Sam had had no idea until now how keenly interested she was in an era so long gone by.

"You realize you've not moved in near three hours? I've come from the room and back in several times, but you only looked at me once. I find you quite interesting and amusing, Sam."

"How do you know that? Do you have eyes in the back of your head?"

Ali laughed. "I knew you would be spirited as well as special. Yes, I have eyes in the back of my head. I have children. They grow there on all parents when our children are born. Or so I have been told by my very own now departed parents."

Sam set the book down gingerly and stood, wincing as both legs quickly cramped. "I don't know. I do not have any of my own. Kids that is. But I always heard it was true. That lurking beneath the hair of our parents were two sets of rear eyeballs. Darn annoying."

He covered the article with a velvet cloth.

"How's it coming? I did not even see what it is."

"You will when it's done. Then you may start to get more interested. Besides, the room is at a perfect temperature and will remain that way until the late night descends upon us." He glanced out one of the side windows. "Which should not be too long. I see you found what you were seeking, at least in the way of that book."

"You scare me. How were you aware that I would be looking for this?"

"You know there is more to your quest than just returning some stones to me. Almost everywhere you go the journey is electrified by multi purposes."

"So you are one?"

"I was until I retired. My wife as well. Alas, my son cannot carry that tradition on. He is indeed a great lad. Very smart. Perhaps someday if we ever move from Mecca to the west, we can get him one of those boxes so we can hear his true voice."

"Can't you reach out to one of your former colleagues and see if any modern operation will help?"

"I have to be very careful, Sam. Everyone here has known him since birth. Should he suddenly speak, they may wonder what else I am up to."

"But they have hospitals here. Can't you use one of them? Oh, Ali, I am so sorry. Naturally, you would seek all possible cures for your son. I apologize."

"Your compassion is nice to hear, my dear Sam. The doctors are convinced internally he is structurally sound. He's never uttered a sound since birth. But they could not find anything wrong that would prevent it. They all think he's 'challenged' and does not want to talk. Another group of skilled doctors told us that it is the will of Allah."

"But he's married and happy, right? So, really it is all okay."

"Yes, but you know as a father I would love to hear him call me or my lovely wife. I'm sure his two young boys would as well."

"I could ask you a hundred questions. But I will mind my business." She glanced up at the old antique brass clock above his work table. "You will need to go home soon and we to our apartment. I have not even engaged Anne all day in conversation. What time can we come back?"

"I have a meeting at a synagogue in the morning. Come anytime after twelve noon. That will be fine. I think tomorrow it will just be you and me." He winked, bringing a profuse grin to her face as Anne came back into the room.

"I put away the dishes we used, Ali. I hope they are in the right place. It seems my friend, who has abandoned me all day, is finally up and alive? Well, that's good to see!"

Sam smiled warmly and took her by the arm after putting her boots and burka back on. She noticed Anne was fully attired and ready to head back to their shared apartment. Sam set the book upon the table next to where she'd spent most of the afternoon. "Is it okay there?"

"It will be waiting for you when you come back." He walked them out of his room, through the shop and opened the door to that now familiar chime of the copper bell. "Good night, ladies. Go right to your apartments. I give you permission to leave here without an escort. If anyone delays your return home, you advise them I allowed you to go."

Sam clasped Anne by the arm and the ladies quickly walked down the alley and around the corner, up the few steps and into their apartment building. Not uttering a word, she unlocked their door and entered, sliding the bolt. She half expected an immediate knock from Clash. But it did not come.

Both women made quick work of removing the burkas.

"He will let us know when he's back, I'm sure."

"You caught that. I need to start hiding my emotions and what I am doing a whole lot better than I have."

"You are still learning. Hell, so am I. No problem. Anyway, are you hungry? I can't believe I had my nose in that book for so long. I am absolutely starved. How about I see what I can rustle up for food in case he is delayed?"

"Tomorrow when we go I need to bring some things. I did not want to eat the food he had. But I sure drank enough of his tea."

Sam laughed. "Okay, and make sure I eat. The last meal I had was on board the ship. Oh shit, I can't believe this. The refrigerator is completely empty. Not even a water. Look up in those cupboards and see if there is anything."

Anne flung them open and then shut. "Nope, not a morsel even for a mouse. Now, what do we do?"

"Crap." Sam peered out one of the two large kitchen windows. "Two blocks down appears to be a small market. Do we dare?"

"We must. I can't be held up here with no food or I'm going to be looking for one of your arms."

"Okay, let's get dressed. Check your purse and see if you have any local currency."

Sam finished dressing. Anne was well ahead of her. "I do! Grab the keys and let's get the hell out of here. I'm not joking. I really am hungry."

One head above the other, streetside door partially cracked, they peered out towards their route. Sam spoke softly. "Thank heavens it is quiet this evening. We need to rush or they may close before we get there."

They scurried like two river rats, darting looks back and forth, arms clutched tightly. They finally turned a corner and went down an alley that brought them straight into the square where plenty of stalls were still present.

"What if they are men? Do we engage them in conversation?"

"I doubt we will see anything but men. They don't let their women do a damn thing here. I'll take control. Point at what we want."

They passed through as Sam did indeed do that. Anne had her wallet out, ready to hand over the money. As they accumulated several paper bags of food, they stopped and eyed each other, nearly breaking into giggles. When the apartment door closed, only then did they dare to speak.

"I felt like we were going to be halted at any second. Oh, my God. That was fun. Truly my heart was pounding so hard I could feel it clear to my throat."

"Oh, Anne. We need to go out together more often. Truthfully, I felt the same way. I would not have been able to speak if we were stopped. I did not even know what I would have said. Damn that Clash for abandoning us." She laughed, heaving the burka onto a chair and not caring as it slid off down to the floor. "Let's get this put away and start cooking. At least we have food for tomorrow morning to take to Ali's."

"I've learned another really big lesson today, Sam. That's not to leave your future to any man. He would have us starve to death. That damn jerk."

"I'll remind you of that when he does come by and your face flames pink for what you are thinking."

"Ignoring that. Wish we had some wine. I could sure use a glass about now."

Sam pulled it out of the last sack, saving the surprise. "Get a couple of glasses. If we can't find a corkscrew, I'll break the damn top of the bottle. This will not stop us."

Anne's hand shot out. "Give it over. I have one."

Sam started cooking vegetables, rice, and lamb and when they sat down half the bottle was gone. "I should have gotten two but I did not want to push my luck. He'd better show up sooner or later. I'm going to need something much stronger than this."

But later, when dishes were done, wine finished and they said goodnight at their bedroom doors, Sam really had to wonder where he had gotten to. She knew he was working the story, but they had not heard from him at all. She hoped he was okay.

Getting up out of bed, she opened the room-darkening shade, pulling it to the side. What was wrong with her? Twice now she'd felt strange. As if a possession was taking place. She dared not mention this to anyone again. She needed answers and needed them soon. Or face the fact she was slowly going insane.

Chapter Nine

"Good day, Ali. I hope we are not too early? I woke with the birds this morning." Sam knew it was just before noon.

"This is perfect timing." He glanced over, taking in the somewhat anxious look on Anne's face. "Go ahead, dear, make a pot of tea for all of us. Make yourself right at home. I bet your friend is going to ignore you again today." His smile engaged both ladies as he watched Anne leave the room and turned back towards Sam. "Having trouble sleeping? Anything you want to talk about while I work?"

"No, nothing in particular. I'll just grab my favorite book and keep reading. I'm nearly three-quarters through and getting to the good stuff."

"You go about it then. A few more days and this will be done. Then you can pick up and continue along on your journey."

She smiled, shifting her boots off and settling in as Anne produced mugs of the hot, sweetened tea for them. "I'm going to be in the courtyard if either of you needs me." The room turned silent with the exception of slight noises coming from Ali's direction. Soon, she heard nothing at all as the words of the book enveloped her thoughts.

It was well after the lunch hour had come and gone when Sam's breath caught in her throat. It was only an artist's rendition, but the soldier drawn encompassed a full page. He did not just appear larger than life; he *was* larger than life. Her eyes misted over. Those eyes bore into her soul, penetrating so deeply, suddenly, she was gasping for breath.

She glanced up briefly to Ali, who had turned around and was looking at her questioningly. She nodded she was fine as the book slid from her hands to the floor.

Yet, it remained on that very page housing the artistic rendition. Her eyes raked him over. In her mind's eye, he was clear. About six two, dark, cropped hair that bordered between brown and black. But it was his eyes. Handsome, sinful and gorgeous. Or dark orbs of destruction. Oh yes, she knew him and knew him well. What had happened to them? Gingerly picking the book back up and flipping to the next page, she continued reading.

Ranofer Aiemapt was better known as Rano the Mercenary. One who moved quickly through the ranks and into the household as a second general during the reign of Thutmose III, his allegiance was never in question and his intelligence far outweighed all that would see him thwarted. His creation of the mighty sword of power brought Egypt's army from strong and mighty to mighty and supreme. This sword, his creation, changed the way armies fought from that moment onward.

Although the picture was a rendition, she honed in on how the stones were aligned. Raising her head up, eyes boring into the back of Ali, her mouth moved but no words came out.

"You reached it, didn't you?" Not halting his progress, he continued placing the next stone into the setting. It was indeed beautiful. A large lapis lazuli.

"Yes," she stammered out.

"Have you figured out any more?"

"I know him, or, I did."

He turned then, walking towards her, and stopped, hovering over her, glasses sliding down his strikingly crooked nose. "You did. Keep reading. If you feel like you need something strong to drink you let me know. I keep it in my right draw over there."

She nodded as he went back to work.

She read on. "General, mercenary and charioteer, Rano's mighty ability to lead the Pharaoh's armies was unparalleled by any other. He commanded respect from all his men and delivered uncanny results in battle. Some say he was a god himself, for who could be so powerful and live through so many battles?

"But Rano was not invisible to enemy eyes nor their spies. His mortal blow came at the end of Thutmose III's reign when a poisoned arrow took the soul from his body as it pierced straight through his heart.

"Sages and alchemists tried in vain to save him. But they could not. It was later documented and word of mouth stories handed down through the generations that this monumental occurrence was caused by his one true love. During his final breaths, in a horrific moment, she had cried out in anguish. Then rose, they said, as if in a dream state and removed an article of great importance from the fierce warrior and left him there, vanishing into the night.

"It was claimed she never returned to see him wrapped in true honor. She never returned to mourn him properly. She never returned to give him peace. It is said that his ghost still haunts the lands where his body was wrapped and laid to rest in *Wadi el Muluk*–The Valley of the Kings."

Oh, my God, she thought, *this was me. I left him. I fought with him about his last battle. Telling him if he led, he would die. I had seen a vision of him lying on the ground in his own blood surrounded by his men. A large arrow protruded through him.* She gasped out loud, standing, grasping the book in her hand. It was him. He was speaking to her. Commanding her to this day, this hour, to come back to him. All these thousands of years he had been waiting for her before he could have a final rest, a peaceful ascent to the heavens. Damn it!

"Ali, how soon can you finish? I really need to move on."

"Yes, I know. Now you know. He will wait a few more days if he's waited this long, my anxious friend."

"I can't stand here and just do nothing. Can you finish it and have it sent to me? Can I see it now? I know what it is; it's his sword. Do you think if I touch it I will perish right into dust before your eyes?" Her voice was close to breaking as Ali clutched her shoulders in his strong hands and gave her a solid shake.

"No, you will not perish. You must bring this to him. All the rest is up to you."

A potent shiver ran right through her body electrifying the entire room as Anne appeared with Clash in tow. "Hey, look who's decided to come back."

Strained eyes looked over at the two of them. Sam felt faint. She let Ali keep a tight grip on her as the blood started pumping back from her heart through cells to her brain.

"Hey, I had no idea you had missed me that much." But Clash's voice did not hide his deep concern at what was going on. "Sam? What is it? Is it happening again?"

Ali stepped between them all, putting up a physical barrier.

"We'd better let her have some time to herself. I'm going to walk her out to the courtyard for some fresh air. Why don't you take Anne out? I'm sure she'd like to get around a bit and stretch her legs. Everyone has been cooped up. I'll make sure she gets back when it is time. Don't worry about her. She has had some startling news today and just needs to digest it."

It was as if Sam was in a trance. Head bobbing, she nodded in agreement. The book tightly grasped in one hand, Ali's arm draped over one shoulder, he led her firmly from the room and outside into the hot day. Sitting her down in the protected courtyard, his right palm rested upon the top of her head as if it was vaporizing out any unwanted thoughts. Straight out her crown chakra all negative energy.

***

As they walked out toward the courtyard they passed into the book room. Clash still could not get out of his head what just occurred. "What the hell is up with her? Has she been like this since I left?"

"I don't know and no. That was damn weird. But what I can tell you is that she has been reading this book she had seen back at the monastery and had wanted to get her hands on it. Something spooky about it, I must say. She had a strong reaction to it when she was looking at it back then. Strangely enough, Ali has a copy and she's been reading it for days. She's been fine up until now. Something today must have stirred a memory for her. But I don't know any more than that."

"I think I need to find out what that book was. It's this room, right?"

Anne nodded.

"Come on, let's see if they put it back."

They had, but hadn't pushed it all the way in on the bookshelf. Clash took it out and leafed through it after reading the title. It meant nothing to him, nor did holding it cause any strange internal messages. "Well, I don't know. I guess we wait this one out. Do you want to go back to the apartment and do anything before I take you for a stroll around the old quarters? That may be more enjoyable than hanging out in the courtyard. She's in good hands. It seems Ali needs to spend some time with her now, not us."

"Well, okay. I'm just a bit concerned. But I agree that Ali is who she needs. I'm all set. We do not have to go back to the apartment. I'd like nothing more than a walk. I sure do appreciate my freedom now that I've been here a few days."

He led her outside and down the alley into the light crowd moving around. "Sorry about abandoning you ladies, but Sam's ideas on a storyline paid off big time. I got some interesting details and private film. Once I head out of here, I can combine it with my story and get it out to the proper people. Did you guys manage to get some food? I never checked if you were stocked before I left."

"We were fine venturing out to the market. There were a few women there without chaperones, so we felt comfortable enough. But both of us were concerned at not hearing a word from you."

He took her arm over his. "You both were?"

She smiled up into his dark eyes. "Yes, that is what I said. Stop fishing. It's just a matter of time before I tell you this, so I may as well be brazen and do it now. I like you, Derek Clash. So there. Out of my Victorian shoebox and smack into this century."

He chuckled. "Not bad. Leave you for a few days and you grow a few. I should have stayed away a bit longer. Who knows what I would have gotten?"

"I have not grown a few, as you say. Well, maybe I have! But all the same, I'm more open to seeing a bit more of you so I can decide, if I ever run into you again, if I might be interested in other things."

She grinned as he stumbled slightly. "Missy, you watch it. In public, we can't have that kind of talk."

"You started it, but yeah, I know. It needs to be saved for another time. Heaven forbid we actually look like we are having a good time in this very old-fashioned male dominated country."

"You've been around her way too long. We need to get you away before any more rubs off on you."

"What we need is to get her along on her journey. But after seeing what little I did this afternoon, I wonder if mine is coming to an end and Sam's is just getting more intense."

"You could very well be right. I think it's concluding for us both. I can feel it. So we'd better spend as much time together as we can."

"Well, let's start with hunger. I want food. Sam has been so caught up, Ali along with her, that a full meal has passed. I dared not leave her and go back to the apartment to eat. Glad I did not, or I would have missed you coming over that wall."

"I knew that was a better access in for me than the front one. It was closer. I had no idea you would be sitting right there waiting for my arrival."

"Man, you sure do have a big ego. I was not waiting on you nor pining away. Just glad to see you. Does that deflate it now?"

"Nope. A man knows what he knows."

"No comment. There is a local eatery up there. You think it is okay for us to go in since we just heard the evening call to prayer?"

"If they are open then they are not doing it either, so let's go for it. I hope you like traditional Middle Eastern food."

She wanted to punch his arm but he held tight. "I'd say something, but I am too much of a lady for that. Although under this full burka I could; they would not see my mouth moving."

"Look at that woman over there." Clash found this strange. "She's not in a full dress. But with a male. That's odd. They are so strict in Saudi in general, but especially in Mecca."

"Her head scarf is beside her purse on the next seat. I thought the same thing. Must be in here things are a bit more relaxed. I'm not going to remove mine just in case."

"Never know. Especially hearing about those women from Nigeria that were detained at the airport. They were in full burka but none traveled with male escorts. No one could find any fault with their documents, but they were detained for four days at the airport and not allowed out at all. They were cooped up like savages in one small room and had to have someone go with them to the lady's room. They had no privacy. Then, they were put on board a plane back to their country with a warning to never come again without a male escort."

Her jaw dropped open. "I have to watch what I say, but Derek, that's just awful. Even in my time women are treated a thousand times better than in this day and age. Why, look back to ancient Egypt. Cleopatra ruled with an iron hand. People worshiped her. You have to wonder where it all went wrong."

"True, so what do you want to eat?"

"Anything. I am starved. Just order for me."

The waiter appeared and took care of them. He brought a pot of tea and pita with hummus. Once their meal arrived they ate in silence until the bill was paid.

"It's dark; let's head back. Saudi has a complete ban on alcohol. It is strictly prohibited. So we are out of luck in having any after-dinner drink."

She smiled. "Is that so? Dictated according to the Koran, right?"

"What are you up to?"

"Nothing, well…" As they reached the busier street and the final call to prayer came, she leaned closer to him. "When we went to the market we were able to secure it. House made. I know the man we bought it from near the market. Want to stroll there?"

"And get arrested?"

"Well, want to try? I'm escorted by my husband, right?"

"Bold and brassy. What the hell, let's give it a whirl."

When they neared the stall, Anne stood back as Clash spoke in Arabic to the gentleman. Some currency was exchanged and then all she could see was a large paper bag. Out of the top was a large bunch of greens, which she recognized as he came closer. Brilliant, she thought.

"Wow, that was great. See, told you it would work. But I have to admit the spinach out the top is a perfect touch."

She walked slightly behind him, not speaking until they passed into the apartment corridor and reached her and Sam's door. Sliding in the key, she closed it but did not engage the lock in case Sam came.

He secured two glasses, popped the cork and poured each of them a glass. "Hey, check her room and see if she's just lying down."

Anne rapped lightly on her closed door. There was no reply so she opened it slightly.

"She's not back. I'm worried, Derek."

He handed her a glass. "Me too. But I believe in her and Ali. They must be going over something of importance or he'd have brought her here by now. Let's see what tomorrow brings. Especially concering breakfast. If she's not back by then we can stop and get some food and tea for her. That may help her out, plus it is right on our way. I stopped in there the other day."

They walked into the living room and sat side by side on the sofa. Anne slid off her boots, burka long gone, and curled up her legs, turning toward him. Together they clinked their wine glasses. "To Sam, this passage and that it brought me a new friend."

"I agree."

They sipped their wine, settling in, quiet for a few seconds. Setting his down and going over to the writing desk, Clash took out a piece of paper, hastily scribbled down a few things and came back, handing it to her.

"Here, my contact details. You never know. When you get back that cellphone will surely disappear."

She slid them into her pants pocket. "Do you have someone special back in England?"

"Nope. Long ago I did, but she's relocated for good. The other one was not one of us and that got ugly real fast.

You know how it goes. You can't explain why you are away so much and how you don't know when you will be back. She naturally figured I had women all over the place."

"And you could have. If you move between several of the same places often enough. Like today's pilots, right?"

He laughed. "Yeah, I guess I could. But I'm never anywhere that long to get a chance."

"So we have reached the awkward time, I think. Well, not that, but strange. What do we do now? We could be parting ways as early as tomorrow."

"Yeah, and since I can't just pick up a phone and ring you, things stay status quo."

"Oh well." She finished off her wine and picked up his glass. "Want another?"

"Sure, why the hell not just in case she does return tonight. You mind?"

"Nope, not at all." She rose, took them to the kitchen and refilled them. "It's near eleven. I almost feel like she's ditched us. Something of the utmost importance must be going on with her."

"Yeah, I think so too. If nothing after I finish this, I'll head."

But Sam did not return.

He rose, setting down his empty glass on the tabletop. "I'll see you tomorrow. What time do you want to go over?"

"Nine, if that works, and let's stop at that shop before we do."

"You got it." He leaned down and planted just one slight kiss on her lips. Smiling, he closed the door behind him and grinned as he walked the short distance to his own door. He heard Anne slide the deadbolt in place.

Chapter Ten

"No Sam at all. I sure hope she had a good night. Perhaps it just got too late and she did not want to come in, thinking she'd wake me."

"We hopefully will soon find out. Here we are. Hang out just inside. I'll order for us all and we can get over to Ali's. I'm sure you want to see what's up just as much as I do."

It was a busy place this morning as Anne leaned against a vacated wall. All the women that came in were in full burkas. *Good*, she thought. *If I am forced to suffer with this awful thing, then you should too.* As the second call to prayer resonated throughout Mecca, the shop suddenly emptied out.

Clash appeared before her with a couple of white paper bags. "Normally I would not ask, but do you mind opening the door?"

"What happens if they are too sick to get up in the morning and can't make it?"

"They slide to the floor on special rugs and pray there." As the bell chimed their arrival, she followed him, nodding to the son, and kept on going.

Already at work at his desk, Ali stopped to greet them. "Shalom. It was a rough night, but she's better this morning. I stayed up with her until she demanded I go upstairs. Regardless, I am sure she will be happy to see you both. You brought food. Good. She hardly touched anything my wife sent down last night."

Anne nodded, leading the way into the courtyard. Sitting in a corner facing one of the fountains, burka nowhere in sight, Sam seemed at ease with her feet up. Placing the bag down and removing tea and bagel, Clash nodded Anne over to another table in case Sam wanted to remain alone.

"How was your night?"

"Pretty good. You want some company?"

"Love it. You both sit down." It was as if a light switch had been turned on, illuminating the room. She was better now, as if she had settled comfortably on a massive conclusion.

"This is the ticket. Thanks, guys." She lifted the lid, smelled the lovely Earl Gray she loved so much and tipped it up in acknowledgement of them thinking about her.

"You two are headed out today."

"We are?"

Sam grinned, slanting her upper body closer to them both. "Yup, both of you. You got a surprise awaiting as well. But I can't give that away. When you are finished with breakfast, head back, pack and go outside. A car and driver will be waiting. Just go with the flow, my friends."

"But what about you? What are your plans?"

"Ah, you know I can't tell you. But I'm here one more night and then I am on my way as well." She locked eyes with him, "You got your business done, didn't you? It's great, I can tell. I think you need some time off to play, don't you?"

He grinned. "Kind of wish I was hanging around. I want to know what you are up to. Seems right suspicious at this time."

"That's the journalist in you. Let him sit back for a spell. You earned it."

"Still, how come you know where we are going and I don't yet?"

"I did not say I know exactly where you are going. Just that you are going. Both of you."

"You mean we have a passage to take together?"

Sam shrugged her shoulders, not being able to confirm that it was a passage at all. "Don't rightfully know.

But you two will be leaving in the same car, I know that much."

"What was in that book? Can you tell us about it now?"

"Nope, it's baggage from long ago. Now, I have to head in that direction and see what turns up next that needs addressing."

"You are not making sense."

"Actually, it's more sense than I've made in a very long time. I don't expect anyone to get it. Hell, I just figured out a lot of it myself. At least I know, and neither one of you had better laugh in my face or add a comment, that I am not crazy. Finally, I see closure on the horizon."

"Shit, it can't be Lord Griffin that you are talking about."

Clash eyed Anne, amused by her language. Yes, the lass had changed.

"It is like a teeter-totter. Yes, it is all about him, yet it has nothing to do with him. That's the best explanation I have right now. Anyway, enough about me. When you get back, go around the rear of the cottage. Take a walk on the path I had cleared until you come to an opening. Go and sit quietly by the statue. I have a hunch you will hear something special."

Anne's eyes pleaded for more. Her mouth opened to follow through, but Sam held up a hand, signaling her to not go there.

"Stop. I know that's a bit strange to say. Just do it and see what happens. You are extremely perceptive. If you are uncomfortable doing that, take someone along you trust to make you feel more at ease. Take that unruly mutt you have at the bakery."

They all laughed. "Okay. That's it. You two are finished here. So, leave me the hell alone." She grinned, rising, and went straight into Clash's strong arms. Hugging him tightly for a brief instance, she moved from them into

Anne's. "I like the fact that I will see you eventually and this is not goodbye."

"I hope you do what you need and are successful so you can come back to us all."

"None of that mush, don't worry. It may be a while. Can you....?"

Anne nodded as Clash picked up all their trash and was holding the door to the inside for Anne to come along. Hesitating, she glanced back over a shoulder as if memorizing Sam's features. "I think I can tell him that. At least he will know I saw you and that you are well."

Sam nodded, sitting down in the chair, waved over her shoulder as the door closed and put her boots back up on the opposite side. Breaking through thick cloud cover above in the sky, the sun streamed down, shining a pure golden beam down upon her. Eyes squinting, it was what she felt more than saw.

His strong hands grasped her waist, thumbs softly caressing bare skin, pulling her closer against his strong, muscular body. She could feel him, his breath warm against the crook of a shoulder. Closing her eyes, chin raising, Sam wound her arms up around his neck, waiting for that kiss to transpire.

Her nostrils flared, inhaling. He smelled of Oud. The familiarity stirred her senses deeply. Yet it had been thousands of years since she had inhaled it. Smoky and strong, the scent wove a sultry net, luring her closer. He was reaching out, reminding her of all the passion they had shared. How could she have buried it so deep? What had happened that caused her to become so possessive, demanding he not fight for his Pharaoh? Do what he had been born for?

A shudder passed as the sun slid back behind a cloud and the lovely warm beam evaporated off her body, up and away, vanishing in the sky. Then realization struck. Again.

What to do about Adam?

She prayed silently to Isis and Thoth that their paths not cross until this was resolved. Hell, she had no idea how it would end. Would she wind up with Rano, dancing on the heavens? Or back in Victorian England dancing in a ballroom? Leaning back and resting her head, she could hear off in the distance car doors opening and closing. *Good*, she thought, *they are now on their way.*

***

Sliding in beside her and closing the rear door, Clash signaled to the driver that they were ready to head off. They drove on, silence resonating throughout the car as Anne looked at him apprehensively. He shrugged, apparently not having a clue what to say. During the drive to Jeddah it continued. Each contemplated the exact second when they would be parted.

Against both their wills.

The driver dropped them off at the same docks, where a smaller vessel awaited their boarding. Climbing the gangplank, still having not spoken, they were greeted by the first mate. "Go below deck. The other travelers are already on board. Your berths are marked. We are preparing to shove off straight away."

Anne muttered a soft "thank you," feeling the pressure of Clash's hand against the small of her back as they descended and stopped at their doors.

Clash halted, leaving just a few inches between them. "I'll throw this stuff inside and come and get you in a few minutes."

Anne nodded, opening her door, and was instantly engulfed in total darkness. As she reached for the battery lantern and turned it up, she saw that a door off in the corner was ajar.

Walking over, she moved through it into a long, mysterious hallway. Glancing back, she gasped. The other door had vanished. A single tear slid down her face to the wooden flooring below. "Damn," she softly mouthed, moving until she saw another door looming up ahead. Turning the knob, she sighed. She was now back in the kitchen of Sam's cottage on Lord Adam's land. Back in her era.

"This must be the first time I'm not happy to actually be home." She spoke with sadness.

"I was hoping for a more optimistic reply from you. I guess I actually have my work cut out for me."

Anne spun around, dropping the bag to the tile floor, and swung herself up into Derek's arms. "I can't believe you are here!" She grabbed his head and pulled his lips down to hers in a searing kiss.

He pulled back slightly. "Wow, well, okay then. Dammit, woman, that was quite a surprise. Now, where the hell am I?"

"You are in my world of 1865 England. This is Sam's cottage. I think someone up there or someplace else is up to monkey business, Derek. Why would you be here with me alone in her cottage knowing full well she will not be returning anytime soon?"

He grinned, and boy, it was a big one. "Who cares? So, this is Sam's, eh? Well now. I guess we should be looking around for the spare room and getting ourselves cozy, don't you think?"

"I do not! I need to go to the village and let my parents know I am back. You will stay right here, and I mean that, and not cause a ruckus until I find Lord Griffin. Imagine what he would think to suddenly come and find you here and Sam having been gone for so long? Think about it."

"Wow, woman, you make sense. But where is all this bossiness coming from?"

Leaning up, she kissed him again. "As soon as I return it will be opened up for discussion. Now, promise you will not even go outside until I do. Any noises, make yourself scarce. I don't care where you hide. Just make sure it is secure. I can't have you found."

"You have my word. Now get your cute ass in gear. Hey, do you mind if I scavenge about for some food? Any idea if there is any alcohol?"

"I know her servant keeps things rotated. She is quite reliable. A local girl that's paid well and does not ask any questions." She opened the cupboards. "Looks like she's been here recently. So, I'll see if I can find her to make sure she stays away until I can figure things out. As for drinks, I don't know. Look around. If not in here, try the study."

"Bossy, beautiful and smart. I think I'm off to a good start here. Now go."

Anne waived him off, already thinking about her parents and Lord Griffin. "Just remember what I said!"

"Yeah, yeah, okay." He was rummaging through the cupboards already.

Reaching down and lifting the hem of her dress, Anne raced toward the estate, recalling a specific path Sam had mentioned before they left her behind. Later, she would seek it out and show Derek as well, when there was more time. Hurrying up to the rear kitchen doors, she threw it open in a mad rush.

Yelping at Anne's entry, Mrs. Lilly's bucket of flour was knocked over. Mrs. H yelled at her, "Girl! Settle down, I say! What's gotten into you? Where the dickens have you been?"

"Sorry, oh, so sorry, Mrs. Lilly, Mrs. H. Really, I am. But I need to see Lord Griffin straight away. Is he in? I also need to make sure Abbey does not come to the cottage for a while." She smiled at the return of Victorian manners.

"Indeed, he is. But this is most unexpected and peculiar. Do you have a purpose in seeing him yourself?"

"Yes, and it is rather urgent. Do you know where I can find Abbey as well?" The room filled with electrifying intensity.

"Yes, now come quick. He is scheduled to go carding tonight with Mistress Sam's brother. So, both are here. Hurry along and follow me." As they reached his study, Mrs. H stopped, tone hushed. "Is she okay? His Lordship has not been quite right since she's been gone without a word."

"Fine, just busy. Seems she has quite an agenda on this trip."

Mrs. H nodded, opening the door. "Pardon, Lord Griffin, but Miss Anne has news that I think you and Master Savoy will want to hear. Girl, when you are through come back to the main entrance before you go to the village. I'll be outside waiting."

Swinging the door wider, Anne entered but was quickly met by Lord Adam's brisk steps in her direction. Not to be halted, Anne maneuvered about and headed straight for his desk. With quill and paper she wrote fervently, blew on it and handed to him. With a quick curtsy, she quickly exited the room and headed back to find Mrs. H.

Pacing back and forth under the scrutiny of the doorman, Mrs. H stood still as Anne arrived. "I found Abbey. I told her I will be back to speak with her. I don't need all the details now, dear, but I will surely want to know why, at a later time. What do you want me to say to her?"

"Please tell her to stop down this evening at six o'clock to see me. I will be preparing for Sam and staying at the cottage until I, well, know more. I, umm, have a visitor there, Mrs. H. He came through with me and I thought you should know. I realize that's quite scandalous, but there is a reason and I must keep him safe while I find out."

"Oh. How absolutely interesting." A quirky smile appeared. "These scenarios continue to intrigue me. Okay, I will tell her shortly. You will of course keep this from your parents?"

"Yes, I am going to tell them I am here for a short time only. Then they will not worry or come up looking for me. Only you will know. When I need something from Abbey, I'll send a note with the money and you can have her take care of it. You are our go-between. Are you planning on traveling yourself anytime soon?"

"You've changed, Anne Baker. A lot. I like it! No, I am not traveling. I've just recovered from my last trip and a sore leg. I've been given my recuperation orders, so to speak. Let's hope that lasts long enough until you get things in order at the cottage. Now scoot, I'll take it from here and, Anne, glad our girl is okay."

"Me too." She started to run toward the side path, taking a quicker way to town. "Thanks!" she threw over her shoulder.

***

Adam and Victor were outside his study enjoying a smoke before leaving. Victor's curiosity got the better of him. "Come now, here. Hand that note over."

Adam laughed. "Fine. Here. At least I know she's okay. I've never known anyone like her. She is unique. Unfortunately, I won't be headed that way when I leave day after tomorrow."

Victor nodded, taking the note and reading it out loud: "*She is well. Lively and spirited. In the Middle East, 2016 and taking care of more than one thing. It will be quite a while before she returns. All I can say. I have no more details*".

"Well, I agree. That is good news and long awaited. Now, I can let the wife know and she and the kids will stop the nagging. I know better than to be specific. I'll just tell her you've had news and she's detained longer than expected. If she wants to hound you for more, then so be it."

He slapped his friend on the back and set the note down on the desk..

Adam laughed. "I'll be bugging out myself soon enough. So, that will wait."

There was a knock at the study door. Both men glanced at it simultaneously as Adam spoke. "Enter."

The groomsman came just inside the room. "Sir, the coach is ready."

"Very good, we will be out shortly." Adam slid the note into his top drawer and locked it, sliding the key into a hollow book on the shelf behind his desk.

"Ah, so that's where you keep it."

He laughed. "Good idea you know. Sam does not. In fact, although I can't confirm it, I bet Mrs. H does. She seems aware of everything that goes on around here. It makes me wonder if Anne told her more and she's not relaying that? You know how these women are. They like to keep things from us men."

"Ah, my friend, I know. But you do miss her and I'm sure she misses you as well. Maybe when she gets back this time, you two can come to an agreement and keep yourselves living together in one house instead of two?"

"It was never my idea that she moved. I'm damn sorry that I even allowed her to override good sense. But, as I've met up with in you, there is a stubborn streak that just rises when it feels like it. You two are quite alike. Perhaps if she's still disagreeable to living here when she gets back, you can give me a hand with her?"

Both men climbed inside the Barouche carriage as the door was closed by the driver.

"I will. I can see what this has done to you even though you would not admit it. But I won't tell my sister how it affected you. I'll do what I can. I tend to agree.

Although, even if she agrees to move back, she won't let go of the cottage so easy. She really loves it down there and I can't quite figure out why. My wife said she talks about the back woods frequently."

Adam knew why. "She likes a good country walk, that's all. She always has liked the fields. Being out there is extremely therapeutic for her. She truly loves nature and all the elements. But it is not getting her to move up here that's really got me bothered. It's getting her to marry me. She's so dead set against it."

"It's that bloke she was previously hitched to. She admitted it was her fault as much as his and does not think she's the marring sort. But we can work on her. Better yet, I'll have the wife work on her when she gets back. Women normally only listen to other women. She possibly will scoff at the idea of listening to me. Her brother."

"Damn if that's not the truth. Anyway. About tonight. We need to keep an eye on Lord Horsworth tonight. I know he is cheating the Simpsons and heard they will both be there. I want to see if we can call him out in a diplomatic way. That pompous ass would not think twice of demanding a freaking dual. I'll have none of that bullshit."

"I'm on it. He's close with that notoriously conniving Langdon Group. I'm not too snobbish to think they are beneath my boots because they combined their resources in industry. It's just that with the dwindling economy in some areas, they are taking advantage of families with lineage and birth that go far beyond their families' years. It's a disgrace."

"Agreed, so let's make quick use of our time there. They have no idea that the chief magistrate will be our special guest. I want to make sure they don't think along the road they can use an upper hand and add blackmail to their list."

"You got him to come?"

"I did. There are times when old family names do mean something here in England. Knowing his father owed my father still rings loud and clear. I called in a marker."

The coach stopped as the two got out, set their top hats on and were ushered in to the awaiting tables. Griffin sat down opposite David Langdon, taking out his wallet and placing it, bills overflowing, beside the drink a waiter had just set down.

The table filled as Barclay Simpson sat down, glaring at Lord Horsworth. He had a hunch he had been swindled during last week's games, but lacked proof. It was when Lord Griffin approached him in town earlier this week that it was discussed and this plan was born. Sitting this round of cards out, Victor was off the side enjoying a good smoke in conversation with a group of local bankers. Facing Langdon, watching every move intently, he quickly realized the pattern.

Two hours passed. Many got drunk as stupidity set in at last.

"You ready to hang your hat now, Simpson?" Lord Horsworth asked. "Looks like you are lacking enough for the next round. Sorry, my friend, appears your ill-fated luck continues to haunt."

"Horsworth, I must admit it. Your streak is quite the opposite. But, the hell with it. At any second my luck could change. I still have ten percent shares in the bank. Dammit, yes. I'll see your stake and raise."

Suddenly boots scraping along the marble floor could be heard. Men not participating looked at each other as Lord Horsworth shuffled the cards and spoke to Simpson. "How many?"

"Two." Flipping them over, he laid them out. "I'll steady here."

Throwing his own cards down in disgust, Griffin rose, chair scraping against the Italian marble floor. "I'm out. You two have at it."

He stood over next to Vic, nodding. "You ready?"

"Indeed I am." He walked over to two gentlemen engaged in conversation. "You had enough?"

"Indeed, I have. Proceed."

Vic walked over, standing at the shoulder of Horsworth and placing a solid grip upon his shoulder. "Care to take a stand up from your game for a minute, Lord Horsworth, so we can look what's up your left sleeve and right inside pocket?"

Horsworth's face turned red. "What the bloody hell? Do you understand what you are saying here, Savoy?"

"Indeed, I do. For starters, let me introduce you to a couple of very special guests who have come all this way to see your prowess at the gaming tables. Lord Horsworth, this is His Lord Magistrate Wellington Stokes and his first assistant, Montgomery Ayers."

Horsworth glanced anxiously around for some kind of backup. Some assistance from the group in the room. But not a soul moved. The room went silent.

"Sir, would you be so kind as to come with us? A private conversation with you and Lord Simpson is desired."

Horsworth seemed to realize that he had been set up. He glared at Griffin and Savoy before glancing around the room and landing on the slight grin on Langdon's face. As he was escorted out the double wide doors, he started to spill the beans. "Sir, I can explain…"

As the room cleared, Adam and Victor shook hands. "Now that's a good night's worth of work. I claimed back what he took and I am assured Lord Simpson will not only recoup what he stole from him this night, but also from the last two occasions. Right order will soon be restored."

"A good deed, I agree. Now, shall we go? I'll drop you off at home so your wife won't send me a nasty note tomorrow about keeping you out late gaming and smoking the night away."

He laughed. "Agreed. That was well done, Adam, well done indeed."

"Two heads, remember. Good for a change we had something to take care of locally."

"Agree. But I see it in your eyes. You are still worried about her."

"Shit, I know."

"Okay, well keep me posted."

"I'll get you a note when I'm back."

"You know where you are headed?"

"Indeed, I do. A change of scenery is all I can say and it will be well wanted since I know she's not returning any time soon."

The coach halted and Victor got out. "Take care, mate." His eyes bore into Adam's just a bit too long as the door was closed.

Chapter Eleven

Anne stopped momentarily at the fork in the paths, eyeing the direction toward the area Sam had mentioned earlier. Instead of taking that one, she quickly continued to the back door of the cottage.

"We are in the clear. I took care of everyone that needed to know. They only have details I wanted to provide. It felt powerful, I must say, to be in charge like that. I liked it. So, watch out."

Clash grinned. She and Sam were so much alike. There was always more to come.

"Sam's employee's name is Abbey. Should she turn up I wanted you to know her name. Although Mrs. Hoyt up at the great house said she'd try to make sure that did not happen. All the same, she will be our go-between. I don't suspect she'd come here. She's a bit timid and not likely to poke her nose around where it does not belong. It's all good."

He moved a bit closer. "I found a spare room and threw my bag in there. Do you have any notion why I came back with you? I have no clue right now."

"I'll make us a pot of tea, unless you want something stronger. We can put our heads together. I have a hunch it is to do with that path Sam mentioned to me. Remember, she said to go down it, find the statue, sit there and you will know what needs to be done."

"I heard her mention Lord Griffin to you once. I take it this is the guy she's involved with here? The one that lured her to this period?"

"Kind of like that, yes. It's a long story. I don't know a lot of it. Of course, he does. Do you think your reason to be here is to help him?"

"I don't know. Just as a precaution I'd better be introduced. Can't have him getting the wrong impression. That would not bode well for me if I was in his shoes and something like this occurs."

Anne thought about that. "Yeah, I agree. I can't have him thinking ill of me even though I know him as quite a modern Victorian gentleman."

Sitting down at the table across from him, she poured the tea.

"I see that look on your face. The wheels are turning. Maybe it's not that reason at all, Anne. Perhaps like Sam, I've been given the chance to stay and work from here. Or, maybe it's to have more time with you. Choices may be being offered to us both. Would you consider returning with me to my period?"

"But I could not just up and go. I'm close to all my family."

"You know you would not have to actually leave them for good, right? You can move between places and stay when the timing works."

"How come I don't know about this?"

"You are still new, that's all. I wonder if Sam does. Those travels are a bit more advanced than what I have even done." He picked up the dishes, pumped the water into the basin and cleaned them, leaving them on the rack to dry. "I bet she enjoys it here, doesn't she?"

"Yeah, she told me she feels like this was where it is most comfortable. I must admit, I found the future interesting. Not how women are treated in the Middle East, but the rest was cool."

"Then modern day England may well be to your liking. I have a feeling our lives are going to intertwine more than we could have realized back in Saudi. What do you say to tomorrow we pay a visit to that statue? See if it 'speaks' to us? Now my curiosity is piqued."

He extinguished one of the two gas lanterns, taking the lit one up along the flight of stairs and glancing back over his shoulder.

"You get those thoughts out of your head right now, mister."

He broke out in laughter, stopping as she went into Sam's room. "We will get there. I'm in no hurry." He leaned down and placed a kiss on her lips. As she walked in, he pulled the door shut.

***

Lying in his comfortable bed with the moonlight streaming in, Clash stood, restless, and walked over to the window. He followed the light with his eyes to where it shone brightly from the back door toward a clearing. There was an undistinguishable large gray object, but from this distance he could not make it out.

His journalist nose could not stop itching. Tugging on his boots, he walked softly down the stairs and outside. Following the glow, he arrived in the clearing where the light was shining in a halo orb around a statue of Isis.

Someone was sitting on the bench.

With apprehension, not truly sure if it was man or other, hesitantly Derek continued over. Then he knew who it was as he sat down.

"I contemplated if you would be here."

"I had to wonder what all the fuss was about regarding this piece of granite. Now I'm getting the message." His sideways glance held many questions. "Why are you here and who the hell are you?"

"Derek Clash. I was recently in the company of someone you know. Then when my requirements were completed, I found my journey took me in an entirely different direction—one I can assure you that has nothing to do with Samantha. Instead, it appears I have much to discover here with that pretty little baker's daughter Anne."

The two shook hands.

"I'm going to take a chance here. You are Lord Adam Griffin?"

"Correct. I'm on my way to Ireland tomorrow. I have no idea how long, but it does not feel like it will be lengthy. Something is strange. Can't figure it out and wondering if coming down here would give me any damn answers. The only other time I felt this out of whack was when I unknowingly lured Sam here from modern day Venice. My life has not been the same since I laid eyes on that woman."

Clash chuckled, giving him a pat on the back as their eyes locked. "I can see why. In all my adventures, I've never met a soul like her. She is different. I don't even think she realizes how very special she is. I've never seen such a free thinker. Not in anyone. It blows my mind away how she evolves."

"Well put. Suddenly, I find even the allure of a mistress unappealing. Damn woman, she's evil."

They laughed.

"I tried to get her to discuss you, but there was no participation on that end. Anne, on the other hand, obtained more information after spending a few days with her. Sam made sure Anne would let you know she was at least fine. Are you okay with us being here?"

"Yes. You two do what you need." He glanced at Clash. "What's your deal?"

"Journalist and filming. Yours?"

"Country gent. Aristocrat. All that interesting bullshit."

"Ah, but you like it. The top coat, horses, the hunt and gaming, I bet. And a mistress or two before Sam."

"I can see you are good at what you do already. Yes, to all of that. Full of tradition and frankly I do enjoy it. If you are still around when I return, I'll have you come up and play a round with Victor, myself and a few other associates you will like to meet. Victor is Sam's brother. One she did not know until arriving in this time."

Derek's pause lengthened as all this was digested. "Now it's making sense. You were the person used to lure her here. But there's a lot more to the story, right?"

"A hell of a lot more. Interesting enough, we have a past going back much further than either of us want to delve into right now. I could have turned tail in Venice, but for some strange reason it did not seem like an option. I had to help her out of a predicament. I know now my course of action was predestined. I've done this a time or two with her. She's some damn hold over me, the wench."

"As men, we know what that is. Some say it is lust, some love and others just outright stupidity. Only you can decide which it is."

Adam stood, nodding. "If you need anything, send Anne up to Mrs. Hoyt. She is my housekeeper and knows the goings on when the rest of us have no clue. I'll tell her we met. Stakes are high she already knows." He smiled, clasping hands as Derek also stood.

"No, you can stay. I just wandered down here as if the goddess herself was calling me."

"She was. Same with me. Another powerful female. You have to be cautious of beautiful women even if they are from our past."

They continued along the moonlit path until Derek reached the rear door of the cottage where Anne was standing just outside, looking nervous as hell.

"Lord Griffin, please let me explain...."

He grinned, patting her arm gently. "No need. I've met your gent and approve—in case you feel like you even need it. You two take care of your business with no need of a rush." He continued along, sliding his hands into pants pockets.

Closing and locking the door, Anne turned the knob on the gas lantern sitting on top of the counter and increased the light within the room. "I heard you go. But I was not fast enough to stop you. Now I'm glad it all happened the way it did. How did you know to go to the statue?"

"If you even smile I'll kiss you until you beg for mercy."

"Fine, so, what happened?"

"She called me. It's as simple as that."

She bit her lip. Then bit it harder. In the light he thought he saw a flicker of a smile. Keeping true to his word, he grabbed her, pulling her close and kissing her potently.

His grip was firm on the curve of her waist as she tried to pull back, unsuccessfully. "Okay, don't do that. It's distracting as holy hell! Now tell me. I have to know and wipe that smug smile off your lips." She jabbed a rib.

"Ouch! Okay, well, she did call me. The moonlight guided me and when I arrived there it was to meet Lord Griffin. He's a good sort, I can tell. Honest and honorable. A quality highly prized in any era. He gave his blessings to us and if we need anything to let Mrs. Hoyt up at the house know and she will take care of it."

"Was he okay about Lady Samantha?"

"Hard to tell. He hid behind that staunch aristocratic air. But, Anne, I could feel it. His heart and soul are longing for their reunion. That was clear as hell. He's off to Ireland shortly. Unless Sam's journey is redirected, there will be no chance of them reuniting anytime soon."

"Damn. Oh, well. I was wishing…"

"Same here. Anyway, I don't know what drew him to the statue but part of it was so we could meet. I'm not clear on why. I did not really tell him anything about what Sam's doing in Saudi. Regardless, my gut tells me I'm not involved with that portion again, nor are you. I have a feeling I'm going to be here quite a while."

"Oh, I forgot to ask. Who is the statue of?"

"Isis."

"From ancient Egypt? I don't know much about her."

"I can fill you in. Why don't we venture back down in the morning?" He glanced down at his watch. "Or, later in the morning. I guess I had better keep this tucked under my shirt sleeve." They headed up the stairs and then stopped as he ran a gentle hand along one soft cheek. "I think I can actually sleep now." He pulled her close briefly and placed a kiss on her lips and then opened up her door and swatted her ass towards it. "Sleep well, Anne."

***

A cloudy mist produced dripping dew on the grass as the sun's warmth quickly pulled the moisture into the clouds. It was going to be a glorious, bright day. Stretching, bare feet meeting the cool floor, Anne journeyed over to the window, inhaling the fresh, clean air as the warm rays reached her skin.

Washed and dressed, she sauntered down to the kitchen and pulled open the back door, knowing there would be some goodies sitting there. Indeed, it was a basket of fresh muffins, crumpets, butter and jam. She felt Derek suddenly tug her against him and let his head rest on top of her hair. She handed him over the basket and he placed it up on the counter.

"The tea is ready, I'm starved. Let's eat so we can go see Isis. Then I think I'll take you to the village."

"Better yet, why don't you point me in the right direction? Then we can suddenly meet and become acquainted and your family won't be suspicious. I do not want you compromised."

"I guess I'd better get my head back in the Victorian era, eh?"

He stuffed a big bite of warm, buttered crumpet into his mouth. "Oh, this is good. I wonder what lunch will be?"

"You know my parents own a bakery. There is a vacant room above the shop. Maybe you will move in there so you can be fed constantly. I'm warning you. They are talented. Wait until you get a whiff of what they can conjure up."

"They always have said throughout all of time that a way to a man's heart is through his stomach. Can you also cook like this?"

She shook her head in disbelief. "Yes, I can. Now don't go getting any ideas." She sat back as he gathered up the leftovers. "I have no doubt you will be back attacking them soon."

He grinned.

"Ready?" She was at the open door as he passed through. Quietly, deep within their own thoughts, they walked side by side down the path.

Suddenly, a faint voice spoke to Anne. Quickly glancing over, she knew he had not heard it. Now it was clear why he was here with her and what needed to be done. Decisions to be made. She bit the inside of her mouth, hiding a smile. It had nothing to do with the cute boy in the village.

Sitting down on the bench, their eyes raised up to the beautiful statue of Isis. Silence continued as she reached over, placing a hand on top of his. Nodding, he rose, clasping it strongly as they retraced their footsteps. Up ahead the path divided into three choices. *Interesting*, Anne thought. Indeed, various choices loomed ahead that would affect both their lives.

"Straight leads back to the cottage, left to the great house and right to the village. Take that one and just keep following until you come to the churchyard. The smithy and green will be next. Then you will be on our main fare. I'll be coming along on the road. My arrival will be a good fifteen minutes later than you."

Her eyes gave him the once over and she nodded with approval. *Yes*, she thought, *he will do*.

He chuckled. "Are your standards met, miss?"

***

All business she was, but he knew as her smile appeared that something was playing around in that mind. Boldly he patted her bottom, turned and headed down the path. Eyes gazing skywards toward the church spire, he soon passed the old graveyard. Not planning on dallying here looking at each name engraved while passing by, a set of old engraved stones nonetheless caused some mirth.

"Rarely is it that I see someone stopping here looking at tombstones and smiling. Usually it's tears, sniffles and tissues."

He hesitated before glancing toward where the voice had come from. One intricately etched name held his interest. Clashton. At some point the ton had been dropped from it and he had no clue why. "Oh, Father. You appeared so fast I had to wonder for a split second if you were indeed a spirit yourself. But, here I have a twisted sense of humor. I was thinking of something else while I was reading the names while passing by."

Both men broke out in laughter.

"You're passing by? A good one, young man."

"Well, you got it. Which proves you are also quick of whit."

Hand extended, the priest said, "Father Godwin at your service. Or, Father G, as I am otherwise known, Derek Clash. I was expecting you."

He was not taken aback. "Why did I not think it was a coincidence? Little is in our world, right?"

The good priest nodded. "You cannot delay longer. I believe there is a young lady I know that will be looking for you on the main fare shortly."

"You know that as well? Do you by chance know why I am here then? Is it for her?"

Father G patted him on the arm. "You already have your answer. I'll be seeing you soon." His toothy grin had Derek smiling as he located the smithy and turned off the stone path onto the dirt street.

Derek was taking it all in as the aroma of a small shop close by lured him closer. Above the door he read the sign, smiled and walked in. She was already there, engaged in conversation with whom he believed were her parents. So, the little chit had said she would arrive later than he. A smile could not be hidden, for he knew she purposely had lied. Or else ran the entire way.

As Derek walked closer to them, a man spoke out. "My daughter will be right with you."

Derek watched on in amusement as Anne eyed her pops quickly and then moved ahead. He could swear the pulse in her pretty neck was thumping as her skin turned a cute shade. Quietly her parents shuffled backward and left the room.

"I need your recommendation for lunch, Miss…?"

"Miss Anne Baker, sir."

He nodded, smiling at her heavy use of the word miss. "I've already been told the selection here is exceptional. I must say I surely agree." She turned a slight shade of pink but kept her eyes locked with his. Daring him to say more.

They both heard the door beyond close.

"Put together a box of your favorites and we can meet back at the cottage. Does that work for you? Do you need to hang around here for a while?"

"Nope. Now that they know I am home and safe I can roam. I can assure you they are already plotting our engagement. Did you catch all of that? Shit, I apologize. But, I do love them so."

Laughter rang out from both. "I know you need to come back at night. But mark my words I'll be making quite a nuisance of myself and your father will know I mean business soon enough. Perhaps that will give us freedom to figure everything else out." He was sorely tempted to kiss those perky lips but had to refrain. "I think you'd better get used to my being here, Miss Anne."

She slid by him and he felt a lone hand run along his arm and chest before quickly moving out of his grasp. "I happened to run into Father Godwin on my way here. That's why I was a bit delayed."

"I suspected as much," was all she said while boxing up the food and tying it with string. Paying, he nodded, clicked the heels of his highly polished boots and left, closing the door behind him.

Halfway down the street, a large sign piqued his interest. As he opened the door to the local office, Clash's mind filled with nostalgia at how far his industry had progressed. Yet, from his modern day to this time one thing remained the same: how information was gathered.

Unannounced, sporting an infectious grin, he walked over, extending his hand to a tall gent who had rolled-up sleeves and a long, feathered quill in hand.

"Might I have a word with the proprietor?"

"You have him. What can I do for you?"

"Well, good sir, it's what I may be able to do for you."

Chapter Twelve

"Looks like that redhead over there has taken quite a fancy to you, Adam."

"Yeah, I've noticed. But now is not the time. We have business to attend and need to discover who sold you out on that gun shipment. Even though it is the 1960s and this rebellion has been going on for years, the IRA does not stand a chance against the Brits and a peace process down the road unless we get this process more structured. I'm here to help, not to reflect in those eyes, which are a striking green even from this distance away."

"I'm afraid you may not have the option to ignore her. She's O'Finnigan's daughter. Shannon."

"Frig, you have to help me out. I do not have the luxury of tampering with her while in these parts. I left some unfinished business elsewhere."

"If there is someone else, you had better put her in the back of your mind. This lass is an asset. She can bend her old man's ear quite well. Don't sell her short, believing she's simple of mind because of her attractiveness. Conniving and convincing she can indeed be."

"Grand, she's headed right our way. Thanks a bunch, mate. I don't stand a chance."

"Yeah, I can see she would definitely make you suffer in one manner or another. Suck it up, my friend. Sometimes a man has to do what a man has to do just to get the job done."

Conversation halted as Adam rose, properly acknowledging her. The grin on his friend's face clearly indicated he would do no such thing and could give a shit about propriety.

"Sullivan, my father has asked me to invite you and your friend here to supper with us tonight. Eight. See you then."

Both men stared at the other. How the hell would she know where Sully was going to be? The scent of fresh flowers evaporated from the air around them as she moved away. Watching the sway of those hips, Adam indeed let his mind wander.

That same devil-may-care attitude had been his best friend since his passages had begun. Then came Sam. But now those old feelings were rearing an ugly head. In former days, it would have been a no-brainer. But with Sam still lingering on his mind, somehow even the luscious redhead's appeal was losing its charm. Although, he considered, who the hell here would ever run into Sam and tell her? Perhaps it was time to test the waters and see how much he truly wanted her in his life.

An old thought occurred to him. Women were usually of two ways: clingy and dependent or independent and headstrong, taking control of a man's life and commerce quickly. Ironically, neither fit the description of Sam. No, she was entirely different.

She squashed talk of anything too permanent. Perhaps the writing had been on the wall when she'd moved out. This could be a doubled-edged journey for him: one to help the IRA gain a stronghold over the British and test his true feelings for her. He rapped on the table top and ordered up two more Guinness as he grinned to Sullivan.

"Shit, why not, right? If you think about it, this is the early 1900s and who I'm thinking about is in fact not actually born yet."

"Now you got a grip, mate!"

Adam took a deep swig of the brew and set it back down. "Damn, these never get old. This and whiskey are a man's best friends."

"And occasionally a pretty woman does not hurt either, my friend."

"I'll drink to that." He raised a hand up to the bartender. "Two more over here."

Adam chugged down a second and made quick work of a third. "Sully, I don't know where O'Finnigan's place is. Do we need to hitch a ride?"

"Nope, don't suspect so. He keeps a place here in Belfast since his wife died. It all happened suddenly. But heaven was not done with him, striking a second blow. His son was caught by the British and exiled."

Adam leaned closer after glancing around the room to see if anyone else was listening in on their conversation. "Go on."

"Besides, his errant daughter is a known wanderer. He likes to be here. Keep an eye on her and all the dealings. In fact, she's a bit like you and your old ways, mate. Neither faithful nor the marrying type. Seems to me you two would make a perfect pair if you were sticking around. But I do see one difference."

"Oh, great, enlighten me."

"You like your mistresses. She likes to be the only mistress. Plus, she's been involved in a scandal or two since coming back from a jaunt to mainland Europe. You, my friend, seem to slip under the radar when it comes to avoiding pissed-off husbands and local newspapers."

Adam pondered that, grinning. "Then maybe she's the perfect diversion for me while I get this job done here." He was glad for the distraction and the warming from the strong brews certainly did not hurt his emotional cause much. Yeah, this was just at the right time.

He paid the tab, sliding some greenbacks the bartender's way. "Give 'em a round on me."

The bartender nodded, smiling and showing a few front teeth rotted out. "Fine. But you two blokes get the hell out of here. Things needs to be taken care of and won't happen if you keep your sorry asses around."

"Keep your ears open. More than just my arrival signals things are going to happen fast here."

Adam was suddenly aware of who this bartender was: the carpenter's son who'd worked on Sam's cottage. Their eyes met and locked momentarily in complete understanding. His passage would soon be completed while Adam's was just beginning.

"Word will reach Sully. Rest assured."

Adam turned and joined his mate outside. Removing a cigar and striking a match against the stone building, Adam lit it and expelled three consecutive perfect circles of smoke. "Lead on."

"When we get there, keep watch on what you drink and how much. The jury is still out in that household on who you really are and what your gig is all about."

"Your advice is appreciated, Sully, I'll pay head. Anyone up front I need to focus special attention on?"

"None that I have been able to sniff out. Perhaps you will have better luck." Adam nodded as Sully rapped his knuckles on the large wooden door dented with bullet holes.

They smiled at each other.

"Ass, the door knocker works just as well."

Sully gave him a solid shove just as the door opened to a large, orange-haired, burly old sod.

"Sullivan, O'Malley. They are waiting on you. This way."

Each knew what the other was thinking while they looked at the giant's rugged frame. He could put a man's light out with one blow. It would take more than the two of them to take this beast of a man down and then keep him there.

"Ah, gents, good to see you. Come, sit down. We were just having a glass of whiskey. Gal, don't dawdle. Fill two more for our guests."

Adam's eyes locked with O'Finnigan's daughter in a clear message as he picked up the glass.

"I hear you secured a fine keg in the last raid," Sully said as they all raised glasses. "I'm ready to give you my opinion."

"Sully, your opinion matters in all but spirits. This whole room knows, probably your friend as well, that you don't care how it really tastes so long as it's bought for you!" The room filled with laughter as they all sat down.

"Shannon, ring the bell and take your seat so we can get these gents fed."

So, that was her name. Shannon. Good Irish name for a true beauty. Adam felt bold as he raised a glass in salute. "Thank you for the hospitality and providing a lovely Irish rose to sit with us to take away from the ugliness of the rest of us."

"Here, here," the other men chimed in, raising glasses to her. She smiled softly. Her ego had been properly fed and the fires stoked. Adam was appraising her as well. Clearly, she was strong willed. That was apparent in the boldness of her actions earlier at the bar. But would she use that beauty to gain an advantage? What advantage was she looking for?

Then again, using her wits and wiles to seek out personal pleasure was never a bad thing. Just what were those? A dalliance here and there behind her father's back? Why was she not married? Certainly, her age was ripe, if not slightly over the proper age decorum of this time. Maybe she was and her gent was a hostage with all the hostilities over the years? A secret held from her very own father?

Yes, he was interested. Not in having the answers to all that shit, but in perhaps burying into her softness to release a demon inside. One more time.

The Irish stew with fresh sourdough bread was served. Talk turned to smuggling firearms and ammo across the Belfast city limits to their stronghold on the Irish Catholic side. Somehow, even in the dead of night and months of careful planning, the scheme had been compromised and lives lost. *Damn*, he thought, *there already has been too much bloodshed*. But it would be years before a true cease fire would commence.

"Damn if we know who the mole is. We have one or more possibilities. No witnesses or exchange of notes. I've the whole area under surveillance and nothing is turning up. Sully, have you had any success?"

"Not yet, but I'm digging. We need to find out who it is before the next shipment. We sorely need to keep this going. I'm headed out tomorrow on a couple of fresh leads."

He nodded. "You need any backup?"

"No, not now. It is easier to slip around alone than in a group. My friend here is visiting only for a short time. If I need anyone I'll take him along. I trust him with my nuts."

O'Finnigan grinned. "That's good enough for me. Mike, how's the exports coming along?"

"Good luck there, boss. We managed two wagons full of whiskey and beer the other night to the shore. They are on the mainland now. I gave your porter the money. Was a hefty sum this time."

"Good. Phinney, when's your next contact with the gunner?"

"Three days." He glanced at Sully. "You want to tag along on that one? Could use an opinion on what you think of him. I don't think he's our traitor but want to make sure."

"Yeah, I'll go. Adam here can find something else to do while I'm away. Is it in Belfast we meet him?"

"No, about five kilometers just outside in a safer location. I'll come by and get you from the back alley of the building. Just be there at six o'clock in the morning."

***

The men rose and Shannon stood, taking their hats off the hallway bench as she and her father saw them off.

"Gal, you watch it with that one. He's handsome for sure but smart. I take it he'd not settle for your antics."

"You keep me cooped up under your nose so much I need diversions. Since Quinn was taken away you make me feel like a prisoner rather than him being the one held by the Torries."

"You keep your sassy mouth shut or I'll lock you in your room again. I mean it. I can't have your swishing skirts dallying about all around town. The next time you ditch your guard and head to the tavern, you'd better think twice about it. I sent you there with a message. But did not tell you to go alone!" His skin turned bright red, voice angry.

She had to be careful and knew it. That temper could hurt more than a smoking hot iron from a fire. "Sorry." She glanced down to the shoes peeping out from her fine, simple, cotton dress. "I will take the bloke next time. Just that I don't feel comfortable around him. That large, ugly scar down the side of his right cheek is hardly appealing."

"He got that defending your ole pa, so you just remember that when you look at him with distaste, girl."

She moved ahead of him up the stairs as he turned and left toward the study—no doubt to drink further into the night.

"Good night, Papa."

"Good night, girl."

Girl. Was that the best he could do? He hardly ever called her by name. As she shushed away the one lady's maid in the household and undressed herself, she smiled. At least there was fresh blood in town and even if he was only staying a short while, perhaps he was just the diversion she needed. His arrival fit in perfectly with her plans. Climbing into the bed, she drifted off to sleep, hearing the distant fire of shots ringing out. It was another normal night, she thought, in Northern Ireland. The Protestants were at it again.

***

As the two men walked the short distance back to the Inn, gunshots rang out in the distance and the sky lit up briefly with the flaming hues of orange and red. Adam looked at Sully. "That's planned. We had to do something to them since they confiscated our last shipment."

"What do you expect I will do with my time while you are off with his man?"

Sully grinned. "You need me to help you to figure that out?" He slapped Adam on the back as they exited and separated toward their own rooms on the second floor. "It's noisy on this level, but easier if you need to flee. Jump down one level to the ground and run like bloody hell."

"Ah, practical I must say. You do this enough, I gather."

"Always a good practice to be prepared. Don't you think? They don't come up here often and raid. Then again, after tonight they will be pissed off, looking for revenge."

"So, hanging out at the city border causing a ruckus would not be in our favor about now."

They laughed, closing both their doors. Locks slid into place.

Hands tucked beneath his head laying on the pillow, Adam could still catch a faint whiff in the air of her soft perfume and see the gleam of her red hair off the lighting in the room. He smiled. Yes, this would work for him. Sully had his mission and Adam had his. No one knew they were one and the same.

Now that O'Finnigan was aware of his arrival, he could go about his business of seeing which side was up to what and his end of the deal taken care of. If in the process the redhead was a diversion; he'd not pass that by. As Sam said on more than one occasion, if it was necessary to sleep with the enemy to get to the end results, then so be it. At this juncture, all the booze collected in his system was taking a toll.

His lids finally lowered. But his ego was still engaged with a strong need to settle a score with her and the control she held. Damn, he was pissed off! He kicked the rough woolen blanket toward the floor. He'd settle this. Starting tomorrow. Finally, he gave in and slept.

Just as the sun was rising the next morning, they met in the downstairs breakfast room. "I've secured a van so I can take you along the border. It has reinforced metal but the tires are still subjected to bullets. I want to scope out the perimeter and give you as much detail on the area as you need. It may come in handy later. Keep your head low." A grin formed across Sully's features. "Or it will be in the line of direct fire."

"I wonder what happens if I die here? Do I remain? Or am I automatically transmitted back?" They eyed each other as the jalopy sprang to life. Greasing the gears along, Sully shifted. "Fine time to be thinking about that, mate."

Adam chuckled. "Don't rightly know why that came out. Ah, I see what you mean. The wall is high enough no one could repel over it without being seen. No shit. This is heavily fortified. I'm sure it's the same on the other side. How the hell do you get over?"

"It is tricky, but we do have ways. A few tunnels are still usable. The good holy people are allowed to flow between the sides to collect those that met their maker sooner than they thought."

"Are there any friend or foe there?"

"No, they were all investigated by both sides thoroughly before it was even considered."

"What about country road access or the shore? Other possible choices?"

"They have us pretty heavily blockaded. Forcing us to bring goods in from the other side of the island. But it works. See that area sectioned off?"

"With the barricades around it?"

"Yeah. That's where our guns were ambushed. We no longer have access."

"Someone must know the layout of this land pretty well. One who is local with means to work all sides."

"What are you thinking?"

"Not clear yet. I'll let you know."

"Not much firing goes on during the day. It is nightfall when you must keep your guard up. Not only do we use the tunnels, they do as well. There are spies on both sides, Adam. Of that we are completely sure."

Arriving back, Sully pitched the keys to a heavy-set man whose Irish wool tweed cap was pulled low over his eyes and they headed in the direction of one of the local pubs. Adam surveyed the smoky interior as Sully nudged his arm toward a set of rickety steps leading down into a dank smelling basement. Rapping twice on a completely hidden panel, it was slid open as two bright blue eyes squinted at them both from behind the opening.

The door swung open as Sully walked in. But Adam hovered a moment, allowing his eyes to adjust. *I've been in more than my fair share of smoke halls*, he thought. But this was ridiculous. Not a damn soul could be identified in its thickness. Any soldiers from the other side would blend right in. Stupid. This was just plain stupid.

"Shit, man, this place is like the thick fog over the English Chanel on a fowl night. I don't sense a high level of security here."

"I know, man, but it is what it is."

No one stopped unloading crates and checking weapons as he passed by. "We have to get this shipment distributed; there is another coming in by ship. We are running out of fortified places to keep them."

"Okay. So the underlying issue is not where you store them, but it's your onshore distribution. We need to find out who the mole is and keep them from squealing like a stuck pig. How long was this successful before the last incident occurred?"

Sully thought about it, taking a swig from the flask he'd suddenly produced. He handed it to Adam, who shrugged it off. "About four or five months. Quite a while, come to think of it."

"Anyone recently pissed off? Ego out of joint?"

"No, most of us band together thick as thieves. Maybe tonight at the pub something will stir our curiosity. Good probability we run into O'Finnigan's daughter. Sure, as it rains on these very shores every day. He has a meeting. When he's off she wanders."

"Shit. When's the next boat shipment coming in?"

"Four days. That's all we got. This time the boss has only told myself, Phinney, and Carey about it. He's tightened the circle."

Adam nodded. *And now me,* he thought. But he was brought in to get this crap figured out and had only a few days to do it.

"You have got a hunch, don't you?"

Adam smiled.

"Fine, you do what you want. Meet me at the pub at seven-thirty. I have a few places to explore. Do you have the lay of the land?"

"Well enough, Sully."

"All right. Go get it done. Catch up with you later." They exited out a rear entrance where children were kicking a soccer ball off the brick walls. He smiled. He'd never have his own kids and that was fine, but he enjoyed the enthusiasm they had all the same. Even with war going on all around them, gunshots and bullet holes all over the place, they still had light-hearted fun. It did not matter if they were Protestant or Catholic, black, white, Irish or English.

What the hell had happened to the world?

He passed a bakery and saw pasties in the taped window. He stopped and then went inside, paid for one and ate away as he sauntered farther into the darker parts of Belfast. Laundry hung between the buildings, billowing in the salty air as the excited voices of those kids receded. Around the next bend, sitting low with an AK47 poised and ready, was a masked IRA man on patrol protecting his quadrant.

They exchanged quick glances. It seemed even newcomers like himself were already identified. Otherwise he would have been detained for questioning. Thank heavens his accent here was Irish and not British or what would be the point?

For over forty years this conflict would continue before a treaty would be signed. Later, a sense of order would be returned and people would live in a somewhat peaceful, yet restrained society. But that was a start. He remembered reading in the Guardian in 2013 how that was progressing since the signing. But he could not tell these people that. Or the other side, for that matter.

Would anyone believe it if he told them that the Queen's flag would fly at half-mast several times in later years? In memory and honor of an Irish Catholic who was killed in Iraq or in a bus crash? Sure, some areas would see mild conflict continue, but it would become sporadic. Even when it happened, the incident would be blamed on a different form of terror: one that came with transients from the Middle East and not their own local-born blood. *So,* he thought, *it changes, but never really does.* Kicking a rock up ahead, he kicked it again.

Stopping, he sat watching boats pass along the River Lagan. Even as the sun had long set and the gas lights were coming on, it was busy. He glanced over on the other side, toward a long row of fancy homes, and scratched his chin. Having it all figured out now, he had to put thoughts into action and snuff out the viper that was hurting these people.

Two drunks passed by, precariously close to launching each other into the murky waters of the river, and he chuckled out loud. Yeah, he'd seen that a few times, being a part of it as well. But damn, current thoughts suddenly interrupted past-memories.

What the hell was she doing? He'd thought it would be just fine between them, but this distance was not suiting him at all right now. Even with news from Anne that she was okay, it still did not change the way he was feeling.

Shit, why the hell could they not communicate? Why did some other governing body have to decide even that? This was the very reason he'd kept those mistresses. Now it was too late. He'd have to slow things down when they reunited. Period. Damn that woman! Dictating to him what she would and would not accept. Where the hell were his balls?

Punching at the air, he marched several blocks straight into a pub. Anger increased with every step closer to the bartender. "You want to start a tab?"

"Damn straight I do. See that bloke over there?"

"Sully? Yeah, I'd call him a bloke. You got a beef with him?"

"No, add his to mine. I'll pay up when we leave. If O'Finnigan's lovely daughter saunters in, add her to it as well."

"Feeling a mite generous tonight, are you?"

"Nope, pissed as bloody hell." He grabbed the pint, swigged it in two gulps and slapped it down on the greasy wooden bar top. "Another."

The bartender returned at a slower pace. Deliberately.

"Thanks."

He took it with him and went over and sat with Sully. "Nearly watched two drunks take themselves both into the Lagan. Made me laugh bringing back some fond memories, old chap."

"Only two on your way here? Well, that's not bad. See anything else of interest?"

"Nope, but it's well guarded, that I can say. I saw a few out in the open but more placed around the neighborhoods. Good protection."

"We need to add more and make it a tighter stronghold. You, my friend, can make it happen."

Adam nodded, lifted the pint up and glanced around when the thick wooden door opened. Shannon had arrived. In tow was a man and woman. "Who's she with?"

"That will be her cousin Molly and husband Liam. Both suit each other. They are of simple minds and harmless. Basically just keep each other company. If she's with them and spotted, it filters back quickly to her father. He then turns a cheek to her being out and roaming. He knows what she's about, but still refuses to acknowledge her deceptive nature."

"If she's not with them?"

"There is hell to pay for us all. He has a real sour disposition when crossed even by the likes of his handsome daughter. You always know when she's done it again. She vanishes for days. He must lock her up."

Adam stood as she came over. The other two paid them no mind and settled at a table and chairs close by. They certainly kept in conversation range.

"Hello, Miss O'Finnigan. It's just the two of us if your party cares to join."

She smiled at them both. "I'd love to."

Adam pulled out a chair next to Sully and waved a circle toward their waitress, ordering a round. "Beer?"

"Yes. I am surprised to see you both. I believed there to be a meeting. My father is gone for the night."

"Not sure about what your pops is up to, but we are not involved with his business matters. I take it he approved of your coming out since you brought your friends. Don't you want to invite them over to join us?"

Sully raised an eyebrow at Adam's use of 'friends.'

"Ah, no. They are fine. Newly married and all and kind enough to get me out of the house this evening. I'm tired of being all cooped up. I'd rather be the third wheel here than with them." She smiled, leaning ever so slightly towards Adam, cloak slipping off and onto the back of the chair.

Venom spewed from the otherwise lovely eyes of the waitress as she brought over the drinks. Clearly, she held Mistress O'Finnigan in contempt.

"Diedre. Good to see you."

"Shannon. Not surprised to see you." She slammed the brews down as foamy drops spilled over. Both men took in the exchange with mild amusement.

"Well. Not sure what her problem is, but who cares? So, no work to do tonight, guys?"

"Nope, nothing is brewing. Are you positive your father knows you are out? I do not see anyone else here I recognize that may give you away. But, all the same."

"Sully, he did tell me it was okay. Sure, he was in his cups but when is he not? Be a good sort and just let it be and not remind him. Will you?" She patted him on the arm.

Adam hid his mirth. How easy she was to read. But those luscious green eyes belied the workings of a mischievous, educated, spoiled brat. Of that he was sure.

All of twenty-five, she was quickly approaching the unmarriageable age. Suspicions about her grew.

A small trio filled the stage with lively music as she eyed him. Only an ass would miss that blatant of a hint. "Come along, I know you would you like a spin on the floor." Adam had to admit her smile was seductive as he winked, passing by Sully. As they moved about the dance floor, the sound of the music increased, as well as hoots and hollers. Grabbing her by the arm in a quick spin, he actually abandoned reason and enjoyed it. Her. The alcohol in his system.

They stayed out there through two more before the inevitable happened. They started a slow, melodramatic folk-song, rich with lyrics of mayhem, whisky and women. He'd had enough. "This is not for me. Besides, our beer will get too warm."

He showed her back as another round was placed before them. Tonight, there would be no shortage of brew. He was going to make sure.

"Mike's giving the nod. A card game is set to begin in the back room. You up for it?"

"Yeah, I am. Got some cash burning a hole in my pocket. Let me settle with the bartender and meet you in there. Save me a chair. I see quite a few heading that way."

He stood, taking Shannon towards her escorts' table.

"Oh, no way. They are boring as hell. I can go in there. Look. Other women are following."

He laughed loudly. Did she realize who those women were? "Well, if you insist, sure. I'll get us each a drink before we do."

The bartender came over.

"Settling, but add two more beers to it."

He nodded, returning with two Guinness and the coinage. Adam pushed it back towards him. "You keep it." He took Shannon by the arm as they weaved through the smoke-filled room and found his chair next to his good friend. "Where will I sit?"

He glanced about. "The women don't sit in here, Shannon. They maneuver around the room. Probably best if you do not do that in case someone makes you out when the smoke settles. Safer to stay close to our table."

Their dealer appeared and sat on a tall stool. "Irish Switch, gentlemen. Place your bets up. Keep your hands where I can see them. Any problems and it just takes a nod and your ass will be thrown out of here. Money then stays." His smile grew bigger, showing crooked front teeth.

"Ready?"

The room filled with lewd conversation as men got drunk and women became friendly. Hours passed. Neither Adam or Sully gave Shannon a sideways glance. Both were having quite a stroke of luck at this table.

In the distance outside in the street, a gunshot rang out. Simultaneously, a few of the women ducked and hollered out. The men could give a shit and continued playing cards. It was just the signal that morning was soon to dawn and they had to clear out.

Rising, Adam looked for Shannon. She had found a vacant chair, removed it from a table and was slouched over, sound asleep in a corner. "Look at that. I should leave her here. But being the good sort I am, I'll wake her and take her home. Let's just hope her father is still away. I have no notion to lock horns with him on this day."

"I have it on good authority he will not be. Due back sometime this afternoon. So hoist away, my friend, and good luck to you." Sully swatted him on the back and then lit a cigarette. Swigging back the mug of beer, he slammed it down on the table and headed out into the bright daylight.

"Shannon, hey girl, we have to get you up and home before your father gets back. Can you hear me?"

She groaned as her eyelids fluttered open. "Oh, I was not dreaming. I am still with you. What did you say about my father? Oh!" She stood quickly, smoothing out her dress. "I need to get home. How late is it?"

"Rather early, my dear. The sun is about to rise high in the sky. Is there an entrance you prefer to use this time of the morning?" He stepped aside, allowing her to walk ahead of him outside, where they viewed a dark, angry sky. Clouds prepared to dump a stream of water down upon them. "We'd better get a move on. Or, we get soaked."

Quickly she glanced up and back towards Adam. "Yes, yes, this way. We can go around behind the neighbors. I can climb over a small fence and up through a back window. It goes to the laundry room so no servants will notice. It's too early. Besides, it's not laundry day."

"Got it all figured out, do you?"

"Well, sometimes I fall asleep like last night and don't get home in time. I know my father won't bother me if he raps on my door and I don't answer. He does not always know if I am really in there or not."

"Well, hell will pay if we don't get you back in case this is the one day he decides to find out for himself."

"Oh, I can't have that happen."

She halted suddenly, taking him by surprise by placing both gloved palms on his chest. He'd take the bait. When their lips met, he could feel that tremble, her tremble.

"What? No apologies?"

He bit back a retort. He was merely taking what she offered. It was her own action that brought this about. Not his.

"Nope, not a damn one."

He released her hand as they moved silently around to the shaded back entrance. "Shannon, I'll be by later today. Your father will not care. Five o'clock. I will stay for dinner."

One leg was inside the window and one dangling as she smiled. "Yes, do that." Then it was shut as she peered through the dirty pane and he could have sworn she waved before disappearing completely.

Eyes narrowed, mind clearing from the alcohol-induced night and that kiss, he walked back and entered his room. He washed up and changed into a fresh set of clothes, ridding himself of the odor of booze and smoke. Then he laid down and allowed sleep to claim him. It was twelve noon when he rose, headed out, grabbed a bite to eat and sauntered back toward the docks.

That redhead was full-blown on his mind.

Chapter Thirteen

"Miss Shannon, this is not something your father would approve. I know he messaged a later return, so I have prepared a letter to give to your gentleman caller waiting out in the foyer."

"Give me that letter." Her hand was out waiting. "It will be fine. I will be fine. You will be right here. Besides, at my age, I should be able to have a daytime caller. Don't you think?"

Her servant was indeed displeased. It was written all over her face as Shannon stared her down, daring her to overstep her boundaries. "Okay, you are mistress of the house. But I strongly disagree. I will show him in but I remain here with you. I won't have your father finding out. Last time was my final warning and I can't afford to lose my position in this household. Your antics have landed me in enough hot water with him. I've covered for you too many times."

"Okay. I won't give you any trouble. Is it Mr. O'Malley?"

"Yes, so sit and look like a lady. Over there. I'll go and show him in. I have a fresh pot of tea brewing. I will fetch that and be back directly. Until then, no unorthodox business. That is all the time I'm going to give you to be alone with him and there will be no argument."

"Fine. Go get him. He's been kept waiting long enough."

Narrowed eyes pierced Shannon's as a cold chill snaked its way up her spine. That woman, she thought, sometimes seemed like pure evil, seeing through her every move.

"Sir, Miss Shannon is right in here." She stood aside, allowing him entry into the small parlor. "I have a refreshment tray ready. I'll return to join you both in a few minutes."

"I understand." Adam spoke back to the servant before entering the room and glancing at Shannon.

"You don't look yourself this morning. Are you feeling well?"

"Tis true, I am afraid after our tea I will beg off and lie down."

"I can leave now. I don't want you to wait if you need to rest."

"No, it would not be hospitable to do that since you came this way. Plus, I have no desire to piss off my servant. If I bug out now, she will surely be put out at having prepared us a tray."

As if on cue, the servant appeared. She set the tray down and moved over to a shadowed corner near one of the few windows in the room.

"Please sit down." Shannon spoke softly, glancing up and locking eyes with him. She could feel the intensity of his gaze even with a safe distance between them.

"She's on to you, I take it?"

A slight grin formed, followed by an even slighter nod in confirmation. "Yes, and I'm about to wring her neck. But she needs the work and I'd feel horrible to have Pop let her go because of me."

"I take it a few have gone that way over the years?"

She moved a bit closer, which brought an immediate "ah-hum" from across the room. "Yes, the last one butted in a bit too much. I had a good suitor. But it appears she knew more about him then I did. He ended up being on the other side. A planted spy. When he disappeared, so did she. I've never seen either around the city again."

"Exiled, jail or worse?"

"I don't want to talk about it. Okay?" She tipped back her cup and set it down. "Do you want a refill?"

"No, I've trespassed on your time." He stood, placing his hat back on, "Thank you. I hope you feel better so we can see you out and about soon." He took her hand in his gently and then released it, nodded to the maid and left the room.

***

Just before closing the outside door, he stopped long enough to hear their voices rising, chuckled then closed it firmly. Yet, he thought, something was nagging at him. He continued walking along the busy street and stopped in front of the bakery. Then he walked up onto the sidewalk and went inside and purchased a sandwich. Back out onto the street, he moved away from the people and off to one side and hovered in a side alley stacked high with dilapidated fishing traps.

As he bit into it and chewed, crumbs from the bread fell to the cobbles at his feet. A rat scurried out, grabbed them and disappeared into a crack in the building. Finished, he reached into a jacket pocket and removed a match, grazing it against the cold stone and lighting a cigar.

His eyes remained watching down the street. Then, there she was. A hooded, cloaked figure. He scrutinized her more carefully as she got closer and closer. Her eyes flickered in different directions as if she was looking carefully to make sure the coast was clear.

As she approached him, Adam lowered his gaze and inhaled on the cigar, blowing out a puff of smoke just as she passed by. She was so close he had no issue placing in her slightly opened receptacle a small listening device. As she moved on, he adjusted his stance toward her retreating back.

Suddenly she stopped a bit further up the alley, a hand resting on the handle of a heavy metal door. She darted one more quick look around and then opened and closed the door behind her.

He kept a safe distance while inserting a mic inside his right ear. Tugging up his collar and down on the Irish cap, he slouched against the side of the building and relit the cigar.

A fully masked IRA soldier came by, stopped, stepped back, then glanced down at him. A gun was poised ready to unload right at his head.

Adam nodded once, staying put.

The soldier passed on.

He tuned in and listened.

"Jaime, no one followed me, I promise. I've found the perfect decoy. Honest, he's the one. Nearly your build and coloring. If anyone saw you side by side they would think you are brothers."

A strong British accent replied. "Excellent. Now, how are we going to make the switch so I can take his ID and cross back over the border? I need his along with my own so I can get these details of your father's operations back into my commander's hands. Especially before that next shipment. Have you gotten into his office yet to get those papers?"

"No, it's locked. I don't like this at all. I think he's starting to suspect me of something. I'm hoping it's just stepping out without a chaperone. I thought he would have me followed by now. Maybe he thinks there are enough people here that would turn me in if they suspected foul play of any kind."

"Then we must move soon. When will you see the bloke again?"

"I do not know. I could get word to him. I need to be careful. I don't want a paper trail to get back to me when he disappears. He does frequent a couple of the pubs along the waterfront. I know a few of them and can get in there with my cousins. They are useless and have no clue what I am doing. No one would suspect a thing. Including my father."

There was silence.

"What about Sully? He could identify me. I need to make sure he's not around."

"No, he's doing something else. The time is now."

"Good, the sooner the better. I'll have my man Reardon follow you. All you need to do is locate him in the room, make contact and he will find me. I can wait in the darkness, close by until the time is right for us to dispose of him. I am fully aware of the weakest section of the city. I'll cross there. You remember what he looks like, right?"

"I do. But what about me? You said you'd take me this time."

"I had not finished. Be ready with a satchel. Take only what you need. I can't be carrying several cases."

There was silence as Adam drew in his brows. *Women*, he thought. Beauty usually meant two things. Dumber than dumb, or into something way over their heads. Then there was a third category. Sam.

"Okay, I'll go tonight and look for him. You be ready. Is there ample time to get word to Reardon?"

"Consider it done. Now go and see if you can gain access to your father's office. If you can't, what I have from the last two times should give us a good idea of where the next shipment is coming in from."

The grating sound of the metal door against the stone, followed by her shoes against the rickety stairs, alerted Adam it was time to shove off. Into the shadow he moved, quietly monitoring her exit.

He watched her peer in every direction to ensure the path was clear as she hurried up the street. He stepped out in plain sight then, watching her go. She never looked back.

He dislodged the wire, placed it in his jacket and took off in search of Sully. Laughing, he crossed the street and found him with a shoe up on a crate hanging out with a group of guys outside of Paddy's Pub. He nodded him over.

"What's up?"

"Come with me. I've got to fill you in on what I've just learned. We've got our mole."

***

Several blocks away, Shannon rushed into the house and threw her hood back and cloak off, missing the hook entirely as the servant looked at her sternly. "Not now, sorry. I forgot something in my father's study and I need to get it. I must have left it there the other night when he and I were talking about him going away for an overnight."

"Now you know I can't open that for you. He gave me strict orders that no one was to get in there at all. That, my dear, includes you."

"Surely you are mistaken. He did not specifically say my name. I mean, I'm what's left of his flesh and blood here in this house. With my poor mother passing away last year, God rest her soul, and my brother in exile who knows where. It will only take me a second, I promise."

"If you get me into more trouble… well, I do not know what I will be able to do. Jobs are tight here, Shannon."

"I mean true to my word. I will not tell him."

"Well, all right. But be quick. He may be home anytime. We have both seen how angry he can get." She pulled the key's cord up and out from beneath her dress top. Quickly unlocking the door, she allowed Shannon to pass inside.

"I'm going to stay right here until you retrieve it. Now make quick work of it."

Suddenly, sounds of successive knocks were heard by them both toward the lower back door. "Oh no." She glanced down at her pinned watch. "That's the delivery boy and I can't make him wait. Last time he left it all on the doorstep and some of the meat spoiled. You get it done, miss. I'll come back in a few minutes and lock it up and no one will be the wiser."

She rapidly turned and left as Shannon moved over to the bookcase and took out the one hardback she knew was hollowed out inside. Glancing through the contents, she smiled, quickly scanning. Yes, this was what he wanted. Moving the books around, Shannon made sure it did not even look like one was missing at quick appraisal. Good. Running over, she closed the door just as the servant appeared.

"A book? You wanted a book?"

"Yes, it was my mother's favorite of myths and legends of Ireland. I wanted to take it back to my room." She hurried by her up the stairs, calling over her shoulder, "I won't be here for supper. I am going out with my cousins. If my father returns, please tell him I'm sorry I was not here and why. I did not want to cancel on them. It is their first-year anniversary and all."

She did not wait for a reply. Dashing, she washed her hair and changed into a dress more desirable to maneuver in tight spots. Pinning her damp hair back up, she removed all her jewelry and jotted a quick note to her father. Packed, she lifted the satchel, left the room and eased it down the laundry shoot. Turning an ear towards the funnel, she listened. The soft sound of it arriving below into the basket was final confirmation.

Fingers crossed, she hoped the cook did not hear it. The kitchen was a floor up from the laundry room. Cloak over an arm, quietly she walked down the stairs and out the front, gingerly closing the door. Rushing quickly around the back, she used a stashed window hook to reach in and grab the bag.

The streets were filling up with men returning from work. Burly longshoremen returning from the docks, masked IRA members and drunks picking themselves up from the washed-out gutters looking about for their next drink. The sun had set and along with it the artificial light of the gas lamps illuminated every step. Finally, she arrived at the front entrance of the bustling Salty Dog.

The door swung open and two drunks sauntered out as Shannon rested her eyes on Reardon. She knew he would not be here unless her gent was. Trying to gain further entry, a hard shove had her reaching for the bar rail while dropping her bag down beside his boots. Rising, her eyes locked with Adam's.

"I did not think I'd see you in a place like this, Shannon."

"Well, I was just passing with my cousins. They are headed across the street to eat. When the doors opened, I saw you and thought I'd stop in and apologize for my rudeness earlier today. I'm feeling better. Although unladylike, I wonder if I could buy you a beer."

"Against my better judgment and the wrath of your father, sure, why not? Bartender, two our way when you can."

"So, do you have plans tonight with anyone?" She glanced quickly around the busy, smoked-filled room. "That you are meeting?"

"Nope, solo. Glad, though, to see you are feeling better. You decidedly were peaked this afternoon."

"A good rest was all I needed. I have an idea. When we have finished our beer, do you want to have dinner with us? I told them I'd be along in a little while."

"Good of them to hold off until you arrive, I'd say. I'll come along. I could use a good bite to eat."

They both finished their beers.

"Shall we?"

"Yes. Oh, I left my bag over by that man near the door. I did not want to carry it all the way in. I will grab it. I'm spending the night with them."

"Here, let me." He picked it up, grin hovering. "Light as a feather. Are you sure you have enough for the night?"

Was he joking around with her? Damn, for a split second she felt nervous, knowing there was no way he would have let her carry the bag. "Here, it's just down the street and around that bend. It's a local place. You probably don't know about it, having not been around that long. But the food is really good."

***

As they turned the corner, something hard hit the side of his head. All Adam could recall before falling to the hard stones below was that stars did indeed explode in front of his eyes. He laid still, motionless, faintly hearing boots, hard and fast all around him. Then loud voices, a muffled scream, and silence.

Stone cold silence.

Was he dead?

Slowly, his head was raised by strong hands. It hurt like bloody hell. Groaning, he held that arm with his hand to keep it from moving him further. He winced.

"Mate, hey, come on. They did not hit you that hard. Shit, are you going soft on me now?" Adam opened his eyes up gingerly, feeling the lump on the side of his head. "Yeah, well I guess I will live if I'm seeing your ugly face. Unless we've both gone to hell."

Sully laughed. "That's more like it."

Standing, Adam squared off face to face with Jimmy O'Finnigan, who was next to Sully.

"Nice work there, lad. I had not wanted to believe for a moment that it was my very own flesh and blood selling me out. I guess I need to admit it now. I've been ignoring the signs for a long while."

"What will you do with her? Did you get the Brit?" That made O'Finnigan flinch. Shannon had sold him out to the very enemy they had been fighting all this time. "She is being taken to a secure place so it can be decided. I'm stepping aside on this one, letting Sully, Phinney, and Carey work it out."

"The satchel, it holds more than her clothes, do you have it?"

"Nope. The bloke got away with it."

"Damn, that's not good. There was more in there than her clothes."

"I know, son, I let it go. It's got bogus paperwork that will keep those bastard British turning circles while we move our cargo. I planted it where I thought she'd look. I was right about that, unfortunately. But can't stop a father from trying."

Adam shook his hand. "I got a bit of good news for you, though. While I was hanging out doing Sully's work for him—" He eyed his now good friend with a glint in his eyes. "—I got you something back in return. Coming straight at us now."

Walking towards them with a gimp was someone very dear to Jimmy O'Finnigan.

"Oh, blessed on us all by the Holy St. Patrick himself. Quinn, is that you, son? I can hardly recognize you with that beard. Dear to your mother's soul. It is you," he muttered, tears filling his eyes.

"Yes, it's me. I don't know how you managed to get this done but I am so glad to see the likes of you, Pops!"

They hugged. A father and son had been reunited as Sully watched Adam slip off into the night out of his sight. O'Finnigan turned towards him to thank them both.

"Where the hell is Adam?"

"He had to go. He does not care for reunions of a gushing type. That's all."

They laughed as he took his son by the shoulder. "Home. We need to get you bathed; you smell like the Lagan."

"Yeah, a good bottle will follow that. I stayed back, Pops, and watched. I am sorry about Shannon."

"I'll deal with that later. She's in a safe spot while we figure out what will be done. If it was anyone else's daughter she'd be dead now. This is under tight wraps. Nobody outside of our small group knows. I'm thinking about a monastery in Spain, son."

***

As Adam picked his moment to exit, moving through the alley to sounds of gunfire growing softer and softer, another sound became stronger.

It was the call to prayer.

Coming out of the cobbled alley, he smiled, looking down at his Arabic dress and the pouch crossed over his body. It had been a hell of a transit this time. From Ireland to… where?

Glancing around at the surroundings, drawing in both brows, he knew he was a stranger to this foreign land. A horn honked as he stepped back up on a curb. All the signs were in Arabic and English. In fact, they all pointed to the center of the ancient city, or what remained of it.

Mecca.

What the bloody hell was he doing here?

Feeling for the lump, he shook his head to clear his thoughts, but it was gone. Well, it sure as shit should be. How could a lump on one's head last for that many years? He grinned, moving with a throng of Arabians across the street and toward an opposite alley. Pausing, he glanced above at the shingle over the door as his eyes brightened. Placing a strong hand on the handle, he gave it a turn.

Chapter Fourteen

"In all that's beautiful, Ali, I've never seen such a piece that could bring a person to their knees, yet yield such hope at the same time. It's beyond words what you have done."

"My work here is finished, Sam. You are now ready to leave and continue along on your journey. Here, come over and touch this. Hold it in your hands. I want you to know the power it generates. As no two but you and he would ever be able."

Sam understood without a doubt the turbulent emotions exuding throughout her insides. Yes, she was afraid. Each step was a struggle. Yet it was tugging her closer, the need to reach out and grasp it so powerful her knees nearly buckled. She held the tip with a velvet cloth, the handle pointed directly towards her heart. How ironic, she thought as the internal dialogue began in earnest.

"You have no choice. The sooner the better. Or I will put it down. For it is quite heavy. Too heavy for this old man to hold much longer."

She did not smile. "I'm scared, Ali."

"Yes, I can see that. Do you want me to put it back in its box and close and lock the lid so you don't have to think about? Giving you time to prepare if I do that? It will delay what you need to do next. Keep that in mind."

She rose to the bait, never having been one to back down from any kind of a challenge. He released it just as she took it into both hands. "Oh, my God," she softly muttered, feeling the full force of the beautifully carved metal sword.

A torrential gale-force wind blew, lifting her hair up as it swirled around her. Raising it higher, not feeling its heaviness at all, she turned, slicing the air as voices penetrated. Too many of them. Women, men and children. Then she heard the one that resonated above all the others.

Ranof.

Strongly he spoke, "Come to Luxor. Come to me."

Ali grabbed the sword just before she dropped it to the hard floor. Wrapping it securely and placing in a long protective box, he closed the lid and snapped the bindings shut.

She gasped for air as her eyes locked with his.

"I've never seen such a sight as that. It will stay with me for the rest of my days. I almost wish I was going with you so I could see what happens next. But alas, that is not my task."

"I cannot possibly carry that box any lengthy distance. I will need help. If it is not you, then who is it?"

"I think that's where I come in, mistress."

Her hands crossed over her heart as she closed her eyes. Exhaling deeply, Sam turned around slowly, her lower lip dropping as her eyes swallowed him whole and then filled with tears. It could not be helped.

"For real?"

Adam stepped close, nodding to Ali, who quickly exited the room, giving them complete privacy. He stood a foot away, clothed in traditional white Arabic dress, head wrap, black shoes and a bag slung across his handsomely rugged frame. Even his face was slightly tanned.

"Yes."

A shaking hand reached out and touched that white robe. Followed by the other until her feet finally closed the distance. He did not move, giving her time, until his index finger raised her chin. Thus, her eyes to his. That's when he lowered his lips to claim those which he had sorely missed. Weeks of pent-up frustration, longing and desire emerged as she returned that kiss with a passion that neither had experienced with the other before.

Was that even possible?

He clutched her tightly, feathering kisses over her eyelids and down her tear-streaked cheek. She felt his hand maneuver an unruly strand of silky hair back behind an ear.

"Still not believing?"

"Oh, you have no idea how much I have wanted to see you. I have missed you so much. I wanted to chuck this all in and just come home to you. But I could not. I knew I would not be allowed there until I completed something of great importance here."

He let go of her waist and moved over to pick up the box. "We need more privacy than will be afforded here. Where have you been staying?"

"Just two minutes away outside and around the corner. But wait. I need to write a note to Ali. He was magnificent in taking care of this for me and hospitable to no end." She knew where he kept his stock of paper and pencils and retrieved one, writing a thank you. Placing it on his first shelf so he'd see it when he did come back, she slid her hand over the top of this master's bench and sighed.

The book was back where it belonged and so was her lover. Her real lover. What was she going to tell him? His hand came out in mid-air, waiting on her. She reached over and took it. The warmth spread through her like slipping into a much anticipated soothing bath.

He would not let her release his hand when they were out in public. She took him and their precious cargo around the bend, into the building and up to the second floor. Unlocking the door, she slid in ahead and secured it as he entered. He set it set down on the settee.

"Nice digs."

She gasped, turning straight into his arms.

"Oh, my God! I left without even putting on my burka! I need to go back and get it. Shit, I can't. You will go. Can you please do it now? Things just seem to evaporate around me."

He grinned. "You have to let me back in, you know. When I knock. You need me to transport out of here."

She melted into his warmth. "I'll let you back in. I never wanted you out."

***

Ah, his Sam was close to returning to him fully. He shut the door and headed back to the shop as Ali met him at the front door with the garments in his hands, holding them out. "How do you just know things?"

"No different than you. I did not want to keep you two apart for long. See, even old men still have a bit of romance left in them. I think I'll go find my wife for a few minutes…" He smiled, shutting the shop door and moving the sign over to CLOSED.

She had the door slightly ajar as Adam came in, setting the burka on the chair. "You must not have liked wearing that at all. I can only imagine the things you were muttering behind that full veil."

She handed him a glass of wine, grinning. "Sorry, we don't have anything stronger than this. We secured this locally from their black market. Even that was sketchy because we had to use two male sources to acquire it."

"You managed in the time here to find someone to sell you bootleg alcohol in a land steeped in suppressing women? You could have been set up and stoned to death, you know."

"Would have been worth it. We wanted booze."

He laughed, feeling her anxiety in the few inches separating them. She needed time and he would give it to her. At last, they were united and right now that was all that mattered. Almost. Except for what he'd witnessed minutes ago in the shop.

"We? I am taking it that it was Anne and Clash?"

Her eyes brightened up considerably. "You saw them then? They are both back there?"

"Yes, and establishing quite an 'Oh, look who've I met recently and I'm interested in' scenario. It's quite amusing, I must add."

"Are they at the cottage? Any news you can give me?"

"Well, I found your statue and Clash there in the same evening so we talked as much as we could. You know how that goes. But these two seemed headed in the same direction we are. Or perhaps they are going to reach 'that' before we do. I don't know." He swigged back the dark liquid. "It's pretty good. I'm going to refill. You want a tap up?"

***

"Bring the bottle back in with you; it's small."
She rose, moving over to the windows and opened them slightly, listening to the last call to prayer. His arms came around her waist, pulling her tight back against him. How she loved the feel of this man.

His chin rested on top of her head. "There are two bedrooms, I see. If you feel more comfortable, I will stay in the other one tonight. We have a vehicle being left tomorrow so I can drive us to the coast. We are avoiding Jeddah. It is too busy. Instead, we are driving a bit farther north, where a small ferry will be awaiting us for a transit over to Egypt. We have to be very careful with our parcel and how we cross."

She wanted him to just keep on talking. Forever. The rumble of his voice from his chest through her back was heavenly. "I'm ready. I can't wait to throw the damn burka into the sea when we hit the other side. I've seen more suppression of women in the last few weeks than I ever want to see again in my life. The one saving grace for being forced to wear one was that veil you alluded to did indeed hide the movement of my mouth. The robe some pretty nasty hand signals."

He chuckled.

"Absolutely you will be staying in my room tonight, Adam."

She turned in his arms and moved away, taking tight hold of one hand. Glancing at the box, she silently asked him to take it along with them just as a precaution. He carried it into her room, setting it down on the tile floor.

***

She closed the drapes as he removed his headdress and robe, laying them on the back of the chair. The atmosphere electrified. Sam flicked on the bedside lamp as the room radiated in soft light as her eyes devoured him. He felt her need straight through to his soul.

Standing before him was the woman he loved without end. Call it what you want, he thought, soulmate, life mate, love of his life, it did not matter. Those were only words. None of that compared to the churning emotions building as she pulled the crisp white shirt out from his pants, unbuttoning one at a time. He let her do what she needed. He was giving her the chance to set the pace. Hell, the longer he had with her, the better.

Her warm lips pressed against his muscular chest as a soft sigh rustled the hairs on it. Sliding hands to his belt, unbuckling it and sliding the zipper down, he pushed his pants down and stepped out of them. The shirt was soon tossed aside. Stopping, she raised her top up and hurled it away, pressing into every bit of him, wrapping hands around his neck, pulling his lips to her own. Gentleness now gone, she claimed him with such force that he pitched back and they landed on the bed together.

He thought he knew every move of those sweet, gentle hands, but a moan escaped when she clasped his swollen manhood. Eyes drifted closed, lips locked as the fire from her damp body sent his blood surging. Already holding tightly to such a mighty need, Adam was sure as soon as he entered her it would all be over.

"Oh, my God. I've felt your heat before. But never like this, Sam."

"You have no idea how urgently I want you inside of me."

"Then do it."

She slid him in, pausing.

One hand clutched a mass of long, silky tresses as his mouth simply devoured her lips. Then they both lost it. Swiftly turning her over onto her back, legs high, there was not a fraction he did not take in his thrusts. Her moans echoed off the walls as with one final plunge she cried out, nails grasping his back, digging in nearly breaking the skin. He did not care. It was the reminder that she was here. Beneath him. Still desiring him.

Lowering her legs, he kept her pinned as his mouth claimed hers in a final exclamation point.

She was his.

Minutes later, her breathing finally normalized as he moved, taking her into his arms.

"Adam, if I die right now, it would be okay. I got to see you again, lay with you again."

"What the hell are you saying that for? You are not going to die. Is there something you are not telling me?"

He leaned onto his side as she matched his move and put her hand on the curve of his neck. They both could feel the moistness there.

"I don't know. It's going to be hard to explain this to you when I don't understand it myself."

"Why don't you just start by trying? I'm all ears. We have all night."

"It may take that long."

He waited. He'd keep her here. Damn the people upstairs, the sword and their assigned tasks. Suddenly, all that mattered was what she had to say. "I know the rules, Sam, but this time I need to hear it all. Forget about all of 'them' right now."

A shudder passed through her. She was worried.

"I'll do my best. When I arrived in Egypt I met Clash. We each had our own agenda so you know how that goes. Then he helped me get to Yemen, where I stole some gems from a private collection and was assisted by him and some associates over the Yemen border to Saudi. That's when I met up with Anne and a group of nuns who helped by stowing me away until we were ready to move on. While we were there, I found myself in their library and picking up a book I was extremely drawn to. That was a very strange experience. It definitely had a power all its own."

His gaze never left her eyes, or her beautiful face, as she paused to compose herself.

"It was when I read about Ranofer Aiempt that my body began to shake and for the second or perhaps third time since leaving England, I heard him speaking to me. He demanded, Adam, not requested, that I come to him. It seems we have some unfinished business and it involves the sword and reuniting him with it."

"And with you."

She exhaled. "Yes, I know that now."

He ran a hand through his hair. "I remember you saying you are an old soul and go way back. What's this man to you and you to him?"

"I do not clearly know that part yet. It seems I must have suppressed parts of what happened back then. Which frightens me. People only do that when something horrible has taken place."

"Was he a Pharaoh or someone of importance? What era was this?"

"He was known as Rano the Mercenary and the very inventor of what is in that box. Hired to instill some menacing tactics to regenerate a dying Egyptian army. Quickly, he moved up through the ranks, along with training charioteers and the infantry. He became Thutmose III's second in command of the army."

"That sword. I saw it and what happened to you when you held it. I've never seen anything like that. You were completely possessed by its powers."

Her eyes welled up as she stoically tried to suppress the tears. "Yes, I don't know what hold he has on me. But it's potent. I must go back. Give him closure. Closure for the both of us. For all of us."

"God, Sam. If I even had a hunch back in Venice that my kiss would have brought you to this, I think I would not have done it." He smoothed a hand over her dampened cheek.

"Yes, you would have. We were meant to do this. I was meant to have your help to help him. I'm thinking once I get back there and see how I can fix this, he can rest in peace and we can move on."

"That's a very dangerous time. War, acts of treason, poisoning."

"Sounds like our modern world. But it was also a time of amazing growth. Egypt's peak was reached during this time and I read women were placed high up on a pedestal and worshiped. Some, anyway. Look at Thutmose III's wife. I read she took over the throne before their son came of age and ruled for a few years. Then, there is Cleopatra and Mark Anthony...." She smiled softly, leaning in to kiss him.

"You don't know what you were to him, but his voice has been in the wind asking you to come back? This is too damn bizarre. Yet, I think I know more myself than I want to realize. This is stirring memories for me as well."

"I had a dream last night when I was at the shop. I must have dozed off while Ali finished, coming to cover me up. When I woke this morning I was still there. But in my dream, I saw him walking towards me with concern on his face. He was dressed for battle and I clearly was not happy. I was in a palace. But not as a slave. I should have thought to look at my hand to see if I was married. I don't even know if marriages took place back then. A ceremony and all and exchanged bands. I was also sure I saw you. But we were not as cozy as we are right now." A smile hovered.

He slid from the bed and walked over to his slacks, taking out his cellphone.

She laughed. "Are you going to Google it?"

"I certainly am. I'm curious and I'm sure you are too." He sat on her side of the bed as she leaned up, resting her body against his back, arms curled around his waist, hands settling on his stomach.

"Okay, here we go. If you are of standing in the community, your plight goes in front of the Pharaoh and his wife. If they agree, it's settled. Simple as that. No rings, no bachelor party, male strippers or any of that." His grin was devilish. "I can't recall what happened at the last bachelor party I attended."

"Oh, cut it out. But look there. If the female simply moved her things into his household, they were considered married. Done deal."

He put the phone on the bedside table and claimed her into his arms. "That means you and I are married. You moved into my house and rooms."

"That also means we are divorced now since I moved them all out into the cottage."

"Glad to see your sense of humor has not abandoned you."

She grinned. "How much simpler those times were. When you are bad and she's had enough of it, all that is necessary is to just pack it up and move on to the next dude. Sweet."

He pushed her onto her back. "Take me seriously just for a second. When you do come back we are going to have that talk again. I mean it."

Suddenly Sam looked a bit solemn.

"What is it?"

"I'm afraid I won't come back. I'm not sure why. He's long dead but haunting me. Why? Was I supposed to die with him? Be buried in his tomb like a mummy?"

He pulled her close, shutting off the light.

"I'll come and find you. I'll haunt you there. As sure as you feel me breathing and skin warm. I'll come and bring you back. Should I pass on before that happens, we shall meet out there somewhere and settle this. If he thinks he has claims to your very soul even from the dead, he's wrong."

A lone tear dropped onto his chest. Slowly it absorbed into his skin. "That was your mark. You are mine. No matter what, I will find you."

Chapter Fifteen

As she rolled, he did. She stretched, he did. She moved one arm up into the air and he matched her motion. They both broke out in laughter. .

"For one split second I thought we were back at home in England and it all had been a dream. What time is the car being left for us?"

Swinging his legs out of bed, feet touching the floor, he looked down at his watch. "In about ninety minutes. We should get something to eat. I need a cup of coffee or tea. You have anything here?"

"No, but there is a shop real close that does. They have a mean bagel with schmear and their beverage choices are excellent."

He laughed. "Schmear. I'll leave that one alone. I suggest a quick shower and get your mind around putting that burka on again." He was dressed in a flash and out the door, not even asking her if that was what she indeed wanted as she stared at it.

"Nope, not yet my friend," she softly muttered, running hands lovingly over the rumpled sheets, recalling his proclamation before they finally slept.

The door opened and he put the large bag on the circular glass table. "You were right, quite a joint. But I hope to never be back here again. The women were huddled in a corner waiting for their men to get their orders and then they could sit and eat. I see what you mean. I think Saudi is the worst place for women's rights on the face of the planet."

"But it's what they know, the women. It will be a very long road for them even if changes were allowed. Hmm, this is good. See, told you so. We'd better hurry up and get outside so we can head out. I feel as if we are carrying a Tommy gun or something in that box. Looks mighty suspicious, if you ask me."

"I'll bring it down. You grab your bag. Anything we need to get from here that is tucked away? Where do we leave the key?"

"No, I have all that's important to me now. I have no idea about the key. When we got here they were given to Clash. I guess I'll just leave them on the table."

"I see you made the bed."

She laughed. "Yeah, if someone came in and saw the sheets crumpled in a heap like that they may wonder who exactly was in here. I'm ready, let's go. I need to get out of this place as soon as we can."

The car pulled up as they came outside. Adam placed the box in the trunk and made sure it was locked. She climbed into the passenger's side as the man that brought it to them silently got out, nodded and walked across the street, disappearing into the same bagel shop.

"What about that? Funny how they just show up on time and don't say a word. I want that type of a job next go around."

"I hope when you get back your jobs are few and far between so we can get some things in order."

"You are going to persist in this, aren't you?"

"Damn straight I am."

"I have to wonder why they picked you to come and help me. There must be reasons beyond our tumble last night. Was it so I could actually tell you what was going on so you'd not just replace me back there in a few more months with another mistress?"

"Shit, that's not fair and you know it. But who the hell knows?"

"I did not really mean it the way it sounded. But I have to wonder why."

"If they want us to figure it out they will let us. Otherwise, it's just the way it is. Look in the glovebox, will you? There's got to be instructions somewhere on what our direction is. I can't just sit here with the car idling all day."

"Nope, nothing. Oh, wait, here it is." She flipped down her visor, removing a folded piece of paper clipped to it. "Yes, we are to head northwest on Route 5 to Yanbu. Shows where the street is located where we park and leave the car. It is the vicinity of where the boat is that will take us across to Egypt. It is above the Sudan border."

He put it into drive and pulled out into the early morning traffic. He glanced over as she was doing something on her cellphone.

"I just Googled the distance and it's under four hours. Damn, I can't say this enough: I can't wait to get out of this bloody outfit and on the other side."

"Not like we are just taking a drive in the country and looking for a place to picnic. More like we have a dead body of sorts in the trunk and we are a couple of renegades."

"Yeah, like a couple of Jersey mafiosos on a run from the big guy. Your name could be Nick."

They broke out in laughter.

"We need a couple of the AK47s like the ones I saw when I was in Ireland."

"Was that where you were before? Did you come directly here?"

"Going to have to marry you so you never repeat the things I say to other people. Code of honor and all."

"I think if any of them were monitoring us last night, they gave up on trying to make us conform to their code. Don't you?"

"Hopefully they were not watching. Let's not even go there. That's weird enough."

Route 5 was basically a steady paved dual access road that paralleled the Red Sea, the mountains, and the desert. It was neat to be on it, Sam thought, as the scenery went from busy to somewhat pretty in just a dozen miles.

"I'm going to visit that gypsy woman of yours when I get back and see if she can tell me more about how to treat old souls like you."

"Didn't see that coming. But she's a cool woman. I can't imagine since they've been allowed on your property for a lot of years that you have never come across her on your rides. Besides, Adam, I have no doubt you are one as well."

"I completely tried to avoid them is more like it. But I don't mind them being there at all. I know that sounded snobbish. But, I just have this vision of when I was a kid of always being beaten up and robbed by them."

"That's crap. You need to reach inside yourself and let go of that baggage."

He laughed, grabbing her hand.

"She may prove to be of interest to you. Perhaps as an old soul, you had your own house of concubines in Egypt during the time I was there. Too busy with all of them and twenty-seven kids, all with the name Mariam and Omar, to know what was what."

He laughed harder. "You are killing me. Stop it. I've had my share of fun with you, I know. But your sense of humor this morning is over the top. Aren't we supposed to be on a passage and not a vacation?"

"I'd rather take the vacation, thank you very much. Which makes me think if we can take these and travel around in time, why can't we do it for personal pleasure as well? Say I'd like to go to the Swiss Alps in the roaring twenties after the First Great War and have a ski. Then take an elevator to sunny Spain for the running of the bulls. Why can't we do that? Or can we and I did not get the memo?"

He smiled.

"I wonder if Anne and Clash will be all hooked up before I get back. I could see that coming. He tried to ignore it. Oh, and you should have been there to see how much she's grown up and gained confidence. It was a blast to watch. I hope I've not been rubbing off on her."

He did keep track of when she took a breath and what she said to make sure he was not asked to participate in the lengthy commentary going on. At last, the signage for their next destination began to appear.

"In all that's holy, why did you let me go on like that? Look at that sign. We are only six miles from Yanbu. I've talked for nearly three hours!"

"Madame, that was extraordinary. I must admit to never having been a non-participant in a one-way conversation like that ever. By the way, it was four hours and thirty-seven minutes, to be precise."

She glared at him and then spewed out in laughter. "My mother always said I talked too much. But really. That's going to bother me. I'm more anxious than I wanted you to know."

"Cat's out of the bag, little one. I knew way back about one mile into the ride. It's okay. It was amusing how you shifted gears. I thoroughly enjoyed it."

"Oh, that's our ramp. Let me look at that paper. Yeah, it is the first left off our exit. Then, two lights down and a right where the lot should be."

He maneuvered around some traffic and got the car parked and the trunk popped. He threw the keys back onto the front seat as she grabbed her bag and shut the door. This vehicle had served its purpose.

"Okay, this is interesting. Look over there. Two ferries. Which one do we take?" They both looked at each other and at the vessels. "I'd say it's that one to the left. The writing translates to Yanbu Passages. I'm going with that one."

She nodded. "Okay, let's go. You get the tickets and I'll hover with the goods."

He spoke in fluent Arabic to the man inside the wooden kiosk. "Two, is this crossing to Janbu?"

The man nodded, taking his payment and giving him two vouchers. "Boarding is taking place now."

He waved, then realized she'd struggle with the box. So he jogged over and lifted it as she was trying in vain. "Sorry about that. They are boarding. We'd better get a move on."

"I put inside your pocket this morning my Saudi and Egyptian passports. So, master, you have total control of my world right now."

He laughed. "I'm sure that's not for long. I'll take it while I can. Let's go." They walked up the plank as he lowered the box and handed over two tickets and passports. The security officer quickly examined them with a side glance at Sam, and handed them back to Adam.

Lifting the box, they went in search of two secluded seats near the first door. Sitting down, they did not speak as he put those passports in her outside zipper bag and then checked to ensure the other two were ready.

"Going to the lady's room. With all this garb, it may take me up to five hours to get back. If we arrive before, come and find me."

He chuckled; she was still at it.

***

But it did take her a while. She sat on the closed lid, mesmerized. A sudden journey flashed before her eyes. A papyrus ship, oars raised, with a tall, muscular man at the bow, glancing up the Nile towards other ships. Suddenly he turned towards her as if she was on board and filled her vision. Ranof.

The walls of the stall vanished.

Hands planted on solid hips, his eyes bore right through her as darkness threatened to engulf. Steadying, placing both hands on either side of the stall and feeling the coolness, finally her true vision returned. "Damn," she muttered, resting her face down onto cold palms.

The toilet next to her flushed, bringing her back to current surroundings. Wow. She had really left the playing field this time. Standing, she walked out, noticing no one waiting, and went and sat back down beside him. "I need to get the hell out of this outfit as soon as possible. Especially before we land. I can see our approach out that window."

"Yeah, you need to change before we hand over proper documents. Why don't you come with me for a stroll towards the rear of the ship? I have a bag we can dispose of it in."

The stench of diesel filled the rear as they glanced about. They were alone. "Go ahead. I'll keep watch. Our view is really blocked from here. But hurry just in case." Hastily she removed it and stuffed it into the bag. Rolling it up tightly, she eyed him.

He nodded and she dropped it over the edge. Quickly it was sucked up, churning in the wake, and was soon fast from view without a trace.

Heavy voices reached them as ropes were thrown ashore to be tied to the large pier. "Good. Let's wait until everyone exits and we will move to the door and get off." Sam peered into the seating area. "It's clear."

As they came off the gangplank, there was no place to go except directly into the customs building. Adam took out their ticket and Egyptian passports and handed them over as the officer looked up, briefly comparing pictures. Then he handed them back.

"*Mutasakkir.*" The officer nodded, glancing over their shoulder to move them along.

"You are quite handy to have about, you know."

"Keep that in mind. Especially if we are forced to split later. What's the plan? This is your gig. Luxor? Where specifically?"

"I'm thinking the museum. I believe I need to get in after dark. Which may prove to be quite tricky. I'm sure, though, you can figure something out."

"Oh, how interesting this has become."

"Well, someone's got to do it. I had heard at the gaming tables you are often referred to as a smooth criminal."

"That bastard brother of yours. He told you. Well, I have very good luck at it, that's all."

"Call it what you will…"

"Yeah, whatever." He grabbed a hand, pulling her close, causing her bag to hit the ground with a thud.

"Hey."

He leaned down and kissed her. "I can do that here, mistress. We will not get thrown in jail for my display of affection towards you."

"What the hell has gotten into you?"

"It's not what got into me. It is what I got into. Or, rather who."

She blushed. "Bring you over the border and all hell breaks loose. Okay, we need a place to stay near the museum. We won't have time to get in and do a thorough review of it at this late hour. So, we may as well settle in for the night and go eat. I know this area well. Let's get a cab."

He laughed, raising a hand and hailing one. "Lead on then, madam. The sooner we get to that room the better."

She spoke to the cab driver through the passenger side window. "Hotel Nefertiti, please. Can you pop your trunk so we can put our luggage in?"

"Absolutely, miss. Please let me take that from you." He quickly got out of the car and took her bag and the box and set them in the back. She was not worried about it. Ali had wrapped and packed it so snugly. It would be fine on their probably fast and bumpy ride to the hotel.

They slid into the back seat with Adam close to her side. Sam pressed the window button down and grinned as it halted of its own accord half way. "I feel like I'm coming home at last, Adam. I can see a whole lot more now."

"How many times have you been here?"

She laughed, leaning towards his ear as he lowered his head. "Why not ask how long I've been here instead of how often? Then I can say thousands of years…"

He kissed her cheek. "You look amazing for your age."

She gave him a sweet smile. "I wish we could just stay here. Then move on when we grew tired of it to someplace else. Maybe northern Italy. I love the Lago de Como area. The cycling is amazing."

"I am surprised you have not tried to sneak a bike back to England. Except you would have caused a scandal. Possibly talked about across the entire country and thrown in jail for having such a contraption. You must be in complete withdrawal by now."

"No shit, I sure am." She saw the driver's eyes crinkle in a smile. "Here there probably won't be an opportunity. So, it will wait until some other time, I guess. You now know one of the few reasons I get cranky."

The car stopped and Adam climbed out, extending a hand as the driver put their things on the curb in front of the Nefertiti. He paid the fare and then they walked into the hotel and directly towards the front desk clerk.

"A suite on the upper floor if you have it available."

"Yes, we do have one. How many nights will you need it for? Your credit card and passport, please." The openly appreciative gaze of the female clerk was not missed by either of them.

"Let's start with two. Are you booked after that if I need to extend it?"

She glanced at the computer monitor. "No, we have five consecutive nights available before our next booking arrives for this suite."

"Great, two then."

She handed him the room cards. "Fourth floor, Valley of Kings Suit. Can I send up anything for you?"

"No, thank you."

Sam stepped up. "Ah, actually I just Googled your site and you have bike rentals on the property. Is that correct?"

"Yes, we do. The concierge over there can arrange that for you. It's going to be a bit cooler today and hot tomorrow. Today you may enjoy it more."

He eyed her. "Really?"

They were on the way over to the concierge. He followed; she lead the way. "Hello. We are staying in the suite and I wondered how soon you can arrange two hybrid bikes for us to rent for the afternoon? If possible with locks and helmets?"

"Yes, we can do that. I can have them ready and outside the lobby in thirty minutes. Unfortunately, we do not have helmets but do provide locks. Are you in need of a basket on either?"

Sam smiled up at Adam. "Just one. Is there someplace close by where we can purchase food and beverage?"

"Yes, the Aladdin Café can take care of that. Shall I charge the bikes to your suite?"

Adam nodded. "Go ahead. She's going to go with or without me. I may as well tag along."

He smiled. "I have a wife like that. I feel for you, sir."

She was about to pipe up that they were not married but he tugged at an arm. "Thank you. It may be forty or so minutes. But we will be down as soon as we can."

He nearly dragged her and all their possessions up to the room. He inserted the room key and opened the door. She slid in, setting the bag down on a side chair and stood with hands on hips, glancing around. Whitewashed walls were adorned with replicated Egyptian art as bright-colored fabric lay invitingly on the oversized bed. The suite had a real Middle Eastern feel.

Walking over and swinging open the double-wide doors, she stepped outside onto the large balcony. "Oh, come and see this. It is going to be fantastic to see the lights come on when it gets dark. They also have a great rooftop terrace that has excellent local dishes. I like this hotel. When I stayed here I was in a single room. I'm stepping up."

He came up beside her. "What's over there?"

"That's the heart of the historic district. Just off to the west is the Luxor Temple. We go in that direction. Then it follows the Avenue of the Sphinxes to the Nile and finally into the West Bank Mountains off there in the distance."

"So where is the museum?"

"Close by. Can't quite see it from here. We probably will when we eat tonight up at the terrace." He pulled her back into the room, leaving the doors open so they could enjoy a slight breeze. "Did you have something in mind that would delay our going for a bike ride?"

"I can't believe you did that." He was pulling her top up over her head. "To pay me back, and you are going to do that right now, you need to allow me to do what I want to you."

She had already removed most of his clothes as her panties slid to the floor and he lifted her up. Well before they hit the bed, she took him right into her.

"Okay."

He slid out of her, to a loud moaning complaint which brought a smile to his face as he took one of her nipples into his mouth, massaging the other. She squirmed, neck arching as he left that perked nipple and moved south, stopping where he would himself make a feast.

His tongue tasted gingerly, then shot inside as she clutched a handful of his hair, holding on for dear sweet life. Then the flow of emotions rocked her, shattering all thought except the immense pressure that was quickly building inside.

As she released, her body broke out in a sweat. He took her hands in his and kissed her deeply, wanting her to know him as no other had or would ever again.

Plunging inside of her, it began. Molten fire exploded around them both while she dug her nails into his skin.

"Adam."

He remained silent.

The quickness of their breath did not settle for several minutes. He leaned up, removing strands of wet hair away from her lovely face as she pulled on his lips. Finally, he relented, leaning down to kiss her.

He got up, taking her by the hand and leading her into the bathroom, where he turned the knobs. Water spewed from the large showerhead. He soaped them both while she washed her hair. Smiling, rubbing against him, she had to silently admit a great enjoyment in this manner of getting him cleaned.

Pulling closer, he kissed her as the water of its own accord rinsed them. He turned the stream off and handed her a towel. As they both dressed and finished, finally he broke the silence just as they were leaving the room.

"Do you want to go and wait at the bikes? Dreaming of riding off into the Egyptian sunset while I go into the café and get us some things to take along?"

They were now down to the lobby. "Yes, I'll make sure we are good to go. Can you get me a bag of something sweet? I don't need anything too sticky." She grinned as his eyes lit up. "Stop it. Any small bag of treats will do."

He nodded, continuing on.

Then there they were. Looking somewhat beaten up, but oh, so beautiful. Trek bikes. Eyeing her green one with the pretty basket, Sam adjusted the seat, removed the locks and stowed them away with the keys.

"Did you manage to fix my seat as well?"

She laughed, taking the bag from him and putting it in her basket. "You know, once I was in Greece on the Island of Poros. I rented a bike similar, except it was a three speed. I went to the market and filled up with goodies and headed up a long, steady climb for nearly six miles to the Sanctuary of Poseidon. When I arrived, not a soul could be seen. So, I took in the beautiful hilltop view of a harbor below, walked through the ruins, then peed on a tree. I thought, what the hell. No one is lurking about. Then it occurred to me exactly what this spot was used for when I read a plaque. He brought unsuspecting virgins up to have his way with them."

He finished fiddling with his seat. "So, you felt obligated to piss on him, did you?"

She giggled, heading off right out onto the side of a somewhat bumpy old, cobbled road. Thankfully, most of the traffic was elsewhere. He started pedaling and caught up with her. "Yeah, it felt quite neat to do it. No lightning bolt came from the sky or an ugly beast from the sea. I think I got away with it and it needed to be done."

He had absolutely no comment about that at all.

They continued along the Avenue of the Sphinxes and down to the Nile, where she found the bike and pedestrian path. Stopping, she leaned the bike up against a vacated bench. "Good place as any to eat. I'm hungry."

"Good, so am I." He took out two sandwiches wrapped in pita and handed her one, along with a coconut water. "I know you like these. Thought I'd try them out. You know, when-in-Rome kind of thing."

She chewed, nodding quickly that it was good. Drinking up, she handed him everything and he deposited it into a nearby receptacle. A bag of sweets appeared before her eyes. "Hummus candy? I've never even heard of this."

She unwrapped one, plopping it into her mouth. "Oh, these are sticky, gooey good. Some sesame and almond. Here, try one."

She could hardly talk without making a sucking noise.

He chewed while attempting to speak and they both nearly choked, laughing out loud. "Don't ride and eat one. It could be the end of you."

"No kidding, so come on. I want to get over to the museum before they close. I need to case the joint. Your job is to report on how many surveillance devices there are and how we are going to disengage what we need so I can get in with that big box."

"Why don't I just call a man that knows a man who knows another man and he will just let us in after dark?"

She skidded around a cat chasing a mouse and put her foot down to stop from falling, then moved it up and continued. "Oh sure, go ahead."

They rode around the complete perimeter of the building, staking it out. She lost him at one point and pedaled on, waiting down in the front of the large building. Now off the bike, she ate three more of the treats.

Finally, he came around the corner and waved upon approach. "Getting the hang of this, Sam. Kind of fun being back on a bike."

"I can see that. Do you think you want to push on up that hill for a better view of the surroundings?"

He was off before she could close the bag, throw it in the basket and pedal off. She did not catch him until he reached the top of the road and turned, but she had been close on his heels.

"Bloke, that was not fair."

"It was. You were too busy filling your face with candy. Now turn your ass around and look."

She maneuvered the bike and gasped. It was beautiful. With the sun setting and the sky bold colors of red, orange and yellow dancing, displaying off the Nile, it was indeed a gorgeous sight to behold. "Oh, it is lovely here, Adam."

He came a bit closer. "I got a bigger surprise for you. I made that call. Tomorrow we are going to meet that man that got a call from another man that got a call from me."

Chapter Sixteen

They got off the bikes and the attendant took them, but not before she removed the bag that held the candy. "Well, I'm not going to give them up. I like them!"

He took her hand as they strode into the hotel and up to their suite. "I can't believe you actually meant that about calling a man that knows a man. I thought you were just pulling a Pink Panther on me."

He chuckled, opening the doors outside to the balcony. "Want to get changed and go up for a cocktail before we have dinner?"

"You mean a grown-up drink?"

"Yes, I sure do. How much time do you need?"

"Well, I've not really come with much more than casual clothes unless my bag is restocked with goodies I am not aware of yet. Anyway, I won't be too long."

She took her bag and went into the bathroom to wash up. A devilish grin hovered as she eyed the contents. Zipping it up, she put it on a chair and sauntered out. He was putting on his shoes when his head raised, eyes fully appraising. "You packed that?"

"Nope. But someone sure has it in for one of us. I wonder who planned this portion. Do you think Nefertiti or Isis had anything to do with it?"

"I'm going to have to find out more about these ancient women of Egypt. That dress, or rather the lack of it, is going to distract more than me tonight. I'm glad it came with a shawl. Put it on instead of just carrying it."

She nearly threw it at his head in humor. "I'm so hungry. Shall we go?"

"Yeah. Hang on a second let me get a weapon. I'm going to need it."

She smiled warmly up at him as the elevator door opened at the rooftop. "Yup, you were right. Good call. This really is a pretty decent view."

***

"Table for two?" Adam requested, hand possessively on the small of her back, keeping her very close. She was warm to the touch as the wrap slid off those creamy shoulders. His eyes followed the movement. "Warning you…"

A shoulder shrugged nonchalantly as the waiter seated them. "No worries. I am in the city of warriors. If you can't keep them all at bay, someone will."

He leaned forward, not really liking this distance between them at all. "Who is going to protect you from me?"

"We should have ordered in."

"Too late; now you have to wait. Serves you right for punishing me with that outfit. Besides, I am hungry. Look at this menu. It is a virtual smorgasbord. I'm going to order a bit of everything so we can try it all out. Unless you have any suggestions?"

"The *fatta, kushaini* and *medames* would all be great. We can mix and match. Order some pita if they don't ask you to sop up everything. Yum, this does sound good. He's coming now. I'll pass on alcohol tonight and just take a cold tea."

The waiter took the order and returned with a warmed dish of *medames* and a basket of bread. They both took no time in placing the napkins on their laps and digging in.

"I like the food in Egypt. It is a melting pot of cultures all rolled into one. The *medame* graced the Pharaoh's table. If it has withstood all this time it must be delectable."

He stared at her for a moment, waiting for a reply. Then realized by the glazed look in her eyes that she had not been listening.

"You just had a recollection. What was it about?"

"Um, well, I think I actually remember it now."

He watched as her words faded and mind drifted off. Quite a few seconds passed by as slowly she started to speak, eyes squinting, indicating she was still deep in the moment.

"*Medame.* It means buried. Which really refers to the manner which it was cooked in those days in ancient Egypt. The pot was buried in hot sand or beneath hot coals. I remember seeing it once when I was on some type of a journey. I was with a large caravan and we had stopped to camp. I do remember more! There were camels roped in a makeshift corral and I had quite a large, colorful tent. I can see the colors flying. There were servants, two of them. I was of importance."

He listened intently, watching emotions display across her face that he'd not witnessed before. "Was he with you?"

"I don't know. I can't see any more. I don't think I was on the road with the army. But who knows? I could have been."

"The saying that we all come with baggage will never hold the same meaning for me after hearing all of this."

She laughed as their platters were set in the middle of the table along with new plates. "I know it is kind of funny, I think. I wonder if that was my origin and I just maneuvered around after that. Pretty damn mysterious and frustrating at the same time."

He leaned over with the *kashani* and she tasted it. "Oh, that's perfect."

He was chewing, nodding. "You think you want to take a walk after? We may need to with all the food we are shoveling down. You'd think we had not eaten for centuries."

His eyes were on her. A silent message passed between them. It was one only true lovers share.

Settling the bill, Adam rose, helping her up. "Hang tight here for a moment while I ask the waiter a question." When he had finished he walked over to her and together they left the restaurant. Out on the street, their hands clasped as they walked onward peacefully towards the Nile. Sitting on the same bench they stopped at earlier, she leaned in and tucked her head on his shoulder as an arm came around.

"Feels like a honeymoon right now."

He squeezed her. "We can have one when we get back."

"Maybe. I'll consider that."

He would let that go. There would be no considering it at all. Either she'd marry him and move back into his home or he'd pack up his things and move into her cottage. There would be no negotiations on it.

The moon was fully exposed, shining on the river and displaying sparkling ripples as the ships steamed on in both directions. The air was cooling off now as they rose and walked over toward the oldest Mosque in Luxor, the Al-Mukashkish. It was beautiful at night as people were still coming out after finishing the final call to prayer.

"When I was in Istanbul on a personal trip years ago, I went to the Blue Mosque and noticed all the men had full rein to roam freely inside. But tucked in a small corner, a large wall with a dark screened door was the only place for the women to go. Even in praying, they are considered inferior. I took a picture through the screened door and obtained a faint outline of a woman dressed in a full burka. It both tantalized and spooked me. It was a moment that I always remember. Women there seem well settled with this, but it still unsettles me."

"She was probably from Saudi. They are the strictest of all Muslim countries about how their women dress and are treated. I've never seen women suppressed and dominated as there. Even in Afghanistan, it's not as much."

"I quickly realized that when I arrived in Yemen and my bag carried the full suit."

"Well, you threw it in the river so maybe the Nile goddess will smile on you and what that meant."

She grinned up at him. "So, you believe in gods and goddesses? I know you sort of believe in Isis, right?"

"We have to believe in a lot of things. Otherwise, how could we grasp what we ourselves do?"

"I agree. Here we are. I'm tired and looking forward to sliding onto those Egyptian cotton sheets."

He hit the button and they rode up the elevator in silence. As he opened their door, simultaneously they glanced over to the box just sitting there under the bed. "Yeah, my thought exactly. But if it had been taken while we were gone, then we'd not have a reason to go to the museum tomorrow and back tomorrow night."

"Mission aborted? I doubt the people up there would think that's just okay and let us pack it all in and return to England."

"Never had that happen. Their plans always provide a course to a successful end." She removed her dress, letting it slide to the floor, and picked it up, placing it over one of the chairs. "My bag did not have any night clothes. I think they did that on purpose."

"Someone is surely just saving you time. They must have known I'd be here and it would be a waste."

She called out over her shoulder, "You don't even have a big bag. Makes me believe you will not be here very long at all."

He knew that. But he did have a few items of necessity in his man bag. Two pairs of socks and boxers.

She came out naked and climbed into bed. Right into his arms. They were both beat. She nestled in and sighed. In two minutes they were both fast asleep.

The room was light as he opened his eyes and glanced at the clock. Eight-thirty. Holy shit. She was wrestling awake herself. "Is that the right time?"

His hands were on the roam, over a hip. "Yup, we don't have to be at the museum until ten. It is a short walk. So, we have plenty of time to relax right here and then eat and go."

She smiled, kissing him on the lips as she slid beneath the covers. Her breath was warm on his skin.

"Sam...."

Her tongue did a fine job of taking him to the very place he had brought her yesterday. Complete and total surrender. As she threw back the covers, her hands moved up over his rippled abs, chest and clasped hands with his. She lifted her hips with his hardness poised and ready as their eyes locked just before she leaned down, grabbing his lips with her own and slid him fully inside.

"You own my soul," was all she could get out before he rolled her swiftly to her back and brought them both to a pulsating orgasm. She arched with him as their sweaty bodies finally melted together. He scooped her into his arms, placing her on his chest over the strong, steady beat of his heart.

He glanced over at the clock. "It's nine. I guess we did pass the time well enough. Let's get up, shower, dress and eat."

Disengaging, Sam pointed directly at him. "You stay right there for five minutes. If we shower together, we will be late. I'll be quick and then you can have it."

He smoothed his hand over her backside as she left the warmth of his bed and body.

He stood, removing what he needed from the bag and walked over, opening the drapes to let in the light of the day. It was another one filled with the sunshine. Glancing at the box under the bed, he frowned. What would happen tonight when they went back?

"It's all yours." Her voice brought him out of dark thoughts and he was in and out of there in five. He dressed as she sat on one of the chairs out on the balcony.

"You ready?"

***

As they left the room, she could feel something was wrong with him but was afraid to ask. Right now, she was hovering on the brink of something startlingly important. Her mind was engaged up there in the spheres. Maybe he was just doing the same. They ate with little conversation passing between them as the tab was paid and they walked to the museum.

Adam glanced at her as they continued along. "Things are changing. I can feel it."

"I know. It's unsettling."

"I agree. I am not sure what the next few hours will bring. You just need to remember what I told you earlier."

"Yes. That if I don't come back you will come and find me."

He laughed. "That and when we do get back you and I are having that conversation."

All too briefly, an intimate smile was shared.

"There he is. I recognize him from my associate's text he sent yesterday with a photo attached. Let me do the talking until I know what exactly is going on."

They approached, exchanging handshakes as she stood off to the side. "Jairo, this is the one we are helping tonight. Where do you want to do this?"

He shook hands with Sam. "Come with your item at nine-thirty and meet back here at this door. I will get you inside. The guards change shifts at ten so they tend to be sleeping right up until their replacements arrive. We will need to be completely silent. All the halls and rooms are lit only with exit signs and diffused lighting. So if we need to duck into anyplace no one will see us. I've arranged for your room of interest to have the cameras suddenly have a glitch. It won't be permanent. It has an auto-program which will reset after five minutes."

He stopped, glancing about. "That's all the time the system gives. Then it will commence a full reboot and auto-start up. I can't control that portion. Once you are through, meet me outside. We will go out the way we came in. Should it all go as planned, we will be in, done and out in less than fifteen minutes. Well before the new shift comes through to do their final check of the building for the night."

They both nodded.

"Take this map of the building. The X marks your area. Familiarize and keep handy in case you need it. Just one more thing. Be on time." He glanced about, nodded, and then left, disappearing around toward the front of the building. When they reached that area to go in and pay for an entry ticket, he was long swallowed up by an influx of tourists just getting off two large buses.

They hurried along ahead of them. He bought two, handing her the map. "This way." She wanted to stop and take plenty of time in each area. Everything was so fascinating. But, more than anything else she needed to reach that location and see what it housed and more importantly, where to leave the object.

"Pretty cool place, I must say. How about on our way out, after we scope things, we take a good look? I've never been in here before and I positively love museums." Sam spoke with enthusiasm and Adam smiled.

"Sure. We have the rest of the day, why not? Give us a longer opportunity to see what else is around here in case we have to come up with our own plan."

They followed the map into a middle foyer as she spotted the sign taking them to the New Kingdom Exhibit.

As they entered she lost him, yet remained fully aware he was not too far off, examining a large oil painting. Continuing along, her gaze moved toward the end of the room.

There it was. Straight ahead.

Suddenly, her mind halted, feet frozen.

At the end of the wing, directly in the center of a tall white wall, it came straight into view.

Walking on, she stood before it, paralyzed, not even sure if a single breath had been taken. The room suddenly closed in and then faded to gray just before she slid to the ground. His strong arms came around her, pulling her back up.

"Oh, my God, Sam, are you okay? I've seen the damn strangest things happen to you since I've been here. Talk to me."

Softly she spoke. Barely a whisper. He had to move his head lower to actually hear.

"Yes. Well, I think so. Adam, look at this. It is him. Rano."

His statue was well over six feet tall, excluding the two-foot pedestal it was resting upon. A single bronze loin cloth draped down to his knees and thick bands adorned his massive upper arms. The brilliant blood-red tunic was laced with threads of gold and lapis. Resting between chiseled, strong legs, tip nestled on the base, was a beautiful replica of the very sword he had created.

He was magnificent. It was magnificent.

Totally breathless, she wanted to run all the way back to the hotel and open the box and look at it more thoroughly. It had to be his actual sword. The placement of the jewels on the one before her were exactly the ones she had stolen from the private collector.

"He's a fierce man. Look at his eyes."

"I can't seem to take mine off his sword. That's what is in our box, you know. Now I get it. I must return it to him so he can have peace. He's its creator, Adam. He needs it back."

"You must be right. I feel like he's looking down at you right now. Although, there is something familiar about him."

A shudder passed through them both.

"Do you want some time alone with him? Are you strong enough to stand on your own?"

She nodded and his hand slid away.

"I'll be back over at that painting. Come and get me when you are ready."

There was a bench a few feet away, but she could not move. She wanted to put her hands on the coolness of the sculpture and feel what she already knew. The rugged handsomeness of his muscles. The strength that was beneath it. Oh. He was a sight to gaze upon and he had loved her fiercely. All the women who had thrown themselves, begging for him to take them as their wives, he had discarded.

Instead, he had chosen her.

A gush of wind swirled around, unleashing her hair and forcing it to flow gently around her face before laying to rest down her back. He had always loved it down. Eyes raised, she swayed slightly. He was potent. Her own delicious drug that she had never wanted to give up and had fought tooth and nail to keep. But she had not been successful. There was more going on here than just returning a sword. Something else needed to be done. Or perhaps undone.

A group of rambunctious Asian women rushed over, gushing over him. One tripped, not paying attention as her selfie pole nearly hit the statue. Somehow, it seemed to bounce off just before making contact. Steadier now, Sam looked over her shoulder toward Adam. He was still engrossed with that painting.

Walking over, she stood next to him. "It's beautiful and bloody at the same time. What draws you to this?"

"I am not sure. I've seen this before. Could have been a replica at the British Museum of Art, or the Louvre. But I can't put a place to it. I am familiar with it, though, and you are right. It depicts both of those images." He turned, taking her by the hand. "Come on, let's move out of this area and go look at other things. I don't know about you, but something is in the air in here and I'd like to get my mind off it for a moment."

She glanced over her shoulder at the women, who were still taking turns with their cellphone cameras. "The artifact wing is back the way we came. I think we should go in there."

"Okay."

"What happened to your hair? Did I miss something else?"

"Better not to ask."

He shrugged and they entered another area, where they spent the rest of the day until her belly rumbled rather loudly.

He laughed. "Yeah, my sentiments exactly." He patted her flat stomach. "There are plenty of small local places along the Nile. I think we should eat before heading back there to wait it out. Unless you want to actually go into a restaurant and sit down."

"Nope, the vendors will work. The more I can keep moving, the better it will be for us both."

They stopped as he ordered two *kebabs* rolled in *baladis*, and they continued to walk and eat. Finished, he deposited both wrappers into a receptacle as they re-entered the hotel.

Up in the room she headed over to the box, slid it out, struggling, then managed to get it up onto the settee. Snapping back both latches gingerly, she lifted the lid as a force of adrenalin suddenly coursed through her veins.

He stepped next to her, removing the soft cloth to expose the magnificent sword in all its glory. "Shit. This is exactly what he was holding. It's really his. I truly do not dare pick it up."

"Probably not a good idea. I do tend to believe in curses, you know, and always have. I don't want you turning to dust before my eyes. I don't have a magic potion or the gypsy woman to guide me in how to bring you back if that happened."

There was no joke in that statement.

He wrapped it back, securing it in place. Leaving it on the bed, he followed her out onto the balcony, where they both sat staring into space. Time passed as they remained in their own worlds until the sun finally vanished over the horizon.

Standing, he extended his hand to her. "We have to go."

"I wonder if our exit out tonight is our journey back to England."

They were walking down the stairs and took a side door outside into the busy nighttime street as he carried the box. "I don't know. Can't see that part of it yet."

"Me either. Damn it, Adam, I feel weird. I've felt this since I've been on this forsaken Middle Eastern soil. But right now it's escalating. I can't get a grip on it. I've been in uncomfortable places and circumstances before, but something is amiss."

"Yeah, I feel it too. But we must do this, Sam. We have no other choice."

They reached the designated rear entrance, where Jairo was already there awaiting them.

"Okay, let's go over this. Silence is key. Watch where you walk and be mindful of your motion. Always keep moving. We are limited with time."

Sam and Adam both nodded.

"Okay, this way."

He unlocked the back door and quickly punched in the security access. They moved swiftly down the corridors to the wing and met Jairo just outside the room. Adam and Sam walked farther in as she stood in front of his glowing form.

The dimmed lighting lent an eerie feel to the statue's eyes. They seemed to be beckoning and bright as her wild imagination saw an arm raising, extending, willing her to grasp it. She bit a knuckle to prevent any sound escaping her mouth.

Adam opened the box, unwrapped it, as she quickly pushed his hands away from having contact with the metal. Honestly, she could not take any chances. Straining, body tensed, face constricted, she lifted it up with both hands.

Suddenly, powerful energies weaved through as she pushed the sword higher, closer, finally resting it against the replica. A mesmerizingly bright beam shone in from the windows high above, encasing her inside, forming a brilliant canopy.

Body and head turning, lips moving, Adam could not hear her. Extending a hand, she tried in vain to move as her vision blurred. The sound of rushing boots echoed in her ears.

Adam panicked. He could not lose her like this! Rushing forward, he leaped, grasping those fingertips just as the last of the beam enveloped them both.

Then nothing followed but a sweep of darkness.

End of Book Two...

Passages Book Three

The Circle Ends

Sandra Waine

Dedication:

To all my family and friends. Especially those that know I
am a bit nuts but appreciate me just exactly as I am.
Thank you.

Chapter One

Where was the light? His arms moved about, feeling the rough sand against his hands. Where the hell was Sam? An old face he did not recognize placed a foul-smelling concoction under his nose, speaking in Arabic. Fuck, this was not what he had expected. Through hazed vision, he could see he was still in the Middle East.

Damn, he thought. He had not left the country.

Had she?

Ears perked, Adam listened as background noises were identified. Women with hushed voices were coming closer to him, along with the sound of shuffling feet. Off in the distance he could hear the flap of a tent billowing in the hot desert wind.

Then someone yelled. It was a faintly recognizable voice. But Adam just did not have enough mental strength right now to figure out who the heck it was.

"Come, girl! Get over here now with that stronger potion. I need to get him up and onto his feet before anyone comes snooping around. I can't lift him alone. He's too tall and muscular. Damn it, girl, has your head stopped working? Hand me that. Quickly now. We must get him hidden!"

Something more obnoxiously rancid than the last concoction was placed under his nose just as he inhaled a deep breath. Rapidly, his head turned away from it, eyes flashing open to glare into the dark orbs of an Egyptian woman. Dressed in ancient robes, she leaned closer, clutching a hand-carved walking stick. As his focus cleared and eyesight returned, he glanced at the circle of women surrounding them, a grin starting to form.

Well, if he had died this was not too bad, he thought. They were all mighty attractive. Ironically, it appeared he held more interest to them than the small group of old men hovering off in the distance. Relief spread through his body. None were carrying any weapons.

"Who are you?"

"Do you really not know me? Honestly? Take a closer look at my face."

Recognition dawned bright as he maneuvered and stood. Quickly, he took her rather roughly by the arm, eyes boring into hers. "Alwen? Is that you?"

"That took you long enough. Now move along and come with me. We need to get you inside a tent before any of the common traders come by on their route to the palace. I'm not prepared to lie for you just yet. As to why you are here and who you are."

He moved about, stunned, yet fully aware now of this new environment. "Is Samantha here?"

"Absolutely. Where is not clear. Although I can confirm she is definitely not in this encampment."

"Shit. I think I screwed things up. I followed her. This is not good. I am damned and will not be able to return unless circumstances are changed. Someone will need to intervene for me. Is that you? This is no time for secrecy. I must know what the hell is going on. All of it."

"Now calm down. You are getting way ahead of yourself. Right now you need to step back. Take a deep breath and try to relax. Do you feel different? Is this all new to you? It is for me. That I can assure you. I believe it may be for many of us that are locked in this circle with your Samantha. So, consider this. It could be right this time, Adam. We have no choice but to go with it."

He raised a skin-roughened hand over his face and through thick hair. "Okay. Give me all the details you can."

"That a new addition would be arriving with her, but not that it was you specifically. I'm here to help two transients. Now that part fits together. Regardless, I am fully prepared to take you where you need to be."

"That was a bit much to follow, but I think I get it. Just where is my next destination? Why can't I remember everything? I know I came through the passage with her, but things are hazy. I don't know why I am here. I've never had so little control."

"There is another woman who is expecting you. We will remain here until nightfall. Then move under darkness to her location." Stopping suddenly, she turned abruptly around, as if she knew what was maneuvering around in that mind of his.

"I see that expression in your eyes. Don't get it in your mind it's her. It is not."

"I don't suppose you have any idea who she is and what she wants with me? This other woman?"

He sat down on a plush cushion as a plate of food and a brass jug filled with wine was set before him. He smiled up into the comely lass's pretty face. One eyebrow shot up as he noticed Alwen's disapproving glance over a fully robed shoulder.

"No, I think you already know the answer to that. When the time is appropriate, you will be made aware."

His gaze lowered, evaluating this new attire. Or rather, old attire from centuries ago. "What is the meaning of this bar and chain I wear? I know I've seen it before. But, can't say when."

"Oh, yes. You are going to want to conceal that. I nearly forgot to tell you. I have a different robe for you to put on. Problem is I can't hide your sandals. We have no replacements for you here."

"Woman, you have been speaking nothing but gibberish!"

They were both getting agitated.

"You can't remember yet, I know. Your contact tonight will enlighten you more than I can provide. That is not the reason I am here. It's only to keep the grass from growing beneath your feet, so to speak. And perhaps—" She glanced at the young, pretty girl eyeing him. "—to keep you out of mischief."

Slugging back a large gulp of the pungent dark red wine, he shook his head in frustration. It was true. His memory was only providing bits and pieces of his life here. *Why?* he internally wondered, trying in vain to find the key to answers burning in his mind. But they would not come. The key was hidden from him this time.

Alwen watched the emotional upheaval wash over his features. "Adam, this is good. You are not quite sure of things. This is indeed a good sign."

She nodded toward the girl, signaling her exit. "Go easy on that. It is important to remember every word spoken to you this evening and after that. I can tell you feel strange. But take my last words of advice. Let everything and everyone flow as they must. Do not get in the way."

"Fair enough to it all. I can already feel my insides on fire from this potent drink."

She rose, preparing to leave, but then turned, clutching both flaps. "You are known as a philanderer here, my friend. Take care with whom you dally. Let it not be any of the handsome girls. Be warned."

He grinned as she shrugged and let the flaps fall into place. Her voice, loud and commanding, could be heard while walking away. "Girls, girls, come along. We need to gather wood and get those sheep tended. I don't see the water jugs filled yet!"

He laughed, listening to the tirade. How long was she here? Probably only until tonight and then would disappear back to Baglen. Leaning back on the cushions, he rested his head on his hand as eyes drifted closed. His mind wandered back to their last few days in Luxor. Only bits and pieces came back. But one part he recalled with clarity. Their lovemaking.

He opened them back up and stared at the pitch in the tent top. "Why" he mouthed softly, "are you trying to vanquish thoughts of Sam from my mind? Already the curve of her small waist is disappearing from my sight. Would you have me take another while I am here? Is she already engulfed with someone? I now forgotten?"

Adam listened intently but there was complete silence.

No one was going to answer his question.

Darkness descended as he finally gave in to the potent wine and drifted off. When he woke, a plate of smoked meats and more of the wine he now had to be careful with had been placed on a mat next to him. Suddenly he was hungry. Grabbing a few juicy pieces, he chewed rapidly while reaching for fresh figs and grapes. The noise level outside was gaining momentum as it got closer and closer to his tent. Taking one final swig of the wine, he set the goblet down, not wanting a repeat of a few hours earlier.

One of the tent flaps slid open and Alwen stood just inside, hands raised resting on wide, maidenly hips, just as he'd seen her do a dozen times back in Shropshire. Funny, he thought, he could recall more about Alwen than Sam right now.

"Gather yourself up. The time is ripe and we are ready to go. Come along."

Once outside the tent, it took a few seconds for his eyes to adjust. It had been a very long time since he had been engulfed in such total darkness as this. Out in the desert with only the stars and a quarter moon, they set out on foot as a very small band. Two men, Alwen and Adam.

High up in the sky, the constellation of Orion was their guide as he followed them along in silence. Adam had read about this cluster. In fact, the journal of a famous explorer's recount of how it had aided in their group's direction when they thought they were lost in the desert, forever still fascinated him.

The recount claimed that it was the same exact distance as the Giza pyramid complex. Depending on which theory you wanted to believe, it was said that the full Milky Way correlated along with other pyramids and the Nile. If that indeed was the case, then he was south of Cairo by quite a distance. Or rather, Memphis, which he recalled was the old name before it was changed in later centuries.

Frivolous information like this kept his mind engaged as they trekked on. It also allowed thoughts of her from creeping back in. They walked on for several more hours before distant speckles of light finally flickered on the dark horizon. Yet it was still the middle of the night.

Alwen motioned him up to the front as the two men stood opposite, preparing to head on in a different direction. She nodded to them both in thanks, taking Adam by the arm. "We will now go to her cave. It's a short distance. Then I will leave, my task completed. Just a bit more advice for you that was requested I pass along. With her, you are not to ask any questions. She is, as they say, gifted. Therefore, a bit peculiar, if you know what I mean. Just pay attention. Listen. Watch. Especially her facial expressions. There is much to be learned by this visit."

"Okay."

As they neared, his eyes were drawn toward the outline of a series of famous porphyritic caves. Even in this era, they were considered quite a natural phenomenon. Centuries later, archaeologists and geologists alike would find many hidden treasures that would shed light on the type of people that dwelled in them, thrived and survived.

The torch lights grew in intensity as he noticed a few men cloaked in robes, hoods pulled up, stationed at various locations for protection. The goat path they climbed was narrow and rocky, making it tricky for him to keep his footing while attempting to absorb the area.

At the largest cave they paused. Adam accidently bumped into Alwen's plump form. Reaching out just in time and clasping an arm, he prevented her from tumbling down to the dirt.

Smiling, she silently motioned him ahead.

Pausing and turning slightly to thank her, Adam met with thin air. She had already disappeared to God knew where. He hoped it was back to Baglen.

"Enter." A strong female voice beckoned him further as the light flickering off the walls gave a clear depiction of the hieroglyphics. A great battle was taking place. Halting, he stared at it, totally engrossed. Someone, somewhere, from another time, had once said it was both bloody and beautiful. He racked his brain, trying to recall who that was and where he had seen this before.

"Prince Jared Malik, come and sit with me. You will not be spending that much time here. So, I now require your full attention."

He sat opposite the woman, trying to decipher her dark facial features from the poor lighting inside the cave. "I am listening. Go on."

"Your people need you from a distant land. They are expecting your return to them shortly. Are you aware of what has brought you here? Whom? Why?"

His brain started to work again. Prince. Did she say prince? He readjusted on the beautifully woven eastern rug, its roughness scratching his legs where they were not covered by the robe.

"You do not remember, do you?"

"No. Nothing yet. What am I to see?"

"Many things. Here, take this orb and hold it with both your hands. Now sit still, relax and glance into it. Tell me what comes into your vision."

It was cold to the touch as he cupped it. Both eyes suddenly started to blur. He blinked rapidly for several seconds, before at last images flashed into play. "A beautiful woman. I am drawn to her. But she's dressed differently. She's not a Hyskos. I think her name is Sam. I see a burning village and a bloody, fierce battle. Has this happened already or is this something that will happen again?"

The woman did not answer the question about the battle. "Here she is not spoken of by that name. Caution yourself not to use it. She is referred to as Nofret Qalhata, the beautiful one of ancient Egypt. She is a healer. Highly esteemed in her village, the valleys and with the queen."

"Go on."

"You will be taken to your village shortly, where all your memory will return once you drink the wine. Do not be concerned it is poison. Do not fight your destiny again, Prince Malik. May my warning be clear. This is the final time. If you both do not correct the past changes in history, it will never be right for the rest of us. This circle will continue. The very last time you sat here and we spoke, about her and all that has occurred, you did not keep your word. You must this time. She needs your strength."

This time? Last time? His mind bolted into a frenzy of thoughts.

"What did I do wrong? I can't remember. You have to guide me better than this if we are to succeed."

"I cannot. It is against the order. But mark on this day my words. Keep them circling around inside your head. Especially when you see her again and your heart has different ideas. A whole gathering of people anxiously awaits a different outcome. An event of great magnitude is coming again. This time you need to get it done. At all costs."

A cold, penetrating shiver passed through him. What had he fucked up previously? Damn. He was frustrated, lifting a hand up to run it through his hair. Then it stopped as it met with a turban.

"You can remove that once you are in your tent. You will not need it after that."

He stared down at the orb again, seeing additional details. Flashes of her. Leaning over him. But why were they not kissing? Prince Malik knew the reason.

It was Rano blocking the way.

He stood tall and arrogant in his chariot, sword drawn, strong hands holding the reins and keeping the horses at bay. Then Prince Malik saw and heard a scream. Yes, it was a piercing, wrenching scream followed by the low chant of distraught women.

Something of great sadness had occurred. Then the prayers followed. He tried to look away but could not. Was he dead? Some members of other villages were being herded onto barges and moved. Although they were not family, he knew them from trading and recognized clearly the weaving on their blankets. They were Hebrews.

A stronger force lifted his face to the woman's as he reached out, handing the orb over.

"Ah, yes. Now you are truly beginning to see more clearly."

"Yes. Enough. I know what will happen when I get to the village. I am now prepared."

She nodded, handing him bread, ground olives and chickpeas. He scooped it up and gulped down wine from a rawhide flask.

"What do you need to remember this time that you have ignored all other times? This is important."

"I will listen. Give her room. Be open when words of great revelation come my way."

"You understand the gravity of this all? This time?"

"Yes. Fully."

"Good. You will go now. There are men waiting who will take you by horseback to the village. They are your people."

"Can I ask your name?"

"Can you not see me clear enough to know?" She raised a torch and kept it to the left of her face, showering it with strong light.

His jaw dropped. "Gerda? You? Do you go by that name here?"

She laughed softly. "No, it's hardly Egyptian or even Hebrew. But that matters little, for I leave soon. If I should see you again, back in our correct century and all seems as it was, then you were not successful." She rose, placing the torch back on the roped loop. Then she walked back into the darkness of the cave, disappearing from his view completely.

"But wait. Don't you mean if I do not see you again...?" He took a few steps toward her, but already knew it was futile. She was long on her way to somewhere else.

Walking outside to the waiting men, he glanced off into the horizon and wondered how the hell this time he would make Nofret realize what she needed to do. Could he keep his word? He kicked a stone and watched as it launched over the trail down into a rocky ravine.

His mind went silent. No one was going to give him any help here.

One thing was very clear: what Gerda said and how she said it. There was no mistaking the gravity of it all. Thankful for the interruption, he turned toward one of the men.

"Your horse, Prince Malik. We must ride hard and fast to arrive in the village before the sun brightens the day."

He mounted and they rode at breakneck speed through the darkness, the moon and stars above providing a soft light. As the sun was breaking the horizon with its beautifully colorful display, they arrived at his village. He jumped down, handing the reins over, and entered what he knew instantly was his own tent.

Immediately his eyes scanned over a battle tunic, shield, knife, and a menacing, deadly spear. He knew these weapons well.

"Brother, why do you ride out into the very desert we prepare to battle the Pharaoh's army on this day?"

He turned and clasped both of the man's hands with his own. "I needed a visit with the crone, Gerda, my brother Ahmall. I wanted to see if their camp lights shined from high above. But they were only a distant flicker. There will be no full moon to guide tonight. The men are ready?"

"Yes, and the women have all gone to the caves under the protection of a few of our Hebrew brothers. I saw to that myself in your absence."

"Excellent. Come. Sit. Let us break bread and drink. Then we will prepare for battle."

They sat talking as his mind wandered, recalling Gerda's words earlier this day about seeing more after drinking the wine. He took a full cup, finished, then waited.

It happened in a quick succession of visions. His tribal brother had risen to get another jug and did not notice how distant his prince had become.

Ahmall reached over, taking his arm. "Should we meet our maker this day, know that I love you. You are a fierce warrior and welcoming friend. I have no doubt we will meet again in another lifetime."

Oh, Prince Malik thought quickly, silently, *if only he knew how true that could be*. Now he knew who this was: Sam's brother. But apparently, Ahmall had no recollection of either of them into the future. This, Prince Malik found very strange, as the air inside the tent suddenly crackled with an unknown force.

Both men turned in fascination as a cold breeze flew through, lifting the tent flaps for a few seconds, then dispersed without a trace.

"What the hell was that? It's hotter than hell outside right now. The noonday sun is not even high in the sky yet."

"I have no idea, Malik. Never seen anything like it. Do you think we are cursed? That it was the cold winds of death coming now to mark our souls?"

Ahmall was clearly spooked, but Prince Malik shook it off. "I can't explain that. But we will not bow down to such a force as that. Will we? Our people deserve a chance. If we cower before even reaching the battle, what kind of men are we?"

That brought him around.

Ahmall stood. "God will not see the destruction of good people this day at the hands of those that would diminish our worth. We are a powerful nation. More powerful than their enemies in the east and south. We will win in the end, brother. I know it."

Prince Malik had to wonder if he was referring to thousands of years down the road of time. "It is no longer in our hands. Now, go and prepare yourself. We must ready as the camp rises." Ahmall thumped his chest with an iron fist, nodded and left the tent.

Jared reached out, gliding strong, darkly tanned hands over the beautiful weave his mother had sewn for their father, the chieftain of this village, who, along with Jared's mother and two sisters, had been ambushed in a village bordering theirs on a raid by the Pharaoh's men. Yes. He wanted their blood on his hands this day.

Revenge.

Yet as he prepared, voices from thousands of years streamed throughout his tent. His mind. His body. All carried a different message and clear warning.

He could hear Sam. The men he'd met in Venice. His own dearly departed parents from England. Mrs. Hoyt. In a rush, he stopped, lifting eyes to heaven. Then he caught the deep voice of a formidable warrior. One who ushered all others from the tent by his mere mystical presence.

"You are not as you seem, Prince Malik. Yet I know all your secrets," was all he could make out as the sound vanished along with the wind.

"Shit. Who was that? All of them? My ancestors?" Prince Malik spoke out loudly as he paced frantically for a few seconds before words from the old crone penetrated his mind, bringing immediate calmness. Then the adrenaline started flowing through as his gut tightened. Apprehension filled Jared's entire being as something yet stronger, more potent, took over.

Excitement. The excitement of the battle.

Placing the tunic over his head, he affixed a woven golden belt around his waist, then strapped on battle sandals. Pulling the knife from the sheath, he ran a finger over the blade, drawing first blood. It was time. His eyes narrowed as he picked up the sword. Everything else would be left behind.

He exited the royal tent for what would be the very last time. He hoped.

The Semite Nation would be proud this day. One way or another. This time he'd follow his instincts instead of ego. It had to turn out differently. Walking over towards the large group of soldiers, he did not pay any heed nor try to comfort with words the sobbing women.

"Men, our choices have been made clear. As we march to battle, keep in your minds why we do this. We will not be held captive, our children segregated, our women scorned and our elders stoned. It is with them in our hearts that we claim back our territory and lives."

Mounted, reins in one hand, he turned and led those on horseback as hundreds of others marched behind, ready to engage their enemy. As the sun moved higher and darkness gave way, they trudged. Up ahead, such a sight came before their front lines.

Charioteers.

Strong, fearless soldiers tightly holding the reins of strong, sleek horses whose hooves pounded the sand beneath them, eager to engage in battle.

It was such a masterful display of strength that hardly a soul with Prince Malik did not envision being trampled to an unmerciful death. Never had any but one seen such a mechanism as this before.

Fear temporarily immobilized their forces as Prince Malik quickly glanced left and right, knowing swift words had to be spoken.

Ahmall spoke, his voice laden with awe. "Brother, that is the mighty wheeled apparatus Father spoke of when they entered the village. I now know it was what left those deep marks in the dirt we could not identify upon our return."

But Prince Malik knew what had to be done.

"Yes. We will be no match for the likes of this contraption or their swords. Let us not share our thoughts with the others." He glanced around at the men. Those he'd planted fields with, yielded good times, shared a few large jugs of wine and a few women now and again.

"Ahmall, ride to the rear and up to the caves. They must be warned to move on. Do not stop. You must reach them, for there will be carnage and slaughter on this day. Tell them it is my wish they go to the Hebrews. I command it. For word has it they will not be engaged in a battle such as this. They will not lift weapons against Pharaoh's army. Rather, they will be rounded up and expelled. Go with God's speed and be quick."

***

Dust drove high as the single rider could be seen from atop the Egyptian army's encampment. Rano's eyes squinted.

"Awaiting your command."

"Let him go. He will not be able to ride to get reinforcements. There are none. He does not know we made work of them all on the way here. Nor that these are the last remaining villagers alive under Prince Malik's reign. Soon, it will all be as it should."

"It is said he is a great fighter, Prince Malik. But none can match our great charioteers and your sword and brilliant tactics."

Rano nodded, walking along the ranks at the front lines. But that beautiful little Nofret was on his mind and she had no place there as he prepared for battle. Knowing he had a few minutes, he let his thoughts drift to their last encounter. Her sweet voice had been reliving a tall tale of a great warrior and had held them all spellbound. He soon realized she was talking about him.

For ages, he had tried to get her to pay closer attention to him. Now, he thought, smiling devilishly, it was time. It would not be denied any longer what was between them. They would marry this time. Perhaps she'd give him strong sons and daughters and they all would be taught the fine art of warfare.

So her aloofness had turned to interest and now he was sure it was much more. Good thing. His libido had been sorely tested. Enough was enough. He would have her. No, not by commanding charm as he had done with other women. She was different. With all his tactical training, he knew a better way to get what he so desired from her. Besides, time was running out.

Again.

He kicked a rock, launching it out of the way. "Damn you. Even on the battlefield, you encroach on my thoughts. Be gone. For I proclaim on this day I have no time for you, woman!" His words were harsh as he spewed them into the air. Raising his head high, the fierce mercenary returned, shoving her into the recess. Glancing off at the Semites, he never felt a twinge of guilt at the slaughter that was about to take place. Stepping up onto his chariot, he removed his sword from the sheath, letting it drop to the floorboard, then turned toward his army, honing in on the figure of his rival.

***

Prince Jared's horse stomped its front hooves into the sand, chomping at the bit to start the pace. Even the horses could feel it. He reined him in and then kicked his sides, raising his spear and shield. The desert sand parted beneath such pressure, leaving a sure imprint on it and the events to follow. It would tell a great story of this fierce battle.

"Attack!" he yelled. His horse and army gathered momentum as the two sides moved closer and closer. As they clashed, he fought on until an enemy soldier's sword clipped his wrist and his sword dropped to the ground below.

Then, as if in a dream, Malik watched one appear as if out of thin air coming straight towards him, smiling to heaven. A large steel handle slid into his palm. It was not one of their own. Quickly, he looked up at this powerful sword, appreciating the fine workmanship before he used it to take down several soldiers, falling to their desert death.

A white-hot sensation suddenly engulfed him as a sword pierced his right side clean through and was pulled out. The reins slipped from his grasp as he lost control of his body. He dropped to the ground even as his mind screamed at him to get up. But it was of no avail. Prince Malik had little strength left now.

The sand absorbed the growing pool of blood, seeming, like Prince Malik, to know it was a losing cause as it streamed around his body. The stinging turned into an ache as his eyes fluttered closed, his body now completely motionless. The pain overtook him and he saw nothing more than a glimmer of her beautiful eyes before blackness flooded his soul.

***

The battle raged on for a few more minutes until the very last Semite left was Ahmall, standing over the lifeless body of his brave, fallen brother. That was where Rano pulled back tightly on the reins of his horse and leaped down, blood dripping from his sword.

Marching straight towards Ahmall, he mercilessly sliced his sword straight through his midsection, pulled it out and wiped it on the tunic of Prince Malik. Not bothering to watch the body fall to the ground, he quickly remounted and circled them both. Brazenly, he reared the horse up on hind legs, released a curdling, victorious battle cry and then riding over the bloodstained earth toward his main army.

"We are a mighty force, men. Work through the village and take what is left. Burn what remains down to the sand before we look in those caves for survivors."

"What are your orders for them?"

"We have done what was asked of us on this day. Gather and keep them alive." He glanced about, nodding as he whirled his horse and entered the village.

"Commander, only a few old men and women remain. I'll take a small band with me up to the caves, by your order."

"Go ahead. Make quick work of it. I do not see much that will be needed here. I will allow those old people to be brought back and settled with the Hebrews. I have seen enough blood today, in truth. I will advise the Pharaoh myself upon return that I made that choice. If he wishes to be angry, he can direct it at me."

Hell, and be damned, he thought. Nofret was back in his mind. How could he slaughter these people and expect her to come to him? She was a healer. It had been very clear to him how appalled she was when they first met and shared a few words. It became important that she realize he was not filled with evil. Perhaps those lovely powers could redeem him. Fill a void no other female had before or since.

Word would spread of this deed. A goodwill gesture towards the old. When she heard, it would be different between them. His horse whinnied as he took the reins in hand. Where had she originally come from? He was fully aware her current village was just downriver on the Nile. Close to one of the palaces. But she was reckless, he knew, traveling often alone from village to village. Healing those in need. Why no husband? Lover? He silently scoffed, thinking *Good thing*. Or he would have had to suddenly make them disappear.

She had visited the palace recently. One of Rano's women had reported back that she had not seen the queen. Instead, she had visited a local sage. He wanted to get back and delve into this, into her, more as the thrill of the day receded.

Pulling back on the reins, he dismounted. Taking a torch, he ignited the prince's tent. *Bastard*. Finally, he was out of his life and his sight, he thought as a sly grin came across his devilishly good-looking face.

"Have fifty of the men gather the livestock and prepare the caravan for departure. Abbore, take twenty to the caves and confirm they are indeed vacated. Then, we move out."

In less than an hour the village was burned. Those foolish enough to run for it or remain hidden in caves were surrounded, surrendered and brought around to see reason. Everything was looted and claimed, including the animals, as they marched back toward the barges that would take them all to the other royal palace at Memphis, upriver on the Nile.

***

As the ravens started to peck away at the dead bodies, a small group that had avoided detection by Rano's army started their descent from the caves. In utter disbelief they met, staring down at the horrifying sight below. Rushing, they began the awful task of checking each fallen soldier from their village.

"Over here. This one is alive. Barely. I just heard him groan. Help me get him up and onto the cart. Maybe the healer can help. Hurry."

"We've checked," another replied. "There are no other survivors. I have given instructions for several to remain behind and start the burial process. What shall we do after that? Follow the army back toward the Nile?"

"No, we shall go and blend in with the Hebrews and perhaps another time we will rise up again. We are not finished as a race. Not yet."

Chapter Two

"I need you to use your knife and cut away the cloth. I must see how much blood he has lost and if I can save him. Someone was watching over this poor soul. That is for sure. If he was not so well draped with this linen, he would have bled more and died on the battlefield. The weave staunched the flow."

"Healer, I am afraid to pull on this piece. It is blended with the blood and wound. It has dried on. If I do, it may start again."

"Put your finger on the edge, here. I will pull as hard as I can. Better be prepared for a struggle if he has an ounce of life left in his dirty, battered body. You ready?" The woman nodded, placing a knee over his legs. "Yes, do it now while I still have the nerve."

Nofret lifted the edge with a fingernail. When she had enough in it, she tugged with lightning-quick force. The man launched straight up, knocking her backward onto a hip. Then he fell, moaning in pain.

Nofret took in his appearance. His beard was thick and heavy, encased with dirt. Quickly washing out the wound, she had no choice but to scrub it with sea salt. That would sting like hell, but it needed to be done. Prepared, she took a deep breath and began.

"Quick, put a glob of the aloe and olive treatment onto the wound. That's good. Now help me lift him so I can look at his back."

The two women struggled but managed to get him upright. "It is as I thought. It did penetrate through his shoulder and out the back. Hand me the bandages. Now hold him tight while I wrap these around. We need to get

Sandra Waine • 476

him as comfortable as possible before he wakes up. That is, if he wakes up."

Gingerly, it took them both to settle him back onto the makeshift blankets. "There is no doubt that a fever will be forthcoming. How long, I'm not sure. But we must be diligent and keep a watchful eye on him. Bring me the jars. I'll mix up what I need and see if I can get some of it into him in a drink. I want you to come back in two hours and relieve me, Dahlia. I feel sad he's the only one that survived out of them all. Surely it was for a reason unknown to us. If he does pass, at least we can ensure he's as comfortable as possible."

"Healer, I will. If anyone can work magic and save him, it is you. I'll go now and take care of things. Then I'll be back. The guard is outside the flap if you need him. Rapidly news is passing around the village. Someone is here who witnessed the battle from a secluded cave. It is true that this was at the hands of Rano the Mercenary. The king was not there during the assault."

Nofret glanced up, nodding as her eyes glazed over. "Stories of his great battlefield skills and tactics do not hold any favor with me, Dahlia. But yes, I am fully aware he shows an interest in me. Now go. Stop all this jabber. We will not be discussing him further while we care for this poor, sick old man."

Moving over to the jars, she mixed a powder for him to drink, adding it slowly to the wine and watching as it dissolved. *That should assist in it going down easily combined with a concoction of dill, apple, and balsam. Plus a bit of honey and mint to ease any discomfort that may arise in his stomach.* This mixture would work well to aid in the release of any fever. But she had no doubt one was to follow.

It was going to be a tough stretch for him over the next several days. She'd do the best she could, she thought, nodding over at the statue of *Sekhmet*, the healing goddess of Upper Egypt. "Please help if you can. You know how I feel about all of this. If you can hear me, know I am sincere for his sake. Surely, he must have been saved so this story could be told for generations to come. I give you my plight."

She lifted his head and got him to drink the wine without spitting it back in her face. Every few minutes she repeated the process until the goblet was emptied. "There, that will help you, Semite." She mixed up another one and set it aside. Later, this routine would continue until she was relieved.

Stepping out into the open, Nofret nodded at the guard, who she now knew had been there for two days. A special appointment by the great wife of Thutmose III, Satiah, who by special courier had requested her presence as soon as duties in the village allowed. The guard would then be Nofret's guide and protector to the palace. Unclear as to why, the note had not revealed what the queen wanted. It only read: "Nofret Qalhata, Healer, come to me. I have a need of your workings. Be here as soon as possible."

Two men had arrived. One stayed and one was sent back with her hand-written reply advising of the sick that needed attending. She would rush there as soon as it was clear whether one requiring constant attention survived or not. Until then, she remained the queen's faithful servant.

She burned the original note. It was partly in disgust at such a random command, when the queen housed her own sages and mysterious healers at the palace. Nofret was fully aware, from having been in that vicinity, that the queen had an entire entourage that followed her every step. But also for privacy. No one else needed to know her own private business or that of the queen's.

Continuing by the guard and inhaling a deep breath of fresh air, her mind drifted to a sage that had lived temporarily up in one of the caves who had also sent a cryptic message warning Nofret to pay attention to everything happening around her now. To not be stubborn about the advances of one man and to keep distance with another. Properly forewarned and forearmed, Nofret felt as if she was walking on hot coals. Who was the second man? She truly was not aware of another that sought her out so blatantly as Rano during the months she had been here.

A soft moan from inside brought her back in a rush. Taking a linen cloth and saturating it in fresh well-water drawn just that morning, she sponged his clammy brow.

Already the mixture was working to expel the fever from his battered body. She glanced back at the partially open flap and saw the sun had set. Dahlia would be returning shortly, so she held his head up again in her hand while managing to get a second goblet finished.

Mixing another, she set it down as Dahlia entered. "Right on time. I have given him two doses. That will ease through his body and calm his mind for a few more hours. When the sweats and shaking begin, give him the mixture in that goblet. Then pat his head, neck, and chest down with cloth and water. I'm pretty confident that this will see him through the night." She scooted a scorpion under an opening and back outside.

"Damn things, never liked them. Anyway, stay with him. We need to find out who he is and what we are to do with him. His recuperation will take quite a while. I think possibly six or seven days. Don't relay under any circumstances what he tells you or mumbles in a heightened fever. I trust you, Dahlia. Don't let anyone persuade you that our business with him is also theirs."

Nofret brushed a hand against his beard as a slight tingle weaved up her spine. She stood, glancing down at him with her eyes narrowing.

"Healer, you have my word."

"Good. I am on my out of the village. I have been requested elsewhere. Four times over the next several days remix the drink and herbs. Change his dressing and reapply new salve twice a day. I will let one of the younger girls know they are to bring you food and drink. You can step outside. But stay close in case he wakes. We don't want him being injured further. Also, make sure the crawlers keep out of the tent. They seem to always locate the sickest of the sort and sting them with their poison."

Dahlia nodded. "When will you return back to us?"

"I don't know. Once I am there and hear what is needed of me, I will have a better understanding. I know you figured it out. Some of the others here have as well. I can tell by their glances at the guard. His uniform clearly gives it away. But let's not discuss that. We know he is the queen's. The less speculation involved will benefit us all."

A sly grin appeared on Nofret's face. "Has he even blinked?"

The two women smiled.

"Yes, he let one of the women bring him food and drink. He's staunch, I give him that. He has only left his post toward the bushes a few times. He's a man of steel."

They giggled.

"Okay." She picked up her carpet satchel. "I'm off. I entrust him to you. If for some reason things turn out bad, make sure they bury him and not burn him."

Dahlia nodded. "Safe travels there and back, Nofret."

"Thank you. Good luck with him. Pray to Sekhmet while I am away." Her grin grew as she nodded, hand holding the tent flap open. "Oh, and Dahlia, if anyone does come snooping about, we do not know his identity. We are waiting for his fever to break so we can discern who he is. I made sure to dispose of certain things already." With that, she walked out of the tent, the flap dropping behind her, and stared straight into the eyes of her new companion.

His stoic face, leathery, tanned and lined with tell-tale creases around his eyes, told her he was indeed a weathered soldier. Hardly acknowledging Nofret at all, he was standing by, prepared to help her mount if needed. As if on command, the camel knelt and she climbed on, grabbing the ropes. As the bag was secured, she patted his long neck and the animal slowly rose.

Nofret smiled. The slow and gentle pitch and rocking sensation swayed her around. But she enjoyed it. Camels were a necessity in the deserts of Egypt and the Middle East. She had always loved these gentle giants of the desert and was very much at home on them. From here they would trek a few miles, then board a beautifully crafted wooden boat bearing the queen's crest as they sailed up the Nile. She knew their arrival would be at the second largest of their royal palaces in Memphis.

Of course he did not speak. He rode beside her, never taking his eyes off the areas they passed through, vigilantly ensuring no one would halt their progress. She doubted any group of bandits would even try. Indeed, he was hardly a regular foot soldier. As she glanced more than once over at him, she knew he would be nearly as formidable as Rano.

Quite handsome, his tunic was of red and gold. Sandals, partially covered with royal armor, ascended up his legs, stopping just below his knees. Yes, he was indeed privileged. But she was sure he had earned it through blood, sweat, and determination. She pondered how the women would gather around him when he arrived back to where he was stationed. This type of man never had lonely nights. Of that, Nofret was sure.

He did, though, glance her way just once as a slight flush crept into her cheeks. Steadying her gaze ahead, Nofret watched the brilliant blue of the Nile become clearer as they reached the thriving village where the boat was awaiting their departure. As the camel kneeled and she slid off, the soldier took her bag and motioned with one hand for her to proceed him up the gang-plank.

At the stern on the top deck, she sat, noticing the bag had been set down close by. He remained near, leaning against a railing as his eyes searched the snaking river.

"How long will the journey on this vessel be?"

He turned, coming over. "Through two sunsets, then we will arrive. The winds feel strong against our back. Look at how the reeds bend over on the other shore. If it remains that way, we will have a quick sail."

She smiled up into those handsome features as one of his brows raised in silent amusement. She kept it to herself that she was amazed he had disclosed so much. The entire camel ride he had not uttered one damn single word. Indeed, men here could be harder to read than in the future. When had things changed?

Over his shoulder she surveyed a woman heading toward them, carrying a very heavy wooden tray. As she neared, Nofret's stomach grumbled. Laid before her were meats, fruit, two wine goblets and bread. She motioned her closer. "You can set that down next to me."

"No, she won't. Woman, don't listen to her. Set it by my side. Then go. We will not be in need your services until I advise."

The servant quickly scurried off.

Interesting, Nofret thought. She was a pretty woman. But he had treated her like she was beneath his feet. "Why did you do that? If I may be so bold to ask."

He lifted the wine, pouring a small amount and tasting it. Filling the other goblet, he handed it to her. "To ensure you are not poisoned."

"Oh. Did the queen request that of you?"

"No, Rano did."

Drinking down more than she should have, Nofret spewed out a small amount that landed at his sandals.

"Something wrong?" His mirth was clear.

Damn ass, she wanted to say. "No. Just a bit bitter, that's all."

She watched as he tasted everything off the platter and then set it down on the cyprus wood stool at her feet. "You can eat."

"Won't you have any?"

"I just did."

Once again, he was baiting her. "Are you looking for some kind of an argument so you can report back to your commander what a nasty woman I am?"

"He would not believe it so. I'm testing you for my own knowledge. He only speaks highly of you. Only here I doubt him. Surely, no woman could manipulate the greatness of Rano the Mercenary."

"Oh, you are so full of shit."

He laughed so loud it brought several glances from those working on the ship. "Now that's better. He said you have a quick tongue and sharp mind."

"I think you got that backward. Just wait until some woman gets into your head and you lose all rational thought. I'm going to make sure I see this happen."

"Healer, the sun will stop shining over Egypt when that occurs."

They both laughed.

"Don't be so sure. Someplace out there she exists. It's only a matter of time before you two meet."

He leaned down, resting an arm on a strong upper thigh. She truly had to lock eyes with his to not look at what might lurk beneath his clothing.

"I've been through almost all the household women in the palace and I can assure you she's not there."

Nofret popped a grape into her mouth. "Nope, you are right. She is not. But she does exist. I can see her. You will fall to your knees begging for her attention one day. Mark my words." It was bullshit, but she wanted to tease this soldier a bit longer.

His grin was devilish, and now inches from her face. "Woman, you lie. Now I am beginning to realize Rano's torment."

She smiled up seductively, eyes ablaze. "I was just delaying your exit from my company to make sure the food and drink are safe. That's all."

He slapped the railing, grinning all the way to the ladder below deck. There, he would indeed eat and drink. Just not in her presence.

She ate, enjoying the journey on this fine vessel. The simple, smooth rhythm of the oars being pulled up, over and down into the water in a repeating pattern, was soothing her mind. She watched with eager interest as a group of men raised the sails. The wind took them and they billowed out.

Bread raised to take a bite, she halted, recalling a larger, sleeker ship that she had seen in a recent dream. A skull and bones flag flew high above a lookout point. Then it was gone.

How she loved life on the Nile. It was her home. Her lifestyle was gentle, being a healer. But she did have to leave at times the comfort of her village in Middle Egypt and go where no healer lived. She had to wonder why Queen Satiah wanted her when there was a full host of sages, alchemists, and herbalists at her disposal in the royal household.

She set the goblet down, never partaking in that much drink, as she nodded for the hovering woman to come and take it away. She rose, stretching her legs as the vessel cut swiftly through the darkening waters of the Nile.

He was back up on deck, having finished his meal, Nofret assumed, as without hesitation she approached him. "I don't suppose it is allowed to ask if you have any idea why our queen wants to see me?"

"No, I do not know. I just follow orders."

"Well, it was worth an ask." He seemed preoccupied now as his gaze glanced back towards the vacated chair and then towards her. "Oh, you don't want to talk now. Is that it?"

He started to open his mouth to speak, but she was quick to interrupt whatever he was going to say. "All right. I shall go sit. On second thought, I won't. It looks like one of the servant women is trying to get my attention."

The woman nodded her toward a partially tented-off area in the middle of the boat. "We have made a make-shift bed for you. It should be comfortable. I will stay here with you. If you need anything just ask. Tomorrow we will arrive at the palace and the queen would wish to see you refreshed."

"Oh, that's sooner than I was told. Okay, good. Thank you. If you do not mind my asking, what is your name?"

"Ospera, and yes, you are correct that we will arrive ahead of schedule. This journey is blessed by strong winds."

"That's pretty. Your name I mean. Do you happen to know why the queen has asked for me? I inquired with my escort, but he is not aware."

"I do. But it is for her to tell you. Not me." She swept a single hand around the small enclosed area. "Will this work for your needs?" She had moved the draped linen panel down so they were indeed enclosed. Nofret settled on the cushions and was covered with a blanket.

"Yes, with this pitching of the ship and listening to the oars and the wind, I think I will actually sleep. Thank you, Ospera."

"Good dreams to you, Healer Nofret."

"Thank you." Within minutes she dozed off, falling into a very deep sleep.

Suddenly, men's voices alerted her that she must have slept longer than she realized. Glancing over, she saw that Ospera had left a damp cotton cloth. Nofret reached for it and washed hands and face. She would leave her hair unbound, never having been one of those that wore the popular black wigs of this period.

But she did reach inside her bag and apply her very own mixture of alluring scents and oils where the wind would catch it just right and take it upon the breeze. Perhaps all the way to Rano. Shaking her head at such frivolous thoughts, she tied up the bag and sat quietly for a few moments in contemplative meditation.

But it was short lived.

Ospera poked her head inside. "It is nearly mid-day, healer. You slept longer than I thought."

She grinned. "Yes. You should have woken me. I feel like I wasted part of my day."

Ospera shrugged. "You needed the rest and may not have as much once we reach the palace. So I left you alone. Besides, there is not much one can do on this ship but watch the water, birds flocking above or the men."

"Ah, there are indeed some interesting options, then."

They laughed softly.

"There are food and drink where your chair is and the sun is bright and warm against today's breeze. We still have a strong one and expect to be arriving as planned when the sun sets."

Ospera held back the makeshift drape as Nofret stood, walking out into the bright sunshine. It took a couple of seconds for her eyes to adjust. "You are right. Indeed, it is a lovely day. I'm not familiar with this area of the Nile. Where do we pass?"

"The shores of Herakleopolis."

She sat down, taking food off the platter to her left while sipping on the wine. That was why she'd slept so well last night. It was probably due to the two cups she had consumed. Although not drunk, it was as if she had taken a sleeping draft and it had mellowed her mood.

She turned to say something, but Ospera had returned to the draping. With the assistance of one of the men, she took it down and folded it. She then disappeared once again below the deck.

As the current, wind and men manning the oars moved them farther up the river, three hours later off in the distance, she began to see the brilliant torches signaling the end of this journey.

It was as if she was in a dream observing the cool shades of marble and granite steps as they rose from the waters of the Nile. Appearing to be suspended from the very heavens, pools of flowering lotus blossoms danced across the ripples of the water stirred slightly by a light breeze. Their heavy scent wafted up just as her first sandal stepped onto the marble.

Two women were awaiting her arrival. She took in the sheer gauze wraps that tried to house their bodies, but in the disappearing sunshine, they were clearly outlined for all to see. Did they expect her to dress like that? She grinned, knowing that would have quite an effect on Rano the Great.

They rushed down to take her bag, clutching both her arms as they ushered her up the stairs and onto the landing. As they walked beneath four grand pillars, Nofret glanced about, marveling in true awe at what was before her. Halting them both by her quick stop, she was allowed a moment to gaze at all the glory and splendor around her before their giggles motivated her to move along with them.

Rapidly, their infectious laughter gave way to seductive smiles as a small band of soldiers exited the king's wing just as they passed.

"Good to see you, Healer Qalhata."

She nodded at Rano, eyeing him skeptically at this impeccable timing. Then she kept right on walking. *Damn,* she thought, *I should have acted more politely*. But the truth was women were not allowed in public to openly display any emotions in front of the men. *Especially that man*, she thought. One thing was clear. She'd not be able to avoid him now.

In truth, she did not want to.

"We have your rooms ready, healer. There will be a massage later. But see here, there is plenty of food, drink, and music to keep you occupied. It is imperative that you have a good night's rest before your appointment with the queen scheduled for later in the morning tomorrow. She rises early to take an oil bath in the private pools. After that, she will want to see you."

Former kings and queens beautifully carved out of stone lined the final three steps up into her rooms. The double-wide wooden doors suddenly swung open as women of various ages rushed out towards her. Hands. All Nofret could feel were hands all over her. Pulling, tugging, removing her clothing, pushing her down onto a set of oversized plush silk pillows.

Those hands continued, removing the silk band from her long hair. Another took both of her sandals. Then off in the distance, growing louder, was beautiful music being played by a lone woman with a golden harp. Each stroke of the strings brought Nofret to a quieter, more gentle place inside her head. The sound was positively lovely.

Yes. She could get used to this. Being in the desert all the time with constant dirt in the teeth did not always sit well. Or taste well. Then again, out there she was with her people. Those that could not ever dream of this and who needed her special healing magic to help them just to survive.

But it was a lot more than that.

Out there was freedom.

Rising naked, unabashed, her beautiful body was exposed to strangers, a hand clasping one of hers as she followed in a languid trance.

"Healer Qalhata, come into the pool. We will wash your hair, set it and then massage your body with essential oils. You will have the very best of the queen's delights tonight."

Running the clear water through her hands, she let them do just as they would. When those subtle fingers began easing tired muscles, Nofret fell into a deep, sound sleep.

Giggling woke her. *Damn these pesky people*, she thought. Could they not leave her alone for two straight minutes?

"Healer Qalhata, we are sorry. You must get up so we can dress you."

She eyed what one of them was holding. Was that slim, soft, pink gauze material going to cover her enough? She'd need more clothes than that to see the queen, that was clear. "Will I have something different to wear tomorrow?"

They appeared to be amused by her question. Did they think her just a simple healer, not caring about what she wore because she lived predominantly in the desert?

Oh, she thought, finding amusement now with their lack of her background completely. *If they only knew*. They were basing this on that ugly tunic she'd used to arrive in. A sly grin passed by her lips. She let them dress her in it and then slid under the soft, smooth sheets. A sigh escaped of its own accord.

Two very young maidens stood outside the silky mesh drapes surrounding the oversized bed. As her lids drooped, she shook awake, remembering they were still there. "You can go. I will not need you to stay here all night." At their hesitation, she persisted. "It is my wish. Queen Satiah will be fine with my decision and should she question me, I will let her know I felt so safe I did not believe you were needed to watch over me. Good night, ladies."

A bit later when she rolled to a side, one eye barely opened. But it was enough to know they were gone. Early the next morning, just as a phoenix flew over the wing of rooms, Nofret woke. Stretching languishingly like a sleek, satisfied black cat, she opened her eyes to scan the area. Six women stood around her bed, ready to pounce and prepare her for the queen.

"Okay. So here you are." She did not know what else to say. Had they arrived with orders not to wake her? This moment was a bit embarrassing, even for her. "I'm all yours."

With all tasks completed, Nofret's eyes roamed over the flowing aqua silk tunic tied snugly with a glistening gold belt. A small shudder passed through her, though, as she noticed the mesmerizing blue lapis lazuli stones encased on her leather sandals.

It was his stone. A stone of royalty. Visions of long ago, yet they were now, beamed through her third eye like she was watching it happen live. In a split second, she saw a quick flash of a strange wooden object suspended off the ground with legs then vanished. "What the..." she started, and then stopped as a soft gasp from one of the women reached her ears.

A potent internal struggle then began in earnest. Shrugging, she smiled, acknowledging the hard work they had just put into making her more than presentable for the queen. They had made her beautiful. Later when there was more time and privacy, Nofret would do a card reading and see if what she had just experienced could be made clear. For now, she had to let it go.

As she followed one of the ladies out of her room, the breeze from the open corridors weaved through her garment, gently caressing her skin. A soft quiver of delicious delight ran up her spine. The scent of lotus, rose and jasmine assaulted her senses, the queen's own special scent. Its arrival announced her long before she made her grand entrance.

"Ladies, we will need some time alone. Go and bring us back our meal and then leave us. I will let you know when to return. Healer Qalhata, come. Sit opposite me on the pillows so we can have our much-needed talk."

Nofret lowered herself and got comfortable. "Is it permissible to ask you a question?"

"Of course. Here we speak without barriers."

"I must admit at wondering why I've been invited to see you with all the excellent people you have here, my Queen."

"You shall have your answer. Word has spread to me of your amazing uses of the herbs. There are those here and in the caves high up in the hills that cannot replicate some of your idolized potions." She leaned closer, taking both of Nofret's hands in a tight grip. "My king and I are having a bit of trouble producing our first heir. I had my sage provide my forecast and she talked of Nofret from the middle village of Amama, who has special gifts blessed upon her by the Goddess Hathor."

Nofret had heard these rumblings even within her own village and others during the last moon cycle. "You do indeed honor me with such talk. I am your servant, always. What would you ask of me?"

"The king is preparing to march with the charioteers and army to western Asia. When their business is concluded, they will continue to Ethiopia in three moons. It is my hope that when he leaves, I will have blessed him with the news of an upcoming child. A son. Tell me you can make this possible."

This powerful woman, strong of spirit and heart, fair and honorable, was asking her above all others for help.

"Yes, I can. I have seen this in a vision before leaving my village. I am prepared to assist. We can begin right away. I brought my herbs and oils in the carpet bag." The healer leaned closer to her to ask, "When was your last bleeding?"

"Five days."

"Excellent. I will need some glass bowls and sticks. Where do you want me to work? I will require a room with a plentiful breeze so I can capture the wind off the Nile. Also, along with that, I ask for lotus and jasmine buds. Unfortunately, I used my supply and did not have enough time to gather more to bring."

The women returned with food and drink and set it before them. "Meliah, stay and get a papyrus, reed, and ink. Write some items down for me. Then go to the market and secure them. When you have gathered the highest quality, bring them to the small chambers behind my quarters and come and let us know. We will be here or at the pools."

When she returned with the writing materials, Nofret dictated a list of exactly what was required. Promptly, the servant left the palace toward the village market.

"How long will it take before we have news?"

"Well, I can tell you that before he leaves we will have an answer." She would not insult this woman by asking if she had been praying to the goddess herself. Of course, the sage would have suggested that a long time ago when they had been unsuccessful. Although they had only been wed two years, it was a bit unusual that she had not successfully conceived by now. Then again, Nofret had seen visions of a future filled with difficulties for them.

"Shall we swim?" the queen asked. "The waters today are warmer in the pool as there was no chill last night." They talked easily along the way.

"I would like that. I noticed how beautiful it is here. When I was in the village near the palace at Thebes, I did not have a chance to see all the temples. There are quite a few here. There their numbers are greater. Is that correct?"

"Yes, more than any other city in the New Kingdom. When you wish to come back, send a note ahead and I will welcome you into our palace so you will not have to stay in the village. Although it has been advised to me that you much prefer the dust of the desert and a simpler way of life."

"Indeed, I do. But at times like this, I am also happy to be out of them." They both laughed. "Yes, one could truly get used to this, my Queen."

They were assisted in disrobing and quietly slipped into the pools overlooking the Nile. Adorned with her luscious glittering eye makeup and dark wig glistening in the sun, Queen Satiah was indeed a beauty that would stop any man in his tracks.

Over her head, Nofret caught sight of the one she now knew as Meliah approaching at a near run. She tried not to break out laughing. Bowing to them both, Meliah looked at Nofret. "We have gathered everything on your list and are ready. Would you like to begin now?"

"Yes. If my queen will allow me to leave her company?"

Her response was a simple nod followed by a gentle smile.

Nofret snapped her fingers and her wrap reappeared as she climbed out of the pool, was dried off with rough linen and flax and dressed. Bowing, she left the queen, who was now resting her head back on a pillow, eyes searching the heavens above. Or perhaps beseeching. Nofret was not sure.

Chapter Three

She was brought into a pair of large rooms that were wide, open and airy. Outside, abutting both, were several beautifully white-washed patios. Further, she had her own pools and garden, overflowing with various herbs and flowers. It was lovely and Nofret sighed, wishing she had such extravagances back in the village. There were times when this would indeed be useful in healing those that required it. Supplies here were more abundant.

Walking back inside, she saw that two women stood, intently watching her every move. The sheerest of drapes hung to keep some of the flying insects out as her eyes drew to the cushions where she would spend the next several nights. Turning back, she smiled at them. "This will do very well. I know I am not too far from the queen's rooms. Which will prove vitally important when I have the potions ready to deliver. Go ahead and unpack. I'll let you know where I want my supplies. It will be in the other room. I can work in there away from my night chamber."

Her few articles of clothing were neatly folded and set into a bamboo basket. How ironic that she carried more herbs and oils than clothing. The other woman picked up her carpet bag, setting things in their proper place, and nodded for Nofret to follow.

"I think you will find everything within close reach. We are now ready. What other requisites do you have?"

"A large jug of water from the Nile. But do not have it drawn until just as the sun sets. It is imperative that the timing is exact. Not one minute before or after the sun disappears into the water. It must shine as if diamonds glisten upon it." Nofret glanced up at the sky. "There is still some time prior to that occurring. You will need a reliable man for this. The quantity expected necessitates a big, strong man for this task. But you must be right there with him, making sure it is not removed one minute early or late. Then bring it back to me. I leave you with these instructions to take care of when the time is right. In the meanwhile, I would like some soft music played outside these rooms. But no singing, please. All I desire is quiet distraction."

Nofret pointed toward the other women. "Please do not move the palm fronds any longer. The breeze coming in is sufficient. Shortly I will be grinding powders. I do not want to take a chance any of it is displaced by such a motion. If you want you can sit. When I need your assistance, I will ask."

She lined up all the soft and hard ingredients and began moving about the chamber mixing, grinding and adding them into a larger mortar. When the correct level had been reached, she placed them into a black cauldron suspended over a wood-burning pit. "I also ask for blocks of myrrh and cedar resin along with three bundles of papyrus. Go ahead now and retrieve them."

The woman in the chair rose and Nofret caught a brief glimpse of dissatisfaction upon the younger girl's features.

"I apologize. That was rude of me. Please tell me your name?"

"Asofia, healer."

"Pretty name. Thank you for helping me."

"It's for our queen. For her, I would move heaven and earth." She started from the rooms but Nofret halted her. "The other woman is Meliah, I believe. Am I correct? I heard her name spoken by the queen and previously when I saw her in the market. But want to make sure."

"You are right."

Nofret looked closely at her now. She seemed anxious to move on.

"Anything else? If not, I will go."

"Nothing. Thank you."

When all was in order, Nofret moved out to glance at the Nile. The sun was starting to set and Meliah was down on the steps with the soldier, a jug between them, ready to be filled. *Good*, Nofret thought, satisfied at their progress while moving back in. Asofia returned shortly with all the other items. "I will have food and drink brought when you are ready."

"Thank you." At the pit she stacked the wood and resin, having them touch at the top and fan out at the bottom. Smiling, she recalled back in Norway how she had learned this from that rogue, Gunner. It was the surest way to keep a fire going. Shaking her head and shoving those thoughts back into the recesses of her mind, she manipulated the papyrus into a cone shape, keeping it adhered by a bit of spit.

Moving the cauldron's arm, she knelt, eyeing the distance from the flame. *Yes*, she thought, it would work. Removing mixtures from all three glass jars and emptying them into the bottom, she turned, raising eyes to the heavens and silently offering up gratitude at the success of this ceremonial process. The timing was perfect.

The guard, followed close at hand by Meliah, parted the draping and entered with the jug filled with the water from the ancient Nile.

"You can set it down right next to me. You are free to go. I will need you to meet Meliah over the next two nights. The exact same time and procedure. If you are unable, let me know now. I must have someone completely reliable to assist her."

"I am at your service, healer, by orders of the queen."

"Excellent. Thank you."

He bowed, thumping his right fist on his chest, and left the chambers.

She ignited the wood and resin with sage brush and set it into the center of the circle on top of the blocks. It exploded to life, crackling sparks flying upwards. Stepping back, simultaneously mesmerized, mouths agape with eyes wide, both women watched in complete concentration, totally drawn in by the healer's display of magic. It confirmed all the stories they had both heard.

Reaching for the large, blue jar, Nofret immersed it into the jug filled with the Nile water and spilled it into the cauldron. Hissing smoke billowed straight up, then dispersed on the breeze and filled the room. Repeating the whole process two more times, she then mixed it slowly. Using the long glass rod, she stopped intermittently as if in a trance. Then inhaled the thick concoction while softly chanting words neither girl would understand.

"It is ready. Bring me that glass vial and remove the stopper. Hurry now. Time is of the essence."

She dipped the blue jar into the cauldron and quickly filled the vial, sealing it immediately. Walking over to the edge of the patio, she held the vial up to the moon, her body swaying back and forth. Turning, she nodded to the women.

"Take me to her now."

They walked silently at a quickened pace, together.

At the queen's doors, Nofret met with no delay and was immediately allowed entry.

Getting ready to meet the king for their evening feast, the queen stopped. She never took her eyes off the healer as Nofret approached.

"Accept this now. Before your meal. You will find it is bitter but palpable."

"Taste it before me. I have to be sure about you."

Quickly uncorking it, Nofret took a tiny amount onto her tongue and swallowed it. "You are safe with me, my Queen."

The queen's fingers clasped it firmly, tipped the contents back and drank until the glass vial was empty. "Do you want this back?"

"Yes." Nofret took it. "Tonight you will make love with your husband. We will repeat this entire sequence in the exact order over the following two nights. Then you will go and visit the sage to be delivered your awaited news."

Nofret took a step backward to leave. "I will then depart for my village. You will send me word of confirmation. The Pharaoh will know before he travels that you are expecting your first son. All the land will share in your joy. He will be healthy. He will sit on his father's throne when the day comes."

The queen nodded. A lovely, knowing smile hovered upon her face. "As you say it, so it shall be. It is now declared by you, Healer Nofret. You may now go."

The ladies escorted her back to the chambers. "I wish to have a platter and drink brought to me shortly. I will not need you both until tomorrow. Later in the afternoon. As I mentioned to the queen, I say to you both as well. Same time, the same process. See you tomorrow. Thank you."

When the food arrived, she ate and walked out from the rooms laughing to herself. For the queen indeed trusted her. But not completely. Just outside was an assigned guard to keep watch on her comings and goings. *Fine,* she thought, reconciled to the reasons why. But she'd not stay put. If he was to guard her, then he was going to go on a nighttime stroll. Like it or not.

Coming across a beautiful marble pond, she watched, enchanted by lotus dancing animatedly against the vibrantly lit stars in the sky above. Sitting down and crossing her legs, she glanced off into the distance. He was there. A gray silhouette against the darkening night. Closing her eyes, she fell deeply in prayer. Holding palms up, facing the fuller moon, she spoke with the cat-faced goddess of fertility and motherhood, Bast.

Even deep in meditation, Nofret saw visions of her guard appointed by the queen watching her every move. She was fully aware his eyes were gazing upon her lightly clad attire. The moon shone down upon her, revealing to his eyes all her curves.

She suppressed a grin, took a deeper breath and settled more deeply into prayer. After nearly thirty minutes, she finally lowered her hands and opened her eyes to see he had now moved from the shadows and was standing a few feet in front of her leaning against a closer pillar.

Nofret rose and they walked side by side. "I think you would be better rid of me now for want of food, drink, and other pleasures?" She smiled up into his handsome face and ruggedly chiseled features, seeing desire in those eyes. "I know you are ordered by the queen to watch over me. But you could visit the ladies down the hall in my wing. I'm sure they would enjoy company this night. I doubt they are allowed to take of such pleasures with their current responsibilities. This could prove to be a satisfying situation. If you know what I mean?"

They arrived back at her rooms, where she lowered the flimsy drapes, providing some privacy. More than that, it also seemed to keep the night creatures from paying an unwanted visit. Damn, how she detested those pesky scorpions. She watched on in amusement at what he was doing.

He surveyed the interior rooms, checking for ghosts lurking in the shadows, she imagined. Finally satisfied, he spoke at last.

"It was my orders to stay with you until daylight when they join you. I cannot disobey those."

"Ah, I see. I shall not compromise you then, but have an idea." She came out, then marched down the long, quiet hallway. Halting at their shared chamber, she opened one door, rather boldly, to the two ladies' startled expressions.

"I have need of volunteers to come and pass the evening away with my guard. I can't have him bored all night outside my rooms. I have two separate chambers opposite each other. If this warrants your interest, ladies, please come and help him out."

She turned, leaving them as four jumped to their bare feet and were quickly on her heels.

Walking over and parting the sheer gauzy drapes, she motioned him inside. "Over in there. You will not have abandoned me. In fact, being inside puts you closer to protecting me than out there. Enjoy your night, soldier."

Could a man's grin be bigger than that? Nofret thought.

He nodded, glancing back only once at the wisdom of her words as with purposeful strides she watched him move out of sight and directly into the other chamber. Rich, deep laughter followed by soft sighs and giggles was all she could hear while climbing back into the plush bed.

Gentle hands slid over supple silk sheets as she released a truly contented sigh. For once, it felt good to send a bit of pleasure their way. For once it felt good to not have to heal someone who was sick. For once it felt good to not see glimpses in her mind's eye of another who still haunted bits and pieces of her life here.

Listening to the babble of a fountain off in the distance, Nofret allowed her tired mind to claim her tired body and sleep.

The next morning, she rose to sounds coming from their direction. Catching sight of him before he disappeared, she gave him a knowing smile. Without a doubt, he would have a good day and quite possibly look forward to leaving his regular military duties to come back again the next two nights.

As she was bathed in the pool and redressed, she noticed something behind one of the lady's backs and nodded her over, extending a hand.

"You have a note from the village, Healer Nofret." The rolled papyrus was grabbed, opened and the script read. "In a feverish state, he has spoken. It is not broken yet. But it should this night or by the morning. I have news for you. When shall you return?"

She nodded at one of the girls. "Bring me a reed brush and ink. I will write a reply and have it taken back to my village. The delivery needs to be quick. It must be handed to the same person that sent it to me. I need your promise."

When she returned, Nofret wrote the reply: "Two more nights and my needs here will have been met. I shall see you the day after tomorrow. Give him an extra dose this evening and tomorrow if needed. I assure you that will flush the fever from his body."

She let it dry in the sun, rolled it back up and handed it to Meliah. "Please see it is brought there now. By the way, how was this delivered? Surely not by the same river route I took to come here?"

"No, healer. By courier on horseback. He rode straight through to you. He has been replaced by a fresh rider and horse awaiting your return note, should there be one. I will make sure he is on his way in minutes."

"Thank you." She took it as Nofret glanced at Asofia.

"You have a question for me burning on your tongue. Do not be afraid to speak. What is it?"

Asofia came closer, glancing around, ensuring no one would be lurking in the shadows. "You are very young and quite beautiful. How did you learn all the trades of one that should be an elder?"

That brought out a laugh. Sometimes stories had to be embellished. "By birth. I was born with special talents that I noticed when I started to walk. My instincts are in line with the gods and goddesses. I can hear those from the heavens. They help me heal wherever I am at the time. They guide me. But we are all special, Asofia. Give this some thought. If you were not here right now, doing as I request, exactly in the proper order, things would not have the same outcome. Would they? You are equally as important. Our queen needs you just as she needs me. Not one sitting above the other."

"Oh. I had not thought of that." She lowered her head, blushing. That flush creeping up her cheeks certainly had not been caused by Nofret's reply. That was apparent. It was the remnants of what had occurred during the passing night.

"You had your fill of him last night. I can see it written all over you today. Well, you had better rest until I need you again. For I have it on excellent authority he will return tonight. Plus, one more following. I am sure he will be searching you out again."

"Oh, healer, if I may be so bold. Indeed, he is a handsome man. Full of energy, strength, and stamina. We all enjoyed him."

Nofret smiled. For indeed it had been a tidy sum of days and nights since she had been near any man that had aroused her to want him again like her young friend here. There were a couple of handsome men in the village that she enjoyed talking to, but no more than that. Here she was still a virgin. Well, sort of.

A wry smile hovered on her lips as she recalled a woman a bit out of luck recently who needed tender healing. She was a belly dancer. Rather than accept her coinage, Nofret had asked her to teach her the fine art of this exotic dance. Readily she accepted and the two had become fast friends over the weeks.

***

As time progressed, she became quite proficient. Then it dawned on her why she wanted to learn. A warmth spread through her at just the thought of how much she would enjoy taunting that great warrior. Again. She glanced back at Asofia, who was staring at her with a puzzled look on her face.

Nofret bit back a laugh. "Go ahead and rest until needed. I am going to start mixing my powders." She turned and got to work. When the fire was ready, the water was brought and the liquid put in the vial. Shortly after, the ritual walk to the queen's chambers commenced.

After she drank and handed it back, the queen spoke, halting their exit. "Healer, just a moment. I must tell you something of urgency. In confidence." The others moved away, turning their backs to them. "Last night was different. He was different. I was different. Today I am different. I hope sense is being made of this."

Nofret smiled up into her eyes, nodding, already aware of what would happen. "Yes, and so it shall be. Remember? I declared it." The queen clasped her hands tightly and they both softly laughed. "Go on then, healer."

Onward into the next day, night and following night, not only did the queen feel altered, but her appearance did indeed take on a distinctive appeal that had many glancing in her direction. Now she did indeed have that decided glow of a woman that held a child growing inside her womb.

Life was good in the healer's world.

The soldier was more content than ever before.

As the day of departure dawned bright, hot and clear, Nofret packed up her carpet bag and left toward the queen's quarters. Immediately she entered, passing her sage, who halted and grabbed both her hands.

"You are indeed a gifted healer. For you have done that which no other has. Now go ahead in. She is excitedly awaiting your arrival."

The queen's eyes were pooling as Nofret swiftly eliminated the short distance between them. Taking one palm and placing it on her abdomen, a quivering smile appeared upon this lady of royalty's lips. Nofret raised her hand up from her stomach and touched one tear before it fell to their feet.

"Nothing but joy, my queen. I see nothing but joy. As well as a strong, healthy son. He will bear the name and resemblance of your husband, our king. But your true beauty will shine in his eyes always and his heart will know the pure, true love of you both. He will be a commanding and fair ruler. If ever you are in need of my services, please send word. I shall come as quickly as possible."

"Wait just a moment longer. I know they prepare for your departure down at the boats." The queen drew off a table a small silk parcel and unwrapped it. It was a beautifully forged gold and silver cat, sitting upright with a basket of papyrus reeds popping out of the top.

"Oh, this is lovely. I shall put it on now." The healer removed the tie over her shoulder, looped it through the brooch and tied it back. Indeed, it held an important meaning which the healer would not recall until much later. In fact, several lifetimes later.

"It is just as special as you are, Nofret Qalhata, the healer." Her face suddenly turned stern, eyes drawn as if she was angry. Nofret stepped slightly back, not understanding this mood swing as apprehension weaved through her gut.

The queen stepped closer. "Now you must listen and listen well. If I never give this to you again, it means the gods have smiled on us all. At last. Go. I will be in touch soon. You will find the same boat will take you back down the Nile. There is a surprise awaiting you, perhaps more than one. May the heavens always smile upon you, healer, as they smile upon me."

Nofret was temporarily paralyzed. Her mind wove between the here and now and a vision of a handsome man dressed in strange clothes sporting a tall hat of some kind on his head. His voice held an accent she was not familiar with and he seemed to be standing directly in front of the queen.

"Come home. I need you to come home." was all she heard as the vision evaporated.

The queen's gaze questioned her. "Are you okay?"

"Yes. Yes, I am," she lied. "I saw a wonderful glimpse of your future. It is filled with bounty." She nodded, bowing slightly, then walked out of the chambers. But the strange man's words resonated inside her brain. Her heart. Something was stirring there that she just did not understand. Had she been hallucinating? Inhaled too much of the liquid in the vial?

Her eyes drifted towards Meliah carrying the carpet bag. Without distractions on the trip back, she would have time to filter out exactly what her intended message truly meant.

"It is a wonderful day for your return, healer."

She glanced down the few remaining marble steps towards the plank, taking the bag. "Indeed, it is. Meliah, thank you for all your help. I am sure our paths will cross again. Until then, be well."

The sun was bright, too bright, she thought, raising a hand to shield her eyes. Then she walked straight into a wall of iron.

Chapter Four

"Oh." The bag dropped as her hands slid up a walled chest of muscular strength. She let out a gasp. It was someone she knew quite well. He leaned down, picking the bag up with one hand while clasping her petite one in his other. Moving slowly for one so tall, he escorted his lovely guest the rest of the way up the plank onto the ship as the clouds continued to shroud the sun above.

It was him.

Damn, what the hell was he doing here? Did he not have an army to train, someone to irritate or something to burn?

"Healer No fret."

Why did he bother? Why did he not just throw her down on the ship's deck and have his way with her in front of these men? Why did she feel such strong stirrings radiate throughout her being in proximity to this guy? Sure, he was handsome as sin. Sin being the key word here. She did not want to provoke him at all. But no matter how hard she tried to dislodge her hand from his iron grasp, he would not accommodate.

"General Aiempt." The deep, dark urge to kick him in the balls, or give him a good, hearty shove backward and have his ass land in the shallows was overtaking common reasoning. But she refrained and it was a tough task to fulfill. They walked side by side as she dropped down into what was now that familiar chair adhered to the deck. As the plank was removed and the shore began to recede, her hopes of ignoring him went down the river along with the current. Fast as hell.

He left her and was engaged with someone, but her eyes watched him like a hawk, mind wandering. There had been many times of late when their paths had crossed. Especially recently when she had been visiting a sage in the village near the palace. He'd shown up when she was heading out on her camel. Oh, how his eyes had burned into her very soul. A gruff voice verbally warned her that chasing off by herself could prove to be detrimental. She had lowered her eyes, thanked him, and then moved on. But in fact, she had wanted him to assist. Give protection. A few extra moments in his company. Damn. That arrogant bastard had launched an attack on her heart and was winning.

Eyes seductively drifting closed, head lifting toward the warm breeze, a not-too-subtle emotion was generating from the inside out. It caused scandalous feelings where her skin was exposed.

His eyes devoured her and she could feel it.

"Trying to ignore me this time won't work, healer. You are now my captive. Unless you can walk on water, as I've heard claimed, then how about we start with something simple. Would you like a drink?"

A smile hovered as a soft sigh escaped her lips. His hand extended, producing a goblet of wine.

"Yes, thank you. I will go easy on this, though. Every time I drink it strange things occur."

Their eyes locked. Seconds passed by. She did not even know if her lungs were working.

"You were successful with the queen?"

"I'm not sure I'm at liberty to discuss that with anyone. No disrespect to you, General."

He leaned down, putting one sandal up on the rise beside her chair. Unlike another circumstance when her eyes had refused to wander, this time she had no choice but to allow them to drift up that leg.

"You do not need to fear me. Nor put a wall between us that will surely come down. I know my reputation sparks anger and disgust in many, but I would not wish it to be so with you."

Her heart skipped a beat, lower lip dropping. She'd have to be very careful with this mighty man.

This time.

"Well if you are honest, then so shall I. Your prowess on the battlefield speaks volumes. There is not a man near or far who can beat you. Of that I am sure. But your willingness to burn, pillage and kill using your mighty sword and chariot will be your downfall. You seek to destroy anything and anyone that steps in your way."

"I see you are not fearful for your life, having proclaimed such about me."

She did not flinch, nor feel threatened by him at all right now on her second goblet of wine. "Not one bit."

He laughed. It was hearty. Enveloping her. Bearing charm and arrogance. "Perhaps I am all of those things. But not at the same time. Remember, little one, I follow the orders of my king first and foremost."

"Okay, that may be true. But your journeys have been many and your successes great." She pointed to that glorious sword attached to his belt. "You created that. To many, you are one step away from being a god yourself. Years before you pass on."

"Do not humor me, woman. We know again and again what this is all about. Why don't we just cut to the chase and put all in a right order?"

"You speak of that which I am not clear on. What would you mean to have me say, warrior?"

He was getting pissed off. "But in those that seek to glorify me, I do not cast a glance. There are only a few that truly matter You are one. So here is your chance. I cannot rip you in two and cast you out to the Nile gods, as you are under the protection of the queen. What do you think of me, really? I will not have you hold anything back now so we can avoid a repeat. I want to know."

She shrugged, trying, as with the queen, to fathom what exactly he was saying. But he stood fast, not moving an inch, awaiting a reply. His eyes would see right through to her soul if she attempted a lie. Her hand went up, pleading.

"I have no wish to anger. Are you so very sure you want to hear my words? I am by nature a healer, not a vengeful person."

His turn to shrug, anger giving way to apparent annoyance and frustration.

"It is not clear to me if you will tolerate my company, or allow it out of true feelings. Perhaps I came upon your good nature for a reason. As you are here to heal me in different ways than the queen."

There was a pause while neither spoke. Then it occurred again. The wind was warm on her body but it was not filling the sails above. Her eyes fluttered shut as her fingers clutched tightly to the chair.

"Nofret?" He was down on both knees, hands cupping her cheeks as she opened her eyes.

"I am afraid of you. I've been lying to myself. You are more potent than any potion I could make. I think even from the grave you would haunt my heart and perhaps you have done so."

His hands stopped. He did not look at anyone but her. "I would never hurt you, love; it will be you that does it to me."

Her hands went over his. "I believe I know and I am very sorry." She refrained from adding that another from the heavens or the grave was seeking her out as well.

He stood, refilling her goblet as her breathing returned to normal at last. Those visions finally evaporated. "Will you be riding with me to the village?"

He nodded. "I have received word that there is one close to your own who wishes to speak with me. I used that as my excuse to be with you on this return. Also, it suits me to go there rather than hold this particular conversation inside the barracks or at the palace."

"Are you testing me?"

"I have no need. It is not I that does not trust. It is you. But it won't be long now. At last, I feel the tides shifting."

She eyed him skeptically. "You know more than you are telling me, Rano, and I do not like it."

He leaned close, too close.

She wondered why he had not kissed her yet.

"Ah, I see that look in your eyes. It's coming soon, woman, so you best prepare. Once I do, there will be no turning back. I leave you now. But I want you to understand one thing. I never quit. This time, Nofret, we will do things my way."

"Why does everyone keep giving me..." Her words trailed off as he stalked away. "Warnings?"

"Damn," she spoke out softly as he disappeared. "I really need to get back to the sanctuary of my tent so I can put this all together."

Her eyes constantly searched for him. Her mind was convinced that he was a demon in a handsome man's body. She would not want him. No, not even if it took a special potion to stop the thoughts of him that were running through her head.

Yet a searing heat, hot and unstoppable, spread through her lower body as her upper lip broke out in a sweat. She swiped it aside with a finger, resting the other hand on her abdomen. But it increased. Closing her eyes, she felt the pulsating invasion increase, forcing her chin up and her head back onto the cushions. She grasped tightly at her tunic, lower lip dropped, until the feeling finally started to drift away. *Oh, my God*, she thought, opening her eyes and staring at him across the deck. Yes. He had done that. Just made love with her body from over there. With his powerful mind.

He grinned, resting a strong hand on the railing, refusing to come closer. How in hell had he done that? But more so, why? That had been extreme torture. Yet somehow pleasurable at the same time. A shudder passed as she lowered her eyes, knowing he had felt it too. Even from where he stood.

Resting back, she allowed the retreating sun to soothe her invaded body and mind and drifted off into a deep sleep.

He lifted her up as if she was a sack of feathers, while she tucked her head under his chin. Her hand wound its way up behind his strong neck, feeling the warmth there as a sigh escaped her lips.

She felt him set her down on the cushions, cover her body with a rough blanket and speak quietly to someone close to them. "You let her sleep. But when she wakes, make sure you have food and drink ready. She did not have much today."

Nofret listened to his retreating footsteps, wondering if he was going to the helm to be with the captain. Then she fell into a deep sleep until stirred by loud voices. Eyes opening slightly, she watched a hand appear, tying back the draping. Moving onto a side and sitting up, she felt a bit dazed while glancing into the eyes of the awaiting servant.

"I must have been quite tired last night. I have no recollection of getting up from the deck chair and walking in here. Strange." It was a small fib and she knew it, but she had to make sure it had not been a dream with Rano.

"You did not. It was the General that carried you in his own arms. It was with great care he decided to not wake you as you were sleeping so sound."

"Oh."

"Here is your food and drink. You must be hungry. When through, I will remove it. Today we dock and you move onward into your journey."

As Nofret ate, she glanced quickly at the retreating back of the servant. Those last two words echoed around inside her head. *Your journey.* Who was she? Someone from long ago or into the future? Upon closer scrutiny, she realized it was a woman from a place that appeared in thoughts and dreams from a distant land. A modern land of cars and trains. Yes, it was that same attendant from the Exeter BritRail Station.

Then he came into view, walking closer as she squinted, making out his shape through the flimsy curtains. The acute disappointment was clear when he did not halt. Rather, he continued along. Nofred shook her head and finished the food before stepping outside and into the bright daylight. Instead of going to that chair, she continued along toward the rear of the ship.

Stopping, she reached up and removed the gold rope from her hair, running fingers through it as waves of tingles weaved up from her toes, prickling her skin along its journey.

He took the cord from her hand while taking in his own a thick mass of her wavy hair. Weaving the band around its silkiness, Rano secured her hair at the bottom.

A pulsating need ran rampantly through her as his rough hands gently caressed her neck.

"You slept well. Did you eat?"

Her voice was faintly soft, filled with unchecked emotion. "Yes. I understand you carried me last night. Thank you." She had wanted to chastise him for not waking her, but those words remained dormant.

"We will make land later. Would you like to stretch your legs and come up with me to the first oarsman? He is steering us. Perhaps you may like to give it a try?"

"Won't that upset him? I don't know if we should ask."

"It's only for a few minutes so you can feel how powerful the boat is. I already inquired while you slept and he agreed if the timing was right that he would allow it."

"You mean most of the men are below deck preparing for our arrival?" She grinned up into those penetratingly dark blue eyes. When had they become blue, anyway? Last she remembered they were black orbs of destruction.

He took her by the hand, grinning. "You have things figured out before they become a fact. Yes. You are correct. Do you want to take this opportunity?" But they were already walking hand in hand toward the first oarsman before she realized what had occurred.

"Stand here and hold the tiller exactly as I do, with one hand over the other. Keep your eyes focused toward the front statue of Anuket. That will keep the ship toward the middle of the river where the water is deepest."

She placed her hands on the tiller exactly as he instructed. A strong tug from the current pulled against the sails and caused her to lose her footing. Rano steadied her, hands on her hips.

She did not care that he took such liberty. This was fantastic. The gold cord in her hair undid itself, releasing up into the air as her hair took to the breeze. He caught it just before it went airborne while keeping her firmly footed.

"You would make a good sailor, healer. How does it feel?"

"Strong, Rano. I can't believe how much it wants to pull against me. This is amazing." She was laughing, trying to stay upright while feeling his hands tightly against her hips. Then the captain was back, taking the tiller from her hands and nodding that it was time for them to move along.

She skirted quickly around as he laughed at the burst of energy. "That was so wonderful. How did you know that I would like that so much?"

He placed both of his hands over hers and lowered her right one over his heart so she could feel the beat of it.

That worked.

Her eyes lowered, as did his lips, onto her plush soft ones.

He did not plunder or punish or command. Instead, he let her take the lead as their tongues touched. She rose on her tiptoes as their bodies melded together, a soft moan escaping from her into his mouth.

Settling her heels back down on the deck, he swiftly swung her around, taking her hand. "I will leave you here and go prepare my things for our land journey."

She did not sit on the chair. Instead, she chose to stand and watch him walk away. At the railing she pulled her flowing hair to one side, holding on to it and wondering exactly when it had come undone. "I guess you have it now, don't you?" she whispered out over the Nile.

He came back up, setting his bag down, but did not move over toward her. As the ropes were being thrown to men ashore, she walked back to her bag. She reached down just as he did and their hands touched. Eyes locked, his roguish smile weaved warmth around her heart.

"You are too powerful for me, mercenary."

"No, you have that all wrong. It is you that is too powerful for even a great warrior like me to resist."

Her eyes glazed over. The shouting voices receded and as if in a trance, she leaned in and kissed him again. Then moved slightly back.

His smile grew.

She walked slowly down the plank, knowing he was directly behind. They moved away from the bank and up towards the awaiting camels. His hand suddenly halted her progress. She glanced up at him, her eyes questioning.

"This way. I brought along a chariot with us. The men assemble it now. I thought you may like to ride in one to see how fast they move through the desert in comparison to the camels."

She grinned, not being able to hold it back. Yes, she liked to try new things and this contraption was all the talk. They had used it in several conquests in Ethiopia and word of its success had spread like dry reeds on fire.

He helped her up and put the bags between them as he took up the reins and steadied them off. It was bumpy and fast at first and she slid into him. Quickly he stabilized them both with his right hand. "It is like being on board the ship with the ebb and flow from the waves. Think of it that way. You have no trouble on the seas. Your legs need to adjust. That's all."

"I like this. I have heard about them from villagers and even saw drawings being carved on some of the caves I've visited."

"Yes, they are not what any other army has. Egyptian advancement is far superior to all others."

"I agree with you. That, along with the sword and speed of the horses, well, you could run right through all enemies."

"That's the idea. Supremacy."

"But how long in this heat can those animals go without water? Surely not as dependable as a camel."

"For true your words are accurate. The camel is used for longer journeys when we do not know where our enemy is. These are used for the final battle when the horses are freshly watered, fed and rested. We plan ahead. Our routes are known in advance. We send a group of men in a water caravan and they place the jugs several cords apart. They submerge them into the sand where only tops are seen. We know from our shared maps where these locations are along our routes. It has proven to be very successful."

"You are giving away your battle secrets, Rano." Her mood had lifted. The way he dealt with people was not her concern. But at least like this, they were equals and she could move those ugly things he was said to have done to a place in her mind where she'd not resurrect them. This time.

"I will share a truth with you. It really was my choice to have the camels unavailable. I wanted to have you to myself."

She remained calm.

"I'd like to know why you wish to keep a distance between us. Or, if that has changed. If it has not, then I want to know why your eyes and kiss say something completely different than your words."

Her cheeks flushed. "I have no wish to harm you with words that I cannot back up any longer."

"But there is more. Something lurking in a dark area of your mind. Ask me. There can never be any barriers between us, Nofret. Now nor in the netherworld."

She hesitated. "All right. But this is not easy. Why did you have to slaughter all the Semites? I heard even the children and women were not spared from your wrath."

"That is not an accurate statement. The men, yes, were slaughtered. Especially those that chose to run instead of halting. But we did go in with a delegate from the Pharaoh asking them if they preferred exile. To work for him or choose death. They chose death. We did give them a choice."

She was silent for a few minutes as the rocky hills up ahead signaled they were fast approaching her village. "What happened to those that did not fight?"

He shifted the reins, pulling them back, slowing their progress. "They are encamped with all their belongings in a segregated area outside of the walls of the palace. They will set up trade markets, work and earn a good living. Under the rule of Thutmose III."

"What was done with the bodies? Left in desert sand to be eaten by the ravens?"

"You have heard grave stories, have you not? No. We did leave them there while we searched the hillsides and areas around their encampment and villages, making sure we took care of everything. Then their own people, who we knew were still in hiding but were left unharmed, went back to bury them properly. They were by then under our protection. We had guards observing. We even allowed those chosen few to leave unharmed to a new location."

Her heart was softening as his rugged, muscular, tanned arm brushed up against her bare one. "I have nothing else to say."

"Oh yes, you do. I know there is more. Speak of it now before time runs out for us on this day."

She hesitated. How the hell was she to explain to him about visions of another whom she was not sure was a demon or dream? About knowing things in a time that did not exist from sages and scribes? He surely would think her crazy. Hell, she thought, it could be true. Perhaps she was going crazy.

"Nothing."

Screeches of delight from the children lifted towards them as they came running at top speed. He slowed the horses down to a trot. "I don't want you to think any more or less of me. But I will share this with you. I am not a gentleman. I am a soldier. A mercenary. Hired by Pharaoh to come and train his expanding legions to conquer. But I would never hurt you or those you care for. When you come to me, there would be no other. With that, I promise. I am always a man of my word."

He stopped close to a large group of people. Young and old alike circled the chariot as two buckets of water were brought over for the horses and placed beneath them so they could drink.

"Your people are quick-witted and thoughtful."

"Yes, they are. I have perhaps wronged you, mercenary. I think more than once. Yet I am thankful you brought me back so we could talk." There was a double meaning to that which she did not realize right away. He got down, taking her bag in one hand and hers in the other until her sandals were back on the sand. The horses finished and were standing at bay.

"Healer, our paths will cross again and quite soon. Mark my words, you will not be able to dismiss what is between us from now to then. What has happened and what will." The back of his rough hand smoothed over her soft cheek, lifting her chin up so their eyes locked. "There is no place you will be able to hide from me, Nofret, until this is resolved."

When his hand dropped, she grabbed for it, momentarily holding on, and then let it go. Smiling, she stepped aside, the bag now in hand. Her eyes never left his as he climbed back on the chariot. Pulling sharply on the reins, he spun the horses around and rode tall and proud out of her village.

"That was quite an entrance."

She smiled. "How is he, Dahlia? I am anxious to see him."

"His fever broke late this morning and he's resting soundly. He's able to get more liquids in him and I gave him another dose at mid-day. Here, let me take your bag."

They walked through the village, where voices could be heard discussing who had brought the healer back. She grinned, letting the flap down and inhaling the scent of sandalwood. "It is always good to leave. Better yet to come back. I appreciate it much more when I do."

"So, what did the queen want? Can you tell me? I swear I will not breathe a word of it to another living soul."

She shook her head, letting the backside of her hand touch his now cool brow. "No, but perhaps a word of what happened will reach us in a few months. I suspect so. It should be good news."

"Ah, I get it. Since she tried to conceive and lost the child called Amenemhat, successor to the throne. I think that's what you are talking about without committing any words to it."

She grinned. "It won't work. Now, I'm going to bathe down at the pool. Want to come with me? When I come back, I'll assess him and see what is next. He will need a shave as soon as he's well enough to sit up and realizes what we are doing. Can't try it now. If he suddenly moves, his throat could well be sliced before he even knows he has survived."

They laughed and Dahlia decided to join her in the water.

"The coolness of this pool always feels soothing. Tell me what you know. You mentioned it in your scroll."

"At first it was just mumblings of a sick man. Then, there was one name he repeated several times. I believe he was asking for someone very important. Someone he knows well. A woman, I think. But I have never heard a name like that before. It was Samantha."

Stunned, Nofret felt her heart stop beating for a split second.

"He did? Was there more?" She submerged quickly, rinsing her hair of goat's milk and honey wash. "Was his accent from afar? A land we are not familiar with?"

Dahlia shook her head. "No, it is Egyptian. Who do you think he is?"

"Well, we will find out. That is a strange name indeed. I wonder what land that hails from."

"It can't be any place around here, I think."

"Anything else transpire while I was away?"

"No, all is well. We heard about the massacre of the Semite nation."

"If word of what I am about to say gets out, I could be labeled a traitor. I do not agree with the tactics of king and warrior. But I had it from Rano himself that they fought a fierce battle. They were outmatched by the charioteers with their mighty swords." She knew Dahlia was not prone to gossip. But she had to be careful all the same.

"So he happened to be your escort back. Why was that? Surely you must see, as we all do, that he means to have you. You are very fortunate, Nofret, that he has not just taken you as he has other women."

"Not yet, anyway. I have no notion to allow it either. I am now under the queen's protection. If all goes well, he will not want to cross those boundaries with her." She grinned. "I have just realized that. He has to tread carefully with me." She smiled, wondering who was going to protect him from her. She had been quite bold and brazen with him on the ship and the journey into her village.

"That puts you in a better spot with him if he does try anything. I think I'm through here. My skin is shriveling. I will go and replenish the herbs and oils and have food and drink brought to you soon."

"Thanks, Dahlia. I won't be much longer." Resting her head back, his parting comment resonated through her mind as she whispered, "Maybe I shall steal your heart, great mercenary. You had better be on guard at all times." Feeling smug, she rose, dried off and dressed, taking the supplies inside the tent. Setting them down, she moved back and lifted one flap to ventilate the interior.

Although large, today it felt decidedly small with this patient in it. As she stood glancing down at him, he mumbled something. Then he swiftly turned his head toward her. Suddenly bolting upright, he sat straight, staring at her, eyes boring into her soul. She eyed him suspiciously, not quite sure what he was up to.

She took one step back. "You are feeling better. We had thought you for dead. Mind you to say what your name is? I am the village healer, No fret."

She sat down on the cushions next to him and was mesmerized at how his eyes swept right through her. "Have we met before?" He sat up further, leaning close. "No, we have not. I am indeed in your debt and should not trespass on your kindness any further." He tried to get up and then winced, sitting back down.

She laughed. Already it was apparent he was another stubborn man. Did she need two? "It's not the time for you to go. The wounds are not healed. Perhaps in a few more days. Although you have taken to our treatments nicely."

A needed breath was taken. By them both.

"Where is your village? How is it you happened to be brought here? The old man that came in with you cannot speak. Only sign. We were hoping you would recover so more details could be obtained."

"I was in the Lowers moving with a caravan of goods when we were accosted by desert bandits. They must have thought me dead, for surely they would have finished me off if they knew I was still breathing."

"Who is the old man? He dragged you in on the backside of a mule. He clearly was nearly dead on his own feet and quite sick. We have nursed him back to health by another here in the village. He did not need remedies. Only food, rest and time. Shall I have him brought to you?"

"Who was nearly dead? The mule or the man?"

She had to laugh at that. "The man. Do you want him brought in?"

"Yes. If you would. Or I could go to him when I am stronger."

She straightened. "No need. I will see to that now. I will have a platter of food and drink brought in for you both and will allow plenty of time for a reunion."

Without warning, breathing became an issue. Inexplicably, it was apparent she needed to get the hell out of this tent and away from those penetrating eyes. Her brain was trying desperately to give her a message. A message she simply refused to allow.

"I'll return later. Someone else will show your friend in."

Silence permeated around them. Shaking her head, Nofret turned and left the tent. Quickly she found an older man. "Will you please go and get the other one and show him into the invalid's tent? I must attend to a pressing matter."

"Yes, healer. Right away."

"Thank you. No need to stay. They need to converse with privacy."

He looked at her skeptically and went to do as bid.

***

When his friend walked in using a cane, Jared tried again to rise. He glanced around, dropping the tent flap, knowing they were secure for now. "No, my son. Stay put and gather up your strength. We have work to do." He stopped talking just before their meal was brought and continued when they were again alone.

"How are you feeling?"

"Gaining strength. Her treatments are potent."

"That they are. You were so very close to death. I did not think I would see you sitting up. Let alone the two of us having a conversation."

"How did you find that mule and get me here? You are, after all, a very old man, Jacob. By the way, none of them believe you can speak. Until we leave, you had better continue that ruse. This is not the time for us to be brought under suspicion."

They both glanced over at the opening. "It was roaming up near one of the caves. I had to chase the beast down. You can only imagine the discussion I had to have when I finally caught it. I felt like a wild-west cowboy, for heaven's sake. Roping then tugging it under dire protest until it finally figured out who was the boss. But joking aside, I did what I had to do. You were lying there dying, my friend."

He stopped, head turning toward faint voices and then continued as they faded. "It was even harder to lift you onto it. But I had to. I hid us when the army came back with the captives to bury our dead. They lie out there in marked graves. They allowed a decent burial."

"It was to be an equal fight. How truly little we knew about their charioteers and those swords. But we did engage hard. Did many survive?"

"Out on the battlefield, only you. Others in the caves ran and were soon caught and captured. The ones that did surrender are outside the city under custody, working for the Pharaoh in the markets and fields."

"We have to come up with a plan. Give me a few more days and I'll have it. Is the mule still around?"

"Yes, she is well enough now to travel, having been well fed and watered. What about the healer?"

"You know about her? Did I talk in my delirium?"

He nodded. "Yes. You love her. I will help you get back to her. You should not have reached out when she was disappearing. That is the very reason I was brought here. Then spared in battle. But, my friend, our work will not be easy. You still have choices to make. The wind needs to blow in a different direction than in both our pasts. I have seen a glimmer of hope this time. Together, we need to see this through."

Jared sighed, feeling strength return after eating the food. "Yes. I will take you up on that. Two are better than one, they say, and I know already what challenges come before us. Old man, we have to succeed this time."

"I will not argue with you on that score. Quiet now, I hear footsteps fast approaching. I had better go."

Jacob rose, passing Nofret while exiting the tent. Their eyes locked momentarily as he smiled at her as if he knew something.

***

Nofret was about to turn around and demand he give her answers, but then thought better of it and continued inside the tent.

"He did not need to leave. I was coming to just check if you two required anything. I see you ate well. That is good. Your strength will soon return. Now you just need time to fully recover."

He leaned back against the rough blankets, eyelids half closed. "Thank you, healer. I will rest now. Feel free to do whatever is needed in here. The noise will not bother me."

She smiled. Two handsome men in one day being nice. Surely all was well in Egypt on this fine day. Or all hell was about to break loose.

As she mixed up new remedies, restocked the jars and put the lids on, another beastly scorpion pissed her off. Shuffling it away with the end of a reed broom, she lowered the tent flap and ushered him out with a hearty bout of swearing.

"You are probably more danger to him than he is to you."

She laughed. "Those damn animals are a nuisance. I have yet to find one good thing that they are here for."

"You know, that's a good point. Unlike the snake or scarab."

"Sometimes I wonder about them as well. I do not like anything that can crawl around me."

"Seems ironic that you are in such a climate, then."

She turned. "Do you have some kind of a message for me?"

That halted his next random comment in mid-stream.

"Why do you ask that? We do not know each other."

She turned back away from him, placing the last jar up on a wooden box. "Sorry. Don't know why I just blurted that. Are you in need of anything else before I bed down for the evening?"

"No, I am fine."

She checked her bedding one more time and slid in, snuffing out the candles. During the night, she was the one that tossed and turned. In her deepest sleep, she uttered just one word.

Adam.

***

He was watching her, eyes raking over her darkened form while he stood over her. Stopping abruptly, just before leaning down and taking her in his arms, he silently cursed towards the heavens and laid down on his blankets.

"Damn, this is not going to be easy for either of us. But this time, love, the struggle will be worth it. You just don't know it yet."

Chapter Five

"Do you want to bathe and take fresh clothes before we load your mule up and send you both toward your destination? I think your friend agreed. Well, he nodded as much. Besides, well, how can I put this delicately and not offend? You both could use one. Anyway, I have a question and I hope you don't mind my curiosity. Where are you two actually headed?"

"Towards Memphis to join others. I'd appreciate your assistance. I am not offended, healer. I do not believe my clothes will hold together if we do wash them. They are close to rags at this point. I don't want to look like a bandit as we enter the city." Jared glanced down at his clothing, knowing they needed to be replaced.

"Go ahead then down to the pool. I will make sure fresh garments are brought. When you are through, one of the ladies will bring you up. Look." Nofret pointed over his shoulder. "I see your friend is already there."

He left and walked on, noticing that it was not the first time today something odd was occurring inside his gut. It was time to move on. But he had one thing he wanted to do before they walked out of here. Down at the pool he allowed the soft enticing hands of two beautiful women to disrobe him, wash his body and dry him off.

Then they dressed him in a long tunic belted with a handsomely woven leather cord. Its status immediately alerted all who took notice that it was designated to the middle-class. Good. With a haircut and the long, dusty old beard shaved off, he smoothed his hand over a clean-shaven face, satisfied.

He glanced over toward Jacob, belting out a laugh. "Go easy on him, ladies. He is old! I need him as healthy as he can be along on our journey to follow. He has a big job to perform, pulling the mule."

They giggled as he was dressed, feet oiled and sandals put back on.

"You can't take this from me. It could be several days that I am stuck in your company and they are ten thousand times prettier." Jacob glanced around as they moved ahead of the women out of earshot.

"Agreed, old soul. Now come along. We have to set out and I have one last pressing detail to take care of."

The women caught up. "Ladies, we are very grateful." He bowed, placing his right hand over his heart. "If we ever return, we will repay your kindness." He let those words trail off, knowing by the brightness in their eyes they fully understood.

They climbed back up the rocky path alone as the women went a different direction.

"She won't recognize you."

He ignored the comment, taking the reins of the pack mule and surveying the area. There she was, picking up two sun-dried sage brushes. She was clutching them tightly in one hand and reaching for a third when his strong mind willed her to look his way.

She did.

***

Dahlia was saying something as Nofret's eyes locked with his. The ground beneath her feet trembled, branches of the remaining sage crushed beneath a tightening grasp. Her lower lip opened, eyes raking him head to toe. Twice. At Dahlia's curious look, Nofret shoved the brush into her hands and began a slow, arduous walk towards him.

She did not know why. But she stopped short of actually reaching him. Oh, but she did know why. She was afraid if she wove her hands up through his hair and found the indent she had felt in her dreams, she'd know.

Somehow, the universe was testing her. A distant face from a distant time.

She shook her head, causing her hair to spill out of the woven band. Now she could tell by the look in those eyes that he was sorely tested. His fingers flinched as she imagined them reaching out and touching one of her unruly curls.

"Jared Malik, you look very different. Almost like someone I thought I may know. But it cannot be. He does not live around these parts."

"Who was that?" He stepped closer, taking both her hands in his. Glancing down at them, she let them rest there as tingles heightened.

"I cannot say. I do not remember. It was a different time in my life. Damn, you have unnerved me. A stranger from the desert whom I brought back to life."

He leaned down, kissed both palms, released them, and stood back. "When it is clear, find me. I am most curious. You will know where that will be when the time arises."

She stepped back, perplexed at his boldly spoken words. With great relief, she saw that Dahlia was now at her side. Mule in tow, the two men set off out of the village toward their next destination with no backward glance. Both women stood rooted to spot and watched them leave.

"Healer, there are times when we block things that have happened to make our life more manageable. Then, there are times when it hits us like the sting of a scorpion from the desert. That is when we can no longer escape it."

Stunning her, Dahlia's words of wisdom penetrated fast into her confused mind. She was unable to halt them and the result hit its mark. It was as if Nofret was in the middle of a blinding desert storm. When it finally moved on, the only thing remaining was a hole where she had been.

She shook.

"You are wiser than your years, my friend. Go back to collecting brush for me. I require a moment to gather my thoughts."

In a daze, walking along a little-used path, she left the village. High above, there was a special location she used for intense meditation and reflection. It overlooked the Nile and desert beyond. The view itself provided the perfect backdrop for thought-provoking memories.

For Nofret, it was a highly powerful, spiritual place.

Sitting, legs folded, eyes lowered, she began softly chanting in prayer to the angels above, asking for guidance. Something. Any sign that would help her understand what was going on all around her now. Rano, Malik, the mute and what the village sage had told her.

As her own internal chatter stopped, a soft voice grew stronger. More explicit. High above, a raven's screech seemed to put the exclamation point at the end of all the visions dancing around in front of her eyes.

"Oh, shit!"

She rose, running down the path around the other side of the village to look for them. They were nowhere in sight. She spun in horror. How could she not have known him dead on the spot? For all that was holy in the heavens, she had let him slip off into the approaching night! "Oh, my God." She fell to her knees, lifting the cooling sand as it sifted through opened fingers. "I screwed it up."

Yes, it was Jared Malik, Prince of the Semite chieftains. But it was also Adam. Lord Adam Griffin. He had not let go of her hand quick enough at the Luxor Museum. "Oh, my God," she repeated over and over, yelling skywards as more memories flourished. Lowering her head to her hands and bending at the waist, she let it all come, unable to suspend it.

"What have I done?"

With strong, purposeful strides, she walked back into the village and right into Dahlia's tent. "You knew."

Dahlia nodded, patting the cushion next to her. "Yes, and I had to keep silent while you figured it out or you would have thought I was mixing the wrong herbs on purpose again."

"What am I to do now? I could not see them. I do not know what way they took."

"You will not do anything. It will be done for you. You will have choices to make. That is why you are back here again. This time, someone else is in control and has intervened, enabling what several of us hope will be a successful outcome."

"Choices between him and Rano?"

"Yes, and they will not be as easy as you think."

"I thought I could not do that. Come back and repeat as that could alter history. Isn't that against the sacred rules of passages?"

"With you, Sam, nothing is as it seems, is it? You are different. Do not be afraid. Trespass where you have been told not to go. This is not your first 'repeat' here. You just had chosen to ignore all the other times. Suppress it from memory as it suited you. And it seemed to have suited you often."

"Hey, you just said my name from the future. Isn't that dangerous? Or, at a minimum, bad?"

"Yes. It will be the only time you hear me say it. I know all about you. I am not the only one here to help. When you leave the village it will be for a new home. You must remember that you have a haven here if you need it. It is better to sometimes take a deep breath and halt progress before you rush into decisions that may lead you where you do not belong. From here on you will remain Nofret until this passage is concluded. We all hope successfully."

She raised hands to flaming cheeks, tears filling her eyes. "I have mixed feelings about them both. I'm probably not knowing it now, but I am glad he is not here. If he was,

I'd make a mistake." Rising, head slumped, she headed toward the tent flaps.

"I will see you tomorrow, healer. Pack your bags, jars and anything else of importance. Use your time wisely to stock up. It is important you gain back full energy. Clarity of thought. Make sure you are of sound mind before leaving."

Trying desperately, Sam let one more thought of Adam stay before clearing it away. Would she have to work through all her other lives before they were truly reunited? *Crap*, she thought, sadness filling her soul. If that was the case, then thousands of years would need to pass before he held her in his arms once again.

Feeling positively miserable, she was aware of a soft emotion spreading through her body. A faint voice followed it and as she listened intently, the message was clear. Finally, a slow, steady smile emerged.

All was not lost.

Back in her tent now, a diversion was in order. She lit the sandalwood paste in a golden plate and sat down with a statue of the Goddess Tawaret, who protected women during pregnancy and childbirth. Raising the incense in front, she blessed this statue and chanted until sure the great goddess would give the queen a healthy, strong son and easy birthing.

Wrapping the statue in silk, she placed it in her carpet bag and set about taking stock of what was needed. Tonight when the moon was full, she'd walk the path and gather. Tomorrow it would be finished as the new day dawned. It would not take long to finish bringing together all that was needed.

Grabbing a basket, she set off out of the tent and through the silent village. Singing locus and chattering sheep were the only sounds her ears met on the walk up to the hilltop. Now full of future remedies, she sat down, glancing up into the heavens just in time to catch a streaming, falling star.

"Back where I come from if you see a shooting star you have to make a wish right away. Or you miss the chance."

She expelled a deep breath as her lids closed.

He took one small hand into his strong one.

"I heard you on the wind calling me back."

"I did."

She set the bundles down and moved in front of him, shifting the tunic sideways, and sat on his crossed legs. She had to know. Then again, she already did. Reaching behind his head, she felt the indent. Then she pulled his lips to her own.

He moved back slightly, leaning his forehead against hers. "I am to take you to Memphis with me. The queen's courier met us along the route. Since I knew the way, I was given two camels and instructions. They took Jacob with them to board the ship and await our arrival. It was by order of your Rano the Mercenary."

"Oh." Lifting off him, she stood, hands on hips. "Why did you let me kiss you? Damn, you are an ass. Even here."

She moved toward the trail, feeling a bit humiliated, but would not in ten thousand years show it.

"Because I could. Because I wanted to know if you still had some passion in your body for me before I bring you to him. If you had not, I would have."

Her nostrils flared, her mind reeling. This was probably why she had not wanted to be fully committed to him in the future. "My guess is this. You are a rogue. Throughout all of history. If I am here to do something of importance with Rano, why are you here? To slip off into the city and have your way with dozens of mistresses? Probably, since you did that where we just came from."

"Stop that shit. I gave them all up once you came around."

"Well, here I may not come around." This time she meant it.

"Look, it was not my idea to come back. This is all pretty screwed up, if you ask me. Anyway—" He stood, not bothering to take her hand, but he did take the basket. "—until we completely understand why we are both here, we'd better keep our distance. If Rano even sees there is anything between us, he will not think twice about killing me. Healer, I need to know why I've returned. It is not all about you and a coincidence that you took my hand and we both made it across. You were destined to drag me with you and I am at a loss why. I have tried without any luck, but my mind is blocking much of this period. Even some stuff regarding you."

Inhaling sharply, air finally rushing out, she had to admit at being pissed off too. "Okay. I am not going to fight with this right now. I am already packed. We can leave when you wish."

She turned to go as he dropped the basket.

"Fuck it. In case you are between fences, let me just remind you who I really am."

As he pulled her hard against him, she could feel his underlying frustration. The passion between them, between all of the time, flared up. Immensely.

She pulled roughly away. "You have to stop that. If you tell me to keep my distance, then you'd better not do that again. I am not always as strong as you. But right now, you were not strong at all."

***

"*Touché*, mistress." He laughed, enjoying the changing of the guard. "It seems you arrived here with even more gusto than you had with me previously. I can't wait to see what happens next."

"Oh, shut up. Now, where are these transporters of ours? What specifically did the courier's letter say? Do you have it on you? I'm quite sure if it was from the queen herself, that I am the one who should be reading it."

"Yes, it's for you." He chuckled at her arrogant display of superiority. "I have it in my pack down below. The camels will be set to go after sunrise. You already know the route, don't you? A boat will be awaiting us. But worry not another thought my way. Once we arrive in Memphis, I will be joining the army. You may not see me at all."

He was trying to get her goat and she'd not have any of it. "It will be as it is and no more."

He softened as the moon glowed from above, all but melting the silk from her luscious curves. "Maybe we just stay right here, you move in, finally confirming our marriage and we have those twenty children."

She spun around, bursting out laughing. "I certainly will not." But her smile lit the sky.

"Then maybe in our next life, after our last life, that's not related to this one. Oh hell. I will shut up now."

"Yes, please do."

***

As they came back into the camp, she left him without another word and spent a few minutes packing up the last needed items. A small batch of flowers could be gathered upon their exit from camp. He would have to stop and that was that. Lying down, she felt the need to speak with Dahlia one last time. Rolling over, she hastily wrote a quick scroll, tied twine around it and left it beside the rug. She'd see it when she came in tomorrow.

Curious, crawling on hands and knees, Nofret flipped one flap partially back a few inches and peered outside. He was sleeping on a carpet just a few yards away. Both camels were sitting down in the sand, eyes closed and making some unusual grunting noises. Or was that him, snoring? Dropping it back down, she stood, laughing all the way back to her cushions at what she had just done. Perhaps it had not been to spy on him, but to make sure he was indeed there.

***

Jared's eyes went from slits to closed as he smiled. He'd seen what that chit was about. But quickly it was replaced by a frown, arms tightening across his chest. Rano. What was to be done about him? He knew part of the story from her before this happened. What was the rest? Was he here to protect her? Lead her like a lamb to slaughter? Bring her back? Make her stay? Or worse of all, let her go for good?

He shook his head. No. He would not let her stay. But if she had to, he would too. It would break all the rules and alter his destiny completely. For her, he would do it. Only for her. Although, perhaps her true destiny did not involve him at all. Just Rano.

"Damn," he muttered, shaking his head. "Enough." He delivered his final thoughts verbally up into to the heavens above in frustration.

As the ravens flew overhead, his eyes fluttered open and he glanced at one that landed in a sagebrush damn close. Those penetrating black orbs mesmerized Malik for a few seconds. "What message do you bring me, my friend? Just an alarm to get up?" He rose, rolling the carpet and securing it on one of the camels. Taking out two flasks, he drew water from the well just as a hand appeared, opening the flap of her tent. Two carpet bags now secured, one in each hand, she walked towards him as his gaze honed in on her face.

"Good morning."

He nodded, settling the bags securely in place. "You need to relay anything to anyone before we head out?"

"No, all taken care of. I am ready." She slid up on the sitting camel as Jared took the ropes and the gentle creature stood. He noticed she seemed well at ease in the whole process.

***

Mounting, they headed out of the village before anyone else woke. "Did you read the scroll?" Nodding yes, she sipped the cold water inside the flask. "Thank you for filling this. I'd prefer a cup of English breakfast tea filled with organic sugar, cream and a scone from the bakery. Is there any possible way you can fetch that for me and arrive back before we reach the ship?"

He grinned as they continued along side by side. "Yeah, I can just portal there and back before you reach that fork in the path up ahead."

"Oh, thank you. It will make my mood brighter."

He laughed. "Did you not sleep well, healer?"

That was a reminder to refocus her thoughts and curb those comments. *Damn*, she thought, *he is straight to the point this morning.* It would take away their few minutes of fun banter before 'all eyes and ears' would be upon them both.

"I did not. My mind was busy trying to put things together. I guess this is when I just let the wind blow the direction it will and take me along with it. I don't know, Malik. I am really baffled."

"So am I. We won't have much of a chance to engage in conversation like this down the road."

"Are you joining the army so you can be housed closer to where I'll be?"

"And closer to where he will be."

"Ah, a bit jealous, are you? I thought that never happened inside your heart."

"A word of caution here. Just remember all the women I will be around. I should not want for anything should I ask for it."

A sandaled foot shot out but was inches from making the mark.

"Don't say it. Ladies do not speak like that here."

She wove some silk up over her hair and around her ears to keep the dust from coming into her mouth. More than that, to keep it shut. As they approached the outskirts of the port, she saw the familiar sails and crest of the queen's ship awaiting them.

As they arrived, both camels lowered as two soldiers walked, faces stoic and unreadable, over to her. One took her bags and the other motioned with a hand for her to follow toward the plank.

Nofret dared not glance back to see if he was in tow. But from the intense feelings toward her back, it was clear his eyes were on her. Halting a few feet onto the plank, both soldiers stopped behind, one speaking. "Healer, he's waiting."

Oh shit, she thought. One love of her life was behind, ready to board, and the other ahead, looking like he was about to have lunch and dinner in one meal. Shaking her head slightly, determined, Nofret walked into her future and past, combined.

What a sight he was, that commanding figure of her mercenary. Indeed, he was handsome as she pondered if any woman would be able to resist his charms for long. He was at the helm talking with the captain when he caught sight of her.

His strides quick with purpose, Malik passed by them both, nodded, and then continued.

The emotional ties between them she could feel straight to her toes. Not with Rano, but Malik. Yes, he was jealous. Jealous of a man from her past that had loved her perhaps as much as he had throughout the rest of the centuries. They had seen much between them. But now he was not in control. He glanced above, beyond the clouds to the heavens, shook his head in arrogant dismissal of their reasons for him being here, then disappeared to a section no longer viewable by her eyes.

Chapter Six

"Healer Qalhata, welcome back aboard. It seems we have good timing. I just finished my affairs and was advised to hold our sailing for your arrival."

Rano took the two bags, tilting his head to the side for her to pass ahead. As if on queue, the sun suddenly shone down upon Nofret, illuminating her body. Rano's smile increased as he raked her backside head to toe. He housed no doubt she had dressed like this today just to entice him further. *As if proof was needed*, he thought, she glanced back with an inviting smile that matched his own.

They both broke out in laughter, ignoring the looks that came their direction. He leaned down, settling the bags as she suddenly surprised him.

"I am happy to see you again, mercenary."

"What are you up to now, woman? Trying to tighten the strings around my volatile heart further?"

She pushed up onto tiptoes and kissed him quickly. "Could be I am. If that is even possible."

He groaned. "You should be in charge of my army, not I. You by far prove to have more tactical skills."

She giggled. "All women do, Rano. It's just a fact we arrive on the earth with more of it."

Settling back, he motioned the servant over with a tray. Pouring only one goblet, he handed it to her.

"What, not joining me?"

"No, I need to keep my wits about me. Possibly later I will when I can't sleep."

"Well then, let's change the subject. The wind is with us, it is a fair day, let's hope it holds until we arrive. Was your business successful?"

***

Small talk. She needed lots of small talk now to keep from throwing herself at his feet. Yes, she was somewhat aware of a future with Adam, but that was a long, long way off. Right now, things had to be put into perspective. Keeping Malik at a safe distance was necessary. In fact, out of sight out of mind was what she was wishing for.

Her eyes drifted over towards the twosome as Rano's eyes followed.

"Ah, the old man. Yes, he was with your escort so we provided him safe keeping until you joined. If we had not, he would have detained your arrival. He does not speak, it seems. But is proficient in herbs and remedies. Although not as knowledgeable as you. One of my soldiers needed something done of a delicate matter. So he proved his worth straight away to relieve some of his sufferings."

She laughed. "Ah, I see. He was visiting someone in the village and took away more than he paid for."

He joined in, placing a sandaled foot up on a stool, signaling to the captain to prepare for immediate departure.

"Well, he's feeling a lot better now. I suspect he will be right back at it by our next night on land."

"I bet he will. Will you consent and call me Nofret? 'Healer' puts me on a pedestal and I'd prefer not to be on one."

He handed her a small platter of fruits and meats and she ate. "I can do that."

"What will you do with our voyagers when we arrive in Memphis?"

"Jared of Mykonos will join my legion. He's strong and smart. I've already received a needed dispatch about his background. He is of good heritage. I find myself in need of another formidable strategist."

She blinked quickly, staring down into the dark purple wine in her goblet. Jared of Mykonos? He must have come up with a valid story. If Rano had any idea that he was dealing with the chieftain of the expelled nation of Hemite, his blood would boil and he would make quick work of killing him.

She grinned up at him, finding true enjoyment now in both men's maneuvers.

"And the elder, do you have any use of him?"

"Not at all. He can do as he wishes when we arrive. He seems sturdy enough. Just unable to communicate."

"He will come with me then, so it will be settled. I will take him under my guidance. I could use a learned man who can use the herbs. I will discuss him with the queen. I am sure she will allow it. Especially with his skills. I will tell her you consented."

He raised a brow. "As you wish. There is a storm brewing. Our arrival will be sooner than planned. I will have you there before that comes about. The river will rise overnight with strong rain."

"It will be a blessing for the grains and to fill our wells. So tell me, where is your next conquest? Will you be off again as soon as we land?"

"No, not right away. We have preparations to make and reinforced training to take care of. So you see, you will not be able to elude me much longer." He leaned closer, his lips just a few inches from hers as they lowered, anticipating that kiss. "Perhaps we shall become more deeply acquainted, healer. It is time."

Seconds passed.

"I would like that." She lowered her eyes from his heated gaze, feeling a pulsating warmth in her loins. If he could make love to her without touching, oh, what would he do to her when they did?

"Ah, the interest grows, as does the need. I feel what you feel, love. You want us to be alone and naked. I match that. No point in hiding it any longer." He moved closer, sitting on the platform beside her chair. One strong tanned hand rested over her own. "I am to move my quarters closer to the palace when I get back. The Pharaoh has ordered it. There are warnings from trusted advisors that someone may try to kill him or sabotage the army."

"Are you telling me this to test? Surely, this would not be discussed with anyone except whom you have the utmost trust within the upper levels of your liege."

His fingers were weaving through her soft, wavy hair. "I have excellent instincts. You and I have a purpose, little one. Things need to be different between us this time. If it means giving up all the other pleasures I've taken, then I will do it. If it means allowing all the ones you have taken, then so be it."

Her mind wandered a moment. Was that it? Last time he had too many women and she was pissed to not be the only one? No, for some reason that did not seem to be it. Fuck. She needed to remember but was deathly afraid to use her own potions to delve into the darker side of a thought-induced trance to figure it out.

This was a deadly formula from the Book of the Dead. She had tried it once and the ramifications had been awful, practically causing her mind to shut down for nearly three days. It was as if it had cursed her for using it. Body fine, mind paralyzed. There was no way she was going to do that again.

His voice broke into her thoughts at last. "I trust you to not discuss any of what I tell you. It is between a man and a woman. Not healer and mercenary."

She sat back, placing the cup on her lap. Oh, this was a turn of events. She had not expected this man, soldier and sometimes killer, to have such a soft side and affect her inside and out so intensely. "I pledge my silence. You have my word."

He stood, taking one hand into his and placing a kiss there. "I will leave you. I need to speak with my men below deck to prepare for our arrival." He tapped his chest and walked off as her eyes followed every step of his way.

Damn, she thought. This was going to be a big test of strength. He was intriguing. It was just so frustrating only recalling bits at a time. So far it was of little use. She needed more. There was someplace she had turned her nose to near the palace that she was going to visit as soon as time allowed. There, answers would be found.

Everywhere she turned the same words plagued her. Something had to be different this time. Did the lives of many hinge on her? Would he continue to haunt her from the grave for lives to follow if it did not? A cold shiver ran up her spine. No, this time she would not wilt under this enormous pressure.

What about Adam, England, Norway, the Great World War, Anne, Clash and suddenly finding out she had a brother? Would it and all of them simply evaporate from time? Or just from her existence? She was upset. Her insides pulling out, she spewed up to the heavens, "Too many freaking questions unanswered. Can't you do better than all of this shit?"

Jacob, standing quite a few yards away, glanced at her with a smile. There was something in that smile that had her stomping a footed sandal down hard on the deck. No. It was not going to be this time. Period. Samantha Arnesen's courage filled the body of this Egyptian healer.

Rising, she marched over to one of the railings and clutched the wood with white knuckles. A voice penetrated her dark thoughts. "Healer, your bedding is prepared for the night. Would you like to stay here or follow me?"

Nofret's eyes relayed a potent message, but she softened her words, recalling what occurred last time she'd remained on deck. "I will go now. I am tired. Please make sure I am not disturbed. I don't care about the noise out here, but I need privacy."

"As you wish it. Come this way."

Lying down, she moved the blanket, tucking it under her chin as the servant took a place on the opposite side and closed the drapes. "We shall be there by early morning with this wind."

Nofret smiled. "This pitching is not quite as soothing as it was the last time I was on the boat."

"If you need the jar, let me know. I have it ready for either one of us." That caused them both to laugh.

"Good thinking." Nofret rolled to one side and drifted off, listening as long as possible to the voices inside her head. But they did not stop as tossing and turning ensued. Well into the night she suddenly bolted straight up. Glancing at the still sleeping servant, she sighed softly.

Throwing the blanket off and crawling on hands and knees to where the draping split, she peered out. A few were about up at the helm. But the only other noise was the oars' steady rhythm in and out of the water.

"Oh, screw it," she mouthed softly. Then she stood and walked out, venturing toward the closest railing. She gazed up to where the angry storm clouds were gathering, hiding the expansive sparkling galaxies in the sky that she loved to view in the darkness of the night.

"You could not sleep?"

"No. Not really. I thought a bit of air would do me well."

"You care for some company?"

There it was. The moment of truth.

"Yes."

The boat pitched and he grabbed her, pulling her back tightly against his chest while holding the railing with both hands to keep her safe and secure. "What's on your mind that has you unsettled, healer?"

She smiled. Was he ever going to address her informally? "Could be why you have a hard time calling me by my first name, Rano."

He chuckled, the comforting sound reverberating from his chest into her body. "I would call you many things. Should I say them now you may hurt me in your attempt to move away."

She liked this side of him. A bit on the frisky side. "Well, let me be frank then. It appears I do want more of you. There. Said and done." Silently she knew the line had been crossed and she was ready to play at this game.

"It is inevitable, little one." One hand started to roam from holding her around the stomach. It massaged over a hip and then halted briefly before embracing one firm breast. She leaned further into him, head tilting back, wanting to turn straight into those arms and make love with him right here, right now.

"Let me assure you again. Once we are on dry land, you will not get rid of me until the king declares our next conquest and my army and I are commanded to move out."

She was forced to lighten the mood. "Well, you will not be in my wing of the palace. It is a large place. Besides, if you are near the king I assume you will be farther away. Which is much to my delight. I will then have run of the place and can scurry around in the dark corners of the corridors and avoid you. Those that you set out to spy on me will have their hands full. I will give them a good run for it. I know what you are about, Rano. You will have me watched."

His fingers tweaked the taunt peak as a wanting sigh escaped her lips. Increasing this irresistible pleasure further, he applied pressure to her lower abdomen just as she felt his firmness against her backside.

"Oh, mercenary. Yes. It is true I desire you."

"And there will be a time when you will come to me. The pleasure we will have then will be like nothing else you have ever known. Nor I."

Yes. It would be true. She knew it. Until another time well into the future and another man. "A bit cocky, aren't you?"

"Interesting you used that word."

They both broke out laughing. "Oh, stop it."

"You did set yourself up for that one. Unfortunately, I have to attend to a few things. I'm going to attempt this and see how much stubbornness I am met with. Will you come willingly back to your bedding? The waves and the wind are kicking up. I'd prefer to know you are safely tucked back in there and not overboard where no one would know until it was too late."

She turned into his warm strong embrace at last. Yes, it was clear the love they already shared. "I will. I think all this gibberish has tired me out. I will go willingly so you don't throw me over your shoulder like a sack of grain."

"Well now. A small victory for me on this night for sure."

She poked him in the side, letting go of his hand. "Good night, mercenary."

"Sleep well, healer." He dropped the draping, leaving her as she maneuvered back, dropped down, covered up and did indeed regain sleep. It was a peaceful, dreamless sleep that left her completely invigorated the following morning.

***

"Healer, I have your bags ready. They are about to hoist the ropes so we can go ashore."

Nofret was awake and had remained quiet, making a mental good/good list comparing Adam and Rano. Sitting up, she combed through snarly hair. "Thank you. Take those out toward the chair and I will join you in a moment."

Checking the surroundings, she left to join the gathering group. Malik and Jacob were well behind her as Rano slid his hand down an arm and encased her hand.

"I have appointed one of my men to escort you to the palace. There is a rather urgent business matter I must attend to in the village and then with the king."

Good, she thought. *I now have time to put some ideas in motion.*

Strange, though. His next comment made her think he was indeed reading her thoughts. "Don't go off and get into mischievous dealings. I now have those that will hide further into the dark shadows where you will roam and report their findings."

She giggled. "Shut up."

"That is hardly any kind of commitment."

"You are a clever man."

His shoulders shrugged as he released her arm. He nodded to the soldier assigned to her as the plank was placed against the ship. It was as if this protector's eyes bore into her soul with a warning that he would not be so tolerant as his commander would.

She was first off the vessel. Onward they walked as she followed him through the cobbled streets and up the marble steps to her now familiar access into the royal palace. As he drew the doors open, she continued in as he sat the bags down, banged his chest with a fist and left.

She smiled, both at his action and at who was awaiting. "Meliah, Asofia, hello to you both. Are you here to settle me back in?"

They embraced. "No, we are officially assigned to you by our queen. Your quarters have been extended now that you are a palace resident. You still have these three rooms but now two more have been added. Plus a private balcony, gardens, pool and a maid to prepare the meals."

"Well now. That truly is splendid. One of you can unpack the larger bag. I will take care of the smaller one. It houses some delicate items and I wish to inspect them to ensure they fared well during my journey. I have a special gift for the queen. I know it is late now, but am I scheduled to have a visit with her soon?"

"She is already aware of your arrival. As soon as the ship was viewed and you were spotted on land, a dispatched courier brought her the news. Later tomorrow morning we will go and see her after she rises. Her health is good. But she has been feeling a bit strange over the last few days. That is why she requested your urgent return."

Nofret nodded. "That's to be expected. I will reassure her then. You both will have some free time. You probably recall how I like to venture off alone. But this time I return knowing we are now friends. It will be nice to have your help preparing my remedies. I will put my services out for the villagers if they wish to use me. I don't want to be idle."

Now she got down to the real work. "Has that handsome soldier been visiting while I was away?" The threesome all giggled, coming closer, clasping their hands together.

"Yes. He can't decide which of us he likes the best. But we do know he's not visiting any other."

"Well now. Does that mean I may lose you both from living inside the palace soon? I understand if you move your possessions into his quarters, you will officially be his wives."

They laughed as Asofia declared, boldly reminding Nofret suddenly of Anne, "I'm not sure I want to be his wife. I'm young. I may quit our gatherings and let Meliah have him." She poked fun at her friend. "Then I can resume my other pleasures."

"Do you want that, Meliah?"

She smiled coyly. "I would not mind being his wife. But could just one please a man like that? I don't think so. He would be free to take others if he chooses."

As Sam she was laughing inwardly Nofret the Healer was smiling outwardly. Yes, men and women in this era were allowed an open policy on mating, marrying and staying faithful.

There was no cheating here. *Why not let the good times roll?* she thought.

It was a love free-for-all without paperwork, money-hungry lawyers and nasty divorces. How much more simple it was. She grinned, letting go of their hands and opening up the small bag. It was a good thing she had not married Adam. She'd feel a bit of remorse here even though nothing was binding in this period.

That grin expanded two-fold.

"Would you like a pool bath or an indoor one tonight? You are invited to dine in the main area any time you wish. We were asked to tell you. You are not off limits anywhere in the palace by order of the Pharaoh."

"Wonderful. Outside at the bathing pool will do. It is warm and the waters will feel refreshing." She knew the routine even though she was quite able to do this alone. They would hover, assist and then she'd dismiss them for their evening of pleasure. "Well, I am unpacked and you have finished the other bag. Shall we? I'd like to wash off the dust from my trip."

They lathered and oiled her body and hair and then towel-dried her. She was wrapped in a new outfit and belt with matching silver sandals. *Hmmm*, she thought, *not Versace or Louie but sure would do*. Both those designers would cry out to heaven to have such raw materials at their use.

"Thank you, ladies. Come when the queen requests me tomorrow and we shall go there together. Otherwise, you both enjoy your night." She smiled as they parted, walking around a band of soldiers having just come from the corridors of Thutmose III.

Rano stopped, nodding for the others to continue along.

"Heading to dine?"

"Yes. Care to join me?"

"I will." He took her hand in a gesture that was not common in this period. He should have taken her arm. That was two or three times he had done that now. They walked into the great room, where the chatter minimized as Nofret walked by the queen's table and nodded, smiling warmly at her. It was returned by one laden with relief.

"You are a favorite now. Everyone here will want to get closer to the queen's new healer." He sat her down on a pile of cushions and waved for attendance.

"Well, it will pass. I live quietly. I came in here tonight so I could see her. Otherwise, I would have taken food and drink in my quarters. I do not prefer to be in the limelight."

He drew in a brow. "Limelight? What does that mean? I am a learned man, but do not know I've heard that."

"It was a word a passing tradesman used in our village a while ago. According to him, it means one does not like to be in the center of attention from others."

"Where was this tradesman coming from?" He was getting nosy. "I am not sure, since many pass through the village on the way to the Nile. I could be right in saying he was from East Asia since his robe looked like it was from a distant place."

That settled it nicely.

But there was something Nofret needed to know right now. "Did you move your quarters?"

His mouth was full of food and she hid a grin, awaiting his reply.

"Yes. We had just come from the Pharaoh's area having just finished. I have rooms close to his now. So the royal palace has two new residents. You and I."

Oh great, she thought. He'd be under her nose until whoever had threatened Thutmose III this time was caught and executed. "How does your search progress?"

He leaned closer. "It was rumored that suspicion was being housed on that man Jared of Mykonos. But an additional dispatch has arrived confirming what I already know. He is no longer being watched. Did you settle the elder?"

"He is in a guest area until I can speak with Queen Satiah tomorrow. Surely you do not suspect him? Granted he is older, but surely…"

He held up a hand. "No. He was also listed in the dispatch. He is no harm here. Mykonos has joined my legion and is in training with my men. He has already shown to have superior skills close to mine. So this process will continue until our next campaign. I have placed him under my second-in-command. He has intelligence and I plan to use it. Some of his ideas are more advanced than we are using."

"Isn't that odd that he has superior knowledge?"

He eyed her suspiciously. "What are you saying, woman? That he could be an implant, a spy? Or set here for high treason?"

Her voice shot up. "No, of course not. I guess I am not understanding how his knowledge could be greater than yours."

"You have the mind of a general and the smooth talk of a snake in the Garden of Eden. It is possible no person is here to threaten our king. Perhaps it is just that you are here to threaten me."

"I'm ignoring that. But surely you won't go on that campaign until the person is located and disposed of?"

"I see and hear more now, Nofret. It could have been planted as a rumor to get me into the palace and away from the army while a spy is routed in. This is now merely a precaution. I do not think a threat is posed on Pharaoh at all. Nor do I believe this person has anything to do with Malik and the elder."

She smiled sweetly, as he had used her first name. "How wise of you. So by removing yourself, that person may feel more comfortable and drop their guard down and be exposed. You should have him taken to the priestesses.

It is known their charm could work any words from a traitor's lips."

"Or I could send him to you. Perhaps you have a serum you could give him?"

They both leaned in as his tanned muscular arm heated up her right side, resting possessively against a hip. "Sorry, what did you ask me?"

He leaned in then and kissed her sumptuous lips.

Her hands wove up around his neck, clasping, taking him prisoner completely. As their mouths parted, softly she spoke. "I hope you don't leave too soon."

He stayed close. "Long after the rising of the Nile from heavy rains and when the grain is harvested, then we will be going. As to where I will not say. For you may decide to follow."

She smiled as the musicians began playing. The exotic scents of the scantily-dressed dancers arrived long before their bodies. Dancing seductively around their table, one got bold, leaning over and letting her breasts spill nearly out. With a flicker of a hand, Rano moved them along.

"You insult them by your quick dismissal."

"I will do as I please. They do not hold my attention this night."

There it was again, gruffness. Or was it frustration? Was he trying to make a bold statement to all that were watching? Was this just a show and later on when he retired to his chamber others would be there taking care of his needs?

"Do you dance like that?"

Their eyes locked. That was normally a question not asked by a man of a woman at all. It was just expected she 'knew' how to please him in every way. Women here learned from their mothers and it was passed down for many generations.

"Yes." She was getting as bold as he was.

"I am intrigued by you. Again."

"Yes, I am fully aware."

"I will have you, you know."

She shook her head slightly. "I am aware of that too."

"On top of being a healer, do you also possess the same gifts as the Goddess Maat?"

She giggled. "Truth, balance, morality, justice and can see the future? No. Well perhaps a little of each, yes." That was true. For she was already special, wasn't she? How many here in this room right now were involved in a 'passage' of some kind? That intrigued her. Indeed, she thought as she glanced about the room, she'd never know the answer to that. Perhaps Rano was as well? No. He was a man who needed her for some very special reason and she was here to know why and help. So if that involved being in an intimate relationship, then who was she to scoff at the gods' requests?

His eyes were intently upon her as her mind had wandered. His voice brought Nofret back to the present. "You were distant. What words were taking place in your head?"

"There will be times when a woman will share that. This is not one of them." She reached over and touched his bare forearm. "But it was not dangerously bad, I can assure you."

He put his other hand over hers and let it rest on top. "Of all the forces I've fought against, you will be the toughest, healer." He rose suddenly and she glanced up into his eyes while he extended a hand.

"The hour grows late, Nofret. I will walk you back."

She took that hand. "I bet you already know where they are, don't you? My rooms."

He laughed. "You have a ready answer. So why have you asked it?"

Along their walk she glanced around, noticing changes since she had last been in the palace. "There seem to be more guards posted. Is that because of what has happened?"

"You really don't miss a detail. Yes. We are taking all precautions seriously. But relax. You are free to move about as you wish. Just don't be surprised if you are followed. Under the queen's protection or not."

"Ah, here we are. I hope to see you soon."

She felt bold. It was probably the pungent wine. Two goblets of it.

"Yes."

He pulled her roughly into his arms against that rock-solid chest while grabbing her long, flowing hair in one hand. The other slid up the warm skin of her neck, tilting her chin up as he lowered his lips, claiming hers.

Lifting on tip toes, she did not want to let him go. His kisses were passionate and consuming as all chatter in her brain subsided. He pulled back as her feet lowered down onto the marble floor. "It will not be an easy night to sleep for either of us."

He let her go and she opened up one door, turning toward him. Her body was screaming to grab him by the arm and bring him in, but that hand rested on the frame. He shifted closer, placing his hand over her heart, cupping a firm breast. She swallowed hard as he nodded, gaze not disentangling from her eyes.

"Yes I know," she whispered. Then she closed the door.

***

Slowly he crossed the corridors as his mind demanded an immediate turnabout. Marching back and just taking her. Hell, they both wanted it and knew it. There had never been a time in his life where his mind had to be stronger than his body. Things had to be different this time. Perhaps it was one more venture to the temple? Frustration finally gave way to common sense. Instead, he went back to his own quarters and stayed there. The whole night. Alone.

Chapter Seven

She was roaming the streets outside the palace with her trustworthy guard at hand when she spotted Malik with a herd of women gathered all around. It caught her by total surprise when jealousy and anger did not rise up within her chest.

As if from a distant body, housing a soul that did not know him yet, she looked on with mild amusement. Was this where he started to gather those mistresses? An old saying rang through her head. The apple really did not fall far from the tree. Giggling, she recalled how that was not old as of yet. In fact, not even quoted. Basically, she silently acknowledged what happened in Egypt stayed in Egypt. Okay, she concluded. It worked for her. Winking at him from afar, she waved her shadow to come up beside. He was indeed a handsome bodyguard from the palace assigned by the queen. But she also knew he reported to Rano.

"Do you want to go over and have a jug of wine? I'm just going to look at purchasing some seeds and herbs. Just keep an eye on me so I don't get into trouble."

***

They both shared a grin as he set off, giving her a few megalithic yards of freedom. Hell, he knew this was time off with perks. Each night was a heck of a lot more enjoyable than the last. Finally, he had given up on the women in the village. The ones in the palace really did hold magic in their hands.

As he drank his first goblet down and refilled, she disappeared around the back of a stall, but quickly reemerged with a bunch of some darn thing in her hand. He moved back, leaning comfortably against a stall pole.

"That's Rano's woman, I see. So you were the one chosen to guard her?"

He nodded. "Malik. I see you've taken a handful of my former women. Well, keep them satisfied, I say. There is an abundance at the palace and I am enjoying their delights. So tell me, how are the plans coming?"

"All is in order. Although we may well move out before the queen births. You may find yourself staying behind and missing out on all the action, my friend."

He refilled the goblet. "I don't think so. This is a big campaign and Rano will need all of us on that one. I think I should take the old man aside and show him how to use a sword and spear so he can protect the healer. He seems strong enough. Just looks old."

"Jacob is strong of body and mind, I assure you. His only issue is that he cannot speak. Use him. I've known him quite a while and he's honorable. He'd give his life up for her. He is appreciative of what he learns and already follows her about. Look."

Alioss glanced over. The twosome were nose deep, engaged in some type of an animated conversation. Tucked neatly into his hands were her purchases. "I swear he's a ghost. I did not see him anywhere near us when we left and I've been keeping a keen eye on her."

"Alioss, he has her back. Speak to Rano. We need your strength in the camp to finish training the new arrivals."

He nodded. "Jared, do you know she does not even ask my name? Don't you find that rather odd?"

"Some are like that. It's not always the men who care less about the woman's name. Two can play at that game and I've heard she can play it very well. I've run across a few along my journeys. Then again, perhaps she already has from Rano and has no need to ask you directly."

Alioss shrugged, patting Jared on the shoulder. "I'll see if I can get her back to the palace so I can send a courier to Rano. Unless you mention this first. I don't think it will be an issue. Although he is mighty protective of the healer."

"Consider it done. Let's see if I can have you back amongst all the other women by nightfall. They are exhausting me." Malik punched his upper arm, gathered his flock and disappeared into the thriving market. "Ladies, I leave you here. I have business to attend." With no further explanation, he strode off.

***

"Jacob, will you take these back to my chambers and leave them in the alchemy? I have someplace I will go and you will not come." Nofret grinned, not divulging any further details. "The guard will follow me on this venture, I assure you."

Nofret did not glance back as she wound through the crowded market toward her protector. She halted as a group of priests blocked her way. This was perfect timing as excitement rose up in her veins.

Maneuvering to the right and slipping down an alley, she quickly glanced over her shoulder and saw daylight. Locating the building was easy when all of a sudden the air misted over, vision blurring as a cold wind rushed and swirled around her. Then it spoke. "You must release him." But as she swung around anxiously, not a soul was there.

"But which one are you talking about?" she asked as the noise of the busy alley emerged back into her ears. Glancing up at the steps, she released a frustrated sigh and then continued up, softly rapping on the door. It swung open slightly and someone Nofret did not know spoke to her. The woman seemed to know her.

"Ah, healer, what do you do here? I do not think anyone has need of your services in these parts today."

"Correct. But allow me entrance. I need to see who is in charge. I have a special favor to ask and it is rather urgent."

The woman glanced about quickly. "Yes. Come in. I will go and advise her now. I am sure she will see you shortly."

Nofret stood just inside the corridor, time ticking away, when finally a stately brunette approached. She was dressed in what seemed like gold particles instead of a proper day tunic. "What services do you need from us, Nofret the Healer?"

Nofret moved closer. "This is a bit delicate. May we speak in private? Is it safe enough?"

"Yes, it is."

"Okay. Well, there is something I want to do for a special man. Can I enlist your help? I know those that come from leagues away to see you perform."

She laughed. They both actually laughed. "I know there is a strong man of great worth that has his sight on you. So there is a true purpose in your arrival. I knew of it before. Now the time has come. You are here."

"Ah, why yes, of course. I should have realized you would already know."

"Come along. I will instruct you myself. Then you will have a chance to practice with some of the girls. We have a group coming in a short time. Shall we?"

"Yes. Oh, please do not call me healer. Nofret will do."

"I can do that. I am Aeroella. Now, let's get you properly attired." Together they walked into a rather large and formal dressing area housing quite a selection of garments. Glancing further, Nofret could see additional rooms.

"Oh, I should like to try on all of this. Which do you suggest?"

Glancing at the color of her eyes and skin, Aeroella handed her something that should prove to be of benefit.

Changed, Nofret swung around several times, glancing at herself in the glass. "This is just what I was hoping."

"No other has worn this. It was made by a passing gypsy woman who instructed me to hold it aside until the right moment arrived. I guess you are that moment."

"Do you know her name?"

"Unfortunately, no. She showed up on our back doorstep as I was entering and handed it to me with those instructions. Then she disappeared into the market. Never have I seen her since."

Nofret engaged her in a sly smile. She knew who it was. Glancing up at the ceiling, she felt the smile grow. "Are those other rooms yours? They look comforting and lovely."

"Yes." They continued along to a different area. Stopping, Aeroella snapped her fingers and the music began, along with the sway of her hips. "Join when you are ready."

Two hours later, sweat beading an upper lip, Nofret was moving about the room with Aeroella, very pleased with her reassertion into the fine art of erotic dancing.

"You are a natural. He will not stand a chance. For you possess skills that take some years to learn."

They laughed.

"By then women are usually a bit heavier in the hips than a man not into a drink would want. Are you ready to try the results in the big room this afternoon? No one will know you there."

"I do. But feel I may be recognized. I was under the protection of one of the guards appointed by the palace. For some strange reason, I lost him on my way here."

"Oh, I see." She grinned. "I like you, Nofret the Healer. How about we use these and cover your beautiful face. But let them see your lovely eyes?" She held out a gorgeous gauze face veil.

"Yes, this will do. How many will be out there?"

"Peer out that curtain and you will see. They come eagerly. After the performance, they normally walk off with a few of the ladies or head back to the village to their normal flock."

Nofret's jaw suddenly dropped. He was out there. Malik.

Oh, how she was going to enjoy this. When she'd overheard him proclaiming to his women he had business to attend to, he had meant this. *Typical bloke*, she thought.

"I hear the music beginning. I'd better hurry."

"I think we can take our time. Let them begin without us. I want to have the pleasure of you and I entering in together, last. Here." Aeroella handed over a small goblet of a dark, aromatic mixture.

Sipping, Nofret felt immediate results. "This is a potent mix I've tried a time or two myself. But never in the company of overeager men. How did you know it? Exactly what else are you besides the proprietor of this lovely establishment and an amazing dancer? Come now. Tell me."

"There are secrets neither of us can disclose. Right? But you are correct. I also have a list of other qualities I bring to the table. Let us forget about that for now. There is fun to be had, healer. Why not jump right off the bridge and go for it?"

They laughed.

"*Touché*, Aeroella."

"That's our drum beat. They are ready. As I heard in another time, let us go and knock them dead."

***

Nofret knew in that instance Malik did not stand a chance. She housed the element of surprise and damn if she wasn't going to use it until he begged for mercy. *Well*, she thought, giggling wantonly with the effect of the powerful elixir, or until he realized just exactly who he was really dealing with. Here and in England.

Cymbals snapping, they entered the room together and Nofret wove her way around the performers that had stopped, parting like the Red Sea, giving them a perfect lane. The twosome broke apart, dancing, displaying flesh and charm between the men sitting on plush cushions.

Circling around Malik, Nofret did not care at this point if he recognized her or not. She lifted her arms high, breasts heaving over the skimpy blue silk fabric. She watched as his eyes roamed over her entire body, heating it further. Yes, it was there. Obvious desire for them both.

Abandoning all sense of propriety, her hips swiveled right in front of his face, spinning, then slid away just out of reach of his grabbing hands. As she seduced him, arms motioning for him to come and then saying no, she glanced over his shoulder and caught sight of her bodyguard.

An extremely pissed-off bodyguard.

Shit, she thought in a haze. The attempt at ditching him had not been successful. How the hell did he know it was her in this outfit? *Fuck*, she internally screamed, *it was the earrings!*

Then she let it all go. Cares all but forgotten, she moved toward him, leaned on him, smiling and hoping he would not believe her this bold. As he grabbed her close then set her free, he whispered roughly into her veil-covered ear. "Rest assured he will find out about your antics, healer."

Laughing up into his face, she met Aeroella and they strutted away, settling into an alluring pose just as the music ended.

Quickly, she disappeared out into the corridor and hastily changed, handing Aeroella the garments. "I'm screwed." Nofret was laughing. "That damn guard found me and my cat will surely be let out of the bag."

"I can perhaps get you safely out of here if we hurry. One quick question. Which one were you trying to torment?"

"The first. The second was the bloke I ditched when I came in here."

"I am familiar with him. Yes. You are screwed. He's as loyal as they get to the great general."

"Don't I know it. I'm sure I'll hear an earful when I see him again. But, oh what fun that was! I can't thank you enough."

"I could tell. Anytime you want to step out of your world and into ours, you just pop right on in. Now come. I will wrap these up. They are more fitting on you than anyone else inside these walls. My gift. Well, actually by way of the gypsy."

"Ah, but you danced beautifully as well. I sure hope our paths cross again. We made a great pair out there." She took the parcel tied with a leather strap, smiled, then went right out the front entrance, knowing he was there waiting.

"Alioss."

He turned abruptly, eyeing her with a devilish smile. "That was quite a performance, healer, one I should not soon forget."

"Glad you liked it. Any chance you would keep that to yourself?"

He grinned, taking the parcel from her hand. "No. He's going to find out, I'm sure. You don't have a prayer's hope in hell at this point between those that I recognized from the army, including Malik. What possessed you to do it?"

She stopped so suddenly he nearly knocked her down. "Your commander or general. Whatever it is you call him. He is what possessed me to do it."

His brows shot straight up. "If they get drunk today they may forget. But in truth, the only two that know it was you is myself and Malik. I will take care of this."

She turned, smiling, knowing this day she had won. "Thank you. Now I have another idea. I was wondering if perhaps Jacob could take your place. I truly believe I am safe under his care and if you spend a bit of time to show him how to defend with a spear and knife, that would be of a great benefit. I do not think he would like to carry a sword."

She turned forward and broke out in laughter. For ahead of them, leaning against a wooden stall, was Jacob the Elder. "Is that right, Jacob?"

He had listened to their conversation and his eyes lit up, head nodding approval.

"He is of keen strength, I can assure you. I've had him moving heavy objects without anyone's assistance."

"You can stop now. No need to convince me. I agree. The final word will come from Rano. If he says it is okay, Jacob, someone will come and bring you to the encampment so we can begin work. I will personally train you. Now that I am familiar with her comings and goings."

Jacob produced a grin, nodding.

Malik continued on. "As I suspected, you are probably more aware than I am of these constant antics."

They had arrived back at the palace. "Thank you, Alioss." But his attention was quickly diverted, handing the parcel to Jacob. Several lovely ladies were sliding into the wading pool, naked.

She grinned, taking Jacob by the arm. "Come along. We have some mixing to do. I have half a notion you brought that all about. Making sure they did that just as we arrived. You are by far, Jacob the silent, much smarter than I."

She gave him instructions and he worked on one side of the room while she ground up seeds, started the fire pit, unwrapped the Goddess of Tawaret and placed her on a golden plate.

"By the way, I know. But I will never say a word to anyone." She smiled slyly at him as Jacob turned around, throwing his hands up in the air and then bowing in a grand gesture.

"Bring over the mixture." She had the pit blazing, throwing a handful of the sage mix on it as the air crackled with sparks, producing a quickly evaporating white smoke. He stood back, mesmerized by her magic.

"Oh, great Goddess Tawaret, I ask you to bless this statue that we honor this day with great protection over our Queen Satiah and her son to be born as next ruler. Please bring him into our world with intelligence, strength, and humanity to all peoples." She threw another handful in and the statue was engulfed.

Quickly she wrapped it for the final time and put it in the silk pouch. "I will give this to her tonight. This is all she needs. I really could leave now, for my task is done. But I doubt that I will be allowed. I am sure there is a bigger task than this in the form of Rano the Mercenary."

He smiled, shaking his head affirmatively.

"Yeah, I knew it. It's always easier to see things from the opposite side. Like yours. Anyway, will you be with me the whole time until I am finished?"

He nodded yes.

"Can you write any little bit of detailed information down? Something that I could really use? I feel like I am stubbing my toe one minute, then getting a wonderfully relaxing massage the next."

Chagrin was all over his face.

"Oh, whatever, Jacob. I am fully aware I should not have asked. But I had to give it a whirl all the same. Can't blame a girl for trying."

His eyes belied total merriment as he left her rooms and took leave.

She bathed on her own, having advised her ladies tonight they were officially free to do something else. With all this unabashed lovemaking going on all around her, it was starting to wear her thin. The less she saw the better. At dinner she knew it would be the same. Both the Pharaoh and the queen liked the dancers and music.

That was fine, but it was what was going on all around the tables that was severely grating on her delicate nerves. More and more thoughts of Rano ran rampant through her mind. She'd not seen him in a few days. With the silk pouch in hand, she gained entry into the queen's quarters and approached slowly as her ladies in waiting were getting her ready. Bowing, she extended her hand, holding out the pouch.

"I have this for you to put on a shelf over there."

The queen took the pouch and opened it, unwrapping from the fine cloth the six-inch statue and allowing her fingers to glide over its beauty and coolness. "How did you find one so small? All the ones I've seen are of course larger than life itself."

"I had it made for me before I left my village and just finished the blessings. You do not even need to say a word to her. Just smile and place both your hands on your swelling stomach and that will be all that is required."

The queen stood, walking over to put it on the gold shelf. "Thank you, healer. I still want you to stay until I deliver. You and the wives will be here. But if you want to return to your village to help them or other villages near, I give you my blessings. A ship and crew are at your disposal."

Nofret smiled warmly, truly liking this intelligent and beautiful creature.

"I will let you know. For now, I have someone at my village who meets my qualifications and she is taking care of all their needs quite nicely. She sent me a scroll telling me things were fine. But yes. I would like to help those in the villages near here. Do you have time to post a courier out with messages that I will be free if anyone requires my services?"

"I will, but they already know of your special gifts, Nofret. Your history came before you even arrived for the first time. That's how I heard of you myself." She smiled, taking her hands. "You do not wish to dine with us this night, I can see it."

"I am not the only one that has special gifts."

"It is not a special gift to see the yearning in the eyes of another woman and know that it's not for female companionship, but a male. He will not come this night or for several others, as he prepares for our next campaign. He has asked for the Pharaoh's permission to assign you Jacob the Elder as your guard so he can claim all his soldiers for duty. My husband has approved this request."

Nofret gazed at her questioningly. "Was that movement I just saw at your stomach? The baby moving?"

Both women smiled as the queen continued. "Have him go to the encampment at sunrise. He will stay there for a few days in preparation for his new service toward you. When Rano is satisfied, he will return. In the meanwhile, the two palace guards outside your chambers will remain there and you will promise me that you will always be with Meliah and Asofia. I know you like to go off by yourself, healer. Word has gotten back to me of certain events that took place."

She grinned and stepped back, unable to hold in a laugh. "One would think in a palace this grand and large that one could maneuver without much notice. But that is not the case. It is the truth you speak, my Queen, that I do wander off. But I give my word to abide by your full request."

"As you say by my full request, I will wonder if you will find a hole in those words that you can use to your advantage later."

Nofret raised both brows. "I will do my best to live by them. I promise."

"As it is said, so shall it be. Ladies, you are my witness of what this woman is all about."

They all started laughing.

"You are in great health, Queen Satiah, I can see it in the twinkle of your eyes. They are bright and your tone of voice is light and happy. You do not need me any longer. Of that I am completely sure. But I will stay until your son is born and then will leave. On that, you do have my word. Unless, of course, something else of major urgency takes me away."

She bowed, leaving the chambers truly feeling of light spirit herself. *Excellent, s*he thought, for having Jacob the Elder. That brought out a smile. For they would indeed find some mischief to get into for sure. He'd not be able to berate her when she pulled him along on her adventures.

She went into the dining area, took a spare platter and filled it with food. Quietly, she left the room not engaging anyone in conversation. Thankfully, the room had not filled yet, as it was still early in the evening.

She nodded at the two soldiers posted outside her chambers and they promptly opened and closed her doors. Setting the food down, she walked straight out onto the balcony, immediately disobeying orders. With the ladies off tonight and Jacob the Elder doing his own thing, she was free to move about the country, so to speak. Jacob would be searched out shortly and handed that all-important scroll. Tomorrow, his day would begin entirely differently than today.

So her first course of action was the pools. It was perfect timing, as most of the palace would be joining the Pharaoh and the queen for food and entertainment. Then it struck her as she was walking through the garden area to her private section overlooking the Nile, that she'd not actually engaged him in one word. The Pharaoh. Probably never would, she thought. She'd seen him with Rano, some other guards, his servants and leaving the palace on his grandest of grand chariots. But not a syllable had passed between them.

Slipping out of the silk, allowing it to drop onto the cold marble at her feet, she slid into the crystal clear water and let her head rest back against the linen pillows. A raven squawked above her, but her eyes remained closed as she tried to disengage body from mind to see with her third eye what was to happen next.

It came to her. Not in the way of a vision, but in the way of a strong calloused hand sliding over her silky wet shoulder, cupping one breast.

Chapter Eight

She moaned as his body slid up against hers while his lips kissed the curve of her neck. A weak protest nearly formed at his lips not touching her very own. Moving her head to the side, her eyes opened.

"You!"

"Yes. Who else were you expecting?" His voice was gruff as he waded back just enough.

"I can see I will need guards to accompany me even to the water. I was believing you were fully engaged at the encampment."

"You will never need them here. I only have those keeping an eye on you when you leave since it's clear you like to roam, healer. When inside the walls, I have no need of knowing what you are about."

"So what is your business with me? State it. You know perfectly well I am naked. Did you come carousing thinking I'd just fall into your arms because you are leaving soon?" She wanted to bite her tongue for the bitterness in her tone.

He grinned, splashing water up on her shoulder and watching, mesmerized, as it slid softly down its silkiness. "What concoction do you use on that lovely skin to keep it from turning brown in this desert heat?"

She did not move. "You will not distract me. I keep my wits about me unless you prowl around when I am dozing. It will not happen again until I know you are off." She was grinning, daring him to come closer.

"But you were not safe, were you?"

"That's only because they know you are here and allowed you entry to my areas."

"Why would I not be allowed here? I am the Pharaoh's general. I can go anyplace I choose. There is no section that is off limits to me." His knowing grin matched hers.

"Well, that may mean places, it is true. But it does not mean people, as in me. I am a favorite of the queen and you and I both know you will not just take me as you do others."

He did not budge.

But she did. Swimming close, she stood, allowing the water to swirl around her breasts. His eyes blinked twice but never left her face. Oh, she thought. He did have a will of iron.

"Your fiery tongue is anticipated and enjoyable. I will like doing battle with you verbally and between the blankets, I assure you." He rose in all his naked splendor, as her eyes and mouth dropped.

"You see? You are not indifferent to me, woman of mine. But I have known that throughout time. I wanted to come and tell you myself that Malik and Alioss are both training your Jacob the Elder. He will be back to you in three days. Should you find yourself wandering outside the palace against orders, I have those that will keep watch on you in case you decide to go where you do not belong or decide to entertain my men with your exotic dancing."

Every inch of her exposed skin turned a soft shade of pink.

"Oh. I knew someone would tell you. Who did? I was promised no word of this would reach your ears." She was grinning, unabashedly coming up the steps one at a time. Then she wove her way around him, keeping out of arm's reach while placing on her robe. It clung tightly against her wet body.

"I was there."

She stopped dead in her tracks. "You were? I did not see you."

He pulled her close, letting his hands run inside that robe against her still dampened skin. They both felt her quiver. "I was retrieving a few items left there from a previous visit, healer, and stopped when I saw Aeroella dancing in the great room. She only does that when something is amiss. I wanted to see who she had it in for."

"Shit."

"That word I understand, Nofret, and I must say I will look forward to you dancing solely for me. I have never seen a woman move as you did. Even Aeroella was second to your swaying hips and overflowing charms."

He all but ripped the silk cloth from her body, dislodging the robe. It pooled on the marble at their feet. As he lifted her up, she wrapped her legs around his naked hips and he brought them both back into the warm waters. As he moved them toward the center of the pool, the atmosphere around them sizzled.

"I will dance for you, mercenary. Before you go to battle." She pulled his head down and kissed him wantonly. It was just not fair. He was in her blood and bones. Tonight, if he even hinted, she'd say yes.

He pulled back, releasing her and shaking his head. "There is no hope for me as a man keeping my strength with you about, love. But I would have it no other way. Will you not be more cautious when you venture out until Jacob returns?"

She shook her head no. "So you have not been told, have you?"

He left the pool, put his tunic on and fastened the gold belt before he slid into his sandals and tied them up. "What?"

"The queen this very day gave me leave to move about on my own until he does return. If I wish to go into this village or another I am free to do so."

"I think you missed something there, my lovely. There was an entire message you are leaving out in this conversation. I know it was if you would wait until Jacob the Elder returned and take him with you was what she had suggested. If I am not right."

"Damn it."

He laughed, his eyes warming tremendously as he gazed down into the pool.

Oh, how bold he was. She wanted to splash him and stomp her foot in the water, at the same time making him take her here and now. But it was futile. He waved her off and departed.

"Arrogant ass," she muttered into the darkening sky as she glanced about, noticing that the torches were already lit. When had that happened? How dare that bloke touch her like that and then depart with such indifference? She placed a finger gently on her swollen lips and smiled.

Damn! She had no choice but to take this into her own hands. Time seemed to be running out. Drying off and dressing, she pulled her knees tight against her chest and stopped, quietly listening to the locusts off in the reeds singing their nighttime song. The wind picked her hair up, moving it across her back. She had refused to wear the wigs and, seeing as they thought she was already an eccentric healer, she knew no one would demand it.

One lone fishing boat was being rowed towards its shore. She envied the fisherman's freedom. She had to know what to do next when her responsibility to the queen had been met. Was it possible that she could leave before the baby was born? Would Malik? For a long while she just sat there, not thinking of either man but listening to her inner voice prescribing a plan.

The wind blew again as she stood with a firm idea in place. As soon as Jacob returned to her they were going to set out on a mission of their own. She went back and slid into her bed, forming it fully in her mind.

When she rose the next day, she set about preparing. She did indeed not leave the palace grounds nor go to the pool without her ladies. As she gathered up supplies in the herbal room, she awaited the arrival of Jacob. At last, one day later than planned, he was allowed entry into her chambers.

She waited for the two guards to close her doors before rushing over to him. "So, was it good? Are you a full-fledged Egyptian hitman now?"

His grin produced a set of white teeth as he nodded, thrusting his mighty arms up and exposing them, to her great joy. "Excellent. Where are your weapons? In your room? Did they test you to your limits? I heard from Rano that both were training you. For their own devious purposes, I am sure. Were they like two bantering elks?"

He moved two fists towards each other and back again.

"I get it. They were. How funny that must have been. But look at you. Tanned and not looking the worse for wear. I'd say you are stronger than you want us all to believe."

He touched the side of his head.

"Yes. I agree. Smarter as well. But I'm on to you, Jacob the Elder."

He grinned, enjoying that name.

"Well, we leave at first light. I have two camels ready. I want you to go back and get your gear prepared. We are going to visit some of the villages outside Memphis and see where we can be of service. Has the army left for their campaign?"

He nodded yes and held up two fingers.

"Two days ago? What the hell. Where have you been?"

He grinned, obviously glad he did not have to reply on that one. He might look old but parts of him were still apparently quite young and arduous.

"Really? You? Without potions or magic? Oh…"

He left her then, sporting a wide, toothy grin. It was during the night when she was sound asleep and the wind blew her drapes around that she heard Rano's voice. It was as if he was leaning over her whispering into her ear.

"Valley of the Kings."

Her eyes flashed open, sitting straight up. "Oh, my God," she said into the darkness. "But we can do it. I have a ship at my disposal. Shit, yes, we can do it." She felt it. Closure was on its way of some type. She wanted to jump up and down on the cushions. Was it going to be that easy? What was she to do there? That was a burial ground. Rano was not dead yet. Why was his voice so clear in her ears when he was still alive? How could that be?

This was getting a bit too surreal.

Lying back, she tried to sleep. But a million things needed to be prepared. How was she going to get the queen to let her go that far? She could not lie; that would not be fair. Besides, before they even left port she would have heard of it from someone and prevented it. Damn. She'd have to abort her earlier plans and think about this.

Rolling over, she plotted, sighed and then gave up. It did not matter. If she was supposed to go there then the green light would go off and there would be no obstacles. Were they not headed in that direction to Lower Egypt to squash the Kush uprising that had grown momentum and now was on a big push into the territory? Had she heard Ethiopia? Shaking her head, she let it all go. It would sort itself out when it was time.

But she was so impatient. It was not like any other passage, that was clear. Nor was she the same person who had left Venice on that fine day and found herself in Victorian England.

The next day when Jacob the Elder arrived with a scroll in hand, she was eating outside. His face said it all. He was anxious. Glancing at him while unrolling the parchment, she read the bold and now familiar script of their queen.

"You must leave at once. My sage had a vision that someone of great importance may need your healing at the impending battle in the southern lands. Go quickly. Take your man and what you need, but hurry. Time is of the utmost. The ship is readied and awaits your arrival."

"Crap. This is both good and bad news. She does not mention who the vision was about. Surely it can't be the king, or even in her pregnancy she'd travel to be closer." Nofret rose, sending the goblet off the table. Jacob leaned down and replaced it. "I know. My nerves are rattled. This is exactly how I felt when I arrived in another time and did not know how I got there or how to get back home. I was lost."

He patted her on the back.

"Okay, enough self-indulgence, right? Are you ready?" He nodded, pointing to a large carpet bag, weapons protruding out. "Wow, do you have ESP? Do you know what that is?" He ignored her just then as he quickly went about gathering up jars, herbs, salves and jugs.

"Okay, you keep doing that and I'll grab better clothes for the desert. I can't go scampering about on board that ship and probably a mule or camel looking like Queen Sheba of Arabia," she mumbled to no one, for as she turned to look at him, he had vanished. "Well, what the hell."

He reappeared from another chamber, motioning rapidly at the scroll and moving his finger quickly.

"Of course, I will write a reply." Dipping the reed in ink, she hastily scribbled a note back to the queen advising they were preparing to depart on the awaiting ship shortly. "Just hand this outside the door to the guard and we will leave out through my balcony. It's a quicker route down to the docked ship."

She hoisted one bag onto her arm and the smaller one as well. Jacob took three and they walked rapidly down to the awaiting crew. Indeed, they were prepared to shove right off. The second her sandals hit the deck, the plank was pulled away.

She was shown below where she could store her items and spend the night. She stayed there, not bothering to unpack or go up. She had changed hastily back at the palace and more than a few male eyes had squinted at her adjusted female attire. But she cared not.

So what she had a male tunic on over her wrap? It was a hell of a lot more practical. Especially if she had to run or rip the damn thing off and still have freedom to move. This was not modern day Saudi. It was ancient Egypt. She could actually get away with this. Particularly under the blessings and protection of Queen Satiah.

A rap at the door got her attention and she opened it to a tall man with a small tray of food and drink. She took it, kicking the door closed with her foot and feeling some semblance of courage since Jacob was on board. Until she needed him again, or he decided to have one of his strange conversations, she'd leave him to his own devices as he would her.

Restless and eating little, she drank even less, as her stomach was in upheaval. Not by the pitching of the ship, but by a clear internal message that someone was in trouble and someone else was going to die. Who was it?

She could hear men's voices in her head and stopped to wonder if she'd just imagined something going on between Rano and Malik? Or was it just the voices from above or below where the oarsmen were being urged on by the helmsman to row harder until the wind hit the sails?

She had no clue.

Opening the door in frustration, she moved up to the deck and stood the night away with the working men until sunrise. Finally, she strode over to the closest one.

"How far down the Nile have we come?"

"Between Beni Suet and El Minya."

She nodded, moving back when she saw Jacob heading her way. Damn, even silent, she was happy to have his presence. He looked none the worse for wear, so obviously, he had received a good night's sleep. She nodded him closer. "We are nearer now to El Minya. The battle I overheard was to be near the Valley of the Kings in Edfu. That means we are on the river another twenty-four hours. I heard them say a strong northern wind was starting to blow and would move us faster. This is good, look, the oars are raised and sails full."

He made a small pyramid with his thumbs and pointer fingers.

"Exactly. That's what I think too. We will get off in Luxor if the battle is in Edfu. Then we can set up a camp of some type. I still am not sure why I'm needed specifically. But we are both headed in the right direction."

She grasped for a quick breath. "Will I ever hear your voice, Jacob the Elder?"

He nodded yes.

"Good. I want to know what you sound like."

She was done talking. Standing there at the railing, she only left it to relieve herself in the pot below and eat. She did not sleep. He did not sleep. Together they stayed side by side, watching the shore get closer and move away as the Nile weaved like a snake through the land.

She watched the captain's approach.

"Healer, here are your items. We are landing shortly. The ship will stay as most will go ashore to ensure your safe passage to Luxor. There you are to set up camp."

"Do you know for how long?"

"No, you will await orders."

"Thank you. We are ready."

Chapter Nine

The drums could be heard, their steady rhythm growing louder and stronger as they approached the enormous encampment. Her eyes bulged out. All she could see in every direction was thousands of soldiers and tents. *Oh, my God*, she thought. This was just what a blockbuster movie set would look like in the future. Mini camps inside the larger-scale one were formed for provisions, horses, and camels. As well as continued training and sleeping quarters.

As it grew larger and larger, Nofret and Jared were met by a familiar face covered with desert dust and a warrior's helmet. She knew him well enough.

"Healer, Jared the Elder."

Nofret spoke for them both. "Alioss, hello. I don't know if it is good to see you or not. Where are we to go?"

He turned his horse around. "To where the other women healers are. They have already established their supplies and are readying for our battle."

There was no reply. She did not have one in her right now, realizing that of course there would be injuries and death.

"Rano himself will not come. Explicit instructions will be handed down and brought to you. Set up your own tent as you see fit. It has been raised over there with the flying colors of the House of Rano. This will keep you both safe from any internal camp strife. I wish I could say the same to you, healer, that it is good to see you. But perhaps more men stand a chance of survival with your skills."

She was indeed touched by his proclamation as he turned and pulled the horse's reins, leaving them in a cloud of dust.

She turned toward Jacob. "So you are to stay with me. Good, I am glad to have heard that. I have never seen anything of the likes of this. Jacob, have you?"

He shook his head yes.

"Oh my, poor you." Then she halted their progress. "Was it because of me?"

Again he shook his head yes.

"Come on." The camels lowered, kneeling on the dirt. "Let's get in there and see what we are dealing with. At least here we are actually doing something of use. Look way over there in the distance. I can see the tallest of the pyramids. Even from here they are indeed an amazing sight."

As the camels brought them the short distance into the encampment, they remained quiet until their feet were back on the sand and they walked side by side with their bags.

"I overhead a couple of the women assigned to me back at the palace gossiping. Anyway, they were talking about the Pharaoh. I was not really paying it much attention at the time, but then it dawned on me. Now I understand what I heard. I guess he has several wives. But Satiah is his first one. If she bears a son she will potentially rule should he pass on. Until the boy is of age. Now it truly becomes imperative she bears a healthy one that rises to power. Or she will be moved down in the wife rankings. Imagine that."

He touched her arm, possibly hoping to alleviate all that pent-up nervousness.

She smiled at him. "I know, I am rambling. Once I get busy, I will shut up."

That toothy grin appeared.

She went inside the tent and was surprised at how roomy it was in comparison to what it looked like on the outside. "We'd better set up what we can. Can you move that damn scorpion out of here? I have no patience for those ungodly creatures. Anyone who's crazy enough to worship them is positively nuts. Surely he will just get in the way and I'll have to kill him."

Gently, Jacob prodded him along, using a long-handled reed sweeper.

"That's better. Now take a look around and see if we can keep those dang things out. I can deal with many creatures, but the thought of those moving about while I sleep is disturbing enough."

He roamed about, nodding that the coast was clear. She finished unpacking their supplies, laying them out for quick access. "We'd better prepare some ointments for wounds, rip up some of that linen for bandages and mix up some powders in case they need a swifter means of leaving this earth."

Three hours later they had established an advance on what they would surely need when the battle started. "I'm going back out there and see who wants to talk and find out what they know. I smell food being cooked. I don't know if we have to get it ourselves, or someone has been appointed. This does, though, seem to be a well-oiled machine."

Nofret approached several women dressed in multi-fabric tunics, which dictated the village they hailed from. They were not Egyptian.

***

"Healer Nofret, a welcome to you and Jacob the Elder. We watched your arrival and were notified you would be joining our group. I am here to advise that you are in charge of our quarter. When you are fed and have had water, come with me. My name is Neira. Unfortunately, we do not have the luxury of much time for me to tell you who everyone else is. I'll leave that up to you to discover if you feel the need."

Nofret nodded. "There are many. How many healers do we have gathered in total?"

"Sixteen, including you. The rest are from other villages who were brought along due to the massive size of the king's army alone. Someone thought ahead and gathered more to help."

Nofret glanced around at the large gathering, noticing the frightened look on most of their desert-weathered faces.

"Are they here with full knowledge of what may not only happen out there, but to them as well?"

Neira's reply was a bit to clipped for Nofret. "Does that matter? They will do as asked. They have not been given any other choice."

"Ah, I see. It's just easier if someone wants to help instead of being held in bondage. But I do understand."

Neira eyed her skeptically as Nofret withstood the appraisal. "You are not Egyptian? I was under the impression that you are since you came from the palace."

"What, because I dress differently? Well, let me assure you that I am. Also here under full blessings of our queen. Anything else you want to know? I am not opposed to you asking now while there is still time. After that, it will be too rushed for such small talk." Her own wall was up and it would stay there. This woman did not need to know any more than was told to her in the way of instructions.

But Neira was ballsy and persisted. "And the man?"

"He is Jacob the Elder. He is my assistant and extremely capable of taking care of anything asked of him including drawing a sword if necessary. He may look like an elder, but he is quick of wit and strength. He does not speak. But let me assure you he does comprehend with utmost intelligence everything that is going on around him."

"Ah. I understand. So I recommend you keep him with you."

This woman was starting to piss Nofret off. So she pushed back. "Just so I am clear, where do you come from and what is your role in all of this? Are you a healer?"

"I am Hebrew. My village was destroyed, my girls sold off and my sons bore into labor over there building the final pyramid." Her voice was tinged with sarcasm.

Her plight did not touch Nofret's heart. Something about her warranted closer examination. "Your husband, where is he?"

"Bondage like my sons. I was told I could work in the village. There were no other choices offered to me. I am merely a slave under the king."

"How are you a healer? What do you know?"

"My grandmother and my mother were both gifted with special healing touches and a mind to know how to help others discovering what ailed them. I also have this. Why don't you come with me to my tent? I will show you what has been prepared."

Following along, Nofret could not resist the urge and stuck her tongue partially out at Jacob. He shook his head back and forth, trying to hold back a laugh at her bold sassiness.

Nofret surveyed the scene inside Neira's tent. "I see potions and dried goods mixed properly. Your oils and tonics are the correct color, mix, and quantity. You are indeed good at what you know, Neira. When you decide to say my name it would be easier to use Nofret and not 'healer,' as I think others here would look to answer you as well."

"But you are above us all and we know that."

Their gaze steadied. Neither one was willing to give a fraction of an inch.

Nofret needed to straighten this out right now. "I am not of higher value than anyone else here. Man or woman. In my eyes we are equals."

Neira released her gaze as Nofret continued. "You seem to know what's going on all around us. So, when are they marching to battle and where is it to take place?"

Neira hesitated a second and then answered. "The Kush army is already encamped in Kom Ombo. They will meet the army somewhere in between Luxor and there. The Egyptian army stretches from here to near the border of Edfu."

Nofret was a bit taken aback by the details. "That's incredible. I would think it uncommon for a healer to know who is where and when they will battle. Especially knowing how your people can be treated."

Neira bristled at the reference to how she would come to know such things as Nofret watched her closely. "I was taking care of a man that had been injured during training and was brought to me. He eventually took fever and rambled on like I was his companion on the battlefield. I do not think he realized what he was saying."

"Oh, so it was just talk? The ramblings of a sick man?"

Neira seemed to be very careful. "It could be. Why don't you ask the commander? You are under his protection, are you not?"

"What gave you that notion?"

"The stripes on your tent. They are the same that are found in high ranking people that show allegiance to the king and queen."

"Now, how would you know such things? More rumors?"

"I apologize, healer. I got carried away. Having been out in encampments before, I was quickly educated on where I could and could not go and was warned to never go into the area where the larger tent with yellow markings was."

"No apology needed. But you are correct to acknowledge that those words may get you into trouble someday. I will not, though, be a part of that process. Just be careful is all I can say to you now."

"I know," Neira stuttered. "We should go out; the food will be ready." She held her tent flap open as Nofret passed outside, noting where it sat in the midst of this part of the encampment.

Eyeing the much-talked-about striping, a slight grin formed. She still did not know precisely when they would do battle. Well, perhaps those in this section were not allowed to go further into the encampment. But Nofret sure as hell would if it became necessary.

"Healer, I am four tents down from yours."

That brought another smile to her face as she stopped and was handed a plate of cooked meat. "You did mean to say Nofret, right?"

Neira eyed her with a grin, locking horns with those dark brown orbs once again. "Yes, exactly."

They sat down opposite as she joined Jacob. "You lucky man. I will not hear a complaint coming from you ever. Especially now that you are surrounded by all these women. I hope you have been making yourself useful."

He bit off a piece of the meat and drank of the water, watching her closely. It was still ninety degrees even at this time of the afternoon with the sun beating down on them in full force.

She glanced over to the viewable tip of one of the pyramids off in the distance and was sucked into a moment where she saw a procession of heavily decorated soldiers carrying a box encased with...

Jacob nudged her, holding out the liquid.

"Damn, I had something going on there before you interrupted me. But thanks. I am parched." She drank deeply of the coldness, quenching her thirst. Then she rose, washing her plate and stacking it back with the others. "I'm going for a walk. Make yourself useful and come along with me."

He held up his hand and shook his head.

"Why? Can you sign me on this one?"

He pointed to the ground.

"You want us to stay right here?"

He nodded yes.

"I can't sit still. I'm filled with anxiety right now, Jacob. I have to move. What do you suggest I do, walk in circles?"

Again he nodded yes.

"Damn it," she whispered close to his face. "Okay, fine."

She had pressed down a good inch of desert sand, forming a large oval behind her tent. Then she looked up and saw Alioss coming toward her with a horse in tow. He leaped off, leaving the ropes dangling. Walking over, he picked her up and set her up on the other, handed her the reins, and climbed back on his.

"He wants to see you." They trotted through the enormous encampment as it spread out in every direction imaginable to the naked eye. It took nearly thirty minutes by horseback before she reached what she knew was the center of the army. Sliding off the mare and walking behind him, she noticed the colors of his tent matched her own.

Her heartbeat increased.

He was indeed a smart man. Being in the center of several tents all flying those exact same colors would outsmart any that were bold enough to infiltrate and think they could sweep in during the darkest hours of the night and kill him.

She locked eyes with Alioss, noticing he seemed restless.

"What are you waiting for? Go in. Don't keep the general waiting. I will be right outside ready to take you back."

She moved hesitantly through the flap and halted just inside. He was pacing about, similar to what she had been doing making her steady circle in the sand just a while ago. She glanced over to the makeshift bed made of woven blankets. In one corner were his battle armor and that glorious sword that she was extremely fascinated by.

"Woman, you can touch it. I'm quite sure, though, that it is too heavy for you to lift. You may have a recollection of seeing it before."

"I know."

He turned his body right behind hers. "You do, don't you?"

"Some of it, yes. Some of it, no. I am still trying to figure out what the bloody hell I've done wrong so I can right it. Only you and one other would understand that I am not a raging lunatic right now."

She slid her hand over the coolness of the heavy blade, knowing the death that it would bring. "This you made. I know that. But where did you get the jewels? They are exceptional."

"I believe someday you will have them if I am not mistaken."

She shook. Did he understand? She would indeed someday have them. But why? Did he take them off before battle and give them to her? Was that why she was here now?

Something was truly screwed up.

"You once said some women will not share their thoughts when they look as far away as you do right now."

She moved closer, only a few inches separating them from the much-wanted contact. "Yes, I did say those exact words."

He moved so only the thickness of a thin thread separated them.

"This time I will share them with you. But rather than with words of which I can produce too many, I will use my touch."

His eyes turned dark as he stood still.

"Mercenary, I did not bring my costume to dance for you. There was no time. If you want me to not do this, you must tell me to stop right now."

He did not move. Nor speak.

She untied her belted robe, letting it drop, followed by her heavier tunic and lighter wrap. Before him, she stood naked.

His muscles tightened as she moved forward, untying his gold threaded leather belt and letting it drop to his sandaled feet. His breath was deep on her face as she removed the clasps holding his custom tunic and it slid down into a heap.

All they both had on now were sandals.

She moved into his arms, strong arms that encircled her slim waist. Slowly, she slid palms down his rippled chest, memorizing again the firmness. His skin was warm. Her heart was pounding rapidly inside her bosom.

Eyes locked, he held her spellbound. Without knowledge, one hand glided down, resting gently against his raised manhood. He moaned but remained still.

Oh, she thought. *What control he has!*

"You brought me to this, mercenary."

"We should have had more time at the palace, Nofret. I had not requested you here for this in truth, my love. I wanted but your company. To make sure you are settled."

She tilted her head back as one of his hands wove through her silky hair, down her back and over the curve of her buttocks. She felt their roughness wanting more. But then stopped when she felt something familiar against her skin.

"You have it?"

He smiled into her eyes. "Yes, when the wind would have claimed it, I decided it would be mine."

"Oh, Rano." She let those lips take hers as she moved one of his hands between her dampening thighs.

His finger went inside. "Woman, you have no idea how I have wanted our reunion."

"Oh, there you are wrong. Yes, I do. Your voice has been calling me back for a very long time." She moaned, arching as his strong grip kept her upright when her knees threatened to buckle. "I wish I could have danced for you."

He chuckled, taking her with him to the rough blankets. "I will not die this day, my sweet. You could dance for me right now. But in an entirely different way than the one you shared with that room full of men."

She turned, kneeling in front of him. Her heart was already shattering and there was no way to stop it. This was when she became completely aware of what she was doing and thinking.

At last.

Gently she touched his heated skin to discover how ready he really was. A strong gush of wind suddenly threw apart the heavy canvas tent flaps, swirling around them both. Then it evaporated back out the way it had come, closing them shut.

He pillaged her lips as all thought in both shut down. Her nails dug deep into his strong muscles as he lifted her up and took what was rightfully his. All of her. She moaned as he sat up, holding her tight, forcing a union so powerfully potent she started to cry, having never been filled with such love before.

They both shook, releasing, as he kissed each tear while it fell streaming down her cheeks. No man who called for death should ever have such a gentle side, she finally thought, as her breathing slowly turned to normal.

"I think I may have left my own special brand of marking on you, mercenary." She looked him square in the eyes. "I love you."

"Yes, you do. It took you long enough."

She tried to jab at his ribs but he caught her hands, shoving her down on the rough blankets, hovering above as she felt him grow inside again. When he released her wrists, she grabbed his neck, tugging his head down to hers and kissing him deeply.

He pulled back. There was something very important that needed to be said. "Woman, you know I am in love with you. A hundred years before I was even alive, I knew I loved you."

Her voice was raspy, barely above a whisper, struggling to get something out as he watched her intently, waiting.

She finally managed, "Thank you for not giving up on me." Her hand was over his heart as one last tear fell.

Leaning down, he scooped her tightly into his arms.

Her unspoken words nearly mirrored his. Soon, she would have to let him go for good. But this was not the mood either wanted in his tent right now.

"I think I'll tuck these clothes of yours away and keep them. Forcing you to ride through camp on bareback. That should fire up all my men."

"Smart ass."

"Ah, my sweet. You are my life. I should have just taken you back at the palace and forced you to be my wife."

"Never mind that. Ask me now, here. We do not need the blessings of the Pharaoh to know we belong to each other."

"I will do no such thing. Yes, we do need his approval and you know that. Otherwise, you are no more than my mistress, since we do not share common quarters back at the palace. Perhaps you would not mind that at all?"

There it was. That damn roguish grin reappearing.

"Fine. I was never one to like things nailed down in writing anyway. Must be some kind of commitment issue I have."

They both laughed. "You sure do."

She scoffed, feigning indifference without much success. "Anyway, you have something of me. What shall I have of you?"

Oh no, she suddenly thought. *Is this when he will remove the jewels from his sword and give them to me?* Thankfully, he did not budge.

"Women. Always wanting more. Did you not just rake my body with yours? Do you need to have me again?"

She laughed up into devilish dark eyes. "Yes. I want more. A lot more. But we are out of time right now, great mercenary."

He reached for her but was met with thin air. She was now out of his arms and searching for all her belongings, laughing. "If I can find everything I came with, I will dress and go back to my people. If I stayed any longer, they will all know what went on here and who summoned me to do it. Although I care little for idle gossip, I do care if it involves me."

He stood, taking her roughly against his nakedness. "Fine, go. But come back before we go to battle. I will send someone else next time. Be prepared. I won't keep either one of us waiting long."

***

She tied the belt around the final layer, turning as he lifted one side of the tent flap. "I will come whenever you ask it of me."

He partially blocked her exit. "Wait, one more thing."

"Yes?"

"Did the queen truly believe it is the king that's in danger?"

Her eyes locked with his while she blatantly lied. "I do not know. But I'm here in case anything like that happens."

She dropped the flap, quickly locating Alioss chewing on a reed. Her demeanor altered slightly as along beside him was Malik. She refused to look at both but addressed Alioss while staring off in the distance.

"Are you coming?" Even to her own ears her voice sounded agitated.

Alioss shook his head. "Malik will bring you back. I just received special parcels that are in need of urgent review with the General."

"Which is it truly, Alioss? Commander or general? Anyway, never mind. But he said it would be you that does it."

His gaze roamed over her swiftly, apparently wondering why she felt bold enough to question his judgment in this trifle situation. "Go, healer." Alioss stood back, letting Malik take control.

Who put his hands on those all-familiar hips and slid her up onto the horse as she took the ropes. As they moved back at a slower pace, she looked down at her own white knuckles and tried to get her brain engaged.

"It's all right," was all he said as they wove through the encampment. "It has to be. If it is any consolation, I was told only that which we really needed to recall would remain in our memory after we move on.

"It will all become very clear to us both when it is necessary, Healer Nofret. Until then, I ask you to bury all those worries away. They are not needed here right now. Neither of us have been angels and were not asked to come here to do so. But, before we close this subject for good, I'd like to ask you one question."

"Go ahead."

"Do you recall all the details of being here before?"

"No. Not all of it. Truth is, I do not know what is in store for me this time. I have just a brief recollection of knowing you here. In the future, well, that is a different story. I know we have a strong connection. Here, it is Rano. I am truly sorry if that hurts you."

He smiled. A very genuine one. "I am not sure I was here when you and Rano originally met. I am convinced this time I came to make sure something happens differently. What that is I am still not clear about."

"Again, more damn gibberish. I am fully aware you can't just tell me what's important to know and be done with it. I get it."

All of a sudden something violently flashed before her eyes.

***

He was caught off guard at what he was witnessing. Again.

"Oh my God, Malik, how many times have we done this?"

He was so relieved she had asked. "Enough. We have both been allowed to remember certain things so that we can change what was and fix this for good."

That got her attention.

He grinned. "Well, if we can recall any of this when the timing is right, we can compare notes. Now enough. Here you are, Healer Nofret. Back within the safe confines of your site."

***

She slid off the horse, tossing him the ropes. He tossed them back. "You may want to keep her handy in case you want to jaunt off later. I think you know the way by now and certainly, do not need a chaperone." He tugged on the ropes, moving his own horse around, and then disappeared.

As she tied it up, a stranger, somewhat resembling Mrs. Baker, brought water and feed. She was too beat to stop and evaluate her more closely. What the hell? Everyone seemed to either look familiar or were trying to push her in this or that direction. Enough. She was tired.

Slipping into her tent, she did not bother disrobing. Tugging the blankets up, she closed her eyes and drifted off into another troubling sleep.

As the next day passed, she knew he would not come to her. That would cause too much of a commotion. After putting in a full day of preparations and meeting others inside their special area of the camp, she finished cleaning the dinner plates.

"Jacob, I am going into the encampment. I will be back later on." She ignored his knowing smile while untying the rope attached to the brush. Grabbing the horse's mane, she swung up and took the most central path deep into the camp. When she arrived at Rano's tent, he was just walking back from where most of his lieutenants were encamped.

A wide grin lifted light up into his handsome features. It was clear. He truly was glad to see her. She slid down off the horse as he took the rope and tied it to a branch. Opening up the tent flap, she turned toward him just as it fell in place, giving them some much-needed privacy.

"Wipe that satisfied look on your face. In here, or wherever we do this, we are equals. May I repeat what I said to you earlier since you forgot those words so quickly? You do not own me."

"Yes, I do."

"No, you do not."

He reached behind his tunic and removed a scroll from his belt. "For you, woman."

She read the document. One hand clutched it tightly while she lifted on tiptoes, kissing him as strong arms encircled her petite waist.

"Husband?"

"Signed by the king himself."

"You really must think pretty highly of me then."

Clothing now off, he slapped her naked bottom. "And I shall properly claim my bride now." He gallantly brought her into his arms as if he was crossing a fictitious threshold. The special one reserved for newlyweds. Then he set them both down onto the rough blankets.

Now he would know her just as well as she knew him. As he moved his tongue and lips down her neck, pausing only briefly at her luscious breasts, she seized an abundant amount of the blanket, hanging on for dear life as her back automatically arched.

Oh yes. He had found her out. She was indeed his.

But he was not done.

He lifted her legs up over his shoulders and plundered her with such might her back felt sensitive from the roughness of the blanket. Neither cared.

Upon mutual release, he lowered, encompassing her body, mind, heart and soul with his entire being. She gazed in wonder as the muscles in his arms contracted. Their eyes locked as a silent message carrying the weight of more than passion passed between them.

His voice was deep as he spoke first. "I had a vision of you long ago."

"You did? Why did it take so long for you to come?"

"I do not know. I am trying to figure that out. As we prepare for battle, I also had another vision that you would be here to heal me."

"That's the queen's vision. She told me in a scroll that she saw danger for someone. It must not have been Thutmose III, but you."

"Or both."

"No, it must be you."

He kissed her, again running one hand through silky, long hair. "You are not a conformist. You do not wear a wig nor parade around with glitter on your eyes. I was drawn to you even in my dreams. Our time here will not be long. But it is a love that spans many centuries. When it is time for me to leave you, Nofret, for good, I want you to remember these moments and then let me move on."

Oh, how she loved him. No wonder she was here. It was to give him final peace at last. To ensure the correct future for her and a whole lot of other people. To stop being selfish, arrogant and willful.

His eyes pierced beyond her heart to her soul. It was as if, she thought, he could read her mind and knew the struggles she had been going through.

"You are right. I do not own you. Equals we have been and shall always be. I just do not have any will left to be kept your prisoner any longer."

She released a sigh inside their tent. Hope rose. He gathered her up into his arms and they made love one more time.

Chapter Ten

"You will take leave of me now, woman. Very soon I will have a tent full of men and I won't have any snide retorts against you. Not as if any of them would dare, but you never know with this crew. At least they should not be so lusty, having been entertained very well before your arrival."

"So you say this was not planned? That you knew I was coming here all along?" As Nofret dressed he attempted to pull her backward against his bare skin.

"You must, as you say, let me go now. I will not have them seeing me like this." He laughed loudly as she jumped up and completed dressing in quick order. "You had better get a move on. I hear them coming." He reached over and swatted her ass.

"Shit. You are right." They both laughed as she slid to her knees and crawled out the back, letting the tent drop into place just as they walked in. His grin was engaging as the men eyed each other, glancing about the otherwise empty area.

"Commander?" One stepped forward, "Unless you have her hidden, what the hell has gotten into you?"

He turned, filling a goblet and motioning them all over to partake. Not a sign of her was left except the rumpled blankets and no one would give a care about that. "Did you bring the maps, Malik?"

"Yes." He rolled them out, indicating the area around them and the latest movement of the Kush tribes. "They are on the move. I just rode back into camp and have left behind two spotters and a relay so we can have updated details this evening. I highly suggest that we prepare to move out and begin our preparations across the encampment. You advise and I'll dispatch a courier with details to the healer's area."

"How much time do we have?" He rolled up the maps, putting them back in the camel leather pouches. "Three days, if we want to ride out night after tomorrow. The perfect location has been assigned. It is on the lower grounds of the desert."

"Excellent. Continue training those that need it. Make sure it is properly coordinated with supplies to the men. How many did you calculate?"

"Approximately ten thousand, commander. I did not view any superior weapons. But I am sure they would not be so reckless and expose those. Behind their encampment there were caves. I have men going in tonight to investigate and report back by tomorrow."

Rano patted Malik on the back, nodding for the other men to leave. "Go ahead and send that dispatch to the women. Did you eat and drink yet?"

"No, I reported right in. I'm headed to bathe before I visit anyone. I can't have them turn noses up at my stench." Malik grinned. "You know where I'll be if you need me." He turned, the last to exit.

"Wait." Ranof halted him. "I want to run something by you."

***

That surprised Malik. He sure as hell hoped it was not about the healer. He was not in the mood to hear about her right now. He had reined in his emotions. Locked them up and was not going to release them for any reason. Now or later.

Besides, he had found solace in the arms of a very pretty village woman who had lost her husband last year and was in no way going to make demands on him or produce any offspring when he finally left here. It was common knowledge she was barren.

Rano handed him the goblet full of red wine. "The truths will be told this night. Sit. It is not a command, but a request. For you see, Jared Malik, Chieftan of the Semites, I am fully aware of who you are. Now I mean you to know who exactly I am."

The two stared, neither giving in. Some major conclusion was drawn as Jared relented and sat down on one of the rough blankets. "How in the hell did you find that out? It has been a well-guarded secret."

"Simple. I was the one that left you for dead. I knew you'd be found and cured by the healer."

"How did you know that? Her? I thought you had not met yet." He paused, shaking his head back and forth, listening to a soft voice clearing up a few things inside his brain. "I see. You had met her before. She arrived long before I did."

"Yes. She and I began again our relationship prior. You were delayed in coming for a purpose. An important purpose. Now I will fill you in."

Apprehension filled Jared's gut. It was the same feeling he'd had in those fleeting moments back at the museum before he found himself down in the sand. His brows drew in. Frustration mounted, followed by acute anger. Was he being played for a fool now?

"I will not mince words with you just days before a major battle. What are you specifically referring to?"

Placing his hands on broad hips, Rano stepped closer, taking a moment to listen to sounds outside the tent. When satisfied, he continued. "We are brothers, Jared Malik. At birth. Born as twins. Our mother feared for your life. You were not as strong as I and her body tired after producing many daughters. Much to the disappointment of our father. She was worried. Or so I have been advised since my recollection of her is so vague.

"Choices had to be made and she did it after hard deliberation. Our father was never to know that two of us were born. One being sicklier than the other. She sent you away to a healer woman and her husband in the Semite village nearby. You were raised as their very own. They already had five healthy boys. So you blended right in. Eventually strengthening and thriving."

Jared ran a hand up through dark, thick hair. "More and more questions I've had are now being answered. This is making sense. You were meant to be with her here. I later. But how did you find out? How long have you known?"

"I just recently found out."

"When? How did you know it was me out on the battlefield? Why did you not reach out to me during all those years like you did her?"

"I did. I don't think you were paying me much attention. Nofret was your main focus. Regardless, it was the old woman that raised you who found me prior to that last battle. She was brought to me in a frenzy and told me about your past. She was not a lunatic at all, although close to hysterics. She described you down to your weapon, clothing, horse, and, most important, the indent under your skull. I had to pay attention. The gods were willing it. If she had not done so, I would have just killed you and left you for your people to bury. It appears we were both robbed by our mother of a brother."

He felt under his back neck. It was unique.

"There is no way you would have seen that under my hair."

He laughed. "True. I hold no magical powers like our healer does. I cannot see through anyone. It was the stripe on your garment. She sewed it on when she gave it to you. The care you needed to survive would come from Nofret. Especially that you would live and we would meet. Although I was not aware of the circumstances that would bring us together. Just that it would happen. Here you are."

"Was she an old woman living high up in one of the caves outside my old village?"

"No, I was told by one of the queen's."

"Did she see my Semite stripe? Did she know I was coming without knowing why?"

"No. It had been removed and replaced with plain clothing. She did not know what you were. How you were raised. Only that my brother from afar was going to join me here. When I was told that, I set up a few men outside the village to make sure when you left I had the right man. Once I laid eyes on you myself, I knew it to be so."

He extended his hand.

Jared glanced at it long and hard, and then reached and clasped it strongly. "Brother."

"Yes. You will fight alongside me in battle. But there is something more. Of utmost importance. Much more so than what we will see out there. As I know it, I will not live much beyond that. Even the gentle, loving hands of Nofret will not be able to save me."

"What are you talking about?"

"I've made the same mistake over and over again by loving her and not letting her go when I die. Did you not know you've been here before? Several times? She as well? We are almost a love triangle except I marry her. I know your memory has been tampered with and why. Yet I am fully aware of your buried feelings. The eyes see it and do not lie, brother."

"You married her? When?"

"Ah, there it is. Pain. Don't hang on to it. For it will be short-lived, as will I."

"You seem to know so much more. I have started to have visions of things I've not seen before since I've been here. I know I have to finish something, but it's not clear to me what that is. Yet I definitely have a hand in it."

"Yes. When I die do not let her mourn. Because she will. Again and again. It is important that she not be allowed to remove even one of the jewels off my sword. Although she will think about it and try. Removing them all and storing them in a special pouch. That healer of ours is a fighter to the last breath. Hers, yours or mine. You have given in all these times. Hell, so have I. But now neither of us can. I am tired. I am ready to let her go so she can know peace and a future with you. I've seen it."

Jared stood rooted to the spot, mesmerized, as a blast of cold wind carried thousands of voices around him. Voices he knew. Alwen, Mrs. Hoyt, Father G, Victor and a whole legion of others. Swirling before his eyes, it finally subsided as a true strength rose up from inside. Yes, Malik was determined as never before.

They stood, clasping hands again. "Rano, I will make sure. I vow. Now, I must go and bathe. I will return shortly and we can eat and discuss our plan. As forewarned and forearmed as I can be against her, the better it will be for us all. I shall not think about the love you share and pray that in the future I soon let it go and forget it all."

"So be it, Jared. Now go. This time we do this together."

"Will she return back to you soon?"

"Yes. At dark. When the camp settles for the night. This time, my brother, we are going to do this right."

Jared went to his tent, brought out a fresh tunic and went to the pool and bathed. Swimming in the cool water felt refreshing after eating for two days the dust of the desert. As he looked up at the galaxy, brilliantly displayed above, it all came back as the floodgates opened wide. He rose, dressed and on his way by his tent, threw in the dirty garments and headed back to his brother's. Not even pausing to announce himself, he strode right in.

The food and drink were prepared. He sat down and ate with a hearty appetite. "Tastes a damn sight better than what I took with me." The wine dribbled down his right side and he wiped it away with the back of one hand.

"Damn nuisance of a woman, isn't she? Haunts you, haunts me."

Rano sat down, laughing. "You got that right. It's high time she let go of me so I can roam the heavens. I hear there are some mighty fine wenches up there."

"The results are going to be different this time. Damn, but something has been plaguing me. Why has it taken so long for us to get this right?"

"Her. She does not like to let go of that which she loves. Do you not know that even back in England?"

"Oh, my fucking word. Can you see the future? Strange how hard it has been for me to see the past. Anyway, it's the opposite there. I'm the one that has been chasing her around. I assure you. Since the moment I saw her in Italy. She's different there than here."

"Nope, you are wrong. She's got control of you there like she has control of me here. She is a powerful healer and a sorceress rolled into one gorgeous woman. She uses all her lovely vices to keep us both under wrap."

Jared thought about that. Times and places were layering one over the other as he recalled how she'd acted so indifferent to him when she first moved into his estate. How she used certain moments out of the public eye to make sure he partook of her womanly pleasures. But then she'd meandered off, not wanting a commitment.

He grinned. "There is a man's sturdiness inside of there, isn't it?"

Rano matched his grin with a laugh. "Nope, her strength surpasses even toughened warriors such as us. Using her brain like a man and her body like a woman. Deadly combination. But we've got her all figured out this time. It's only taken three repeats."

"So what will happen if we are successful?"

"You are going to have a merry chase on your hands in earnest. As she will be pissed to high hell over the fact that I'm no longer accessible."

"But I still will be, won't I? I'm not quite finished with her yet."

"All yours, brother. You may find yourself spending the next century trying to lure her back to you like I've been. But for entirely different reasons."

"Well now, maybe then it's time we just go our separate ways so I won't be tortured for as long as you have been?"

"You have to decide what's better. I can't answer that. So, just in case she does an about face on us both, I've got a plan. Now listen, I was talking with the sage before we marched out and here is what she told me specifically we must do together and what you will do after that to make sure this is the last time."

***

Their two voices could hardly be heard, muffled as they were, just outside of the tent to anyone passing by. Jacob had monitored the entrance to the general's tent, knowing that Prince Malik had re-entered, but had not come back out. Moving closer, he was met by immediate resistance when he stopped to strengthen the straps on both of his sandals. Dumbfounded, he was quickly picked up by two strong-armed guards posted nearby and moved a good forty meters ahead before his sandals hit the sand.

They caught him by such surprise, he had a hard time keeping loud, rude comments from streaming out of what should be a silent mouth.

"You move along in the night to your healer, Jacob the Mute. There will be no information passing from you to her this night. We know about you."

Several times he glanced back over his shoulder on the forty-minute trek back to their tent. Entering, he lifted the flap up in a huff, placing his hands on his hips. She turned, taking in right away his clearly displayed irritation.

"What do you have?" She turned, wiping the remnants off her fingertips onto a cloth.

He shook his head negatively.

"Nothing? Nothing at all? They are up to something. I can feel it in the pit of my stomach. You need to get closer to them. Listen. Watch."

His head shook harder as he knelt down and drew two stick figures with swords.

"Oh, his guards moved you along? They are suspicious of you. Is that what you are trying to tell me? Did they say as much?"

He nodded yes several times.

"Shit. Okay. Damn, they are on to you. Which means they are on to me. Do you know where that sage is that Rano uses?"

He smiled, motioning with his head.

She dropped the cloth and Jacob the flap as they followed the moonlight through their part of camp. He halted, pointing inside a small tent. From its depths, a voice rang out, startling Jacob and Nofret.

"Stop lurking in those shadows, girl, and come in. I have a notion to speak with you and you have made me wait long enough. Time is running out. I grow impatient. Now get your bony ass in here."

***

Nofret walked in, letting her eyes adjust to the softly lit tent. Then she halted, feet embedded into the sand, unable to move any farther.

"Yes. It is me. Sit before I pin your ears back. Now let's get things straight right off the bat. I will not answer any of your questions just yet. You will listen and that's that. It is time. Again."

"Hello, Gerda. How have you been?"

"Smart ass still, I see. Sit. I have been well enough. But tired of seeing you time and again."

"Oh shit, Gerda, I feel really weird." Nofret sat quickly down. "I see things now. It is starting to come back. Unravel."

"It does every single time, dear. But we have to put a stop to it once and for all. We must."

"How? I want to. I really do. I know we have had this conversation before. Each and every time. By the way, how many has it been by now? Oh, don't answer. I am afraid to hear the number. What am I supposed to do?"

"Stop fighting it. Rano wants to move on and you need to move on. I'd think a future with Adam would be a bit more promising than repeating this over and again, missy."

A wan smile appeared and then turned into a full-fledged grin.

"This is not a time to be impertinent. I've got other things to do too, you know. Every time you refuse your true duty, you bring us all back. Don't you know that?"

That did it.

"Oh, my, I had not, well, I've not actually ever stopped long enough to think of anyone but myself."

Gerda nodded, watching closely.

"How many are here because of me and will finally have closure when I go back?"

"Adam, Rano, me, the queen and Pharaoh—and that's probably why he avoids you like the plague. At this juncture, he'd probably like to have you tortured and beheaded and just let the universe destroy him later. There are others as well. At this point, I can't keep track of them all. One of the guards, the master craftsman, you know he's got things to do too, and Clash. Is that a good enough list to begin with?"

"Clash too? Oh. Then I am affecting his life with Anne as well. Oh, my God. How come no one has explained this to me with such thoroughness before?"

"Oh, that's precious. I have. Every single time we sit in this tent, in the same desert, under the same sky and time of night and have this exact conversation."

"Oh damn."

"Yes, you even reply with that."

"I guess I'm not much of a healer here if I keep dragging souls back to a time they want to exit from."

"Well, that's new."

She did not smile, standing. "I'll go now and spend some time up in the cave. Have I done that before? I don't remember if I have."

"No. You go do that. Take Jacob with you. He's one of us as well. He'd probably like to go back to where he was. Enjoying a conversation with a pleasant and charming tavern wench in Boston. Sure as shit smells from a donkey's ass, he was engaging her in a truly animated conversation. He probably would like to use his voice about now and give you a decided piece of his mind. Rightfully so."

"Okay, okay. I get it. Again." She exited the tent, scuffing up a large swirl of desert sand as her companion stood close by, waiting.

"I'm sorry, Jacob. I knew and pretended every time it did not matter. I'm going to fix this somehow."

Jacob's brows drew together in concern. He also had heard that before.

"What is it, Jacob? Do you have something to do?"

He nodded.

"Can you do it quickly?"

Again he nodded.

"Okay. Meet me in fifteen minutes. We are going up into the cave to spend some time before the battle." She turned to say something else, but he had already disappeared from sight.

As they met outside, Nofret watched Jacob hand a guard something rolled up but forgot to ask him what it was as they proceeded on together.

On their trek to the cave, she kept glancing down to see the torches of the camp and how it spread out for miles. Twenty minutes straight up and she finally halted as he lit a fire and settled his blanket to keep the scorpions at bay. She squatted down like a monk, folding her legs resembling an oasis lotus.

Her eyes fixed on the encampment below.

For twenty-four hours they sat, neither sleeping, as he kept watch. She did not utter a word as nightfall began. At last, she rose and rolled the blanket. "I'm ready, Jacob."

He nodded, following the goat trail back to the camp. She did not wonder if Rano would be concerned that she had not come to him last night. Tonight she would. She had to. At her tent, she opened the flap and set her things inside, nodded to Jacob, and then left.

It seemed strange to her that the horse was all prepared. It must have been for someone else. Or, had an unknown indeed been made aware of her last minute travel plans and their only passage was to come and make sure it was ready?

Now her mind was really beginning to engage.

She glanced up to the stars. "How do you know this? You must be pretty sorry to see me again. Well, this time I am going to work my hardest."

A roar of thunder echoed angrily across the nighttime sky as she ducked, then smiled. As she approached his tent, sliding quietly off and handing the reins over to one of the guards posted, he lifted the flap and she walked softly in. Rano's trained ears had already known, before he'd even turned around, that she had arrived.

"I did not come last night because I had to go up to the cave and think."

"It is okay."

She steered into his arms.

Suddenly, he had to wonder if it was he who had been holding her back. "You will stay the night."

She nodded, not disrobing him. Rather, she took his hand as they sat down on a pile of blankets. "When do you march?"

He pulled her closer, leaning back on his side. "Tomorrow as the sun sets. We will meet them in the southern reaches on the following day. You will stay here. Do as I say, wife, I mean it."

Alas, they both knew better.

"I will remain with you, then, until early morning. We will not make love. I want you to remember more of me than just your lust for my body, Rano the Mercenary."

He polished off the wine and dropped the silver goblet into the sand. "Unless you change your mind during the night, healer."

She grinned, always loving that name, while tugging his head down to a kiss. "We shall see."

In minutes they were both sound asleep. As darkness gave away to a lightening sky, she opened her eyes and felt if her clothing was still in place. It was. Moving softly from his embrace, she stood to smooth it down.

"I will love you forever," she whispered. Then she raised the tent flap and walked towards the waiting guard and horse. Mounted, she glanced back only once, nodded thanks at his early morning duty, and then rode off.

Within minutes of departure, the entire encampment was up and awake. Men emerged, dressed in their battle tunics with gear prepared to deliver a decisive blow to their enemy. Moving through them as they assembled to march south to meet the Kush army, she felt shivers go up her spine.

Sliding off the mount, she handed the reins to Jacob. He walked the horse off toward where the others were corralled, tied the barrier, and returned.

She was deep in thought. "Well, now we wait. Did you eat? You are up early. I guess everyone is. You can feel it in the air, Jacob. Death. Death is coming."

Gerda's hand slid on top of her right shoulder. "Death and peace, healer. For some, it will be both."

Enlightening energy raced from her toes to her head as she spun around to reply.

But there was no one else there except Jacob.

"Did I just imagine her?"

He nodded, pointing to the telltale footprints her sandals had made in the sand. Retreating from them both.

"I don't think I can stay here. I wonder if I may have a better advantage moving to higher ground. What do you think about that bluff?"

He shook his head sharply back and forth. But she was already ditching him, heading inside her tent as he closely followed.

"Jacob, I have to go. I can't wait here for word two days from now and wonder what the hell is going on."

"For all and damnation, girl. No, you cannot go. I repeat this every single time. Precisely at this moment. Yet you still refuse to listen. Stubborn as bloody hell and go anyway. If you do, it will distract him. Do you want that?"

Their forward progress halted immediately. He looked apprehensive. The very fact that he spoke, Nofret realized, repeating past warnings, and the fact that she was still going to go, had her wondering what to really do. No, she had to. The deliberation and decision were made and firm. No backing out now.

"I must. You stay here. You will be safer. Did you come with me all the other times?"

"Yes."

"Then stay. It will make a difference."

But as she left and began the climb up the rocky terrain, she knew he was right behind, close on her heels. It did not matter; she kept right on going. It was easy to locate the army at this height as they kept pace with the dust cloud down in the desert valley.

When they halted at nightfall to rest in the desert, eat and drink, she noticed no tents were put up. No fires were lit and silence filled the darkness. No conversation could be heard echoing up to them high on the hill.

She took out bread, pulled off a chunk and handed it to him and they ate and drank in silence. Both of their minds were locked into their own world. Nestling into a ball, head resting on her arms, she drifted off to sleep. Jacob was but a few feet away. As her lids dropped, she thought he was already asleep.

***

Later a boot nudged Jacob. Eyes opening, he watched a hand lower a scroll down beside his side. He turned his head quickly toward Nofret and back again. But the person had left quietly back into the dark night. Leaning up on one elbow, he glanced over at her sleeping form and waited a few minutes before unraveling the scroll and holding it up into the moonlight to read.

He smiled and folded it, tucking it inside his pouch. Then he went back to sleep.

***

As the heat of the sun beat down on them, they rose. Each disappeared for a few minutes before returning to eat and drink prior to their final trek. Nofet broke the silence. "We have not seen any of the Kush soldiers up this high. But I see tracks. They are not from wandering animals. They are from sandals. It must be that they have trackers up this high and soon enough they will head back down to where it is safer and report their findings. I don't think we need to worry about them spotting us. Those tracks must have been from yesterday before we arrived last night."

Jacob kept his mouth shut.

Throughout the day they kept pace until the sun was lowering into the desert and the large army finally stopped.

The footsteps of the trackers headed up and out of sight as they spotted men Jacob recognized pointing over towards their area. They were posted sentries. She nodded, knowing full well those below knew they were up here. She was pleased that they were being left alone.

Stopping, crouching down and biting on a balled-up fist, Nofret remained there silent.

"Are you okay?"

"I did it again." She kicked at a stone sending it flying over the path's edge.

"Yup, you sure have. You never learn, do you?"

"Apparently not. So mind if I ask what is next?"

"Does not matter in the least what I say now. I'm going to save my words. You will end up doing what you always do."

"I can't help myself. What's wrong with me? Is it all about him?"

"Nope, you are selfish. It's all about you."

She shrugged, having not recalled hearing those words from him before. But sure she had heard the others. "How far are we from the Valley of the Kings?"

He pointed in front of her nose. "There. We are practically on sacrilegious ground right now. If we even wanted to get there, it would involve us going down this steep hillside, into the valley, right through the heart of the army and up over that hill. It would take us probably all night and into tomorrow."

She nodded at his lengthy description. She liked a man that spewed out a good sentence. "Okay. Then let's go. Standing around like this means we are wasting precious time. I've got a plan and it is going to work."

"What?"

"If up to now most everything is status quo, then I know going there is not. So it's like I said—" She was already up and moving down the trail, eyeing the best way to cross the valley to the other side. "—get your ass in gear or you won't get back to that wench in Boston, England, Jacob the Mute."

All the way down he kept muttering, "I hope you know what the fuck you are doing. This can't be right. I should have tied you up back at the tent. Oh, I don't like this. It is not good."

Every word he uttered simply egged her further on. She turned, walking backward just before they hit the rear of the army, much to the amazement of several soldiers. But she kept on.

"First you would not speak for days. Now it is clear that I can't shut you up. Come on, old man, keep pace. A lot faster steps and a lot fewer words would work for me about now."

She spun around as a massive wall of chest smacked her right in the nose. "Ow, that hurt! Step aside, I say. I am on important business for your General Rano. I am Nofret Qalhata the Healer."

The soldier paused, looking at his men, perplexed. Then he stepped aside, allowing the unlikely twosome to begin their long trek through their massive numbers.

She did not care as she wove through hundreds of them if Jacob was still with her or not. She'd never turned around again to seek him out. When they reached the other side it was dark. But the sky was bright enough to light their way.

"You doing okay back there? Are you even still back there? I've not heard you in hours."

He laughed, catching up with her. Then he stopped to take a much-needed piss. "You hardly knew and did not care. But just so you know, I am fine. You want to stop for a minute, or keep moving?"

"No and no. I have a plan. Let me ask you how many times I've repeated this little maneuver?"

"Zilch. So I must admit I'm intrigued and actually plan on observing through the duration."

She smiled to no one but herself. "I think I calculated the distance right. We should be well out of reach of the battle but close enough to watch it from over there. I could see from that ridge we crossed before sunset. That location was partially vacated. I am thinking only soldiers are guarding it now and the slaves have been moved to a different location until this is over. Again."

"Well, toots, we are soon to find out."

She let that slide. Onward they trekked throughout the night and into the better part of the following morning before the pyramids loomed larger and larger. She saw that she'd been right as they watched a small band of armed soldiers on camels trot out towards them. Suddenly Nofret was confused. It appeared to her as if they had been expecting her and Jacob all along. For in tow they had two extra. Just as they arrived, the beasts were commanded to kneel.

"Get on," was all the conversation she received. Her gut instinct was that she had fucked up even more. Otherwise, how the hell would they have known?

"Seems as if they were awaiting our arrival, Jacob. I think I've done something wrong. Yet you said we had not done this before. Could I have been with someone else another time because you were someplace else?"

"That is correct and no. I can pretty much recite your exact moves and words as if I wrote the script myself. You know, perhaps this time the gods are working with you and not against. Maybe they are just tired of seeing you in this era."

She glanced over at his amused look and relaxed, staring straight ahead. The final resting place in the Valley of the Kings of Thutmose II and many others finally came into clear view.

"Someday, his son will be there as well. One of the last ones."

"Yes. Before the looters get to them all."

She slid off the camel and stood. "Now I am not sure what to do." She wove around in a circle, trying to decide on a direction. Then she halted, realizing that the soldiers and camels had disappeared.

"What the hell? Where did they go? Did you see?"

He glanced around. "No. That is strange, Nofret. What are you thinking? Feeling? Take your time. This is a very important moment."

Head lowered and eyes closed, she breathed a steady rhythm in and out, feeling and listening to all thoughts around her. "That I need to pee. Then maybe I will think better." She grinned, walking behind a bush. Finished, she lowered her tunic and returned. She tapped him on the right shoulder but appeared on his left, startling him.

"Stop being naughty. Did that little excursion exercise your brain enough to give any ideas?"

"Yes." They both glanced towards the large opening and tunnel inside the massive pyramid. "Let's go inside. It will be cooler and we can eat and drink. Maybe that's where they disappeared to."

But there was not a soul to be found in the chamber they entered.

"I can't even find tracks from them. Oh my God, Jacob, I feel so strange. It must be getting close because I don't normally feel this very way. In fact, I do not recall ever feeling this way. I'm a bit frightened." She rubbed the skin on both of her arms as numbness wove its way up.

"This is spooky. I've never been in a pyramid before when it still housed tombs and rooms not yet sealed. Oh my, look at the drawings above this entrance. You have to come here now. It is Rano. Oh God… yes. Now I know I have been in here before. I think."

"Do you feel it? Hear the voices off in the distance? The battle has begun."

Nofret lowered her head and looked at him, feeling sheer panic grow inside of her in a split second. "Yes," she stuttered out back to him. "I do."

For hours they listened as the ground beneath their feet rumbled with the vibration of thundering hooves and chariot wheels as the battle raged. Neither spoke as outside from high above, the vultures and ravens circled in anticipation of fresh flesh and blood to gorge themselves on. The screams and yells of men fighting and dying echoed through the walls of the great pyramid.

Nofret sat down on a gold bench and felt the coldness of the mineral penetrate through her clothing.

"How long?"

"Any time now."

"Will you help me?"

"No, you have to do this on your own. But, if you need guidance, glance at me. Hell, yell at me and ask me if you should or should not do something. As long as I don't lay a hand on you and halt you physically, we are okay."

"You were with me last time and the time before that and I can see your mouth moving, yelling at me. But, I don't know what you are saying." She looked down at her left hand. "Is it starting to get see-through?"

"You hang on. Listen. Something else has occurred and here the soldiers come. Get prepared. Every time you see this, it is like viewing with fresh eyes."

She had no idea what he was talking about. His mouth was moving but no words reached her ears. Suddenly she saw what was causing all the commotion over Jacob's head as four men carried on a slab the lifeless, bloodied body of their great leader, Rano.

Gasping, rushing to stand, she hurried over to Rano, utterly horrified. His tunic and robe were saturated with blood. "Quick! Put him down!" She glanced up, momentarily locking eyes with Jared as he set her bags down hastily. They both opened up and the contents spilled out. Swiftly, she reached for ointment.

"Take that robe off. Here, you." She pointed to a soldier. "Give me your knife. I will rip it quick so as to not cause him undue pain." She finished, throwing the bloody clothes aside as everyone inside the tomb of the pyramid closed in around her and Rano.

That's when she saw Jared holding Rano's sword just as Rano's blood squirted, splattering out all over her face and eyes. Hastily she cupped a large amount of the green salve onto a palm and filled the wound. He moaned as her heart filled with pure agony, trying to absorb all his pain. Willing it to become her very own.

"My woman and wife. You are here. As this was prepared for me, for this day, I will be at my final rest. But only if you let me go." Rano's eyes fluttered, closed and opened again.

She leaned down, pressing her lips to his as tears streamed down her face onto his cold skin.

"Be brave, Nofret. No matter what. I will always love you. Now, we must part."

She clutched one of his hands tightly with a bloody one and yelled out in agony. The tormented sound echoed around the large chamber as her gaze, through tear-streaked eyes, saw others already down on one knee.

"Malik, bring me that sword!"

He could not disobey her. She took it from his hand and laid it on top of Rano's cold body. Moving his hands rapidly, she forced them to grasp it tightly along the handle. Momentarily her mind shut down. Her hands now rested on top of his, her own head lowered.

A beautiful lapis stone dislodged and popped into her hand. She turned it over, staring at it, crying, as one other came out.

She stopped.

Reaching down, she took some salve off his drying wound, put some on each of the stones and placed them back where they truly belonged. Somewhere in the recesses of her mind she was aware that when it dried they would adhere.

For an hour she sat with him until his body was stiff.

As if in a dream, she felt a hand press onto her shoulder and she raised her eyes to Malik's. Standing, ripping a section of her own tunic off, Nofret placed it over Rano's closed eyes and then looked again at Malik.

"Come with me."

She glanced around the room. All others were gone except two guards and servants from his household. They would take care of him properly, she knew.

"Please make sure no one removes those stones."

They nodded as she passed through the chamber, noticing that items of his were being moved in. That quick? How could that be? Glancing down at her feet, she was momentarily horrified to see that they were not touching the dirt below. Slowly she raised a fist and bit on it, not feeling the sensation of pain.

"You did it."

"What?" Her voice was hardly recognizable, even to her own ears.

"You did not take the stones. That was what caused him to always seek you out. He needed you to love him enough to leave all of him behind. That included them."

"I was the one that stole them when he lay dying?"

"Yes, out of love, Nofret. You loved him very much and he you."

"Can you still see me?"

Malik smiled, taking her by the arm. Above them, the sun hit a global opening, producing a glorious sunbeam that shone brightly upon them.

"Yes, I can see you and I've got you now. At last."

Then suddenly, angry voices were growing louder and louder.

"There they are!"

As Sam and Adam turned toward the growing sound, he grabbed her hand and the bag on the floor as they sped out of the museum and through their emergency exit, vanishing into the night. The guards were fast on their heels when they hit the outside.

***

"What the hell? Where did they go?"

"Shit, we need to get back in there and see if anything was taken." The museum guards quickly returned to that section, checking over every square inch thoroughly. "It all seems in order. That's strange."

One pointed over at the life-size statue of Rano the Mercenary. "I don't recall that sword standing out so much. I wonder if it is a copy and that's what was taken?" He glanced quickly around the silent room. "I'll make sure to ask the curate and verify its authenticity just in case. I'll get him on the phone straight away."

"I think it was replaced with a replica earlier this week when you were on vacation. Yeah, check with him and make sure. I think we scared them out just in time. I'll go back to the control room and make sure all the monitors are working. You do a door-to-door sweep and keep your radio close in case you find anything at all out of sorts."

But they found nothing wrong other than a magnificent addition to the great statue of Rano the Mercenary. His sword was mighty indeed and gloriously encased with gems and jewels that no one could explain, but they later proved to be authentic. Nor could any discern anything else amiss. Including the cameras, which had malfunctioned for eleven minutes.

Chapter Eleven

They both laughed all the way back to the Nefertiti Hotel. Finally, he slowed down to her panting words. "I am so happy to be done there! How did you know? You have a lot to tell me, mister. How many women did you indulge with? What did you do with your time?"

He pulled her close and kissed her. He knew what would happen next even if he'd never seen it before. She was going to feel his soul leave her body soon. It could be tonight or it could be in three days. But it was going to happen. She needed to know right now, remember right now, the love they shared here before mourning Rano.

Releasing her, he took her by the hand and led them away from the hotel door and up toward a chapel. She glanced up, stumbling slightly. As he righted her, both laughed. They were headed directly into a small church.

As soon as they opened up the doors, she was sitting in a small boat while he rowed them through Meuse. A lovely canal through the old City of Brugge. She dipped her hand into the cool water and splashed him slightly. He raised a brow.

"They say the chocolate here is molded into several different styles. I think we'd find something for both our tastes and desires."

He grinned and kept rowing.

"Looks like, by our attire, we are in somewhat older times. I truly hope we are between all the wars and well after all the plagues."

His smile grew. He loved having her back with him. Just him.

"Did you lose your tongue in Egypt?"

"No. Just listening to your voice, Sam. I missed just hearing you."

She moved gingerly. The boat was sturdy enough but rocked, precariously close to allowing water to spill in.

"Careful."

She kept on creeping until she was kneeling on the bench in front of him as the oars came inside the boat.

They both released a contented sigh at the same time.

"I can see it on your face. Are you feeling a bit strange?"

"Yes. Am I that transparent to you, Adam? What is wrong with me?"

He kissed her lips softly and pulled away. "He is releasing your soul now. I have no idea how long that takes. But you will be solemn while it happens. Or, so the gypsy advised as well as Gerda."

"I feel it now. I look at you one minute and I want to crawl into your skin and the next I want to be alone."

He did not fully understand but was willing to try. "I won't interfere with this process. But I will stay close in case you need me."

She nodded as a tear formed and dropped. "Bugga. I don't like feeling this soft."

He chuckled. "Don't suppress it. That is all the advice I'm allowed to give. Oh yeah, and do not try and drown it out with alcohol or a good smoke was the other."

"Shit. Who comes up with these bloody rules anyway? Some eunuch with no body parts to know the pleasures we experience?"

He lost it, laughing out loud. "You do come out with really interesting sentences sometimes."

She wiped the wetness from her cheeks. "So while I was busy doing other things, tell me what you were up to."

He shrugged his shoulders. "Ah, you know a bit of tactical maneuvering and all." He knew now was not the time to tell her that he was the twin of her Egyptian mercenary lover.

"What about the women? You telling me you did not have any kind of enjoyment? The man of mistresses?"

"Why are you pushing this? I happen to know that before you two were officially acknowledged as man and wife by the Pharaoh, that you spent a few times in his tent. At least once I know you had intercourse with him. Hell, Sam, you two were in love. Even I recognized that and had to try and reconcile for a spell why I was there. I was sure it was not just to watch it happen and be so punished by it."

"Nice diversion. No need to answer. You are right. I'll shut up about that area henceforth and vow it shall never be brought up again. How can we be accountable for something that was going to happen before this happened, right?"

"Well said, my dear."

"Oh, sod off."

"Now that's better."

The dock attendant secured the rowboat as Adam stepped out, turning to extend his hand to her. She clasped on to it so tight he could feel it up his arm.

"Sorry, really did not feel like falling in right now. I'm hungry for some good old-fashioned food. Oh look, see? It's like I said earlier, there are chocolate concoctions to suit all desires."

He stood in front of the lavishly displayed store window lined with row upon row of chocolates in all sizes, shapes, and color. "Oh, I see the ones. Ah yes, the very ones. Look, all I can say is a set of those would do me well except I like the real thing and they belong to you."

Glancing at her face quickly, he stopped his comical banter when he noticed her discomfort. "Come on. Over there is a nice little restaurant. I see quite a few ladies and gents going in."

She adjusted her plumed hat and took his arm. "I think we are somewhere between the Great Wars. It looks like down a few of the alleys is still some rubble."

He nodded as they were situated at a nice table by the windows.

"Please just order for me. Do we know where we are staying?" The waiter approached as Adam spoke to him and then looked out at what she was glancing towards and realized she was gazing awkwardly at her own reflection in the window. The silence grew between them.

As their food was brought over he noticed she hardly ate. He knew the whole process of her much-needed release from Rano, and his release from her was taking place. Paying the bill, he rose and extended his arm, bringing them out into the old cobbled streets.

"I bet a good bike ride would lift your spirits. How about tomorrow? I can locate one with a bell and basket and set you off on a proper jaunt. Some time alone. What do you think?"

Her eyes lifted in genuine happiness. "Yeah, that would help. Thank you. Is this where we are staying?"

He opened up an exterior door and motioned her inside ahead of him while producing a key with leather ID attached. "Yes, it says so right here."

She jabbed him in the ribs as they walked up a flight of steps. He unlocked another door and pushed it open while they both viewed the small apartment.

It was cozy with plenty of windows. He twisted on a light switch, and the bulb came to life, but barely produced a dim return. Sam was at the window looking out over one of the many canals in Brugge.

"It's lovely here."

He glanced about. "One bedroom, Sam. I'm sorry. I can sleep quite comfortably on the sofa."

She took his hand as he stepped beside her. "I don't think you should. I need to feel your life as his leaves mine. I know that's selfish, but I can't help it."

He squeezed her hand. "I've seen something."

"Already? We just got back. Where and when do we leave?"

He put a hand to the window pane, feeling the coolness. "Not you, just me. I leave tomorrow."

"Oh."

"It's for a good reason, I'm sure."

"Perhaps you are right. I'll know when it's time for me soon enough. Do you know if you will be coming back here?"

He shook his shoulders. "Can't really tell at this point what will happen after that. I wish I had more to give."

She moved away from the window, sitting down on a chair and unlacing her boots. The leather was soft, and she let her hands weave over the top. "I had a pair something like this back at the cottage. That seems like thousands of years ago now. I think those planners upstairs know exactly what they are doing. No sense in you being around a mope like me while this all transpires. Good move on their part, I'd say."

He stood back, feeling a bit uneasy. This was new for them both at this point.

She turned. "Well, I need that kind bloke that was so patient with me back in New Orleans to unbutton me. Tomorrow I'll go and see if I can secure simpler clothing or hire a part-time maid."

His fingers fumbled with the tiny buttons. "Or get a few gowns where they button down the front. These are a royal pain in the ass."

She laughed as he nudged her forward toward the room. He could see her washing in the tiny bathroom and then wiping her face with a cloth. He watched her walk back into the room and climb straight into bed.

"I'm not sure I can sleep in this after the bedding I had back in Egypt or at the cottage. I am spoiled, Adam, that's for sure."

He walked into the bathroom and leaned down on the ceramic sink, running the water and splashing his face before glancing up for a few seconds at his reflection. He shook the uncertainty from his head. But not from his heart.

***

Moving the pillow to the center of the bed, Sam fluffed it several times and settled onto it. Turning the switch off, he got in as the darkened room filled with streaming moonlight.

"Already feels like we've lived together in a hundred lifetimes, Adam."

The back of his hand slid softly down one cheek as she kissed it. He leaned in, touching his lips softly to hers and pulling her onto his chest. She listened intently to the steady beat of his heart and the rhythm of his breathing, allowing both to soothe her tired mind, body, and spirit into a beautiful, deep sleep.

She was so glad someone upstairs had planned on one bedroom and not two. For if there had been two, he would have been the gentleman and insisted on being in the other one, knowing her pending condition. Together they drifted off to sleep.

As she turned over in the morning, her hand instantly went to his spot. One eye opened, followed by a second. He was not there. "Adam?"

No answer.

She glanced over, frowning. His clothes were gone from the chair. He had left her already. Lying back down in bed, she fell back asleep. When she woke, she rolled over and glanced at the small wind-up clock, which displayed nine-thirty. A soft knock slightly rattled the door. Rising and walking over, she moved up on tiptoes and peered out through the keyhole. It was a woman she had not known before. At least she did not think so.

"Yes?"

"Ms. Arnesen, I'm Lucy. I know your gentleman has left for business. He stopped into our company this morning and has contracted me to come and assist you twice daily should you require it."

She opened up the door. "I sure do. Especially with my dresses. I was going to do that myself this very morning. He's a thoughtful man." She closed it. "Would you be kind and advise me on where I can get a pot of tea and breakfast? Something close by. I am not in the mind yet to wander off too far until I take care of a few things."

Lucy grinned, stepping farther into the room. "Yes, I will write down places you can visit while you are alone. I have already stopped at the bike shop on the corner. When you are ready, they will fit you with a fine model. Many are new. So few survived the Great War. But you will be right at home here in Brugge. Almost all of us ride. It is just a lot easier to get around with the small lanes and cobbles. Plus, petrol prices are more than most of us can afford."

Cobbles. Her mind went to 2015 and the Tour of Flanders. It was one of her favorite one-day professional cycling classics. It was housed every year from this very location in Brugge.

"Miss?"

She spun around, facing her new acquaintance. "I am so sorry, Lucy. Please call me Samantha. I'd like it very much if you could come in the evenings around eight to help me get out of these dresses. Pretty as they are, I really need your assistance."

"If you are not here long and want more ease in your clothing, I can recommend a shop two blocks down that may have a few dresses in your size. They open later today. I've seen a few in their storefront window that have back zippers. All the rage and fresh in from the fashion pages of Paris."

She actually felt the smile starting deep within. "Zippers, you say?"

"Yes. They are all the talk now here in Brugge."

"Well then, I'll stop in this morning. Previously, you were trying to gain my attention. I apologize for woolgathering. Is that the list?"

"Yes. There is a lot in this general vicinity. Let me recommend the purchase of an umbrella. Although it is warmer now, it rains frequently here in the spring. I also listed a few markets where you can stock up if you get tired of eating out. The agency's name and address are on there as well. I am only a few minutes away."

"Great. What is your rate so I can pay you now?"

She put up her hand. "No need. Your gentleman paid for several weeks. If you depart sooner let us know and the difference will be returned."

"Excellent and you don't have to do that. Let's just call it a bonus that's between you and I, shall we? There are times when I just decide to move on and take the next train someplace. I will leave word at your office. But you keep the difference should there be one. I much appreciate your help and all the detailed information. You have already done me a great service."

Sam opened up the door for her, smiling as she left. No further small talk was needed. Enough was enough. She grabbed her reticle and looked inside. As usual, it was filled with plenty of the local currency. Belgian francs. So she slid it up her wrist, placed the key inside and closed it.

Humming an Egyptian tune, she left and was outside in short order. She stopped to glance up, the warmth of the sun's rays penetrating to her soul. Yes, she concluded. It was indeed a fine early spring day in Belgium.

Crossing those very famous cobbles, she felt a vigor in her step as she found the shop and engaged the clerk. Indeed, they had a spiffy black bike complemented with a bell and basket. How dandy.

"I shall keep this for at least a week unless my plans change. Just as a precaution, I will pay you for two weeks up front in case you do not see me." She filled out the verification card and signed it. "Will this be enough?"

"Indeed it will. Good thing you are paying for two. Later this week the racers are in town and the streets will be a throng of bustling activity. My supply will dwindle. I may not have rentals at the end of this week."

"Racers? You mean the Tour of Flanders racers? You see I am not from here. But from England and a big fan."

"Your accent gave you away, madam." He grinned.

Sam thought he was quite a nice man and a bit on the handsome side. Amusing enough was that his wife kept glancing out from behind a curtain keeping an eye on them both.

"What is the race route? Where from Brugge do they leave?"

"The center. Where we are right now. If you want to come and stand outside on Saturday, my wife and I would be happy to hold you a spot so you can watch them. They do a few laps through before heading out on the actual course."

"Oh, I will be here. I'd love that. Can I bring anything to celebrate? It would be my pleasure."

He laughed at her enthusiasm. "Anything you wish. We will supply paper cups. No sense in having anything finer than that."

"How old are your children?"

"Eight and ten and yes, of course, they like chocolate. Especially the pastries."

She nodded. "I shall bring wine for us grown-ups and goodies then for them. If I do not see you before, I will see you on race day. What time?"

"Earlier the better. We actually do that so we secure the best spots right in front of the shop. If we do not, then we lose out and watch from the upper windows. That's no fun."

"Wonderful. Thanks." She waved, mounted the bike, lifted the hem of the dress up a little, and pedaled off. She had no particular route in mind and just kept going until she stopped to let a lorrie pass. Glancing over, she saw people coming out of a small alley carrying large totes overflowing with exposed vegetable greens and fresh bread. Yeah, that was her direction.

Following tiny local signs, she stopped in wonder, gazing at the thriving marketplace next to the Belfry of Brugge and The Basilica of the Holy Blood. Jumping off, she walked the bike the rest of the way before resting it against a gas lamppost not in use yet. Then she started maneuvering through other people gathered to shop.

Stalls were filled with needed staples of nutritional value and delicious pastries that were not, Sam noticed. Eventually, she had the basket full, retrieved the bike then rode back to her temporary digs and unloaded it all. That finished, she took what was needed and went downstairs.

Back outside and on the bike, she started out again, this time with a small picnic already in that lovely, tidy basket. Weaving over the famous cobbles, her energy level rose as her muscles balked at the excessive pedal strokes.

She spoke out loud to no one. "I must be getting soft. Or need more gears than this." She laughed, continuing on.

Because Brugge was referred to as the Venice of the North, she had no trouble finding a beautiful bridge to cross. Breathless, she lowered both boots to the ground as she moved off the bike, setting it against a building. She then located a vacated bench and ate lunch. Relaxing, she watched a steady succession of boats and barges come into view before disappearing up the waterway.

She glanced to the heavens, speaking softly. "This is so beautiful. I'm not happy you took Adam away, but if you had to put me someplace where I needed reflective time, this works." She smiled into the fluffy white clouds floating by.

On her way back, as the sun set, the streets came alive with musicians playing mixtures of waltzes, polkas, and even very Parisian music. Setting the bike inside the building, she went back out and just walked until she came to Damme.

Turning, she crossed over one of the canal bridges and came back along the opposite path, stopping along the way at a café to sip tea and watch people stroll by. Rising, she paid the waiter and continued, heading upstairs before realizing she had forgotten to stop at the dress shop. What time was it?

She glanced at the small wind clock. It showed eight o'clock. As if on cue, Lucy's knock came directly after.

"Come on in. Perfect timing. I just got back. I was so fascinated by this area I lost track of time on my walk."

"My apartment is just across the street. I was watching for you."

"I'm sorry you had to do that. You probably have other things you may prefer to be doing. I forgot today to stop in that shop. But I will tomorrow before I leave. Can I see your place from up here?"

"Yes." Lucy was unbuttoning her dress. "Right across, see? I left a light lit."

"Indeed I do. But now I am having a thought. Should I find a few dresses of use that I can get into and out of on my own, I will not need your services. In exchange, would you be free to give me more advice on where to go and what to do outside of Brugge? I would love to take full advantage of my bike."

"But he paid me for so many more days."

Sam scoffed, waving both hands. "Not an issue. Having a local tell me things I'd not know is worth a lot more than you having to bother coming here for only a few minutes in the morning and evening to do these silly buttons."

She had finished. "Absolutely I can. Tell me what you are interested in and I'll bring a new list with me tomorrow morning. If you have left, I will slide it under the door. Will that work?"

"Perfect. I'd like to know more about Damme and other towns near here. I like to ride, Lucy, so if it is fifteen kilometers or more I'd be happy to jaunt off. I also like history, architecture, art and old churches. Now don't go laughing at me, I know what you are going to say. But this is Brugge!"

"I can't help it. I enjoy your enthusiasm. I'll set you up with an interesting list. Some areas are still being rebuilt after the Great War. But there are places the Germans actually did not destroy for its architectural grandeur. I will take care of this and see you in the morning."

"Thanks very much. I look forward to what you come up with. Have a good night." She smiled and closed the door.

Sam washed up and went to the window to watch the people stroll by, feeling better. She opened one as a cool breeze wafted in off the canal below. Turning and climbing into bed, she laid a weary head and body down on the pillow. A quick roll-over left her improving mood diminished as she threw the second pillow out of sight onto the floor. It was the noise of the street below that proved to be a needed distraction, finally shutting her brain down so she could fall asleep.

After Lucy left the next morning, Sam sat down with a pot of tea and reviewed the list. Cool stuff. She had definitely a future in the travel industry if she ever wanted one. Glancing at the clock and then jumping up, she quickly washed the dishes and left them to dry on a wooden rack before dashing from the apartment to the shop. Lucy had been right. It took Sam only a few minutes to find the shop door.

"Hello, Miss. What can we do for you?"

"Well, I hear that you may just have what all the ladies around are buzzing about. The new style from Paris and it involves dresses and zippers. Would you happen to have one that may fit a lady of my size?"

The dressmaker eyed her. "I think I do. Why don't you come with me to the back and see what we can come up with?"

One hour later Sam left the shop with one of the shopkeeper's sons close in tow. They carried five boxes between them up to her apartment, where she slipped a sizable tip into his hands. The door could not close fast enough for her to begin opening the boxes. At the shop she had the clerk help her to change into one. Now all that was needed was some snacks and her bike. There was exploring to be done.

Taking her reticule and umbrella just in case, she grabbed the premade picnic and loaded up her bike. Forty minutes of steady riding later had her stopping beside a field and glancing around. A happy smile lit her face as she spotted a graveyard and spire of a ruined church dating back to the year 504.

Oh, how she longed for Father G about now.

Hopping off, she walked the bike, finding the perfect picnic spot. Setting it down on the grass, she took the food and drink and enjoyed this tranquil, peaceful location.

Softly the words just came out. "I've not heard your voice, Rano, for a few days. Are you done with me and now chasing those wenches up in the heavens?" Lips quivered as the first tear dropped. Then, quickly, several more, until a steady stream flowed.

"I don't understand. I let you go. Why do I feel so empty without you? Are we not finished with business?"

She slumped slightly, crossing both hands over her heart.

"Open your eyes, woman."

She shook her head, placing it in her hands, and then brought her legs up, tucking them under her chin.

"Open them."

"No. I am not going to see you. You are gone. I am here. I do not hear you."

A warm breeze lifted her hair and removed her braid. It sprang to life, swirling around before lying loosely down her back. She pulled it to one side in a bunch, her eyes opening slowly. There on the ground, right beside her left hip, rested the gold hair thread.

She gasped.

"You are releasing me?"

She picked it up. As it dangled she tried to smile but was in so much anguish. "You kept part of it, this is only half."

A powerful bright light surrounded him as he knelt before her, raising his palm. She lifted one of her own toward him. His other hand gently caressed her cheek as all the wetness simply evaporated. Their hands touched as, mesmerized, she felt a lightning bolt of intense energy surge through her being.

"Yes. It is time for us both. I have loved you throughout the old. Now, my brother will love you throughout the new. As our souls move on, my lovely, you will heal. I will heal. Eventually, only bits will be in your memory. It is time."

He released her hand as the sun's rays diminished behind a passing cloud. He faded, disappearing in seconds. Struggling, she reached out into the air and then stopped. Tying the cord back into her hair, she curled into a ball and broke down sobbing.

Racks of pain seared her soul. But slowly her heart began to mend. Heal. Just as he said. It left her weak as she unfurled and reached into a slit pocket, producing a cotton hanky to wipe her eyes and blow her nose.

Then her mind went blank and nothing followed but silence.

It was welcoming.

Time passed unnoticed until she realized the sounds of the approaching night were fast upon her. Sitting up farther and crossing her legs, she started to gain control. Lifting her eyes up from the green grass and glancing around, she felt bereft as images of Rano quickly disappeared from her vision. She closed them tight and let the coolness of the stone against her back weave around her, bringing her slowly back to reality.

Not a soul was around at this hallowed place. She rose, grabbed her hat, put it back on, took the picnic bag and walked back to her bike. On her short journey through the graveyard, a warming inside her soul started to take place. Yes, his exit was painful. Years of being pent up in there due to her own selfishness. "Oh, Rano. I am so sorry I held you for so very long. Find peace, my love."

A cool wind lifted her hat up off her head and swirled it around before dropping it to the unkempt grass a few yards beyond. As she leaned down to pick it up, she saw his face looking right at her. He did not say a word but smiled. It was that special smile that spoke volumes about how he felt toward her when no more words would be allowed. It was a love that spanned time and space, just like her love with Adam. She reached a finger out magically just as did he. In that one brief instant, they touched.

Then both were free.

For several minutes she absorbed it all until he passed from her thoughts completely. It was as if someone from the twenty-second century had taken the motherboard out of her brain and deleted most of him from it. Shaking her head at the sound of children laughing in the distance, Sam walked back to her bike and sat with one foot resting on the ground and one on a pedal as she looked around.

"Of course there is no one here but me." She smiled, pushed off and started the journey back to the apartment. A soothing breeze was at her back now. Yes, she felt whole again.

"Now, Lord Griffin, where shall I find you? Do you think any of you up there could lend me a hand now that I've done right by us all? You owe me for finally smartening up, you know." She giggled while reaching the cobbles at the outskirts of Brugge. Then she took her sweet time putting the bike away. On the slow climb up the stairs, she suddenly broke out in a dash, hoping that someone had told him the good news and he would be waiting for her when the door opened.

A brief flicker of sadness passed through her when it was flung open and the rooms reviewed. He was not there. *Oh well*, she thought to herself. Tomorrow was the race and she was eager for this day to pass so that the rest of her life, wherever that was going to be, could commence.

Then it dawned on her. Feeling bold, she made one more request. "Oh, shit. Can you also do me one more favor and not shuffle me from here tomorrow? If you could make it the day after. I want to see the race."

She laughed softly, hoping she had not pissed the people upstairs off. But in truth, she really did want to be here. To be that close to the racing and disappear would just not be fair. "Please?" was added as an afterthought.

Chapter Twelve

"You've been seen all around Brugge's countryside. Do you know what some of the locals in the neighborhood have taken to calling you?"

"Yes, that damn crazy dame from England. I rather like it." She grinned ear to ear. "Oh, don't say it. I do not want you to ruin my mood. Look, here comes the first group. I am so excited I can hardly stay inside my skin."

"Yes, stop flailing your arms. Or you are going to do bodily damage to my entire family."

Sam laughed a bit too loud, her enthusiasm getting in the way. Glancing down, she made sure her boots were not extending over the curb as the gust of heavy wind came by them with the first group of cyclists.

"How I wish I could ride like they do."

"That would be scandalous and you know it. They will be by three more times. But not for about thirty minutes. Now, where is that wine?"

She reached behind into the bag and produced the bottle and cork. "Where is your husband? Oh, I see him. I'll get him to open this." Mary was smiling at Sam's enthusiasm. Since arriving, this quarter of the neighborhood had lightened up at the wonderful atmosphere she brought every place she went.

"No need, we are women. Surely together we can get it opened. We don't have to worry about the kids. Look at them filling their faces at this time of day with those treats you bought. Which will bring a tongue lashing from my lovely mother-in-law, I am quite sure."

"Well, I may add, look at us for drinking this early in the day before most people have had a proper pot of tea."

They giggled, heads together, as the cork was removed with a thud and flew across the narrow street. "Oh, my, good thing they had already passed. Look, here he comes now with those parents of his. Quick, fill my cup so I can drink it and have another. Then it could actually be possible that I may like them more."

"Oh, I got that a few days ago. They are not your favorite apples in the bunch."

"Sour grapes are more like it. There, I feel the warmth. That's much, much better. Now drink and fill me up."

Sam hid a smile behind her hand as they indeed descended upon them. "You seem to have the best spots already taken, I see." She shook her head in disdain. "I guess I could go upstairs inside of the shop and watch from the windows."

Sam nudged Mary.

"Oh, Mother, my apologies. I got caught up in the moment. By all means, have my spot. I am a few inches taller and can see over your head." She moved back, grabbing Sam by the arm and giving it a mighty tug. If she had to give up her spot to see them, so was Sam.

"I would have bit your hand if I had known what you were up to."

"Shush, she has the ears of a predatory mountain lion on the prowl in the wilds of Africa."

They chuckled. "I just saw Arthur trying to hide his grin. I think he enjoys my having a poke of fun with his plump, old, nosy, meddling mother."

"You did not miss any adverbs there, did you? I noticed they are both good to the kids. I've seen that with my own two eyes. Where are your parents?"

"Abroad in Germany. They have a joint business. With these grumblings of unrest making headlines they decided to go back. It is time to sell and cut their losses."

"You are German?" The concern could not be kept from Sam's voice. She was fully aware of what would transpire in the next twenty-plus years.

"Nope, Austrian and French. But all the same." She touched her shoulder fondly. "I know, Sam. Thanks for your thoughts."

"I'm glad to hear that. Not that I would not like you all the same. I know how Brugge is somewhat of a melting pot with Germans having stayed here after the Great War and all. You did not even sound like you had that kind of an accent and your name is not German. Anyway, I digress. How's your stomach? Time for a pastry to absorb your early morning courage?"

"Yeah, I'll have that chocolate one. Can't seem to keep them off my lips nor what eventually forms on my hips."

"May I recommend renting a bike for a day and coming along with me? It would ruin any extra calories from having the idea of settling where you prefer they do not. Besides, I visited Damme the other day and was taken aback. It is so beautiful. Surely you must have been before."

She nodded. "Yes, we have. Walked and taken a picnic last summer." She leaned closer. "I heard somewhat bizarre gossip late yesterday. Some passers-by at the cemetery saw a woman curled up in a ball crying her eyes out. Those that came across her did not even bother to see if she was sick or needed assistance. I guess they thought she was crazy. Some people. Willing to tell a good tall tale. Indeed, I know these two blokes. They are always in their cups before our eyes are even open in the morning. I put quick work to their story. Told them if I heard it about the neighborhood, I'd tell both their mothers where they really go every night after work. It is sure as hell not to chapel to pray."

Sam smiled, realizing the special message. "You are indeed a good sort, regardless of what she may think." Her finger pointed to the mother-in-law. "I wish I was here longer. I'd like to get to know you a lot better."

"Yes, you are in transit, I know. When will your man come back and get you, or are you leaving here to meet him? You seem well enough to travel on now, don't you think?"

"I'm really curious about you. What do they call your type?" They both got closer.

"Watchers."

"I think I read long ago there are two types. You are clearly of the warm-hearted version. You do not assist like I do? But observe and lend a hand as needed?"

"That's right. There is a pecking order so to speak. You are pretty close to the top of the pyramid, Sam."

She watched her closely, having chosen that particular word for a purpose.

"Pyramid. You knew."

"We have to know what we will to help you when the time is right."

"Do you know where Adam is?"

"He's here."

"What?"

"You did hear me. He is here. I could not out and out tell you. Against protocol and all. You had to ask me first for me to give you a correct answer. It was not possible for you to heal properly if he was to stay with you. Would you honestly say you would still have broken down like you did if he was?"

She shook her head roughly, polishing off her wine. "No. I would have buried it. Where exactly is he right now?"

"At the Basilica of the Holy Blood in the Old Center. He did have to take care of some of his own personal business. That is why he returned from the East with you here. I think you two basically punch your own time travel cards."

She handed her the bag and bottle along with the remaining goodies and nodded, lifting her dress hem and bolting quickly across the cobbles. Glancing nervously, she half expected one of the abundantly placed police guards would halt her progress. Waving over a shoulder, quickly she disappeared into a throng of people on the opposite side of the street.

Not giving a bloody damn what she was leaving behind, she rushed on. Lucy could have it all if she so chose. A brick wall of gatherers halted her forward progress. Would these people ever get out of her way? She was growing impatient, giving a good shove to a tall gent that seemed to want to block her as he tipped and spilled his beer onto his shoes.

"Damn, hey you! Stop!"

But as he turned toward her, she moved around and was on her way.

At last, it loomed ahead. It was a beautiful chapel. Used formerly by the Count of Flanders, it was said the very cloth held in such high esteem there had the blood of Christ on it. It would have been quick of her to forget why she was there, as it was such an architecturally inspirational small chapel. But as her steps moved on, her heart began to beat like it had the morning after he had given up his room in Venice and then stole that infamous kiss from her in the breakfast room of the *Pensione*.

"I bet I know where your thoughts were and wonder if this is the most appropriate place to have them?"

She spun around so fast she had to grab his lapels to keep from falling down at his shoes. "Well, it's not entirely improper." Her heels went up as her toes lifted.

"Really. I don't believe you." His hands moved to hers, holding them tightly.

"Well, it is, of course, all your fault."

He leaned closer, moving her toward an alcove away from the few eyes there who were not out watching the race. "Of course, but why?"

"You caused my heart to race wildly back in Italy. Now again. I happened to just learn where you are. I came to find you as fast as I could."

"You must be wrong. You just exerted yourself, that's all." His eyes were so dark, and a dangerously handsome smirk creased the sides of his mouth as he leaned down and kissed her gently.

She softly moaned into his mouth as their tongues touched. He pulled back slightly and then placed a gentle kiss on the curve of her lusciously warm skin.

"If you let go of me now, I will slither down to my boots." Her breath was shallow. Words hardly heard.

"I'll always be here to help you. Carry you. Always."

They stood, eyes locked, as he kissed her again. This time was not so gentle or quick.

"Ah, hum."

No response.

"Ah, hum. I assume you two are here to ask me to write up and post bands of marriage for your upcoming nuptials?"

They pulled apart, smiling.

"Father G! Can we get back to you on that? Oh, and it's darn good to see you again." Adam shook his hand.

"Still not ready, are you two? I would have thought this last big one would have sealed the deal. Well, you know how to shut the door on your way out and where I am when you are ready."

He disappeared into the sacristy.

"I need some time alone with just you. What about we sneak to the cottage and hide out there for a few days?" He had just closed the outside church door and was taking her hand in his.

"I checked my schedule and I'm free for at least a week." They continued along the path, both spotting that exact location where once, not that long ago, they had made love and nearly ruined the baker's new pie concoction.

"We have memories all over the globe, Adam. But I want to make sure we have more here than anywhere else. I don't know how you could have known what was going on back with Rano and not come and dragged me away. Then flogged me."

"You have to keep it in perspective. Someday that role may be reversed. We can't always remember every bit of all our lives until it's time. Or it would simply be too easy. I did know you and he were in love. But it was a different one than what we have."

"Yes. Before we get there, do you have any questions about it, him or me? I want to get that right out of the way now. It seems some of my memory of that era is quickly fading."

"Nope, I'm good. Anything you want to ask me?"

She shrugged, and then gave into the jabber inside her mind. "Yes and no." Her eyes remained steady with his as they continued to walk along. But she refused to ask the question burning on her tongue.

He spun her around to face him. "Then I will answer you so we can put all of this to rest forever more. One. Do you need to know more?"

She giggled and then laughed out loud, nearly doubling over.

"That's funny?"

"You have a will of iron then, Lord Griffin. Because I saw many lovely women all around you. Must have been a few broken hearts when you disappeared."

He kept them moving right along now inside the cottage and shoved a boot against the door, closing it with a thud. "I bathed at the pools on my own after that. Although I visited their houses a few times later, it was to gather up some errant soldiers and get them back to camp in one piece. That was not my agenda on this passage. As I found out after. And may I add, that a certain beautiful erotic dancer stole my heart. Teased me relentlessly. Then simply disregarded my existence and vanished off with another?"

She blushed sweetly as he swept her up into his arms and placed a solid kiss on her partially parted lips. "I fully expect you will remember how to do that here. Right?"

They both inhaled the sweetness around them.

"Smell that? Fresh pie, bread, and meats. I think someone else knew of our arrival today and planned. We have to thank Mrs. H at some point."

"So, what was it then? I have a feeling you need to tell me one more thing. Something you have deliberately not told me since we arrived in Belgium."

"Damn you are so perceptive," he laughed, smoothing both hands up her ass as they headed up the stairs.

"Well?" They were now in her room, both of them releasing each other momentarily from a locked gaze to look at the bed.

"Fine. I see no other way around this except to tell you straight up front that Rano and I were brothers. Twins, separated at birth because our mother thought I may not live. She did not wish to give a sickly child to her husband as the heir apparent first born."

"But you two must have been fraternal then, right? As you were not identical. Wow, now that I think of it, you would pass for brothers."

"Correct on both. We shared the same indent on the back of our necks."

"I know that now. But never put the two together for some damn reason. What happened?"

"She gave me up to a nice settled pair in a neighboring village."

"Semite village?"

"You are smart. Yes. I was raised by them. I did not know I was to be reunited with my brother until I met you and we started out on this long journey from Venice back to here. Several times. You see, part of the reason why he could not settle his soul was his love for you. Also, his love of me. He had found out later in life about me and worked tirelessly behind the scenes so no one would know, to make sure we met—even going so far as to fight me himself in battle knowing I would be saved by our healer. You. But that was not all. Apparently our meeting there was always preempted by your choice to change the ending, so to speak, so I was never allowed to know. I am not telling you this to hurt you. But to help you realize how all our past actions can really cause a dissatisfying turn of events to occur in our futures."

"Wow. This is a lot more than I realized. I truly am so sorry. I hope it is all finally settled. I truly think it is. Believe me, I will keep this in the back of my mind. To make sure I really think about my actions before moving forward."

"I know you will. Until he is removed from your memory for good, you may still go through some strange feelings. Now I understand the voice that I heard from time to time. It was him. He affected you in an entirely different way."

"I'm sure we can agree that's a good thing."

They both smiled.

"He would somehow speak to me at times and make sure that we stayed on track in getting you and the jewels back to the craftsman and he reunited with it. He needed it all in place to rest in peace. You letting him go, the sword intact and seeing me one more time. I did not actually figure out it was my brother guiding us back in time through it all until he approached me in the encampment and told me everything."

They had crawled in bed naked, each on their side facing one another. "Adam I know it was me trying to save Rano. That I had pried the jewels off the sword as some kind of a remembrance and took them. That was eye-awakening to know it was me that was making us all keep repeating the same scenarios over and over again. The strangest part was that I never remembered meeting you until it was over and it started again."

"Yes, you have been playing with a lot of people's lives for a very long, long time, Sam, including ours."

"What happens now? We are both here. I have not been given a choice to return to my modern Exeter. What happens next?"

"Your original time is now. I don't think it all has settled in with you yet."

"I don't quite understand."

"Love, you dragged your heels in letting go of things and people, that's all. You made the choice long ago to stay here. But then you got confused and left. Over time you moved on to 2015 England and for some strange reason, those up there permitted you to remain for a while. That's the best explanation I have."

"As long as I don't do that all again, all will be well in the world?"

"Yes. That's your final step or stop. You already completed half of it by not taking the jewels off the sword and keeping them. The other part was you believing in being here. In other words, don't get restless. If you do, it will reverse what was done and lots of people, including me, will be quite angry with you."

She settled back on the pillow. "So how can we make sure I don't get restless? What can we do that we've never done before to ensure I always return here? Can I just go back and get my bike and ride it in secrecy?"

He slid on top of her. "You could do that. I will go with you to make sure you come back, mistress."

"Can we go in a few days? I need to make sure I have a list of what I want to bring so I don't have any reasons at all."

"I have another idea to throw into the mix. This will ensure we've done something that we never did before."

"What is it?"

He smiled. It was the most touching emotion that she would ever know. In this lifetime. That itself was different.

"Will you be my wife?"

She wove her hands up into his hair, feeling that notch once again. "Yes. I will. The sooner the better, please, and Adam?"

"Yes, love, I know. It's time to stop talking."

Chapter Thirteen

"Did you see the look on Mrs. H when she caught sight of my bike at the cottage?"

He laughed, pulling her tightly into his arms. "How do you like your wedding present? You are causing quite a stir all around the village. The paper wants to do a story on you."

She laughed, running her hand over the leather seat of the Velocipede, a very special ladies' bike he had imported from New York City. It was the height of fashion for women's two-wheeled transportation.

"Oh, I love it. Wait until I create ladies' pants and ride with those. It could launch a new style of clothing and make us rich before the rest of the world catches up years later."

He shook his head. "That's the last of your things from the cottage. You know I'll miss not coming down here for our afternoon trysts. Are you sure you want to give it up?"

"Absolutely. For Clash and Anne, I'd do anything. I can't wait for their wedding. You like him, don't you? I hear he gives a fair shake at your loot in cards."

"A shark, that's what he is. Even Victor has conceded that he's outsmarted us on more than one game. He fits in with our type. I'm glad you are happy giving up this place to them."

"Well, that's it then. Shall we?"

"Yeah, I also had one other thing done. The statue of Isis has been moved to our western garden. I thought you may like to still visit her. It is quite nice when the sun sets. She really does light up. I think she'd miss you not coming around."

She leaned over, kissing him while never missing a step wheeling the bike out. "I like that you had a shed built for this right outside the back. Being spoiled by you works for me."

He took the bike from her and kept going. "Well, we agreed as long as I keep you occupied and happy you won't get bored and go away." His voice was light, holding no uncertainty. Finally, it seemed they both were beginning to relax into this new marriage, believing it really was over.

"One area we certainly have diversity in is our sex life. I should be all set. That and the bike rides, of course."

He swatted her on the ass as he closed the shed door, eyeing the other bike in there from her Exeter cottage. She was still adamantly using it on the sly, even though the tires were small for the dirt-packed roads. Sliding the lock in place, he instantly felt the mood swing before she even opened her mouth.

"I'm a bit anxious to go to sleep tonight, Adam. It is six months to the night and the Tinker and the Sage both said all will be decided on within this timeline."

He knew.

"So you can wake up tomorrow and be assured that this is all real. That you were not transported back to 2015 England and start this all over again. I know. I have taken it upon myself to have Mrs. H serve us out on the patio. Winter is nearly upon us and it will be colder soon. I suggest we eat early then call it a night. I admit I feel the same. I want to wake up tomorrow and know you are still here. I'm sorely tempted to chain myself to your body. I should have taken that extra duct tape from your cottage before we returned here. That stuff would work for sure. I've never seen anything like it."

Hand in hand they went together to eat, both keenly noticing that even Mrs. H seemed unusually quiet this evening as she brought their dinner and left them to converse privately. Moving her foot out of a pump, Sam slid one silky foot up his leg as he eyed her suspiciously. Actually, a bit on the lusty side was more like it.

Mrs. H reappeared. "I'll just clear this off and you two can sit back and relax."

"Mrs. H, that was fantastic as always. Would you like to take a chair and have a nightcap with us? A bit of a catch-up?"

She shook her head "No, I'm ready to call it a night. Albeit an early one. Everyone has taken off already. Seems there are a lot of anxious people across the land. Good night to you both."

They both watched her leave.

"She thinks so too?"

"Yeah, we all are wanting this night over."

"What if it's the wrong one and it is actually tomorrow?"

"Can't be. It's on the calendar. We all cross-checked each other to make sure. Besides, that gypsy woman's readings have all been spot on, remember? Considering how much of what she said has come true. Like all of it. We can't just stop believing her at this juncture."

"Of course, you are right. Okay." She rose, sliding her hand over his shoulder and ruffling his hair. "You going to stay and smoke?"

He nodded, taking it out of his inside jacket pocket and lighting it up. "I won't be long." He watched her go, knowing the last time he saw this much anxiety in her, they were in the car on the way out of Mecca.

***

She went up through the main stairway, slowly, keeping a hand gripped tightly on the brass rail until she reached the third landing. Apprehension filled her entire body. Stopping, she leaned against the wall, glancing up at two of Adam's ancient ancestors and sensing they were anxious too.

"Okay, let's do this." She spoke directly to them. "It's now or never."

The long walk down their hall toward the double-wide suite doors seemed to take an eternity. Anxious as all hell would be an understatement. She stopped, gazing lovingly up at their newly painted wedding picture just before entering their suite.

"I love you, Adam," she whispered. Slowly pushing down on the handle, she entered, closing the door behind her. Undressing, she washed up, slid on her silk robe, and opened the balcony doors to step out where the sun had set. The last of its glow shone on the top of Isis.

The wind rustled her robe, untying it, but she did not notice. Nor the chill that wove up her spine. She closed her eyes and leaned slightly back, the robe billowing in the wind as his hands slid up her thighs, cupping her breasts, pinching both puckered peaks.

Sam released a moan into the night sky.

When his lips touched hers, she knew it was different.

"You are here."

"Yes, I saw this brazen woman exposing her luscious skin, like an angel, high up on my balcony and had to come quickly before she disappeared." He turned her into his arms and kissed her with torturing passion as she felt him against her thighs.

"You are naked."

"Absolutely. I could not come out here with such intention and not be. Being the goddess that you are, you may have turned your nose up at me."

"I thought you were a dream and he had returned. Ironically, your voices are so much alike."

"Nope. I am your barrier now. He will not get to you, nor would he try. He made me the promise that when you finally did this right, that throughout all the rest of our time, I would be the one. He gave me his word."

"Oh, how blessed I am to have the love of two great men."

He picked her up and slid her down on him as the robe fought fiercely to be released. She raised her arms and it released up and off, blowing out into the sky. He sat on the balcony bench as she arched back, taking him in deeper.

"You own me."

She had heard him say those words as well.

"No, I do not."

Their breathing was heavy as the raven passed by, adding his comments.

"Yes, you do."

He plunged so deep into her their release brought a moan from their lips. As the kiss deepened, so did their shared release.

He pushed hair back from her face, tucking it behind both ears while her nails dug into his back. "You are going to leave scars, woman."

She smiled. "Take us to our bed, husband."

It was the first time she'd said that. To him, no words could mean more except when she said she loved him.

"As you command, mistress."

"Oh, I shall always love that word."

"I know you will. But you are so much more than that. You are the trifecta. My wife, mistress, and soul mate."

"Adam, I love you so. Please hold me tight all the rest of this night until the sun rises into tomorrow's sky. I cannot help it. I still have doubts."

He allowed no distance between them as he covered them with the sheets and blankets. "I'm right here."

She tried so hard to stay awake, chattering away. But even he could not, Sam noticed, as he dozed off. But she did remain stuck to him like glue throughout the night.

***

Then the dream started.

She tossed and turned and was in and out of his arms. He felt her restlessness and pulled her back against him. Finally, she settled something inside those dreams and slept again.

Damn. Was this right?

As the raven flew by along with a few of his friends and the sun shone, he turned over. Her spot was warm but vacant. Jumping up, he could not see the balcony. Yet, with each purposeful step his heart was moving further and further into his throat.

He stopped, stepping out onto the balcony and grabbed her tightly into his arms. She was here.

"You thought so as well, for just a second, didn't you?" Her smile was warm and inviting.

"Did you do that to me on purpose? You wench."

"I like the trifecta. There is no more room to add another."

"And smartass as well."

"Yes, and this smartass is going to be harassing you for a very, very, long time." She turned and kissed him, and then flexed out over the balcony. "Look over there. I could not stop laughing earlier. Surprised I did not wake you."

"What?" He looked out over the west garden and could not believe his eyes. Her robe had not only taken flight last night, but it was draped around Isis.

"Shall we leave it there?"

"Hell no. I want it back here with you. That is the most bizarre thing I've ever seen."

"It was your brother. You two still work in cahoots. He removed it and you plundered. You damn thieving men."

He burst out laughing. "Who knows, you could be right. But, all the same, I'm going to throw on some trousers and boots and run down there and get it before anyone else sees it and wonders who the hell it belongs to.

Then, we have to start to explain. Or in your case, create such a story no one will believe a word either way." He turned, dressed and dashed out in a flash.

She watched his strong form run down the path and untie the robe. Then he threw his hands up in the air in mock victory, looked around, and ran back up the path into the house. He was not even breathless as he came into the room and out onto the balcony to show off his prize.

***

"Okay, where the hell are you?"

Silence.

He turned into the room and saw her. How the hell could anyone do that? She was in what would be described as a position straight out of the ancient Asian Kama Sutra. "Is that comfortable? How the hell are you holding that position?"

"Stretching. In the future years, I did a lot of yoga. I remember the poses. Want to come on over and see what happens?"

He threw the robe toward one of the chairs, but it missed and slid to the carpet. "Yup, sign me up."

She maneuvered him inside of her as his roaming hands halted. The heat quickly engulfed them both as an intense tremble followed.

"Lord Griffin, I like that. I think you should come into the future to learn yoga."

He laughed, sliding a hand up her curvy waist to cup a firm breast. "Perhaps a trip to the future, yes. But to a bookstore to get a copy of those poses in print."

They both laughed harder.

"I think a while back I made mention of our meeting again in our next life. Instead of doing passages we just get married young, have half a dozen kids and a very normal, British life. What do you think?"

"Did that come out again because of what I did?"

"It sure did. It is not just what you did, it's wow, what you did. If you owned a brothel and taught all your women that move, men would be lined up for miles to get in and would pay any sum to stay."

She smiled warmly. "I have a few others to try out on you. We don't need that book."

"Oh, I like this being married stuff."

"Like I've said all along, we did not have to marry to have this. But now that I am married, I'd not give it up for anything."

"I know you are happy. I feel it."

She leaned in, kissing him. "Yes, I really am. Thank you."

He tugged her down. "Unfortunately, I am completely wiped out. So, unless you have some secret Chinese medicine tucked someplace in your herbal bags, healer, I need to have food and drink to sustain me. I doubt I can even rise from the bed and get dressed, I am so expended."

She grinned like an alley cat. "I'm hungry too. I wish you had a bike as well so we could ride together. Set a new trend. Start tails a wagging and all. Then all the aristocrats that stick their noses up at us will want to copy."

They both rose and dressed and then headed out of the room to eat while chatting away.

"I did. I ordered two of the ladies' bikes and the gypsy's son is rearranging it for my size. You know, he's quite resourceful with designing. While I was there, he showed me some of his ideas. I am going to sponsor him to full University in this upcoming winter session at Oxford. I had to pull in some markers to get him accepted, but he's going. I could not let his talent go to waste. Not like he was not using some of it on the road, but now he can look at some options for a future if he chooses to."

"Oh, Adam, that is fantastic."

"They are going to stay the winter and make sure he's comfortable before moving on."

"Can't they stay longer? I like spending time with her."

"I know you do. It did not take much to persuade her. This will be a first. Her youngsters are going to go to school. But she does not want to give up their caravan. I'll make sure they are all comfortable. She's done a lot for us."

"As long as she feels like she's contributing. You know how they abhor charity."

"Her son is going to work while in classes. I have arranged it with an associate's agency. He can start from the ground up learning about design properly. He will earn a modest wage and have to work his ass off. But he was keen enough when we talked about it in length. He has potential. I'm just giving him a hand up, that's all."

"I always said it. You are a good bloke, Lord Griffin."

He laughed, reaching for her hand. They entered the breakfast room but then halted.

"What's all this? Are we expecting company?"

Indeed, they were.

Mrs. H came in with Anne, Clash, Victor, her sister-in-law, the kids, the gypsy, her kids as well as her husband and Father G.

"Mrs. H?"

"It's time to celebrate, Master Griffin. We made it. All our lives are going to get a bit easier now that the mistress has settled in."

Father G took Sam by the arm, bringing her over to sit beside him and Victor. "She means you are..."

"Oh, Father, I know what she means. I more than you all am overjoyed at still being here this morning."

"So perhaps I won't see you two so much on the back path heading behind the cottage now that you are properly married?"

Sam blushed as Adam grinned. "Now, Father, you know how we both like to take in a bit of fresh air. This English weather is more temperamental than the spirited woman I met long ago in Venice."

"Stop it. Don't speak around me." She eyed the children, grateful they were having a hard time following the adult bantering. Father G seemed to read her mind and silently agreed, nodding at her. "If I may steer this conversation, which I started, back to a more serious note. You did it, Sam, finally."

She grinned, lifting her juice glass. "With a lot of help from all of you and a few others around the globe. This is to us all."

THE END... Perhaps.

About Sandra Waine

Sandra Waine currently resides in central New Hampshire with her cat, Irene. Along with writing, she also enjoys cycling, hiking, traveling and photography. As well, she is a Level 2 Usui Reiki Practitioner.

Social Media Links:

Author website: www.sandrawaine.com

Facebook:
https://www.facebook.com/profile.php?id=100000005071 04

Twitter: https://twitter.com/@slwaine777

If you enjoyed this story, check out these other Solstice Publishing books by Sandra Waine:

Passages A Trilogy Book 1 Touch Me From Afar
It only took twenty-four hours for Samantha Arnesen's world to change drastically and there was no logical explanation for it. Divorced, forty and needing a complete change, she ditched a logical, safe world back in England and took off exploring other parts of Europe.

A rather embarrassing circumstance in Venice propels Sam into a bold interaction with a handsome stranger. Had she left things alone her safe little life would have continued. But it was not her destiny. A passionate kiss transcends her right into his world of 1865.

Was it irrational, destiny, or a bump on the head?

With no apparent possibility of returning back, it all simply starts to unravel.

https://bookgoodies.com/a/B01N9PXR7N

Passages A Trilogy Book 2 What Have You Unearthed?

As book two continues, Sam finds herself thrust into an uprising in modern day Egypt with bold, daring cameraman, Derek Clash. They team up brilliantly. But it's clear he has an agenda that extends beyond just helping her. Somehow, he's entangled with more than one person from her Victorian past.

With assistance from strange outside sources, a small group of ex-military men turned mercenary and the good sisters of a small leper monastery, Sam and Derek soon discover how intense their connection really is.

Separately, Adam moves on a different path and passages. But along the way, he realizes how important Sam has become to him. Finally, they intertwine on a journey that brings them both to internal discoveries that are far beyond anything a great imagination could ever conjure.

But her past won't lay silent. In fact, it's drawing her closer and closer to an event that will take them both down the dark tunnel of their soul's journey. Back in time to a powerful Egyptian dynasty. Their future, their love, and the existence of others hinge on how they both act and react during this period.

https://bookgoodies.com/a/B06XXPJB4R

Passages A Trilogy Book 3: The Circle Ends

Book three continues with Sam and Adam in Ancient Egypt. Separated. He has his own past to delve into and repair as well as a major task in subtly assisting Sam to accept a reality that she has up to now resisted exists. To deal with a love that transcends all time and to ultimately face her choices, hopefully making the right one. For all their sakes.

Then, there is one more thing that he has to contend with. Ranof. Alive, well and has a purpose with Sam. A purpose that Adam can do nothing about but watch it unfold. Or, remove himself from their volatile relationship and find solace in the arms of another.

Figures from the first two books keep reappearing in her lifetime and Passages, even in Egypt. All with special messages connected to an important event that this time she cannot ignore.

As all these people intertwine with purposeful missions, slowly, Sam realizes what it all means and that she has indeed been controlling all of their lives for centuries. If there was ever to be a future for them all, she had to find the key to what needed to be done in Egypt. Now.

CPSIA information can be obtained
at www.ICGtesting.com
Printed in the USA
LVHW081611270119
605414LV00028B/447/P

9 781625 265937